Jumpseat
A Tale of Twisted Fate
E. E. Valenciana

D1707475

Mahalo to kokua wahine
Judy Ruiz Verhoek
Rebecca Jane Verhoek
&
Nancy Stek

.

Special thanks for your assistance
Joseph Grady

In memory of
Robert Gallegos
12/14/51 – 10/31/79

Inspired on the journey by the music of Giuseppe Mango

There is no greater agony than
Bearing an untold story inside you.

                                    -Maya Angelou

Prologue

Anyone who says that time will lessen the deep-rooted pain in one's soul, lies. Those who preach patience and perseverance do so for their own peace of mind. Their words are a cruel excuse, a mere ploy allowing them to step back from the circle of plague of one who is damned, lest they be tainted by the misery apparent to all who gaze in. These were the thoughts that consumed my mind as I stood at the end of the Manhattan Beach pier. I searched the coastline northward a few miles toward Los Angeles International Airport (LAX), the home of my beloved airline. There was a brisk chill in the air that November morning in 1986. Winter had come early.

They called me a hero. A miracle. I became the poster child for the airline and eventually, the target of the angry. You see, I had the good fortune and the bad fortune to survive.

"Bury it away," my own mother constantly urged. "Just don't think of it."

"That's fine for everyone else," I whispered to no one and everyone. They, the entire world, were safely outside the grasp of this vicious anxiety that continually tightened its grip on me, crushing my hopes and dreams. Its source was the first thing I thought of the moment I awakened on any given morning. Its agony was my last companion at night, always engaging to rob me of badly needed sleep, delighting in my imprisonment of relentless taunts.

Suddenly, I spotted an aircraft soaring skyward just seconds after take-off from LAX. It was a Boeing 747. It was soon followed by a 737. I was very familiar with the characteristics of that aircraft. I was a certified Flight Attendant, a professional crewmember of my airline, one who saw to the safety and well-being of my assigned passengers. These were the golden days of aviation travel, pre 9/11, when a company identification badge and a gentle smile afforded a well-respected crew-member undeterred access from the employee parking lot, aboard the company crew bus, straight to the terminal building and appropriate departure gate. There, an unsold comfortable seat would be offered to an off-duty employee.

My hands firmly gripped the metal railing of the pier as my anxiety grew. Then a McDonnell-Douglas DC-10 shot into the sky. I focused in on its large red logo, the same trademark was planted in the center of my precious flight wings. I would be boarding such an aircraft later this night, bound for Minneapolis, (MSP). I could stand it no more. I was intent on ending my despicable dilemma. I was a trusted associate of my airline; my true intent would have been unthinkable. Now, unexpectedly, this posed a *big* problem.

"Forget about it." My sweet mother's voice filled my head once more.

"Don't you think I would if I could, Mom?"

Everyone around me desired that this wicked quandary be controlled like a light switch, as if one could just turn the torment off. The psychosis convinced me that the rest of the universe believed I wished to embrace the ungodly pain and suffering. Like some masochist the emptiness became my new-found love. The malignant tumor in my soul denied me the ability to rationalize. The need for survival created the set of skills I needed to become a master of pantomime. No matter how grueling the anguish became, the smile would not fade, the consequences be damned.

God was to blame, leaving me to do a job *He* should have taken care of that dreadful Halloween morning so long ago. The airline, the governments in all their hypocrisies, and all the corrupt little assholes looking to make a fast buck on the misfortune of others – they all shared in this hideous fiasco.

"How in the hell did I allow myself to be reduced to such a level of disdain?" I asked myself. I slowly gathered my emotions and tried to recall the pathway, the people and events that had led me to this miserable point in my life. I recollected the years. God, I so enjoyed the thrill of flying. I drifted back in time to the day I entered the company's headquarters, the executive offices on Avion Drive, at LAX.

Muerto: Death himself. A common element in culture and history personified in male form. He may cause the victim's death by coming to collect him. One may hold onto life by avoiding Muerto's visit, or by fending him off with bribery or tricks.

Part I
Earning My Wings

Chapter I

It was a more simple time, the 1970's. The nation was healing from the hangovers of Vietnam, Watergate and the oil crisis. An unknown peanut farmer from Georgia was hailed as a breath of fresh air in his bid to capture the White House. Freddie Mercury and Queen were rising strong on the rock music scene and The Sex Pistols sang of anarchy in the U.K.

The employment department of the Los Angeles based airline was having a busy season. With the oil crisis receding, both business and commerce in general could focus on the future. Cheaper oil meant cheaper airfares. Cheaper fares meant more passengers and more money with which to purchase cheaper jet fuel. This meant a profit which led to the purchase of more aircraft and that required a need to hire and train new recruits as flight crews.

What had primarily been accepted as a "woman's job" prior to 1973 was now, by the opinion of the Supreme Court, being pushed by the aviation human resource offices as a career. "Stewardess" was no longer an acceptable term. "Flight Attendant" was the phrase of this new age for aviation. With strong federal government regulations in place at that time, the future looked bright indeed. The industry seemed to reconsider its initial push for the male candidate by concentrating on the professional attributes of the vocation. It had become evident that there had been a shift midstream to change the image of flight crews as a whole.

Arriving in the early morning at the executive offices, I signed in and was ushered into a large room with the other eligible candidates. We were advised to sit on one of the many basic black office chairs, with partial tabletop: the type one might find at a community college. They were all arranged in neat equally spaced rows. Some overly anxious prospects quickly moved to the front of each aisle. To these young individuals, this was more an audition than an interview for a job. The well-dressed young men and women were of a variety of backgrounds, ethnically and economically. A fashion model aura seemed to glow in all of them.

An office worker passed out company employment applications. I looked down at the request for the names of the schools I had attended. As I emerged myself into the petition for details I reflected on my past, my upbringing, and the events that led me down the road to this day, this airline. I thought of my parochial journey.

I spent nine years attending Our Lady of the Rosary of Talpa School learning from the priests and nuns the morals and faith of my family, my heritage. Along with that, at a great sacrifice to my parents, I studied four more years at a prestigious all-boys Catholic high school. Then there was college, all in the hopes of my parents that I would make something of my life, have better opportunities than what was presented to them. How would I ever find the words to tell these two hard-working people that all their sacrifice and all the education was so I could seek a position as a flight attendant.

My mother, Alicia, was initially a stay-at-home wife, as were most Hispanic women of that time. Later, when we were older, she became a valued sales associate for J.C. Penney. Her first duty was always to the children, the family. I was the second of three siblings. I had an older brother, Miguel, and a younger sister, Alicia Jr. My father, Reynaldo, had come out of World War II taking full advantage of the veterans' education benefits offered to those who served. They struggled greatly in the beginning, my father doing whatever it took during the day and studying in the evenings trying to get ahead. His fortitude paid off as he rose to the position of an esteemed Engineer with Lockheed Aircraft Company, working in their highly secretive Skunk Works Program in Burbank, California. Once firmly established at Lockheed, my father made many attempts to tempt my mother to consider the possibility of relocating the family outside the boundaries of East Los Angeles. He suggested we move to the more suburban neighborhoods in the San Fernando Valley, closer to his work. My mother firmly resisted, opting to remain in the only way of life she knew, where she was comfortable.

Like my father, I too had studied Mathematics, Physics and Chemistry and was enriched by the high quality of education made possible by the sweat of my parents' hard work. The result of this, in their minds, was their belief that I would embrace an occupation of importance, something they could be proud of. Once established in such a profession I was expected to remain in the Southern California arena, stay close to the family, perhaps marry a local Hispanic girl -- preferably one from a family they were familiar with, one they had developed years of friendship with. I would have none of it.

The first real indication that I was dead set upon another path came when I was a teenager. My brother Miguel, who was always called Mike, had made the decision that many young Hispanic men make after high school. He joined the military, the Air Force to be exact. Although his enlistment was right at the height of the Vietnam conflict, the family was much relieved to learn that he was to be stationed at Torrejón Air Base, just outside Madrid, Spain. I recall my mother in joyous prayers to all the many statues of the saints that were displayed throughout the house. I was surely happy that Mike did not have to go to Nam but I also saw a bigger picture. There was a dream I always had since childhood, an ambition to travel, venturing out into the glorious world. I was determined to escape my surroundings. I felt my excellence in athletics and studies would guarantee my parent's approval in traveling abroad to visit my brother in Spain but NO!

"Why can't you stay with your own kind?" My mother's voice pleaded. That is when I realized that my mother's reluctance to move from the neighborhood was not so much a matter of dealing with distance but a real fear of other cultures. Growing up in a time of segregation in Los Angeles County, there were few opportunities for either my mother or father to intermingle with others of different races, religions or lifestyles. This revelation gave me a better understanding of my parents. I approached my father, who sternly dictated the more logical argument of economics.

"Do you know how much such a trip would cost, and who is going to pay for it?" But I was resolute; I was not going to lose this chance. Then along came Stephanie Rhinehardt.

East Los Angeles Travel Agency was but a few blocks from the family home. I figured that every proposed trip had to have a starting point. I tried to develop a plan for an overseas venture. Stephanie, a tall blond woman from Germany was the proprietor. Her thick German accent was unusual for that part of town, but she had built a strong clientele who trusted her for all their travel arrangements. I would speculate that ninety percent of her business was in arranging trips to Mexico or other Latin countries, but her knowledge and experience covered the globe.

I was an adolescent of my time and surroundings. I studied in an advanced curriculum at my parochial high school but when it came to international travel, I was truly naive. I explained my dilemma to a very understanding Stephanie.

"I wish to go to Madrid and at the very lowest, rock bottom cost. Can you help me?" I was about to get a lesson in travel 101.

"Do you have a passport?" The smiling German woman asked.

"A passport?" It never occurred to me that such a document was needed when traveling to another country.

"Oh yes," the travel agent continued. "And you will have to be immunized also."

"Immunized?" I was stunned. "You mean shots?" Stephanie simply nodded. Gosh, I hated shots but at that time travel to Spain required the forms documenting that such inoculations had occurred. I don't know why but the knowledgeable German agent took pity on me. Perhaps she saw the resolve in me to see this trip through no matter the price. She became my teacher, a mentor in some ways. I believe she respected my drive, my curiosity to see the world outside East L.A. I made a dear friend that day and she went to work to help make my trip a reality.

I wrote my brother informing him of my great plan. After some time, I received a positive response. We determined that the following summer, when I was out of school, would be the best time. My excitement grew. The first obstacle to overcome was applying for a passport. Getting the primary documents, birth certificate and proper identification was no difficulty. The real problem was that I was a minor and I would require the consent of one of my parents. The possibility of accomplishing that goal continued to look bleak.

Stephanie came through tremendously, informing me that a flight to Paris and a train ride to Madrid would be the cheapest way to make it happen. The entire round trip would be under five hundred dollars. Yet, it might as well have been five thousand for someone without the funds. I resolved to work and beg if I had to. I was determined to get on that silver bird and fly away.

I continued to seek the blessing of my parents for my endeavor, but they were solidly against what they saw as just a fanciful fiasco by their disobedient teenage son. The months passed and I continued to make my plans with the aid of Stephanie. With continuous conversations my mother began to see my deep desire for this trip.

"Why don't you wait 'till your brother returns and then plan a trip with him," she recommended.

"No." I insisted. "He is there now. This is it; I go now or never." I was appealing to a mother's inner sense of her son. My father remained adamant.

"No!" He insisted. "No way, no how." As time went on he resisted even more. Hispanic children do not defy the wishes of their father. That's the way it had been and that is what he expected, total submission to his will.

Finally, there was a break several weeks prior to the planned departure date. My mother relented without consulting my father. She signed the needed document of consent for my passport. We both immediately agreed to keep the information from my father until the proper time. I endured the needed inoculations and paid Stephanie to the penny for the airfare and train tickets. Word was sent to my brother of the date and time of my arrival in Madrid.

Later I returned home to find my father in a rage. I knew that he must have found out I was going. My mother reasoned with him as much as possible, but he would have nothing of it. He felt betrayed and held my mother accountable. For several days he would not speak to us but one night after supper, there was a phone call for him. It was an old family friend, making a social call. Such conversations at the time always included an inquiry as to how Mike was doing since he was so far away from home.

"Well you know," my father began to say. "Eddy is leaving next week for Madrid to see his brother." I was shocked as he uttered the words. There was even a positive tone to his voice. This man was suddenly proud of my decision? I thanked him in my heart as I was relieved and grateful. Now I knew that my instincts were correct. This trip was the right thing to do at this pivotal point in my young life. I was home free, or so I thought. The next day the news on the television reported an outbreak of cholera in a small town in northern Spain. Anyone traveling to that country would now require additional inoculations against this very contagious and deadly disease. I gritted my teeth and endured the painful shots just days prior my departure.

On a beautiful summer morning in the L.A. basin, I took a ride down the Santa Monica Freeway on what was to be my first visit (but certainly not my last) to Los Angeles International Airport. Because I spent almost all my money on the airfare and train ticket, I was leaving for an extended stay through France and Spain with a total of ninety dollars in my pocket. But I couldn't care less. I was certain that Mike would take good care of me because that's what brothers do for each other. As a teenager traveling solo, I was about to take my first ride in an airplane. I left my tearful mother at the gate as I boarded a Pan American Airways Boeing 747 jumbo jet. I gawked and wondered with amazement at every aspect of the spaceship that would transport me halfway across the world. A great new sensation filled my being. I did not realize it at that moment, but I had been bitten by the travel bug. I felt a rush of elation as the mighty craft lifted off over the Pacific, turning north toward the pole and on to Paris.

In the employment office of the airline on Avion Dr., I had just completed a written exam. This was monitored by a well-dressed, professional woman I assumed was the office manager who had been assessing all of us every minute we were in her presence. I was overcome with a feeling of confidence when I was told I had passed. I felt very fortunate when I was selected as one of a few who were asked to wait in another smaller room, which seemed like some type of first-aid station. We were informed that we each would be weighed and have our height measured. At that time the airline industry had strict weight limits. While it was essential that one be fit in case of possible emergencies, some flight attendants believed the weight/height issue was just a tool used by the airline to conform to their vision of a perfect crewmember.

The ideal weight for each perspective trainee was determined by a calculation involving one's height. No one was ever told how the company settled on the accepted guidelines, but it was a rule that put the fear of God into the person who presently stood on the medical black and white scale. Tears flowed down the cheeks of an auburn-haired girl who, to her great disappointment, registered two pounds over her designated limit. She was not plump nor gave the appearance of needing to slim down. At that moment I was introduced to the airline culture. Its regulations manifested complete dominance. Rules were rules and the young girl was informed in a cordial manner "better luck next time."

"You're next Mister...Valenciana," the office lady hesitated in pronouncing my family name. I hopped upon the scale as she read the specifics on my sheet. She nodded as she began to extend the handle of the scale. My height was measured at 5'8". At that stature my maximum weight was placed at 175 pounds. I began to worry. She slid the weight along the vertical unit until it balanced perfectly. "Let's see, you're one-seventy-three," she stated in a somewhat disappointing manner.

"Give me one second," I requested. I jumped off the scale and removed my suit jacket and when I turned to face of my evaluator, her mouth dropped open in surprise. Wearing a short sleeve dress shirt, I could see I had made my point. Sure, I was just two pounds shy of the maximum weight, but I carried a slim waistline and a low percentage of body fat. This was the result of years of sports and weight training.

"You know, if you were to be hired there is a weight check each and every month for flight attendants." I would soon learn that violating the weight restriction meant automatic suspension and removal from the flight line for a month. "Would you be able to maintain the weight?"

"Ma'am, I assure you, I'm in control of it. Also," I added, "Think of the advantage in the rare case of an emergency inflight." How unknowingly prophetic I was being. She nodded in agreement.

Once the other candidates had completed their turn on the scale, they were graciously thanked for coming and informed that they would be contacted soon concerning the airline's decision. I naively followed the other candidates and began to exit when the kind office manager asked me to remain.

"Valenciana? Is that Italian?"

"Spanish," I responded. She again glanced at my application. She spoke as she read the details.

"Ethnicity, Hispanic. Have a seat Mr. Valenciana and someone will be with you very soon." I could hardly maintain my excitement. The possibility floored me. I relished the opportunity of having the ability to travel the world as a crewmember of a respected company. The deco-style room displayed hanging posters and photos reflecting the airline's long and esteemed history. First mail service from Los Angeles, circa 1927, a photo revealed. There was a colorful poster boasting the upcoming anniversary of the company with the magnificent McDonnell Douglas DC-10 Spaceship displayed proudly in all its glory, right in the center.

"There is my magic carpet." But now I would have to make it happen.

"Edmundo Valenciana," a call rang out. I looked up at the sprite blonde who got my name wrong. I quickly rose and replied.

"Eduardo, it's pronounced E-d-u-a-r-d-o." I made sure to throw in the Latin accent in my pronunciation. I firmly rolled the "R". In an instant she widened her eyes and gave a big smile. I sensed her acceptance. I read her thoughts.

"Yes, Hispanic." I stepped forward and was ushered into her office, thinking back to a decision made by my mother who, along with my siblings, had registered our legal names in Spanish. Eduardo is who I was christened, although I preferred Eddy.

"Why do you want to be a flight attendant Eduardo?" Ah, here it was, the all-determining question.

"I truly enjoy assisting people. I would relish the chance at making sure our passengers received the best flying experience they deserved." It was the right answer for that moment, place and time. She asked about my background, where was I raised?

Although Boyle Heights is not far from LAX, more than likely few flight crews would ever intentionally seek it out. Unless the crew member was of Hispanic heritage and had family ties like I did, there would be no reason they would venture into our neighborhood. The exceptions were the restaurants. Where better to find the best Mexican food but in a town that is 98% Hispanic?

The blond interviewer seemed pleased. My education was in private Catholic schools. My base support was a strong family structure, fifth-generation Mexican American, salt of the earth.

"Would you be willing to trim your mustache a little?" she asked. "Trim your hair some?"
I assured her that I absolutely would. I told her I would be committed to do whatever was required in maintaining the highest standards, dedicating my loyalty to this airline." In that last part of that statement I vowed to remain steadfast. I left the executive offices in a gleeful mood. A victory on one side also produced an obstacle on the other. I would have to explain my choice to my parents, my family. I wasn't sure they'd be as happy as I was.

I was beaming with pride while driving through Los Angeles' freeway system. I exited at 4th Street in Boyle Heights, the place of my birth. The multicolored billboards not found anywhere else in the Southern California basin advertised the products most desirable to the Hispanic culture, many written in Spanish. Many homes throughout the neighborhood displayed the flag of Mexico together with the flag of the United States. It is a known fact that there have been a multitude of Mexican American recipients of the Medal of Honor in the history of military service of the United States. There is no doubt of the population's commitment to our nation, yet they also honor the country of their ancestors. I returned home to await my start date of my new career.

It greatly surprised me that I had been assigned to a flight attendant training class that was starting so soon after I was offered a position. The process, I'd heard from others, was usually much longer throughout the industry, though I was not complaining. My parents, as it turned out, were really not surprised by my choice but I could sense that becoming a lawyer, a dentist even a position with the county would have been preferable. At that time "Flight Attendant" was still registering in their minds as "stewardess."

By the time I began training, I had traveled to many foreign countries since that first flight as a teenager. My father took to calling me "the wandering gypsy." And so with my parent's semi-blessing I traveled to the Airport Park Hotel in Inglewood, California on the day the trainees were required to report. We would be housed there during the scheduled six-week training period. I checked in, was assigned a room and told that the company bus to the first day of class would depart the facility in the morning at 7:30 A.M. with or without me.

That morning I got my first glance of fellow classmates, hopefully soon to be fellow crewmates. All were bright, energetic young men and women who would represent "our" airline. I also recognized there was a definite ethnic balance.

"Let's see," I thought to myself on the ten-minute ride to the training center at LAX. "There are two African-Americans, one Asian-American, fifteen Anglo-Americans and one Hispanic, me." I discovered that in later training classes there were candidates who had interviewed months before I had but had their training dates delayed. It became obvious that each class was intended to contain the same type of ethnic balance. Maybe that sprite, little blond in HR that hired me really did need a Hispanic that fateful day. I was just happy to be there.

Flight attendant training would become one of the most cherished periods of my life. Class "2" of that year's program brought together many faces and personalities from many locations and cultures. By the end of the six-week training period, I would be blessed with bonds of friendship that would remain with me always.

We all were aware that acceptance as a trainee was no guarantee of a position with the company. There were classes to attend, exams to pass and more scrutinizing by the management of the airline. If all tests were satisfactorily completed then there would come the promise of a graduation ceremony, presentation of my flight wings and I would become a federally certified F/A.

They would then present me with a ticket to one of the yet-to-be-determined "base" cities in the airline's system for a six-month-on-the-job probationary period. During that time, an F/A could be terminated for any reason.

Introductions were exchanged on the bus ride as the new kids grinned with excitement. Arriving at the Avion Drive offices, I stood to exit the bus when a young man sitting a couple of rows behind approached me.

"Man, you're built like a brick shit house!" You could say I liked Kyle Tillman from the start. He was a muscular, athletic individual from the Midwest. He had attended a prestigious Big Ten school and his chalky-white skin was a complete contrast to my olive complexion. Kyle and I bonded quickly and shared our hopes and concerns throughout the stressful training period

On the first day, the "children" were ushered into the company's "Champagne Room." Formal introductions were made by each of us and our instructors. There were papers to read and sign. Class material was issued and upon opening the "Flight Attendant Manual," I was enlightened as to what was expected of me. It immediately informed me that my life was no longer just mine.

Kyle had taken the desk next to me and we both showed signs of concern as we briefly glanced through the manual. A regulation entitled "Flight Attendant Conduct While in Uniform," laid down the law. I had attended Catholic school for over thirteen years and this seemed no different. If any of the trainees objected to what they were reading it was not made evident. The students all seemed as clean and innocent as the company's image. One thought filled our minds: we all had come too far to screw up now.

Every weekday morning, we pupils would promptly rise at 6 A.M. and dress ourselves with our regulation pants, regulation ties and regulation smiles. From the start it became clear that Class 2 had been reduced to children attending their first day of kindergarten. That bus to the company's headquarters was always on time and the students were expected to be also. Missing the bus was a sure sign to management of future problems.

"MIA, is the airport code for Miami."

"Hurray! Toddlers must learn to walk before they can run," I thought. And so it was with us that first day in memorizing city airport codes. Any second grader could have mastered the exercise. Each correct answer was followed by jubilation and a show of tremendous pride by the person giving the answer. The reality was that each new associate knew that failure in a discipline that even a parrot could master could get you booted out. I went along with the program.

"SEA is Seattle,"

"Good job, Eddy," the raven-haired instructor commented. The kiddies of Class 2 studied those codes as if their lives depended upon it. One of our four instructors at any time might throw out three letters to challenge our memories and immediately hands would shoot into the air.

"LAS is Las Vegas," proclaimed a self-assured respondent. It was Janey, a snob of a lady from Northern California. She made it clear that she had all the answers. Even though she felt the disdain of most of the class, Kyle and I knew we would have to play it cool when in her presence. She sought to be the teacher's pet and certainly would be willing to inform them of any violations of the numerous restrictions that had been placed on us. The most obvious and the one Kyle and I intended to test was our nightly curfew. A good flight attendant takes full advantage of getting the proper amount of rest on a layover, so as to perform to the highest standards during the next day's duties, or something of that nature. Kyle and I knew instantly that Janey would have taken great pleasure in seeing these flyboys bounced out of the program.

An obvious addition to complete our motley band was a freckled face, red-haired, saucy fellow from Minnesota, Mark Matsen. Four-eyed and white skinned, he even made Kyle look tanned. Mr. Matsen displayed a wit about him that had the class in stitches. The exception, of course, was Janey who saw our antics as mere childish pranks.

"Why did you join the airlines?" Mark asked me one early morning. I hesitated, uneasy about whether he was being serious or setting me up for one of his now familiar pranks. To get to this point, every F/A candidate knew the reason like a catechism. I pondered then said, "I enjoy helping people." I gave the standard interview response. My face registered no reaction as my eyes stared locked into the impish face of my friend. "Why did you join?" I countered. There was a long silence.

"Why the fuck do you think?" he replied. "So I can get free flights." We paused in minor shock at his words then broke into laughter. Hilarious but true. We reminisced later that evening with Kyle over a couple of cold beers, which were strictly forbidden during the training period.

"The flight attendant is responsible for the passenger's comfort, welfare and safety, performing all cabin services in accordance with company policies and procedures, as specified in the Flight Attendant Manual." So read our Job Responsibility. Comfort and welfare were obvious to me, but the word "safety" seemed to cause confusion. In classroom conversation, it was an accepted fact that if anything seriously went wrong on the aircraft while as a crewmember, and it "went down," safety would be irrelevant. Nevertheless, all of the kiddies in Class 2 were anxious to view the films the company kept on file for the emergency procedures training. Watching those films was a taste of reality. Although classes on uniform regulations and food service had been received and performed by rote, Emergency Procedures training was dead-serious and some of it was in living color.

A soon-to-be-familiar sight of twisted metal and charred seats jumped right off the screen. Almost like a taunt, the pictures challenged us in an effort to destroy our dreams.

"So, you want to fly for free?" The metal carnage could not easily be dismissed. I gazed over at Kyle and could see that the broken fuselage of an airline embedded in a forest somewhere had struck him. Even Mike was made speechless, a rare occurrence indeed.

"What were the odds?" My final reaction was just like every other mind in the room. "It will not happen to me. Someone else maybe, but not me." Then there was the fire. Always the fire. So you're lucky enough to survive the initial impact, rarely in one piece, but if you did you most likely won't escape the fire. Remember, a jumbo jet essentially is a flying bomb. And if the unthinkable happens on take-off, like some have in the past, it's instant incineration.

Mari was our feisty little instructor. A flight attendant for over ten years herself, dark hair and angelic features, she was dead-serious while teaching Emergency Procedures. Her little nostrils would flare open in accompaniment with her piercing eyes as she related the gravity of the material she was preaching.

"If the oxygen bottle is not properly stored on the aircraft it could become a deadly M-I-S-S-I-L-E, missile in flight during an emergency." She presented material of what was left of a Southern Airlines jet after falling from the sky as a result of a terrible storm. We all lied to ourselves after viewing the films and photos made available to us by Mari. It was the only way to keep the dreaded possibilities at bay.

Weather. That was one issue flight attendant training could do very little about. Turbulence became a new word in my life's vocabulary. There was light, moderate and severe turbulence. Once on the flight line reality re-teaches you what you thought you learned in training. When the pilot informs the passengers that we are experiencing light turbulence he really means moderate. When he mentions the word moderate, he really means severe. The worse scenario is reserved for when the captain asks the F/A's to remain strapped in their jumpseats for the remainder of the flight. The procedure is to sugarcoat the seriousness of any intense situation. As a crewmember you really do not want the passengers to know what you know and there is a legitimate reason for that.

"No matter what, you must survive." The command created a chill running right up our spines. Mari continued. "If *you* survive such an incident, many others will have a better chance of surviving." That was the real reason for our existence. I knew that if that awful day came when I found myself in the cauldron of such a chaotic mess, I had to make it through. This training experience, Mari's flaring little nostrils and all, would help me be the means by which others could be saved. That made all the jokes and jests seem infantile. I would be on the plane so others could live. Somehow in between the skepticism, I listened. In retrospect, Mari's persistence paid off on my behalf. I owe her a great debt.

"The P.A. system is to be used on the aircraft to communicate accurate information," so regulation dictated. In the "real world," one would hear various interpretations of such celebrities as Donald Duck, Richard Nixon and John Wayne in English and Spanish. During one training session on the DC-10, two of our fellow classmates decided to emulate the voice and setting of an episode of the Twilight Zone. Kyle and I opted to take the service elevator to the lower galley where our instructor was conducting a serious discussion and explanation of its function.

"Gaze upon one Mister Otto Beamer, a little man of little consequence." For those of us in the lower belly of the craft it was as if Rod Serling, the creator of the historic popular show, was now in command of the massive jumbo jet. The look on the face of our business-oriented teacher was one of astounded shock. Yet, from a different station above in the main cabin another member of our scalawag pupils picked up where the first impudent young man left off.

"Mr. Beamer has just boarded an unfamiliar DC-10 Spaceship bound for a uniquely unconventional destination we call the Twilight Zone." The instructor had enough. Her face reddened with anger. She turned and quickly hurried into the service elevator and up to the main cabin. Kyle Tillman broke into hilarious laughter as the other students in the lower galley feared getting the boot. The two pranksters were verbally reprimanded and given a stern warning, but even this did not deter the mischief makers from seizing the P.A. system at every chance. One often fantasized having a captive audience on the DC-10.

No matter how hard I tried to enjoy myself in the various activities in the classroom I could sense a seriousness, a shadow on my soul when the safety issues were continually brought to the forefront. Regulation after regulation dictated your actions. Care and tools were available for every conceivable situation except one: the procedure for an emergency landing with no time to prepare.

"Grab ankles and stay down until the plane stops," Mari's persistent voice rang out. If one were lucky enough to run this gauntlet of horrors and come out alive there would be more regulations. There was Regulation 8.12-6: *Do not make any statements to the press concerning the probable cause of the accident.* Public Relations releases this information. It reinforced the realization that I was expected to be a company man to the end. I wondered out loud why these words seemed to continue to nag at me. Mari was efficient at her task, handing us special safety cards inscribed with the instructions on assessing the situation after an emergency landing. Mark took one such card and inscribed his own philosophy on the subject that seemed more realistic concerning the physics involved in such an event. He turned and flashed the content of his perceived judgment concerning a fatal crash.

"Get your own ass out," the message read.

After reviewing the various potential accidents, it became evident to me that surviving in such a critical situation was similar to enduring the environment I grew up in -- the Eastside. One had to use common sense and sharpen one's skills.

By day, our trio were personified gentlemen, but by evening the nightlife that surrounded LAX became our playground. The age of disco and such clubs were the rage after hours in the basin of the City of the Angels. At many a sunrise, the taxis brought the intoxicated cadets back to their dormitory. Kyle and I usually accepted the task of carrying the lightweights through the kitchen entrance past the smiling hotel help and up the stairs to avoid any company spies sent to check up on the mischievous children.

The introduction of males to a workplace that had been exclusively female for half a century brought about interesting situations. The feminist movement of the late sixties was being played out in reverse now. The boys would never have to experience the brief terror of enduring moderate turbulence in high heels. While housed overnight in a major city on layover, I was not hesitant to leave the safety of the hotel to partake of the local culture. The ladies rightfully had to be more careful. "All the women you want, a decent salary and free travel. It beats working for a living," roared Mark with laughter. With a little boyish grin and a flattering word, Mark, Kyle and I got away with murder during that training period. One could say that our actions away from class were far less than professional. Fortunately, our trio's conduct was never looked upon as anything more than boyish behavior by our superiors. We assumed they were not fully aware of the depth of our rogue antics. If there had been a question concerning our qualifications it was quickly swept away by the quality of our performance in class. The high scores we achieved on the federal and company exams were solid testimony to our commitment.

I also began to recognize another development that quality and professionalism are aspects of an airline culture, but warmth, understanding and true compassion are bonuses, rarely found in the corporate world. The people of the airline, the everyday workers from crews, mechanics, office people to ship cleaners, it was evident that this was as good as it gets in the industry. I truly had been permitted to be an employee of a great company. I was very grateful for the opportunity.

The Airport Park Hotel, our temporary home, had an efficient enough weight room. Right after the company bus returned us at the end of a class day, I would seek the solace of the gym.

"Turn negative energy into positive." My high school coach taught me a very basic and logical lesson. "Keep a clean and healthy diet," he always advised. That part was always much more difficult to maintain. The headquarters of the airline contained a decent cafeteria that all the employees enjoyed, including the new hires. Being two pounds shy of my maximum weight limit haunted me. I was having too much fun and eating too much junk. Although I did not look over-weight, I was sure I was right at my maximum and would be weighed again before being fitted for my F/A uniform. Unfortunately, like anything one becomes obsessed with, there were days of great discipline and days of total failure.

Back in the classroom Mari introduced us to the possibility of our worse fears. There had been a massive airline disaster some years prior on the runway at the main airport on the Spanish territory of the Canary Islands. Fog was a dreaded obstacle for any aviator. A fateful decision by one of the most respected captains of KLM, the Dutch based airline, was a major contributing factor. The Cockpit Voice Recorder, otherwise known by the public as the "black box," revealed his impatience. With zero visibility and without final clearance from the tower, he took the Boeing 747, filled to the max with passengers and proceeded down a fog-shrouded runway. It remained unclear at that time whether he realized that a Pan American Airways 747 had just landed and was taxiing on the same runway heading to turn off to its assigned gate. The photos screamed it out loud. Over five hundred perished in the impact and inferno that followed. I got lost in the minor details. There were rows of blackened seats. An emergency procedure placard lay on the foam-filled tarmac. There was a suitcase here, a shoe there, and metal contorted by massive forces seared inside and out. Then there were the bodies, some covered some not. Some whole, some not.

"Eddy, are you okay?" Mari snapped. Perhaps she noticed I looked mesmerized.

"You know, I have not felt well since breakfast," I stated.

"Maybe you should go back to the hotel," she suggested. Having had enough time in the presence of Death, I jumped at the opportunity to play hooky.

"I don't know if I can make it back to the hotel," I played the part. "Perhaps Mark can come back with me?" Mark did not bat an eye. He picked up on the deception.

"I'll see he gets back," he retorted. The company bus was brought to the main entrance, we boarded, and the charade was continued until it dropped us off. "What's up?" Mark asked. A huge grin appeared on his face.

"I'm gonna give you a personal tour of the scenic highlights of Los Angeles," I told the freckled-face boy from the land of ten-thousand lakes. We broke out in laughter. The prankster from Minnesota was up for whatever shenanigans I had in store. Now, when anyone imagines the sites a visitor to Southern California would wish to see, Disneyland certainly comes to mind. The Hollywood Bowl, Grauman's Chinese Theater and the Sunset Strip are other popular sights to be visited. I, on the other hand, had a completely different itinerary in mind for my red-haired compatriot in mischief. Mark was going to experience the majestic environment that is East Los Angeles. Since I was in my hometown, I was one of the few trainees who had the availability of a motor vehicle. Like two impish children playing hooky from elementary school, we gleefully zoomed onto the intertwined system of freeways. Boyle Heights and Whittier Blvd. is where the center of the Mexican American community congregated. Mark's eyes widened with amazement. He was all at once transported into some distant land, a completely different world. Many residents were black-haired, dark-skinned and alien in their features and mannerisms. Beer, and lots of it, was first on the agenda of our unique personal tour.

The "Par-a-Dice" club is a hole in the wall bar on Atlantic Blvd. near where my parents lived. Its small billboard sign was truly unique: the artistic rendering of the biblical Garden of Eden, book-ended by a pair of dice revealing 'snake eyes.' The graphic was amateurish at best. Some people may have called the establishment a dive. I chose to look at it more as being a place with its own flavor.

It would have been a good bet to say that Mark Matsen might find himself out of his comfort zone. The mariachi music blared as I opened the door. The bar was crowded for an early afternoon with many individuals wearing the typical white cowboy hat worn by the hard-working migrant society.

"Buenas tardes," I greeted. Several of those drinking at the bar turned their heads slightly as they focused in on my face without any reaction. But a split moment later their heads swung around again, this time with their eyes wide in amazement. They caught a glimpse of Mark.

"Weeno diiaaas." The smiling white boy stated. Oh God, was I making a big mistake? There had been some local men playing pool when we entered but now the entire premises became motionless and the air filled with dead silence. Like an episode out of the Twilight Zone, where all the inhabitants are frozen except the primary characters, I began to worry. I instantly moved about as though there was absolutely nothing wrong. Silently, I worried that we would be knifed and thrown out the back into the desolate alley.

"Dos cervezas Mexicanas, Bohemia por favor," I requested calmly. We slowly approached the counter. One of the young campesinos (Native Latin-American laborers) sitting at the bar continued to stare intensely after the others had slowly returned to their prior activities. I could read his mind. "What's this gringo doing here?" I quickly approached the stern, weary young man and nodded towards Mark saying, "Está bien'. He's good." I quickly turned my attention to the man behind the bar, "Otra cerveza para mi amigo aquí," referring to the campesino.

Conversation slowly started up again. I became worried that possibly they might think we were policemen, since we were still dressed in our regulation trainee attire, dress slacks, shirt and tie. The majority of the patrons of the club wore cowboy boots, tapered jeans, big belt buckles, buttoned down long sleeve work shirts and those white hats. The exception was the bartender. He had a lime green polo shirt with a name embroidered on the left side of his chest. The two wannabe F/A's took a seat at the far end of the bar. Mark was amazed. The decor, the mariachi sounds and the establishment's customers, the entire setting blew his mind.

Initially, we were pretty much isolated from the rest of the patrons at one end, but as time went on the atmosphere became more relaxed. Suddenly, Mark nearly fell off his stool and displayed a strained look. My heart jumped wondering if there was some immediate threat I was not aware of. The black-rimmed glasses came off his face. He quickly cleaned them and put them back on and stared again.

"Look," he pointed. We are being served by Jesus himself!"

"What?" I was confused.

"Eddy, the bartender's name is Jesus."

"No Mark, it's *Jesús,* pronounced (hay-soos)," I said emphasizing the Latin accent. "There are a million guys around with that name." The campesinos became alerted by my classmate's animated behavior and wanted to know what the white boy was raving about? I explained the situation to them, and they began to laugh. Words like "tonto" and "pendejo" popped out but there was no choler behind the comments, only jest. Mark became curious as to why this guy had the name Jesus? There were a few guys there that spoke some English and graciously engaged in small talk with the fair-skinned stranger. With time it grew to real conversation. "Look at him work the room," I stated to myself. Mark was showcasing his charismatic personality and winning these tough guys over. Soon there was no concern whatsoever that there was a gringo amongst them. I could see why the airline believed Mark would be an asset.

One Bohemia came and went, another was served. The blaring sound of the mariachi trumpets echoed through the smoke-filled room. With the influence of the beer, Mark joyfully tried to join in on the lyrics of the music. I was not sure at this stage of the visit whether he knew that the words were in Spanish. He really didn't seem to care as he mimicked what he thought were close enough sounds. He shot pool with a few of the guys, continually called the man behind the bar Jesus (the English version) and emphasized it with a sense of reverence. The jester of F/A training Class 2 was having a good time.

When it came time to leave there were sincere invitations from the frequenters of the establishment to return anytime and soon. Mark had developed a special interaction with one crusty old "veterano" who soon was treating the white boy from the North as an adopted son. The man's leathery skin and dark complexion spoke of a life of hard work in the hot sun. Taking me aside as we were departing, he informed me in Spanish that the reason for the uneasiness upon our arrival was not due so much to my friend's ethnicity. Because of our professional attire the crowd inside believed we were agents of the immigration department. I chuckled and understood very clearly what he meant. I didn't see any reason to tell Mark about the revelation. I turned to him as I unlocked the door to the car.

"Now you can say you've been to the Par-a-Dice Club." He snickered like a little girl.

"And I got to meet Jesus," he insisted. From that point on the saucy fellow also acquired a taste for Mexican beer, Bohemia in particular.

Olvera Street in downtown Los Angeles is the city's historic representative of old California. I wasn't going to take Mark just to the shadier locations of the East Side; I wanted him to get a better understanding of my rich culture. Feeling hungry after the beers, we ate taquitos like nowhere else with their spicy green salsa and sampled a combination of additional tasty delights. The air was filled with delicate aromas. Enchiladas verde, carnitas, pollo con mole were some of the dishes sampled for the first time by my excited companion. He particularly relished the sweetness of Pan Mexicano (Mexican sweet bread) for dessert. Once done filling our stomachs, guilt due to my ever-mindful F/A weight limit persisted. I thought to ignore it by dashing along the cobblestone thoroughfare alongside Mark, amusing ourselves by zigzagging through the various shops that lined the oldest street in Los Angeles. Leather goods were the specialty of one, while authentic and colorful sombreros, hats for all Hispanic occasions were neatly displayed at another. Multi-colored wrestling masks, like the popular "luchadores" of Mexico, hung in rows. There were piñatas in all shapes, colors and sizes for any festive occasion. Some stores had rosaries, religious medals and statues of every saint imaginable. At the old church in the plaza there was holy water for the faithful and an offer of redemption for those souls that were lost.

One shop that caught both our eyes was the one that was dedicated to "El Día de Los Muertos," (The Day of the Dead). It was filled with "calaveras," skulls of all sizes and made from every possible material thinkable. Skull stones, skull posters, skull rings, skull belts and even skull candy. Mark's initial reaction was to think that the display of such items was morbid. I tried to explain to my hooky-playing comrade that we Hispanics do not always see death as an abstract.

"We garner the greater image of Muerto, Death himself," I explained. "Being skeleton-like and sometimes referred to by other cultures as the Grim Reaper, the Spanish version plays a much more active role in the daily lives of the people, a life that is much more burdensome than we here in the States could ever know. Therefore, Death could always be near, perhaps just around the corner."

It was renowned Mexican author Octavio Paz who wrote:

"The word Death is not pronounced in Los Estados Unidos because it burns the lips. The Mexican in contrast is familiar with Death, jokes about it, caresses it, sleeps with it. It is one of his favorite toys and his most steadfast love, but at least it is not hidden away. He looks at it face to face, with impatience, disdain or irony."[1]

Mark became intrigued. I knew there probably were not many stores in Minnesota dedicated to the Day of the Dead. My friend wandered through the shop with greater interest after my explanation. The design of the various artwork projecting the theme, and Muerto (Death) in particular, was amazing and well done. We envisioned showing up to our F/A classes with a

---

1   Octavio Paz: Labyrinth of Solitude

skull-latent black t-shirt but determined that it would not go over very well.

"It's not regulation," Mark joked.

It was getting late and we would have to deal with rush-hour traffic to get back to the hotel.

"What is the Day of the Dead?" a somber Mark asked as we moved slowly along the Santa Monica Freeway.

"At the end of October, you have the three-day events of Halloween on the 31st, All Saints Day on November 1st and All Souls Day on the 2nd. Halloween is a day dedicated to the mischievous ways of Muerto, a celebration of the macabre, one might say. All Saints Day is more religious and honors those who have achieved the salvation of Heaven. All Souls Day is related to Purgatory and is the only day in Roman Catholic belief one can actually pray a soul out of its bondage. The latter two days were initiated into the celebration after the Spanish conquest of Mexico and today festivities and dates vary in different parts of the country depending on culture and location. In some areas the Day of The Dead covers a two-week period. In other parts it may be confined to three days. To the religious it provides hope in combating Muerto. "If you ever want to experience the bizarre and the macabre, Mexico City on Halloween is the place to be."

Suddenly, a rusty old two-tone car cut right into my lane on the freeway. I frantically blew my horn and drove around and pulled up beside the driver. I glared through the side window at a strange and defiant face that seemed not to understand what he had done. His wide sunken eyes locked with mine. They were void of compassion.

"You asshole," Mark interceded. I drove away shaken.

The traffic increased and we worried that our classmates would wonder why we were not at the hotel. I was supposed to be ill and Mark was supposed to be tending to me. We tried to think of some excuse to use if questioned. Mark suggested that we simply tell the truth.

"We'll tell them that we went to go have beers with Jesus," he stated as he grinned widely. I could only shake my head.

During the coming weeks, Class 2 continued to excel as we got the opportunity to get hands-on training in the various airships in the company's fleet. There were the Boeing 720, 727, 737 (dubbed Fat Albert by flight crews) and the DC-10. The "10" was used on longer flights over the Pacific, up to Alaska and down into Mexico. Each of the tri-jet's exit doors were classified with a number and letter referring to which side of the craft it was on. 1L and 1R were just aft of the cockpit at the head of first class. 2L and 2R were at the mid galley. 3L and 3R were adjacent to the wings. 4L and 4R were in the aft, with another small galley and lavatories. At mid-galley was an elevator that led down below to the galley where all meals were prepared and sent up the elevator to the main cabin in carts. Of course, at the end of class the elevator became a plaything for our amusement.

Nestled in between first class and the mid galley were a few rows of coach christened "El Segundo" by flight crews. El Segundo is a quaint little community that has the distinction of being bordered on the south by a huge Chevron refining facility, on the west by the Pacific Ocean and on the north by Los Angeles International Airport, thus isolating the town in its own unique section of the basin. Since the coach section was also isolated and many crew members lived in the community, it was dubbed El Segundo and the name stuck.

Kyle, Mark and I gathered in the aft section and were examining the jumpseats at 4L and 4R. Rear facing with its bottom folded up, it appeared as one solid unit.

"Doesn't look like much to save your ass if the plane goes down," Mark stated. "Why are all the jumpseats positioned to face aft?"

"Probably so the flight attendants can have a better view of the passengers," Kyle remarked.

"Not really," I said. "Actually, a person has a fifty-percent greater advantage of surviving a major crash if facing aft. (I had spoken to aviation experts in my former travels). The "G" forces involved in an aircraft incident do major damage to one's body, and by facing aft you lessen the chance of having your head snapped off." Mark and Kyle looked shocked.

"Why don't all the airlines have their passenger seats facing aft?" Mark inquired.

"Because it is not marketable," I explained.

"You know this shit and still want to do this job?" Kyle asked.

"I like to travel."

"How many types of fire extinguishers are available on the 10?" Our instructors tested us constantly. "Where are the life rafts on the 10 located? How do you secure and arm the door at 2R on the 10? What exit would the F/As at 4L and 4R direct the passengers to if their exits were blocked in an emergency evacuation?" We all studied the diagrams in our flight manuals over and over.

"Hey Kyle, what rows of seats are restricted from children or the elderly on the 727?" I tested my friend.

"Rows 14 and 16 are where the over-wing emergency exits are located."

As the weeks passed the material given by our instructors increased and so did their expectations. It was a common occurrence that classes would lose a trainee or two during the process due to poor performance or personal reasons, but as we celebrated our midpoint after three weeks, Class 2 remained intact.

Each student was assigned a pair of mechanic overalls with the airline logo on the front and massive lettering on the back. We wore them proudly as we practiced evacuation drills on the aircraft, jumping onto the inflatable slides attached at each exit. Some were detachable to use as flotation devices in the rare occasion of an emergency water landing, or "ditching." The swimming pool at the hotel was reserved and utilized one afternoon so that the new kids could practice these water procedures. After a while, as was predictable, we no longer wished to take the drills too seriously and eventually turned the experience into a pool party.

With the use of the hotel gym I was able to maintain my weight and was fitted for my flight attendant uniform with its various color schemes and mixed accessories. We all looked so elegant and dashing as we paraded about with pride. All that was missing was our flight wings. The second-to-last week of training we were advised that the following day we would be guests at the executive board room where we would meet and interact with administrators of the airline. Up to this time we may have passed inspection by the company's Flight Attendant Training Department but the powers-that-be wished to have a closer look at the new young faces that were to represent their airline. In an effort to prepare her students, Mari assigned each trainee the task of presenting before the administrators an oral history of each executive. I was presented with a folder. The contents contained a biography of Mario Reddick, the Chief Executive Officer of the company.

"Oh shit," I muttered. I had been assigned the top dog himself. Kyle and Mark just shook their heads.

"Good luck," Mark stated as he rolled his eyes. The others had been designated various vice presidents and senior managers but everyone from mechanics, reservation agents, fuelers, baggage handlers, ticket agents and gate agents were all under the command of Mr. Reddick. The more I thought about it the more resolved I became to succeed in my introduction.

"Obviously Mari had a reason she matched me with Mr. Reddick," I thought. I took it as a sign that she had confidence in me to entrust me with such a responsibility. A summary of Mr. Reddick's life and accomplishments jumped off the pages as I stayed up late, reading and preparing.

Before the era of deregulation men such as Mario Reddick were considered giants in the industry. He was there at the onset of the modern age of air travel. A graduate of a noted Big Ten university, he had worked his way up in the industry. He was also a member in good standing of the prestigious Conquistadores del Cielo club, conquerors of the sky. The organization was an all-male exclusive organization founded in 1937. Only those individuals of high esteem in global industry were ever considered for membership. It was a way to develop friendships and share a camaraderie at dude ranches and annual meetings in New York.

Every detail was seen to in the preparation of the board room the following day for the appearance of our nervous class. There was the airline's special first-class china, set upon a large polished wooden table, although it was kept informal with just snacks and drinks. The finest products one would find in the first class cabin of one of our magnificent aircraft were on display. The students of Class 2 all knew just how important this day would be.

The Flight Attendant Training Department was headed up by one classy lady named Barbara. Professional on every level, she also displayed great insight and understanding. She had a willingness to work with any of us whether on specific material in a class or just lending an ear. I will always maintain my deepest respect and gratitude for her guidance. Her style was to mostly stay in the wings and allow her instructors to be upfront and personable. There was no doubt that she had seen to the detailed decor of the meeting room that day.

At a pre-ordained time, the doors opened, and the executives all entered the room. I immediately sighted the silver-haired distinguished figure leading the group. Tall and fit, the icon was in his mid-sixties. Mr. Reddick carried himself with a confidence that radiated throughout the room. His navy-blue double-breasted suit spoke of his impeccable taste. He seemed a bit taken by surprise as I seized the moment and stepped forward to personally welcome him and the other leaders to our gathering. It was more impulse, an act to squelch the anxiety in me, but as I glanced over at Barbara, I could tell that she seemed pleased. The other trainees took note and advanced to greet the specific individual Mari had assigned them. There was initial small talk and both bosses and new hires settled down into a more relaxed atmosphere. Barbara and her crew, at the appropriate time, invited the leaders of each department to sit and allow the students to present themselves and express their wholehearted desire and pleasure at being part of our airline family.

With only knowledge of my own interview process weeks prior, it became evident why each member of Class 2 had been selected amongst the numerous applicants that entered the offices of human resources each and every day. When the time came for my presentation, I was determined not to let my teachers down. My oration on Mr. Reddick was spot on and well received. Each introduction by fellow classmates motivated the entire group. Heck, even the rogue trio was rooting for Janey when her time came. I believe this was felt also by the executives themselves, acknowledging their approval and proclaiming Class 2 to be a fine example of what they desired the flying public to encounter when boarding one of our aircraft.

One executive who expressed his personal commendation was a tall, lean gentleman who was introduced as the Vice-President of In-Flight Services. Barry Lane was well known in the company for being a person who would lend his ear to the common worker. Barry started out as a ship cleaner in the early years, dealing with the messes left by the passengers. He had experienced getting dirty with all the rest of us little guys and giving his all for our company. Now, through hard work and education, he rose to lead the cabin crews of our airline. His gentle manner and willingness to remain with the class when the other managers had departed said volumes about how he cared for his own. He earned my trust and respect that day.

Barbara and her staff were also well pleased and that was a bonus because we all had developed a tremendous liking for her. Each trainee left the meeting with the powers-that-be with a great deal of satisfaction. Things were going so right for all of us.

There remained one important question for us. Once we graduated, where in the airline's regional system would we be based? This would be determined by company need. Rumors abounded; some said it would be Seattle, others said Minneapolis.

"I hate the cold," I complained as both mid-western boys laughed. They were used to frigid weather. One reason I applied with the west coast carrier was in the hopes that I could be based right here in my own hometown. Such a possibility was nonexistent in other airlines. Most of their new hires were sent to some city with difficult weather to be endured until an appropriate amount of seniority was acquired to get you back out to the west coast. As I would come to learn, seniority was everything. Seniority determined where one was based, what flight assignments you were issued each month, when you took your vacation and what position you worked on the aircraft.

I had one ace up my sleeve as the day arrived and the bases were to be announced. I thought of testing to qualify as a Spanish speaker, requiring I be based at LAX. My family roots were planted deep. I wanted to have my cake and eat it too. The price for a locked-in slot at such a senior base as LAX for a Spanish speaker was banishment to the world of Mexico flights.

Every F/A certainly looked forward to experiencing the festivities and historic locations to be found down south but flying to the same destinations day in and day out could get tiresome. I made the fateful decision to bypass the opportunity to apply as a translator, gambling I would be selected to remain in Los Angeles anyway.

Seniority again would be a determining factor, but since everyone in Class 2 had the same date of hire our personal age would regulate the selection. The eldest would have first choice of available bases and the youngest would be assigned what was left. I was third eldest and knew that the two older students, Kyle being one of them, were from the Midwest and therefore would want to be based closer to their home towns.

Barbara arrived at our classroom to find us filled with anticipation, yet something was up. She got right to business.

"Okay, I have the information on your base assignments." She paused as she enjoyed seeing our expectant faces listening to her every word. "There are twelve of you going to Denver and three of you staying in Los Angeles."

"Yeah!" I had beaten the odds. I realized that being based at LAX meant years of flying on reserve, having to remain on-call by a telephone so that scheduling could assign me at their discretion to whatever flight needed me at that moment and that was just fine. I thought it a small price to pay for being given what thousands of flight attendants throughout the country wait years for; I was going to remain home. There was a sense of sadness though as Kyle and Mark both opted to go to Denver as most of Class 2 would. There would be little chance of seeing my fellow rogues as we flew to different destinations, but it would happen. I would be on my own at LAX having to meet other flight attendants, make new friends and develop relationships.

Once all the details of issuing our base assignments had been completed, Barbara steadied us for more developments. The airline had currently been in the process of having three new 737s scheduled to be delivered from the Boeing plant in Washington State within days. As is common in corporate deals, there was a snag. The three aircraft were going to be delayed by a period of three months. That meant the airline not needing us for that period of time. Class 2 was to be furloughed. Of course, we would be eligible to apply for unemployment compensation but that was little solace for the dejected new crew members. Our graduation would still go on as scheduled but then we would be released to go our own ways and nervously anticipate when the airline would recall us, or if they ever would.

But Barbara had saved the very best for last. She announced that in a gesture of good faith and as recognition for our dedication, each of the graduates of Class 2 would be granted full flight benefits during our layoff period.

"What?" My body jerked with excitement. "What? What?" Had I heard right? Every new hire must complete a six-month probation, on the job training, before being fully accepted and granted such benefits. We all jumped for joy. Some of the ladies in the class hugged Barbara and the other instructors. Of course, this meant one thing in the minds of the majority -- free passes to Hawaii.

Chapter II

Our commencement ceremony was filled with so much promise and hope. We had made it through one of the most important times in any of our lives. Every F/A remembers and cherishes the day of his/her graduation from Flight Attendant Training. The photos and diploma would come to represent a precious time in the lives of all those entrusted with the safety of the flying public.

Barbara had done it up right. Representatives of various companies respected highly in the airline industry were on hand to officially pin our flight wings on our freshly pressed company uniform. The ladies were also presented with orchids. A wonderful lunch was served, and a child-like thrill was felt by the F/As of Class 2. There would be no drunken festivity after the formal event. No, Waikiki would be our next port of entry and once there we would have plenty of time to celebrate on the white sandy beaches. We already had our regulation suitcases packed.

I said my fond farewells to my classmates, vowing to remain in touch. My plans were to visit with my family, then prepare to return to LAX the following morning to stand-by for a seat on a flight to Honolulu. Yet, I had one more obligation to meet. I drove to the offices of the East Los Angeles Travel Agency. I paused outside dressed in my airline uniform, flight wings glistening in the sunlight. I slowly opened the door and walked right in to see Stephanie Rhinehardt.

"My, my indeed," she stated. "We have come a long way from the boy who did not know you had to have a passport to travel abroad!" I could tell that she was pleased. I would call upon her for guidance in my many travel plans, each trip becoming longer and bolder. She had truly opened up the world for me and now Hawaii awaited.

Some people believe that airline personnel have the ability to just get on any plane, at any time. The truth is, there are different degrees of what is sometimes called a "pass." A request would be submitted by an employee and someone in the general office would type up a ticket with at least three copies attached. Within a short period of time, a crew member would visit their official mailbox in the flight attendant lounge to check if the desired ticket had arrived. Of course, checking the passenger load on any given flight was vital in planning your adventure. There were regulations covering the use of the pass and more regulations on how to dress, how to act and what not to say when traveling virtually free. I would become a walking encyclopedia on these rules and regulations, not just of our airline but the multitude of airlines throughout the world that had reciprocal agreements with our company.

Once arriving at the terminal gate of your desired flight with plenty of extra time to spare, you presented your pass to the agent. This person then became the gatekeeper who determined whether you would be allowed to take a seat once all the paying passengers had boarded. If you were well-dressed, very patient and developed a connection with the agent, there was the possibility that he/she could assign you a seat in First Class if available. That was the hope and dream of every employee traveling on a pass, whether on your own airline or that of a competitor. The selection of which passes had priority was of course determined by seniority. All passes were on standby status with the exception of the "A" pass. The holder of an "A" pass was a "must fly," even superseding a paying passenger. These magic coupons were reserved mostly for top executives, important business clientele of the airline or political allies in the ever-changing climate of the airline industry.

I made sure to tell the agent at gate 57 that I was a newly graduated flight attendant. Airline employees make extra efforts to take care of their own. Not only was the lovely lady gracious in her effort to accommodate me but she handed me a boarding pass for First Class.

My first experience in flying with my company was everything I had hoped for and more. The flight crew made the new boy feel just like one of the family. They gave me tips on what to do and where to go in Hawaii. I had my eyes set on the remote island of Molokai, off the beaten track from the hustle and bustle that was Honolulu. But to experience Waikiki and see the sights of Oahu would be a great introduction to the new cultural experience I was undertaking.

I picked up my rental car at the airport and was surprised by another airline perk, a reduced rate; all I had to do was show my airline ID with my smiling photo and employee number: 21196-1. Pearl Harbor and the Arizona Memorial brought to life What I had only seen on TV or been told about by my father who served in the Navy during WWII. The beautiful sunset at Waikiki revealed the radiant colors of sun, surf and sky in a way that a boy from smog-ridden Los Angeles never envisioned. Wanting to venture out and experience the true beauty that is the island of Oahu, the next morning I headed out around the back side of Diamond Head and up the coast looking for some good surf, the road leading me to Makapu'u Beach.

The setting was thrilling. With Rabbit Island in the backdrop, eight to ten-foot waves were breaking nicely on the clean soft blue water rushing to shore one right after another. This was definitely a body surfer's dream. But even though a novice, I would enjoy an exhilarating afternoon riding the waves.

Being pounded by the surf, I soon became exhausted and happily crawled onto the dry sand. I lay there soaking up the radiant sun and breathing the fresh salt air. The waves only grew bigger and stronger as I gazed along the shore. I spotted two individuals about thirty yards out in the water, right at the very linear area where these vicious waves were breaking. At first, I thought I was seeing double as the figures were identical to each other in every respect, even wearing the same color swim trunks. Their glowing white, sunburned skin attested to their being visitors to the island as all the locals have a golden-brown complexion. It was evident that I was looking at identical twins. I became concerned as the two men were getting battered by the walls of water time and time again. Even though they had muscular builds I believed they may have been in some danger. Though a novice, I could see them doing all the wrong things. They were turning their backs to the oncoming waves and by their floundering I got the impression they were limited in their swimming ability. But by the look on their faces they seemed to be okay and enjoying themselves. I leaped up and dashed into the surf to get their attention and suggested that they either go deeper into the water or just come out.

The Byron twins were visiting Oahu from Minot, North Dakota which explained why they were not ocean savvy. They greeted me with great enthusiasm, and they explained that they were on the island visiting a former classmate of theirs who had moved to Hawaii and now made the beautiful shores of Waimanalo his home. The pale, sunburned young men were carbon copies of each other in every aspect, even their mannerisms were the same. I couldn't tell one from the other.

"Do you know the word of Jesus Christ?" One brother asked excitedly. I immediately recognized that the two brothers carried a tremendous exuberance for their faith and belief. Being raised in a Roman Catholic home and schools, I had come to a comfortable understanding of religious theology and different spiritual institutions through my travels. The likable boys quoted scripture and were happily sharing their knowledge with me when a 6'5" lanky figure appeared. His sun-bleached hair and tanned lean body revealed that he was a local to these beaches. Lonnie Grimes was the North Dakotan native the Byron boys had traveled to visit. I recognized Lonnie as one of the figures who was expertly ripping up the surf on the massive waves at Makapu'u. The twins introduced us and invited me to have lunch with them.

Four figures politely bowed their heads at the seaside cafe as the twins solemnly thanked the Lord for the delightful meal placed before each man, hungry from bodysurfing. Lonnie seem to take the prayer seriously. I assumed that he shared the same convictions as the Byron twins. The boys were men of good character and that is all that mattered. The twins wrote down their address and promised to continue to pray for me, an offer I never reject, no matter the faith. Then they were off, leaving me with the tall local body surfer.

"Where you going now?" Lonnie inquired shyly. A little embarrassed, I hesitated.

"It's been a hot day; I think I'll grab a brew somewhere." At first Lonnie's face registered a bit of confusion.

"You drink beer?" He asked. I began to feel embarrassed, but then he said. "Heck, I was dying for a drink during lunch."

"I thought you were as straight as the boys," I stated. We both started to laugh. He in turn believed that I was religious like them. "I'm just a regular, ordinary sinner," I replied. I had made a new friend.

Lonnie made it a point to mention that there were only seventeen kids in his high school graduating class. Serving a term in the Navy on a submarine introduced the landlocked lad to the beauty and aquatic pleasures of the islands. The champion bodysurfer and artist owned a pool-servicing company. With hard work the self-made boy from Minot had done well on Oahu. In our conversations I explained my background and my newly acquired position with the airline. I mentioned that I was off to Molokai, anxious to experience the world's tallest sea cliffs. The night before I left, Lonnie presented me with a gift. I opened the aged, wooden box and was pleased to find a wonderful unique instrument. It was an elegant knife, beautifully shaped in its design, with exceptional balance.

"Every Hispanic needs a knife," my smiling tanned friend said. I saw that the blade had been forged in Mexico and also that there was one obvious problem. The nice polished handle was married to a row of very menacing brass knuckles.

"Oh, this is so illegal," I said while still mesmerized by the craftsmanship of the handsome weapon.

"I really don't need it," the North Dakotan said. "I thought maybe you would appreciate it more."

"Ah, I will my friend, I will," I replied still fondling the menacing implement. I considered the gift a generous act of Aloha and was very grateful. With the fine instrument buried deep in my regulation suitcase, I departed Oahu and flew to the tranquil isle of Molokai, filled with excitement and anticipation of all the wonderful experiences she had to offer.

Among the students of Class 2, I was fortunate in that I had savings available to me when the furlough came. I could sustain myself and if I went broke that was okay because I knew the gift was a once-in-a-lifetime situation. If I became destitute, I could always catch a flight home and be fed. With the flight benefits I explored the far reaches of the airline's routes. To the east I flew to Miami and experienced the richness of the Cuban culture. I traveled to Minnesota, to visit Mark and meet his parents. There would be ventures to Seattle and Juneau and, when I was running out of money, I carefully selected flights in which the load of passengers was low so I could enjoy the journey, get a free meal and sometimes see a movie. On all flights I studied the activities and work ethic of my fellow flight attendants. One day on an impulse I caught a flight at LAX to Anchorage. When I arrived, I just remained at the airport and proceeded to stand by for the return flight back to LAX. A round-trip, just for fun.

As promised, in three months Class 2 received the call and reported to our assigned bases. I relocated to the seaside community of Manhattan Beach, just minutes from the airport. "Junior" became another important word in my life's vocabulary. When it came to seniority at LAX, I was at the very bottom. Noted as a senior base, it was very clear to me that I would be on reserve, waiting by the telephone for a long time to come. If I wished to secure a line of Honolulu-bound flights I had to have at least 30 years of service under my belt to bid for a position. But every once and awhile, employees called in sick, opening up a spot on the DC-10 with a 28-hour layover at the Beachcomber Hotel, smack in the middle of Waikiki. Schedulers would hasten to find a replacement from the reserve list and one who was nearby, hence my decision to relocate to Manhattan Beach.

Of course, the formula did not always work. I could be called out for a Honolulu-bound DC-10, dressed in my regulation Aloha shirt uniform, suitcase packed with trunks, snorkel mask and sunscreen. At the last minute, they would pull me off the flight, still attired in Aloha and put me on a 737 hopping across the Rockies, ending up in Pocatello, Idaho in the dead of winter. Still, that was okay because I thrived on the unexpected.

Reality soon set in. It was time for my first monthly weight check. Fate had it that I was assigned Shana James as my F/A Supervisor. Even before I reported to LAX, word had reached the kids of Class 2 on who to avoid in the supervisory staff at the base. The petite redhead's name came up more than once. I fasted for two days prior the weight check and limited my liquid intake. I arrived at the Supervisor's offices adjacent to the flight attendant lounge below the passenger area at Terminal 5. My uniform was immaculate. Shana held my file trying to gain information on her new hire. This first meeting was extremely important as I was just at the start of my probationary period; I could be released from the company for any infraction. I stood on the scale and was a bit relieved to hear her say that she would deduct 2 pounds from the final number to allow for the weight of the uniform. The scale balanced at one hundred seventy-three pounds.

"My, my Edmundo, we are putting on a little weight," scolded the supervisor. I did not respond. I was happy just to make weight for the month and made no explanation concerning my body structure. I shook my head like an obedient employee indicating that she did not have to worry about me. I would have done back flips for her if she had asked at this point in time. I silently vowed to disappear from her view until the following month's weigh in. Besides, I thought if she was in any way displeased with me she would be looking for a fellow named Edmundo. I did not correct her with regard to my name.

Once on the flight line, you realize maybe for the first time that the position is a job. Flight attendants tend to avoid reality because there is nothing normal in the workplace 30,000' above the ground. It becomes easy to create a fantasy in which F/As live a virtual vacation or so they would lead you to believe. The glamour is on the surface. The truth is, the vomit and trash are a part of it. Another fact that caught my interest early on was that Los Angeles International Airport was not a pilot's concept of the perfect airport. During the Fall, the facility could go for days bathed in fog causing delays or making flights divert to alternate airports.

One night we suffered a delay in Acapulco because we had to wait for the Mexicans to supply us with jet fuel. Our 727 was late coming into the air space over LAX. The thick fog had rolled inland from the Pacific and it suddenly became clear to the crew and me that landing was going to be risky. On final approach, at the very last moment, the aircraft lurched back upward, engines roaring. The cockpit crew decided to abort the landing. We made two more approaches with the same alarming results, turning for final approach and then suddenly dipping into the soup of clouds, making it impossible to see. The craft's lights projected out only to be reflected back into us as blinding white glare. The engines would go silent as we sat in our jumpseats, gripping and waiting for that moment when the wheels find the pavement. All at once the roar and high shriek of the jets kicked in, pitching the fuselage upward. I knew darn well that the captain pulled the plug on the deal at the very last second. On the fourth approach, the wheels touched down and the cabin erupted with applause. I was the perfect picture of cool and calm as I thanked the passengers for their patronage as they deplaned. They did not notice that my heart was stuck in my throat. Once the last passenger was off, I approached the cockpit wanting to know more about the situation. The captain's face was ashen as he rose to leave.

"Thanks for getting us down captain." He didn't even look at me when he spoke.

"Don't thank me, in fact thank the first officer," the sullen aviator walked off. We had come close to becoming a major headline on the morning news.

A junior F/A "on reserve" learns to listen and take directions. With the overwhelming number of flight attendants being women, it paid off to listen. Not only did one learn the tricks of the trade from one more experienced, but after the meal service on a six-hour flight from Honolulu, the gathering at mid-galley produced the most interesting gossip one could ever hope to hear. There was the story of little Susie who had been dating a certain pilot based in Seattle. She was thinking of putting in a transfer from LAX to SEA to go live with him but now word had gotten back to her that he was messing around with a young new hire from MSP, Minneapolis/St. Paul. Susie was devastated. Of course, that pilot's name was mud among the cabin crew. Poor Susie was a wreck, or so the gossip related, and she didn't know what to do. I had to admit that the stories were better than the soap operas on daytime television.

Then there were the diamond rings. They might as well have made it a regulation because the mark of a successful "stewardess," in a few people's eyes, was measured by the size of that rock on her finger. Many a young lady came to work on an airliner in the hopes of finding that Mister Right. Numerous doctors, lawyers and wealthy executives flew daily on the company's air routes. If the stars happened to be aligned perfectly an F/A just might happen to be at the right place at the right time and attract the attention of a good catch. Some prospective boyfriends had other incentives besides just a beautiful fly-girl. Spouses of airline employees also flew virtually for free. At the conclusion of a successful mating ritual there was always that ring, the one the flight attendant would flaunt for all in the cabin to see as she worked the beverage cart.

Sometimes it would be an aviator in the cross hairs of a stewardess, preferably a Captain. But since most of them were senior, a First Officer would do. Because the introduction of men as flight attendants was relatively new, serious relationships between fellow crew members was limited to mostly junior crews. There would be F/As who found true love, married and would bid flights together as a husband and wife team. The aim of a young lady working a flight in pursuit of a serious beau was also shared by some of the gay flight attendants. Their hopes also lay with finding that doctor, lawyer or wealthy executive to court.

Of all the people I worked with I was most fortunate to fly with Michael Lottergan, a blonde-haired, gay crewmember who was filled to the brim with personality and a good heart. He treated all cabin crew members with respect and made every effort to make the flying experience one the passengers would remember. He was a riot, quick-witted and always ready to explore. I had taken a lot of flak, mostly from my brother, about the image of the male flight attendant when I was accepted for the position, but homophobia was never an issue with me. I may have been confused about many things in my young life but sexual orientation was not one of them. I was heterosexual and the way I looked at it, having gay co-workers was less competition for us straight guys.

"Haven't you ever wondered how it would be with a guy?" Michael asked me in mid-flight, while positioning the meal carts onto the elevator of the DC-10

"No, I like the soft feel of a woman's bosom," I relied. He instantly threw out his chest and said,

"That's because you never experienced the pleasure of a man's firm pecs." He was so animated in expressing his opinion, I started to crack up. There were those in the company whose religious beliefs cast the gay community as a whole in a negative light. When I saw Michael, I saw another child of God, one who was most likely a person of far better character than I.

One of the unforeseen results of choosing this occupation was the flirting I would receive from passengers, both female and male. Of course, the female interactions were more easily dealt with. In my best professional manner, I politely told the male admirers thanks but no thanks. One has the picture of a lovely female flight attendant being courted by a handsome young professional man upon arrival at any given destination. More often than not it was the male F/A who rode off into the sunset with the handsome, young professional man.

What can one say about the boys in the cockpit? Because many of the cockpit crews were former military there was a mannerism that reflected that culture. There were many captains I found to be magnificent aviators, responsible to the utmost, utilizing their skills in assuring the safety of their crew and passengers. Some even were not too "high and mighty" as to acknowledge a lowly junior flight attendant, have a conversation or share a meal with them on a layover. Then there were others who believed themselves to be second only to the Almighty. They reeked of narcissistic self-glory and used their rank to make sure everybody knew it. The majority of pilots, though, were boys with only three stripes on their sleeves and shoulders. They spent every waking day waiting, dreaming of the time when they would be the one to be promoted to that left seat. Until then, they minded their business and did what was told by their Supervising Check Pilots. I knew many aviators who were happily married and respected as good family men, people of great character and in good standing in their communities. I also found others who were referred to be "horn dogs," as the ladies I worked with used to call them: using a nice layover at an exotic location, a free hotel room, a couple of drinks and an uninhibited desire to tell an unsuspecting pretty woman what they do for a living.

I, for the most part, kept my head down while in the flight lounge, scanning faces lest Shana find me. I would spend a great deal of time reviewing the pass benefits manual for as soon as my probationary period was over, I was planning to bid a monthly schedule grouping all of my ten days off together and take off on another adventure.

As I viewed the pages, I noticed that Iberia Airlines of Spain had an agreement with our airline and I could use them to get to Madrid. Trans World Airlines had deals that opened the way to Rome, Athens and Cairo. London was available through Pan American Airways or British Airways. KLM, the Dutch based airline, had a history of treating crew members very well. They could transport me to Amsterdam and beyond. Air France to Paris, Lufthansa to Frankfurt and Berlin, it was all there, tremendous benefits for a pittance. This job truly did offer me a magic carpet and I licked my chops with anticipation.

"Just lay low, keep a clean record and make weight check," I murmured to myself as I closed the manual and went to work.

Month after month I starved myself to make weight but other than that life as an F/A was good. I was living in a great beach town community minutes from the airport. Many a time I could be seen rushing down Pacific Coast Hwy., hurrying to catch a flight I had just been assigned minutes before and destined to go who knows where.

Soon, six months had flown by and my probation period was ending. That meant the time to escape was near. I made my plans very carefully. I could catch our airline to Miami with a 4-hour layover, then hop on an Iberia jumbo jet to Madrid, total cost round trip LAX – MAD – LAX only eighty dollars. Yes, it was a gamble involving stand-by status there and back. But what the heck, I was young, strong, single and I had ten free days.

Word got around concerning my planned venture and another F/A who had been a classmate in training was interested in coming along. Alan was a tall, good-looking, dark-haired man. In his uniform he looked striking enough of be on the cover of GQ. The ladies adored him, yet he never flaunted the obvious. He was a down-to-earth guy who had aspirations of becoming a high-fashion model. He eventually succeeded.

"You can come if you like but I know exactly where and when I am going," I informed him. I also mentioned that my one carry-on bag rule applied. I never took the chance of having my suitcase stored below, thus delaying my well-thought-out plans.

Alan was well aware of my travel experience since training and he agreed to the terms.

Finally, the day of our liberation came, the day we became "real" flight attendants. All the employee benefits kicked in: health insurance, dental plan, life insurance and membership in the credit union were all available to us now. One other change was that we were now members in the Association of Flight Attendants union with the proper dues to be deducted each paycheck. During training we were given the application forms for the union and told that whether one joined or not the fixed charge would be deducted. Everyone filled out the forms except me. I suppose it was done as an act of defiance against those in authority. Perhaps I was just being a rascal; it never entered my mind that it would make any difference in the long run.

España, and Madrid in particular, had become a much-desired destination for my early adventures. Over the years friendships were made and nurtured and the Spanish capital made a fine jumping-off point for traveling farther east or to the south. Eating fried calamari and sipping sangria, Alan and I enjoyed the fruits of our vocation. Heading south we experienced the beauty that is Seville. Catching a ferry at Algeciras, we explored the wonders in Tangiers where every merchant professes to be your best friend to entice you into their venue. Returning to Spain we sunned ourselves on the exquisite beaches of Marbella before driving up the Costa Brava to Benidorm. Alan and I were intoxicated by the depth of our curiosity; our eyes open wide in amazement. Finally, we had our fill and boarded a DC-10 at Barajas Airport. I was exhausted yet exceedingly content with the outcome of my first adventure as an F/A.

Arriving back at LAX I felt a sense of achievement and was not hesitant in sharing my first adventure as an F/A. Relating the details and highlights of my recent journey, I encouraged my co-workers to see the world as I had.

"It's all there in the pass manual," I said to my fellow crewmembers. "Where to go next?" I wondered out loud. If planned correctly with my reserve status I could literally do an exotic jaunt every month. Let the senior girls have their fixed trip. I was enjoying myself. More importantly, I was understanding the systems, culture, pace and face of my beloved airline. These were the keys to ensuring a successful job experience.

"Eddy, I have sequence 190 for you tonight." On a day that was like any other F/A Scheduling needed to fill a position. I would have to check my F/A bid sheet to see the details and destination.

"Oh no!" It was the all-nighter. LAX – MEX, nine o'clock report time. I was not pleased. The aircraft was the 10, probably eight flight attendants, three-and-one-half hours flight time in the middle of the night, arriving early morning with limited time on the ground before we return. That morning flight back to LAX was always full and would include a meal service.

By the time we arrived in El Distrito Federal, the only thing I got to see of the Mexican capital was through the windows of the aircraft at Benito Juarez International Airport. I was tired from being on duty all night. My spirits were lifted when informed I was allowed by customs to bring back one bottle of liquor into the U.S. each flight. My selection that morning and for future flights was a fine tequila, Centenario, but there was little time to relish the joy of my acquired bottle as the passengers began to board for my return flight. After working through the night and "busting my butt," that second leg was a real backbreaker. Exhaustion set in along with irritation as a result of a woman with her crying baby in my section of the cabin. Just as the upset baby began to cry at an even higher pitch, and while trying to recover a food tray in light turbulence, I of course spilled remains on the aisle floor and myself.

Relief set in once we landed and the craft was secured at the gate that led to U.S. Customs. The experience of coming back from Mexico as a crew member was different than the passengers. We were allowed to bypass the main crowd, but those custom guys sure did like to look through the suitcases of the stewardesses. I have truly seen some of the strangest and most interesting items while accompanying crews through customs; all one has to do is use one's imagination. In pre-9/11, with less security, much more contraband boarded the planes every day at the hands of both the public and the flight crews. Passengers also took more liberties in the amount of alcohol consumed on any given flight and the messes they created were cleaned by the F/As. It was not an easy job. Flight after flight made me realize that I was going to be made to earn those benefits I cherished. I would be disposing of dirty diapers one minute and helping the anxious try to relax the next.

A flight to HNL with a nice layover is what every reserve F/A desires: roll the dice and pray it came up ALOHA. It was important to develop a relationship with the flight attendant schedulers even if it was only by telephone. Be nice, considerate, responsible and maybe when that Hawaii trip popped up they would remember me.

Names and faces were becoming familiar and the more I flew the more I learned. Because of the time I had committed to working out in the weight room, I wasn't one to hang around the flight lounges. I formed few real relationships at the airline, opting to stand in the background. I did attend a few crew parties but was always there more as a spectator, not one of more colorful actors at these functions.

My work month always focused around the day I had to report for weight check and Shana continued to address me as "Edmundo." Always just making the cut, I would hurry away, rushing to find a decent meal after days of starving myself and hopefully avoiding Shana for thirty more days. One morning I strolled down the aisle of a 727 that was just about to board for a flight to Guadalajara. While checking the over-wing aisles where the emergency exits were, I turned and spotted a person sitting in the back row.

"How did that passenger board?" I was puzzled and concerned. Perhaps it is someone needing first aid. I hastened aft and when I got closer, I realized it was Shana. My loopy supervisor was all dressed up with clipboard in hand.

"Hi, Edmundo!" Her voice shrieked. "I'm here to do your check-ride." A flight to Mexico with a full load on the return in a few hours, two complete meal services and Shana James on board to judge every minute of my performance. I wanted to cancel sick.

The flight was predictable. Over a hundred hungry, tired, anxious people, mostly bilingual, were being served drinks and a meal in mild but bothersome turbulence. The women always wanted Cola, the men a cocktail or beer. We struggled to balance the meal trays, the money and the drinks as we inched our way down the aisle from row to row. Then there was the dirty clean up, with your bare hands. Some passengers were demanding, while others were just trying to sleep without having their seat belts fastened. There in the aft with a stern eye on me was Shana, head swaying in and out of the aisle. One second my supervisor was gazing, another second, she ducked back behind the seat in front of her as she wrote down notes on her yellow legal pad. I spilled a drink on a man, apologized and went off to get a cloth soaked in soda water, the flight attendant's all-purpose cleaner. Shana scribbled down more.

Once the cabin was clean and secured for descent, a Spanish-speaking woman started to complain of problems with her ears. This happens often, mostly to young children when the airplane is descending. The other two F/A's tried to assist but they did not understand her as she only spoke Spanish. The assigned Spanish speaker for this flight was positioned in First Class and had her hands full. Shana stood up and joined the rest of us in the aft galley deciding what to do as the woman's agony seemed to increase. I informed them that I spoke Spanish and would speak to the lady.

My efforts were made a bit awkward as she occupied the middle, seat B, of a 3-seat section. You must be tactful when there are other passengers on each side. I bent down and explained to her in Spanish that what she was experiencing was very common. The woman took comfort in what I said and the fact that it was in her native tongue. I demonstrated for her how one opens the mouth wide to help the ear adjust to the sensation of descent. She began to settle down as I turned to ask if anyone had a stick of gum since chewing would relieve her ailment. Someone obliged as I left the sweet lady calm and satisfied, pleasantly chewing on the gum for the rest of the flight.

Shana was indeed pleased. One of her charges had taken control of the situation and saw it to a successful conclusion. She would make too much of it.

"Great job Edmundo," she gloated once we had arrived and the passengers had deplaned. The cabin crew remained on the craft as we were scheduled to turn right around, back to LAX. From that point I became relaxed. The return flight went without a hitch. Back at LAX Shana James had given her full approval of my abilities to do the job. That was fine by me, but I was leery for I knew there would be more check-rides to come in the future.

I settled into a comfortable routine, grabbing my share of Hawaii flights, mixed in with a combination of layovers to all sections of our company's route system. On one flight I found myself in sunny Miami; a few days later I got to see the glaciers of Juneau. Just when I thought I had it all together, a flight to Kodiak, Alaska in the dead of winter made me remember all those little prayers the nuns in elementary school said might save my soul one day. Every F/A was strapped tightly in our jumpseats from beginning to end. The turbulence was so severe that passengers were heaving to the left and right. It made me wonder what was keeping the airship in one piece as I began to plead with God, making promises I knew I would never keep if only we arrived safely at our destination. Once on the ground all the F/As strode about calmly, acting cool and collected in front of the shaken passengers.

"Yeah, it's a piece of cake. We experience this all the time." It's better to lie even to ourselves than contemplate reality. Yet, in between the messy food services, missed connections and mechanical break downs, I was given the opportunity to literally escape every month. Ten days of wild escapades at the festival in Avignon, France diminished the thought of nail-biting approaches and fog-ridden landings. A couple of months later I was drinking crystal liters of fine German beer while dancing at the Oktoberfest in Munich.

The highlight of those first few years of flying was having the opportunity to escort my 48-year-old mother on her first plane trip, carefully planned with Honolulu as our destination. For a woman who worked hard all her life and rarely set foot outside East Los Angeles, a whole new world was about to be revealed that day as we boarded the DC-10 at Terminal 5. For her it was the same sheer excitement of a child's first trip to Disneyland. With the majority of the First-Class cabin all to ourselves, we sat comfortably in the lush seats. My mother, Alicia, clenched my hand tightly on take-off, unsure of what to expect as the large metal bird did its magic and lifted up over the Pacific. Sitting by the window she seemed concerned because she continually looked out upon the vast ocean below then back into the cabin. Finally, she leaned over to ask a question.

"Eddy, you mean we have to go over water to get to Hawaii?" I was stunned. Of all my ventures throughout the world, that trip with my mother remains the fondest memory. Yes, things were going pretty darn good and I was grateful. And then there came a change.

Chapter III

It arrived like a chilled breeze, unexpected and all encompassing. Something was not right: as though someone was supposed to come and deliver some stunning news or make a relevant announcement. I was on edge without knowing why. My routine remained constant through the months, yet little things started to occur. I was assigned more of the less-desired flights, or so it seemed to me. Honolulu almost became a distant memory. The passenger's demands seemed greater. That nice flow and rhythm of our inflight services began to be interrupted by unforeseen incidents. Mechanical problems caused hours of delays. On layovers I would be assigned a hotel room next to elevators continually in use, the traffic and ding-ding-dinging keeping me up all night. Then an early morning report would follow, with a grueling six legs across half the country.

Right out of training, my uniform was kept impeccable. Now, I began to slack off. My shoes no longer had that mirror-reflective shine. Even my usual workouts in the gym suffered, my motivation being sabotaged. It came to a head when, after days of starving myself, I barely passed weight-check having one pound to spare. Shana warned me of the serious consequences and possible suspension, scolding me like a child. I retreated to one of the many sofas in the flight attendant lounge to think about my predicament.

"Maryann, hey are we on the same flight?" A familiar face of a well-known F/A rushed to greet a friend. They were both dressed in their regulation Aloha uniform. That fact irritated me as I was due to land up in Idaho Falls with a very short layover. Rocky, another charismatic young man, entered the lounge and was received with great excitement by a few of my fellow crewmembers who were happy to see him. And so, it continued as dear friends arrived and left, greetings were shared and best wishes given. I sat, a virtual unknown to the crewmembers based at LAX, yet I accepted responsibility as that was the way I initially wanted it to be.

"I bet they would notice me if I survived an air disaster." The outlandish statement just came out. I had not contemplated such a thought before. I felt ashamed that I'd wish to be recognized by my associates at the cost of such a terrible event. Fortunately, no one had been sitting near me when I voiced the unthinkable.

And so it began. It lodged itself deep in my soul and I made every effort to deny that it was with me. Foreshadowing? I carried it on each and every flight I boarded and into every hotel room where I hoped for some peace. It would soon manifest itself late into the night, invading my somber sleep, like a thief coming to rob me of my very dignity.

"Perhaps it is just the job?" I began to avoid the airport on my days off. I tried to get my feet solidly planted on the ground, spend more time with my family. In reality my actions were a vain effort to hide the deep fear I could not shake. Of all the airline companies, all the daily flights and all the flight attendants working the skies, what were the odds such an event would strike me? I quickly dismissed the warning as nothing more than anxiety and forced myself to devote more time in the weight room. I would drive my body to exhaustion, seeking repose. I became isolated in an attempt to simplify my life. I postponed any future adventures and concentrated on performing my duties inflight to the best of my abilities.

Finally, Scheduling gave me a prize assignment. It was a flight on the 10 to Mexico City with a wonderful extended layover and lodging at a first-class hotel, the El Presidente at Chapultepec Park. The thrill of exploring the Mexican capital would lift my spirits. Perhaps my luck was changing. I day-dreamed about venturing into the renowned Zona Rosa, enjoying fine cuisine, savoring Mariachi music, meeting new and different people, and getting myself back on track.

The cabin crew was assembled in the briefing room where each F/A would choose a work position according to seniority. Some faces I recognized but some were new. My eyes fell on a lovely Hispanic "señorita." I determined her status because the tell-tale diamond of every married F/A was absent from her ring finger. Like the blooming roses my father had nurtured at our home in East Los Angeles, Reina Patricia Torres was as precious in God's creation. Olive-skinned with radiant black hair, I could not help but be dazzled by her. Once on the plane and on our way her elegance glowed as she walked down the aisle, performing her tasks and seeing to everyone's needs. I was hypnotized. My eyes continued to follow her as she moved forward up the aisle, vanishing behind the curtain into First Class. I had no intention of trying to make a play for her. Yes, she was extremely attractive and possessed a bubbling personality but my emotions for her were motivated by a reverence. Reina was something special, yet peculiar. Hispanic culture admires honor and respect above all and Reina possessed an inner splendor that vied with the physical luster, if that were indeed possible. This creature was far more worthy of esteem than any silly flirtation.

I got to spend some one-on-one time with her in the aft of the cabin once all the services were complete. She expressed strong family ties, having eight brothers and one sister. Her family had been fortunate to escape the ravages of war in El Salvador. Coming to the U.S. as a young child, she spoke about always wanting to be a flight attendant and named all the airlines she had applied to. I felt that our company was indeed fortunate to have her. Then she said it.

"I believe one day I will be killed in a plane crash." The words came so easily from the same mouth that seconds before had displayed such a radiant smile. I was stone-faced. Then my jaw dropped, and I turned away in disbelief. I had flown with other flight attendants who spoke of having a bad feeling, yet that is all it remained, a feeling. All at once that chilling breeze returned causing me to feel insecure.

"Come on Reina, how can you know such a thing?" I tried to appear composed.

"I just know," was her simple response. I looked right into her face. She was calm, she was cool, and she was real. "I've had dreams of the event since I was a child," she continued. My mind went numb.

"This knowledge, it doesn't bother you?" I asked in bewilderment.

"If it be God's will, I accept it," she whispered, releasing the full effect of the grand innocence of her soul. "I even know the flight numbers, 2-6-5." I had to admit that I was shocked. Uncomfortable with what had just been said, I made the excuse of seeing a passenger needing assistance and escaped up the aisle. I would have no more conversation with this woman.

"Man, this is nuts," I thought to myself as I worked my way up the aisle seeking the refuge of the mid-galley. As I moved forward, I imagined a tugging at my apron strings pulling me backward, a physical presence requesting that I return to Reina. It was in a way enticing, the temptation to seek more information from this lovely angel, but I was not that brave a person. I didn't want anything to do with what she claimed to have hidden in her thoughts. Once on the ground and in the safety of my room at the luxurious hotel, I checked a company timetable involving every flight in our company's system. Flight 2-6-5 was not to be found anywhere. Perhaps her premonition involved another airline? Perhaps a flight she may board one day on holiday? Finally putting that aside, I proceeded to explore the wonders of the Mexican capital that evening, to enjoy myself and block out that disturbing conversation. Over a magnificent dish of pollo y mole and a cold bottle of Bohemia, I firmly decided to avoid Reina Torres in the future.

...

In December of 1978, a plane glided down below the clouds, and through the mist. Silently, it descended toward an airport. Out of fuel, out of power, the commercial flight crashed into a countryside. "Only ten" people died. The coroner, the investigators for the National Transportation Safety Board, the Federal Aviation Administration and the news media all came. The latter scavenged fact and fantasy to make the next day's newspapers scream at a shocked flying public.

Gliding into 1979, my daily ritual of physical training had become a novena, forging discipline in place of a less-than-noble past. It seemed strange to me because I had always enjoyed a quiet yet disorderly sort of life. Formally, stability had not been important or appealing to me. Slowly, I began to look upon my job as a punch in/punch out sort of existence. It was becoming obvious to me that something had to happen to allow me to break free of an ambivalent life that had slowly crept around me. Perhaps my workouts could offer a solution?

Prior to the transition period in which hard core bodybuilding transformed itself into the purported "health industry," I busted my butt in the gym. At first it was to satisfy a craving for continued challenges in athletic activities. One day I accepted an invitation of a friend to work out at a facility aptly referred to as the Animal House. There I found myself surrounded by energetic new comrades. I realized I had discovered a valuable tool. Among the serious-minded athletes there was an abundance of great knowledge.

As time sped by, the initial training routines given to me by far wiser colleagues at the gym were not enough to satisfy my acute hunger for change. In one of the many fitness magazines of the period I was caught by an advertisement for a physique competition located in the Midwest. I realized I had not the knowledge, the genes nor the "pharmacist" to be competitive in Southern California, the mecca for the sport. With flight benefits however, I could give my best in a different venue, without possibly embarrassing myself. I knew very few people in that region of the country. Such a venture would demand great dedication, an opportunity to shake the precariousness that filled my life.

...

In February of 1979 an aircraft from the United States was on final approach at Benito Juárez International Airport in Mexico City. The blue and white jet flew over the now dried lakebed, once described as a water haven by Hernán Cortés in 1519 when he first entered the largest city in the New World. Much had changed in 450 years.

The plane was directed to Runway 23 Left, the more often used of the two runways at the airport. The plane glided down under the midday sun, the wheels touching the pavement before a multitude of people. They stood on the fringes of the airport hoping to get a glimpse of the festivities that were about to commence. The aircraft, designated Air Force One, had arrived in Mexico carrying President Jimmy Carter.

Once the craft was parked, a red velvet carpet was laid at the jetway stairs where President and Mrs. Carter would descend to a military band's rendition of the Star-Spangled Banner. The Carters were officially greeted by President José López Portillo, the leader of the United States of Mexico. Carter was visiting Mexico in hopes of re-igniting stalled negotiations between the two countries over natural gas and the newly discovered rich oil fields of Mexico's eastern border. The negotiations had been going on for over two years and an energy-hungry United States wanted to gain a share of that abundance. The care of the oil was under the control of Petróleos Mexicana (PEMEX), the publicly owned oil company of Mexico. The gist of the disagreement was that Mexico wanted the help of the U.S. to develop and industrialize the country in exchange for oil and natural gas. The United States represented by the Carter Administration wanted no part of any industrialization of Mexico, and simply wanted the gas and oil. Mexico's representatives in the dialogues had backed away in disgust, seeing just another insult on top of numerous others since the U.S, in Mexico's eyes, "had stolen" half of their country 150 years earlier.

Now Carter had arrived to try and get the deal sealed. His plan was to work with López Portillo personally, win his trust and build on a newly developed friendship. If that was what he had in mind as he stepped off Air Force One, he instead abruptly put his foot in his mouth. In his remarks in front of the press at Benito Juárez he chastised López Portillo and the Mexican Government for what he interpreted as their dismal human rights record.

I recall viewing that evening's news report on the TV as video of that speech was broadcast. I focused in on López Portillo's face, which looked as if he wanted to run up and strangle Carter.

"What an idiot," I thought. "You arrive in a foreign country and instantly insult your host." The U.S. purchase of natural gas was completed by the two countries but the damage had been done and the visit will always be remembered as just another black eye in U.S./Mexican relations.

My uneasiness had returned and continued to grow, an intense preoccupation with being right in the middle of a major airline crash. Of course, I was expected to do my duty as a professional should it ever happen. It seemed to be something in the back of the minds of all flight crews, the last thing there is to experience: fearsome yet enticing.

By March, I had become "obsessed" in the minds of some of my family. The dedication to workouts at the Animal House had become a religion. Even without realizing it, time in the gym soon became my most important daily activity. The big payoff would come in some ordinary Midwestern town I had never been to, participating in a Mr. "Whatever" competition later that year. It made no sense to my parents. It made no sense to anyone, but as my body reaped the benefits of my commitment, I became more in tune with myself. Change was taking place. This drive - I would not be able to escape it. It was all-consuming.

In May, a Los Angeles bound DC-10 crashed in Chicago. I really should say "incinerated." My warped fantasies placed me on that flight. While on duty, locked inside the McDonnell-Douglas jumbo jet, I would look up and down the rows, seeing a typical passenger load. I became breathless knowing that to the very end one had to remain totally professional. Logic dictated that as a flight attendant in such a tragedy, I would be instantly destroyed. Honor and respect, the first rules by which one survived in my old neighborhood, would demand that an F/A play out the entire scene to its conclusion. Being a Hispanic, Roman Catholic, and male, whipped up a sense of martyrdom in my young impressionable mind.

The possibility of "Muerto" (Death) boarding an aircraft was always there, but now it had become a reality. Since our company flew the DC-10, it brought the horror home. The insider jokes throughout the industry were rampant. DC-10 flights would be dubbed the "barbecue" flights. I became one of the most notorious at such sick humor but that was all on the surface. Inside I was dealing with the conflicting rumors of the craft's capabilities and its purported shortcomings. Now when one rolled away from Terminal 5 at LAX, the feeling was different than before. That positive attitude the company staked its claim on was gone; a wary business attitude replaced it. I began to ponder the possibility of my flight being the next casualty and wondered how I would handle it. How could I seat someone who was going to face such a horrible demise? I did not want to cope with such thoughts, so I blocked them out with jokes.

More and more the thought of what Reina said came to mind. My initial decision to avoid her wasn't necessary. One can go years without running into a specific flight attendant. Our encounters were no more than an occasional glance across the lounge. But now I found it far more difficult to shake her words.

Reina had shared her premonition with others. The fearful consulted the company's flight schedule, as I had, to discover with relief that the airline was void of any flight #265. Yet, by the quality of her character I took to heart that she indeed had these deep feelings and even more importantly put stake in them. Something told me that perhaps I should, too.

The occasional flashes were becoming more detailed: a scene of an air crash with me in the middle of the chaos. The daydream assigned me a seat as a spectator, although I was well aware that I was a participant in the tragedy. I would be observing the tail section of a plane, an interior view. Forward was the normal image of the cabin with seat backs, escape doors, windows and a few passengers standing in the aisles. Suddenly, in an instant I found myself separated from the main cabin. At the conclusion of the vision, I would retain only one thought: that I had escaped "completely clean." I received no injections from the assisting medical personnel, a relief from my childhood fear of needles. That was truly coming away clean. In hindsight these visions should have been taken seriously but at the time I was determined not to let such warnings interfere with the day-to-day dealings of my life, including flying on the DC-10.

In reality, my immediate future presented great opportunities. I had interviewed for and was selected to participate in one of television's favorite game shows, Joker's Wild. With my workouts going very well and a strict adjustment to my diet, I was able to focus on the show. Luck was also on my side as I was faced with questions from categories I was familiar with. I played up to the audience by hesitating in my responses, but the reality was I was dealing with subjects like politics, geography and history, which were my strong points. The show's host, Jack Barry, was pleased with my progress as he emphasized the amount of my winnings up to that point. Defeating my opponents qualified me for the bonus round. I was required to pull down the lever of a huge slot machine, trying to accumulate more money and prizes before a menacing dragon appeared on the panel. Each time I pulled the bar the cash and prizes piled up. Then the host, relishing the buildup, would ask if I wanted to take yet another chance. If I did and the dragon appeared, I would lose all the booty I had accumulated to that point. The studio audience became involved in the frenzy as I continued to win round after round. A trip to the Galapagos Islands appeared on the slot. I jumped for joy and my confidence was pumped up even more. A cruise down the Amazon, a beautiful camera and more wealth were added to my winnings. The host and the audience continued to egg me on.

"Eddy, do you wish to try one more time?" Jack Barry created a hysteria with this question. Suddenly it struck.

"Stop," a voice within me whispered with assurance. I could see the dragon coming up on the next pull of the lever. "I know what's next," I stated to the host. The crowd insisted all the more for me to continue but I was done. "I have a feeling," I nodded to the host who jumped on the opportunity and used it to create more excitement.

"Oh, he has a feeling," he repeated with sarcasm. "Well Eddy, try it one time just for fun. You will retain your winnings, but I want to see how accurate your feelings are." I stepped up and yanked the bar. Round and round sped the dials and in an instant, the dragon appeared. The crowd was stunned and roared with relief for my good judgment. "Do you have these feelings often?"

"All the time," I responded. As the program broke for a commercial, he asked,

"What's your feeling on the stock market?" The clever host of course was joking with me. I walked away that day with a nice bankroll and some fabulous prizes thanks to my inner sense. One thing was true in that I indeed had always had such feelings, but fear forced me to suppress them. My Roman Catholic upbringing certainly conflicted with this supposed ability to sense the future.

"Who is God?" I recalled my dear second-grade teach Sister Therese asking of her precious little students at the parochial school I attended.

"God is the supreme being who created all things," we excited children shouted out word for word straight from the catechism book. Once out in the greater world I began to question the specific, rigid wording that implied that this greater being was one to be feared if you failed to walk the straight and narrow. Certainly, my mother Alicia and her sister, the highly respected Sister Marie Inez of the Sisters of Carmel, would be the first to warn me against putting any value in these strange premonitions pertaining to the future, especially concerning a terrible airline crash. Unquestioning submission, through the guidance of the Holy Church, was the one and true way to find peace and salvation, or so they said.

I was sure Reina was a devoted Catholic, placing far more faith in this all-knowing God than I. Her premonitions dominated her life as if they were directly sent by God. I had never had a problem in developing a relationship with this silent God. It was the "guidance through intercession of the Holy Church," that truly bothered me. I would be reminded of this influence in my life on a four-day trip I received from Scheduling.

The bulk of the journey took our crew through Utah, Wyoming, Idaho and Montana with a final layover in Arizona. Working the first-class section of our Boeing 737 aircraft I embraced the position of Senior, as the rest of the cabin crew was very junior. It was a rare opportunity to work in the forward cabin and have the time to develop a better rapport with the passengers who preferred our airline, our service, over our competition. The very last legs of Day #4 took us from PHX to SAN (San Diego) where we would sit for an hour or so before returning home to LAX and well-earned days off. Our crew of two ladies and two gentlemen was very anxious to complete the twenty-five-minute flight leg that would take us home.

Finally, the gate agent boarded the plane and delivered the passenger manifest into my hands.

"You have some VIP's occupying the first-class section on this flight," he announced. As I gazed down at the rows of passengers and their seating assignments, my eyes widened. Timothy Cardinal Manning, Archbishop of Los Angeles and his entourage were about to board my aircraft.

"Holy crap." A Prince of the Roman Catholic Church was headed down the jetway and panic set in. I rushed into the first-class lavatory to check my appearance. I stroked my hand through my hair while still holding the manifest list. I quickly gazed at the rest of the names. There was a Bishop, a Monsignor and four lowly priests rounding out the group. With the exception of His Eminence the Archbishop, none of the names were recognizable.

"Boarding!" I informed the rest of the crew as the distinguished men in black approached. They seemed too preoccupied with personal conversation to readily acknowledge me, the representative of our airline standing in the forward galley to greet them with the most sterling smile I could produce. Certainly, the group's focus was on the slender, senior official with the red cap and red sash.

The Archbishop occupied the window seat in the last row of the first-class cabin. I immediately saw to the storage of the delegation's very formal black briefcases, filled, I imagined, with all the business of one of the largest archdioceses in America. I carefully and efficiently went about my professional duty of listing their preferred beverage to be served once airborne for this short hop to LAX. With the task completed and the shepherds of the Catholic Church settled in, the rest of the passengers began to board.

"Welcome aboard." My greetings were sincere to each and every traveler entering and retreating to the coach section, yet my mind remained centered on the Cardinal. My mother would truly be amazed if she could have seen me at that time surrounded by what she regarded as the cream of the crop of her precious faith. She saw to it that her children had only the highest esteem for such "men of God."

Once we were in the air and leveled off I was able to deliver the requested drinks. The group relaxed and took very little notice of the sole F/A in their midst. There was a very handsome and self-assured member of the entourage seated next to His Eminence. He took the Cardinal's soft drink from my hand and placed it upon His Eminence's tray table while the Cardinal enjoyed the vista outside his window. I returned to the galley and checked the manifest again. The tall, confident man seated next to Timothy Manning was a full Bishop, but I was not familiar with the name.

Curiosity began to get the better of me. I was sure that my dear aunt, Sister Inez, might be familiar with one or two of these distinguished guests. I hesitantly approached one of the seemingly lower-ranking clergymen sitting forward, farthest from His Eminence.

"Excuse me Father," I asked the thin, balding, bi-focal man of the church, who then put down some reading material. "I realize you probably know quite a few nuns in the service of the church, but I was wondering if you know any from the order of the Carmelites?" The stern-looking clergyman asked for her name. "Sister Mary Inez." He thought for a moment then shook his head. I was not surprised as there were thousands of women who had dedicated their lives in service to the church. I headed back to the forward galley when suddenly I heard a strong voice.

"Sister Marie Inez?" I turned and saw that the tall bishop had overheard my inquiry.

"Yes," I said.

"I know her. How are you associated with her?"

"Well, she is my aunt, my mother's sister."

"Your Eminence," the right-hand man excitedly turned to the Cardinal. "This young man right here is the nephew of Sister Marie Inez."

The Cardinal had been caught off guard but quickly replied.

"Sister Marie Inez? What a wonderful woman. My dear Lord, just a marvelous individual." All eyes in the first-class cabin were now firmly fixed upon me. Timothy Cardinal Manning extended his hand up towards me. I grasped it to kiss the large ring, the insignia of his important standing in the Vatican.

"I better kiss that ring," I thought. I was sure that both my mother and aunt would ask if I had enough sense to kiss the ring. I kissed it a second time for assurance. The smiling Archbishop continued to hold my hand firmly as he spoke.

"Your aunt is one of the most precious ladies I know." Now the Bishop joined in on the praises being lauded upon my aunt. Did they assume that I must be a good Catholic young man of outstanding character? I wanted to shy away as the official of the Church of Rome made a fuss over me that I felt was not warranted. Any commendation should be reserved for Sister Inez, and her alone.

"Such a blessed woman," was the last statement I heard as the No Smoking sign came on, signaling descent into LAX.

The cabin was quickly prepared as all unnecessary items were stored away and all trash collected. The landing upon the concrete runway was flawless.

"I'd like to welcome you to Los Angeles and request that you please remain seated with your seat belt firmly fastened until we come to a complete stop at our gate." I was upbeat as I thought that my brief audience with the Cardinal went well.

The agent threw the front door wide open and quickly stepped aside. He was aware there was a VIP on board. The entire cabin was filled with activity as the passengers rose and shuffled about for position, trying to gather their belongings and quickly depart. The lesser clergymen were also making haste to allow His Eminence a smooth exit. I slid into the forward galley and extended my pleasantries and gratitude to those who had chosen to fly with us.

One black robe quickly passed by as another battled somewhat with a heavy-looking briefcase. Then the tall, confident Bishop and Cardinal paused before me. His Eminence faced me with his commanding presence and piercing eyes.

"Well young man, it was wonderful to meet you, and what did you say your name was?" The Prince wanted my name, dear God.

"Eduardo, your Eminence," I said softly. Family protocol required I use my legal name when addressing an authority of the church. More importantly I was very aware that word of this was going to get back to my mother and dear aunt.

"Edw...ard," he leaned forward to catch my pronunciation. "Eduardo," he correctly stated,

"Valenciana," I spoke the family name slowly. I glimpsed past the Cardinal. I could see a huge logjam in the deplaning process and His Eminence was the log.

"Yes, Valencia," the Cardinal stated. I did not correct the mispronunciation. Instead I quickly knelt on one leg, clasped his hand and began to kiss the ring once more. I needed to hasten this meeting of fellow Catholics and get these people out as I spotted the ship cleaners waiting patiently in the jetway. The gate agent was on the verge of panic as he had a tight schedule to keep. Even the Captain came out of the cockpit as he could not hear any passengers deplaning and wondered about the holdup. Finally, His Eminence seemed satisfied with his little meeting and blessed me. I rose to my feet and he was gone. The passengers quickly slid by. I gathered my suitcase and garment bag as the other F/As and captain stood staring at me.

"What was that all about?" The aviator asked.

"Oh, the Cardinal was hearing my confession. You know, I had a lot of sins," I said with a straight face.

The rest of our crew gathered and deplaned. I entered the LAX flight lounge still shaking from the experience. I prayed I had done my mother and Sister Inez proud. Even though I'd just returned from a four-day trip, I headed right for the gym. The experience had created a great amount of anxiety I needed to dispose of.

I was determined to be a good pupil like the most serious bodybuilders who staked their claim at the Animal House Gym. Anatomy, kinesiology and nutrition were just a few areas of knowledge I came to understand under the tutelage of these "muscle men." I had increased my physical size over the months and would be further challenged in the process of dieting correctly. I needed to showcase my personal gains at the Midwest competition and continue to pass my monthly weight check with Shana. Purchasing a pair of military combat boots, I could be seen running along the soft sand of the South Bay beaches to strengthen my legs and burn more calories. The elimination of significant amounts of carbohydrates from my diet made the ordeal even more burdensome and I quickly found myself becoming edgy. Depression soon set in.

In September I calculated my bidding process to create a block of ten days off in the middle of October to prepare and compete in this contest. This meant working long flight days back-to-back while maintaining my strict diet, resisting the aroma of airline food. I spent the majority of layover time in any weight room I could find, at or near the hotel. As the percentage of body fat was drastically reduced, I could see that some fellow crew members wondered if I was okay. There were very few people in the company who knew of my endeavor. In that culture few would have shared my obsession, and in reality I didn't understand why myself.

Once released into my days off, I focused on the latter stages of preparation for the competition. The first part of my plan was to ensure I had the best tan in the competition. I was apprehensive about being clothed only in a pair of Speedos, so I resolved to be a golden-brown stand-out. I boarded a DC-10 and headed off to Honolulu.

Timmy Leong had been Mr. Hawaii in 1952 and '53. His gym was small but unique. Noted names in the field of bodybuilding considered Timmy's a home away from home when in the islands. The old building with wooden panels was lined with memories of glory days past. Black and white photos of a young, Mr. Hawaii in his heyday showcased the road to his current reputation. In these pictures, champions of the day and future cinema stars stood either side of their Hawaiian mentor. I staked my claim at Timmy's Gym, resuming the intense final workouts.

The availability of fresh fish helped me keep to my strict diet. Upon arriving at Timmy's, I was somewhere between 5-7 % body fat, but the day before leaving HNL (just days prior the competition), I had lowered it to 3.2% body fat. Of course, that would change drastically right after the event. I had endured the absence of beer, pizza, French fries, ice cream, greasy burritos and soft drinks of any kind for over six months. I was determined to gorge myself at the conclusion of the contest.

For some reason, while in the training process, I was attracted to the importance of timing: adherence to timing in execution at the airline, in the gym during the workout, and especially in the diet. I recognized it was not a simple decision to go to such extremities. I did not understand how a physique contest could reveal the importance of timing. Yet, something convinced me its relevance would be forthcoming.

The morning I was to leave for the Midwest, I arrived at LAX with time to spare. Standing in the gate area, I heard a familiar voice

"Holy shit, you shaved your legs," came the wise crack. Tommy Acoba is and always will be a gift in my life, my best friend. Our friendship dated back to ninth grade, enduring athletics together, drive-in movie theaters and purchasing at that certain liquor store on Fourth Street that sold beer to insistent teenage boys. Tommy was a mathematician in an important position with a major aerospace company, one of many that dotted the landscape around LAX. We even traveled together in Europe for some time prior to my airline days. My tall, strong structured friend found his discipline in running marathons. He knew the importance of routine, diet and commitment. Heck, he knew a lot about everything.

"Yeah Acoba, I shaved my legs, what of it?"

"What would your brother the cop say?" Tommy sized me up as he had not seen me in a while. He quickly noticed the drastic change. "Shit, you're cut to ribbons." I noticed his flight bag and I became excited. My buddy was boarding the plane with me. I wasn't worried anymore for my dear friend would be at the competition to cheer me on.

In the frigid weather of the Midwest, it became very evident that I had the best tan in the entire state. When questioned how I had attained it, I simply responded, "Tanning booths." I performed with dignity in front of a crowd where I did not know a single soul in attendance expect Acoba. I went for it and figured, what the hell, I will be on a plane in the morning and be gone.

"Man, you are ripped!" A fellow competitor's show of respect added to my confidence. I was asked about my training diet by others attending the show. The boys at the Animal House knew what they were talking about. The diet was the key and everything else fell into place. The stage was lined with competitors who also endured a small hell for the limelight in such a small window of time in one's life. It hit me that no matter what, in my entire life, I would never again be in this fit a condition. I was 27 years old and if I lived to be 100, I still would not be able to attain this level of physical conditioning. I was at a peak and I did not know exactly what made me do it.

"When you see one double bicep pose you've seen them all." Tommy 's sarcastic evaluation of the competition had some logic behind it. But now it was over. The need for pizza and a cold beer took on a new priority. Because of my low body fat, I became intoxicated with one small can of beer. I gorged like a sloppy little pig. When the pizza was finished, I followed up with a cheeseburger, everything on it, extra mayo and of course French fries. It did not take long for the full meal to be consumed but moments of contentment didn't last long; all at once I ran into some bushes by a park and heaved the whole lot. I took a few minutes to clean my face, settled myself down then I was off once again looking for more food. Pie à la mode satisfied me but only for a short time. Mashed potatoes and thick gravy were the dessert. The disgusting cycle repeated itself again. It was time to leave and go back to the West Coast. The commitment was over.

I viewed the setting sun from above as my flight headed back towards the Pacific Ocean. The subtle colors of yellow and orange mixed with the shades of purple on the clouds marked the conclusion of a short period of time in which I was no wiser for all my effort. Nine months of dedication and sacrifice for what? Respect? Hadn't it all started with respect? Physically, I could not have been any better. Mentally, I seemed lost and confused. The event was not the splendid culmination I had envisioned for the better part of a year. In a moment of impulse, I turned to Tommy, and murmured,

"I know you're going to think I'm crazy, but I'm going to be in a plane crash." Tommy gazed at me. I began to feel embarrassed.

"Do you believe you will come out of it?"

"Uh, yeah, I think so." I responded.

"Then don't worry about it, let it go and when it happens that will be one thing you can cross off your bucket list." Tommy turned to pick up one of his technical books (which only someone like him can happily get lost in) and that was the end of the discussion.

That's what Reina Torres was doing. Her acceptance of what she believed to be God's will, allowed her to live in peace. I was no saint, nor did I want to be. I just wanted some serenity. I gazed out the window and saw the last rays of the sun vanish below the horizon.

Down on flight hours when I returned to duty on the 24th. I hadn't yet been called for a trip. Meanwhile, relishing the extra hours of sleeping and eating became the focal point of my day. Soon I was rewarded by Scheduling with a trip and a unique situation. The entire crew of a Miami bound DC-10 flight needed to be replaced. They also informed me that I was to work the Senior/ lead position on the flight. I was shocked because I really hadn't accumulated that much seniority compared to most based at LAX. I was then told that the rest of the F/As assigned were all new, just out of training. The bonus was that this flight sequence also offered a 31-hour layover in the Floridian metropolis. No bossy senior gals on this one, I thought. I then became panicky as I tried to recall the first-class service on the route. I rushed about my home looking for my Flight Attendant Manual. I prepped for the flight.

"The McDonnell Douglas DC-10 has eight emergency exits," I rehearsed with my best disc-jockey voice. "Make sure your seat is in the upright locked position and your tray table in front of you is stored away. On behalf of the entire cabin crew I would like to thank you for flying with us this evening. If there is anything you need please don't hesitate to ask one of our friendly flight attendants."

Once we assembled in the briefing room, I was amazed to find an all-female cadet crew. They were young, bright and willing to hang on their Senior Flight Attendant's every word. Every new hire imagines what the first great trip will be like. I was overwhelmed. This naughty little boy found himself locked in the candy store.

"Respect," my conscience dictated. I would try my best to be a fine example of what a Senior F/A should be. One other factor was that I no longer felt depressed or sluggish and I was ready to work the cabins. A normal diet was supplying me with tremendous energy so there would be no need for coffee on this leg.

The crew worked with precision and the new F/As were on top of everything as we cruised at 35.000'. Some passengers complimented the young and attractive female crew. Everything went more than right, and like my class, they had developed a close bond with each other.

"What's to do in Miami, Eddy?" The ladies wanted to go out, have fun, see and be seen. Some spoke of eating fine Cuban cuisine, others wanted to dance, and all had come with classy attire stored in their regulation garment bags. As each reappeared in the lobby later that evening I was blown away. I had not been around that much elegance in a long time. They certainly turned heads! As the evening progressed some young buck would approach the fillies to try his luck only to be politely dismissed.

This splendid evening out was not about finding a boyfriend or forming a new relationship. This was their inaugural flight and as one crewmate told me, it was filled with hope for a long and successful career in the industry and enjoying the fruits of their trade. They were simply celebrating their recent graduation. Soon I discovered by the evening's activities that I was designated to be their chaperone. Seven gorgeous ladies was a big responsibility. I would never have a moment to focus on any one F/A as it was my job to see to the well-being of all of them. I was the director of this little Girl Scout group and the airline would have my head on a platter if something happened to even one of them. Dinner was first on the list and Cuban cuisine was the star attraction. Although considered adults, some of the ladies were just a couple of years out of high school. They respected me and trusted that I would watch over them.

Drinking for me was kept to a minimum as I still retained an extremely low percentage of body fat. Besides, as the time passed, I became more nervous as suitor after suitor approached only to be rebuffed. Then they would glance over at me and deliver a menacing stare. Why did these seven gals stick so closely to that tanned (Cuban)? Anyway, I was there to protect them. The F/As never realized I was lucky I didn't get my ass kicked that night. There were a lot of pissed off guys when we finally left the disco.

The crew laughed and sunned by the pool the next morning and it was clear that I had made some new friends. That made me happy and the flight back to LAX was easy. The depression I encountered while dieting faded away. I was now consuming a lot more calories and my energy level surged. At the gym I was easily handling sizable amounts of weight while still retaining a low percentage of body fat. Life was good again.

Chapter IV

When I awoke on the morning of Tuesday, October 30th I struggled to open my eyes. My mind caught a flicker of light, a flame. Was I dreaming? Only half awake, I caught the stare of the Virgin Mother, a statue I kept in my room. Her face seemed so peaceful as I studied her features. Mary seemed to be focused on the small candle's flame at her feet I had failed to extinguish the night before. The fire danced a gleeful jig as an act of defiance to taunt me because it had survived the entire night. The Virgin statue had been a gift from my aunt, Sister Marie Inez. She had attained the position of Provincial Mother in the convent of the Holy Sisters of Carmel of the Most Sacred Heart of Jesus. I was sure Sister Inez would have preferred it if I had become a priest, but she got a flight attendant instead. I recalled the time I had just returned from Las Vegas, and she referred to the desert oasis as "that city of sin." I thought the real sin was having to work six flights enduring awful turbulence caused by the hot desert below.

Although I had drifted from my Roman Catholic practice I had not strayed from my cultural beliefs or lost respect for my aunt's and mother's dedication to the faith. I reasoned that if God listened to anyone, he listened to the Sisters of Carmel. Sister Inez assured me that the assembly in the convent was constantly praying for me and, I supposed, the repentance of my wicked ways. Yet, I was wise enough not to dismiss the power of prayer that echoed in whispers through the religious space of their convent.

Now upright in bed, I noticed my suitcase open on the floor, filled with everything a reserve flight attendant needed to cover any flight on short notice. My clothes were nicely packed; there was my flight manual, a flashlight, a wine corkscrew and my passport. All that was needed was for Scheduling to call with an assignment. I glanced out the window that revealed a lovely sunny day in the South Bay. I decided to push the scheduling process in hopes of having the possibility of beach time before reporting to LAX.

"I think I have one, Eduardo," Marlene the friendly scheduler stated.

"I'll take anything," I interjected but was hoping she would say Honolulu. After a moment's pause, she resumed speaking.

"Ah, Sequence 190." Concluding the call, I grabbed my current F/A bid sheet. My finger frantically ran down each page seeking the destination of Sequence 190.

"LAX-MEX," the coded letters jumped out at me

"Shit, the stinking all-nighter." I slapped myself on the forehead and cursed for having forced the process. If left alone, I may have been awarded a Honolulu trip. All that was now settled. It was going to be a long night, a hard-international flight with no sleep and a full service turn-around back to LAX the next morning.

Although there would be no layover, the thought of Mexico City brought warm memories of the Zona Rosa, crewmembers laughing wine glasses in hand. I wanted Mexico to be my next destination for a lengthy escape, a new adventure. The beaches of Acapulco or Puerto Vallarta were tempting. The cuisine, the nightlife and especially the warmth of the Mexican people, all of it was very inviting. But tonight, would just be an all-night turn-around.

Resigned to this fact, I put on my workout clothes and drove inland to the Animal House gym. I suppose my decision was out of habit more than anything. There was no more contest, no more test to challenge my will, no more anything. I sensed a measure of anxiety, a sense of uncertainty lingering in my mind. After a while I tried to shrug it off. I stood in the gym and tried to balance the pleasurable and the necessary for the workout. No matter how hard I tried I could not get my thoughts together. Something was wrong. There was no focus. There was no particular problem distracting me, but nevertheless I <u>was</u> totally distracted. On October 30th, I quit my work out early for the first time.

Heading back to Manhattan Beach I began to get nervous, to tremble. My hand was still shaking as I shut the door behind me. I lay down and sought to rest before my evening report at LAX.

The anxiousness continued to rise and soon turned to anger. My body just tossed and turned as I desperately tried to sleep. The time dragged on with not much comfort, just the gentle look of the Virgin, reflecting sympathy or possibly pity. She didn't have to work the all-nighter, I thought, and I wished I didn't either. I glanced at the clock and it was time to get ready.

I selected the beige shirt with the company logo once I had showered and shaved. Fully dressed, I gazed into the mirror one last time. My dress tie with the airline's emblem was straightened. As I grabbed my suitcase and closed the door behind me, I had a strange thought -- would I ever see this place again? I tried to shake it, I had to go to work. I settled into my vehicle, turned on the radio and headed out for LAX.

"What if the plane goes down?" I whispered to myself. It wasn't the first time I had asked myself this question. I supposed that other flight crews most likely had doubts now and then on their way to work. Of course, others must have such questions. It must be normal.

The radio's music soothed me as my mind insisted that such thinking was silly, at least on this night and as this flight was concerned. I gazed into the sky as I came to a red stoplight on the crowded boulevard. I allowed my imagination to enjoy a recurring dream of a DC-10 ascending into the heavens. I recalled the sensation of sitting behind the captain in the cockpit, a few miles high and gazing out the window. The spray of lights that gathered around a city were always impressive. They seemed to be galaxies, complementing the galaxies above. I would always get carried away with the fantasy that I had transcended the mundane, that in fact I was on a spaceship destined for some remote star.

"Get moving asshole." The car horn from behind broke the vision. The light was indeed green.

"I hope that individual is not on my plane tonight," I expressed with some embarrassment. One thing was sure -- it was going to be a long night.

A day full of unpleasantness convinced me that it might be best if I kept myself busy through the night flight. Work would make the time pass quickly, or so I hoped. Going into the last day of the month I figured that the other crew members would also be reservists. With the addition of the recent graduating class I most likely would have more seniority. Maybe I should bid to work the first-class position? That certainly would keep me on my toes. Arriving at the company's parking structure, I quickly gathered my belongings and hurried to catch the company tram that took the crews to the terminal building.

As the elevator door opened, I heard the clanging bell announcing the tram's arrival. Not wanting to be left behind to wait for the next tram, I began to run. Leaping upon the bus at the last moment, I stopped to compose myself before finding a seat. As the tram sped off, I immediately recognized friends' smiling faces. Tamlyn Surutan Baily was a "lovely little flower" of a lady. In her early twenties, we had shared duty on various flights in the past. Her laughter was always welcome. Becky Devita was another of the new faces on the flight line. Her blond hair and green eyes had such a sparkle. Gary Rollings, Rod Dawn and Jeff Stillwell were familiar faces. Three other people I did not recognize - a young man, a woman and a girl dressed in an F/A uniform who looked as if she could be a student in high school.

"They are sure hiring them young these days," I whispered to myself as I took a place in the rear of the vehicle.

"Maybe you're just getting old." The statement came from the rear corner of the bus. Funny, I did not initially notice anyone on the other side, as my mind had been occupied. The lights on the tarmac outside the vehicle shined brightly through the window of the dimmed tram, creating only a silhouette of the figure that had caught me off guard. I strained to make out a face.

"Well I know one thing, I will be a lot older when we arrive back here from Mexico City tomorrow morning," I countered.

"You're on Flight 605 also?" The figure lurched forward; the airport lights shifted. Out from the shadow emerged the radiant face of Reina Torres.

"We're all on the flight, Eddy. What a great crew," Tamlyn blurted out. "It's going to be a grand flight." The revelation that such close friends were assigned the same sequence lifted the spirits of everyone except me. I glanced back at Reina who had switched on her F/A flashlight to delve into some paperback novel. I was left in silence to ponder my fate.

"Why were we all going on the all-nighter?" I was speaking to myself. What had happened to the regular crew? Immediately the answer came from Gary, speaking to one of the F/A's that I was not familiar with.

"Yeah, they became illegal to fly the trip by five minutes," he stated. (illegal-exceeding monthly allowed work hours. "They," I took to mean as the regular crew.) No wonder the replacements were so junior. Jeff spoke up revealing that he and Becky would be "dead heading" on the leg down to the Mexican capital. That was indeed fortunate for them I thought, and this fact just pissed me off even more. I envisioned them nestled nicely in the comfort of a First-Class seat, sleeping, conserving their strength, to be available to work the leg back to LAX the following morning. I assumed I was senior to most in this group of youngsters, so why hadn't Marlene, the flight scheduler, reserved a dead-head position for me?

The tram made its way around the parked planes that night of October 30th, jet fumes heavy in the air, service vehicles scurrying about, personnel all around. The drop-off point was a ramp that led down to the company's operations center, the underworld of Terminal 5. Upon entering the flight lounge, I had already complained to two acquaintances of the burdens of having to work all night then deal with a full flight in the morning. My miserable state of mind forced me to sit alone in the lounge, wishing I was elsewhere. Suddenly, a gleam caught my eye. It was coming from Gary Rollings' shoes. I gazed in complete bafflement because they were immaculate. In fact, Gary's total appearance epitomized perfection. I was clearly outclassed. This made me feel worse.

It was Gary who herded the youngsters for the pre-flight meeting. As I grudgingly entered the doorway, Gary put a hand on my shoulder.

"Join the fun big fella." My desire to isolate myself became even stronger as I sat at the end of the table, distancing myself from the others. I was physically present, but not mentally. Something deep down nagged at me. I wanted nothing to do with this flight. I tried to hide my foul mood.

All the riders from the tram were present. The adolescent looking young lady was introduced as Karen Smitt, 20 years old, fresh out of training. With dark satin hair, fair complexion, she was the all-American gal, the girl next door. I would learn years later that as a freshman in high school she once informed a senior classmate that she knew exactly what she wanted to do with her life.

"I want to be a Flight Attendant." And here she was filled with enthusiasm wanting to embrace this dreadful all-night voyage. The DC-10 flight would be her first flight into Mexico. Her joy was evident, smiling broadly like a child on her first excursion to Disneyland. I wondered how long that smile would remain once she worked the "slave ship" leg the following morning on the return with a full load and a full breakfast service. My spirits finally improved to some degree when I discovered that there would only be one hundred passengers on this first leg down to MEX. Gary announced that this night's flight would be his first in taking on the responsibility as a designated Senior/lead on the DC-10 and humbly asked for the entire crew's assistance in performing his task successfully. Everyone eagerly committed their support except one. Gary hesitated a bit in his next request. Since the crew was so junior, a volunteer was needed to work the downstairs galley, knowing what was in store for them in the morning. Oh no, I had no desire to spend all night and the following morning wrestling with the nasty food carts. I instantly closed my eyes and pretended I did not hear the request, the actions of a scoundrel. If no one stepped forward, I was comforted by the bottom line. I had seniority.

"Let the high school kid do it," I thought to myself. I found disdain in her delightful manner. I wanted to politely sneer at her, give her a full dose of reality.

"This is not an enjoyable assignment," I wished to tell her. Cary Diller was a new acquaintance, but I would soon discover what a fine lady she was. She eagerly stepped forward to do her part in making this trip successful; she volunteered to be the galley person, thus sealing her own fate. The other face I had not recognized belonged to a wholesome looking young man with reddish brown hair. The name "Skip" was all I could recall.

"Eddy?" The calling of my name startled me.

"Asleep already?" Cary asked. The rest of the crew started laughing. A few seconds passed before I realized I was being asked which flight attendant jumpseat I would prefer thus dictating my duties on Flight 605.

My own bed at home. The thought remained in my head. I found it difficult to choose while also acknowledging that I indeed was on this appalling flight. Wanting to do the least amount of work, I chose door 1R in first class. I reasoned I would be required to serve the least amount of passengers on a full flight in the morning. Reina had been assigned as the Spanish Speaker which was fine with me. I didn't want the other crew members to know that I, too, could speak Spanish, not this night. Reina Patricia Torres' profile caught my attention as she sat content, those gorgeous black eyes still holding that paperback book. If I had been spooked by her stories previously, I was in no frame of mind now to even begin to address her nonsensical little dreams. Fatigue, anger and pettiness brushed aside any fears generated by her in the past.

"We'll see you at Gate 58," Gary concluded the meeting. I waited until all had departed, trying to somehow delay the inevitable. Exiting Operations, I carried my suitcase up the back stairs of the jetway at the assigned gate. No sooner had I arrived when a maintenance man appeared, attired in the familiar red jumpsuit, to depress me further. The DC-10 Spaceship designated as our craft for Flight 605 had just arrived from Honolulu a few minutes earlier and the ground worker shook his head and rolled his eyes.

"Wait till you guys see the mess," he shouted above all the jet noise of the busy airport. Upon crossing the threshold into the belly of the craft, I threw my bag down and stood in astonishment. I just wanted to cry at that point. The cabin section was a disaster. Barf bags full and empty lined the aisles. Plastic cups, napkins, tissues and dirty diapers were what greeted our happy crew that evening. Gary Rollings kept a positive attitude and made every effort to try and rectify the problem, folding blankets and restoring pillows. I, on the other hand, planted my rear-end in the galley, full of disgust. The gate agent boarded the jumbo jet and asked the crew to deplane, wanting us to wait in the jetway. The captain had seen the mess and requested a replacement craft from the hangar. Of course, I recognized there was going to be a substantial delay while they prepped the new aircraft. I was sure the world was conspiring against me.

"This is worthless," was all I could mutter as I huddled with the rest of the crew in the cabin. The gate agent was upset because I believed she wanted to board the passengers and go home. I was upset because there would be less time to do the service and I was stuck with the flight no matter what. But the rest of the flight attendants of 605 took the delay in stride, seeming to be enjoying one another, making friends. How could they be so upbeat?

After some time we caught sight of another jumbo jet with the large red logo of our airline broad across the ship's side. The DC-10's number's, NW903, could be read on its side during the slow journey to our gate. It always was an impressive view. I gazed down the left side of the craft as it was slowly positioned aside us. I was in wonder with the thought that in a short time this enormous vehicle would carry us miles into the heavens.

Once aboard, the crew worked quickly to prepare the cabin. Carts were properly stored. Emergency equipment was checked and double-checked. Blankets and pillows were taken from the overhead cabinet area and placed onto the seats as the majority of passengers on this leg would soon try to get some sleep. Once I had secured my belongings and checked my station at 1R, I walked to the mid galley where a pot of coffee had been brewed. I drank the first cup quickly in hopes of alleviating my fatigue and displeasure. I was pouring a second cup as Captain Carl Herbert Sr. boarded the craft, his craft this night, at door 2L.

"Need a cup of java, Captain?" My personality surfaced momentarily.

"Thanks partner," stated the bigger-than-life figure in full-dress uniform. Captain Herbert took a couple of sips and turned forward and headed to the cockpit.

The flight was already delayed for some time and the gate agents wanted to board the passengers as soon as possible. I returned to my station at 1R to find Gary and Karen Smitt waiting for me.

"Listen Eddy," Gary became diplomatic. "As this is Karen's first Mexico flight, I was wondering if you would switch positions with her so I could teach her the First-Class Service." The request only further confused me, then I felt my temper rise.

"What?"

"Switch with Karen. You go aft to door 4R." Gary was doing what he felt would be of benefit to Karen and thought I would feel the same. He did not realize that this particular night he was wrong.

"You want me to go aft into the smoking section?"

"Hey, it's your call, but I know Karen would be grateful," Gary reasoned.

"Please, please, please," begged Karen. Finding myself cornered I grudgingly agreed and gathered my belongings and proceeded to the rear, to door 4R, whining quietly every step of the way down the right aisle.

"Boarding." Reina's clear voice rang over the intercom, putting everyone on alert. After checking the emergency equipment in the aft I moved forward to where Cary was having a tough time with a stubborn trash cart at door 2R. Glancing across the mid galley I noticed Reina intently gazing down, holding a boarding card which the first passenger entering had handed her.

"Hey, you okay?" I queried.

"Huh? Oh, yeah," She stated. "The flight numbers. I was just looking at the flight numbers." Her voice registered a concern.

"6-0-5, what's the big deal?" I asked.

"No. It's changed. It's now 2-6-0-5."

"6-0-5, 2-6-0-5, who cares, this is still a piece-of-shit assignment."

"Eddy!" Reina was surprised by my lack of concern.

"Well damn it. These passengers should be home, tucked warmly in their beds, fast asleep as I should be." I grabbed the boarding pass from Reina's hand. 2-6-0-5 were indeed the numbers on the card and I started to think back to the flight I had worked with Reina to the Mexican capital many months ago. I pondered for a moment. "Our conversation, your premonition, that dream you said you have." Then I remembered. Whenever there is a change of aircraft the airline must change the flight number. It is customary to just attach an extra digit in front of the original number. In this case, they happened to choose a 2.

"I've had the same dream ever since I was eleven," she insisted.

"And what were the numbers you saw?" I challenged her. She looked away for a moment then replied.

"2-6-5."

"Oh Christ," I thought to myself. Here I was in the presence of a psychic, we were delayed, I was exhausted, and Rebecca of Sunnybrook Farm had just taken away my position in first class. I wanted to plead with Reina not to do this to me. "Was there a zero in your dream?" I asked her. She thought for a while then answered.

"No."

"Then this is not the flight in your vision," I logically stated. She remained silent for a moment, then I saw a smile appear and she livened up.

"You're right, I'm being silly." The bulk of the passengers began to arrive, so I left her and hurried down the right aisle back to my post.

"God, Reina, if you ever have the feeling you are going to be killed on a plane make sure I'm not on it with you." I murmured to myself. How I wished I was somewhere else. The plane began to get organized. I saw the rear section as a refuge where I was determined to remain and do the absolute minimum involved.

In the cabin of Flight 2605 the scene was normal, passengers fussing around, trying to get their luggage into the overhead cabinet, grabbing as many pillows and blankets as lay on the seats. Some moved about the cabin, looking to take advantage of the open seats. They wanted to stretch across 2 or 3 seats once the craft was airborne. They all wished to sleep this flight away, something I could not do. I slowly walked up the right aisle checking to make sure that the passengers I would be responsible for had their carry-on luggage packed safely away. There would be plenty of open seats on this leg, so I expected no difficulties. I noticed a Mexican man with a white cowboy hat. Two Hispanic women, possibly sisters, took seats in the rear section along the side of the cabin and just a couple of rows forward of door 4R, my jumpseat. A beautiful, dark-haired, dark-eyed young lady caught my eye. She was sitting on the opposite side of the craft. The female gate agent came on the intercom to apologize for the lengthy hold-up and hurriedly shut the door.

DC-10, NW903 suddenly lurched backwards. There were a few individuals still standing in the aisles, but the action of the plane made it obvious that Captain Herbert and his cockpit crew had decided that our delay had been long enough. The young, LAX based F/As scurried to their assigned positions, securing the doors and preparing for the safety demonstration.

"Welcome aboard Flight 2605, operating to Mexico City." Gary's voice took command.
"There are eight emergency exit doors on our aircraft. Please locate the exit nearest you." I could see that a great many passengers already had their eyes closed. I thought how confused they would be if a quick exit was required. I went through the motions of showing my aft section how to grab and place the yellow oxygen mask over their face if required. But as I had been explaining to Reina, nothing was going to happen. The flight would be as typical as it was every other night so I could care less if the people were paying attention to my demonstration. Once Gary was done, the emergency information was then repeated in Spanish.

"Bienvenidos Señores y Señoras." Reina's announcement in Spanish was perfect. Her voice contained the confidence I hoped would remain, considering our earlier discussion. I walked down the right aisle as Reina spoke, checking to make sure the seat belts were on, the seats were in the upright locked position and the tray tables were up and stored away.

"Yes, everything is going to be all right," I whispered to myself. I wanted to feel it. I just wanted to get up in the air, get the service done as quickly as possible and tuck everyone to sleep for the duration of the three-and-one-half-hour flight. Cary had secured a liquor cart and a trash cart in the aft galley just to the rear of my jumpseat. In training it was always emphasized that these carts could be a real safety hazard on takeoff and landing if an emergency occurred. I did a double-check on them, making sure they were locked and secured. The last thing I wanted was one of them to shoot forward and slam right into my face while I was buckled to my jumpseat at 4R. Securing the aft galley, I then strapped myself in.

"Flight Attendants, prepare for take off." The command came from the cockpit and the 10 rotated on the tarmac at the end of the runway. The Spaceship positioned itself and started to accelerate.

The fantasy was about to begin. I always found the feeling so ecstatic --a rocket to the stars and being taken away, at the mercy of a force beyond one's control. With the sound and sensation amplified in the aft, I was aware that the craft was turning left as it rose higher into the heavens over the Pacific. This allowed me to see the jeweled brilliance of the Los Angeles Basin. On such a clear night, the stars vied for my attention.

With the DC-10 still ascending, the young crew rose to get organized and prepare for the beverage service. A portion of the passengers were already asleep and the F/As wanted to ensure that the rest would soon be.

"Let's get this out of the way." Finding myself somewhat rejuvenated I donned my blue regulation F/A apron with the company's logo dead center, middle chest. I re-pinned my flight wings onto the apron. My new attitude surprised my co-workers as I energetically arrived in the service galley. I scanned the craft to see where everyone was. Gary and little Miss Karen were taking care of the first-class cabin. Rod Dawn was at 3L and the guy I knew only as Skip was still aft at door 4L. They would be responsible for the service on the left side of the fuselage. Tamlyn, stationed at 3R and I, would take care of the service on the right side. Reina who was stationed at 2L, assisted Cary and serviced the passengers located in "El Segundo." (between first class and service galley)

"Hey, Mexican Jumping Bean," Cary said, "I have the Menudo pot down below ready to go, you want to put it on your cart?" I was surprised, then realized she was poking fun at me.

"Only if you sit up front rolling and slapping fresh tortillas," I responded. Cary laughed at my come-back. She could be seen still snickering as she rode the service elevator back down to the galley.

Tamlyn and I passed out the usual fare: Coke, coffee and peanuts. Extra napkins were given to a little Mexican man and woman, an obvious couple. The dark skin and aged hands testified to a life of hardship. No matter how foul a mood I may have been in, I was always humbled by the sight of such people who most likely had saved up their hard-earned money for this trip. He was a laborer and she a maid, or nanny perhaps. I envisioned them returning to their homeland, a rare opportunity to visit loved ones. I spent extra time with them making sure they had everything they needed, and they assured me in Spanish that everything was just fine. Maneuvering the cart a few steps aft, I came to an aisle where everyone was all asleep, requiring no assistance, yet I made sure that they still had their seat belts attached in case of turbulence. Making sure Tamlyn had finished with her passengers, we again adjusted the cart and retreated a bit more aft. I turned inward towards the center and was met with a bold request.

"Hey man, got any brew?" A young man with a prominent red beard was thirsty. Much later I would discover that his name was Ronald Daily. A handsome young Hispanic man sat next to him. I immediately assumed they were traveling together. I smiled and squatted down to check the bottom of the cart where the beer was kept in some dry ice, ensuring that it was nice and cold. I grabbed a bottle and was quite surprised.

"It's Bohemia," I stated. "This is damn good stuff,"

"Good, huh? Give us six," the red beard requested. I began to laugh. These guys were dear to my own heart.

"How about I give you each two now and the others a little later?" The men were content with that arrangement. As the cart worked its way back, each encounter with the passengers of Flight 2605 began to make me focus, when just a little while before I wanted to hide away. Now I was taking care to notice every little detail about everyone I saw and served. A slight scar on the forehead of a man, a mole on the cheek of a Mexican woman, the torn blue jeans of a young man, and always there was the distinct visage of the Native American that was the foundation of the modern Mexican. The majority had dark, elastic skin, sun-parched, the distinct nose and the deep pool of the dusky eyes. I knew the "sangre," the blood of a rich heritage that ran in their veins also ran in mine. These were the same features my father carried, not just outwardly but deep in his soul, the same spirit he carried intimately inside. I felt as one with the Mexican Nationals who often booked this late flight and who were the majority this night on the DC-10. Some were returning to visit family after long periods of grinding labor in the fields of California's San Joaquin Valley. Some were traveling with forged documents, illegal while in the United States. The one thing they all had in common was that they were simple folk, the salt of the earth. The DC-10's cabins were not occupied by sun worshipers on a fling down to one of the many hot spots on the Mexican Riviera. As I served them, I understood them and was touched by their almost religious kindness. These were the sort of people who were our neighbors while I was growing up in East Los Angeles and represented the very reasons my parents never moved out of the old neighborhood. My mother had taught me to respect and learn from such simplicity. On Flight 2605, I felt a special bond with them.

As the cart reached the aft of the craft, right before door 4R, I came upon the two Hispanic women I assumed were sisters.

"Ustedes quieren un refresco señoritas?" The women smiled and blushed as I offered them a soft drink. They were obviously older married women, yet I addressed each of them as "Miss." My mother had long ago instructed her son on the proper etiquette when addressing a woman, I was meeting for the first time. In Hispanic Culture, it is presumptuous to assume that a woman one first meets is married, no matter the age.

"Whiskey con agua sin hielo." One sister requested a cocktail. I took my time and proudly served the water in a plastic cup and presented her with the miniature bottle containing the hard liquor.

"Dos dólares por favor," I requested. The woman stared blankly. It soon became obvious to me that she was not a seasoned flier, and by her expression did not realize that the alcoholic drinks were not free. I immediately acted to save her the embarrassment. "Me complacería si me deja pagar." I politely told her that it would please me greatly if she allowed me the honor of purchasing the drink for her. The older lady was deeply touched and extremely grateful and held out her hand. I took it and held it graciously to the shock of Tamlyn on the other side of the cart but to the delight of the ladies. With the service concluded I stored the cart into the aft galley just feet away from my assigned jumpseat at 4R. As I turned and faced the cabin I was surprised to discover that a young Mexican family, which included two children, had relocated to the aft sector of the craft, to my section. The young family needed more room for their children to move about.

Rudimentary logic told me to just accept my fate in working this flight. These good people deserved the best service for their hard-earned money. I reworked the beverage cart…arranging the small glass liquor bottles, making the cart look a little nicer to be used as a secondary bar for the aft passengers, those who were unable to sleep. All at once I felt a presence behind the panel, behind me. I turned and glanced down to see a sheepish, funny-looking little face peering up at me, standing in the aisle.

"Hola Capitán," I stated to a small shy figure who I assumed was one of the children of the young Hispanics who had opted to move aft in the cabin. The dark shaggy-haired lad turned his head, perhaps indicating it was his family fast asleep. Instantly I turned back to the service cart, and dug deep through the drawers, feeling for a little plastic bag.

"Ah, this is it." Holding up a plastic pair of junior pilot wings, I saw the sleepy brown eyes of the child open widely. I stopped down and prepared the metal pin in the backside of the wings and was about to pin them appropriately upon his chest when I noticed he was wearing pajamas. "Yeah buddy, I wish I had my pajamas on, too." He glared at my flight wings pinned to my apron and slowly reached out and touched them. He smiled and I sent him off to his sleeping family. The boy hopped away gleefully installing himself firmly by his mother's side, lowering his head to rest.

I would make my rounds in the slumbering cabin, then retreat aft. As I did, I would always refocus myself by viewing the child's smiling little face. I began to appreciate being re-assigned to the back of the plane where it was quiet. The side panel lights were dimmed so that there was a shadow engulfing each cabin. The lit areas by the exits provided enough light for those who wished to walk about. I just sat in my jumpseat, listening to the deep whistle of the air outside. All that remained was the humming of the turbines in the tri-craft's engines as they sucked in the jet fuel that is stored in the outstretched wings, allowing us to streak across the heavens. Suddenly the young child appeared before me once again. I wasn't sure if he needed anything or just wanted to see what I was doing. I believe he had become fascinated with me.

"Quieres una Coca?" I asked.

He nodded his head excitedly.

"Who's your friend, Eddy?" Startled, I rose and turned to see Tamlyn standing in the dim cabin lighting just forward of us. She walked over to the liquor cart to get a drink for a passenger.

"I'm not sure," I responded. I turned to the boy.

"Cómo te llamas?" I asked.

"Javier," he responded as he sipped his cup of Coke.

"There you go Tamlyn, my friend's name is Javier." She stood facing the forward section when she nodded for me to look. I could see the red light that signaled that a passenger was requesting the presence of an F/A. It was actually coming from a seat that was closer to the mid galley but the gals up front were in the service center. I supposed they could not see the aisle light or hear the tone indicating the need for assistance. I winked at my little Mexican friend and he sluggishly turned and walked up the aisle. The angle at which a DC-10 flies makes the aft section the lowest point. Focusing in on the blinking red light to direct me to the appropriate row, I finally made out a gentleman whose head popped about like a rooster, gazing in all directions of the mid cabin. Once I appeared, he released a burst of frustration before I could even fully turn to face him.

"It's maddening, not to mention creating a strain on my eyes. I want it fixed," he demanded.

Hey man, slow down, lighten up, I wanted to say but his strained face indicated that I should be careful, work this matter with logic and concern to satisfy his needs. "I'm sorry for the inconvenience sir," I babbled the usual protocol. "Sir, there are plenty of seats in the aft, the back of the plane." But the gentleman, who seemed to have a European accent wasn't having any of it.

"Did you hear what I said? I want you to fix the blasted light." As I gazed up I saw that his particular reading light was blinking off and on erratically. "Now, get on with it. I don't care what you have to do to get it done."

"I will contact the cockpit and see if they can do anything," I assured him, but really wanting an excuse to get away from him. Picking up the crew phone at 2R, I punched the proper keys of the coded sequence that ensured that someone in the cockpit would answer, most likely the Flight Engineer who handles that duty. I gazed into the mid galley to see Cary in a happy mood sitting on a jumpseat, talking to Reina. A tired-sounding voice finally answered.

"Yeah?" I suddenly found myself unprepared as to what I wanted to tell him.

"There's a guy, midsection, having trouble with his reading light. Can you guys do anything about it?" I sounded foolish.

"Just have him move to another seat," the voice suggested, then hung up.

"Hey, he ain't gonna like that," I whispered to myself. Of course, I was given the most logical answer, but would this guy be willing to endure the minor inconvenience? I slowly returned to the gentleman who had witnessed me talking on the aircraft's phone. I surmised that possibly he would be a little nicer, having seen my efforts on his behalf, but when I suggested he move I saw I was wrong.

"Sir, the Captain regrets that..."

"You incompetent oaf." The passenger cut me off at the knees. "What seat can I move to? I've wasted enough time already," he snapped, as he gathered his things and jumped up. I hopped back a step so as not to get trampled by this raving individual.

"There are plenty of seats in the aft section," I reiterated, standing silent as he hurried off into the darkness of the back section, waving his hands in displeasure. That night, I encouraged him to change seats on Flight 2605, and that fellow is forever indebted to me whether he would want to admit it or not. Of course, no one was expecting an emergency -- not on my plane, not on this night. I turned and gazed across the cabin looking forward. There was no one except perhaps Reina. I shook my head and retreated aft to my little sanctuary.

Suddenly, a dark figure appeared in the aft service center, under the aft galley lighting. I recognized the face as Skip's, the fellow working the left side of the fuselage at 4L. I really didn't know him, nor had the opportunity to fly with him prior. Skip had thick wavy reddish-brown hair with a nicely trimmed thick mustache and, as I would find, an uncanny sense of humor.

"I'm glad you got to handle that guy," he said. He added sarcastically, "I must say you did a splendid job of customer service." I could only stare at him with a blank look and then we both began to laugh. "What was the guy's problem?" I asked. I then added, "Well, if he has a heart attack you are the one that's gonna give him CPR," and we laughed once more. The gentleman's actions had been unusual, but more and more the industry as a whole was experiencing such behavior. It made me wonder what the future of air travel had in store for us. Skip and I formally introduced ourselves and I sensed an easiness in his spirit as we wandered back to our assigned stations.

I rearranged my service apron, binding the ties behind firmly. The stress was getting to me. I was becoming "antsy." I headed forward supposedly checking the passengers, but my real intent was to find Reina and see how she was doing. I approached the service galley at door 2R just as Cary stepped into the aisle and greeted me.

"Hey Mexican, you need a green card to be up here." I liked her spirit. I enjoyed someone who could dish it out.

"I don't know if you realize it white girl, but we are now in el espacio aéreo de Los Estados Unidos de México," as we had long ago flown over the border dividing the two countries. "You're the one who needs a visa." I smiled broadly as Cary was impressed with my reply. Her unique humor was refreshing. "Why are you so gleeful on this miserable night?" I inquired. She grinned a bit and hesitated, her thoughts wandering as if she were recalling something or someone.

"Nothing could get me down right now," the beautiful light-haired lady stated. "I just got back from vacation."

"What? Coming back to work is a joyous occasion?"

"No, you don't understand. My husband and I were just in Yosemite, backpacking. It couldn't have been a better time. We were able to understand and share like a wife and husband should. It was special."

"I'm very happy for you, Cary," It was somewhat annoying that anyone on this flight at this ungodly hour could be that happy. She continued to smile as she entered into the galley elevator. I gazed through the window of the door as her bright face descended into the underbelly of the aircraft. As I turned, I saw Reina sitting and as angelic as ever, her eyes focused on her reading, the same publication she had on the bus ride. She slowly gazed up to see me staring. She was reading a book of religious content and had a peaceful, serene look on her face.

"It must be a bestseller." I stated.

"Number one," she replied, offering up the cover for me to view more closely.

"That little Mexican boy is so sweet," she smiled.

"Yeah, his name is Javier."

"I heard his mother call him by that name when I was back there." she responded.

"Well, I'm sure one day you will have a little guy just like him," I suggested. Reina drew silent and turned away for a second. I immediately took the second jumpseat at mid galley and sat next to her, facing her side profile. I took the initiative.

"This dream of yours," I stopped, then continued. "Tell me about it, honestly." She did not move at first, but I saw her eyes fill with tears as she turned her head toward me and in a shy, timid manner began to speak.

"I've told you pretty much everything. I don't expect you to understand because I don't understand it either." Her voice fell to a whisper.

"Understand what?" I wanted to learn and possibly console.

"A truth I've tried to prepare for all my life," were her words.

"Is this the flight of your dreams?" I pressed her. Her eyes continued to tear up as she shook her head in an uncertain manner.

"I don't know." I sat straight up, contemplating her words. I too had feelings while thousands of feet in the air, but I had been able to dismiss them. That is what someone in this career must do and I wanted Reina to do the same.

"2-6-0-5 is not 2-6-5," I insisted. "This can't be the one because I don't feel like I am going to die this night," I sternly stated. Reina just smiled and replied.

"Then you won't." That was not the answer I had expected and again there was a long pause. I began to feel shaken by her words and panic set in. I needed to change the subject.

"Hey, I can't let all this beer go to waste." In my failed attempt at humor I stooped down and grabbed a couple of bottles of the remaining Bohemia from a cart tray. I could not indulge myself, but I knew that passenger Ronald Daily and his friend would certainly appreciate the cold brew. I arose, breathed deeply and tried to regain my composure. I exited the galley and headed down the right aisle spotting the two young men half asleep in the mid cabin. "Here you go boys, drink up." I placed the cold bottles, one on each man's lap. Ronald opened one eye and smiled as I strolled off. Most passengers were asleep by this time as I walked into the darkness of the aft cabin back to my section by door 4R. I tried to relax and push aside my encounter with Reina, but the thought lingered.

I could have said, "So what the hell do you want me to do, get on the intercom and announce that tonight's flight is going to be dubbed the 'doomed' flight?" What I needed to do was separate myself from the whole world and delineate a boundary between myself and the rest of the crew. I found an empty passenger seat apart from everyone, 33-K, the empty row just aft of the two sleeping Mexican ladies and forward of my jumpseat. I dug into my suitcase and removed a magazine and tried to force myself to become engrossed in it.

"Muhammad Ali says, 'Stronger boxers make better boxers and they get stronger with weight training.'" So said the cover of the fitness magazine. I had always found peace in the gym and hoped I could find some while reflecting on my recent accomplishments. Yet, no matter how hard I tried the text failed to grab my attention. Instead, I tried to concentrate on the beautiful Sea of Cortez outside the window. The Gulf of California below presented a tremendous show. The image of the moon in the heavens shed some light, revealing the glory of the terrain. I followed our line of flight up one hill and down another keeping pace as we raced over that sparsely settled region of Mexico. But still I remained impatient. Fear again gripped me as I began to look up and down the aisle and occasionally glance across the cabin. Does someone need assistance I wondered? Was I ignoring my duties? All at once, something became very apparent. There was an ambiance about the craft, indescribable, yet present and all-encompassing. It perplexed me.

"Is this seat available?" The request disrupted my daydream. It was Tamlyn.

"How is it going?" I forced myself to make small talk as it was evident that the all-night flight was taxing on all of the crew members. Tamlyn took the aisle seat beside me and gazed intently at the fitness magazine lying on my lap. It was opened to a page revealing a photo of the current Mr. America.

"How ugly!" She exclaimed while scrunching the muscles on her face, signaling her disapproval. I quickly put the periodical away in the back pocket of the seat in front of me. She began to laugh, hoping she had not offended me. "You know Eddy, things have been going really great for me." This lovely Asian-American began to express herself in the same amicable manner Cary had earlier. She had recently married, and one could tell she was still in the honeymoon stage of her relationship.

"Just terrific," I stated with a tinge of sarcasm as I rolled my eyes.

"But one thing is new, I'm getting out of flying," she said proudly and continued. "I've applied for a transfer to a ground job as a gate agent." I was dumbfounded since I believed that being a flight attendant was one of the best if not most enjoyable positions within the company, especially at our young age.

"Where are you transferring to? Are you still going to be at LAX?"

"I don't know yet, but I'll take any position that is open," responded my attractive crew member. I continued to express confusion, a contrast to the smiling face of my crew mate sitting next to me.

"What brought this about? We've had some great times on layovers." I wanted to know more.

"Well, there have been some problems," my associate stated.

"What kind of problems?"

"Well, Eddy, it's my mother." I could see Tamlyn found it difficult to explain, hesitating. I recalled she had previously told me that her mother still clung to the old ways of her culture. "You see, she is very afraid," my friend sheepishly said, lowering her head.

"Of what? The long trips?" I was resolved to force the issue. Tamlyn could only shake her head. "The possibility of danger during the long layovers?" I pressed again. This sweet F/A tensed tightly as she now seemed afraid.

"No Eddy, it's kind of silly," she interrupted.

"Of what? A crash?" Tamlyn sat upright and locked eyes with mine in amazement.

"Yeah, that's it! How did you know?" Tamlyn was so surprised that I had come up with the answer on my own. I was shaken. I had to look away, retreating to my window and the outside. I saw the mountains down below, but my field of vision was narrow, and I unconsciously focused in on a vital part of our aircraft in mid-flight - the number-three engine dangling just under the right wing. I felt myself to be a rational human being; after all what were the odds? This was not logical. I sat up to gaze forward through the cabin of the 10. Tamlyn could only be baffled by my sudden actions. An atmosphere filled the cabin of DC-10NW903: unfriendly, wary, foreboding.

"What did Reina tell you?" I asked sternly, poking my head forward as my surprised workmate leaned back, eyes wide open.

"Reina?" Tamlyn was confused.

"Have you spoken with Reina and told her of your decision to transfer out of flight crew?" I tried to soften my tone.

"No," she responded.

"Did you mention your concern over a crash to anyone else on this flight?" Now the sweet girl seemed concerned by my behavior.

"No. In fact, you are the first one I have told about it." She then pulled out a copy of the transfer request from her uniform vest pocket. She opened the company-issued document and placed it in front of me, but I did not want to see it. I was spooked. I shook my head, grabbed the magazine from the seat pocket and turned away from my friend, forcing myself back into the journal. Tamlyn took the hint.

"I've got to finish a letter I started. I'll speak with you more later," she stated as she arose and walked forward to her 3R station. My eyes, hidden behind my periodical, followed her every step. At that point I became leery of everything that was happening. I told myself to observe carefully, be attentive to what was going on.

"Pay attention!" I repeated the command over and over. Feeling rattled by what I was told by my two crew mates, I rose from my seat and slowly walked up the aisle under the guise of checking in on the comfort of the passengers. Instead, I looked at every person on this flight deliberately. I took notice of details: a woman sleeping, two Mexican men conversing, gesturing with their hands, slightly limited by their weariness. The young red-bearded Ronald Daily in a blue woolen shirt was now deep in slumber along with his Hispanic comrade. A campesino slept with his prized white cowboy hat resting on his lap. Even the irritated European passenger had succumbed to fatigue and sat motionless with eyes closed. And of course, there was little Javier and his family cuddled together in one aft row. Forced wide awake by the foreboding words of my mates, nothing escaped my eyes. I tried to calm my nerves with a prayer. Certainly, God in His greatness, the Father, Son, the Holy Spirit, the God of the Sisters of Carmel, the Almighty of the faith I had been raised in, would protect us.

Traversing once throughout the cabin, I again arrived at 4R. I went forward a few rows and found a company blanket lying in the aisle. I picked it up and realized it probably belonged to a slumbering passenger, someone peacefully unaware of my anxieties. Then there was little Javier and his family. Do I wake them up and tell them?

"Wake up! Your lives are in danger!" No. You gather your emotions, refocus yourself and whisper, "Not today." I was possibly taking Reina's and Tamlyn's words out of context. Tamlyn said her mother was fearful of a crash in general. Her words did not necessarily mean such a thing would happen within hours. I turned to view Javier's little angelic face.

You are locked in this metal fuselage and that's not going to change. In the vocation of my choice I had to be professional to the end. *So, I'll go down in a blaze.* The mask of sarcasm softening the fear. I entered the aft lavatory and tried to straighten my twisted apron. I gazed at the reflection and focused in on my flight wings. I had a responsibility to see to no matter the consequence. I was going to go forward, meet up with my crew at mid galley, forget my moodiness and find some of that camaraderie that was so special in our profession. I turned into the galley to find my fellow F/As in cheerful conversation. I froze and slowly backed away.

"How's it going Eddy?" Gary rose up and was very cordial. "Hey, you know anything about real estate?" He raised his hand in my direction then swiftly walked to my side. I stood motionless at the edge of the service center as I was caught off guard by his question. Before I could come up with a response, he was off on a monologue. It seemed as though he really wasn't talking directly to me, but just speaking with enthusiasm in general, as he gazed forward with his large eyes fixed first upon the ceiling, then the walls of the cabin. "You see I've got this chance to buy property in Denver," he stated. "I put in my transfer for that base recently, and I suppose I'm really going to do it. It'll be a big change but I'm excited about it." Gary was a stand-up guy, a person of good character, confident and self-assured and a conscientious Senior Flight Attendant. He seemed to be saying, "I'm ready for whatever is next." As he continued to speak I was puzzled as to why he was telling me these things. We were at best mutual acquaintances among the thousands of other crew members in our company. Then just like that he was finished. He slapped me on the shoulder and then he was gone.

"What the heck was that all about?" I desperately wanted to get away, but where could I go? "The cockpit," I said. Maybe the pilots might need something, a coffee, a soft drink. I can spend a little time mellowing out up front, gazing out the panel windows at the lights below. I retreated aft to ask Skip, who was just reading a magazine, if he would mind covering my station for a bit, to which he obliged me.

Moving forward once again I spotted Gary talking with Cary. How could they all be so pleasant? Passing the brightly lit service center, I encountered the rest of the cabin crew. I felt like a stranger as they were all laughing, having a party that I wasn't invited to. My anxiety escalated.

"I'm going up front to the cockpit, Gary." I announced.

"See if they need anything," he recommended.

"Sure thing." I caught a look from Reina gazing up at me as if she wanted to tell me something, but I resisted the urge, broke eye contact and quickly left.

Arriving at the cockpit door, I casually chimed in the regulation flight code on the admittance panel. I waited for a moment but there was no response.

"Did I chime in the right code?" I was confused and waited a minute longer. I became impatient and punched in the code once again. Still, there was no opening of the cockpit door. "What the hell?" My frustration rose. Suddenly the door opened briskly and then was shut right in my face. Just as quickly, the door opened once again. Bewildered, I hesitated and then entered, closing the door behind me. The sight that greeted me was astonishing. Captain Carl Herbert with four stripes on each shoulder of the pressed white shirt, sat in the left seat and stared indignantly at his first officer. The Captain was extremely agitated and was lecturing the F/O whose back I could only see.

"That's it, damn it," he screamed. "That's it!" The Captain continued fuming. I wanted to get the hell out of there but instead I found refuge by quickly sitting down in the seat right behind him. Dead silence abruptly engulfed the cockpit; only the humming of the engines could be heard along with the whistling of the wind outside of the fuselage. Finally, my eyes adjusted to the darkness in the compartment as I turned to see the Second Officer seated next to me. It was Sam Wells whom I had flown with numerous times. We locked eyes and he rolled his back into his head. I took it as reflecting frustration. Had I found someone who was just as perturbed to find themselves on this wretched flight as I was? I recalled a recent trip to SFO I had with him about two months prior when we had dinner with the whole crew. Sam was a riot, a prankster known for throwing a rubber chicken from the cockpit to amuse the ladies in the cabin. I refocused and looked at him once more, but he did not move a muscle. The S/O sat silent, very aware of his rank and place in the cockpit. In the blackness, the colors of the spectrum radiated from the instrument panels, creating a surrealistic scene in which two men seemed to be facing off - if not in words, then certainly in posture. I remained up front for some time and still not a word was spoken. Wanting desperately to exit, I now found myself too afraid to move. The atmosphere was smothering, but more importantly there were two so-called professionals that were pissed off at each other and I wanted no part of it. Finally, the silence made my anxiety unbearable and I abruptly stood.

"See you guys on the ground." As I was exiting, I glanced once more at Sam Wells, but he remained stoic and gave no reaction.

"Yeah, see you later," was the belated response from the beleaguered First Officer, never turning to acknowledge me. I never got a good look at his face but only later discovered that it was really Dieter Reimann. My palms were sweaty as I slowly stepped back into the First-Class Cabin and gently closed the cockpit door. The whole thing frightened me. These combinations of events that had occurred on 2605 and to which I had been a witness, seemed to foreshadow an impending danger.

"Stop the plane, I want to get off," I said to myself. My emotions were running away with me. I retreated into the first-class galley at 1L. Needing a moment to settle my nerves, I slowly stuck my head out and gazed through the darkness of first class down the left aisle, spotting Jeff Stillwell and Becky Devita fast asleep in almost a doll-like manner. The two beautiful young F/As in their nicely pressed flight attendant uniforms comfortably rested in the first-class seats. I envied them. I looked further aft to the light that was coming from the mid galley. I made out the figure of Reina popping in and out of view as she engaged in conversation at the service center. These happy crew members were all young, bright and promising. I spotted Rod Dawn as he joked with sweet Karen on her maiden Mexican trip.

I stood alone. Dumbfounded. Moving across the cabin I quickly rushed down the right aisle past the sleeping campesinos with their white cowboy hats, past the red-haired young man and his friend who slept contented. I passed the two Hispanic women who remained awake talking of their visit back to their homeland, past the peaceful picture of a young family perhaps dreaming of hope for the future and opportunities for their young sons. I reached the rear, to my safe haven at seat 33-K, slumping down below the light that shone on my seat. Paranoia hitched a ride on my jumbo jet. By a matter of twisted fate was I to find myself trapped in the belly of a beast that was soon to die? The cabin fell silent, the hum of the General Electric engines was dominant. Forward, I viewed the bright illumination of the service center and figures in crew uniforms as they played and laughed. The sight made me conceal myself all the more. There I remained, a coward before the very thing I had professionally trained for, which now seemed inevitable. I tried to remove myself consciously from the situation - a decision made by one who is in denial. I lapsed into a reverie, riding along the jet streams and sensing every adjustment made by our craft that was heading for a rendezvous with uncertainty. After a time, I felt the great bird beginning its descent and I regained my composure, forcing myself to believe the logic that my DC-10 would soon arrive at its destination and all I had experienced would prove to be nonsensical and quickly forgotten.

The cabin's calm was broken by the illumination of the Fasten Seat Belt sign. The intercom at 4R rang and slowly rising, I lifted the phone to hear Cary's voice.

"You have two carts back there Eddy, you want to leave them stored there or do you want to bring them up to have them secured in the galley for landing?" I hesitated. Fatigue told me to leave them where they were, right across from my jumpseat, to be utilized on the next leg, the trip home. My apprehension made the decision and I took each one forward to be secured down below, leaving nothing but fuselage aft of my station. The young flight attendants scurried about organizing themselves for the immediate duties of securing the cabin for the expected landing.

The No Smoking sign lit brightly above the heads of the slow-stirring passengers, signaling the approach through Mexico City air space. The glistening lights of the capital sparkled through our jumbo jet's side windows, then they disappeared in the cloud cover only to sparkle once more a split second later. The whistling sound of the air passing outside became more intense as I struggled with each cart, walking slowly uphill. I then returned downward on the right aisle awaking passengers and making sure their seats were in the upright position with seat belts fastened. When I came to Ronald Daily and his friend fast asleep, lying sideways, I could see that their seat belts were secured across their waists. As I was about to awaken the gentlemen, I stopped.

"Screw it, let them sleep," I said. Tamlyn was right behind me also checking the passengers. "Listen Tamlyn, let these guys sleep," I said adamantly. Tamlyn seemed confused by my request but smiled and agreed. With all secured, I was reluctant to go to my station at 4R and instead I quickly walked forward across the floor of the aircraft. I seemed to want to ensure that all was indeed well stored away and the crew strapped in firmly to their assigned jumpseats. Gary seemed surprised to find me wandering about as the pitch of the engines now dominated the atmosphere of the cabin.

"Better get to the back Eddy," he said. At 2L, I came upon a calm Reina, religious book on her lap. I looked to see that her straps were taut, then quickly moved across the mid-service center to the right side at 2R, the craft sloping at an angle as I shifted my balance. My eyes fell upon Cary who was still standing and adjusting the straps on her jumpseat.

"Better get your ass seated, Mexican, we're almost on the ground." I hurried down the aisle and slipped into an aft lavatory. I gathered some water and splashed a bit of it on my face. I raised my head and in the reflection before me I came face to face with my mortality. Was this night and day going to belong to Muerto? I washed my hands and hurriedly unbuttoned part of my uniform shirt. My chest and back itched mercilessly, irritated by the stubble of hair that was growing -- an annoying souvenir from the recent body-building contest. I may have been rattled by the events of this flight, but if the unspeakable did happen I took comfort in that I was physically strong. Second Officer Sam Well's voice came over the intercom.

"Flight Attendants be seated for landing." We were on final approach. The figures and faces of the passengers became a montage passing as I gazed about the cabin one last time. I rushed to strap myself in 4R and adjusted the belt on my harness, pulling one end as hard as I could, trying to position my body as rigid as possible. Releasing my hold on the strap I realized that the pressure was too great. I could barely breathe. My hands fumbled as I searched for the buckle once more to loosen the harness that was now so restrictive, having a smothering hold upon me. The lights in the cabin went dim as I decided to endure the strain, knowing that 2605 was near the ground.

"This is it," I whispered to myself. The idea came faster, repeating itself, keeping pace with my heartbeat as the aircraft became louder and more prominent in my consciousness. My preoccupations became stronger, the rhythm quickened, and I looked up at the mirror located high on the cabin ceiling, above the aft service center, positioned so the flight attendant seated facing rear can see up the aisle toward the front. I stared at the floor, then quickly gazed at my regulation watch. It was the early morning hours of October 31. I turned my head left and strained to look through the window at seat 33 K just forward of me. Looking beyond the glass I recognized a thick haze, an ocean of fog into which our craft descended.

The majority of the passengers had just been awakened, so there was little sense of anxiousness throughout; mostly there was a quiet, peaceful calm. In the rear of the plane, this silence heightened the awareness of the craft itself as the decisions from the cockpit instructed the mechanical systems in the tail to do their job. The groaning of the equipment was clear, predominant. There were fearful, loud noises, exposing the lie of the aircraft simply as a soaring bird of nature. My heart was beating faster as the plane immersed itself into a deep, thick haze. 2605's landing lights became useless as the beams shot out but failed to pierce the dark ahead. Instead, it was reflected back into the cabin, creating an eerie illumination. Then an unfamiliar calm came upon me.

"Don't be afraid, it's going to be okay." I sensed a protective ambiance that nurtured me.

BAM! The first massive force was unmerciful as I was jolted into the back of the jumpseat and my legs went flying uncontrollably.

"Dear God." My voice broke the overwhelming silence. No one dared say a word as if praying that everything really would be okay.

I turned my head to the right to see Skip at 4L all twisted about like a parachutist stuck in a tree. His eyes were wide open, revealing a specific fear. His hands were clenched around a handle on the fuselage wall. The plane yawed slightly to the right; no one was stirring or panicking. To me it seemed as though there was a total submission to powers beyond our control. I tried to get a hold of myself.

"Be calm," I whispered, breathing heavily. I rationalized that we had just encountered a hard landing. The DC-10 had bounced once and was coming back down again. This was not particularly uncommon. I waited with anxiety, but the craft did not return to the runway nor did it take off again. We merely continued on through the fog, suspended in a thick limbo. "Skip, are we on the ground or in the air?" I shouted across the cabin but received no response. Skip was frozen, unable to speak or even think clearly it seemed.

"I don't know," He finally blurted out. As I sat, I couldn't sense that the engines were delivering much power. There was no sensation of acceleration pushing on me, and there was no roar of the exhaust. Turning back to my left, I gazed out the window and saw a sudden huge flash. For a split second it looked like lightning, but then I thought the craft was striking some debris.

All at once the aircraft pitched violently upward. The raising of the plane's nose caused great relief in me, believing that we were being lifted out of the uncertainty of the mist.

"He's taking us out of here." Suddenly the plane began to swivel once again, and I turned my head to the aft-center portion of the cabin. Looking down, I noticed the floor was cracking open widening and lengthening. The DC-10 was splitting open from within like an eggshell ready to eject its contents. No one around me made a sound. There was absolutely no noise other than the breaking metal.

"This is not really happening." I fell back to my childhood and faced the turmoil in the way a small child might look at a wild animal he's never been warned about, totally in wonderment. For a crazy spit second, I imagined myself on a thrill ride.

The aft, the entire rear of the jumbo jet started to shift away, no longer lining up with the rest of the fuselage. The noise became unbearably deafening. Nothing in training had prepared me for this. A lavatory door blew open and pieces flew, hitting me on the leg and face. Dirt was flying, pinning me against the back of my jumpseat as I was continuously struck by debris. Only my right arm was raised up to protect my face, my head. The aircraft continued forward as the aft section split into two or three pieces. At that moment, the others were gone. Forever.

A massive explosion erupted above me just below the number two engine. I witnessed the fuel line detach from the burst metal, whipping about like a wild serpent striking at its prey. The fuel gushed out and was instantly ignited, the fire dancing along in rhythm with the broken line. In an instant, a huge fireball formed a meter or so above me then shot forward. Leaning to get out of the way, patches of my uniform dress shirt were sucked from my body by the violent energy. The hair on the right side of my head was singed. Then the explosion tried to push me forward but the jumpseat harness did its job and held me firmly. Eldritch missiles then appeared shooting through the cabin. I became frantic and turned inward gasping for air. There was another massive explosion in what I determined was left of the forward section of the aircraft. The fire sucked the air from my body and my lungs which were filled with the foul fumes of jet fuel. Heads and various other body parts flew past, singing a grotesque whistle as the reverberation of the full impact made itself known, revealing the ominous impression of death and misery.

"It's gonna be okay," whispered the voice once more. There was an intense pressure on my head. Suddenly, all fell still and silent. The overwhelming smell of jet fuel and burnt metal started to dominate as this diabolical ride came to an abrupt halt.

Chapter V

The nightly ritual of the Los Angeles County Sheriff's helicopter patrolling above the streets of East Los Angeles is par for the course. I would recall how foolish my brother and I were when as youngsters we would attempt to try and convince the flying bird to shine its great light upon us in our back yard, feeling a sense of accomplishment if we succeeded. In the early morning mist of October 31, as the helicopter briskly raced across the sky, the beam from the spotlight randomly transverses over the bedroom windows of Alicia and Reynaldo Valenciana, illuminating the dark spaces for mere seconds. Alicia awoke, focused on the silhouettes of her statues of the holy saints that stood guard on her dresser. There was Saint Therese, the little flower, the family patron, clad in the familiar dressings of the Sisters of Carmel. She was my mother's favorite. The Holy Mother stood beside her in a crimson gown and a blue mantle ornamented with gold, holding the precious Baby Jesus. The Madonna's glance with her light brown eyes seemed concerning. Alicia lazily scanned the room, sensing an unusual presence but initially seemed out of order. She then strained to notice a fog-like haze outside the window in the back yard. It had a ghostly appearance, a heavy mysterious glare that immediately grabbed her attention. The good woman studied it carefully and could make out a figure with a hideous face and an arm that reached again and again through the bedroom window, as though trying to claim something that belonged to him. My mother's life in this Mexican community and her faith in her church told her it was the ashen face of Death who seemed to desperately want to cross the threshold into the realm of the living.

"Holy God, His Holy Strength, and His Holy Immortality, save us dear God from all that is evil." The words from her pleading, trembling lips were rooted in her very soul. Alicia, with her faith, stood her ground and soon the phantom mist dissolved away. She finally settled herself and eventually returned to a peaceful slumber. Only the hum of the police helicopter remained to break the stillness in the neighborhood.

The phantom was very much present in the Mexican capital that misty morning. My mind was in a daze and I struggled to grab hold of some sense of logic.

"Hurts are where?" I was a battered mess. "The inner right thigh, I hurt in the inner right thigh." My fears were heightened. "My leg? Is my leg broken? Is my leg still there?" I rambled with fear. "My hands? Do I have all my fingers? What about my knees? My back and shoulder are burning with pain." Finally focusing through the debris, I became aware that parts of my F/A uniform were missing. But amazingly I still had on my company service apron. It seemed as though its fabric was more resistant to the fireball than the other materials of my uniform. I desperately reached for the harness release and found it jammed, possibly locked.

"Oh, shit! There's fire all around! I am going to be trapped." The very act that saved me now could became my executioner. I was strapped in the jumpseat as tight as possible, snug enough to survive massive "G" forces which were strong enough to rip the heads from the torsos of some victims.

"There!" I had continued to fumble with the harness belt. The restraints fell loose, and I crumbled from my position. I gazed back up to see that there was no seat, just the backboard of my jumpseat, harness securely attached. I was entombed under a ton of rubble with threatening flames everywhere. My little section of fuselage was intact, and it initially seemed as though I was also. Cement and iron beams were now my companions in an inferno maze that offered no sense of direction.

"I'm standing on tarmac." The entire floor of the DC-10 was gone.

I became frantic as I hoped and prayed in random mutterings that someone would save me. The crackling, dancing flames and blackened smoke were getting closer.

"Damn you God! Why did you save me if I am to burn like a trapped rat?" Fear mixed with anger grew with each precious second.

"I am going to be trapped and will burn alive." Like the Christian martyrs of old, was I expected to accept this? Stubbornly, I fought the urge to cry and tried to distinguish my surroundings. Recognizing iron beams and concrete, I visually placed myself at the base of a building the plane had struck. The light moved erratically as a result of the dancing flames. I could only make out one direction in which there seemed to be a spot of darkness, a possible escape. I staggered between many broken chunks of concrete as I tried to stand up and straighten my sore body. Here and there was blackened chunks of metal and plastic that had moments before been our magnificent DC-10. I attempted to clear burnt rubble away. The air now smelled of poison; much of what I had inhaled was jet fuel. My entire body was saturated with the substance. Miraculously, it had not ignited. I fell and crawled as best I could into the dark spot that looked like a tunnel in the labyrinth of devastation. Could it be a death trap?

Adrenaline gave me the power to stand and move remnants of what seemed like cabin seats and a portion of the aft service center, barely recognizable from the effects of the fire ball. I continued down the "tunnel" and carefully entered its narrowest point trying to be aware of the hundreds of exposed pieces of metal all around, razor-sharp and deadly. About twenty feet in I was blocked by a large slab of concrete from what used to be a building. The block was squared off, but it was not going to be easy to move, not in my state. I gazed around looking for an alternate route but there was none. Through a hole in the concrete I leaned forward and tilted my head up. I imagined I saw stars. I squinted and looked again. It was a star in the early morning sky. I had to move the debris. The potentially lethal smoke persisted as the fire grew and flames continued to feast on the carcass of my aircraft.

My first attempt at moving the slab completely failed. It was wedged into what I determined was left of the interior of the aft fuselage. I was unable to loosen the rock's foundation by any means and the strain only increased my pain.

"Move the slab," I shouted in a panic. I leaned my entire weight into the barrier in one grand effort. It proved to be useless. I broke down and began to cry, teetering on the edge of total despair. Like a child torn from a mother's grasp, I wept. I attacked the slab like a deranged man, clawing at it, increasing the pain of my scorched hands on its coarse surface.

"It's going to be okay." The soothing warmth returned as I gathered my emotions and straightened my posture as best I could. I began to work the problem.

"I lift every day. What is the best way to move this obstacle?" I could hear Mari's voice from training:

"If you survive, others will have a better chance of surviving."

"Use leverage, like in squatting," I whispered to myself. I pulled aside a metal panel and positioned my back against the side, creating a wedge. If I could lift it but inches, I could use gravity to my advantage. I did not have much time left before the fumes induced their own solution to my dilemma. It actually felt good when I lifted. I realized I had just dedicated nine months of my life preparing for this very moment. It gave me a sense of purpose; with support from a Greater Source, the stone began to move. The concrete shifted a foot or so, just enough for me to slide through in a sense of relief and excitement. I climbed upon the slab and emerged at the top of the twisted rubble. What I saw overwhelmed me. There, before me, Muerto feasted on several large fiery heaps.

In the opposite direction in a long ditch, seventy or so yards from me lay the rudder of my DC-10 with its massive lettering.

"WHAT HAPPENED?" I screamed. Suddenly I thought about the crew. "The others? Where were the others?" I frantically began to focus on the flaming piles. There was a hunk of the DC-10 over there-could that be the mid-section? Wait, where was Reina?" I spun in confusion not knowing which direction to go or what I should do. All at once the magnitude of what was happening to me fried my mind. BUT I WAS ALIVE! I hesitated and looked up and acknowledged the true source of my incredible fortune. Then I snapped back to reality. There were others that needed assistance. In the distance the fire's light revealed a mass of dark figures and shadows running erratically in pain and sorrow. I tumbled down from the twisted metal and concrete, landing face first upon the scarred tarmac. I painfully struggled to stand, propping myself on a knoll of concrete and steel.

My vision cleared and I hobbled as best I could to some burning debris in the hopes of finding someone, anyone who I could possibly save. At the base of the inferno, no silhouettes were seen to indicate life. Then at once there was movement, as one body ran in one direction and another body in a different direction. The cries and screams of men, women began to fill the air. The injured passengers were regaining consciousness. A Mexican man wearing a mask of Muerto himself noticed me as I stumbled about. He recognized I was wearing my blue service apron with the company's logo on my chest and quickly concluded that I was a crew member aboard this tragic flight.

"Que pasó joven?" He shouted from a distance.

"Todos están muertos," declared another frantic Hispanic who came running behind him.

"Were you in that hell?" An English-speaking voice caught me by surprise, and I tried to focus on it. A tall, dark, sinister figure moved forward and slowly removed his skull mask. I suddenly remembered that today was indeed Halloween, and some people who began to surround me were dressed in the spirit of the day. One woman wore the hat of a witch, another was dressed as some sort of goblin and of course there were skeletons. We were all gathered together in the sight of Death himself, whose stench was all around, in the air, through our noses and caked in our hair.

The people became frantic and began to surround me with incomprehensible questions. A figure dressed as a werewolf grabbed my arm. Another figure, a hunched back, ghoul-like creature jumped toward me. They all wanted answers, not necessarily the truth for the truth was much more difficult to face. Filled with dread and feeling physically beaten, I hobbled through the crowd to a nearby fence that stood partially upright; the remainder lay buried beneath the plane's debris. I suddenly started coughing and spitting up jet fuel while crouched in pain.

"What happened hombre?" A gentleman in the uniform of a foreign airline squatted beside me.

"I don't know," I stated shaking my head, barely able to breathe. "I don't know!" Although I was injured and severely bruised, I appeared to be in one piece. By the stunned looks around me I must have seemed a Phoenix rising from the vivid, colored flames.

"What of the others?" I tried to compose myself while focusing on the heaps of burning debris all around. There must be people trapped in there. I looked back to where I had first escaped. In the dancing light I could see a hand moving, trying to signal for help. I had to rescue him. The gentleman, who I now determined was a Hispanic pilot, remained by my shoulder. At first, he tried to restrain me as I moved forward toward the flames, fearing that I might have become deranged, a definite possibility considering the circumstances. I was trying to run back into the hopeless inferno, he must of thought. I tugged all the more, finally convincing my new friend that someone was there, possibly dying before our very eyes. I dove to the ground at the base of the flames and started to dig. Soon other pairs of hands joined in. despite their being in danger. Desperate, I crawled about but could no longer detect the hand. I became frenzied. Then out of the corner of my eye I spotted a body.

Lying face down, it twisted and turned in a series of spasms in an effort to free itself from the burning wreckage. Shielding my face, I went forward dodging the flames to reach the figure clothed in a flight attendant uniform, or what was left of it.

"Thank God, I won't be alone." It was Skip and I became jubilant. I tried to lift him to his knees where I could possibly get my shoulder under his arm. Suddenly the Hispanic pilot arrived, and we lifted Skip from under each arm and we quickly dragged him from the flames. I looked down and noticed Skip's foot twisted backwards in the opposite direction.

"We made it buddy, we made it." I yelled. Finally, we laid him down on the tarmac as vehicles started to arrive. I turned and swore at Muerto in all his fiery rage.

"You didn't get us. No! We slipped through and got away, asshole." I began to laugh hysterically as the Hispanic pilot looked at me surmising that I was being driven mad and perhaps I was. I taunted Death because Skip and I will always represent his failure. Other frantic people flagged down a maintenance truck and helped carry Skip to the rear of the vehicle. As soon as he was found, he was whisked away. I once again felt so alone.

"What do I do? Where do I go?" The frenzy heightened.

"Madre de Dios," screamed a lost soul from within the belly of the burning rubble.

"Help me, please help me," cried another. Tumbling over the crushed debris, I scrambled to follow the desperate cries. I viewed a figure moving slowly at the base of some debris. Suddenly a screaming figure dashed from the flames totally ablaze, running and twirling like a Fourth of July[2] explosive. I could not get near him. An airport fire truck arrived, and the crew jumped off to assist the terrified man, first dousing him with portable extinguishers then carrying and covering his blistered body in blankets. The screams within the wreckage intensified in volume and frequency. I froze wondering if these victims had been unconscious, but now awoke in excruciating pain and panic. I witnessed the lamenting of tormented souls in a hell of twisted metal and flames. The air space around Benito Juárez International Airport hung heavy with the smell of jet fuel and burning flesh, grotesquely embraced by desolation.

Shaking with dismay I spotted a charred figure lying alone, isolated on the tarmac, its severed right leg a few feet forward in front of it. There were body parts littered all about, some no more than a lump of flesh with clothing, a part of a sweater on a torso, brown charred polyester on a single leg. I followed a visible line on the tarmac, and then backtracked, trying to make some semblance of the destruction. Suddenly there was a man rolling in the rubble in front of me. I fell forward onto the ground and grabbed his leg. I yanked hard, hoping the limb would not detach. Others quickly rushed in to aid me as we pulled him out. As we lifted the poor soul and quickly carried him to safety I could see that both his arms were severely burned.

I turned to join this vigilante band of brave bystanders who like many that morning risked their own lives to try to save lives of loved ones and strangers alike. Then there were the others, those who were traumatized by what they had witnessed and sat motionless. In morbid irony those affected continued to don the Halloween masks, costumes and disguises, unwittingly resembling celebrants at Muerto's horrid fete.

---

2   Fourth of July, U.S. Independence Day

An ever-growing crowd had initially gathered atop the vast spectator venue at the airport, patiently awaiting the arrival of 2605. Many of the festively clad citizens of El Distrito Federal had been aware of the delayed departure of the flight from LAX and happily passed the time, children playing make-believe and dreaming of the goodies they would enjoy later that evening. Their mother's thoughts were on the family members who were with me inside the jumbo jet, perhaps the fathers of these children who played gleefully about, some being laborers who lived and worked far away for months in an effort to try and make a better life for themselves and those they left behind. Family was there to greet a brother, a mother or sister, while others waited for an associate or friend.

They all had been gathered there when the fog rolled in, partially blocking their view of 24-Left, the main runway onto Benito Juárez. And they were all witness to the crash and horrible explosions that destroyed the DC-10 that carried their loved ones. Instantly there was a mad dash over the balcony wall and through security fences onto the tarmac, dodging airport vehicles, racing frantically to reach that brother, sister, mother, father who was trapped in and under the burning mounds of wreckage. There was the phantasmagoric figure of a skeleton screaming in anguish, moaning words at random, desperately looking for a trapped sister. A woman dressed as what I believed to be a Mother Goose character was on her knees crying and praying for the Holy Virgin to intercede on her behalf seeking comfort from the overwhelming heartbreak and hopelessness that now afflicted her. In a dizzying whirl I once again viewed the werewolf figure scurrying about as he assisted a passenger from 2605 who although was covered in soot looked familiar. I moved in closer to assist and instantly recognized the battered figure as the businessman who had been rude.

Truly, only the innocent die young I thought. The survivor was carried about thirty yards behind where fire fighters were engaged in battling the flames and placed into an emergency vehicle where Mexican paramedics ran amok trying to make sense of the nonsensical. Somehow, deep inside I already knew that no matter how severe his injuries this fortunate soul would survive.

"Por amor de Dios," screamed the chorus of the victims.

"Mother, mother," cried someone running in the darkness, perplexed by the madness. I tackled him around his ankles as he ran past me. I quickly rolled away to avoid any flames as fire fighters arrived and doused him with foam. The wretched soul reached and caught a shred of my regulation service apron which I was still wearing. I rolled away on the tarmac as more people rushed in to take charge. Lying on pavement, I recognized many as airport employees. There was a luggage handler bearing the colors of Aeroméxico. Another was a security man in his uniform, also an agent from an international carrier. Mechanics working long night shifts in the hangars came running, all with the desire to try and help. I painfully sat up to see the man receiving the aid and knew he would not make it. Deep down I hoped he wouldn't; I wished him a peaceful death. Survival would have been cruel.

"Mamá, mamá." I caught focus of a faint cry. A child.

"Ay, un niño," a female voice indicated.

"A child somewhere over there," I yelled to the firefighters who stood over the deceased figure. I painfully stood and hobbled blindly through a maze of twisted blackened metal, trying to locate the faint cries.

"Mamá," the voice persisted in what now seemed like a whisper.

"There, right there," I cried. I spotted the young child, his face framed by glowing hot iron and smoking debris. The boy immediately recognized me as I spotted other motionless bodies beside him in the ever-changing light of the flames. I was sure the trapped figure next to the bewildered boy was his mother. I became like a raving lunatic, scurrying around the inferno to find a way in, but there was none. Burning my hand, I backed away and stumbled. Muerto was repaying me, his vengeance for my earlier taunts. The flames crackled loudly as they danced and shot into the brisk morning air. There was little time left and I had to hurry. Javier was hurt, barely audible. The harder I tried and no matter how hard I prayed, it was obvious that I was doomed to be rendered useless, designated a spectator to the unimaginable. Then I recognized that a third figure emerging from the debris was the boy's brother. I stared in horror as various figures ran about, yelling, crying, grasping at their own throats, trying to rip off their own clothes and asking God to save them. I was among them.

"No God! No God! By the holy name of your precious son, no!" An airport fire truck arrived at that moment and the workers fanatically scrambled to douse the flames, but the old vehicle's pump malfunctioned. The hoses remained limp. Nothing could be done to douse the fires that now began to consume the tiny figures. The child and his brother continued screaming. The brothers wailed their death song like wild dying animals. Then suddenly they were silent.

"How could you?" Devastation consumed me; I went berserk. I screamed in terror. I instantly understood that I would never be released from Muerto's curse, a witness to ruination. Just minutes prior I had been filled with great joy at my good fortune. The bill for surviving had arrived and payment was due in full. I attacked the two firefighters who held the limp fire hoses. I howled like one of the many ghoulish figures I was in the midst of. I collapsed and began to weep overcome with feelings of abandonment and anger. I would struggle with mortal men, but I squarely laid the blame on this all-knowing God who clearly failed in His responsibilities.

Sirens! I squinted into beaming headlights of a fast-approaching vehicle. More silhouettes rushed into chaos. An illumination to my right made me aware of an arm extending from the wreck, hand open, maybe reaching, strikingly rigid. I slowly and awkwardly stepped up to the side of the hot unstable mound. I fell on my knees and reached to grasp a possible friend, maybe another crew member. Death, sadistic and frivolous, arranged for the limb to be severed. I instantly let it loose as it tumbled some feet away and left it resting on the charred debris. The need to survive forced me to become jaded as reality made an unexpected call. If the graciousness of a giving God had planted faith and hope in my precious heart, it was grievously stomped on and tossed to the wayside by a world that can be brutal and unforgiving.

The morning sun's rays began to pierce the heavy fog, the light slowly revealing the total extent of the catastrophe. There was a young girl attempting to free her clothing from a jagged frame of metal. Physically, she seemed unmarked, so I assumed she was one of the witnesses of the crash and rushed to try and find one so dear to her, one possibly now gone. She was screaming and I rushed forward and yanked the cloth. It ripped and she quickly she ran away into the morning mist. I never saw her face. As I stumbled about the wreckage once again, I found a man whose hands were severely burned, the skin failing to cling to the bones any longer. I took the fabric from the torn dress and used it as a wrap. A vehicle carrying paramedics arrived. I turned and stood, taking in the whole scene with little emotion. I saw the hordes running about and for some reason I began to chuckle. Some had suitcases in hand, some a purse. Many items being snatched away from the wreckage had telling scars from the fireballs that torched the cabin. The many shades of gray and brown revealed telltale-signs of the crimson flames that had danced upon them. This was Mexico City, where five hundred years prior thousands had been sacrificed to satisfy the lust of the gods for blood. The crowd surrounding the crash site seemed to be of the opinion that such an ancient ritual had just happened again.

Reina, Gary, the others-they were gone, and I knew it: snatched away leaving me behind. Other than the tail section of DC-10 NW903, there was little that was recognizable. If there was a fuselage it was now in destroyed chunks, covered by the rubble that had once been buildings

People continued to gather, some still dressed in costumes and pointing at me.

"Mi madre?" A woman ran to me, fell on her knees, and grabbed my leg. She refused to let go until I could give her some information concerning her mother, whom she feared was dead. She caused me tremendous pain but as I gazed upon her face, I saw greater pain than mine. I had no answer for her. I could only face this crowd that stared in anticipation. Comfort and care were in short supply. I felt like I had to do something to give them hope. I owed them that. I bonded firmly with the simple people of this great city as we lamented. Their faith and superstitions somehow had convinced them that I could provide answers they sorely needed and deserved. The faithful sought the miraculous "aeromozo" (flight attendant), who had walked out of the madness and stood whole in front of their very eyes. This walking phenomenon certainly must have had some magic, as an old woman rushed forward to kiss my hand as I frantically backed away. One man slowly removed his mask, another a hat in an act of respect, which made matters more awkward. Perhaps I was merely the fool selected to confound the wise. These genuine children of the world seemed temporarily sustained by the fact that I existed.

I could say nothing, and I decided it was time to escape. I had been much too long in the presence of Death. It was at that moment I pondered whether he would let me leave. Shaking my head, I bent over trying to force myself from going over the edge, losing a complete grip on reality. At this point it would have been so easy to do, but I knew I had to regain my composure. Although my uniform was in tatters, I was a crew member of 2605 and with that came responsibilities.

"I need to contact the company, contact LAX." I had to find a way to get to Operations on the airport grounds, a facility that was surrounded by chaos. I suddenly felt my strength abandon my body. I was nauseous and I fell to the tarmac like all the other wounded pulled from the wreckage. Some of the locals around me quickly came to my aid. They carefully lifted my limp body, placing my feeble arms over the shoulders of two hefty Mexicanos.

"We will be your legs, amigo," a good man stated as another assisted in pushing through the crowd. We proceeded quickly, the two supporting an almost lifeless body to get me to a safer place.

"Yo quiero hablar con mi familia, my family, I must get word that I am okay," I whispered to one of the hefty gentlemen, the one who spoke some English. I explained that the company's Operations is where I needed to be. The kind man acknowledged my request and knew just how to get me there. A tug used to taxi aircraft about was brought alongside as a band of helpful citizens gently placed me on the seat. They all smiled once I settled in the compact vehicle. Another man sat on the hood as we sped away. These true men, salt of the earth, were committed to something good coming out of the bedlam for me. They turned to smile and stare, and to them I still express my gratitude.

I could see the fires still burning across the tarmac. As we rolled along the runway, the people continued to stream toward the disaster: men, women and children, some dressed in costumes, others just curious citizens. Some must have been out and about in the brisk morning air walking past the vast airport facility, when their attention was drawn in by the massive jumbo jet descending through the thick blanket of fog.

I could now see that the path of destruction led much farther than I originally estimated. The momentum of the DC-10 had carried it outside the airport boundaries. A neighborhood on the fringe was burning. I shook my head at this unfathomable situation just as the sturdy tug approached the back stairs of the main terminal lobby. I had gained my strength back and with my two escorts in tow I impatiently flung the doors open to the long mausoleum-styled corridors. The howling wails and tear-filled faces are what greeted us. This stone building was equipped with an observation deck on the roof where a great number of the people were witness to the carnage. In one swift stroke they too were branded for life.

The throngs in the hallways and on the main floor were in shock, invoking in loud desperation the names of countless saints. They tortured their own bodies, twisting and flinging themselves upon the marble floor in a painful attempt to break Muerto's grip. They cried and pleaded for compassion. One man in particular, dressed in the skeleton outfit was enormously distraught. I would later be informed that he lost his whole family in the crash. Still wearing his mask, the face of Muerto, he leaped from one position to another and screamed for someone to end his life. The burden he was now to bear was indeed unbearable.

"Maria, José y Jesús!" A small child attired in the garments of a hobo, wept bitterly. Another child dressed like a zombie, a little girl with long dark braids, clutched a small statue of some saint, maybe Jude (the patron of hopeless cases), its garment embroidered with gold. My religious upbringing led me to wonder how so many souls would suddenly be finding themselves at the gates of eternity. Wasn't this indeed the first day of El Día de Los Muertos festivities? The horrible screaming, moaning and crying became more than my heart could bare. Sensing my distress, my Mexican guardians each gently grabbed an arm and continued quickly across the marble floors. One man gripped ever tighter as we tried to navigate around the hysteria. Being supported by others, I raised my injured hands to cover my eyes as I tried not to imagine what torment these people were suffering after helplessly witnessing the airplane's disintegration.

Amidst this incredible chaos, whole families were frantically running back and forth in a desperate attempt to escape the despair that now enveloped them. Once again, I witnessed the distraught tearing at their own clothing or grabbing handfuls of hair on their scalp. Like me, all were hoping to find a way to avoid the terrible reality that lay buried and burning just outside the door.

Some recognized the company logo on my soot-filled service apron and my tarnished flight wings still pinned on the fabric. They determined that I was the person who might give them answers.

"He is from the crash," I heard one say. Heads instantly turned and searched about until most eyes became fixed upon me. "He looks in one piece," another voice stated. I imagined their thoughts. "Possibly, maybe, perhaps by God's good grace, my friend, mother, uncle, neighbor, loved one would also be found in a similar condition." They reached for me wanting a piece of the magic that they surely believed had saved me. I was greatly saddened to think that they would only learn the worst. I cursed God, believing the emotional devastation that was sure to come would take away their ability to ever hope again.

My Mexican guards strained to force me through the collapsing crowd; they would see that I would not drown in this growing tide of human misery.

"Does your mother know you are alive?" A voice yelled to me as I was now lifted above the growing crowd.

"Such clarity of thought," I muttered as we finally arrived at the Operations office. The first thing I had to do was to get word to my mother, my family. This task posed a difficult problem since it was still quite early in the City of the Angels. As the chaos continued in the halls of the airport terminal, I decided to take action. My Spanish came in handy as I frantically grabbed one of the many phones in the airport office and proceeded to contact an international operator, requesting a call to Los Estados Unidos. I heard the ringing on the other end of the line.

"Hello."

"Tommy. Listen to me," I tried to accomplish my goal with the least amount of words.

"Do you know what time it is?" Tommy was rightfully disturbed as he struggled to awaken.

"Shut up and listen," I became very stern, something I never would ordinarily do in his presence.

"I am in Mexico, our DC-10 went down and there are people hurt."

"Holy shit, what do you need?"

"Call my parents, tell them that no matter what they may hear from any source concerning this mess, I am alive and fine. Tell them I will get word to them the first opportunity I get."

"You got it and call us again when you can." Tommy's response gave me a sense of assurance. I knew he wished he could be by my side at that moment; surely, he would know what to do far better than I in these matters. My head lowered as I once more had to get a firm grip on reality. My eyes became fixed as I noticed the amount of blood on my uniform pants for the first time. I had told Tommy to let my parents know that I was okay but were those words true?

People now filled the room and doorway, all silent and focused on my every word and movement. Sitting at a company desk in the operations center, my battered body was wrecked with exhaustion. I held a company phone in my left hand as I noticed the index finger of my scorched right hand shaking uncontrollably. I attempted to dial for a line connecting me with the international operator once again. The task fell on me to call the airline headquarters in Los Angeles. I had a responsibility to inform them of the disaster, the massive inferno outside that had shaken the faith of so many who had believed in a God of mercy.

"Bull Shit!" My frustration surfaced, to the confusion of my two bodyguards who now stood by the doorway, to keep the crowd at bay. Suddenly a woman appeared, anguished and desperate as she frantically argued with the men standing guard. I expressed my desire to speak with her. The woman's daughter had been a passenger on the plane.

"She's nineteen years old," the woman stated. "Her name is Penelope." How was I to know who that possibly could be? All at once I recalled the lovely young lady that had boarded the craft back at LAX. I remembered how I was disappointed that she sat across the aisle in a seat that was not in my section.

"Yes, I remember her." A glimmer of hope crossed on the desperate woman's face. But what could I tell her? I had no idea if she had survived, yet her mother's anguished face demanded that I give her some sense of hope. "She was in the rear section," I said. "Those in the rear like me had a better chance of making it out." That was all I could say. By her reaction I could see that her spirits were lifted as she stepped forward to touch my face. In the depths of her own anguish she shed a tear of joy... for my survival.

"Thank God you made it and are alive." She stated the words I was unable to. Perhaps in her faith she would be rewarded. Most likely she would be crushed. I returned to the phone and proceeded to contact Flight Attendant Scheduling at LAX.

"Hello, what's that?" A female voice, a company scheduler on the other end of the line had answered.

"We crashed," I said in a very simplistic tone.

"Yes dear, we just heard about it," the response came as the grief began to overwhelm me. "How many made it? Ed, where is the rest of the crew?" A male voice had entered the conversation on an extended line.

"Not many," I replied and began to weep. My mind went blank as I could no longer remember Skip's name. He was the only one I knew for sure had made it out. The male scheduler went down the list of the crew manifest but in my confusion no name jumped out at me. I knew Gary, Rod and Jeff. The name Ronald Mitchell, Skip's real name, made no connection. The schedulers concluded rightfully that I was in a bad way. The call was concluded with assurance to me that the full powers of the company would be extended to assist me and others during this painful ordeal. I hung up the phone with a promise to contact them again.

I thought about those who perished, recalling a vision of my childhood. I attended the funeral of my mother's dear Godmother, and was lifted by my mother to gaze into the open casket at the elderly deceased woman. I asked my mother to lean forward so that I might touch her face one last time. I vividly recalled the shock of discovering how icy cold her rose-tinted cheeks were. Suddenly, I recalled the face of Reina and I started to cry.

Those standing about were perplexed, wondering what could be done to ease my pain to alter the fates that were occurring this day. I lifted my head and felt tears running down my cheeks, one falling upon my right arm, upon the blood-soaked pieces of fabric that had become one with my skin. I wanted to go back in time.

"I want to go with them," I blurted out. One of the Mexican gentlemen, the one who spoke English, understood my words. He locked onto my eyes and realized that what I had expressed was a desire to be with my crew in death. He became concerned for my mental state. My throat tightened as I asked the eternal question, "Why?" for the first time and, understandably, not the last. I could only muster one word in prayer, "Reina."

I began to feel my right leg being squeezed and someone applying pressure. Immediately I noticed a tall, dark-skinned figure had squatted down, focusing on my leg.

"The wound is nearly closed but still bleeding slightly," he said in clear English. "We have to clean it and get the swelling down." This new face, a stranger, had entered the office without my notice and was now taking charge. "We also need to get you to a hospital." The man sternly took on the duty at hand, taking care of my obvious needs. I slowly stood and for the first time really noticed the details of the tattered uniform hanging on to my battered body. I also noticed that my new-found friend also wore the crimson and white colors of my airline. I supposed this kind person to be an agent stationed in the Mexican capital. He rushed from the office but quickly returned with a damp cloth and began to wipe my soot-blackened face. I thought "God, could I be bleeding inside?" The friendly Mexican agent continued to wipe my face and neck. Small blisters now appeared in patches on my skin.

"What do you want to do?" The possibility of just escaping was inviting but wasn't it my responsibility to stay? "You need help amigo," he insisted. Here was a fellow employee, someone who was truly concerned and wanted to help one of his own. The strain took its toll.

"What can I do?"

"I can see that you get some help," he said with authority. He purposefully locked onto my swollen eyes as I recognized the same tranquil peace I had seen in Reina's eyes. The Mexican leaned closer and softly spoke. "I can see that you get some protection."

"Where do you want to send me?"

"To the British-American Hospital."

"Do it." This was Mexico and I was very familiar with the modus operandi of the country south of our border. Mexico would be intimately involved in all aspects of the investigation that was to develop very soon, an investigation that was sure to bring Los Norte Americanos from the United States, officials certain to breed contempt in the eyes of the Mexican host, my host. It was evident that I was all alone and would need friends and this Mexican with the rich black hair was my guardian angel. He beckoned those around us, who seemed hypnotized, to help. The agent emphasized that time was of the essence. My new guardian angel was in charge now and he was ready to move me. My time at the Benito Juárez Airport had to end.

I was taken through the one route of the airport terminal that was familiar to me. With a "heavenly" escort, I found myself gliding on a stretcher through narrow corridors, bound for the terminal's main lobby. Again, the sound of the wailing sirens blended with hysterical lamentation that filled the great hallway. The stench of burning human skin and jet fuel hung in the air.

"Reina, help them!" The plea came very easy. I did not wish for God to abandon me yet but I found it impossible to call upon His name. The Mexican agent was positioned at the head of the escort assembly. His deep eyes were focused on the thick crowd that had quickly gathered around me to sneak a peek at this wounded man on the stretcher. Perhaps it was someone they knew? Perhaps it was their loved one who still had not been accounted for? The face of total despair is cruel. The teasing anguish of desperation disguised itself as hope. The morbid procession then became a total haze to me. In my dreamlike state I wondered why I would assume that Reina was now in a position to intercede on my behalf? I anxiously began to wonder if there could be others from 2605's crew who survived! I wanted so badly to believe there were.

"Mi madre!" A woman screamed and I cringed, the tension caused me great pain. One of our escorts leaped forward to block her access to me.

I remember as a child reading about Odysseus strapped to the mast of his wrecked ship, driven mad by the sirens of the forbidden island as the distressing cries echoed off the marble walls.

Of all the airlines, all the flights and all the crews... I recalled Kyle and Mark, my partners in mischief as a slight smile finally broke through the grief. I began to laugh loudly and those carrying me looked at each other, questioning if I had gone mad. None spoke a word as we continued.

"Muy afortunado." An elderly Hispanic businessman gazed upon me for an instant as we quickly passed. I suddenly found myself being lifted into an old 1960's-era ambulance, its attendants rushing about in a panic. I did not want to get involved in any type of detailed discussions involving this accident. I quickly found my wits and thought of a plan.

"Por favor mister, I need, quiero, maybe you, como assistano?" I tried to address the frantic ambulance attendants in a gringo style of Spanish. Yes, I was Hispanic, but if I could solidly create a supposed language barrier, it might offer me my best defense. One attendant seemed to get my frenzied message. The dear Mexican agent standing nearby witnessed my actions and immediately understood. My guardian angel smiled and gave a wink, acknowledging he too would help me in my deception.

"Hey, what's your name?" I shouted at him through the noise of the chaos.

"Hugo, Hugo Garcia." The door shut firmly, then the siren screamed loudly. The driver stomped on the pedal and we took off in grand Mexico City style. My thoughts were with the kind Mexican gentleman.

"Hugo Garcia? Good name." I smiled briefly then settled back, wanting to sleep but the violent turns of the ambulance made it clear there would be no peace.

The city's early morning traffic was treacherous. I was losing hope of getting to the British-American Hospital, as was the original instruction given to the attendants by Senor Garcia. The driver panicked and drove the vehicle onto the shoulder of the road, which furthered complicated the entire situation. The ambulance jerked to a halt.

"Flight Attendant Dies in Ambulance." I shouted the imaginary newspaper headlines that flashed through my weary head.

The two attendants rattled something off to each other and I figured out they quickly made the decision to target another hospital. The driver revved the motor, but we did not move. At that moment a skeleton figure, the face of a calavera, a skull, appeared outside the rear window. A curious array of costumes began to wander about the sitting vehicle, a witch, a ghoul, a grotesque mouse-like figure all appearing as they pressed their gruesome faces upon the glass to get a closer look inside. Their surrounding presence upon the streets on El Día de Los Muertos convinced me we would not be moving any time soon. A couple of the curious removed their masks and made the sign of the cross, a gesture on my behalf. On the morning of October 31, 1979, there were only two kinds of people in the Mexican capital: those that prayed and those that died.

I took comfort in the accepted belief that the company would surely take care of me. Is this not what we were taught in training? Somehow though I could see a more frightening picture developing.

"What a mess I'm in." I was streetwise and well aware of the institutional processes of my host country, Mexico. I knew the true score.

The ambulance driver suddenly gunned the engine and we were off once again. I struggled to hang on as the vehicle jostled from side to side through the crowded morning traffic. I already knew somehow that there would be no company representative awaiting my arrival at the hospital. I was on my own in the most populous city in North America.

"Accept this fact." I scolded myself for if I did not recognize the obvious, I would get eaten alive by the powers that be that were sure to come down on me. The lessons learned from growing up on the East side of L.A., surfaced. "Protect your own ass!" I repeated the phrase over and over. It was finally getting through my clouded head. The tragedy of the plane crash was just the beginning; the true threat to my survival was yet to come.

Chapter VI

The Chief Executive Officer of the airline received the early morning call while in bed at his residence in California. Mario Reddick's first reaction was to curse the timing of the accident. He had secretly been trying to forge a merger of the company with another regional airline based in Denver. Such an alliance would have strengthened the chances of survival in the developing competition of airline deregulation. Now this incident complicated matters. The company had a game plan in place for such a situation and a nervous Mario Reddick immediately gave the go ahead for its execution.

Jack Mckay was a jovial Scotsman who had made quite a reputation for himself in the airline industry for his outstanding diplomatic skills. As a Senior Vice-President, he became Reddick's first choice for the pivotal position of point man in the delicate negotiations that would certainly arise with the Mexican Government. The elderly man who had been born in China to missionary parents was one of the first to be summoned to Reddick's office at the company's headquarters at LAX.

"Jack, thank God you're here," a frantic Reddick stated as he rushed to shake hands with his associate.

"I came as soon as I heard. How bad is it Mario?"

"Bad." He stated. "Listen, Jack, you've got to get on the next flight down there. You understand those people." Reddick tried to remain cool and composed. Mckay could see that the chairman was taking the loss of 2605 very personally.

"Any crew make it out?" Reddick turned his back on Mckay for a few seconds trying to gather his thoughts. Then he turned to face his friend.

"Only one flight attendant that we know of for the moment, ah, an Edmundo Valencia. The Mexicans verified he is alive, but now it seems that they have lost him, can't find him anywhere. See what you can do about tracking him down, Jack."

"I'm already packed, I'll call when I arrive." Mckay left quickly, leaving a worried Reddick to pace the spacious executive office, slamming a fist into the palm of his hand.

Shana James, the slim redheaded flight attendant supervisor had also been summoned to Reddick's office in the early morning. Upon entering she could see the strain on the face of the man she so admired.

"Oh, Mr. Reddick, it's terrible," Shana wanted to be sympathetic while her chief's mind was burdened with a thousand-and-one thoughts. He was caught off guard by her arrival.

"Now Shana, I called you because I need your assistance in a little matter," Reddick stated firmly. Shana eagerly stepped forward. She was proud to have been included in on Reddick's team.

"I understand flight attendant Edmundo Valencia is under your supervision." He enquired.

"Edmundo?" Shanna concentrated.

"Anyway, I want you to pull his file. Find out whatever you can on this young man. I want to know him better that his own parents do."

"Yes sir, Mr. Reddick." As Shana started to exit.

"One more thing Shana, make sure we keep his family away from the media. Pick Edmundo up at the airport when he is released to us. Board the plane and sneak him out before the newsmen know what's happening. Tell the young man we'll take him to his family."

"Yes sir, Mr. Reddick." She was gone. Reddick stood staring for a moment.

"Those families. Those poor families." The reality was registering. He had to keep his composure. He felt the weight of the multitude of issues he had to deal with. First on his agenda was to find out what the hell went wrong. He knew Carl Herbert, and there was no better pilot in this airline. He hoped the findings would lay the blame on Mexican air traffic control. If so, that would create difficult diplomatic complications.

...

As the aged ambulance pulled up to El Central de la Ciudad Hospital there were several nurses awaiting my arrival. The vehicle jolted to a stop and the attendants rushed to the rear to assist me.

"Look! I'm okay. No hablo español!" I pleaded panic-stricken. My charade had to hit everyone firmly.

I thought, "No one is going to come and help me. I must help myself. I am and must be my own best advocate. I repeated this in my head over and over. I took solace in the fact that I could rely on Tommy and trusted him to take care of informing my family.

The nurses, demanding I lie on a gurney, wheeled me through hallways filled with chaos. A man overwhelmed with emotion ran past us. I assumed he was a family member of one of 2605's victims. I was finally wheeled into a small room which was dimly lit, and immediately ushered onto an examining table. A blinding light from a lamp above came, hurting my eyes as dark silhouettes rushed into view. The sound of rapid Spanish filled the room. From other rooms came the cries of tortured pain and anguish. This must be where the more seriously injured had been brought.

A drape on the other side of the room was pulled aside revealing a large window exposing the reception area. People quickly pushed up against the glass. Like a Victorian freak show, whose patrons had deposited a few pence, they excitedly glared at the oddity lying on the table.

"Remove your shirt," commanded a voice in broken English. I froze. The physician who spoke expressed a sign of caring. Handsome in his dark features, he carried himself in a professional manner, wanting to evaluate the situation and select the proper course of medical aid. I sat up in pain and with great care tried to unbutton what was left of my uniform shirt. The fire had made parts of my uniform become one with my skin at various points on my torso. A patient nurse cut away small portions of the garment leaving tiny patterns of cloth encrusted on my arms and upper back where I had sustained most of my burns. As the last segment was removed, I turned and faced the group that gathered as they stood in astonishment, their wide eyes embarrassing me.

"He has no body hair," declared a man in Spanish. I later discovered he was a newspaper reporter who stood looking through the window. The stubs of hair upon my body apparently weren't visible through the glass.

"The inferno was so hot it burned the hair right off his torso," stated a lady in Spanish. The newspaperman quickly dashed away, perhaps believing he had an angle on the story. The pleasant doctor dismissed the nonsensical behavior of the others and began a hands-on examination. I endured the probing as my muscles were bruised and sore just about everywhere on my body. After some time, he asked me if I was involved in athletics. His simple approach in the questioning brought a smile to my face.

"So what will you do with your new life?" His question puzzled me. I was not ready for such a thought and for an instant wondered if I would ever be. I painfully shrugged my shoulders.

"You will be fine mi amigo," the doctor stated as he concluded his examination. "All you will need is a tetanus shot."

"No! No!" I frantically protested. "Yo fue a China para vacaciones." The fluency of the native language I planned so carefully to hide was revealed as I lied to avoid getting an injection. "No shot, I got one." The doctor was startled.

"How long ago?" The physician quickly asked.

"Tres meses, three month ago," I explained in a panic even holding up the same number of fingers in a belief that would convince him. The doctor dismissed the nurse who had returned with the dreadful syringe. I had survived the accident, was injured to a certain extent yet had avoided the shot as I became conscious of a past premonition.

"Is this for real?" I instantly blanked and was filled with confusion. I had enough of this circus ride and wished to just go home, lie down and close my eyes hoping that when I awoke, I would be back in my old life. *What is God's involvement? Is there even a God listening? Why me and not Reina?* I was asking questions that seemed unanswerable. If I persisted in demanding such answers it would only contribute to the pain that grew deep inside me and eventually drive me mad. The hospital staff began to leave the small room; they were desperately needed elsewhere. One Mexican woman dressed in hospital white remained. She stared hard at me, handing me a clean cotton t-shirt and assisted me as I gingerly put it and my tattered uniform shirt on.

"You are very lucky, blessed if I may say." She politely stepped forward and caressed my hands gently as her beautiful face shared a comforting smile. I froze physically. I wanted to scream and crawl into a fetal position. Had my soul vanished? Perhaps it was imbedded into the core of the crushed aircraft.

I turned to see the faces pressed against the window. Was I a saint or a madman? They refused to accept any other possibilities.

"I'm still here," I shouted, the words echoing through the busy halls of the hospital emergency rooms but neither God nor hospital staff replied. "I'm still here!" I screamed louder hoping an intercession would reunite me with my crew once again, for that is where I desired to be. No one came. Everyone just accepted that any bizarre behavior was a normal reaction to an abnormal event. The winds of change were just beginning to stir about.

...

Comandante Primitivo Luis Chávez de León was a stickler for details. The proud policeman's pressed black suit ensemble dictated a man who demanded respect. He and his accompanying cohorts briskly entered the hospital, heading for the emergency rooms. The friendly physician who was seeing to my needs brought in a wheelchair. Perhaps the company called and would soon be there to take charge, for this is what all crewmembers are led to believe when involved in a tragedy of this magnitude. But that thought only led to being blind to the reality of my situation, a complicated scene I wanted no more part of. The Comandante quickly approached the kind doctor and displayed the appropriate papers and identification, expecting the hospital staff to relinquish his prize catch instantly. The medical staff gazed in confusion as this stern, menacing man and his entourage took command, simply sweeping the doctors and nurses aside.

"Por favor Señor, venga con nosotros." The Comandante displayed a deviant charm and determination. I could see that his face was tanned and filled with pockmarks. With his eyes set deep he had the appearance of an Aztec prince or warrior.

"I'm sorry sir, I don't speak Spanish, I mean I'm Mexican, Mexican-American from Los Angeles." I heightened the stakes with a questioning expression. The elegant policeman began to chuckle as he turned to his subordinates, three treacherous stooges ready to do the arrogant superior's bidding. In an instant, one officer stepped forward and firmly placed his right hand on my shoulder.

"Okay, Mr.-Chicano-I-don't-speak-Spanish, come with us."

"Get your hands off of me," I demanded but my battered body was too weak to resist. The friendly physician suddenly stepped forward and courageously confronted the intimidating figure, questioning his authority in this matter.

"What is going on here? This man is my patient." Luis Chávez de Leon was on him like a cat.

"Callate, chueco," the officer got right in the doctor's face. "This man was one of the crew-members in the crash and he is coming with us whether you like it or not." The subordinate yanked me from the examining table as the Comandante directed his cohorts to remove me from the room. Off we went, being nearly carried down the long hallway. The stunned and intimidated hospital staff hugging the wall as our procession passed. By their insistence I was then persuaded to lie down on the floorboard in the back seat of a dark-colored vehicle. These men were Los Federales, the federal police, and I intended to be as cooperative as I could be considering my current condition. The car sped off and I imagined I was now in a different part of this day's eternal maze that indicated no end in sight, revealing a paradox uniquely its own. One resist Los Federales at one's own peril.

A blue wool blanket, the kind found at any local hotel, covered me as the Mexican officials began to joke and laugh. Primitivo Chávez tolerated the lax moment but soon it became very silent. The Comandante spoke firmly and with authority. Smoke quickly filled the compartment, the stench of the cheap cigarettes even overwhelming the smell of the jet fuel that had dried and caked on my pants, my shoes and my body.

"Where are we going?" I tried to sound demanding but failed miserably.

"Do not worry my Chicano friend, we are going to take you to the airport…to home, to Los Angeles," the Comandante teased in delight.

"There's no flight leaving now." I should have kept my mouth shut. The result was a swift kick to my battered right leg. "Okay." I relented. The pain I felt made their message very clear. Suddenly the vehicle jerked to a stop, as one henchman in the back grabbed the blue blanket and threw it over my head. He grabbed my arm firmly and made it clear that I would walk along with him utilizing his support. I graciously went along.

"I didn't do anything," I called through the blanket. Why was I even speaking?

My escort was not interested in listening to anything and I decided that under no circumstances was I to remind them that I was an American citizen.

"Ah, I can't keep up. I'm hurting." I tried to remind them of what I had experienced – a plane crash. They were not sympathetic. The more I resisted; the more force was applied to my bruised arm. Finally, I heard a door open and I could tell we had entered a room. The door was slammed shut. The blanket was pulled off and I blinked and rubbed my eyes trying to adjust to the light. I was told to sit upon an old black wooden milk box positioned in the middle of the floor.

"Do you know where you are?" the Comadante's voice spoke softly as he paced slowly in no particular pattern. I placed my hands over my eyes. The single bulb was very powerful and blinded me. I caught sight of a small table and chair in one corner of the room, but the rest of the floor area seemed to be empty. I recognized a photo of President José López Portillo hanging up on the lime-green wall. The President was wearing the green, white and red sash that is the symbol of his office.

"Yes, sir," I finally responded to the question.

"Where?" the raspy voice demanded. My mind was in a whirl, only one answer filled my conscientiousness

"In deep shit." I softly murmured.

"Speak up mi amigo."

"I am in Mexico." God, I felt like that was such a lame answer. The Comandante slowly stepped forward to again reveal his face at a close range. The thickness of his black hair was distinct. His eyes were like the sudden shine of the sun upon gleaming water, piercing, revealing a sinister spirit, a predator focused on its prey.

"Sí amigo, you are in Mexico." The policeman sensed an opportunity to try and get on my good side. "We do things a little different here and I simply want to ask you a few questions." I knew that any form of resistance was futile; I had to find a different plan. "I want to know what happened to make the plane crash."

"So do I." My smart mouth was not part of the plan.

"What happened?" He demanded.

"I'm cut, bruised and still bleeding." I painfully waved my arms in all directions trying to get my new friend to acknowledge the obvious.

"No, en el accidente," he shouted. I remained stone-face, fatigued.

"What? Oh, the accident, the crash. Well the plane hit hard, then it turned to the right sort of like this." I used my battered hand as a tool trying to indicate a certain angle or motion of the craft. "It just kept banking. I'm sorry, that's all I know." The quick-thinking federal policeman changed his tactics as he retreated momentarily and shortly returned a more agreeable person.

"Only one thing stands in the way of you being released, on your way back to Los Estados Unidos, and as soon as we can take care of that, you are gone." I slowly raised my head. It wasn't going to be that easy, was it? There had been nothing easy all day concerning this tragedy, so I listened with skepticism. Shining gold caps on two of the Comandante's molars caught my eye. A crystal bead of sweat raced down the Aztec's leathery skin on the side of his face, revealing his courtesy as a lie. "We need to take your sworn declaration," he announced. It had become all too apparent to me that I was now in the middle of a complicated predicament that would not be resolved so easily.

"My God, what am I doing here?" I whispered a lamentation.

"Was the flight normal?" Chávez turned to diplomacy in requesting a logical answer which only became fodder for my sarcasm.

"Have you seen what's left of the jumbo jet and buildings? Does it look normal to you?" I almost laughed. My impudence confused the interrogator for a moment, and he strained to calm his anger.

Still sympathetic, he crouched down to meet his captive's eyes. "Yes, I have seen it and that is why I need your help, Eduardo." It was the first time he spoke my proper name, which indicated that he knew way more about me than I knew about him. It scared me. "Help us find out what went wrong in this terrible incident."

"Yeah, I'll help you. That damn thing crashed, don't you get it?" At that moment, discretion became another victim of 2605's demise.

"What happened?" The comandante's posture became rigid, impatient.

"I told you, we clipped. Then we bounced up and there was an explosion, a fireball, and then they were all gone."

"Clipped? Clipped? What did you clip?" Comandante Chávez demanded more and demanded swift answers. I tried to be compliant.

"I don't know. I was inside the airplane. I don't know. Look, I can't say any more until I speak with someone from my company." The cunning officer slowly broke a broad smile as his elegance returned.

"Ah, you do know something after all." He relished my indignity as he favorably patted the top of my head. I had been reduced to being a broken pet with whom he could toy. He then placed a piece of white paper on my sooty lap, tossed a pen in my direction which I was unable to catch. It bounced off the floor to be retrieved by the Mayan-looking officer who then placed it in my sore hand. "Sign this and you can be on your way back to your precious company." I looked at the typewritten letter.

"This is in Spanish." I protested. The Comandante ignored my obvious point.

"Yes, so? Sign it."

"I have no idea what this says," I had to retain my parody. If they figured I understood Spanish, the pressure would increase. The officer's intention was to reduce me to a subservient pawn.

My thoughts spun, perplexed. Surely, this could easily tumble into being one of a great number of "misunderstandings" between the United States and her sister to the south. "Shit, people end up dead for much lesser things in this part of the world." Reality was making its point and I was aware that I was walking a tight rope.

"Come my friend, this paper is merely a routine statement; let us send you back home."
Chávez believed he saw a chance to achieve his goals quickly and I was convinced I was about to get screwed in the ass whether I signed or not. I resolved not to be a passive victim.

"Routine maybe, but...I've told you. I don't speak Spanish and guess what? If I can't speak it, I certainly can't read it." I threw the paper and pen on the floor in desperation. A henchman, who he referred to by the name of Cardosa, was told to pick up the tossed items. Chávez could afford to be patient; he now tried a different approach. The finely dressed Comandante huddled with his subordinates in a corner of the boxy room. My attention was also drawn to the faint sounds emanating through the small upper window, the sounds of the metropolis outside the concrete gray walls. All at once a mid-day's light broke through our space, slowly crossing from one bare wall to another. Then it was gone. My eyes instantly returned to the profile of my nemesis. His arrogance sickened me but also made me realize what a dangerous individual I was dealing with.

"Your name is Eduardo Valenciana?

"Yes." Politely I responded.

"You were the senior flight attendant on the plane that crashed?"

"No." He did not like the answer but pressed on.

"No? You were not the senior?" I raised my head, avoiding locking eyes with my inquisitor, still defiant.

"No means no. What part of no don't you understand?" My host bore a slight smile, if only for a second, lighting another cigarette. Soon the room reeked with the smell of those horrible smokes. If Chávez only knew that all he had to do was to continue to blow that crap in my face for a period of time, that I would have given up, signed any document and admitted to any crime he accused me of.

"Valenciana is a Mexican name is it not?" Pleasantries now returned.

"Yes."

"What is your mother's name?" Why was he asking me that?

"Alicia." I spoke hesitantly. The comandante raised his arms in an animated posture.

"Ah, Alicia, such a pretty name, a Spanish name. But of course, you do not speak Spanish my Chicano friend. "Y sus amigos? Did you see your friends in the fire?" This vicious and cunning man had set his trap, his tactics were obvious, shrewd, and would require I pay a price either way. The comandante was going to play with my mangled mind. Unfortunately, it would not be the last time someone utilized this strategy to try and gain an advantage over me. I would have been safer if the crash had truly driven me crazy.

"Would you like to see your mother Alicia again?

"What do you mean?" I shouted.

"Just sign the paper and I shall have you on a plane back home this evening if you like." I came to a point where I had enough.

"I don't mean to be rude but get this through your thick skull. I'm not signing anything." The comandante exploded.

"¡Pendejo! Do you believe I am stupid? You fake! You liar! I don't believe one word you are saying and now you are going to tell me the truth. You know you served liquor to "Los Pilotos" during the flight, didn't you?" Chávez grabbed me with both hands and threw me off the black box onto the ground. He ordered Cardosa to retrieve the pen and paper which also went flying across the floor. In an instant he regained control, and in a calm manner requested, "Now sign the paper so we can ship your stubborn Chicano ass out of here." Another henchman wearing a gray leather coat lifted me up and slammed me back upon the ebony wooden box that was my seat. Cardosa, once again held up the pen and paper and politely laid them on my lap. The rough treatment had its effect because now I was truly scared. I fumbled as I slowly unfolded the paper and reviewed its contents carefully. I quickly gazed at the bold print trying not to let them realize that I understood what it said. In print Chavez was relating what he demanded verbally.

"This is my sworn declaration; October 31. I Eduardo Valenciana, the Senior Flight Attendant on Flight 2605 served alcoholic beverages to the cockpit crew during the flight."

"Now sign it if you know what's good for you."

"This is not true." I persisted weakly. The comandante quickly rushed forward and grabbed my hair, making me wince in pain. Then he was in my blistered face.

"Let me explain something to you. You are going to give me this declaration or else."

"Or else what?" The comandante instantly whacked me on the side of my head, a payment for my defiance. It was apparent that my Aztec friend did not use all his force, which scared me even more. The Mexican jackal suddenly tried to calm himself as he bent forward and pointed his index finger at me.

"Believe me my insolent friend, you don't want to know. Sign the paper! It crashed because the pilots were drunk! Do you hear me? You served them alcohol and now you are going to admit it." He tossed the paper at me once again and once more it fluttered to the floor beside my right foot.

"Bullshit! This is total bullshit!" I whispered to myself as I slowly reached down to grasp the white sheet, then crumbled it and tossed it aside. Chávez slowly reached inside his tailored black coat and removed a revolver from a side holster. Brandishing the firearm, he reached forward and grabbed me with his other arm, elevating me off the black box. He was rabid.

"You think I am playing a game? Sign the god-damn paper." Comandante Primitivo Chávez turned his revolver in my direction. The henchman in the leather coat standing nearest to me quickly stepped aside, recognizing the trajectory the bullet would take. He had no desire to have his fine garment splattered with blood and brain matter. This action made it apparent to me that the brave Comandante had done this before. Oddly, I wanted him to pull the trigger.

"Go ahead. Do it! Get it over with. I should have died in the crash anyway." The events of this hideous day overwhelmed me. I should have signed the paper and got the hell out of there, letting the diplomats untangle the massive web of complexities that were developing around this horrible event. But then again, "The hell with it." Perhaps I wanted death to win the game, allowing me to rejoin my crew mates and find the peace I believed they had. For the first time, but not the last, I was of the mind that my survival was more an act of rejection from that greater source: that silent God that was indifferent regarding pleas for intercession. I had lost control of the direction my life would take when DC-10 NW903 died on the tarmac. Even if I did survive this bizarre ordeal, it was already clear that any sense of what I regarded as life would never really be mine again. I began to cry uncontrollably as the weary comandante became calm, believing he was successful in breaking me. He slowly lowered the weapon, securing it once again into his military holster. Primitivo began to circle the small room lost in thought, forming a strategy to take full advantage of my obvious vulnerability. My Mexican nemesis began to sneer as he stalked about reminding me of a cunning jaguar, a valiant beast revered by Aztec warriors.

Chávez politely asked Cardosa to bring him a chair, then sat glaring at me. He finally removed the blue pack of non-filtered cigarettes from his inner coat, ceremoniously removing one. Immediately, one of his flunkies offered his chief a flame. I studied the tanned skin and jet-black hair of Chávez's youthful, right hand man. His subservience actions were par for the course in this military-based culture. He was probably biding his time till he would fill the shoes of his superior, the shoes of a madman.

At any time, any place, the walking time bomb that was Comandante Primitivo Chávez could go off and I was well aware that I would be the casualty of such a detonation. The federal officer arose and carefully parked his chair next to me as I struggled not to sob. He took a long draw on the cigarette and retained the smoke in his lungs for a long period of time. His profile was peculiar. I recalled long ago in my youth the story told by my maternal grandfather, Álvaro. The family blood line could be traced to a craftsman from Toledo, Spain, named Francisco. He reportedly was with Cortés when the Aztec empire fell before the foreign invaders. I began to wonder if our Francisco was benevolent and just to the conquered indigenous people, or as abusive as this demonic comandante.

But I was in a no-win situation and Primitivo Chavez knew it. His craftiness reappeared as he quickened his pacing and began to speak in Spanish.

"The carnage must have been incredible." A sympathetic snake is still a snake. "What is it like seeing your friends die? Could you see the flesh melting off their bones?" The diabolical words of death flowed gracefully en Español. Yes, there is good and evil. Perhaps this was the one obvious thing I learned from this catastrophe. Dwelling there, deep in the eyes of this man, was the latter. So I began now to understand how crucial my responses were going to be.

"I understand many of the pasajeros were decapitated mi amigo, crushed. Did you see their heads rolling down the aisles? Could you hear their painful screams? Did you witness their agonizing demise?" The federal officer broke into a smile and shook his head. "What a pitiful piece of meat!" His thoughts betrayed him. It was going to be a long day. Here I was in custody in what I later would discover was a room in the security offices of El Centro Hospital de la Ciudad del Distrito Federal, sitting on a black wooden milk box in the middle of a pit of snakes. Suddenly, another subordinate entered the room.

"Comandante, por favor, teléfono." The chief glanced over at me as I cowered, and he spoke loudly in English.

"Our Pocho friend will be okay. He's not going anywhere. ¡Vámonos!"

They walked out leaving a very able attendant in the form of Cardosa to assure I did not wander away.

An angle of minimal light broke onto the floor from the small window. I estimated that it was already late afternoon. It was Halloween and excited young children were putting the final touches on their costumes.

"On October thirty-one when the sun goes to rest, it's the night of Halloween when fun is at its best."[3] I recalled a childhood song. This was the one period during the year you could live out a fantasy (or a nightmare).

Even in his absence the fear that was Comandante Chávez was gripping. I had to come up with something to increase my

---

3   Bob Hannon 1946

odds, just enough to survive this wicked episode, at least until others with more common sense could find me. The accident, the fire, the grief had to be stored away to be dealt with on another day, another time. Chavez was the problem at the moment, and I had no choice but to deal with this.

…

Primitivo Luis Chávez de León was the son of an aristocratic military career man, the equivalent of a Colonel in rank. The elder Chávez was a bitter man and took his anger out on his young son. Primitivo was reared in a patrician world but only by the grace of his stepmother, María de León Pérez. Born a bastard to his father Ramon's long-time mistress, he was immediately branded with the mark of rejection. The officer's wife who was a devout Roman Catholic decided to do the unthinkable by adopting the young child as her own. From that moment on, the boy became a constant reminder of his father's shame and his stepmother's efforts at becoming a living saint.

Soon after his birth in Guadalajara, the future comandante's biological mother vanished. Rumors persisted that she had been bought off and fled to seek a better life in Los Estados Unidos. Compared to his cousins, who registered the trait of the blue-blooded family with their light complexion and fair hair, no one mistook the source of the bloodline of the young Primitivo. "Indio" was the nickname he carried for most of his life, which greatly irked him. Motivated by resentment, the strong boy scratched and clawed his way to better his lot in life, constantly trying to do whatever it took to be looked upon as an equal. Never mind that he carried the de León name. Because of his lowly birth by his Indian mother, it became apparent that he would never be accepted by the political aristocrats that surrounded him.

"La sangre no es pura." Reality spoke to him every day of his life.

Ramón, the elder Chavez, died an alcoholic, ashamed of the child he had fathered. Señora de León assisted Primitivo in his efforts to attend the best military schools and his maternal grandfather saw that there would be a command awaiting him after his studies were completed. Because of his birthright, or lack of it, he became a loner and seethed with contempt for those who purposely kept their distance. His only companion was the Roman Catholic faith he inherited from his saintly stepmother for it was very clear the patricians would never allow him to become one of their elite.

Primitivo Chávez sought to make his own statement as an officer in the Federal Police. His dress was impeccable, and he became a man of habit. He attended La Purisima Catholic Church in the center of the city every Sunday morning, remained a lifelong bachelor, ate the same meals at the same Zona Rosa restaurant, and developed a reputation as a sadistic bully throughout the Federal District. His appearance at any gathering stirred fear in those in attendance, which delighted the law man: a tool to level the playing field, as he saw it. His stunning career, fueled by the hatred that festered within, made him the perfect man for covert operations against discontented indigenous Indians in the south.

…

On this particular day, the situation at Benito Juárez International Airport office of the Mexican Minister of Transportation had become chaotic. Obviously unprepared for such a disaster, all governmental department heads initially seemed to panic in trying to decide the right course of action to take. Paranoia caused them to cut all communication with the downed airline's head office and/or appropriate U.S. officials. Rumors would persist that Mexican President López Portillo had called diplomats at the highest level in Washington D.C. to smooth over any fears or confusion. If there were a more correct procedure being applied, it was through the efforts of individuals, airport personnel who took it upon themselves to make the tough decisions that were making a difference. Hugo García would prove to be one such man. The Mexican gate agent took command those first few vital hours until company representatives, both in Los Angeles and Mexico City could be brought up to date in the early morning hours.

Enrique Valenzuela was the company's main man in Mexico. The airline's vice president was a veteran with many years in the business and retained the right political keys to run the operation. Valenzuela had the knack of knowing how to deal with Mexico's pirate unions that could go on strike on a moment's notice, shutting down a company's entire operation for a few hours or a few days.

President López Portillo made it clear to the elected officials in the United States that the Mexican Government could ill-afford a nasty incident of this sort. Tourism was at an all-time high and they were very aware that millions world-wide would view the twisted wreckage and fire on the television and newspapers. Mexico needed a scapegoat and the deceased pilots wouldn't render any resistance. If they could obtain a statement from the surviving crew member of 2605 that he had served the pilots in the cockpit liquor during the flight, then the Mexican Government would be blameless regardless of what any investigations revealed.

"Valenciana? Eduardo Valenciana?" Enrique Valenzuela's voice brought Hugo García to his superior's office. "I have not met with any crew members," Valenzuela said to the phone. Hugo was surprised. "I'll get on it right away, thank you." The company's Mexican Vice-President hung up the phone.

"What about Valenciana?" Hugo interjected. Enrique was surprised by Hugo's sudden appearance and thought for a moment.

"Was there a flight attendant from 2605 taken to the British-American Hospital?" He asked.

"Yes, I put him into the ambulance myself early this morning."

"Well, he is not there now, and the company wants confirmation on whether he survived or not." Hugo was dumbfounded.

"Survive? You better believe he survived, and others did too because of him." Enrique dropped his head into his hands and sighed.

"Señor Garcia, I do not need any more trouble than I already have." Hugo understood what he meant as government officials were in the waiting area. There would be no time for employees to search for the lost flight attendant. "What a shit of a mess," the Mexican V.P. stated as he put on his suit coat.

"Ah, Excellency," Hugo García walked past the government official as Valenzuela extended his hand to the Minister of Transportation.

Agent García's thoughts were still on the young crew member as he entered the elevator. He was sure he had given the proper instructions to the ambulance attendants. The elevator door then opened to the terminal level. Hysteria dominated the greater space. Extended families consisting of cousins, uncles, grandparents and friends had besieged "el aeropuerto" to join in on the lamentation. It was Hugo's responsibility to assemble the immediate relatives into one room, away from the growing glare of the frantic news media now descending upon Benito Juárez like locusts.

...

"Valenciana! Valenciana!" A short Mexican man with glasses had found his way to the box room back at El Centro. "Ramón Gutiérrez," stated the man, extending a hand I was too startled to grab. Suddenly, a small crew of workmen hurried in carrying a small wooden desk, chairs, lamp and typewriter. I was instructed by Senor Gutiérrez to sit in front of the desk. Then the workers were gone. A woman dressed in business attire soon entered and occupied the seat at the desk. Her dark hair was worn up, crimson framed glasses sitting on the bridge of her nose. Her makeup seemed overdone, but I was in no position to make any suggestions. In a stern business-like attitude, she proceeded to speak rapidly in Spanish, totally ignoring me at first, setting the tone of her authority. Other people began to enter; the sinister comandante was not among them. The chamber became a cauldron of motion and of speech with everything happening so fast, I could not keep up.

Primitivo once again appeared but totally ignored me. For an instant I felt his scorn as he approached the businesswoman and spoke confidentially. In the rapid exchange of dialogue, I was able to determine that she was from some ministry department and had arrived to make "a damage report." Once the two agreed the room grew quiet and this ministry woman took charge.

"Señor Valenciana, I am Lupe Ortiz Hildalgo," she addressed me in English. "I have come here to make a brief report. Once completed we can then have you back on your way back to Los Estados Unidos." The hours were taking their toll and fatigue was becoming a big problem. I tried to appear cooperative since the alternative would surely put me back into the hands of my dear friend the comandante.

"What would you like to know?" I politely asked.

"What happened?" My eyes focused on the two metal bobby pins that prevented her rich brown hair from falling into her face.

"I'm cut and bruised." I sighed as I ran my stiff hand across my lip, releasing a flake of caked blood.

"No, no, the accidente," the woman insisted, never raising her eyes from the small typewriter as she pounded the keys.

"Look, I'm pretty beat up and extremely thirsty." The lady became annoyed by my answer and gazed at Chávez who then motioned to the solidly built Cardosa. He left and returned with a bottle of soda water. I was presented with someone's handkerchief and I tried to clean some of the caked slime off my face as Chávez and his men once again left the room. This was my opportunity. I would enact basic stupidity; give the impression I had finally gone insane. I proceeded without any gauge as to the real purpose of our conversation.

"The accident? The accident?" I looked about the room at the continuous movement of people coming and going. "Didn't the airplane crash?" I sheepishly inquired, wanting my words to express diminished mental stability. Why not? I hoped no one would deny me the privilege of being deranged since everyone in the room was by now familiar with the scenes being televised from the airport. Deep down they probably expected a lunatic. Lupe Ortiz Hildalgo, the determined ministry woman, continued to type.

"How did el avion crash?" Like a first grader, I used my scorched hand as an aircraft, stiffening it into a plane, gliding it through the air. Suddenly my palm dropped, demonstrating the descent and crash of the DC-10, and then I fell silent. Then I noticed a newsman entering the room. He set up his cameras and lights just feet from where I sat. I began to realize the risk of giving even a hint of having solid information that could be twisted to their advantage.

"I'm sorry, I don't know. I'm sorry, I don't understand." I began to ramble. No matter, everyone was simply waiting for the magic statement that would help them make sense of the devastation at the airport. The ministry-woman became frustrated. I turned to see the menacing figure of Chávez enter the room once again, the hunter seeking his quarry. He walked straight up to me.

"Perhaps you would like to visit el baño my Chicano friend?" His politeness was unexpected. He motioned to his henchmen to assist me. "Llévalo si es necesario," he ordered. The snake's concerned manner threw me for a loop as I struggled to stand. My legs were so painful. Cardosa stepped forward to offer more assistance as I placed my sore arms over one shoulder. Being lifted and extracted from the room, I noticed that the hallway was now filled. People were everywhere, talking, pushing, walking briskly to undetermined destinations. The area had an aura of a central hub. The press by now had assembled en masse: television crews with all their equipment and radiomen with shoulder-slung tape recorders. All raced about in pursuit of any shred of data concerning the crash of my DC-10.

Once in the lavatory, the two henchmen would not allow me the privacy of shutting the door to my toilet stall. The junior cadets, as I started referring to them, did not speak English and I was not about to reveal any knowledge of Spanish. I struggled to undo my pants, or what was left of them. Suddenly, I heard a door open and the sound of quick steps as someone speaking English entered the lavatory and pushed his way through Chavez's henchmen straight into my stall. He excitingly identified himself as "John Smith" of UPI. He was tall and carried himself with assurance, his blond hair being a contrast to all the people I had dealt with this day.

"What happened, Valenciana? Why did the plane crash?" Surprised and momentarily confused, the comandante's henchmen stood and stared in wonder. Sitting on the toilet with some idiot wanting to question the survivor of this horrible incident irritated me greatly.

"Can't you see I'm taking a crap?" I was face to face with what I had been dreading since leaving the airport facility, the press discovering my identity and hounding me. The reporter continued pressing without consideration, as though we were seated in a lounge area or a cafe. I was barely clad in the charred rags, some still embedded in my scorched skin. I became disgusted and felt nothing but contempt for this "fellow

American." I signaled the befuddled henchman, raising an arm for their assistance.

"¡Alto! ¡¡Alto!!" The two stooges finally came to their senses, figuring out what was happening, they became angry and chased the reporter out of the lavatory.

"Was the flight normal?" The American screamed as he was physically thrown out of el baño.

The international media reached and reached to find one piece of dung to banner the next day. Revolted, I decided that all questions would be met with exceedingly soft answers. I recognized blood sucking for what it was and ignored the attempted rape of what sanity remained in my battered mind. I would remain silent through most of this awful ordeal and put aside for the moment what I really wanted to say.

"I am all alone...defenseless." I had to fend for myself. The fact that the ambulance driver had made an instantaneous decision to change hospitals because of the festivities of Halloween suddenly took on importance. Once returned to the interrogation room I began to understand the significance of being in the wrong place as far as the airline was concerned. There was absolutely no way I could get word to them.[4]

The whirlwind of activity continued around me as I sat motionless and silent. I caught sight of the rugged features of Señor Chávez. For the first time, that Aztec face broke into a smile as he caught the gaze of my weary eyes. He would be patient, bide his time. He would have his chance at slowly breaking me down; exhaustion and fear were quickly draining whatever strength remained.

Alone and lost in the most populous metropolis in North America, I was scared and began to feel the ravages of time. I had been up all night, survived a major airplane crash, was in a foreign country where the officials could do potentially do whatever they wished to me. I was in no physical condition to resist. I tried to gather my wits once more. I began to play with the idea of giving them "a story." I knew I could trust no one.

---

4   This was 1979. There were no cell phones, no texting, no e-mail. I was M.I.A.

"I do not speak Spanish. I do not speak Spanish." I repeated the words over and over to myself, hoping to cling to the one possible advantage I felt I still had.

Continually popping their heads into the room, the press recognized me in my tattered uniform and with my identity confirmed, the lights, camera and microphone quickly converged upon me. Now I would be abused once more with the relentless demand for information, far more than I possessed. The bulk of the questions were the same, but each reporter asked them as if his inquiries were a novel, insightful request. The din was intense, and I soon became unable to focus on any particular person. In an instant, I mentally withdrew from the situation and became an observer, making no effort to tackle any of the questions as their faces and microphones all pushed in on me.

The majority in this chaotic interrogation refused to believe my claim that I had little if any knowledge of the Spanish language. Certainly, with a name like Eduardo Valenciana, as it had been recorded on the official manifest of Flight 2605, it was assumed that I must speak Spanish. Primitivo Chávez decided that he would toy with his prisoner for the delight of the press, determined to unveil the farce right before their eyes. The aggressive comandante ordered the crowd back with ease, pausing to light another one of those atrocious cigarettes. Suddenly the federal officer began to cough in a heavy raspy tone which brought a sly smile to my sore face. Gathering his composure, he approached me and softly began to speak to me in Spanish, first in a whisper and then louder so the others could hear. I began to shake.

"¿Que pasó con sus amigos en el avion?" (What happened to your friends?) No reaction; instantly Chávez returned to English.

"Let us see, there was Señores Rollings, Stillwell, y también, las señoritas Karen Smitt, y Cary Diller," his eyes rolled up as he counted on his fingers. The shock registered as the sinister demon played me to perfection.

"Ah, my young Chicano friend, I may have forgotten one señorita whose body was found mangled in the wreckage, just pieces that now lie in the morgue. "¿Que pasó con Señorita Torres?"
Chavez placed his face close to my ear.

"I know everything."

The snake returned to speaking Spanish.

"Why didn't you save her when she cried out in pain? Why didn't you help her when you had the opportunity? You let her die! You failed and you'll never be good enough to make it right again." No one moved a muscle or said a single word, not the ministry woman, not the newsmen not the onlookers who had stumbled upon the scene and watched intently. Intimidated by his presence, they all allowed the comandante to complete his interrogation. The added advantage of his atrocious behavior for the media was that I just might release the information they so desperately wanted.

My reaction was to remain perfectly still. My battered body was sore so I used that as an excuse and deterrent. I also became overcome by a tremendous ringing in my ears. I was struggling to refocus my eyes, awkwardly trying to appear normal.

The sound of the ministry woman's continuing pounding on the keys increased the discomfort in my head. She removed the finished paper and handed it to my impatient interrogator. The sly snake picked up right where he had left off, taking the freshly completed piece of paper and placing it on my lap. I gazed down at the document and discovered that this new declaration was also written in Spanish. I sat motionless, which displeased the comandante who occupied center stage. With a nod from him his goons lifted me and off we went once again right out of the room. Señor Valenciana needed to visit the men's room again, or so it was explained to the media and everyone else.

I discovered that the black wooden milk box was now moved to the middle of the bathroom. One of the officers stood by the doorway to insure we would not be disturbed. Cardosa was given instructions and promptly left the room. I was now all alone with my inquisitor, left to consider my plight. Once again he handed me the newly printed letter as I clumsily fumbled with the sheet trying to rest it upon my lap. Exhaustion blurred my vision and I strained to read the bold print.

"Eduardo Valenciana declares the following to be the truth." The words jumped out at me. I also noticed that the efficient Sra. Ortiz Hildalgo had also prepared a space at the bottom of the declaration for my signature. My mind reeling, I suddenly recalled flight attendant training, Regulation 8.12.8.

"Do not say anything that might imply that the company is admitting liability for injury or damage." I wondered if this asshole Chávez would back off if I began to recite the flight attendant regulation that prohibits me from admitting anything? It was an amusing thought that brought a hint of a smile to my weary face. The reality of these situations could never be fully grasped in training and there was apparently no company representative deployed to come to my rescue. Alone, I continued to decipher the rest of the proclamation: "During the flight, alcoholic drinks were served to the on-duty pilots in the cockpit." My ability to read Spanish was somewhat limited but there was no denying what was staring me in the face: the Mexican government's attempt to completely absolve itself from the crash. It was important for me never forget that I was no longer in the United States. The ACLU was not going to arrive to represent me.

"Don't say anything, you have rights!" No, the only rights I currently had were whatever the sinister Primitivo wished to bestow upon me. At that moment his body was once again wracked uncontrollable spasms of coughing. I thought it futile to remind him that those awful little cigarettes might be bad for his health. But here I was, on a box on the floor of a lavatory of El Central Hospital in Mexico City on Halloween night, totally lost. Finally, I concluded there was only one solution: I needed to get my bruised ass out of that place as quickly as possible.

I refused to admit that Comandante Chávez had me cold. If not fluent in the native tongue of his country, he probably suspected I had some understanding of the language. After composing himself once again he retrieved the sheet of paper I had refused to sign. The henchmen returned and I was taken from the lavatory to the previous room which to my surprise was now empty. I supposed the show was over so the audience left, or so it seemed.

I was back upon the milk box but was surprised to find my escorts leaving. Smoke break? The last to exit, Chávez shut the door so I would not be able to eavesdrop on their conversation. Now totally alone I studied the four walls that constituted my holding cell: concrete blocks. The office desk that had been carried in for use by Sra. Ortiz Hildalgo remained in front of me. I noticed a thin beige cord that extended from somewhere in the desk and out through a hole in the floor. The discovery gave me a surge of strength as I slowly rose, taking a moment to stretch my sore body. I tracked the cord to a bottom desk drawer, discovering a telephone. Both excited and fearful I lifted the receiver. With my stomach muscles tightening I heard the sound of a dial tone.

What number do I call? My panic was rising. What number would be the key to an outside line, to an international line? I struggled to recall what magic number allowed me to make calls on recent layovers, while in the Federal District. I anxiously tried a "9" then an "8." I worked my scorched fingers down the numerical line till I finally tried "0-1."

"Bingo!" I instructed the international operator to request a collect call and recited the number of Flight Attendant Scheduling in Los Angeles. The Mexican operator told me to hang up and she would ring back when the charges were confirmed, and the line connected. I hung up and was shaking with fear. What if Primitivo Chávez returned before I had a chance to complete the call? More vital was what excuse could I give the ill-tempered Mexican officer for not signing the declaration? The phone rang as I swiftly grabbed the receiver hoping the others in the hallway did not hear it.

"Is this Eduardo?" questioned the voice. "Where are you?" The anxiety in my gut was intense.

"Get me the hell out of here," I whispered in a panic. To the best of my clouded recollection, I explained to the female scheduler where this administrative section of the hospital might be.

"In the hospital in the heart of the city." Assurance was given that everything in the company's power would be done to secure my safety as I hung up the phone. For the first time since this mad ordeal began, I felt some relief, if only for a moment, as I suddenly I realized that company headquarters might be under the impression that I had been taken to the British-American Hospital. I had failed to inform the scheduler of the blunder in being taken to the Hospital El Centro. Help would be on the way to the wrong location. Now I really felt like I was about to lose my mind.

"Why wouldn't my interrogators think I was just a step from becoming a madman?" I thought as I gazed upon the declaration the policeman had left on the desk. Suddenly I could hear the sound of footsteps approaching. The comandante opened the door and seemed a bit mystified to see me calmly sitting upon my little black box, my mouth stuffed with and me in the process of eating his prized declaration. "Do you have any beer to wash down this tasty paper? I would prefer Bohemia." The words had come so easily. Maybe I <u>was</u> truly losing my mind!

Primitivo Chávez glared at me, hesitated, then called for Cardosa to get me out of the room. I was taken down the hallway into the main lobby where the newsmen had gathered, setting up their cameras and lights. Frazzled, I was unceremoniously tossed like a rag doll onto a tan leather sofa; I was on display for all to see. Comandante Chávez was indeed sly. He could not get the answers he wanted from his stubborn prey so he would let the press destroy what was left of my will. Primitivo had promised them satisfaction and as the deluge began it seemed he would make good on his word.

"Valenciana! Valenciana!" They screamed. "What did you see? Are you going to make your declaration?" Lupe Ortiz Hildalgo quickly positioned herself behind another desk with her typewriter. Her fingers methodically worked on the keys of the beaten machine occasionally glancing up from her task to meet my frightened eyes. Completing a new document, she removed it and handed it to the nauseous, nervous wreck I had become.

"Sign!" She demanded, handing me a pen.

The waiting room fell silent, just the way it was in the cabin of 2605 before the aft floor began cracking open. I began to hear the shrieking sound of jet engines in the distance, while the bright lights of the television cameras blinded me. The pitch rose greater in volume making it difficult for me to focus on the Spanish words on the sheet of paper. Basically, it was a repeat of the letter I had just devoured. "Alcoholic beverages, drunk pilots," the words were all there. Before I could decide on a course of action, a frantic newspaper boy came running in from the street. I saw the bold newsprint:

149

"¡Error de Piloto!"

Without a declaration from me, the plot had been put into motion and its desired outcome achieved. I knew Captain Carl Herbert Sr. He was a damn good pilot and if mistakes had been made in the cockpit, I knew they surely weren't enough to have caused this catastrophe. It was evident that the Mexican Government was in a frenzy and what better way to settle the dilemma than to point the finger at a dead man? The anger swelled deep inside me and I wanted revenge. I decided it was about time they all felt the disappointments I had endured.

"I want to tell the whole truth!" Like a crazed man I rose shouting, then tumbled to the marble floor. My legs could no longer support me. "I want to make my declaration," I begged while lying on the tiled floor. The room fell dead silent; even Primitivo Chávez looked of surprise. Then the lobby became alive with activity. "This is what the vultures have been waiting for," I whispered in exhilaration.

Will he describe all the gory details? I imagined one journalist wondering. *Was the Captain of 2605 a madman?* I waved to attract the attention of a watchful comandante. When I was sure he was paying attention, I pointed to "el baño" where I wished to compose myself. Chavez motioned for Cardosa and another sidekick to assist me. Once on my feet I pulled away from my escorts. Instead of entering the bathroom, I staggered over to a corner of the spacious room, positioned myself, unzipped my ragged pants and proceeded to urinate right there. Wearing a cool mask of innocence, I looked about and gave an expression of complete ignorance.

"¿Qué estás haciendo?" What was he doing indeed! The assemblage was both amazed and repulsed in one stroke. Once I had relieved myself, I adjusted my pants, turned and prepared to address the gathering, some smirking and shaking their heads.

"You are going to give your declaration," shouted a faceless silhouette as I stood blinded by the lights.

"But I don't know anything," I insisted as I continued to struggle with the zipper on my ragged trousers. All fell silent. Instead of the answers they were promised I presented the actions of a lunatic.

"¡Está loco!" The consensus was unanimous. The disappointed media began to dismantle the lights and the cameras, and to pack their equipment. The proud Aztec Chávez stared intently. The others may have fallen for my ruse, but he was not fooled one bit. Was he perhaps enjoying this game of chess between us?

I had to turn away for I knew I couldn't deal with this insanity much longer. I recalled thinking how stupid someone could be when they admitted to a crime they did not commit. Now under severe interrogation, I was enlightened. I wanted a hot shower, a cold Bohemia, but most of all I wanted to be gone from this ghastly ordeal.

Chapter VII

One moment I was the prized crewmember who'd been the center of attention in the administration's large entryway. Now, after my crude stunt, I found myself being completely ignored. The very journalists who fought to get to me would now walk right past as if I were a part of the large room's furniture. People came and went as the ministry woman conferred with other men in suits down the hallway. Even my captor, Primitivo Chávez, no longer focused on me, and was distracted by others who requested his presence elsewhere in the hospital. Certainly, there were a few survivors, passengers who had beat the odds and needed to be interviewed. Chávez' reaction gave me hope that my desperate charade of losing my mind was having some success.

Another media crew approached. An older Hispanic man introduced himself as a reporter. A younger, tall man carried his equipment. I looked closely at reporter's face, then to his eyes. The obvious struck me; he was blind. My first reaction was to feel a camaraderie with this Mexican man, both of us needing to cope in an uncertain environment. The man could not see, and the injured, exhausted crew member could not communicate. It posed quite a dilemma. The inability to have eye contact with the reporter put me at a disadvantage. In the others, the eyes were the most significant hint of their intentions. Confused, I was forced to deal with him in a straightforward, honest manner. Without hesitation, he respectfully asked for a full interview.

"Interview?" Blind or not, boundaries had to be set.

"No!" I asserted myself.

"Well, can we talk for a while?" The man's thick English accent had a tone of sincerity, so I reluctantly gave my consent. Quickly, cameras shoved their way forward.

Initially, the man presented the same questions to which I gave the same guarded answers. There was no feeling of mistrust, not like I felt for the others. It seemed for a moment that the blind reporter and I were shielded from everyone else in the room. He told me bluntly but honestly that he wanted to know specifics. Although I was not obliged to speak with him, I found it difficult to simply dismiss him. It had to do with Hispanic cultural respect.

I became nervous and my palms moistened. I repositioned myself on the chair to speak softly and close to his ear.

"Señor, por favor, I cannot discuss any details until I speak with a representative from my airline." His mouth opened in surprise.

"You *do* know something, don't you?" I pleaded with him,

"For my sanity, por favor, for my sanity, I need time. I need my company. I cannot say anymore, I can't now." The commentator suddenly backed off: perhaps he sympathized with me and my dilemma.

Unbeknownst to me the cunning Comandante Chávez was observing me from afar, studying my mannerisms. While watching with a dignified, official air perhaps he was worried that things might progress beyond his control. He approached me once again with the ministry woman in tow, but this time there would be no authoritarian manner. Instead, Lupe Ortiz Hildalgo attempted to sweet talk the dazed little lunatic.

"Of course, Eduardo, you could have whatever you desire to be comfortable, even be released to return home." The "gracious" lady offered to bring in an interpreter. We could move to a secure room with no interference, with no pressure. Like sharks, she and the vicious policeman would circle, wearing me down, their kindness but a charade. I turned away wrapping my sore arms around myself and, lay in a semi-fetal position, falling silent. Disappointed, the pair retreated.

"What is my importance?" With each passing second, I grew wary of my role to defend this company, my supposed beloved airline. With the press acting so viciously, I owed them nothing. I wanted nothing to do with the event's spotlight, wishing only to get as far away as I could from this three-ring circus. *Maybe I could just blend in with the chaos.* Sometimes the easiest thing to lose is the obvious. I decided to make an effort to stand and see if it were possible to hobble through the crowded lobby. I strained to stand up and grimaced, using the excuse that I was terribly stiff and would need to stretch my aching muscles.

Over a period of about an hour and with each circuit around the room, I would venture a little farther out. The comandante would occasionally glance my way but paid me less and less heed. My Aztec friend had no idea that his "pocho" would try so bold a plan. Regrouping within myself, I would stop at one point of the floor and then another; one time to solidify my innocence, the other to not-so-innocently case out a possible escape route.

On one of my rounds I slipped into an adjacent small office, unnoticed. I backtracked and made my way to the entrance of the administration offices, gazing through a tall window at the outside world. I pretended I was looking for someone, awaiting someone's arrival. But I was simply staring at the clamor and chaos of Mexico City. Suddenly I felt a hand on my arm, then turned and faced an older gentleman who was dressed in a janitorial jumpsuit. He stared intently at my face. I recognized him as the very man the officials had summoned to clean the puddle, I left in the lobby a bit earlier. Perhaps I should have apologized but I remained silent.

"¿Adónde vas?" He finally inquired. I hoped he wasn't angry about having to clean up my mess and lead me back to my interrogators. I needed an excuse.

"Yo quiero mirar la luna. The moon, I want to see the moon." Grinning, he nodded his head and continued about his business. In this packed room of manic humanity, he was one of the normal people. I had seen his kind at the airport this morning, risking their own wellbeing in an effort to help total strangers. He represented the Mexican people at their best, sharing in the happiness of my survival. The majority of those I was to meet in the capital were of his kind and I will always be grateful for their graciousness.

Finding myself alone once more, I hobbled slowly to the large gold swinging doors, through them and out the building. It was not just my tormentors I was running from, but from the death and tragedy of the day. I wanted to go home. Once outside on the street and in traffic, I realized my escape was poorly planned.

"Right or left?" I had no idea. And the noise deafened me. The sound of the tearing metal and explosions in the fuselage had earlier sent me in shock. But now it was the roar of this city of millions. I saw a main intersection and limped over to the edge of the curb in the hopes of hailing a taxi. A small green creature, teeth in disarray, jumped into my space and shrieked. I had stepped into the madness of Halloween night with Los Muertos, the walking dead. Out of a side alley came a massive skeleton. A pack of intoxicated ghouls were next. There were dead brides and grooms, dead butlers and maids, and doctors and nurses drenched red with the blood of a botched surgery or worse. A seven-member band of gruesome corpses played their instruments, blaring and enticing their followers like pied pipers of the lost. A large flatbed truck turned onto the main boulevard bearing many dearly departed gleeful dancers. At the tail end of this procession of the damned a large white Styrofoam construction of Muerto was carried. It rose high into the black sky, a massive marionette controlled by four demons. I couldn't stand this and hobbled headlong into the frenzied crowd.

The ghouls, witches and spirits of Mexico City ran amok all around me. To them my odd attire became an airline crew-member crash-victim costume and drew no notice. Children carrying "calaveras" (skulls) approached. One white-masked child offered me a clump of sugar molded into a skull. The youthful ghoul popped another skull into his own mouth and smiled. I could hear the last portion of a silly riddle a girl sang about Muerto. Then, the call of many names was in the air. I saw a small boy dart through the crowd, his frantic mother reaching for him as he sped away. With an anguished face she called to him.

"¡Ramón!" High-pitched jets engines filled the air once again. Voices of those trapped in the burning rubble filled my head as they screamed for their loved ones.

"José, Ramón, Julieta, Reni, Francisco......Javier! My mother! Juanita!" The cries of the ill-fated freaked me out. I fell out of the swiftly moving wave of bodies. Exhausted, I leaned on the edge of a building, the deafening noises continuing.

"¡Dame tu alma! Give me your soul!" screamed a red devil, who then ran off. Frightened and exhausted, I sat on some concrete steps and struggled to breathe. I tried to settle myself, then watched people exiting a Catholic church across the boulevard. The three days of El Día de Los Muertos festivities were indeed in full swing. Rising, I made my way a bit further down the road, stopping once again to rest and pressing my face against the window of a small shop that sold religious items. I gazed at the small showcase decorated with golden paper surrounded with "calaveras." In the center stood the figurines of revered saints. Some were familiar since my mother displayed a group of them around our home. Then there was Saint Jude, the patron of the impossible, of desperate cases. Surely a small word or two to this intercessor would help my tortured soul. I pictured the crash site in my mind once more, doubting the intercession by this indifferent God.

"He wouldn't save little Javier, why should he bother to assist me now?" I knew I was doomed, and I began to weep. The tears ran down my cheeks and the glass pane as I cursed God, this day, and the entire tragedy. It was then that I realized this enormous suffering would be a constant companion for years to come. There was no way to avoid it or wish it away. The morning's events had marked my rebirth, but not into a world I was familiar with or could find comfort in. The Eddy I was before had died, and now I was delivered into a cruel limbo of insanity.

"Life is a journey of twisted fate," I decided. I surveyed the crowded roadway. The parade symbolizing the fragile line between life and death pushed forward.

A trio of skeleton mariachis appeared with instruments in hand, singing with gusto for their supper money.

"Una canción? A song?" One thin zombie "caballero" holding a guitar called to the masses as they cheered and cried out for their favorite tune of the season. He began to serenade the crowd with a ballad of wine, women and death, the latter being the outcome of the song's troubled hero, a colorful tragedy. I was a survivor and should be celebrating my good fortune, yet in the same instance I felt like one who was also condemned. The seductive lyrics of the traditional ballad attracted a crowd of witches, goblins and rogue spirits that circled the minstrels as I stood transfixed from a distance. I was spinning out of control. Depression set in, I wished I had died too. I sat on the curb totally defeated as madness and death danced all around me.

. . .

Mexico's population in 1979 was nearly 69 million.[5] It was a time of graft and corruption, and the truth behind the demise of my airline's jumbo jet now lay in the hands of those who were comfortable with protecting their government no matter where the facts lay. In a pact with evil that usually was made at the beginning of their careers, the powers-that-be saw truth as an expendable commodity. If necessary, they might even eliminate those who spoke it.

The downward spiral of Mexico's economy that existed when 2605 met its fate was put in motion during the Presidency of Luis Echeverría whose term lasted from 1970 to 1976. Up until 1970, Mexico had made real economic progress in spite of questionable governmental procedures that had existed from the beginning of the republic. Progress, and a sincere effort to "clean house" in the government, was due largely to the appointment (by two consecutive presidents) of the brilliant and honest Antonio Ortiz Mena as Minister of Finance.[6] Ortiz Mena had twelve uninterrupted years (1958-1970) in which to set the economic course for the nation and he made the most of it. It was Ortiz Mena who conceived Mexico's "maquiladora" (manufacturing) program and gave it life. The system allowed for free trade zones where manufacturers could import material duty-and-tariff-free, for assembly.

When Echeverría took office most of Ortiz Mena's economic policies were abruptly changed. As president he stole a lot and did little. Worse yet, it would be discovered that he had far more blood of the innocent on his hands than any former Mexican president. It is widely believed that Echeverría planned and helped to execute the student massacre of October 2, 1968 prior to the opening of the Olympic Games in the Mexican capital. As the Minister of Interior Affairs during the administration of President Gustavo Díaz-Ordaz, the two men unleashed military troops upon protesting university students, killing several hundred at "Tlatelolco," a student gathering place in the city. Echeverría's own presidential reign included the same tactics of oppression, assassinations, and disappearances as those used by

---

5   Wikipedia
6   New York Times

157

military dictatorships in other Latin American countries but kept largely secret from the general public.

It was Echeverría who set the course for the eventual downfall of the Mexican economy, and the beginning of the most corrupt era in Mexican history. Any opportunity for a true democracy would lie in the hands of Echeverría's successor. Mexicans joked that they lived in a state of hope-they hoped the next president will be better. Everyone hoped that Echeverría's handpicked successor, would be better, since there was no way he could be worse. But it was, after all, Echeverría who did the picking, so it shouldn't have been a great surprise that his choice would turn out to be worse. Thus, José López-Portillo came to reside at "Los Pinos" in 1976, the official residence of the Mexican President.

It was easy at first for López-Portillo to convince Mexicans he was going to be a great leader, they so wanted to believe this. Events, however, would prove him to be another catastrophe. His administration would give new meaning to corruption, ineptitude at managing the country, and recklessness at handling the country's wealth, much of which would find its way into his own pockets or those of close relatives.

When it was discovered that Mexico's oil deposits were far greater than previously believed, providing the country with one of the world's largest reserves, López-Portillo took the country on a wild orgy of spending by borrowing against future oil deliveries. Under his leadership, Mexico would borrow over 85 billion dollars, much of it misspent or diverted into his and his cronies' hands. If anyone dared to protest, their mutilated body would be discovered in a ditch or sewer a few days later. The common citizen learned to stay quiet and go about his own business. The wild spending on every conceivable infrastructure and housing project fueled the inflation which began under the Echeverría administration. The strain on the peso's value reached the breaking point. Within a few years, López-Portillo's house of cards would tumble under the strain.

On Halloween Day of 1979, a telephone call made from Los Pinos to the White House made the situation clear. López-Portillo would never forget the visit to the Mexican capital of the seemingly (in his opinion) self-righteous Norte Americano

President Jimmy Carter. Aware of López-Portillo's true colors, President Carter forced "El Presidente" to endure a tongue-lashing on human rights, a sincere but foolish action. Such behavior would not only sink U.S.-Mexican relations to its lowest point, but also promote a pro-López-Portillo movement by the majority of the Mexican population, who viewed Carter's actions as hypocritical.

Now with the crash of a U.S. airliner in his backyard, López-Portillo had the opportunity to pay Los Norte Americanos back for the insults endured earlier in the year. A well-placed Mexican official who was present during that presidential conversation, stated that López-Portillo clearly informed Jimmy Carter that "the United States of Mexico did not need nor want any assistance with the investigation from Los Gringos to the north." President Carter had taken some flak from the press for his "holier than thou" lecture which had strained relations, but more importantly, crippled business between the two nations. Despite the damage done prior the crash, the United States and Mexico had been able to hammer out an important agreement: Mexico would supply Los Norte Americanos with petroleum and natural gas through the year 2005. President Carter knew how important the agreement was, especially since the oil embargo of the early 1970s had caused such turmoil. Word went out from the U.S. State Department to investigators of the National Transportation Agency: don't investigate too closely, this should be a Mexican show.

While this political jockeying was taking place that Halloween night, I had finally been picked up and was being carried arms-over-the-shoulders, by two young Mexican gentlemen, orderlies I barely recognized from my time at the hospital. My valiant effort to escape only led me back through the streets, through the crowds to the entrance of the administration building of the hospital El Centro. The strong young men spoke rapidly.

"Sí, es él del accidente."

"No se ve muy bien."

"Necesitamos regresar al hospital." I was too exhausted to protest as they believed that I was disoriented and in need of assistance. As we approached the large doors of the building, I noticed some of the comandante's men scurrying about. My absence had been discovered. Chavez himself met the three of us as we entered the lobby. He exploded in rage which was primarily directed at his subordinates to whom he gave no quarter.

"Cabrones!" There were violent threats, then more cursing followed by more threats. He ordered everyone back down the long hallway into the private cubicle. I found myself propped up again upon my little black milk box.

A reporter rushed to the entrance but the angry comandante slammed the door in his face. Chávez continued to scream, first at me then everyone in general. The frightened orderlies stared in disbelief.

Chávez turned and faced me once again, accusing me of the very charade I was playing. He reached far back with his arm and brought it down hard on the right side of my head, knocking me completely off the black box, screaming for answers he wanted. I felt the pain and throbbing on the side of my head.

"You know you served "los pilotos" liquor on the flight and the captain was drunk when he tried to land the plane at the airport. Admit it!" Like a vicious panther he roared while everyone in the room remained silent. Chávez was a cunning man. Even if I were to complain to the proper authorities, who would be able to tell what injuries were from the crash and which were inflicted by this madman.

Reina, help me. This thing is getting out of hand. I offered up a silent prayer. Perhaps the comandante's erratic behavior had embarrassed him? I hoped so, but such optimism was dashed as the snake asked for a chair and promptly seated himself next to me and my black box. I lowered my head and the officer slowly lit another nasty cigarette. The interrogation began once again.

"My friend, your mother's name is Alicia. Your father's name is Reynaldo." This was a new approach by my adversary. I had not told anyone my father's name, or had I? I was too scared and exhausted to think. "Alicia, Reynaldo and Eduardo?" Chávez demanded my attention. "You expect me to believe you do not speak or understand Spanish?" He gritted his teeth. "Pocho pendejo."

Chavez motioned for Cardosa to escort the two orderlies out of the room. I desperately wanted to go with them. One turned toward me for a last glance, a nod and a wink. I sat silent and defeated. There was no way out. Survival again became the primary goal; live another day. The comandante stooped down close to my face and screamed.

"You will give me the mother-f###ing declaration I want." His dark choleric eyes revealed the true depravity in his rotten soul.

"By the time we are finished my young Chicano friend, your Spanish will be excellent." Chavez chuckled mischievously, then turned to a subordinate, "Llame Señor Montoya." The finely dressed young man left the room. The comandante continued rambling as my mind fell prey to exhaustion. I tuned him out and tried to fill my head with thoughts of my family, my mother making her famous red chile enchiladas. What had registered before this day as normal now seemed so distant.

"Tell me mi amigo," Chávez pressed. "Do you have a wife, children?"

"Don't you know? You know everything else about me." My impudence forced a slight grin on the comandante's leathery face.

The room remained silent. Suddenly the floor began to shake under me. The door swung open while I was staring at Chavez's smile of contempt.

"Let me introduce you to Señor Montoya," he motioned his arm toward the door. Confused, I looked up to view the leviathan that was to be my "persuader."

"He has no neck," I blurted out. Officer Montoya was of a much darker complexion, a reflection of the indigenous cultures of Lower Mexico but the prominent characteristic was his sheer size. There did not seem to be an ounce of fat on him. My persuader wore a short-sleeve white shirt with a little black tie that began and ended at the base of his head which seemed bolted onto his muscular body. Disregarding the pain, I stood looking in desperation down the long hallway, searching for anyone. Then the door slammed shut. To the amazement of the federal officers, I began to chuckle. I once again recalled Regulation 8.12 "Do not make any statements concerning the probable cause of an accident."

"Montoya, por favor, Señor Eduardo Valenciana. Oh, excuse me," he said sarcastically, "We must speak in Inglés as Senor Valenciana does not speak Spanish." I was in real trouble.

I am going to be sick.

The Hispanic code of conduct demands that a true man's suffering be done in silence. The good sisters of Carmel always would remind me that I must be willing to bear my cross in moments of personal suffering. *The hell with that* I thought. But any attempt to struggle against my captors would prove futile as my broken body was no match for this gorilla who was about to toy with me. My black box shook once more as Montoya took a position behind me. Looking up, I saw the sadistic comandante nod his head. The first crushing blow was administered to the back of my head utilizing two Distrito Federal telephone books as the tool of persuasion.

"Sign the paper and we will stop."

…

Concerned that I had not yet been located, Gate Agent Hugo García entered the chaos at the office of the Minister of Transportation, located on the grounds of the airport. The media's miles of cables, lighting fixtures and cameras slowed his progress as an exhausted Señor García sought to accomplish what the airline's officials could not.

"Don Diego por favor," he addressed a harried secretary in an office where all hell seemed to have broken loose. "Tell him it is Señor García." Hugo knew something was very wrong. The woman returned and escorted him into an interior office. He made inquiries with the local police concerning my disappearance but felt he was being stonewalled. Now he would go over their heads to find his Norte Americano friend.

A sunrise at the high altitude of Mexico City can be beautiful on a clear day, which is not very often in the smog-choked metropolis. The landing approach into the airport is even more breathtaking as it takes you right over the center of the bustling city.

As a company DC-10 made its final approach towards Runway 23-Right, the cabin was full, shrouded in depressing silence. This was a special flight, for among its passengers were families of the dead. Some of the distraught wept openly, others just stared blankly.

Señora Torres was on board with her eldest daughter Theresa, now her only daughter. As the jumbo jet's wheels touched down, the religious woman held tightly to hope. Perhaps the company had been mistaken when she received that fateful call in the early morning hours. What little optimism remained was certainly snuffed out however as the plane taxied toward the gate. All heads strained to catch a glimpse of the blackened remnants of Flight 2605, outside, scattered upon the tarmac. Señora Torres turned away: she had to and began to cry softly.

There were other passengers with a vested interest in the catastrophe. They too strained their necks against the confines of expensive shirts and ties for time was of great importance to them. One gentleman in particular, Mr. Gerry Downey, projected a cocky self-confidence. His jewelry and tailor-made suit were expressions of success in his chosen profession, a lawyer specializing in liabilities. Gathering his belongings and stepping out into the jet-way his intentions were clear. He had made news in the past representing various interests and had been very well rewarded for his time and expertise. One may wonder what went through such a man's head as the first news reports of the crash were aired on the morning programs. Tragedy or opportunity?

Once clearing customs in the Mexican capital, he hailed a taxi. Downey had grown up on his father's ranch in Texas, worked closely with the migrant hands and spoke Spanish fluently, a tool that would prove to be very useful. Well prepared, he had acquired the names of the few who had survived, and it was just a matter of finding them. His clever tongue would handle the rest as he would dazzle them with promises of justice and, of course, grand fortunes.

There were other lawyers exiting the plane that morning, but their intent was of a different sort. Not as finely dressed they were company representatives or more correctly, representatives of the insurer of the destroyed DC-10. Ahead for them was the slow process of gathering information for what was sure to be a series of lengthy and expensive lawsuits. The lead attorney in this task was Andrew Jawkins, a tall humorous sort, rather young for a position of importance as an investigative lawyer. He had specialized in airline accidents and had helped handle the messy process of a similar tragedy in Chicago some months earlier. On this trip, his briefcase was much heavier than usual. Along with the necessary legal material needed, Jawkins carried a tremendous amount of United States currency. Cold cash. His entourage, too, had a prime interest in finding the survivors and families of the deceased victims as soon as possible. Jawkins' goal was opposite of Downey's. Andrew and his team had "quick settlement" on their minds and the immediate offer of cash would be the bait used to hook the grieving families.

It was assumed that the majority of the dead were Mexican nationals, and Jawkins was counting on that. Poor families could ill-afford the time and effort, not to mention financing legal representation, to hold out for the big money. Another dilemma was that Mexican law places a ceiling of $70,000 in payment for the life of a victim. Although Jawkins was not specifically aware of the presence of Downey in the Mexican capital that morning, he was sure that someone was already in motion trying to secure the American families as clients. In the suit-happy United States, laws capping the amount of a settlement did not exist. This was unfortunate for many a Mexican family, and the money-waving tactics of Jawkins and his team would prove far too tempting to pass up. It was rumored that some families settled for as little as $6,000 cash for their loved one that first day in November, All Saints Day. There were few of the righteous to be found conducting such business on one of Holy Mother Church's most revered days.

According to a pact called the Warsaw Convention, nations of the world agreed that if such an accident were to occur on their soil, such as Flight 2605 in Mexico, the appropriate agencies would be invited to participate in the investigation. And so, also deplaning that first morning of November were experts from McDonnell-Douglas Aircraft Company, the maker of NW903, The U.S. National Transportation Safety Board (NTSB), The American Air Lines Pilot Association (ALPA), investigation experts representing the airline itself; and, as a show of proper courtesy, representatives of the Airline Flight Attendant Association (AFA). Highly motivated and with completely good intentions, the various American groups of experts set about to face their task: seeking the truth and formulating a logical conclusion for the cause of this disaster. What was on no one's mind was that a clause in the Warsaw agreement stated that the *host country* would conduct the official investigation and determine the official cause of the accident.

…

Last to deplane at Benito Juárez that morning was Mrs. Torres and her daughter. Neither lawsuit's millions nor aviation data was on this mother's mind. All the money in the world could not eliminate the horrible pain she felt. Originally from El Salvador, the good woman left her native country before the turmoil of violence fully erupted. She sought a better life and opportunities for her ten children, eight boys and two girls. Limited by a lack of formal education, she still possessed the strength a mother gains through the uncompromising love for her children.

Señora Torres hurried to the customs agent with the hope of having no delays. She sought to claim the remains of her youngest daughter Reina as quickly as possible. The customs officer, upon seeing her Salvadoran passport, requested that she and her daughter step aside. Señora Torres and Theresa were about to be detained in customs for the next four hours. Looking around for the company representative they thought would be waiting at the airport, they saw no one. They felt abandoned.

Theresa Torres was a strong-willed woman. She repeated the reason for their arrival at the Mexican capital, first to one officer then another. They had not come to live in the city. They were not political refugees seeking asylum from the death squads in San Salvador. No matter how many times it was explained, the true purpose of their trip seemed to be swept aside. Señora Torres quietly wept. She simply wanted to be reunited with Reina, her lost daughter.

The airline soon became increasingly aware of the shocking limits that were being imposed on them by the host government. Mexico was calling all the shots, utilizing circuitous political clout. If an investigator wanted to see something particularly relevant, he must first check with the Mexican official in charge of that department of investigation, assuming he could determine who that official was and where he could be located. If a smart Norte Americano happened to make it that far in the chain of command, then he would have to wait for hours for what amounted to worthless answers and limitless excuses.

Concurrently, investigators for the airline focused their attention on the control tower operator who had been on duty the previous morning. Certainly, his part in this affair needed clarification but he was nowhere to be found. No American investigator would ever be allowed to speak with that gentleman.

The Mexican Government reassured all interested parties that the controller's official deposition, given only to Mexican officials, revealed nothing that would determine the final outcome. To the Mexicans it was a clear case of "error de piloto." Simply put, it really would serve no purpose to allow this individual to be scrutinized by foreign agents. It was a cruel joke that was substituted for the truth that first day of November.

At the airport, traffic was at a standstill because of the restrictions placed on the facility due to the crash. Time was of no concern to the customs officials who were evaluating the Torres' visa status. Finally released that afternoon, Señora Torres and Theresa could not imagine that their ordeal was just beginning. The ride from the terminal building to the old hangar that doubled as a makeshift morgue, was a short one. A fragile-looking Mexican man greeted the ladies and politely inquired the purpose of their visit. An awful odor hung heavily in the large hangar, and the curator explained that the corpses had been doused with lime for preservation. He also tried to warn them of the condition of the bodies, for it would not be a pretty sight. Upon entering, what greeted the women was an introduction to their worst nightmare. All remains and parts of remains were laid side by side on the bare concrete, stripped of all clothing. Because of a lack of refrigeration facilities, this house of horrors was created instead. Señora Torres' hope faltered once more as the unthinkable entered her mind: what if she was not able to recognize Reina?

As mother and daughter began the gruesome process of studying individual bodies and parts, they indeed found it difficult to distinguish much. Suddenly Theresa glanced down a row of remains.

"There she is!" The sister cried. There was no way that the older sibling could not recognize her younger sister's legs. The two women immediately raced across the concrete floor, side-stepping and jumping over charred cadavers. The young angelic beauty of Reina's face was at peace. Weeping, the women were at least thankful that Reina's wounds seemed minimal in comparison to the majority of remains. A grieving mother knelt beside her child, her broken heart trying to gather the strength to give thanks to God, for she had her child one last time. In that instant all the lights in the facility went dark. Very much aware of their surroundings, enveloped in darkness in the house of Muerto the ladies retained their composure and held on to a small sense of peace, because they were with Reina. It would take some time before the power was restored, a normal occurrence to the local citizens of that city.

Señora Torres's grief could not be relieved by anything the Mexican Government or the airline could say or do. At that moment she was preoccupied with getting her daughter's remains home. There would be papers to fill out, customs agents to see once more, much to do. The first task would be to recover Reina's belongings. Why had all the clothing been removed, the ladies wondered.

"For sanitation purposes," was the response. The woman asked, "Where can Reina's personal effects be found?" The mother and daughter assumed that they had been placed in a secure place.

"Of course, come this way" The mother and older sister of Reina Patricia Torres followed the little man outside where several large vans had been parked. The curator opened a vehicle's rear door, revealing large plastic garbage bags filled with the scorched, blood-soaked personal items of all the victims. "Your daughter's belonging are in these bags," the little man gently stated.

"Which one?" Señora Torres naively asked.

"Yo no sé," he responded as he shrugged. To add insult to total anguish, La Señora and her daughter were forced to scavenge through all the bags to try to locate and sort what might or might not have belonged to their lost child. Later that painful day, this good woman was again suffered another affliction when the little curator advised them that there were absolutely no valued items such as jewelry, purses or watches recovered from any of the remains. Finally, as the mother could no longer contain the revulsion, she felt deep inside, she fell ill on the spot and began to vomit.

Meanwhile, I lay exhausted in a tightly protective fetal position upon the cold floor of my cubicle. Awaking, I recognized a figure hunched over me. It was Muerto humming a jingle from a morbid Spanish ballad.

"Do you want to go along with me?" He asked chuckling, revealing the large gaps between his rotting teeth. "We belong dead." I screamed and rolled away across the floor. As I turned to view the figure once more, it was no longer present. I wiped my eyes and awoke, leaving one nightmare and having to live in another – the nightmare of reality. The spasms in my battered legs became more frequent as my mind seemed to float in and out of consciousness. While aware of my surroundings I didn't know what time it was. Then I would fall into a light sleep only to be suddenly awakened by the twisting pain in my body. It would paralyze me, then it would be over as suddenly as it began. The blessed sleep would again gain control.

"Eduardo, wake up. Valenciana, please wake up"

Although very groggy I felt the strong hands on my scorched shoulders as I was being shaken.

"Please, please I'll sign whatever you want," I blurted out in a panic as I prayed to be left alone, I was at the end of resistance.

"Eduardo, por amor de Dios, what has happened? It's me Señor García. Hugo García." I quickly forced the confusion from my head and stared into the same pair of tranquil eyes I recalled prior to the rear doors of the ambulance closing at the airport.

"Hugo? Oh my God, get me out here," I croaked. I reached with my sore hands and fingers to touch the compassionate face of my Mexican friend.

"What is going on here, mi amigo?" Hugo glanced about and was shocked to find his flight attendant friend in such a condition. I embraced my companion as I broke down and sobbed heavily, tears rolling down my face.

"How did you get here, how did you find me? I asked.

"We've been searching the entire city looking for you. My nephew Manuel Díaz is an orderly here at El Centro. He called me to tell me where they were holding you. He told me I had better hurry because you were in a bad way."

That final glance of the tall, thin orderly flashed before my eyes.

"They wanted me to say I served liquor to the pilots." I struggled to get the words out as the grief continued to engulf me. "They wouldn't listen to me."

Where just days prior I had exhibited a body that was strong and impressive, now I had been reduced to a shadow of my former self. I begged Hugo.

"I want to go home to my mother."

"Who did this to you, Eduardo?" The gate agent wanted names.

"I don't know. He took me from the emergency room, some comandante someone."

"Comandante Primitivo Luis Chávez de León, a very sadistic fellow," a voice behind Hugo stated. I finally noticed a young aristocratic looking man dressed in a gray double-breasted suit, hair slicked back, a face calm and confident.

"Eduardo, this is Señor Don Raphael Diego Suárez de la Vega, Deputy to the Minister of Transportation. He's here to help us, to help you." Hugo tried to raise my spirits.

"Let us get out of here, we don't have much time." Suárez de la Vega seemed to take control as Hugo shouldered me, taking care as my muscles began to spasm and my body stiffened. My feet left the ground and they hurried me out of the cubicle. The pace quickened through the hallways as we neared the rear exit leading out into the sunlight.

"¡Alto! Stop this moment!" The comandante's powerful decree echoed off the walls as bystanders stopped in mid-stride. As we escapees turned, we faced a formidable force in Primitivo Chávez, Cardosa and the massive Montoya.

"Comandante." The young aristocrat stepped forward to my adversary.

"Ahhh, Señor Suárez de la Vega." Chávez seemed surprised to find the young official on the scene and sarcastically bowed. The jackal continued, "Where are you going with my prisoner? I am not yet finished with the questioning of this man. He has vital information concerning the cause..."

Diego swiftly cut the proud federal officer at the knees, interrupting with authority. "This man is not anyone's prisoner. Senor Valenciana is a guest of His Excellency, the Minister." Don Diego reached into his coat pocket to reveal the official credentials that would keep the predators at bay. I took great delight in witnessing the comandante's glower as he snatched the papers from Diego's hand and carefully reviewed them. I made sure not to react too strongly as I was still in fear for my safety. Chávez's anger released itself in a torrid of curses in Spanish. Diego simply ignored it and continued in English.

"Unless you want to find yourself directing traffic at the Plaza de Toros, Comandante, I suggest you leave us be."

Furious, Chávez crushed the credentials in his hand, threw them to the ground and turned to address his henchmen.

"¡Vámonos!" They then departed.

Diego calmly turned to face Hugo and me, both of us in utter disbelief.

"Except for his taste in tequila, el comandante is a real scorpion. Hurry, let us get Eduardo to a hotel before 'el perro' returns."

Although relieved, I somehow suspected the ominous Comandante Chávez would not give up so easily. As my saviors ushered me through the building's swinging doors, I inhaled deeply and began to laugh and cry at the same time, I was finally out of there.

Once settled into the dark sedan that quickly took us away, I couldn't help feeling some relief. I tried to convince myself that there was now nothing more to worry about, that I would soon be in the hands of my American employer. I was reassured by the fact that I now sat safely in the car, next to another company man and a friendly government official of influence.

I was now in totally in the opposite position than I had been under the control of the comandante and his goons. There, I was the source of information; no one else knew anything. Although it carried a heavy price, it simultaneously presented me with a power over my captors. In the car, I sat without information; I needed to rely on those that sat with me. What had happened to the others? I knew about Skip and somehow was sure about the death of Reina but what about Gary, Cary, Tamlyn and the rest?

Diego Suárez de la Vega sped along on the main boulevard. In a daze I looked at the people in the cars, the people on the sidewalks. They seemed not know what had gone on. The world had stopped for me, yet everyone else went about their everyday business as if nothing had happened. I saw a tortilla line on the street outside a "panaderia," a bakery.

"Shouldn't they stop what they are doing?" I mumbled. It happened in this city. I placed my blistered hands on my face. One thing was sure. Unlike their lives, mine would be changed forever.

In my exhaustion, I began thinking back to my childhood. Sister Mary Corona had made it very clear long ago:

"Those people who are good but still have a little speck of sin upon their immortal souls must first go to Purgatory to be cleansed "snowy white" before they can enter into eternal happiness that is heaven." It was All Saints Day, November 1st. Tomorrow would be All Souls Day, the time when the living could pray for their deceased loved ones to be released from the torments of Purgatory. The children at Our lady of the Rosary of Talpa Elementary School were taught not to question the ideology but I had long ago dismissed the concept. I was sure that somewhere in El Distrito Federal could be found those who would swear by the significance of the accident happening on Halloween. I began to fantasize how the faithful would debate whether God was being merciful in His actions, being that the crew and passengers of 2605 would only have to spend a day or so in Purgatory before the righteous on earth would passionately pray for their release. The only righteous my bitterness would allow me to acknowledge on that All Saint's Day were the Sisters of Carmel, and they were so far away. I drifted into sarcasm and began to laugh uncontrollably, much to the concern of Hugo and Don Diego. The whole religious argument became too much of a joke for me to bear; I simply wanted to be with my departed crew members.

Hugo was staring at me intently and I could imagine his thoughts. What had Chávez and his goons done to this poor little flight attendant? The deeper I looked into his eyes the more I was convinced here was a man who cared deeply for me who had suffered so much. It was precisely that authentic quality that had been so hard to find in anyone since the crash. It would prove to be even more difficult to find in the days to come.

Totally exhausted, I finally allowed myself to relax my guard. We drove by many monuments of the Mexican capital. There were children playing in the streets. One kicked a soccer ball with one knee, then the next, then again. These were real people, alright, and after traveling for some time Hugo spoke up.

"Eduardo, we are going to take you to the Holiday Inn Hotel across from the airport. There are a lot of reporters and cameras around, so we are going to sneak you in through the employee's entrance." I was indeed grateful that my new-found friends were taking care of me while Hugo continued to stare, wondering whether his instructions got through to me. When the vehicle jerked to a stop at the rear of the hotel, I was ready to slowly slip out of the back seat.

"¡Raphael Diego Suárez de la Vega a su ordenes!" Speaking directly to me for the first time, the young aristocrat made a proper introduction as he opened the door for me, extending his hand in friendship. Startled, I hesitated, then grasped my savior's hand with mine, scorched and wrapped. I know that Diego felt my gratitude as Hugo gently put his arm around my hunched body, moving me at a snail's pace.

"No one else in the crew made it except Señor Mitchell," Hugo whispered into my ear. The statement did not faze me; in my heart I already knew. I could only hope they did not suffer.

"They left me behind alive," I murmured. I suddenly stopped and turned to face Hugo. "Did they have to go to Purgatory?"

"What?"

"Did my crew have to go to Purgatory?" I repeated the question but did not really expect an answer. Of course, Hugo had no answer.

As prearranged, I had already been signed into the hotel under a fictitious name. Hugo informed me that only the top officials of the Mexican Government knew I was housed in the hotel, practically right across the street from the wreckage. Without speaking we made our way past the kitchen staff, through dark hallways and finally my room.

I was in the dark once again, the shades drawn, Hugo at my side. When my eyes adjusted, I found myself opposite the mirrored closet doors. Confused, I gazed at the ghastly figure that stood across from me. For the first time the horror of the entire event slammed right into my consciousness, completely overwhelming me as my muscles began to spasm with great pain. The facial lacerations and dried blood were now crusted scabs. The raw blisters attested to the enormous heat, and the remnants of what had been my uniform of distinction were but scorched rags which clung to my body. Grief stricken; I got a good look. I felt every bit the castoff that confronted me in the mirror. What was not reflected were the mental scars I knew would never heal. I began to cry hysterically and collapsed onto the bed.

Part II
Burning My Wings

Chapter VIII

Hugo rushed to my aid, comforting me as we sat on the edge of the large bed.

"I think you could use a hot bath and a nice hot meal, mi amigo," he gently suggested. Diego entered the room and stared, speechless.

Nothing in life could ever have prepared any one of us for such an event, one still in its infancy. There would be many more people to see, a multitude of questions to be answered. Hugo was wise enough to know that I had to reserve any strength that was left for what was yet to come. He began to draw a hot bath for me.

"Eduardo, you must eat. You'll feel better after a good meal."

I tried to grab the lifeline he generously offered, yet all I could do was shiver uncontrollably. But the tall, dark-skinned native also extended his strength. The events had not overwhelmed him. "Comida?" he asked in a teasing manner. My dear friend could still joke, be down to earth.

"Yes, food indeed." I smiled and tried to focus.

"Eduardo, is there anything special I could get for you?" Diego joined in.

"Cerveza?" Hugo suggested, with wide eyes and a grin.

"Can I?" Flight attendants never drink on duty. Looking at my tattered clothes and body I reached for a bit of dark humor. "I mean, technically I am still in uniform, right? I could be terminated." There was a long pause as Hugo and Don Diego shared a look. "Bohemia," I spoke loudly.

I again began to drift. "I mean, yes I survived a crash but am I still legally on duty?" Hugo spoke up, grinning.

"Mi amigo, after what you have experienced, I believe legalities can be suspended."

The first gift I received in my new life was the aid and guidance of this man. I started feeling giddy and spoke the way a child does when he believes he has gotten away with some act of mischief.

"Yeah, Bohemia." I glanced over at Hugo seeking his approval. Diego rose and stood at attention, gave a salute and was out the door. Time passed as I sat and reflected. As opposed to the vultures, the federal police and reporters who were still outside ready to pounce, neither Hugo nor Diego ever asked me a single question about the incident. "What went on Eddy?" "What Happened?" "Did you see them burning?" "Whose fault was it?" I had the greatest respect for their integrity and character.

My thoughts were interrupted by a knock at the door. Hugo cautiously opened it a crack. He unfastened the latch in excitement.

"Mi amigo, we will have to postpone the bath. The beer has arrived."

My eyes widened in surprise. I saw a large refrigerator quickly being wheeled into my room. I struggled to focus on the two hotel workers who had huge grins. The thought pleased me that reporters and officials were desperately looking for me, yet the maids and cooks apparently knew exactly who occupied that room, my hiding place. With the refrigerator placed and running, the two workers reached out to touch me. At first it seemed odd. Was I some holy apparition to them? Taking a second to look deep into their eyes, the lamps of their souls, they sought nothing for themselves. Mexico's common citizens were expressing their happiness at my escape from Death's grasp. I realized that the people who were considered the least in society were the ones who were the most understanding.

Señor Diego Suárez de la Vega re-entered the room and immediately tried to comfort me once more. He came to my bed and bent down to whisper in my ear.

"Mexican hospitality has not been very good so far, eh mi amigo? Let me see if I can make it up to you!" With the grace of a ballet dancer, Diego gently open the door of the recently delivered refrigerator. The light inside caused me to blink repeatedly, but once I was able to focus, I spotted shelves of Bohemia Mexican Quality Beer. I sat on the bed paralyzed, seduced by the cold, wet brown bottles dressed with the noble warrior on the label. Another knock on the door announced the arrival of the cuisine as Hugo did the honors, declaring "¡Una fiesta!"

"For you, happy birthday." Diego handed me a cold bottle of suds.

"We all get one life, you get two." We raised our beers high. "Salud." I gently kissed the mouth of the bottle and the cool liquid relieved my parched throat. Somehow the small act of drinking a cold one seemed new, as if I was doing it for the first time.

"A new life indeed." I began to laugh, to live once more. The first bottle was empty in a few seconds as Hugo wheeled over the dinner plates. "Taquitos!" The combination was too good to be true, then my thoughts fell back to my family home: my father's special salsa on the table; my friend Tommy always arriving with plenty of beer needed for such a delightful meal. These were good thoughts.

"¡Compadres!" After the fourth beer I was joyful and giddy. I pictured my family rejoicing when given word of my survival. "My mother!" I exclaimed. "I have to call my mother!"

"Said like a true Latino," Don Diego exclaimed. Grabbing the phone, I realized I had forgotten the dialing process. Diego took charge, assuring me that he would secure the long-distance call. I was relieved that my family was spared the terrible news that so many others had suffered that day, *one* thing I sincerely thanked God for. The pain and anger restricted any desire to seek further divine intervention.

"Why should you, Eddy? God was obviously absent for Reina or Javier." New-found voices in my head made their point.

"Eduardo, I have the connection to your family." Diego stated with excitement.

"Eddy, are you okay mijo?" The perfect comforter, a mother's expression of concern. It was good to hear her voice and to personally assure the family that I would be returning to Los Angeles very soon. I was really not sure of that, but it was the right thing to say. The rest of the conversation was assuring them that I was physically fine despite the awful pictures being displayed on the news. I thought to lighten the language.

"I'm sitting here at the hotel eating taquitos and everything is being taken care of."

"Aye Eddy, you will never change." My mother now laughed comfortably, filled with faith, believing that her previous night's prayers had been answered. She could never understand just how much the wounds of this catastrophe were changing me. An airline representative had already called my parents and expressed to my mother that she could fly down to Mexico City to be with me if she so desired. My brother Mike, the detective with LAPD, also received the same invitation. But the thought of Comandante Chavez still lingering somewhere there in the shadows sent a chill up my spine. The last thing I wanted was my family to be subjected to his bullying. I was still emotionally shaken, leery of the buzzards that circled, and I wanted my loved ones kept far away from this crazy circus. Mike got on the phone and insisted he fly down, displaying an older sibling's protection of his little brother.

"Are you sure you don't need us?" I laughed and tried to assure them that all was being taken care of and I'd return home soon. Once again, I would be proved wrong.

The call ended. I was filled with gratitude, realizing how fortunate I was to have such a loving family. For the first time I began to reflect on the families of my deceased comrades, the devastation that was eating at their very souls. I felt shame for surviving, for the blind fortune that allowed me to find a passage out of the fiery wreck. I didn't know how to face this second chance I had been granted while so many others had been denied it. There was too much pain, too much sorrow associated with living. Too great a price to be paid.

"You need to bathe, get the grime off you." It was Hugo, seeing to what needed to be done. I struggled to cast off my ragged uniform. With Hugo's help, we carefully tried not to open the sores where fabric melted into my blistered skin, mostly on my upper back and shoulders. My desire was to cleanse myself of everything: the soot, jet fuel, the sweat. But the filth in my soul took precedence. I wanted to relieve the anguish but once again I began to sob. Meanwhile Hugo took to hanging up what was left of my uniform and taking note of the sizes. My dear Mexican friend realized that I was going to need new clothes and he would be the one to see to it.

Finally, Hugo gently assisted me into bed as I had developed a fever. I tried to ignore it, but the chills increased as I wrapped myself tightly inside the blankets. The shaking and sweat overcame me. All at once, the reassuring voice I heard at the moment of impact returned.

"It's going to be okay." I was suddenly in a deep sleep.

I dreamed a lovely lady covered in a finely colored Spanish wrap hurried towards me, joyful that I had being given a second chance at life.

"Whatever you did in your past life does not matter." she explained. "Only what is in front of you is important." Many children passed by playing and laughing. Suddenly noticing me, they began to wave in earnest, directing the smaller kids to my presence. They seemed to be indicating that I was the privileged one who had crawled out of the fire. Momentarily I too felt like a child who had received this precious gift of life. But then I turned to find a tall, menacing figure standing behind me, hunched with a ragged long coat and a brown fedora shielding his face. The sinister being slowly raised his head to reveal a glistening, shining ashen skull face.

"Dead is good…life is bad." The grotesque fiend began to giggle. Fear gripped me tightly as I tried to back away. Death's laughter grew raspy, making me feel once again the pain of abuse, desperation and hopelessness. I realized I was once again clothed in the tattered remains of my flight attendant uniform. I wanted to run away but my injured legs would not respond. Still, I struggled to get away. "¡Espérate! Wait! Stay!" He commanded me. "We belong dead." His words echoed as I awoke in gripping fear.

I took a while to settle myself. I wanted only to remember pleasantries, recalling for some reason Cary Diller's vibrancy and humor.

"What are you doing up here, Mexican?" Her brash sarcasm brought a smile to my face. Then there was the baby of the flight, Karen Smitt, begging to switch workstations with me before we departed. Her fate should have been mine. Guilt and shame again overwhelmed me.

It hurt to breathe. I wondered what was happening outside, slowly edging out of bed and turning on the TV. The crash site was devastating. Suddenly there was a soft knock on the door.

My initial reaction was to panic, believing it might be the sinister comandante. But then I realized that Primitivo Chávez would have been more inclined to break down the door. I was still reluctant to respond and wished Hugo would return. Finally, I climbed out of bed again and slowly approached the door. Peeking through a crack, I focused on a blond American lady in business attire. She looked familiar. It was Daisy Ackley, Senior Manager of Inflight Services.

"Eduardo?"

"Yeah?"

"Oh Eduardo." She slowly pushed the door open as I backed away, wrapped in a white towel.

"Oh dear." She embraced me. "You okay? Is there anything you need?" I was one of her children, one of her flight attendants of our airline. "It's terrible. Are you sure you are feeling okay?" My muscles began to spasm and Daisy saw me grimace. I tried to change the focus.

"I'm glad you're here. Now, can you get me back home?"

"There's a lot to do but I will work hard to get you home as soon as possible." She did care, her eyes said it. I did not envy her role in this madness. There were devastated families and she would be called upon to face them in the airline's name. In my ordeal I thought about how the associates of the company were dealing with the incident as it unfolded. To airline workers throughout the world, a major crash is their biggest nightmare. It would also prove to be what brings them together, what unites.

I don't know why but it surprised me to see the impact of the accident on Daisy's face. She was extremely emotional. I found myself wondering how many of the dead, her other "children," she had personally known. Then her attitude changed. Her back stiffened and she assumed a more business-like posture. She barely had time to prepare me when through the door came men in business suits. The company coming to the rescue. The circus arrived, all three rings: the management types, the lawyer species, and the corporate entities.

Shocked, I quickly hobbled back into bed and pulled the covers over me like a frightened child, hoping they would all just go away. I was firmly loyal to the company, but in these people with their very official looking suits and all, I saw the same thing. The final judgment must come out and it began then and there in my hotel room. Preparations must be made for that day when the multimillion-dollar lawsuits would crop up, for the advertising image, for all the corporate realities by which they would ultimately be assessed. I felt as if the incident was being dehumanized. I could see a time when there would no longer exist a single human issue. It would be government versus airline versus government versus petty official versus pilot versus government, and on and on.

I was holding an audience, but in control of no one. *I was* being controlled, I reflected on the reporters; this was no different. I was still a pawn, but this pawn had a choice, not white or black, but a selection of grays. It was time for me to pick the best chance for survival as "right or wrong" lost its applicability. Only I mattered.

The lawyers, supervisors, management people and investigative pilots were quickly introduced. Both panicked and frustrated, I countered by dealing with them head on, looking straight into their eyes. Just then, Hugo arrived carrying with what I thought to be my new wardrobe. He was taken aback at the proceedings. He hung the clothes in the closet then bulldozed his way through to me. He could see I was overwhelmed so he grabbed a cold Bohemia from the stocked fridge and offered it to me. Certainly, there would be no objection to the "hero," as the Mexican newspapers were now referring to me, quenching his thirst.

"We need to leave Eduardo to rest." He was emphatic. Daisy picked up on my uneasiness and to my surprise the others left.

"My room is right next to you," she said. "If there is anything you need, I'll be there." I was unsure about my senior manager, but I needed all the friends I could get.

"Thanks Daisy. I appreciate your support." Hugo closed the door and I was relieved to be alone with my friend.

"There is much more of this to come." Hugo wanted me to be ready.

"That may be so, but for now grab me another beer." The company agent smiled. With two beers down there was another knock on the door. Since I was in the control of, and therefore in the protection of the company, I wasn't worried. It turned out to be my AFA union representative. She was very reassuring.

"Eduardo, the union is here to take care of you. You do not have to talk to anyone, especially from management. We are here to guard you." A curly-haired young lady who introduced herself as Reva Grayson stepped forward to take charge. I was incredulous. Just where in the hell had all these people been yesterday when I was getting my senses pounded by the vile comandante? I pulled the covers up once again.

"You don't have to tell them one thing. You have rights."

Before today I had minimal contact with either union or management, and now I'm hidden away in a hotel room with both. Who do I listen to? I quickly downed another Bohemia.

Despite the concern they were trying to show for my well-being, their real mission seemed to be the establishment of "proper procedures."

"Time out," I shouted, making the "T" sign with my blistered hands. The room fell silent.

"I don't want to play this game." Not the government's game, the company's game, the union's game and so on.

I lifted my battered body from the bed with the assistance of Hugo. Clad only in a bath towel, I was diplomatic in assuring Reva that all was well, and I led her to the door. Senor Garcia immediately locked it for good measure. We began to laugh and decided the appropriate thing to do was continue drinking.

My mind was in a whirl. I knew that Hugo saw clearly through the "bullshit." We sat in silence enjoying our Bohemia. Without a word about union options and despite the fact that he was a company man, he knew I needed some quiet time to just think and he silently left.

The phone rang. It was Skip's parents. It turned out that he was safe at the British-American Hospital in the city. The damage to his leg was significant but he was in one piece. His parents had arrived in Mexico City and were extremely grateful for their son's survival.

"We want to thank you for saving him." I was confused.

"What?"

"We know what you did." A female voice spoke from the background. "Yes, thank you." My God, people were believing all that crap in the newspapers.

"Skip saved himself, I was just lucky to find him." I wanted to set the record straight. They owed me nothing. My attitude is and always will be that praise is deserved for conscious acts, not instinctual reactions. They were under the mistaken impression that I had sustained a broken leg. They continued to express the heartfelt gratitude until they hung up.

Hugo was now apparently out of the picture. The lifeline that had been so important to me was no longer there and the company was in full charge. I would learn that the management's hotel rooms surrounded mine. The wagons seemed to be circled in anticipation. The media was sure to discover us.

I was in Daisy's charge now. The Senior Manager of Inflight Services had been a flight attendant herself before successfully breaking into male-dominated management. My superior was a strong supporter of Mario Reddick and as his star rose, so did Daisy's. A blond, blue-eyed stern woman, she became known as "mother hen" to her flock of flight attendants at LAX. She took the deaths of the junior crew of 2605 extremely hard and had hurried to Mexico City to do what needed to be done. Later it would be revealed that Daisy Ackley made most of the initial identifications of the dead crew.

Opening my door just a crack, I glanced warily at the company reps coming and going. The airline's emergency plan was in full swing and the majority of personnel would survive on two hours of sleep per day for the next week or so. The wear and tear were evident on their faces. Maybe I should have felt guilty because I was allowed to stay in my room and rest.

I had done nothing wrong, yet I became afraid to stroll into the hallway for fear of being recognized. The phone rang now and then as "mother hen" kept tabs on her flock. On one such occasion Daisy informed me that a meeting was going to be conducted in about half an hour in her room and I was invited to attend. Although not indicating that my presence was mandatory, her tone made it clear that it was preferable.

To kill some time, I turned on the TV. I was shocked to learn for the first time that our jumbo jet had collided with an object while landing. The reporter described how a dump truck on runway 23 Left had been hit and virtually destroyed by our aircraft. I thought back to the massive impact I had mistakenly interpreted as a hard touch down. The report went on to say that a construction worker had been in the cab of the truck sleeping, the first casualty of this horrible incident. It was much to take in and I changed the channel.

On the screen now was a very distraught Mexican woman who lived in the neighborhood adjacent to the airport.

"Nos despertamos por un ruido estruendoso." They were awakened by a thunderous sound. "The whole house was on fire and I thought I was going to die," the distraught woman cried in Spanish. Apparently one of the wings of the DC-10 had been hurled through the air for half a mile, landing in her neighborhood. The fuel in the severed wing ignited and created a furious fire. Fortunately, the woman explained, she and her family were able to escape the deadly flames but others were not so lucky.

"Gracias a Dios usted y su familia están a salvo," the reporter said comforting the nervous woman.

"Pero el fuego se llevó mi perro Sultán y mi gato Mugroso." She broke down and began to weep helplessly. Having lost her cat and dog. I felt empathy for her.

Did Sultán and Mugroso have to go to Purgatory? I wondered in sarcasm. Trying not to dwell on the latest news, I hobbled over to the closet to examine the brand-new set of clothing Hugo had delivered. Fresh underwear, the right size, not the brand I regularly used but I was not complaining. A pair of beige dress slacks, again the right size. There were dark socks, a new black leather belt with the gold logo of a popular brand of men's wear. I noticed the same logo on the long-sleeve dress shirt I struggled to put on.

Suddenly there was another knock at the door. Expecting to see Daisy's face, I was surprised when it was Reva, my union rep.

"I suppose there was a lot going on before; maybe we can get a fresh start?" I was happy she arrived for there was no way I was going to be able to get the new pair of socks on my feet without help. She graciously re-introduced herself. Reva Grayson was a fellow flight attendant based in San Francisco, who smiled as I stood in front of her sporting my new underwear and unbuttoned shirt.

"I need help with my socks." Reva chuckled, assuring me that she was there in the Mexican capital to do exactly that, to help me with whatever I might need. I gained a new friend that day.

She calmly reminded me that I did not have to speak with management if I did not wish. For one of the few times in this mess I leveled with Reva. I explained that I realized I was now trapped on a runaway roller coaster, events beyond my control, initiated when my DC-10 fell from the sky. I'm walking a tightrope and stonewalling management would only create another obstacle in this already complicated situation. Reva immediately understood. I gained a deep respect for my union rep as she reminded me that when it became too much to bear, she would be available to run offense for me. As she left the room I did not have the heart to confess that I had never filled out my union application while in training. Was I really a member of the Association of Flight Attendants? Oh well, I figured I would deal with that matter down the road and proceeded to finish dressing.

Hobbling over to the closet again, I noticed a new dark-blue sport coat and tie hanging, both branded with a now familiar menswear logo. Of course! My considerate Mexican gate agent had thought of everything. And resting on the back wall of the closet was a pair of new crutches. As I took the new coat from the hanger, I saw those scorched rags, the remains of my uniform, arranged nicely upon a hanger. My first reaction was to grab and toss them out. But as I studied my old blue flight attendant service apron, I could see how its fabric resisted the fire much more efficiently than the shirt or pants did. It had indeed protected me. Then I focused upon my flight wings still pinned to my apron. Sure, they were tarnished and battered, just like me. I knew that no matter how long my new life lasted I could never part with them. At that instant I decided to keep the tattered uniform also. I supposed that in my journey through this second

185

chance, whenever I got too smart for my own good, I could look at them and be reminded how fragile life can be.

Now fully dressed, my stomach began to tighten as I prepared to join the body of company personnel. Nervous and unsteady, I placed a bottle of Bohemia in a side pocket of my new dress coat. Liquid courage. I made my way over to Daisy's room on crutches, not caring about being cited for drinking on duty.

They greeted me well, but I felt like a terminally ill relative who just arrived. Thinking better of it, I did approach the mother hen to see if it was indeed okay with the group if I continued to quench my thirst with the cold brew. Daisy graciously obliged me. It seemed a bit unusual as I sat there guzzling cold suds in the morning as the others sped about, earnestly attending to serious issues. I just stared like a curious bystander. There was a knock on her door as 3 pilots investigating the incident for the company entered the room. One tall individual graciously approached, requesting to sit beside me and ask a few questions. Unsure, and with the experience of the comandante still fresh, I hesitated. Then I noticed that everyone was staring, so I agreed. I had overheard complaints that the investigators had been up half the night as their hosts were not providing them access to the crash site, or any information at all. I decided to firmly convince them that I, too, was "part of their team."

Captain Louie was a recognizable face, a senior captain with whom I had shared many flights. His was never one to show arrogance as some captains could. He showed me something he would continue to display in the future, compassion for my plight. The honesty reflected in his eyes made me want to help him. The worry and stress on his face was the first indication I had that the conduct of the Mexican Government's investigation was not to the liking of the Air Lines Pilot's Association (ALPA). Everyone was frustrated, especially Captain Louie. He began telling me about the obstacles they had encountered. One Mexican official oversaw each area of the investigation and each made it clear to the Norte Americanos that they were allowed to see only what *that* individual wanted them to see.

The captain placed a tape recorder on the table in front of me and began his questioning. Because of my recent encounters with the press and Comandante Chávez with Primitivo, I intended to keep my answers short and sweet.

"What do you remember, Ed?" I hesitated.

"The fire, the screaming." Captain Louie's face expressed sympathy.

"Did the approach seem regular?"

"Perhaps, but the landing was anything but."

"What do you recall of that moment?"

"We slammed down, went up again and after some time the engines roared again. The aft floor started to split open, there was an explosion and all hell broke loose." The captain nodded, but then I became frightened. My upbringing had instilled in me the understanding that trust had to be earned, and my company was no exception. Yes, I was an associate of the airline, surrounded by their representatives. But who were they really? I had been taught in airline training that in case of an accident, they would protect me, but they hadn't. I was not about to let down my guard now. I was not going to mention my conversation with Reina, my premonitions, or my presence in the cockpit during the flight. Revealing that would have been enough to labeling me and my information questionable at best.

In one census tabulation, East Los Angeles was said to be the most "Hispanic" community in the United States. I was fourth generation of that community. When outsiders, those being of a different ethnic origin, are seen about the neighborhood, they are labeled suspect. In this group here at the Holiday Inn, there were too many non-Hispanics for my liking. As I said, I wasn't about to trust them with any of the information Reina related either before or during the flight. I certainly was not going to say I witnessed Captain Herbert verbally reprimand First Officer Reimann. No indeed. I determined that I should bide my time. It was now evident that I could use my persona as the company's "little hero" to see how much information these airline representatives would trust me with and if they, the company, pledge to protect me.

After an hour or so and the consumption of an additional bottle of Bohemia, the questioning was over. The investigating pilots retreated for some much-needed rest. Daisy and her staff discussed the day's schedule, including who would babysit me in my injured state. The beer had finally gone straight to my head and I resented the idea that they believed I was not able to fend for myself.

"Where the hell were all of you when I was in the hands of that madman Chavez?" I blurted out. The room went silent as Daisy turned and looked at me in shock. My emotions had risen to the surface and I realized that they had no idea who Comandante Primitivo Chavez was. Considering I was still in Mexico and these associates were my best bet at finally getting home, I decided not to rock the boat. Daisy would escort me next door to my room and see that her prize "chick" got some rest.

Once alone in my room, a disturbing realization occurred to me. To get back home to my family in Los Angeles I would have to board a DC-10 again, enduring another take-off and landing at LAX. I thought about the figure of Muerto and whether he also would book another ticket for that flight. Would he grab the soul that slipped away? I tried to settle my concerns with basic logic.

"People don't survive plane crashes to die in another plane crash." I recalled my conversation with Reina assuring her how I did not feel as though I was going to die that Halloween morning.

"Then you won't," her sweet voice rang clear as I relaxed and fell into a deep sleep which my broken body truly needed.

I sat up in fear at another knock on the door.

What if the reporters have discovered who was in the room? I approached the door and leaned upon it.

"Who is there?"

"It is the Assistant to His Excellency, the Minister of Transportation of Mexico."

"Diego!" I opened the door, grabbed his coat and despite my pain dragged him into the room. He was definitely taken by surprise. My face suddenly went solemn as I reached for the lapels on my Mexican friend's coat. "How about getting me the hell out of here on the next flight home?" Diego understood my anxiety.

"I have been working hard on your behalf, my friend." I knew he was speaking the truth as Senor Suárez de la Vega, my blue-blooded *amigo*, calmly walked over to the large refrigerator to help himself to a cold one. Opening the door, he was impressed by the dent I had made in the original supply of Bohemia. Diego took a seat, popped open the bottle and got to the business of my departure.

"Eduardo, you have a meeting with the Minister of Transportation at noon. You must give your declaration before you leave this country." The word "declaration" brought back bad memories of the cunning Lupe Ortiz, but after a few seconds of reflection I knew that my Mexican friend was looking out for me.

"I understand the investigation is a mess." I fished for answers.

"Two of your company's investigators got a little too nosy about what they suspected was being hidden from them." Diego's honesty surprised me. He took another swig from the beer bottle.

"My government's reaction to the investigators was swift and firm: expulsion from the country." He was obviously disturbed. "Those pilots have been given eight hours to leave the city, but don't worry my friend. You are "el gato," the man with nine lives and no more harm can come to you."

"What?" I didn't understand.

"That is what the Mexican press has dubbed you."

"Well, that asshole Chavez took a few of those lives." I supposed I would need the cunning of a cat to get through this mess and find a way back home.

"I will return at half-past-eleven to pick you up." Just as quickly as he came, my rescuer was gone.

I began to wonder about the Mexican Government's patience, or the lack of it, concerning those American investigators. It was quite evident that my company had lost control of this investigation. I decided to turn on the TV and tuned in to the English language cable channel. An American affiliate from San Antonio displayed the devastation in full color. Amidst the rubble and the cleanup crews, the reporter announced that Mexico was releasing a portion of the Cockpit Voice Recorder, the all-important CVR for the first time. I sat on the bed frozen with anticipation.

"You are left of the runway," the airport tower controller advised to Captain Herbert.

"Just a bit," was the only response from the now deceased Captain of Flight 2605. Clearly, the Mexican investigators were implying pilot error. Was the truth was going to be snuffed out before it could even breathe a moment of life? I worried about my upcoming meeting with the minister. Certainly, it would be a better experience than the one with the comandante? I had slipped through Muerto's fingers and I just wanted to get on with this new life peacefully. Yet somehow, I already knew that nothing would be farther from the truth.

Chapter IX

I readied myself for Diego's arrival. I grasped the crutches
tightly. The escort that accompanied me to the meeting
consisted of Don Diego and his young Mexican assistant Felipe
and, at my request, Hugo García. Deep inside I felt again like a
pawn, claimed jointly by two conflicting interests. Diego
announced that our entourage would first be going to the
company's operations center. I was initially relieved to see that
outside the hotel there were no reporters about. We hurried to
enter a black vehicle and drove a distance of no more than one
hundred yards across the street to Benito Juárez International
airport. As we pulled alongside the curb, I spotted Daisy
returning from the crash site, the strain showing on her face from
having to endure "morgue duty." Hers was the face of despair.
Pain and despair. She briefly stepped forward alongside the
sedan to acknowledge us, then left. The reporters who remained
in the terminal area did not have a difficult time figuring out that
the young man fumbling with the silver crutches probably had
something to do with the "main attraction" several yards down
the runway. All at once our group was besieged.

"Señor Valenciana, por favor." The inquiries were relentless.
Diego acted immediately, the guards forming a circle around me.
I proceeded mostly with my head down, eyes to the ground.
When I did look up out of curiosity, I could see amazement in
the faces of the people standing and glaring at what they
perceived to be a living miracle. A brown-uniformed Mexican
airline agent entered our circle and offered his assistance.

"Are you Valenciana?" A man shouted. "Señor Valenciana,
por favor, hable con nosotros." I stuck to the charade of not
comprehending Spanish, displaying a look of confusion
whenever the requests were in their native tongue. My anxiety
grew as the crowds increased. I had hoped that the company
officials would make them go away. Fat chance! Their game
plan was old but effective: when in trouble, shut up and move

fast, but the moving was something I was having difficulty with. Spasms continued to plague my body.

Once inside the airport, the screaming figures reappeared. This was the third and final day of El Día de Los Muertos, All Souls Day, the only day the faithful of Holy Mother Church may pray to release a loved one from the scorching fires of Purgatory, allowing them to enter with a pure soul into the everlasting peace of Heaven. There were true believers that day at Benito Juárez, reciting the proper prayers and requested intercession from the proper saints. They hoped to leave the airport certain that their loved one. Deceased for only forty-eight hours, had escaped the ages of suffering, slipping through the pearly gates into Paradise.

Don Diego and Felipe practically carried me the rest of the way to the Operations Center. One portion of the secured room was filled with a couple of company pilots, investigators and representatives of the United States Federal Aviation Administration. I had no idea why we had come to this room prior to my intended meeting with the Mexican Minister of Transportation. Diego seemed to read my mind and gave me a reassuring look as if to say all was okay. Then Jack McKay appeared. The Senior Vice-President of the airline greeted me and grabbed my scorched hand. I tried to hold back a grimace.

"Eduardo, you fortunate young man." I could only stand silent, puzzled, with my mouth wide open. "Come over here boy, there is something I want to show you." I was to discover that Jack McKay was a man of action, ready to immediately share vital facts that had come to light.

McKay invited Diego, Hugo and me over to a large table which held a sizable diagram of Benito Juárez Airport. It was all there: runways 23-Left, 23-Right, block images of the terminal and surrounding structures. Someone with a bit of art talent had sketched the outline of a DC-10 and dotted a flight path starting at the nose of the craft, indicating a hypothetical pattern ending right at two blocked squares, buildings I knew no longer existed. McKay seemed like a boy with a new train set as he gazed at the map.

"Here is where you touched down and hit the truck, then the aircraft clipped a tractor off to the side of runway 23-Left." The executive's eye grew wide has he continued. "That turned your plane about 15 degrees to the right, eventually ending up at the buildings." Jack Mckay had a theory he wanted to share with me. Pointing to the map, he traced the dotted line from the nose of the sketched aircraft at the point of first touchdown on Runway 23-Left, a pathway the Mexican Government was now claiming was closed to traffic that morning. He proceeded with his finger to the point that 2605 clipped the tractor on the side of the runway.

"At this location, I believe the aircraft turned. He then continued on an imaginary route, the one that would have occurred if the DC-10 had missed the tractor on the side of the runway. That imaginary path led right to the main terminal building. The man stood straight up. Without saying another word, we all knew what that conclusion would have been.

"The morning of the 31st there were five 747's all lined up, fueled to the max and ready to depart in the next few hours." Jack McKay had just shown that a much worse disaster had been averted. There was a long silence in the Operations room. A chief pilot interceded.

"We estimate that you were traveling at about 280 miles at the point of impact." McKay began to chuckle, not because any particular thing was funny; it was apparent that he was expressing genuine happiness at my good fortune. The airline chief slapped my sore back.

"You lucky son of a bitch!" The jovial Scotsman took a great liking to me, an act I will always be grateful for.

I found comfort in this man as my attitude changed and I realized the thankless job the executive had been assigned. McKay would certainly need exceptional leadership skills to guide them investigation toward a fair conclusion. Maybe he had the skills of a "poker player," a master in the art of winning whether he had a good hand or not. I supposed the company had selected the right man for this almost impossible task.

Señor Valenzuela, the company's Vice-President in charge of Mexico, joined us in operations. Upon shaking my hand, he also gave me an "abrazo," the customary Hispanic hug.

"How are you feeling Señor Gato? Ah yes, we have heard the reports of your heroics." He exhibited a pleasing grin. My face reddened. I was just vaguely aware of the title the Mexican newspapers had bestowed upon me. Witnesses of the cataclysm testified that a flight attendant, despite the injuries, had made a difference in helping others. The airline's corporate office was pleased as they sought to find something positive in this messy circumstance. Any credit I garnered goes to Barbara and the flight attendant training instructors, for my reactions were mainly a result of the thorough training they had given me.

The pain on my blistered back was intense now but I remained silent, just happy to be in friendly hands. McKay began to compliment me on my physical condition, mentioning that it probably helped me survive the initial impact. My desire for drastic change in my life and imposing that change on my body was now seen not as an obsession or freak hobby, but an action to be admired.

"You took a beating. I read all your hair was burned off." I smiled, recalling the reporter at the hospital.

"Don't believe everything you read in the newspapers."

"That is so true my boy." The V.P. again became almost giddy. The public wondered why I had made it through while so many others perished. Was there divine intervention? To me, it seemed easier to accept my physical conditioning as the reason. If not, then why was God favoring me while abandoning Reina, Javier and the others.

"Everything will be okay." That voice from the moment of impact soothed me. I supposed I was spared for a reason and I knew that discovering why may exact a high price.

Diego finally interceded to remind everyone of my appointment with His Excellency, the Minister. I firmly shook McKay's hand, despite the pain. I would need friends in high places. We all exited through a back door that took us past the many conveyer belts that carried the thousands of bags which would be loaded into the bellies of the day's flights. My inexperience with the newly acquired crutches slowed the procession to a snail's crawl. Airport workers looked on as we passed, breaking into smiles. A young luggage loader stopped his task and reached out and touched me. The motivation for his action I assumed was happiness for me, part faith and part local Indian superstition. I cared not which, for the warmth was evident in their eyes. Suddenly, my heart was in my throat as I spotted a plain-clothes federal officer with an automatic rifle in hand.

"Chávez!" I muttered. The anxiety made me panic-stricken. Diego recognized the problem immediately and took charge to assure me that there would be no repeat of Chávez' bullying. Señor de la Vega told me that the nightmare was over.

As we approached the ministry offices, I began to wonder what specifics regarding the incident I would be required to relate. A quick look over to Don Diego told me that the young aristocrat had it all under control. Entering the lobby, I found myself the center of attention once again as everyone seemed to be bumping into each other. Then the media spotted me struggling with my crutches and rushed my way.

"Valenciana, why did the plane crash? Is it true you served the pilots alcoholic beverages on the flight?" The anger in me swelled.

"Who told you that? Who is spreading that lie? Speak up!" The entire hallway fell silent. Intimidated, the reporters now pressed lightly to get their answers.

"Por qué usted no se murió en el avion?" A tall man inquired.

"I don't know. You'll have to interview God to find out why He saved me." He immediately jumped on the statement.

"I thought you did not speak or understand Spanish? Un pocho?" My protector took control.

"Gentlemen, Eduardo has been through a great ordeal, he is meeting shortly with His Excellency the Minister. Please, let me escort you to the waiting area where Señor Valenciana will have a statement before he boards a flight back to Los Estados Unidos." I felt deeply embarrassed for my outburst as Diego quickly ushered me away into Minister's outer office. I was extremely upset with myself as guilt and shame overcame me once again. Hugo stood by me.

"You sure you're okay? I nodded, then noticed another man sitting nearby, a slight looking Mexican man. Hugo nodded to the stranger, "Well, I'm going to get a newspaper as long as everything is okay here." As on cue, Don Diego picked up the obvious sign to also excuse himself.

"I will see if His Excellency is about ready to receive you mi amigo." Don Diego entered the Minister's main chamber closing the doors behind him. Confused, I found myself abandoned by my entourage and alone with this stranger. He looked around cautiously, spent a second sizing me up, rose, then walked over and took the seat next to me.

"You're Señor Valenciana, are you not? I am Victor Estrada." The man seemed deeply disturbed.

"Are you with the company? I inquired.

"I was one of the controllers in the tower that terrible morning. There are things I wish you to know. It was not that poor man's fault." In my mind I assumed he was speaking about Captain Herbert. I sat in shock. For a long moment, we just stared at each other. The Mexican man's face revealed his torment.

"We need to talk," I said, not really knowing how that could be achieved. He quickly scrawled his name and phone number on a piece of paper and gave it to me, his hand shaking. Without another word he rose quickly and took a seat on the other side of the room.

Hugo Garcia was the first to return carrying a newspaper, followed soon after by Don Diego from the inner office. The stranger now arose and disappeared into the terminal, into the chaos.

"Do you know Señor Estrada?" Diego asked me innocently as I sat overwhelmed by what had just occurred.

"No. Why do you ask?"

"He is a good man. I hope his infant son will be okay." The conversation was left hanging as Hugo interrupted, displaying the Mexican newspaper upon my lap.

"Look at this mess. 'Error de piloto.' How can they say that after only two days?"

"Because there is no honor among snakes," I retorted. Diego checked his watch and gestured for Hugo to assist me into the main chamber of the Minister's office. I grabbed my crutches and hobbled my way through the door into a very elegant stateroom. There, seated behind a massive wooden desk, looking very hospitably, was a light-haired, buxom young lady in a red dress with white trim. She arose to greet us and was introduced by Diego as the Minister's private secretary, Raquel. Graciously, Raquel informed the visitors that His Excellency was awaiting our arrival. I struggled with my crutches once more, my attention focused on the assistant's low-cut dress. I almost paid the price for my indiscretion when I stumbled. Luckily Hugo Garcia was there to catch and steady me.

"I'm calling for a missed approach." I stated in a fluster to no one in particular. Continuing to support me, Hugo whispered into my ear.

"Your heart is racing my young friend"

"Madre de Dios." I prayed for strength. Raquel flashed a radiant smile, pleased to see that I had regained my footing, and continued on as she led us into her superior's private office.

"Ah su Excelencia." Don Diego provided a firm handshake then an abrazo.

"Diego, y sus padres?" The Minister inquired. It was evident from the beginning that Diego Suárez de la Vega was well in his element of upper-crust Mexican society. The cabinet minister was a big man, dark hair nicely groomed with a very respectable mustache that curled to a point on either end. He displayed the lighter skin, the trace of the European bloodline that distinguished most of his social class. His dark blue suit was freshly pressed, and he continually adjusted a pair of dark black-rimmed glasses he wore.

"Mis padres están bien, muy bien." Diego assured the minister that his parents were indeed well. With pleasantries concluded the distinguished cabinet head turned his attention to me as I stood, supported by my crutches.

"¿Y este joven Americano aquí? Por favor Señor Valenciana, siéntase, siéntase como si estuviera en su casa." The warmth in his voice hinted that everything was going to be okay, yet a certain look in the seasoned politician's eyes warned me to stay on guard. His Excellency continued.

"Estoy muy feliz de que usted esté con nosotros aquí en este día." Diego politely interceded as translator, supporting my ruse.

"His Excellency is happy you are still with us today." I was surprised by Don Diego's words and responded in a thick gringo accent.

"Muchas Gracias, Excelencia."

"Please forgive me," the Minister spoke in English. "I now recall that you do not speak our native tongue. Please, make yourself at home Señor Valenciana. Do you find your accommodations satisfactory?"

"Everything is okay now, thanks to Don Diego," I stated but continued on. "Things were not so pleasant before." I tried to restrain my frustration.

"Ah yes, I am aware of your mistreatment. We are extremely sorry for your experience with Comandante Primitivo Chávez. How would you say, he is a very loose cannon? But now things are better, no?" My gracious host nodded in an approving manner indicating that he did not wish me to reflect upon my mistreatment further. I gazed up on the wall of the lush office to view another photo of Presidente José López Portillo, This version was similar to the one I saw in my cubicle of torment as I sat upon my little black milk box. The very official-looking photo reminded me that I was still very far away from home.

"When in Rome...." I muttered to myself. "I realize one person does not represent the actions or feelings of an entire country." I said. I got with the program, saying anything that would get me on a flight back home "I too am a Mexican and am proud of my rich heritage."

"Where is your family from?" I explained how my maternal grandfather Álvaro Francisco Cota, originally from the seaside town of La Paz, Baja California, had been displaced like thousands of others during the Mexican Revolution in the early twentieth century. The educated chemist, my grandfather, had immigrated to Los Angeles, worked hard and became a successful member of his adopted community. My mother Alicia was the youngest of five children and was raised in the mainly Hispanic neighborhood of East Los Angeles. My host seemed pleased with the information I provided, for in our culture la familia es lo primero.

"Well, you know you are quite a celebrity in our country now, Señor Valenciana."

"What do you mean sir?"

The Minister removed a local newspaper from his desk, unfolded it and looked for a particular article. Once identified, his plump face broke into a smile as he handed the newsprint to me. At that point I realized it made no sense to pretend any longer; the minister knew darn well I understood Spanish. Hugo leaned over my shoulder. The article reported I had torn open the fuselage of the burning aircraft with bare hands in a desperate attempt to free screaming school children and save blood-soaked women. Although it seemed rude, I could not help but laugh.

"What a bunch of crap." I blurted out without thinking!

"Quite an accomplishment," His Excellency stated.

"Do not believe everything you read, sir." I tossed the paper aside. "There are already enough lies going around concerning the demise of my crew-mates. We need not add another one." I had over-stepped my bounds and Diego placed a finger over his lips, signaling for me to shut up. He was indicating that the smoothest path was the one of least resistance.

"I am sure you are just being humble Senor." The Minister was sizing me up, needing to determine whether the little hero was an asset or a possible liability.

"Are you interested in economics, Señor Valenciana?" His inquiry threw me off.

"I've really never had a reason other than my own accounts," I replied with a tone of confusion. My host paused, then locked eyes with me in an effort to get a point across.

"It is really a matter of supply and demand, Señor Valenciana. For instance, millions of tourists visit Mexico each and every year. They come for the sites, the hospitality and the rich culture." The Minister rose from his large desk and began to stroll across the room. I noticed a shelf of nicely displayed framed photos of people who I assumed were relatives. There was also one of His Excellency with López Portillo. This was a man of influence, a person with important friends, a man who wielded power.

"These welcome visitors contribute greatly to the economy of our country and in return we provide them with a wonderful holiday experience, the product they are seeking. We have many partners in various enterprises that participate in successfully por las turistas, those visiting our lovely country."

At that moment, the Minister of Transportation reached for his inside coat pocket and removed the blue pack of those same filthy cigarettes that the comandante consumed endlessly. I became fearful as the official continued.

"Your own airline, Señor Valenciana, is a working partner with our government in creating the economic success that is our tourist market." The wily diplomat paused and gave a serious glare in my direction. "Do you understand what I am saying, Eduardo?" I glanced at Don Diego who was already looking at me and moving his head ever so slightly in a positive manner.

"Sí senor," I softly responded. I became more apprehensive. "In my position with the airline I encounter those happy travelers on each flight, looking forward to their stay in your beautiful country." The distinguished Minister of Transportation smiled.

"Ah yes, I knew you would be understanding." He seemed delighted and perhaps relieved by my much-improved attitude. "You know, Eduardo, your own company is rewarded nicely by our partnership in this market. Daily flights to our country make up a great percentage of their revenue, our revenue, and that of the lowly taxi drivers, the hotel workers, even the vendors in the streets whether in Mexico City, Acapulco or Guadalajara. That, my friend, is economics. The success lies in all our partners being in agreement, work in harmony and not make waves."

The Minister of Transportation grinned widely, seemingly pleased with himself as he continuously puffed on the wretched cigarette I had come to detest. "Certainly, cooperation must be kept a priority." The Minister was fishing, and I realized that the right answer was not to convince the official of what I knew, but to satisfy him with the belief that I knew nothing at all. It would be so simple to do just as Diego requested of me and play the game, but I honestly believe the odor of the tobacco caused my anger to boil over once more. I grabbed the Mexican Newspaper Hugo had picked up and was now folded neatly on his lap and I shook it violently.

"Error de piloto huh? Where is the cooperation and partnership? It appears as though there is more than just one loose cannon. Your god-damn press is driving me half crazy." Diego, who was cringing, motioned for me to cool it. I stopped and took a deep breath, allowing a smile once more, trying to let my best side show. "My apologies, Señores, the stress and grief of this entire ordeal, it is overwhelming. Please find it in your hearts to forgive my unpleasantness." The Minister paused but then seemed understanding and accepted my apologies. He hesitated for a moment and then turned to look me in the eyes.

"Can we count on your cooperation, Señor Valenciana?" He asked sincerely and with a deep interest as to how I would respond. This was not a question regarding the facts of the incident, what I may have seen or heard during the crash. It was not an inquiry for the truth or whether my recollections would be or could be of benefit in solving the mystery of the crash. It became evident to me immediately that the conclusion as to why my jumbo jet and all those in her had endured a terrible death had already been decided.

"You can count on me explicitly," I stated, grinding my teeth. His Excellency seemed satisfied and approached me. I struggled to stand and shook his extended his hand, the true bond in a Hispanic agreement.

"Just one last thing, mi amigo," he whispered close to my ear. "This unfortunate incident with Comandante Chávez," he paused as I turned to look into his face. "It would be best for all if that incident was not mentioned further." He didn't not have to wait for my response.

"It is already forgotten," I quickly assured him. Satisfied, the chief representative of the Mexican Government regarding the investigation of the crash embraced me in an abrazo, causing much discomfort to my blistered back.

As I lumbered my way out of the minister's office I thought about all I had suffered. I pictured once again sitting on my jumpseat at 4L, the hard touch down, the explosion at the number two engine, the body parts that were jettisoned in the carnage and of course, the massive fire. Diego remained speaking with His Excellency as Hugo gently touched my right arm trying to see if I was okay. I nodded slightly to let my dear friend know that I was fine but deep down I was fuming. It was very clear that I was being told to keep my mouth shut. I did not speak up, how could I ever completely come to grip with this? This is what I was being asked to do – keep it all inside. And if I didn't? That too was made clear without saying a word. Primitivo Chávez could easily be counted on to ensure I remained in agreement.

"Eduardo, is there anything we can do for you before we arrange for your departure?" The Minister was once again diplomatic as he politely asked from the doorway of his private office.

"I just want to go home" I stated. The official began to chuckle, probably relieved that I had not asked for a million pesos.

"Certainly, mi amigo, the very next flight if you wish." At that instant, something nagged at me and I changed my request.

"No, wait! I want to visit the crash site but keep the damn media away from me."

"Of course you may, and Diego here will be your escort, your protector if you will. See to it, Diego." Satisfied that he had achieved his goal, the Minister of Transportation of Mexico excused himself. Suddenly Raquel appeared and approached me. I nearly lost control of my crutches as she leaned forward to gently kiss me on the check and tenderly rub my shoulder. Hugo nearly fell over and Diego cracked a smile. I blushed nervously as we exited. I slowly made my way to the location where a car would be brought around to take me to the crash site, the very place I had escaped with my life on Halloween morning. As Hugo and I waited, he removed a handkerchief from his coat and began to wipe my cheek clean of Raquel's bright red lipstick.

"Viva Eduardo!" Hugo joked as he laughed. Eduardo Valenciana from East L.A. no longer existed. "El Gato," the man with nine lives, the man who saved women and children with his bare hands, the man who swept women off their feet, Eduardo the saint, now took his place. I felt so inadequate and almost ashamed. This is not me.

Will I ever be good enough? An inner voice persisted.

My mind was in a fog as I entered the black sedan. With Felipe at the wheel and Diego in the front seat, Hugo and I in the rear, we headed onto the tarmac traveling alongside airport service vehicles. I took little notice, staring straight ahead. *How had everything gotten so screwed up?* I wondered to myself.

Finally, the black sedan slowed and came to a complete stop. I slowly exited to the sound of mariachi music blaring loudly from two large speakers across the road and adjacent to the Mexican airport and Runway 23-Right. A huge, black gap lay in the middle of what once had been a peaceful, impoverished neighborhood. Diego, Hugo Garcia, the young Felipe and I stood in bewilderment as we gazed at the span of the total wreckage. There was a makeshift security point about twenty yards from the start of the site where Diego and Hugo spoke with personnel and showed their proper credentials. Feeling the strain on my body, I took the opportunity to lean against the hood of the black vehicle as the spasms returned. I seemed to be in more pain now as my body stiffened once again. As I turned my head I spotted two Americans dressed in very official-looking business suits involved in an argument with an on-duty policeman at the edge of the crash site. The Mexican policeman was very animated. One of the Americans waved his hands to no avail as the officer just shook his head no. I grabbed my crutches and hobbled a bit closer to listen in and discover what the fuss was all about. I immediately recognized the badges displayed on the Americans' upper left side suit pockets: the distinct letters F.A.A.

"What's up guys?" I casually inquired. Caught by surprise, they seemed relieved to stand face to face with someone who spoke English. The older of the two, a balding man, was flustered as he took a deep breath, ready to vent his frustration.

"I have never dealt with such stupidity." Never in their illustrious careers as highly regarded aviation experts had the two Norte Americanos had to deal with such disappointment. "The security force won't let "us" onto the crash site but everyone else and their mother is in there." The younger blonde-haired fellow raised his arm, waving toward the vast destruction, directing me to take a look. He did have a point. Although there was an official investigation supposedly going on, half of the population of Mexico City seemed to be mingling about, moving burned fuselage parts, picking up odds and ends, having free reign of the burnt wreckage. "They've even neglected to have the crash site roped off." The exasperated senior F.A.A. investigator was seemingly at his wit's end. I began to laugh, the Americans glaring at me. Perhaps I was losing my mind. The entire scene to me was a macabre traveling carnival that had just pulled into town on the morning of Halloween. I tried to compose myself as I apologized and made an effort to be more helpful.

"Remember guys, you're in Mexico City now." I advised.

"What's that supposed to mean? We have the proper authority." I cut the older official short.

"You'd do better just going out to the street where the mariachi music is coming from and jumping over the wall to get in, just like everyone else is doing." The two men became silent and looked at each other for the longest moment. Then they turned and squinted in the direction I had mentioned. The three of us could see that it seemed as though everyone in town was climbing that same partition, men leaping over first and then assisting the women and children to get free entrance into the "chamber of horrors." The hordes of curious, the press, even small children were running through the rubble for the sheer excitement of it and I was just pointing out the obvious to the Americans. So, what initially seemed to them like an ignorant suggestion was now concluded to be the best advice they had received all day.

"You would be well advised to get rid of those badges though," I suggested. Both men glanced at each other like two monkeys at the zoo and removed their plastic IDs. As they hurried off I began to laugh all the louder.

"Badges? You don't need no stinking badges!" I could not help myself. They were learning quickly. In a similar situation in the United States I was sure they were always treated with great respect and courtesy. Here, they were reduced to having to climb a battered wall in their nicely pressed suits. For the first time since the crash I had found my humor but in retrospect it may have been revealing the first signs of a breakdown.

Don Raphael Diego Suárez de la Vega had the authority to pull the proper strings. Recognized and well-respected by all Mexican security forces around the crash site, we had no problem entering into the zone that had been off-limits to the Norte Americanos. In the vehicle once more, Felipe directed us to one side. Large cranes were just now being moved into place to begin the removal of the twisted metal. Everywhere I glanced, some ordinary Mexicans stood back staring while others continued rummaging through the debris. I lowered the window

204

so I could listen to the sounds and was hit with the stench of the now-familiar jet fuel that filled the air. Felipe stopped the car and Hugo assisted me in exiting. I stood in the middle of what seemed like a neighborhood party.

It registered as a sight from another dimension, this blackened wreckage of DC-10NW903 with the red-and-white tarnished colors of the airline. Next to it was a vendor selling colorful balloons. Some may think it foolish, but I saw the balloons doing what my jumbo jet could no longer do -- fly. Then there was yet another vendor selling yellow rubber duckies in a little makeshift pool he had filled with water. A young man in a striped blue-and-white shirt with the emblem of his favorite soccer club carted a cardboard square containing cotton candy secured in neat rows. At a point farther along the crash site was a woman selling shoes.

"Nieve fría." Cold ice cream for sale.

"¿Quieres globos? Balloons, red, blue or yellow." The vendors proclaimed.

"It's a stinking three-ring circus!" I shook my head and began to laugh for I had become a member of the audience in a sad and sick drama. Yet, as I did a double take of the vendors I realized that they were all at the bottom of the economic ladder of Mexico City's millions of residents. Their waking hours were spent finding work to feed their families. These real people were the ones who were offering me the most genuine expressions of joy for my good fortune.

"Sí, Señor, El Gato. Praise God for your survival and now I must go find something for my children to eat." I clearly understood because I knew I would be doing the same if I were in their position. How could I fault them for their actions? The press was a whole different story. The cameramen were out in droves. Some security personnel were guiding the press as they moved through the destruction. I could only bow my head and was filled with sorrow as I studied the destroyed remains. I determined that there were five different mounds of twisted metal where the fuselage came to rest. The tarmac was littered with cargo from the belly of the plane. Also, I spotted the company placards describing emergency procedures and what exit to use in case the unthinkable happened, useless now and tumbling along the ground in the breeze. These were mixed with soiled and torn pieces of clothing along with ice cream and candy wrappers tossed aside by the growing crowds. Yellow oxygen masks hung in random parts of the mangled metal. The smell of death hung heavy over the DC-10's remains.

Some of the curious studied what they thought might be body parts. Could it have been an arm or a leg? They discussed the angle in which they were gazing and then began to debate whether it really was an arm, a leg? There was the body of a woman caught in the twisted metal. She seemed to be sleeping with her hands gently resting upon her lap. It was evident that the steel from the maintenance building that encased her would have to be cut before her remains could be retrieved. The woman seemed to be one of the major attractions for the crowd and the press as if admiring an exhibit at a wax museum. Her face was serene. She seemed to be enjoying her eternal rest.

We continued to move along, I still in disbelief. In one section, behind the remains of what I determined to be mid-cabin, scavengers were searching for and going through suitcases.

"It's a macabre circus with looters being the side show," I stated. Diego tried to put it into perspective.

"Remember my Norte Americano friend, the crash occurred in one of the poorest sections of the city. These people live a meager existence." I recognized the truth. I had seen similar scenes in my travels, once being witness to hungry children eating dirt in North Africa.

"You're right," I said. "I would be doing the same to feed my loved ones." Maybe for the first time in my life, I understood man's primary need to survive taking precedence over the misfortune of others.

Throughout the massive crowd I could not locate one American face. The curious wandered, the poor rummaged and the press gawked, but all Norte Americano investigators were restricted to the sidelines. Suddenly I spotted a burnt-out section of what I believed to have been the aft section.

"Let me see if I can arrange for us to get through here." Diego offered. The ship was ripped apart and all contents scattered about. My jumpseat may have been destroyed but the safety harness did its job and secured my body as all hell broke loose around me. I nearly stumbled as I tried to avoid all the chunks of concrete and sharp debris.

"Where is this path going?" Somehow, I knew that this tragic mystery was far more complex than my current understanding could fathom. Walking slowly, I spotted Felipe off to the side maneuvering the black sedan around the rubble so as to be available at the other end of the site. All at once my attention was drawn to activity occurring near the one remaining hangar on the side of Runway 23 Right. Were those stacked bodies? Diego quickly returned with a concerned look on his face.

"Well amigo, we are cleared to wander wherever you wish, but I must advise you that things look pretty bad. There are no refrigeration facilities available, the bodies must be piled and covered with lime for preservation, at least until family members can claim them." I was beyond reacting. I just nodded, indicating that I wished to continue.

At that moment I noticed Jack McKay, and an investigating pilot approaching me. By the initial expression on the old V.P.'s face, he seemed concerned.

"Eduardo, my boy," the executive called out, his breathing a bit heavy due to the journey from the operations center. He placed an arm upon my shoulder and motioned me aside. "Something apparently is going on in the hangar, the one being used as the morgue, and I need a translator." He looked at me hard, studying my reaction.

"What about Diego?" I asked. "I am sure his Spanish is quite superior to mine." McKay did not mince words.

"I need someone I can really trust." It was clear that whatever required his attention in the morgue hangar, it was to be kept among company personnel only.

"Certainly, Mr. McKay." Despite what he was asking me, I very much wanted to be a helpful member of our team. The exhausted company point man had taken a real liking to me, and I felt honored that he had faith in my abilities.

"It's an ugly scene in there lad, how much do you think you can handle?" I hobbled up close to him and looked straight into his eyes.

"Haven't I earned the right to decide for myself if I am up to the task?" McKay nodded his approval.

"Then let's be moving." He seemed satisfied.

The scene that awaited us in the hangar had only grown worse since Señora Torres and her daughter had come and gone. We moved alongside a line of hundreds of body parts, covered in a white and green paste-like substance, the lime used for preservation. I had to admit at this point that I was somehow getting used to the grim scene and smell of death. Does that make sense? The supervising pilot who accompanied us walked up by my side to express his concern. He leaned over and asked me if I was okay considering the surroundings. I just shrugged my shoulders,

"Yeah I'm fine, it was a lot worse when they were burning and screaming." The pilot's eyes grew big as he could only guess at what my mental state might be at this point. But did I not answer factually?

"Ah bienvenidos, Señor Vice Presidente." The morbid caretaker approached us, paying his respects. Designated as the translator, I discovered that the problem lay in a certain Doctor Sixto De Jesús. We were led to the rear of the makeshift mortuary where the doctor was standing behind a wooden table covered with a blood-soaked tarp on which two lumpy, gray tortilla-like objects lay alongside a bottle of Jose Cuervo tequila. By the amount of liquor remaining in the bottle, I guessed that De Jesús was drunk. He stood, slightly swaying from side to side, eyes glazed, hair messed, a pathetic-looking human being. His shirt, sleeves rolled up, were sweaty and blood-stained. He wore a pair of tight suspenders which pulled his beige pants way up above his waistline. Despite the responsibilities of his assigned duties, no one dared challenge the obviously intoxicated doctor. Slurring his words, the physician began to speak.

"Por favor Jefe, yo quiero boletos de primera clase, para mi familia a Hawaii." Had I heard right? I was perplexed.

"Dígame otra vez, senor. Please sir, tell me once again." The doctor repeated his request.

"What's the issue Eduardo?" McKay wanted to take care of business quickly, as he was needed in so many other places, other people to see.

"Sir, Dr. De Jesús is asking you to present him and his family with first class tickets to Hawaii," I stated meekly wondering if I had misinterpreted the request. McKay looked puzzled, then a slight smile appeared.

"Listen lad, tell the good doctor that I am sure the company can supply him with a small token for his efforts in this tragedy, but I have no authority to be giving first-class tickets to Hawaii at random." I turned and began trying to explain the situation to Dr. De Jesús when he rudely interrupted.

"No, No joven yo no quiero hablar con usted." He became angry as sweat raced down his swollen face. "El señor, el jefe, Señor McKay de la aereolinea." In the heat of the exchange the words became clear. The bibulous fool stared at Mr. McKay as the curly black locks on his head swayed with each word and his head jerked about tossing beads of sweat all about. The relentless man continued in Spanish. "If I do not have the tickets by tomorrow morning…." The doctor stopped in mid-sentence and began stuffing with old newspaper the first lumpy grey dough-like object as one would stuff a pinata. He locked eyes with Jack Mckay and never broke away or once focused on his task. After a few seconds or so he resumed in clear Spanish. "I will declare that there is much alcohol in this man's blood." Dr. De Jesús turned the newspaper-filled object, adjusting it slowly. All of us looked closely, confused at first, then came the shocking realization that what we were looking at was in actuality the head of one of the pilots.

"I wish to leave now," I politely requested. Hugo immediately stepped forward and took charge of me, trying to help me remain calm as he escorted me out. "'De Jesús,' means 'of Jesus.'" How ironic.

"Everyone is running their own con for whatever they can get out of it," I shouted at Hugo. Disturbed and angry, he said nothing. We exited the morgue and met Don Diego and Felipe waiting with the sedan. We did not speak a word as mariachi music filled the air, serenading the carnival in the background. I leaned up against the car as Hugo told Don Diego what had just occurred.

"Señor De Jesús?" Diego was familiar with him. I gazed out into the horizon, right over the dried lakebed, the same one that Cortés had first seen filled with life-giving water centuries earlier. Now dried and dusty, the grounds held the shanty town, erected by the poor. Those hastily raised cardboard houses stood pretty much empty at the moment for most of the inhabitants were taking part in the given opportunity. In the contents of a travel bag from Norte America could be articles of great value. Hungry people do not ask, they take. At the same time there were other games in a larger scale being played by so-called reputable individuals. Such acts were far less honorable than the need to disrespect yourself to fill your children's stomachs. These power players' behavior was far more deceitful and downright sinful.

McKay emerged from the makeshift morgue, in utter disbelief.

"This is one big shit, Eduardo." He shook his head, but I sensed that there was more on his mind.

"What?" I asked.

"Did you happen to see..." He stopped in mid-sentence. "Did you notice?" He stumbled once more.

"Just ask me," I said softly. McKay ran his fingers through his scalp, raking the few white strands of hair that were left on his sunburned fair skin.

"Your aircraft struck the dump truck up there at the top of runway 24-left," he pointed off into the distance. I turned and followed his line of direction.

"That's the runway the Mexican's claim was closed," I stated as I turned to face him. He nodded.

"Yeah, so they say." His face cringed as he gathered his thoughts. "Well boy, that is where the right landing gear of the DC-10 lies burrowed into the ground and twisted with what is left of that dump truck. But the other landing gear, the left one...." Once again McKay stopped in mid-sentence. I became impatient.

"Just say it Jack, get to the point." I snapped.

"Damn it, we can't find the left gear," he blurted out. I was confused.

"You mean an entire landing gear of a jumbo jet has gone missing?" I was dumbfounded. "Who in the hell would steal a landing gear?" I turned back and looked at the scattered looters just a small distance from us.

"The whole landing gear?" I asked in disbelief.

"The whole thing, we believe," He responded.

"And they got away with it?"

"You didn't happen to notice any removal of wreckage soon after the crash, did you boy?" I looked at McKay seriously.

"Believe me, Jack, I had my hands full that morning with my own problems." The vice-president looked to the ground.

"Yes, you did. Certainly you did, boy." This real gentleman shook my hand and reassured me of his continued support in getting through this mess. I admired Jack McKay and did not envy him as he and the supervisor pilot made their way back to the terminal building. How many more free tickets was it was going to cost the company to solve the next problem? And the next?

Diego was very surprised to find me quite calm after McKay and his group departed. I was just numb. I had to simplify the confusion.

"Tell me Diego, why would the airline's best pilot bring down his craft onto a closed runway?" My educated and logical friend simply shrugged his shoulders and shook his head. "It doesn't make sense; Carl Herbert had landed here hundreds of times." I was puzzled. "I'm sure he was guided by the landing lights." Diego's eyes widen as he looked at me.

"No amigo, the lights on 23-Left have been offline while construction was being performed on that runway. In a meeting last night with the Minister, that subject was raised, and the answer was very clear." I was dumbfounded. Had I missed something?

"Impossible! I saw the runway lights on myself. They pierced through gaps in the fog as we descended. I also saw them illuminated while scrambling about looking for survivors."

"Well there is one way to find out, amigo. The control boxes for both 23-Left and 23-Right are about a half-kilometer from here. Let us go, I have the keys." I struggled to hurry back to the black sedan along with the others. Racing parallel to Runway 23-Right, the one functioning runway at Benito Juárez International Airport, Felipe tried to avoid any debris that still lay scattered throughout the airport grounds. I shook my head as it was apparent that even though landings had been restricted, some flights were still arriving despite the debris alongside: a definite safety hazard to a speeding aircraft. We arrived at the control boxes for the lights located between Runway 23-Left and

Runway 23-Right. Diego was already opening his door and exiting before Felipe could come to a complete stop. I remained in the sedan seated next to Hugo, keeping focused on Don Diego. Señor Suárez de la Vega wrestled with the partially rusted locks and hurried to open the metal cover. Once open he turned to us with a look of disbelief.

"Something is not right, Hugo," I quietly stated as I began to exit the car. I needed to know. "What is it? Don Diego?" I had to scream as a descending jet roared beside us. The Aeromexico DC-9 aircraft's wheels touched the pavement on 23 Right, several yards down from our position. I hobbled as quickly as possible to get to Diego. "What are you staring at?" There was no response as I assumed he did not hear me or just did not know how to answer. Señor García quickly followed. The three of us stared in amazement. A large orange tag was tied around the four thick cables fastened in the metal casing, along with three reddish-brown cloth rags. The tag read "under repair" in Spanish. Equally shocking was the condition of the cables themselves which seemed to have been cut almost in half, hammered with an ax or other sharp implement and yanked from their installed positions in a moment of panic.

"They told me they were under repair. I was lied to." Don Diego's initial disappointment seemed as devastating as mine but for a different reason, he was dealt a crushing blow. His superiors had seemingly misled him.

"Who would be behind such a thing, Diego?" We stared at each other and I recalled what the minister had meant about partners working together in securing Mexico's economic stability.

"Listen, Diego. We've got to keep our cool. Trust no one." Diego could only nod his head as he was still in shock over the idea that he had been left out of the loop. Did no one know or want to know what caused Carl Herbert to guide his craft to her destruction? I thought *my* path was going to be tough. "The captain is going to be made the sacrificial lamb," I stated to Diego as we rode back. Herbert's whole aviation career: his stellar safety record, reputation and respect were about to be discredited. I prayed to this silent God for the captain's family and did not envy the suffering they were about to endure. I tried to trust that possibly upstanding and reputable investigators would gather enough information and facts to exonerate the deceased aviator. Then I scolded myself for even wanting to believe that in this world the airline industry and politicians are all people of noble character. I decided I had better keep my mouth shut for I wished to survive to fight another day, or at least live another day.

As we reached the outskirts of the main wreckage, the vehicle slowed down. Felipe spotted three youths who were running about. As I peered out the window, I noticed a boy in beige shorts wearing white long tube sports socks and a San Francisco Giants baseball cap. He seemed to be dodging some type of object thrown in his direction by a mate. The boy studied the object on the ground, retrieved it quickly and tossed it to a third boy in tattered blue jeans. They all laughed, and some scooted away from it when the object landed on the ground. Suddenly it was snatched up by the third youth who again tossed it high in the air. This time the receiver caught it successfully and once the object was securely in his possession quickly dropped it. Then, in an instant, I became aware of what the "toy" was they had been throwing about. I stared at the object recognizing that up to that moment in life I had been very naive. The rambunctious youths had been playing catch with a severed human hand and we in the vehicle fell silent.

"I am sorry you had to see that my friend. I'll put a stop to it if you wish," Diego offered.

"No. Let it be," I replied. "It just confirms the madness I now discover myself in." I silently hoped this insanity would offer me a point of exit somewhere in the near future.

The black sedan left the airport grounds and traveled the several hundred yards back to the Holiday Inn. I thanked Felipe for his assistance as he looked at me with true compassion. He, like millions of others in the capital city, wished only the best for me in my new life. The car pulled away as I stood with crutches at the main entrance by the roadway. I paused for a moment as a simply dressed woman approached carrying an infant under her wrap.

"Por favor señor, un besito para mi niño." I was puzzled and turned to Diego.

"She wants me to kiss the baby?" Diego began to chuckle.

"You are a national hero, my friend. Señor El Gato, the man with nine lives. Kiss the child. She is showing you deep respect." He directed Hugo Gomez to remain with me. "I am going to go make the arrangements for your return home," he stated. "I will return soon." I slowly bent over to kiss the child on the forehead to the delight of the young girl. I was truly mystified by the adoration she showed me.

"Hugo, why did she ask me to do that?" While I asked my friend, another man, a common person in simple clothing, now approached us. He seemed genuinely happy to see me.

"Whether you realize it or not, Eduardo, there is a great amount of responsibility that goes with cheating la mano de Muerto, the hand of Death." Others wandered slowly by, the curious mostly, to gaze upon the one who had cheated Death. Others would pass by, touch my shoulder, and continue on.

"How does one live up to such a responsibility, Hugo?" Hugo thought for a while, a slight smile on his face.

"Well, mi amigo, that's the trick of it all isn't it? Since you are the one who cheated Death you are the only one who can answer that question."

"He's the one." That's how they saw me. I tried to see myself from their point of view. In a life that was very difficult and unpredictable on a daily basis, they determined that I was one person who beat the odds. Somehow a greater force, whether called faith or fate had intervened in my favor. Perhaps the mystical power they believed was instilled in me could or would be transferable to them. Yet, when they got very close and I looked into their eyes, these simple souls revealed that they were just happy that I was alive, and their wide smiles attested to that fact. My good fortune seemed to regenerate hope in them which I determined was a reason for me to continue on. I realized I could learn much from them.

Hugo saw that things were getting out of hand as the crowd grew and they started to press in on me. I started to lose balance on my crutches. He rushed in to assist me and provide protection as we hurried into the lobby of the Holiday Inn and proceeded to my refuge once more.

Chapter X

Early morning arrivals to the airport are a way of life for flight crews. Kyle Tillman had reported to Operations the morning of October 31, only to find chaos. The teletype at the Denver hub delivered the grim news: a "10," *our* 10, had gone down. Pilots in Denver, as in every city the airline served, scrambled to gather every bit of information they could. It seemed unbelievable to so many when it was first revealed that it was Carl Herbert's flight, and Mexico's initial decision to cut communications stifled efforts to learn otherwise. Kyle, like all the associates of the company, nervously waited and wondered, but his desire to hang around the lounge to see the names on the crew list of the ill-fated flight had to be put aside. He boarded a Salt Lake City flight with the partial relief that nearly all his personal friends were based in Denver with him. Only Eddy from Training Class 2 remained based in Los Angeles and Kyle desperately wanted to believe that his Hispanic friend could not have been on the doomed DC-10.

While working the flight Kyle would check in routinely with the boys in the cockpit during the flight he was working for any hint of news, but nothing was coming in from the Mexico City. Upon landing in SFO, he couldn't get to Operations fast enough. There he found mass confusion. A chief pilot, frustrated by the lack of information, was awaiting the next flight to Los Angeles for a connection to Mexico City. He was visibly frustrated. Carl Herbert had been a close friend and there was no possible scenario that he could imagine that would lead Carl into a situation where the outcome would be what he was being told. As in Denver, Kyle was learning nothing.

The next leg of Kyle's schedule was to take him to Seattle. He climbed the terminal staircase telling himself his concerns were unwarranted, but uncertainty nagged at him. Entering the crowded halls of the terminal building, Kyle noticed a large group of F/As and gate agents gathered in a corner, so he immediately went to see what the commotion was.

"Oh my God." Someone had the official crew list from 2605. They pushed forward and spoke not a word as they individually and methodically ran down the list of names. Sighs of relief were sporadically heard as the names of the majority of junior flight attendants on the list were unknown to most, including Kyle. But then there it was, the last name on the sheet. EDUARDO VALENCIANA. Kyle's heart sank, but he did not give up hope. He refused to.

"Eddy was physically fit. Maybe he had the strength to get out. Oh my God!" Kyle boarded the SEA-bound flight near tears. Real men do cry. He was going to cling to hope until he was certain. Like most flights throughout the company's system, the cockpit was unusually silent as news from the Mexican capitol was virtually non-existent. Once on the ground, Kyle rushed to Operations headquarters, but they knew nothing more either.

More than likely the impact that had destroyed the jumbo jet had claimed his amigo after all. It just might be true. His thoughts lingered on his friend and the colorful exploits they had shared during training and continued as he boarded the Boeing 727 to "deadhead" back to DEN. As they glided over Elliot Bay, Kyle let his mind imagine what it must have been like in the midst of the horror his dear friend had endured until the point of impact.

"Why so gloomy Tillman?" Robin was a lovely, dark-haired F/A who had been a few training classes ahead of Kyle and his friend Eddy.

"Ah, it's the damn accident. My close buddy was on that 10." Robin immediately registered a chill in her body.

"Dear God Kyle, I'm sorry. Is there anything I can do?" But what *could* she do or say?

"I really don't know for sure what happened to him, but it doesn't look good." Kyle decided he needed to let go.

"What was his name, Kyle?" Robin inquired.

"Eddy, I mean Eduardo Valenciana." Kyle stated in a soft voice.

"Eduardo, Eduardo, was he a weightlifter?"

"Yeah, that's him," Kyle replied, believing that possibly she had flown with him.

"Shit, Tillman, he made it, he's alive." Robin became excited as she rushed to find the latest edition of a San Francisco newspaper. Finding one, she rushed back and held the folded page in front of Kyle's face.

"The miraculous escape of one of the crew members. Eduardo Valenciana simply walked away from it." Kyle read the text over and over again, clutching the paper to ensure it would not disappear.

"YES!" He jumped out of his First-Class seat and gave a yell as the newspaper went flying, startling those around him. But he didn't care! Eduardo was alive and he had to share the good news.

...

I lay on my bed in my Holiday Inn hideout, trying to figure it all. Who would want to steal the left landing gear of the DC-10? My thoughts became bizarre as I imagined the gear modified into an elaborate water fountain in the middle of some blue-blooded aristocrat's living room in the city. I pictured it rising into the air as disco lights flashed behind in rhythm. All for the delight of the master of the house and whatever guest he wished to display the ill-gotten trophy to.

A knock at the door broke my daydream. Diego was back.

"You've been given permission to leave. Here is your boarding pass and seat assignment." I could hardly believe it after everything that had ensued the last couple of days. I was astonished how efficient this young Mexican official had been in arranging my departure. Daisy Ackley insisted that someone from the company accompany me on the flight as the airline could ill-afford to lose me once again. A young manager from the Public Relations Office, Robert Collins, was selected. I recalled this man being present during the earlier meeting in Daisy's room. Bob was a good choice and I felt comfortable with him. Maybe he could hold my hand if I needed the strength to get back on a plane once again. I felt fortunate to just be getting out of town in one piece but then that vile inner voice returned.

"You'll be sitting relaxed in the cabin while others would will be in wooden boxes in the belly of the craft." I tried to shrug the dissension off.

"You've got to hurry my friend; the flight won't wait for you." Don Diego smiled as Hugo helped to gather my things. Daisy arrived to send me off with a gracious hug and I thanked her for all she had done on my behalf. Reva also appeared to assure me that she would always be available to see to my needs. She was keenly aware that there were still many obstacles I would have to overcome as a result of this trauma. It was also time to say farewell to my lifeline, Señor Hugo García, who will always be my hero. I fumbled to find the words that could even begin to express my gratitude, yet all that was required was a sincere look into his eyes and a nod, for he understood my heart. Later, I regretted the fact that we had not exchanged phone numbers or addresses so as to remain in contact, but I was satisfied that if the time came, I knew just where I would be able to locate him.

"Vámonos," I commanded as Diego, Bob Collins and I left the Holiday Inn, with young Felipe once again shuttling us the few hundred yards for my departure from Benito Juárez International Airport, Mexico City.

I struggled with the crutches into the terminal building but hobbled excitedly across its marble floor. The three of us were waived right through Customs by a gesture from Diego and headed straight for the departing gate. A makeshift press conference had been set up where the surviving flight attendant of Flight 2605 would give the press a final statement. Word had quickly spread among the press in the capital city and it was "Lights! Cameras! Action!" once again. It was noisy and the initial flashes blinded my eyes as I tried to focus in on the number of the departing gate, 58.

"What will you do with your new life?"

"Relish it!" It was the right answer even if I knew I would not. My life had been changed. I had changed. And this present version of myself was what I was left with. At this point I could barely figure out who or what I was.

But I gave the media all the right "non-liable" answers. Certainly, I would set time aside for my family, maybe take a vacation, when in reality I had no idea what the company had in store for me once I returned to Los Angeles.

Suddenly, from the corner of my eye, I spotted the jackal, Comandante Primitivo Chávez de León. Certainly, he would not let his prize depart the Mexican capital without one last response. First fear and then anger swelled in my chest.

"Gracias a la Oficina del Ministerio de Transportación y también la gente de la ciudad del Distrito Federal." The local press was all abuzz.

"I thought he did not speak Spanish?" All looked at Diego. I grinned as I locked eyes with my tormentor, the calm Comandante coolly lit another of those nasty cigarettes. I was immediately escorted down the jetway along with Bob Collins and company gate agents. Diego was left behind to create some lie about me practicing some Spanish so that I could thank the people of Mexico for their generous hospitality.

While still in the jetway I regretted revealing my understanding of the native language, well aware that at any time and any place, the long arm of the Mexican Federal Police may try to reach me. I scolded myself for allowing my anger toward the comandante to make me reveal more of myself than I wished. Finally, the noble Diego was able to escape the press and come down the jetway on his way to bid me farewell.

"Along with your new life you now have new friends," he said. We finally did exchange phone numbers and he assured me that he would not share the number with the dishonorable comandante.

"Diego, I wish to thank you for all you have done on my behalf." The good official brushed aside any sentiment.

"You have a new beginning, amigo, and may you soon forget all that is distasteful about this incident. Vaya con Dios." His abrazo was deep and heartfelt as Collins and I turned to enter the DC-10. After a few steps inside I leaned back on the crutches. My body went limp as if I had smashed into a wall. Connie, a familiar flight attendant who was working this flight to LAX, quickly approached me. My fellow associate put an arm around me and by her demeanor knew that she too felt the great sense of loss that had spread throughout the company. Once I regained my composure, Connie removed an envelope from her service apron and handed it to me.

"From Señor Hugo García." I winced when I opened it, struck by the familiar odor of jet fuel. I reached in and removed the contents, my charred blue-covered United States passport. I was amazed. It had actually survived the inferno, being tucked away in my regulation suitcase. I suddenly became fearful and confused as I began to weep. Now that I did not have to worry about fending off the comandante, the press or the curious onlookers, the full gravity of what I had experienced was overcoming me and I was soon drained physically and emotionally. Away from the foreign threat my guard let down and I clung to Connie like a frightened child. Her quick action saved my pride and averted a public breakdown as the rest of the cabin crew was very aware of what was happening.

Bob Collins interceded to inform me that we were assigned seats in first class in the front row, but before I could go forward in the aircraft I *had* to go aft. I crossed the service center and turned my crutches sideways, slowly making my way down the right aisle to position 4R. I laid the crutches down gently against some seats and carefully took up my position once again on the jumpseat, strapping myself in and tightening the harness. I sat and tried to imagine how everything I saw around me could have been so totally destroyed in a matter of seconds. After some time, hypnotized by the imagery I rose up and look at the jumpseat at 4R and thanked it for protecting me so well when it counted. Then I grabbed the crutches and began working my way back up the aisle. My thoughts drifted, once again watching Gary, Tamlyn, Cary, Reina, Karen and Rod laughing, joking in the service area. I wished now I could join them, before the disaster, before the pain, before the fireball. Lost in the reverie, I nearly stumble. Looking up I realized that I was the focus of the crew as they stared. I imagined they wondered what madness had sowed its seeds in my mind. I sheepishly continued on to my assigned seat, forward in first class where Bob Collins awaited to welcome me.

"You okay?" I just nodded my head and appreciated that Bob had given me time to settle myself down on my own. My escort from Public Relations did not follow me to the aft to see what I was doing. He waited, knowing there were things I needed to deal with and in my own good time. I just hoped that the company would allow me the same consideration.

The passengers began boarding our DC-10 and it was announced that the flight was oversold. All the regular flight schedules at Benito Juárez had been disrupted by the accident, and fewer flights were getting in and out. An open seat out of the Mexico City became a coveted commodity.

"You know we had to bump revenue passengers to get these seats," Bob informed me. "Thanks Bob, give me one more reason to feel guilt," I thought to myself. It was so strange. There would be moments of tremendous joy knowing I was still in one piece, but that would be immediately followed by overbearing sorrow and feelings of debilitating guilt.

A petite blonde flight attendant I recognized went past me and into the forward galley. I wanted to look at her, get an acknowledgment, say "Hi, it's me, Eddy," but it was evident that she didn't want to reciprocate. When her eyes wandered in my direction she quickly looked away, opting to work the El Segundo section instead of first class so as to keep her distance. This would not be the last time I would encounter such behavior towards me.

The passengers jockeyed for overhead compartment space as every seat would be occupied. One of the pilots that I recognized from the meeting in Daisy's room was also returning to LAX. Since the flight was completely full, he would have to sit jumpseat in the cockpit. They noticed me sitting in the first row with my wrapped leg and crutches and acknowledged me with a nod. Other than crew members, no one else seemed to know who I was as the gate agent shut the door and the crew readied the craft for departure. Unfortunately, we sat delayed at the gate, the wait just feeding my anxiety. The supervisor pilot who had entered the cockpit earlier came out in hopes of finding coffee in the first-class galley.

"What's the hold-up?" I asked as he stood close by me.

"Something to do with the jet fuel," He remarked. I thought nothing of it at the moment as the craft suddenly backed away from the gate and the regular safety demonstrations and announcements began. My mind wandered back to 2605 as I watched the flight crew.

"Gary busted his butt, and for what?" I stated to no one in particular.

"What?" Bob stared at me. "Don't go crazy on me, Ed!" The statement brought me back to reality as I chuckled and shook my head.

As the jumbo jet taxied down the tarmac, I was about to be treated to one more incredible sight. Just outside the airport fenced area, at the head of the runway where the planes lined up for take-off, portable viewing stands had been erected and were filled with the curious who were perhaps awaiting a repeat of the Halloween disaster.

"What have we become?" I wondered as I gazed out the window. This was their entertainment. Then I began to laugh as I recognized the usual vendors peddling their wares to the anxious crowd that physically reacted as each craft fired up their engines and proceeded on their runs of departure, then rising into the sky. Soon it was our turn. The roar of the General Electric engines grew louder, and the huge craft began to roll down runway 23-Left, now available to traffic. As our DC-10 rolled past the crash site, each head in the cabin strained to get one last look.

"I'm going home at last," I thought to myself. "I will finally be truly free." How naive I was.

Once up in the air I was able to relax a little more, knowing that soon I would be home back in the United States. So it was with deep disappointment to discover that the Mexican fuelers at Benito Juárez Airport had refused to fill our jet with the precious substance needed to get back to LAX. The workers' union leaders saw an opportunity to get a bigger piece of the financial pie that resulted from the traffic disruption, so the fuel crew went on a timely strike. I supposed Jorge Valenzuela, the airline's main man in Mexico, had been busy on the phones trying to work out a solution to a problem he was very familiar with. As a result, the cunning chief contacted a union boss in Acapulco and with a bit of persuasion (perhaps more first-class tickets to Hawaii) reached an agreement to refuel our DC-10 for a more reasonable price than the Mexico City union chief proposed.

It was a short hop to Acapulco where our craft was guided to a waiting area on the tarmac away from the main terminal building. Since the auxiliary power on the aircraft had to be turned off during the refueling process, several doors were opened so that fresh air could flow through the tightly packed cabin. I looked at Bob Collins who had endured sleepless nights through this ordeal, now sleeping soundly. Some of the passengers apparently began to figure out who the guy with the wrapped leg and crutches was sitting in first class. I tried to avoid their curious looks.

A portable stairway had to be brought out to our plane and placed at the base of the open 1L doorway. The local fuelers would have to enter the aircraft when their job was completed to give the proper documentation to the cockpit crew. I arose and hobbled onto the top of the stairway just outside the fuselage. I wanted to hide from the multitude of eyes that glared at the oddity that I had become. I wanted none of this as the visual assault fanned the flames of my shame causing me to feel undeserving of such attention. Yet it all seemed familiar. My dreams leading up to the incident had reflected some sense of this current reality. Then there was the fear regarding Reina's prophetic dreams, it all had to have some logical explanation.

Standing at the top of the portable stairway, I was startled by a woman poking her head out the doorway, staring intently at me, then quickly disappearing. I looked inside the cabin only to see some of the curious walking forward to have a closer look at me. Was I so different? Even some of my fellow F/As seemed uneasy. Were they afraid I might try to speak to them? I imagined that I had come to represent a horrible reality that some in my profession wished never to acknowledge. I started to become agitated, exiled out on the tarmac. I now felt like a hostage. I wanted to descend the stairs and hobble away as I had from Comandante Chávez, but I knew I could not deplane because customs would not allow it. We had all been informed that our stay in ACA was not supposed to be this long and it all seemed so senseless. Why couldn't the craft have been refueled in Mexico City? I knew of course. It was all about money. Re-fueling in Acapulco was less expensive.

I was about to re-enter the first-class section when I noticed a Mexicana Airlines DC-10 taxiing across the tarmac in front of us. So sleek and bold, the Mexican colors so bright on her fuselage. Then it hit me. I suddenly believed I knew what had happened to the left landing gear of DC-10 NW903.

Mexico's two major airlines were Mexicana and Aero Mexico and both companies flew the McDonnell Douglas DC-10 in their daily service routes. My theory concerning the detached landing gear was based on airline culture and process of thought. On that foggy, early morning of the 31st of October there certainly would have been numerous airport and airline personnel reporting to work. Did a mechanic from another airline see an opportunity in our wreckage? A lack of parts is a well-known problem in the industry. I supposed that the left landing gear survived the massive G Forces, becoming detached and still in one piece. Perhaps opportunists licked their chops and jumped on the rubble to claim the prize. I imagine it took keen organization, pure physical strength and sheer will to cannibalize the wreckage, snatch that limb, secure it and haul it off to hide it in a hangar somewhere on the airport grounds. Deep inside, part of me would have admired those guys as it would take balls to attempt the theft and complete it in less than an hour. The only difficulty I had was understanding how they may have felt afterward. If that's what happened, they would have had to come to grips with their own conscience, while those around them were screaming, burning and dying. Deep inside I believed that my slate wasn't clean either. I should have done more. It was becoming crystal clear that I had a perilous road ahead of me psychologically.

Finally, a young Mexican in blue pants and red work shirt climbed the metal stairway, rushing toward the cockpit with the proper papers in his hand: the thirsty jumbo jet had been topped off. The flight was now really behind schedule now, but I was definitely heading home. It would not be until we flew over the last traces of the Gulf of Mexico, that I allowed myself to relax. It wasn't long before the blanket of lights of the Los Angeles basin welcomed our approach.

"Certainly, Tommy would be there at LAX to greet his dear friend," I thought. I envisioned the scene with my mother and sister alongside him waiting for the moment we all embraced with hugs and kisses and more hugs. I pictured my father standing by the gate looking for me as the passengers exited from Customs. I hoped that my brother Mike (the policeman) was able to make it to the airport. I was sure the company had contacted them all to inform them that my flight had been delayed. These thoughts comforted me. They were a fitting conclusion to this chaotic episode in my life. I felt like Dorothy returning from a bizarre trip to Oz, as we began our final approach into LAX. There was a huge sense of relief as the wheels of the huge craft touched down, firmly and confidently.

"It's all over, Bob!" I turned to my new friend with great sense of relief. Bob, unfortunately, would be required to take the next flight back to Mexico City. I realized that he had been assigned to be my "babysitter", but nonetheless, I thanked him for his assistance as I started to let go, relax and try and find my confidence in believing that the worst might be over. I still had to wait for all the passengers to deplane, allowing me with my handicap to be the last to exit. Then I heard it.

"Welcome home, Edmundo!" The shrill voice was all too familiar. Shana, my flight attendant supervisor, boarded the aircraft and informed me that she was in charge of reuniting the "little hero" with his family. Whatever optimism and hope I had upon landing were snatched away. The game continued and now, despite all my survivor skills, I was once again reduced to a kindergarten youngster: one who was too deflated to make any attempt to correct the mispronunciation of my name. The last thing I wanted at this point was an in-depth personal conversation with Shana James, so let it be Edmundo as long as I was able to reunite with my family as quickly as possible.

A gate agent who accompanied Shana on board explained that because of the number of press in the terminal area, Customs had agreed to clear me while I was still on the aircraft. Shana had brought her vehicle alongside the jet. I hate to admit it but at that moment I wished for nothing more than to remain in the cabin of the jet. I wanted to go back to Mexico City with Bob Collins.

"Okay, let's get there." I resolved to push my body and endure the pain so I could quickly end this portion of my macabre adventure as rapidly as possible. The Government documents were secured, and I was assisted down the jetway stairs to a small dark sedan, a bit sporty for Shana.

"The company contacted your family," Shana said, "and we arranged for all of them to be at your home in Manhattan Beach." I felt a sense of relief since the journey would be short, but it lasted only for a moment. Shana seemed nervous traveling on the Pacific Coast Hwy for she continually glanced into her rear-view mirror. She suddenly swerved the car down a side street, stopping and turning off the head lights.

"A black car is following us." Or so she imagined. I wanted to pull my hair out by the roots as this experience was becoming torturous. All I wanted was to be reunited with the people I love, who truly cared for me my safe keeping.

All at once a premonition came to me. I saw myself arriving at my home and being joyously greeted by my mother. My deepest desire upon arriving was to forget my terrible experience, and to just relax in my own home surrounded by my family. With good intentions, my weeping mother would show basic Mexican courtesy; she would invite Shana to come into the house and join our gathering.

How can I get word to my family and tell them that I simply wished to be alone with them, that the last thing I want is to have a representative of the company there, sitting and watching us share our deepest emotions?

"Well Edmundo, I think we dodged the press," Shana said with relief. I panicked as she started up the car once more.

"I've got to warn my mother," I repeated the words silently over and over. I struggled to contrive a plan. We would arrive at my home, I would exit the vehicle, gather my things and stand on the curb to thank Shana for the ride. I'd try to force her away before entering the house. That is how I wanted it all to play out but deep inside I already knew that it wouldn't. As the little sports car turned onto Rosecrans Blvd. the tension became unbearable. From a distance I could see a small crowd mingling in front of my home. Shana parked right where they all stood waiting. Both my mother and my sister, Alicia hurried to the passenger side before I could even open the door, my mother crying uncontrollably as she hurried to hug her son, a child she thought she had lost. I struggled to reach for her as the pain shot up my leg.

"Mom! Mom!"

"Eddy, are you okay, mijo?" Both she and my sister frantically embraced me at once, then sized me up to make sure I was indeed in one piece.

"I'm fine, Mom. Listen, please listen," I begged her. Suddenly there stood Shana right next to me, next to us. She had removed my belongings and held my crutches in a picturesque display of virtuous assistance. There was a moment of silence as I spotted my father, my brother Mike, my sister-in-law Connie, Tommy and my three-year-old niece Jennifer, just a few feet away. "Ah, everybody, this is Shana James, my flight attendant supervisor," I stated a bit awkwardly. Then it happened. My mother stepped forward to introduce herself and shake Shana's hand.

"Thank you for bringing my son home to us. *Would you like to come inside and join us?*" Shana became giddy like a little schoolgirl.

"Certainly Mrs. Valenciana, I 'd be delighted." It was inevitable. What could I have done? It was twisted fate once again. My mother led Shana into my home, our home. I embraced my brother Mike. Tommy and my father smiled but seemed to be keeping a bit of a distance. Then I realized they were just in awe of my good fortune, my ability to survive this tragedy. Mike opened a bottle of his special wine from Spain, Diamante, that he kept in reserve for special occasions. He decided that this was certainly one of those times.

Everyone began smiling, laughing, the tension alleviated by the fact that I seemed to be physically okay. Yes, I was injured in the accident and Chavez did not help my situation, but all-in-all my wounds were seen as minor in comparison to the overwhelming carnage displayed for all to see on the television screen. There it was again in glorious color and my eyes were immediately drawn to it. Everyone noticed my physical injuries, but no one could fathom the emotional toll. Mike recommended more wine. I glanced over at Shana who was intrigued with all of this, taking it all in. Up to this point she probably didn't know me from any other F/A in the company, and now she was fascinated, taking mental notes of my personal life. The life of a "hero." I wanted to scream but shame has a way of bringing you to your knees. My friends were dead, any one of their family members and friends would endure a litany of outsiders just to have another hour or minute with their loved one. I began to cry as I hobbled over to first hug my mother, then my sister once again. I continued on to embrace my father in a sincere abrazo and received a high five from Tommy. The men drank more wine and settled down, a celebration of beating the odds and depriving Death of his quarry. But still I remained leery of Shana.

The television projected the image of what was left of our DC-10 on the tarmac of the airport that was now thousands of miles away. The room fell silent as a reporter expressed the grim tally of the dead. "Only a few survivors have been reported," the analyst stated as the video brought the point home to millions of Americans across the country.

"Such a terrible tragedy," was another phrase I picked up on as I tried to turn off my mind. A company Vice-President appeared on the screen from LAX, reminding the viewers that this was our airline's first accident in the last thirty-five years of service. How ironic, I thought as I began to laugh. Some in the room stood open-mouthed as they did not understand what I found so amusing. I was convinced that the loyal executive had taken this opportunity to deliver a commercial message to the public.

"Yes, fly our airline, we won't have another such disaster for another thirty-five years!" How seriously had I been affected by this tragedy? I am sure everyone in the room began to wonder. Tommy immediately rushed to me and joined in on some laughter as we continued to drink the Spanish wine uncorked for the occasion.

"I was really surprised that you called me after the plane crash," Tommy whispered in my ear.

"Why is that?" I asked him.

"Because people don't ever call anyone again after they have been in a plane crash." The wily mathematician smiled broadly, trying to interject some humor into the conversation. The reality of this whole affair, of course, was too ridiculous to look at logically. Shana joined our conversation.

"It must have been a terrible experience, Edmundo?"

"Ah yes, Shana, it *is* quite an ordeal."

Suddenly my niece Jennifer began sobbing. My mother and sister instantly rose to console her. I thought about the other families, those that were not as fortunate as mine. I imagined the weeping and the screaming that was filling the rooms of their homes. Frustrated once again, I grabbed my crutches and made my way to the outside porch. I needed a breath of fresh air and to escape Shana's prying questions which my mother seemed willing to answer. My mother quickly shut off the television, assuming the report had upset Jennifer and me. I gazed back at Tommy and my father who remained silent. I could see in their eyes that they knew. They supposed that I was plain old Eddy who, by some bizarre set of circumstances, found himself wrapped up in one big shitty mess. Certainly, they were happy that I had survived but did not have to treat me any differently or walk about on egg shells, afraid to upset me.

It was late in the night when my father joined me outside. We both stood in silence as the cool autumn air quietly flowed across our brows.

"Hey Dad, remember "Hollywood," the old veterano who used to hang out at the corner store in the old neighborhood?" I had no idea why I had thought about the old weathered Mexican man from the days of my childhood.

"Yeah, what about him?" My father responded, surprised by my inquiry.

"Why did they call him Hollywood?" He thought for a second then answered.

"Well, he spent so much time on that corner, most of it drunk, that we figured he was hanging out waiting to be discovered by Hollywood." I was experiencing a side of my father I had not seen too often. The opinionated senior engineer who worked at Lockheed Aircraft was very familiar with the workings and flaws of commercial air travel. He seemed in awe of what had occurred to his son who had survived somehow and from that day seemed much closer to me. I was extremely grateful for that gift.

"Oh Edmundo?" Shana chirped, beckoning me inside. My brother Mike whispered,

"Hey Ed, you want me to choke her out?" Mike was feeling the wine. The image of his suggestion made me laugh. I began to wonder if I was being too harsh on Shana since she had never really caused me any trouble. Maybe the career airline woman was just trying to fulfill her duties as a supervisor. Is not that what they are supposed to do, supervise?

"You are being rude," the inner voices scolded me.

"What about your work, your job, Eddy?" A mother never stops worrying about her children. "Your position, your injuries, will this be taken care of?" Shana stood up and walked over to my concerned mother. As the official airline representative, she spoke up with confidence.

"There, there Mrs. Valenciana, I'm sure we can arrange to get Edmundo a couple of weeks off work." The statement was expressed with such conviction. Tommy stared in disbelief. Someone sure had little appreciation for what I had just been through.

"¿Mijo, por qué esta tonta piensa su nombre es diferente?" Alicia Sr. had enough. My mother was annoyed at the supervisor's continued mispronunciation of her son's name. I looked up at a gold-tone wall clock, Pacific Coast Time indicating three minutes to midnight. It was still All Souls Day, November 2, leaving just seconds for the faithful to pray for the release of their loved ones' souls from the torment of Purgatory. I shuddered and bowed my head for I desperately wanted someone to pray for me. I realized that my journey through Purgatory had barely begun.

Chapter XI

Will I ever be good enough? The words taunted me. I recognized the sobbing of a young child. I rushed forward into the rubble in desperation and discovered a filthy, tattered Javier, his clothing ripped and filled with soot. The smell of jet fuel filled the air but initially all seemed calm, for there was no fire to be seen or felt. I was in the midst of the crash site but it was devoid of activity, as if the disaster had occurred long ago. I grabbed hold of the desperate child and lifted him, holding him close as I gazed about in confusion.

"Where are the others?" the small boy asked.

"I don't know mijo." Javier fearfully looked about wide-eyed with growing concern, then looked around the rubble.

"Have they left me behind, alone?"

"No, Javier, they also left me."

"But you were supposed to live, remember?" Javier's words shocked me. I asked how he knew such a thing. Suddenly the young boy turned his head revealing the brazen, blanched, bone face of Muerto.

"I don't want to live!" I cried aloud as I awakened the morning of November 3rd, drenched in sweat. I was indeed in my own bed, in my own house. Immediately the grief gripped me as I tried to control my emotions. I struggled to shower and made make myself presentable for the visitors who'd soon be arriving.

"Bonehead!" David J. Brooks' specific greeting reflected our high school days where, like my friend Tommy Acoba, we had endured the pressures forced on us at the all-boys Catholic institution run by the Irish Christian Brothers. "You don't look too bad for what I read you went through." The now-renowned attorney was a graduate of the University of Southern California Law School and I was so grateful that he and his dear wife Kathy were gracious enough to pay me a visit. But Dave soon recognized that I found it difficult to be jovial. Pulling out his yellow legal pad he made it clear he was ready to assist me in any way.

"It was a mess." I tried to find words to explain but failed. Kathy's eyes expressed her emotions. She was an agent for a competitor airline. One company loses a plane and the pain is felt throughout the industry. "What kind of legal scrutiny will I face?"

"There is very little information coming out of Mexico City at this point but don't worry about it, we will take it a step at a time."

"What rights do I have?" Dave thought about my question.

"I will review the contract the airline has with your union."

"What alternatives are available to me in the complexities of international law?" My friend scribbled rapidly upon his pad. "What kind of protection is at my disposal, if any?"

"Do you need protection?" Dave put the pad down as I related my experience with Comandante Chávez.

"It is definitely the responsibility of the airline to protect you and see to your injuries," Dave stated. I wished someone had reminded the airline of this *before* Chávez found me. Then there was the question of liabilities and possible financial compensation. "As an employee your options in this regard are limited." My good friend was being honest. "If your injuries are severe enough you could apply for workman's compensation." David continued, "If, a thorough investigation was conducted and it was determined that the crash was due to an extreme case of negligence on the part of the airline, then you might have a case."

I certainly valued David's counsel for it was evident that I was soon to be thrust into a legal hornet's nest. I already knew that any official investigation would be far from thorough and besides, any compensation was not even on my radar. Still, it was important that I be keenly aware of all my options.

It was common for airline crash investigations to go on for months, even years before a determination of fault would be announced, and that is when the investigation is done correctly by reputable institutions and agencies. The Mexican Government was directing this investigation and few Americans were invited to participate. The only word filtering out was that it was pilot error and that the cockpit crew were drunk, which made me distraught about the immediate future.

"Listen, the main thing is that you have your leg evaluated by an expert physician as soon as possible," David stated. "Tell your superiors what you need, work with them and if you need me to call them let me know." I felt a sense of confidence knowing I had David on my side. As he and Kathy were ready to depart, I recalled that my vehicle was still in the company's parking lot.

"How about giving me a ride to LAX?" My dear friends graciously agreed. Besides retrieving my car, I thought to speak to someone in authority at the executive offices about getting my leg checked out by a knowledgeable physician.

The scene seemed surreal as I slowly approached on crutches the company's headquarters along Avion Drive. From the flag being lowered to half-mast to the expressions on employees' faces, it was clear that the tragedy of 2605 had shaken everyone. Certainly no one ever would think that the young man moving about at a snail's pace through the hallway was in any way related to what weighed so heavily on their minds.

My first duty was to work my way to Barbara's office at Flight Attendant Training. As I entered her eyes widened as if she had seen a ghost. She screamed and rushed to hug me.

"You trained me well Barb." Others had heard the noise and rushed into the waiting area. Word soon spread like wildfire as employees began to realize who I was.

"Are you okay?" Barbara's concern was genuine. The others tried to move closer to get a glimpse of the survivor, the "little hero." I felt embarrassed, unworthy of their attention, so I tried to make conversation. I showed Barbara the laceration I had received on my wrist when my regulation watch had been ripped away during the violence of the crash. Once free from the wreckage I noticed the injury, but my watch was gone. For some reason word of this made its way around the system.

"Are you going to the meeting?" another of my former instructors inquired. I was puzzled, unaware that any type of meeting had been organized. A familiar face now entered the flight attendant training center. Caitlyn was a senior F/A whom I had flown with on numerous occasions. The short, attractive crew member fought back tears as she slowly approached to hug me.

"Oh, that poor crew," she whispered. "Dear Reina, she knew! We had always talked about it and she knew." I backed off a bit and looked around hoping that the others in the room had not heard her words.

"Listen Caitlyn, we need to keep Reina's premonitions to ourselves for the moment," I pleaded. "Others, especially in management, might not understand." I looked intently at her to see if she understood what I was asking. Still tearful, she nodded in approval. "We need to talk later when we are alone," I whispered. Caitlyn wiped her face and seemed to understand.

Suddenly a smartly dressed company man entered the office, Mr. someone-or-other, asking if he could speak with me alone for a moment. I politely accompanied him into the hallway.

"Were there any infants on the flight, do you recall?" Apparently, a lawyer, he asked the question while looking at me intently. I was caught by surprise as I tried to instantly recall the chaotic scene of that Halloween morning. I wanted to say, "Yeah, Karen Smitt was just twenty years old and her life was snuffed out in an instant," but I bit my tongue instead. I hesitated, then simply shrugged my shoulders and shook my head. He thanked me and was off down the hallway.

I stood wracking my brain trying to recall if I had seen an infant on the flight. All at once I felt an arm on my shoulder. It was Barbara guided me into the crowd of people moving through the hallway, then down the stairs to the employee cafeteria where I was surrounded by people and voices, heads turning to look at me. I became dizzy and frightened. Barbara, her staff and I continued on to the large hangar.

"I want to thank you associates for attending this vital meeting today, a display of your support during this troubled time." I heard a familiar voice, then was surprised to see an exhausted looking Daisy Ackley, our Manager of In-Flight Services, standing at the microphone on a small stage erected at one end. I guessed she had returned from Mexico City for this meeting. She was trying to get the attention of the employees, many who were weeping and seeking comfort in each other's embrace. Several of the associates I recognized, others I did not. All were anticipating, of course, new information. Certainly, the headlines of pilot error could and would be corrected.

Daisy began by introducing the other individuals who were seated upon the stage, a team of psychologists. I felt that was a good move on behalf of the company, considering the traumatized individuals I had encountered in the last couple of days. The overwhelming consequences of this cataclysm were bound to push some people over the edge. "I certainly will not allow myself to be such a victim," I whispered to myself.

"The airline is making help available to everyone," Daisy stated. "This type of assistance is unprecedented in the industry." Ackley then yielded the microphone to a female psychologist who extended an invitation to any associate needing aid to speak with her or her colleagues at the conclusion of the rally. The tall woman then looked over to our side of the stage, then directly at Barbara and me.

"As most of you know, there were two crew members who survived this terrible crash and one of them is here today. I would like to ask Edmundo Valenzuela to please come up and say a few words." The professional therapist stopped, turned towards me, and extended her hand. I thought I was going to pass out on the spot. I felt panic and turned to Barbara and her staff who were vigorously clapping their approval. Barb gave a positive nod urging me forward. I struggled with my crutches but was quickly assisted by those close to me in the crowd who carefully tried to guide me to the front. All at once I froze.

"¡Globos! Balloons! Ice Cream! ¡Fruta fresca!" Suddenly among the crowd in the hangar I saw the same Mexican vendors that had been so prominent at the site of the crash. Muerto had decided to bring his carnival into the hangar. I envisioned his menacing figure boldly walking through the crowd and selecting a seat in the front row. I saw him applauding with great enthusiasm, then casually sitting back to enjoy the rest of the show.

"Go ahead, Ed," Barbara was trying to encourage me. I turned back to see friends motioning me to go forward. Hesitant and confused, I slowly approached the psychologist, leaned toward her and whispered,

"It's Eduardo, Eduardo Valenciana."

"What? Oh, Eduardo Valenzuela!" She announced once more. Once the applause had subsided that hangar got real quiet really fast.

"You're not worthy to be alive!" Muerto jumped up and hurled his insults. I just stood with my head down. Ackley desperately wanted to keep the momentum going so she leaped to her feet and joined me at the microphone.

"Is it safe to fly Mexico?" A voice shouted from the audience as an attractive dark-haired lady in uniform stood up. I looked long and hard at her, for in my mind I could almost believe it was Reina. Ackley immediately chimed in.

"Is it safe? Let me reassure everyone. All systems are functioning and working normally. In fact, our Senior Vice-President, Mr. Mckay has traveled to Mexico City himself. But let's hear first-hand from the gentleman we are so happy to see joining us today." Ackley turned to me, their wounded little hero, as I stood frozen and hunched. I tried to clear my throat, then anger began to wash over me.

What in the hell am I supposed to say? I thought as I gazed out over this sea of anticipation. I stared in silence thinking, *What do you want to hear, people? That our best captain slammed his god-damn jumbo jet into solid concrete, and we all cried and suffered and burned and died? Yes! We all died! And they took the damn left landing gear as a trophy.* I was barely managing to control myself.

"Go ahead, say something." Ackley brought me to.

"Take care of yourselves, you are your own best friend," I warned.

In that moment I thought hard about who I could really trust: certainly not the Mexican government, and where really did the airline's interest lie? I knew Ackley and I truly trusted Jack McKay, but that made only two people in the corporate hierarchy.

You can't afford to trust anybody, was the message I <u>wanted</u> to share. But instead I said, "Care about yourself, I guess that is all I have to say." I tried to keep it short. All at once there was a roar of approval. For those gathered on the morning of November 3 the whole affair was personal. I would have previously believed that our airline would, under no circumstances, allow us to ever fall in harm's way. Looking over the crowd I began to cry. Was my beloved airline doing all it could in offering assistance to the associates? Would we be manipulated? I believed the truth lay somewhere in the middle. I determined it was the Mexican Government who so far was in the driver's seat. But weren't we all supposed to be cooperating partners as the Mexican minister had firmly suggested? It was all so confusing, and I was so angry.

Daisy Ackley did not miss a beat after hearing my soft-spoken words, quickly grabbing the microphone.

"Just like Eduardo said, you all have to take care of yourselves. Be strong. You should not call off assigned flights because of groundless fear. We need to unite and help our airline of which you are all a vital part."

"Stand and unite. Unity! Unity! Unity! The chant went up and I stood in disbelief. Totally defeated, I hobbled to the side of the stage. I sat in a fog for the rest of the meeting. At its conclusion Ackley thanked everyone for coming and encouraged them to stay strong. Both her and the female psychologist seemed very pleased with the results of the first of what I would later learn were many such planned meetings. Grabbing my crutches, I was helped down to the floor where Shana was one of the first to approach me, giggling and greeting me with a kiss on the cheek.

"Oh, Edmundo! I can't believe all this time I thought your name was Jose. Are you okay, is everything okay?" She looked closely at my legs.

"Believe me Shana, it's okay. Nothing could really faze me at this moment."

"And it was so nice meeting all your family. But I just want to make sure everything is okay. Is it? Okay I mean?" I could not fault her sincerity, but it was all way too much. I so wanted to escape the well-wishers who surrounded us and made me feel uneasy. Shana continued as more people gathered. "Oh, I almost forgot. This invitation is from Mr. Reddick, our CEO. He would like to meet with you tomorrow at 12:30. Can I tell him you'll be there?" She handed me an envelope.

"I'll be there." I hoped to shorten this madness.

"Great! Oh, by the way, we're all so proud of you, especially for saving those school children." I looked at her in wide-eyed disbelief and chuckled.

"Shana, that never happened." My spirited F/A supervisor hesitated, then gave a wide grin.

"Yes, it did," she insisted, "I read it in the newspaper." In an instant she was gone.

"Hi, Eddy, you don't know me but..." The greetings came from all sides. Although sincere and of good intention, it was all happening too quickly and was overwhelming.

Ken Franks approached. He was a well-known First Officer, who had an eye for the ladies. He pulled me aside and whispered something in my ear.

"Shit, I wish the crash had happened to me," he stated firmly while gazing out at the F/As surrounding us. I stood in shock as he continued. "You're gonna get all kinds of pussy," flyboy Ken assured me with an elbowed to my sore ribs. Then with a wink and a nod he bestowed his approval.

The world had gone mad. I just had to get out of here. I realized that there were only two options my coworkers would accept, hero or crazy man. Yes, I was in real trouble.

Once away from the crowds I was fortunate enough to be surrounded by Barbara and her group. In the midst of conversation, we were joined by Jerry Buntly, a bright and down-to-earth middle manager. It was said that he was influential in convincing the executives to award free passes for training class 2's duration of our initial furlough. He had my respect already.

"Can I speak to you," he asked. "I'm concerned that you haven't received a full physical exam. You might feel fine but what do we know about possible internal injuries?"

"Hugo!" I blurted out. Jerry froze.

"What?"

"Oh nothing, you just reminded me of someone."

We sat in a corner of the employee cafeteria amongst the mechanics, clerical staff, baggage handlers and others based at the company headquarters. Jerry was kind enough to fetch us something to drink.

"What about Skip?" I asked. I had found him in the rubble, his ankle shattered.

"You know, Eduardo, a decision had to be made. The surgery on his leg in Mexico was minimal. The family decided to gamble on returning him to Los Angeles, seeking the best of care. They filled him with scotch, then set up a special rig on a 727 by removing three rows of seats. More scotch kept him calm for the 3 1/2-hour flight back home."

"Good job." I was happy for Skip. "Where's he at now?"

"Saint John's Hospital in Santa Monica." For what he had to endure, there was a true "hero" to be found in this mess and his name was Skip Mitchell.

Suddenly everyone around us went silent. Jerry stood up straight and extended his hand as an individual approached.

"Good to see you, Mr. Reddick." I struggled to stand as the CEO of our great airline silently placed his hand firmly upon my shoulder. His tailored-made, double-breasted navy-blue suit was immaculate. The impressive figure simply patted my shoulder then shook my hand.

"Fine job, son," he whispered. He was visibly shaken; his face was ashen. This affair tore at his soul. Then he withdrew, making his way through the associates who continued standing and sitting in silence. If no one in the large cafeteria had known who the handicapped figure in the corner was before, it was now made crystal-clear by Mr. Reddick's appearance.

"You'll never be good enough." The voices in my head taunted me as I wished for nothing more than to crawl away into some black hole. Normal conversation around me began once again.

I glanced at Jerry's reassuring face. He believed in me. He was a good solid guy, just like Hugo.

"Listen, Eduardo, I'd liked to take you to be examined by the same physician the Lakers use. He's right down the road in Inglewood." Of course, he was right. Jerry had already made the arrangements.

"You took one hell of a beating," the doctor stated as he viewed the results of my X-rays. "You are a lucky man, nothing seems broken." Of course, there was no X-ray taken to determine the damage to my soul. The doctor was optimistic.

"With some physical therapy, in a short time you will be as good as new."

"You'll never be good again." I couldn't silence the voices. On the way back to LAX Jerry and I stopped at a local hole in the wall and enjoyed hamburgers and fries. The kind manager made himself available to accommodate me.

"You know, Jerry, not all my injuries were due to the crash." The good man sipped on the straw of his soft drink, pondering what to say.

"I heard there was some difficulty in retrieving you from the Mexicans." He kept his eyes focused on me as he took another bite from his burger. I didn't need to elaborate. He knew.

"Oh, look here." Jerry lay the burger down and reached for the inside pocket of his sport coat. "I heard the story about your watch." He pulled out a slender box. "Accept this as a reminder of how thankful we all are for your survival." Touched by his generosity, I glanced down at the face of the shiny timepiece with its red company logo in the center. I also noticed that the second hand had a silhouette of a DC-10 flying around the ellipse. Unfortunately, it would only be a matter of months before Jerry Buntly would be unceremoniously relieved of his duties at the airline, an act that really pissed me off. But times in the industry were changing.

...

While in flight, the lights of the cities below blend seamlessly with the stars above to create a sensation of continuity. Mexico from high above reveals a diverse terrain. There are tropical forests to the south, a contrast to the barren northern deserts. The gray mountains surrounding Mexico City form a solid background as most flights glide over the dried lakebed. I took my place positioned in the middle of the asphalt of Runway 24-Left at Benito Juárez Airport. Gazing skyward I noticed a distant glow. Slowly the light in the darkness grew into a visible DC-10. The roar of the engines grew louder as her landing lights appeared and focused right on me for, she was on final approach. My excitement grew when I recognized her numbers, NW903. The jumbo jet touched down at the head of the runway and in an instant was airborne once again, rising gracefully. I decided her captain must have called for a missed approach.

"Wait, wait for me!" I cried as I watched it rise into the heavens. Falling to my knees on the paved runway, I turned to find Javier standing in tattered rags a few feet away. I was extremely confused for I believed that we both should have been on that 10 that was now high above the clouds, abandoning us, leaving us behind.

"Will I ever be good enough?" The small Mexican child asked me once again. "Will I?"

I awoke drenched in sweat from what was now becoming a nightly venture into what seemed unholy. But I was thankful at least for the consolation that this nightmare had no screaming, burning bodies. Gaining composure, I suddenly remembered it was the morning of November 4$^{th.}$ and I had a meeting with CEO Reddick. I purposely avoided turning on the television with its sights and sounds emerging from Mexico. I wanted to focus for this meeting. Mario Reddick was an imposing figure and I was not certain I could withstand any probing questions that I was sure he'd be asking. For my own protection I had considered him a potential adversary. What did I know about corporate dealings and decisions? My encounter with the Mexican minister made that clear. If they could lay the blame on an excellent pilot like Carl Herbert, how safe was I if someone determined I might be a liability? I grabbed the last bottle of Diamante, the white wine from Spain my brother Mike cherished, to give as a peace offering to the CEO. As I left, I noticed a large business envelope at my door, probably material from some attorney anxious to speak with me. Now people knew exactly where I lived? If I was apprehensive about my visit with the CEO, the envelope multiplied the feeling times ten.

I stopped at a nearby thrift shop on my way to LAX and traded my clumsy crutches for a fine green cane made of solid wood. With a brisk limp and with the sound of wood striking the marble floor, Eduardo Valenciana made his entrance into the executive domain.

I was escorted into the elegant office to find that Vice President Jack Mckay had returned from Mexico City to update his boss on his progress. I noticed artifacts similar to those I had seen in the Mexican minister's office. There were also photographs of important people and models of all the company's aircraft. A large window revealed the hustling traffic of Century Blvd., and on the sill was a model of the DC-10.

I hobbled forward to shake the CEO's hand and offered him the bottle of wine. Mario Reddick seemed pleased, closely examining the bottle's label.

I turned to greet Jack.

"How you feeling, boy?" the jovial Scotsman was sincere when asking.

"I'm doing just fine, Mr. McKay. You know, yesterday Jerry Buntly took me to be examined by a top physician, so I am very grateful to the company for seeing to my needs." Jack just snickered behind his hand and Mr. Reddick smiled.

"Well, you know Edmundo we are all proud of your behavior in Mexico and we want to be sure that you receive the assistance you need in your recovery," the CEO stated. All the events that occurred during and after the crash: Reina's visions, the scene in the cockpit, the explosions, the fire and my time with the sadistic federal officer had to be put aside for the moment. The little hero, the fellow described in the newspapers, "Edmundo the Magnificent" is who they wanted, the flight attendant who ripped a fuselage with his bare hands. I was sure the company would spare no effort to promote "that" guy, so that is who I decided to give them.

The three of us sat in our fine suits, creating small talk as Reddick inquired how my family was dealing with the tragedy.

I wanted to say "A hell of a lot better than Reina's family." I bit my tongue, not saying what I felt in my heart. "Certainly, they are extremely relieved and very happy at my good fortune," I said, forcing a smile. My eyes then caught the black embroidered cursive initials on the cuffs of the chief's crisp white shirt. Then looking toward the floor I recognized the same monogram on his high-priced dress socks.

"Well, we are pleased to have you back, Edmundo, and I am sure when you are ready you will be happy to continue your career as a respected flight attendant with us." I supposed the CEO was trying to feel me out. Had my involvement in the accident given me any other ideas concerning my future? If so, did any of those ideas conflict with the interest of the company?

"If anything, Mr. Reddick, I assure you I will always be proud to wear the uniform of our great airline." I turned just in time to see Jack McKay grimacing, not wanting to react to all the B.S. Jack knew how I felt about the whole affair. He was the one who coined the phrase, "one big shit" to describe the accident and its aftermath. I hoped I had found favor in Jack's eyes.

Before I knew it our conversation was over. Reddick seemed satisfied with our initial meeting and now had more pressing issues to attend to.

"Nothing is too good for our star team player," he stated as he gazed down at his watch. I rose to thank him, my supposed benefactor.

"One thing more" he said, slightly raising his voice. I realize you have been asked so many questions, Edmundo, but if I may, one report continues to puzzle me. Why were you in the cockpit during the flight, son? And did you see or hear anything that might be considered unusual while there?" Caught by surprise I didn't know what to say. Feeling tense and pressured, I gazed back and forth from Reddick to McKay, then smiled.

"Well sir, I went up to offer the pilots coffee. You know, the all-nighter is quite a grueling flight."

"What about the activities in the cockpit son? Were there any problems?" Reddick put the squeeze on me.

"Gee sir, I am not knowledgeable enough to recognize what may constitute a problem or anything unusual in the flight procedures of the DC-10." That seemed to satisfy him. I was just a harmless, naive flight attendant who was not going to be a problem. Reddick could now turn his attention to more vital issues in this messy situation, namely the Mexican Government.

"Don't worry, Edmundo, you are among friends now." These were the last words from the chief executive's mouth as Jack and I reached the exit door.

"I never doubted that for a second," I murmured as I turned, and along with Jack McKay limped my way out the door into the hallway. I was about to thank Jack and make my departure when he suddenly removed an envelope from his inside coat pocket along with a pack of cigarettes, handing me the envelope as he searched for his lighter. Lighting up, he took a long hard puff.

This aroma was far better than what I had been forced to endure with the foul comandante. Both of us began to relax as we talked.

"You know boy, Public Relations will be giving you a call. The damn media wants to meet you." He chuckled, then became serious. "Listen, Eduardo: man to man, anything you need?" I was grateful that there was someone in the middle of this insanity I felt I could trust.

"No sir, but this verdict of 'pilot error' from the media and Mexico is disturbing."

"The whole thing was one big shit. You'd be better off just forgetting about it boy and try to get on with your life." These were words I did not want to hear, not because it wasn't the right thing to do but I knew I could never rest until I got answers. But I knew he was advising me with my best interest in mind. I was later to discover that Diego and Hugo García had filled McKay in concerning my time in the hands of Comandante Chávez. McKay was no doubt convinced I had nothing to gain by stirring the pot.

"The reality is, laddie, this airline has no choice. A dead man can't put up much of a defense. Plus, Washington is putting on the pressure to settle this thing. God-damn strong arm tactics." I quickly jumped at the statement.

"Washington? What the hell is their interest? Don't they have the responsibility to seek the truth?" Jack reacted to my naivete.

"Come on lad, I know you are far more intelligent than that. The U.S. and Mexico have been struggling for years over a huge natural gas deal that was finally settled. You think Washington wants to raise hell with Portillo because of one airline's loss? Politics' only responsibility is to cover one's ass. But I've still got a few tricks up this old sleeve of mine." I was impressed with McKay's straightforwardness. He did not have to share this blunt reality with me.

"What about the black box, the CVR recording?"

"Still in the hands of Mexico. They've only shared portions of it with us. Hell, two of our investigating pilots were expelled from Mexico. Damn Mexican officials thought they were getting too nosy. Listen lad, I can't tell you what to do. But as you discovered first-hand, they play hard ball down there." McKay attempted to prepare me for what may lie ahead.

"I want to listen to that tape. I'll be honest Mr. McKay; I did witness something in the cockpit." Jack nearly choked.

"Crap! I don't want to hear this. I'm gonna get going, lad." Jack patted me on the shoulder and started to walk away. Turning back he said, "If there is anything I can ever do, I will. What's next on your agenda?"

"There are ten funerals scheduled that I'd like to try to attend. I suppose I'll see you at one or two?" The crusty old fellow just shook his head no.

"Reddick has already assigned Ackley to that duty," he responded "I guess a man must do what a man must do, Eduardo. God bless you son." I stood gazing at my stout friend as he walked down the marble hallway of the executive offices, when suddenly a thought entered my mind.

"Did they ever find the lost landing gear?" McKay never even broke his stride.

"Nope, probably stripped for spare parts by now." He quickly disappeared into his office. So I was correct in my assumption concerning the fate of the missing aircraft limb. Suddenly, I realized I was still holding the long white envelope McKay had put into my hand. Anxiously I looked around, then slowly leaned on the hallway wall. Unfolding its contents, my eyes jumped quickly to the bold letters on the first page, C. Herbert-D. Reimann.

"Oh shit!" Was I being set up? I turned to hurry away but my body began to spasm as I tensed up. I tumbled onto the hard marble floor but somehow managed to get myself back onto my feet. As quickly but as carefully as I could I hobbled down the stairs with the envelope hidden inside my coat pocket. I had to find a different way out so as to avoid passing executive offices. In possession of the white envelope, I finally boarded the employee bus and rode it to terminal five. Once inside I worked my way to the flight crew lounge, carefully moving through the aisles of stacked crew mailboxes. Ahead of me was a group of four female F/As in a tight circle. One blonde was speaking of the latest rumor out of Mexico City.

"I heard that those idiots gave the wrong body to one of the families of a crew member." Suddenly a tall brunette in the group spotted me approaching. It was obvious she recognized me and her facial expression showed it.

"Don't worry ladies, I am not surprised by that news," I stated casually as I hobbled by. Of course, they were afraid I had overheard.

Notices listing the various memorial services for the deceased crew, along with their photos, had been placed on the Flight Attendant Bulletin Board along with individual photos of the crew. A small group of both cabin crew and pilots gathered to study the memo, looking carefully at each name, each face, no doubt grieving while reminiscing happier times together. I hesitated and moved closer, looking over the shoulders of one senior F/A. Fortunately, no one seemed to recognize me. One name in bold print jumped out at me.

"Reina Patricia Torres, funeral service Saint John's Catholic Church, Hacienda Heights, CA." I lowered my head and moved back through the crowd, leaving the airport as quickly as I could.

Upon returning home I reopened the white envelope. Inside was a copy of what was a company document, the disciplinary report involving Capt. Herbert and First Officer Reimann which was dated October 30st, the day our flight left LAX. I was shocked as I read the report, finally getting up to turn on the television and catch up on the latest regarding the crash. To my surprise the wreck of DC-10 NW903 was nowhere to be seen. On November 4, 1979, all television reporting on the crash of flight 2605 ceased. A new crisis had grabbed the attention of the entire world.

Radical Iranian students had surged into the US embassy in Tehran and had taken 52 Americans hostage. Their actions were part of the Iranian Revolution which had overthrown the Shah, an American ally who had ruled the country with an iron fist for over 25 years. Recently, the deposed monarch and his family had been granted asylum, mostly on the claim that he was suffering from a cancer diagnosed as terminal. The radical students now occupying the embassy demanded the return of the Shah while President Carter referred to the hostages as "victims of terror and anarchy."

I knew now that any reporter or investigator with a speck of interest in discovering why my DC-10 crashed had now either left Mexico City or was quickly preparing to leave. Muerto had abruptly changed the rules of the game. Just like that, another grand spectacle now commanded center ring. The Iranian hostage ordeal would be in the spotlight for some time to come. All the vested parties involved in the death of Flight 2605 were given a precious gift that awful day, a distracted media. Only the process of cleaning up the mess remained. I knew that the final verdict would now indeed be "Error de Piloto." There would be no one left to argue the point.

Then I thought of my crewmates, filled with a zeal for life and performing their duties with utmost pride. Were they now all expendable once the political and corporate battles began? These entities could easily sweep this all under the carpet. The press no longer seemed to care about my crew mates because there now was a bigger story: the United States might soon be at war.

"My God, Reina, how did you know?" I was so determined to avoid her at any cost, but now I wanted to know as much as I could about the dark-haired beauty.

Chapter XII

My drive to Saint John's Catholic Church in Hacienda Heights forced me to deal once again with the rapidly growing feelings of guilt inside me. Upon arriving, I limped with my green wooden cane to the front of the gray stone church where friends and family gathered, greeting and consoling one another. I imagined one distinguished gentleman who caught my attention to be an uncle, the elegant lady with him an aunt and various younger faces I imagined to be cousins. Standing unrecognized, I blended into the crowd that awaited the arrival of the black mortuary limousines.

I was able to come out of myself and focus on everything happening at that church. The limos pulled up and I quickly picked out the immediate family members. Señora Torres dressed in black, appearing as any mother would who had just lost her child, devastated. She was assisted by Reina's sister Theresa and her eight grief-stricken brothers whose faces showed that life had been sucked out of them, a complete submission to utter pain. The procession into the church was slow and solemn, and I took a seat in the rear. The interior of St. John's had quickly filled for so many had come to say good-bye to such a lovely flower. In the front of the altar was placed the white glistening casket, surrounded by tall white candles that illuminated Reina's immediate space. I found the flickering flames to be soothing. How ironic.

My time with Reina had been limited to so few hours. She lay in the casket now and her absence was reflected on each face. Soon the priest appeared on the marble steps of the altar, a beautiful stained-glass window behind him. Bright blue rays filtered through, crossed the altar and came to rest on the casket. The priest stood straight and firm yet could not hide his anguish. His was a heavy heart for Reina had been very active in this church. I began to wonder how the priest was going to try to convince those in attendance not to question the actions of this supposedly all-merciful God? His eyes betrayed him. He was not coming to grips with it any more than the rest of us.

The organist interpreted the grief that filled the house of worship as the "Ave María" echoed throughout. Suddenly, two young ladies carrying candles slowly walked down the central aisle toward the casket. There was something very familiar about them.

"Cary Diller! Tamlyn Baily!" I wanted to scream out their names but in the very next moment remembered they too had perished. I cursed this mad roller coaster of emotions, and the tricks my mind was playing on me. Was this just an awful dream from which I would soon awaken? I became very frightened and began to regret my decision to attend the service.

"Nothing involving Reina could ever hurt you." A soothing voice began to settle me. The words of the priest were elegant and heartfelt, but I continually allowed my anger to overshadow his call for acceptance and faith.

"Don't you understand the circumstances that got us here in the first place?" The sinister voices again. I bit my tongue and glanced up just in time to see Señora Torres rise and approach the altar. She fell upon her daughter's casket.

"Oh dear God, my son, my dear son." But I was hearing *my* mother's voice. It became very clear, I was getting a glimpse of what could have been, perhaps should have been, my own funeral. That poor woman lying across the coffin of her precious child could well have been my own mother.

"You belong dead." Death's inner voice spun a crafty web.

I can barely remember the rest of the service: the eulogy, smell of incense, final hymn. We slowly filed out of the rear of the church. My head was spinning when I spotted Daisy Ackley who hurried towards me. The wear and tear of this whole ordeal could be seen in her face. She hugged me tightly.

"You okay?" I simply nodded as she turned to view the mourners. Neither of us spoke as we silently sympathized with the wounded. Finally, without turning to face me, my superior spoke. "Eddy, you know that the last associates meeting went so well. Would it be possible... I mean... would you like to participate at this afternoon's employee meeting?"

"Well, I don't know." I was disoriented as I tried to envision what she was asking of me. My anger was at a peak now and I wanted to scream out, "Screw you! This damn company is signing a pact with the Devil for which my poor friends paid the ultimate price." That is what I *wanted* to say. But deep down I knew I had just wanted the truth, the cold facts.

"Certainly Daisy, what time do you want me there?"

...

The long procession of vehicles crawled up the rose-filled cemetery incline, stopping at a peaceful little knoll near the top of the hill. All had been prepared in advance. The fake grass carpet lay on the barren dirt, white folding chairs were neatly lined for the immediate family. I lingered behind but noticed that none of the company's representatives who had attended the funeral were at the burial site. The business of running a major airline had to continue.

What had been a sun-filled morning now slowly turned to gray. Señora Torres, assisted by daughter Theresa and "Los Ocho Hermanos" (the eight brothers), carefully took their positions in the front row just feet from Reina's casket. The many in attendance seemed confused about exactly what they should do. Among them were a few F/As who were based at LAX, friends of Reina. Once the coffin was properly adjusted above the grave site the mortician and cemetery director nodded and backed away.

A Hispanic man stepped forward to take charge of the proceedings, his face tortured by stress and pain. He was her uncle, wearing a white, long-sleeve dress shirt with his tie now removed. Standing alongside the coffin he steadied himself and began to speak in Spanish. He spoke about a love like there never was, nor would ever be again for this family. I knew for sure their lives would never be the same. He described the elegance that was Reina and her desire since childhood to fly into the heavens as a flight attendant. All at once he could speak no more. He broke down and another, younger man stepped forward to take over. I learned that this new voice was from one who had hoped to be Reina's husband, the love she would never have.

I recalled the final moments of flight 2605. I imagined how all of Reina's family and friends had their lives altered in that short span of time. I wondered how those final few seconds of that clock were going to affect my life.

The grief-stricken man removed an envelope from his inside coat pocket, opened it, and unfolded a sheet of white paper. It was a letter written in Reina's own hand and he began to read her words.

"Please do not be sad for I will be happy learning new and remarkable things." Reina Patricia Torres requested that a small tree be planted at her burial site so she might be part of life once more in an alternate form. I could barely believe what I was hearing. Those in attendance could no longer remain stoic as the flood gates were released with collective weeping. Her flight attendant wings were embedded into her head stone with the following words:

"She now has wings of her own," were the final words of her heart-broken boyfriend. Suddenly a light drizzle began as if heaven itself expressed its sorrow. As the casket was being readied to be lowered into the earth, Señora Torres could no longer restrain herself. The tortured woman fell to her knees and reached out as if trying to stop the casket from disappearing. "Mi hija, por amor de Dios." She reached out for her child, her baby that was now dead.

"There but for another name kneels my mother." My anger quickly returned. I wanted to rage at the company, the Mexican Government, everyone who I believed had played a role in creating this cruel scene I was witnessing. Unlike the others that wept standing on the lush green hillside, unlike those who had no idea why their lovely little flower had to die, I knew better. They would probably assume that time and a proper investigation would enlighten them at some point. I was already convinced that day would never come if no one challenged the lies, the cover-up. By Reina's grave I swore that regardless of how long it would take and how much the cost, I would return to this site one day and present her with the whole truth.

The Catholic priest stepped forward to lead the crowd in a final prayer and all heads bowed except mine. If the Lord in heaven was not going to seek justice for this cruelty, then I would.

The uncle signaled the cemetery's director to dismiss the ground workers. The Torres family would see their loved one to the end. The brothers each stepped forward to grab a spade and approached the pile of fresh soil they would lay to rest upon their sister's casket. As they were doing some people began to back away, turn, and slowly walk to their cars. I remained, for I wanted to take in the whole affair. The thought that all of this could have easily been my own funeral continued to grip me. My crewmates were sacrificial lambs and I began to embrace the hatred that festered inside me. I wanted vengeance and I saw my anger and rage as perhaps the tool I needed to accomplish it.

Off to one side I could see Reina's youngest brother, a boy about eleven years. He struggled with his shovel as his brothers worked more easily. The boy would never grow up with his sister, never be blessed by the wisdom of her words, never feel her compassion. He would never be a beloved uncle to her children. She would remain forever young, a memory of elegance that in itself could be comforting yet would always be overshadowed by her loss. I slowly removed my coat and stepped forward to assist the boy as I gazed down at my crew-mate's coffin below. To the side knelt Señora Torres. Where was this merciful God? He was painfully absent. I resented God for allowing this wonderful family to suffer needlessly!

Surely there was more to be learned about Reina from those that loved her. But now wasn't the time. I decided that from that moment I was never going to contact them until I fully understood the circumstances that caused Reina's death.

Exhausted by the shoveling, I started to put my coat back on. I noticed that I was being stared at by Señora Torres and her eldest son, most likely wondering who the heck I was. Should I have approached them and introduced myself? Perhaps, but I just couldn't.

I had already committed to attend as many of my crew-mate's funerals as possible. Muerto wanted me to suffer more.

"Why you?" A grieving mother inquired at one of the services. Yes, I, too, wondered why I was spared instead. There I stood embarrassed facing her, not knowing what to say. Did she really think I had the answer? Unable to at least acknowledge my good fortune, she simply turned and walked away.

A female flight attendant at one of the employee meetings suggested that perhaps I was spared so I could be a messenger, the one to bring solace and comfort to their loved ones since I had been the last person to see them alive. This "responsibility" was one that Muerto would not allow me to accept.

I determined that my physical and psychological pain caused by the final impact of the jumbo jet was only surpassed by the sadistic torment at the hands of the evil Comandante Chávez. Yet, I was soon to discover that both ordeals paled in comparison to presenting myself before the parents and loved ones of my fallen crewmates. Muerto loved every minute of it. This soon discouraged me from attending the rest of the funerals.

And then there was Jeff Stillwell. The young man had put all his efforts into trying to secure an airline position and completed training just months prior the ill-fated flight. Tall, bright and handsome like the others, he could easily have been the poster child for the saying, "Only the good die young." While in his probationary period Jeff had qualified as a Spanish Speaker, which netted him an amazing $3. extra per flight. But It was truly his ability to connect with people and help them that embodied his true character. Working mostly Mexico-bound flights, Jeff exhibited the excellence that made our airline so popular with the flying public. Jeff also made it a point to visit friends and relatives to let them see how proud he was to wear the F/A uniform.

His mother, Carolina, had raised the boy by herself. She gladly accepted responsibility when an abusive and alcoholic father abandoned them not long after Jeff's birth. The strong woman's perseverance and unconditional love were evident in Jeff's character, he being her only child.

The call to duty had come at mid-day on the 30th of October. Carolina felt uneasy as she helped Jeff ready himself in the upstairs duplex they shared. There certainly was nothing she could put her finger on as the assignment was simply another Mexico-bound flight like most of the previous ones the 23-year-old had been working. Yet, her instinct told her to hug her son not once, not twice, but three separate times, unwilling to let go of him. Jeff was more than happy to humor his precious mother in what he perceived as superfluous concerns. But then she felt compelled to face her son and grab his shoulders.

"You look so handsome in your flight attendant uniform," she said proudly. He smiled shyly. Somehow, Carolina wanted to shield her child, even though he was no longer a toddler. No matter how old, he would always be her child and she loved him unconditionally.

Jeff recently had some car trouble, so Carolina insisted he take hers. There would be no inconvenience since he was due to be back in L.A. the next morning. But she remained uneasy as she stood on the steps of their home in Long Beach, California. Jeff slowly drove down the street as his mother, still feeling some trepidation, watched him turn the corner. In an instant he was gone forever.

Once in the house alone, she could not shake the uneasiness for the rest of the evening. Then she was startled awake in the middle of the night knowing that something was not right. She sat up in her bed and hesitated, then glanced at the clock by her bed. It was just after 3 A.M.

"Jeff should be landing soon in Mexico City," she said to herself. She breathed deeply to relax herself, but it was to no avail. No matter how hard she tried she could not recapture a peaceful sleep again that night. Restless, she decided to get up early and while dressing tried to fill her mind with positive thoughts. It was October 31, Halloween, and she considered baking little treats for when Jeff returned home. She tidied the house, dabbled in the kitchen doing the things a mother does, assuming that her son would be exhausted from the all-night, turn-around trip. He would probably want to nap, resting before attending some Halloween parties with his friends. Her spirits brightened as she remembered past Halloweens and the variety of different costumes he had worn, especially when he was young. That child was now a man, well-respected and loved by all who knew him.

Suddenly there was an urgent banging at her door. She opened it to see her nephew Roger in a state of panic.

"Aunt Carolina, is the TV on?"

Muerto made a house call that fatal morning. It was undeserved and cruel. The television dwelt on the horrific scene, sights no mother should have to witness. Yet, Carolina gathered herself together and waited quietly for the call she knew would come. It came soon, verifying what she already knew in her heart. Her dear son, Jeff Stillwell, the young flight attendant still in his probationary period, had not survived.

Jeff had kindled a friendship with Judy, a flight attendant in the same training class, but she and Jeff had yet to fly together. As fate would have it on the evening of October 30th, she was released from duty and Jeff was selected to work. She spoke fondly of her dear friend:

"He was planning to buy a Honda Prelude and he loved playing his baby-grand piano. We could laugh at silly things and yet have a serious conversation. I think I teased him for dry-cleaning his uniform apron. He was fastidious and always looked great. Most of all I admired the relationship he shared with his mother: theirs was a true link that transcended the usual. The last time I saw Jeff was when he came over to my home for dinner. He observed that even though we had not known each other for very long, it was as though we had known each other forever. Not long after that I joined five other uniformed flight attendants as pallbearers, laying him to rest on a damp hillside in a cemetery close by. We all removed our flight wings, pinned them to our white gloves and set them upon his casket.

Earlier that day, a large crowd of people had gathered at the Catholic church for his memorial mass. His mother emerged from her limousine, looked around at so many crew members in uniform and stated, 'Jeff is so proud.' I'll never forget that statement. She did not say that Jeff would have been proud but that he *is* proud. Sometime later Jeff appeared to me in a dream. I asked him if he was okay. He said he was, that it was great where he was at and he could not wait for the rest of us to get there. I expect Jeff to be on the welcoming committee when my time comes to cross over. God bless him, my dear and wonderful friend. "2Good 2be 4gotten." Jeff bequeathed the love and friendship of his mother to his dear friend Judy and her husband.

Carolina's sacrifice was most significant for Jeff was her entire world. I was honored to meet this wonderful woman. When others would continue to tell me to "let sleeping dogs lie," I would remind them of Carolina and her terrible loss.

At the services I did attend I saw there were no children present. I knew my fellow F/A's but not that intimately. As I had said earlier, I had always sought to stay below the radar of the airline culture. Not one of the fallen flight attendants left a child behind, yet on reflection I realized that they themselves were but children. At 27, I was the oldest of all the cabin crew. The fact that there would be no children to remember them affected me greatly for some reason and as time went on my desire to have a child grew stronger. I fantasized on this issue thinking that I could still travel the world even with children in tow. At this point I decided my life should change direction.

The atmosphere at the company hangar for the second employee meeting seemed far livelier than the previous one. The large gathering was once again made up mostly of anxious crew members. The F/As by now had figured out that they were putting their own asses on the line each and every flight and they wanted greater reassurance. They demanded to know if it was really safe to fly Mexico.

"United, we can overcome." Those were Daisy's words as the psychologist stood behind her, ready to be available for anyone still suffering undue stress. "We are here to help you." But as the rally reached an emotional peak the crowd's attention turned to "Edmundo." It was him the faithful wished to hear.

"My crew-mates on 2605 were fodder for the corporate entities. Hell, right now there are lawyers trying to buy off as many families of the deceased as possible." But Edmundo would never say such a dreadful thing publicly even though it was the truth. No, I had memorized words that would go over well with the executives. I spoke of the quality of character that my flight-mates displayed, then proceeded to shame my own by preaching the message of unity in support our grand airline. I would have preferred to tell them what I had to go through, how deeply I had been wounded: "Don't trust *anyone*! Protect yourselves from the greedy business interests that are trying to resolve this mess in a way that will only benefit them." But

Edmundo lacked the courage. He performed to the delight of those in attendance and those who oversaw them. At the conclusion, I was once again surrounded by those expressing their appreciation. One excited blond lady spoke up. "God has something special planned for you."

I cringed. The words seemed like poison. They represented a sinister plan that would ensure ultimate failure and despair. Almost everyone I encountered had a different theory as to why I had survived. Any praise for the performance of the harness on my jumpseat at the peak of impact was not what they wished to hear or believe. They wanted a more romantic explanation, and divine intervention was it.

"Hi Eddy, you don't know me but here is my number." It was another perky F/A. If ever you feel you need someone to…." I turned to see if pilot Ken Franks was anywhere nearby. After the event which I took to calling "the dog and pony show," I was escorted to the Office of Public Relations. A female reporter and camera crew awaited to do a story for the local NBC affiliate in Los Angeles. Even though the country was on the brink of war in the Middle East, some producer -- with the company's blessing -- thought it would be interesting to focus on the heroic actions of the airline's brave flight attendant. It was the typical sound bite during which I expressed joy at surviving and remorse for the loss of my friends. I was filmed limping past a DC-10 outside a hangar, while company mechanics just stared.

"I am extremely grateful for all the airline has done for me, seeing to my well-being," I said to the camera. No one was holding a gun to my head, but I was not taking any chances. Edmundo didn't want to be considered a possible liability. The NBC crew thanked me and told me that the piece would be on the local evening news.

Next, I was introduced to a woman reporter from one of Los Angeles' leading newspapers. Right from the start it became evident that the "no-nonsense" woman was not interested in some human-interest story. Keeping a smile and friendly demeanor, I prepared myself for whatever may come.

"Was the flight normal?" She went straight for the jugular.

"I'm sorry but as a flight attendant I do not have the expertise to determine what constitutes 'normal'" or "'abnormal' in the function of the DC-10," I stated with a naive grin upon my face.

"Do you have any idea why the plane crashed?"

"I don't wish to speculate on anything I am not qualified to determine."

"Did you speak with the pilots during the flight?"

"Yes, I did." I turned and could see that the representatives of Public Relations were becoming uneasy as the newspaper reporter saw an opening.

"What was said?"

"I asked them if they wanted their coffee black or with cream and sugar."

"Did you see people die?" The woman would not back off. Suddenly, Edmundo faded into the shadows as Eddy resurfaced inside of me and said, "Yes, I saw people die. I saw people burn and scream. Would you like me to describe the details of severed body parts and my inner thoughts as I saw young boys playing catch with a human hand?" The reporter stopped writing on her yellow legal pad and looked straight at me. "Yes, I saw all those things and more. Now, what good would it do to rehash such specifics? Do you really think this is what your readers want to know?" There was a long silence.

"How does your family feel about your survival?" The reporter got the message. I turned once again and could see the relief on the faces of my company's representatives.

Photos were taken to appear with an account of my actions. Once the interviews concluded I was told to call Daisy Ackley.

"Eduardo, I wish to thank you for your contributions to the employee meetings. You know, the psychologist and I believe that our associates in other base cities would benefit from such a presentation and we were wondering if you would be willing to participate in such an endeavor?" Oh, dear God, the dog and pony show was going on the road. I thanked her and told her that I would need a little time to consider her offer. Having had my fill of the day's events I quickly left the executive offices. Soon I was on the freeway to Santa Monica, to Saint John's Hospital for an anticipated reunion with Skip Mitchell.

Skip's ankle had been greatly damaged, and problems were complicated by the efforts of the medical staff in Mexico City. The beleaguered F/A lay exhausted in the hospital bed. burdened with a large cast on the injured leg. Staring at me he managed to crack a smile.

"What do you remember, Skip?"

"Not much," he replied. "A flash here, debris there and the heat of the fire." I was grateful he was spared my ordeal. Before leaving I shook his hand and was happy for him. We agreed to see each other again soon and drink ourselves silly to celebrate our good fortune.

After leaving Santa Monica I headed to Grunion's Bar in Manhattan Beach where I met up with Tommy Acoba to have a few beers.

"Do you mind if we watch a news report coming on in a bit?" We asked the familiar proprietor.

"Go right ahead," was the reply and Acoba adjusted the television. The NBC broadcast started with the serious events that were occurring in Iran. The condition of the hostages and their well-being was a vital concern of the White House. President Carter would not rule out the use of military action if Tehran refused to release the American citizens. Tommy and I just shook our heads as we both recognized the possible ramifications if such a confrontation was not handled with care. Suddenly, the anchorman announced the piece dealing with the airline survivor. It was done with sensitivity, yet it was the only report that night regarding the crash of flight 2605.

"Why did such an experienced pilot crash his jumbo jet, causing so many to lose their lives? Was he misled by the Mexican Air Traffic Control? Was he misdirected by the Tower at Benito Juárez Airport? Was there a malfunction of the aircraft? Why were there construction trucks on the runway? Was there any information that the airline or the Mexican Government could provide to clarify the reasons for such a tragedy?" No such questions were asked, nor would they ever be again as far as I could determine. The story of the survivor would mark the end of the media's interest as their resources were now occupied in a much more important matter. It played right into the hands of those who desired to conceal the true facts. Again, I felt thoroughly disgusted.

Arriving at home that night I found more envelopes taped to my door. I was right to assume that more legal representatives of the dead and injured had found out where I lived. I shook my head and realized that my future involvement was going to be driven by the almighty dollar. Mexican law limited economic compensation to $70,000 -- a mere pittance in the minds of the "avaricious." Therefore, most of the cases the airline could not "buy off" would be conducted in courtrooms in the United States.

I suddenly noticed that my front door was ajar just a bit. I was sure I had locked the door when I left that morning. As I entered and walked around nothing seemed out of order, but I was becoming paranoid. I went to bed but did not rest easy.

"Why did they leave me behind?" The young Mexican boy asked with a deep desire to understand.

"No Javier, you are not alone. They also left me," I stated, so very much wanting to soothe the child.
The innocent, tear-stained face of the boy turned, and our eyes met.

"Will I ever be good enough?" He seemed filled with uncertainty which perplexed me. The real question should be if *I* would ever be good enough. Muerto had a quick response to that,
"Never!"

I awoke with a terrible anxiety I found hard to dismiss. There was only one solution; the Animal House Gym would be open early in the morning. The hard-core bodybuilders loved to work out with the rising of the sun. Perhaps I could sweat my anxiety out. My body was still extremely sore, but I needed to turn to what consoled me. A good effort at a partial workout would release endorphins to ease my mind.

"There is the luckiest S.O.B.," a future Mr. America yelled as I entered the weight room through the back door. He and a few other athletes present stopped their workouts to greet me graciously. "All those long hours here in the gym paid off, huh?" They reflected on the fact that my condition had played a big part in my survival. I smiled sheepishly but remained silent. I was aware that I was far from healed. Removing my clothing, I caught sight of my image in the large mirror in the old locker room. I focused in on the scabs on my face then closely examined my body.

Both upper thighs were different shades of black and blue. One bruise looked like an ugly plague that crept just below the skin. I had various degrees of deep bruising on my calves and three places on my back. My deltoids had contusions, lacerations and burns. There was a stream of dried blistered skin across my back and my hands had small lacerations and tiny dried blisters. My front torso revealed shades of dark gray and deep blue on both side along my rib cage. The interior of my mouth on one side still exhibited a mark from a blow, courtesy of the comandante. The back of my head was still tender to the touch. Yet, as a whole, I still looked in peak condition, not what you would expect in a plane crash survivor. I completed a workout that morning trying to alleviate the *unseen* injuries in my mind.

Returning home feeling more relaxed, I had a lot of phone messages.

"Hello Mister Valencia, this is Derek Romero. I would appreciate it if you could call me at your convenience." Mr. Romero was an investigator for attorney "A." There was another message from the offices of attorney "B."

"Please contact us during the hours of 8 A.M. and 5 P.M." Then I recognized the voice of Flight Attendant Supervisor Kelly Ryan:

"Ed, please contact me as soon as possible." I immediately called the Supervisor's office.

"What's up, Kelly?"

"Oh Eddy, thank you for returning my call." Kelly seemed upset. "I was the supervisor for Tamlyn Surutan Baily." I was taken by surprise. She never told me. "You see Eddy, I am meeting with Tamlyn's mother and sister this afternoon. They have taken the loss of Tamlyn very badly and I was wondering perhaps if you could come along with me to help the situation." I was a bit confused by the request, but after all, hadn't "Edmundo" agreed to help comfort fellow-workers at the employee meetings?

"Sure, Kelly, I'd be happy to help." I agreed to meet her at Tamlyn's mother's home which was not that far from where I lived.

I knew it would be a difficult situation but felt confident that we could help soothe some of their pain. Arriving at her mother's home I was totally unprepared for the anxiety that consumed Kelly. It turns out she had faced a lot of hostility when she last approached the two ladies.

We entered the comfortable little home naive to the true circumstances. I was introduced but there were no pleasantries. I stood in the middle of Mrs. Surutan's living room and could immediately feel the resentment. I was alive and Tamlyn was not. In the depths of their grief that is all they could understand. They were a mother and sister destroyed by Muerto's handiwork. Both began wailing, which instantly returned me to the burning wreckage on the tarmac of Benito Juárez. Mrs. Surutan's hysteria was mostly expressed in her native tongue while Tamlyn's sister, in English, demanded answers.

"Why did she have to die? What happened? Why did the plane crash?" The weeping sister approached me. "Tell me why?" I stood dumbfounded, unable to speak. Kelly tried to be rational with the mother.

"Mrs. Surutan, please, Eduardo was on the flight with your daughter." The broken woman screamed all the more. Feeling light-headed, I sat on the sofa feeling totally useless in my efforts to provide any sense of comfort. When we could provide no answers, the mother and sister blamed the airline and anyone representing it.

"I don't want you alive, I want Tamlyn alive!" Shouted the grieving sister. Deep inside I sympathized with their reactions. I too shared their frustration, resentment and confusion. It was not long before Kelly found herself completely flustered and overwhelmed, indicating it was time for us to leave. The grieving Surutan ladies finally got control of their emotions and began to apologize.

"I am sorry, so sorry." Mrs. Surutan was genuinely apologetic for her behavior. Hell, I couldn't fault the poor woman. Kelly and I again expressed our condolences and quickly made our exit. The company supervisor presented her own apologies to me once we were out on the street. I assured the shaken woman that there was no need as I fully understood. In reality, I was affected by the encounter much more than I wanted to admit. I recalled my last conversation with Tamlyn in the cabin of the jumbo jet.

"I am getting out of flying, Eddy. My mother is afraid."

"Of what, a crash?" The words were more frightening now considering the scene I had just witnessed. I would later discover that Daisy Ackley laid into Kelly pretty heavy for not consulting with her prior to including me in the visit to the Surutan home.

Returning to Manhattan Beach, I walked along the landmark pier. I stopped and stared out at the ocean. Why? A question that perhaps could never be answered. Like a dog chasing his own tail it seemed like an endless voyage that could only result in madness. Yet, the sinister inner voices compelled me to take that ride. I was losing control. I became almost hypnotized watching the large white seagulls gliding on the wind's current, making their task look so simple.

"Pilot Error." I should just leave this mess the way it stands. I needed to focus on healing and getting on with my new life. Sure, that is what everyone would have done, but doing the logical thing wasn't always my style. I stood for a while facing the ocean breeze and the setting sun, knowing I had to prepare myself for another crew member's funeral. This one was for Cary Diller and would be a service much different than the others.

The Diller family had made it clear that they wished all to participate in a celebration of Cary's life. There would be no shedding of tears, only a heartfelt acknowledgment of the beautiful spirit that was Cary.

"What you doing up here, Mexican?" I remembered her little jest on that flight which managed to bring a smile to my face. Cary had been married for a short time and I recalled how happy she was and how spirited she was in expressing it. I tried to remember the exact words so I might relate them to her loved ones, to share with them how upbeat she was that night.

Entering the Diller home, it was quite evident that they had prepared for a party. There were colorful decorations, snacks available, soft drinks and a whole lot of liquor. The crowd was just getting started as I said hello to familiar faces. Someone informed me that there was a keg of beer in the backyard so that is where I immediately headed. As I drew a plastic cup, a familiar voice shouted from behind.

"Can you believe that there is a crash in Mexico and who in the hell walks out of it but the Mexican?" I turned and was surprised to see Skip Mitchell sitting on a small white chair. He wore gray dress slacks, a long-sleeve white shirt and a maroon tie. The slacks had been altered on his injured leg to accommodate the large, white cast which reached from his ankle to his knee. He dragged on a cigarette and had a sly smile on his face. He felt no pain.

"Dear God," I shouted, "it is so good to see you." There was a party inside the house, but I needed to remain outside with Skip. The quick-thinking survivor hadn't lost his sense of humor and I needed that right now.

I would have the opportunity later in the night to speak to Cary's grieving husband, trying to comfort him as best I could. But I felt so inept at this, and after sharing with him my conversations with Cary, I walked out of the room hoping I had helped him in some way. I wandered through the house, viewing photos and personal items that once belonged to Cary. At times I stopped and imagined I could hear her voice.

"Don't steal anything, Mexican." I chuckled and chose to believe she was happy in her new surroundings, sharing joy with everyone she met. As I turned, I noticed a tall, well-dressed figure coming through the front door. He looked around with a slight smile; it was our V.P., Barry Lane.

"He is one guy who cares about the working man." I recalled those words of so many associates. I pressed forward through the crowd to say hello. Somehow, I was drawn to him.

"Eduardo." He was taken by surprise as he firmly shook my hand then looked around the room again. By this time the memorial for Cary had turned into an all-out party. Flight crews were cruising high on the fuel of alcohol. The music was blaring and flight attendants, all friends of Cary, had abandoned their inhibitions as they danced wildly to the pulsing beat. Some associates raised a yell in memory of their lost friend, a reflection of how well she was loved.

"This gathering seems to be a little more upbeat," Barry Lane observed with some surprise. I stood by his side for some time but remained silent. I was just content to be in his company. I After a while became hypnotized by the festivities and slowly began to wander about. The beer started getting to me as I was being approached by co-workers.

"We're so happy you made it out, Eddy."

"Good job, Ed." I pretended to dance as my body was still too stiff to fully embrace the rhythm. Slowly, the atmosphere and liquor loosened up the rest of the partygoers who otherwise might be shy. A lovely, smiling redhead approached me.

"You don't remember me Eddy but we flew together last year and…" I thought to try and be polite, but an invitation soon followed.

"Hi Eddy." A smiling blonde associate suddenly embraced me in a bear hug.

"Eddy, come over here." I broke loose and tried to limp to the middle of the dance floor. The attention soon began to overwhelm me. A brunette F/A approached me and asked me something, but I claimed I could not hear her because of the music. Most encounters were sincere friends expressing their joy at my good fortune but as the liquor flowed the missives continued. I was not Pilot Ken Franks ready to take advantage. I was still trying to deal with all that happened in the last week.

"You don't deserve to be happy." The voices returned. "You have no right to relish life." I hurried away into another room to be alone, biding my time, leaving when I thought no one would notice.

…

"Will I ever be good enough?" The young child asked this once more, staring and standing in the blazing wreckage. I awoke gasping for air, confused and panicked. I dressed and hobbled out of my house, tossing my cane aside. Trying to find solace, I limped along the Manhattan Beach pier, stopping at intervals to survey the endless blue green of the sea. I followed the waves as the tide and winds shaped them into almost-perfect funnels before collapsing on the beach. I breathed the salt air and was grateful for nature's ability to soothe. I was learning to appreciate it now, recognizing what I had taken for granted prior to the crash. Then, in an instant, I was gripped by so much shame and began to cry. I really did not want to be a part of all of this. At this moment Muerto was standing next to me again.

I glanced down at the water as the light of the sun's rays glistened off a wave and momentarily blinded me. I saw the werewolf, witch and goblin from October 31 approaching on the tarmac. Suddenly the figures stopped as one slowly reached out to touch me, then they were gone. Their presence lasted no more than a few seconds but was as real as the massive ocean that lay before me. Once again things were becoming very complicated.

Returning home, I listened over and over again to messages from investigators and legal representatives wanting to speak with me. I was a wreck and feeling paranoid about being alone. I remembered the slip of paper on the bedroom dresser I had been given by a woman at the company meeting. I made a phone call.

"Hi, this is Eddy."

"I'll be right over," was the only response.

Chapter XIII

Mario Reddick, CEO of the airline, wanted to express his personal condolences to the families of the deceased crew members. The plan was to have the airline host a religious memorial service for all who may have had some connection to the tragedy. St. Anastasia's Catholic Church was chosen, located right beside LAX in nearby Westchester. Daisy contacted me and made it clear that it would be beneficial for all if I was in attendance. She continued, "Have you thought about joining us for the associate meetings at the other bases?" My anger rose again, but I realized I was also to blame. Had not the Magnificent Edmundo been part of the presentation? I certainly wanted to appear as part of the team, but I was also recognizing that such cooperation had consequences. But a refusal would perhaps make it more difficult to get the answers I sorely needed before I could ever heal.

"So much is happening and so fast, Daisy." I wasn't yet ready to commit. "I will speak to you at the company service."

"So, I can rely on you being at the church." Daisy stated.

Arriving at St. Anastasia's for the company memorial service, I was surprised to find the grounds of the church empty. Had I gone to the wrong place? I waited in front of the church, still unsure I wanted to be here.

What good did prayer do for Reina? I recalled the religious periodical upon her lap as she sat in her jumpseat while we descended. Now we were to pray once more. Why? They're already gone! Around five minutes before the service was scheduled to start, everyone seemed to arrive all at once, exiting their vehicles at the same time. Daisy Ackley caught sight of me.

"Certainly, you'll sit with me, won't you, Eddy?"

As I stood in front of this house of worship I hesitated before entering. I studied those around me and began to recognize the faces of the family members of 2605's crew. Since I had attended several of the previous services, I sorted them out and began to wonder why Reddick thought holding *this* memorial was a good idea. I focused on their eyes as they moved about and wondered, did they hope to get some answers today? Was there anger mixed with their sorrow?

Señora Torres entered the church with Reina's brothers, sister, and the uncle who had delivered her eulogy. Feeling guilty for being alive, I wanted to slip out unnoticed.

"May I sit here, Edmundo?" Mario Reddick, dressed immaculately, wanted to share a seat with the survivor.

NO, damn it! Go hang yourself. The words almost came out, but I caught myself and said, "Certainly," as I slid further into the pew. Daisy joined us from the other end. There I remained, stuck in between Mario Reddick and Darling Ackley. How in hell did I end up here? I wish I were dead.

As the service began, selected flight attendants in dress uniform carried lit candles down the central aisle of the church, placing them before the altar and then taking seats in the first row. A finely printed card of remembrance was passed out to all. It said, "To the families and friends of the crew and employees of flight 2605." A poem followed which was titled "God's Calling." I took issue with it. The "black on white" printed card was signed, "The people of our beloved airline." I thought hard about the big brass mingling with the workers in saying farewell. Either by choice or persuasion they were suppressing the truth. But for the moment, I had to remain silent.

You can always count on a priest stuck in the old theology to remind us that in the eyes of God, we are His imperfect, ungrateful children. In a homily lacking in graciousness and void of forgiveness, we were reminded of this Deity's swift judgment upon us. I am sure the sermon did little to soothe the seething anger in the hearts of the stoic family members. I wanted to tear my hair out. When the ordeal was mercifully concluded, the F/As marched out of the first row, up the aisle and out of the church. What remained were the lit candles and the battle lines drawn by the hostile families and friends. Positioned on one side of the house of prayer was management, chatting and socializing. On the opposing side were the destroyed loved ones in total silence, glaring across the aisle with scorn upon their faces.

At the service I discovered that two company ticket agents who were on board 2605 also perished. My guilt returned, shaming me for not being aware of this. They were seated in first class and became Karen's responsibility when we switched stations.

"You worthless piece of shit!" The voices laid into me. I recalled Karen's lovely face. Spotting her mother, I rose to pay my condolences. I had not attended Karen's funeral and felt guilty for that. I never mentioned that she had saved my life by switching stations and was not about to, ever.

"Hello Mrs. Smitt, I was with Karen on the flight that night."

"Did she suffer?" The lady just blurted the words out. I was caught off guard but recovered quickly. Logic told me that Karen was right at the impact point, so I was pretty certain she never knew what hit her. I hoped telling her mother this would give her at least some comfort. Ackley then appeared and mentioned that there were other families she wanted me to meet. The Rollings family had chosen seats right up front. Daisy tried to introduce me but they took little notice. Besides being grief-stricken, they were pissed off, exhibiting downright hatred for the airline. I hadn't expected such silent hostility but sympathized with them. If I had been taken, I would have wanted my brother Mike and my friend Tommy to react in the same manner. I wondered on whose behalf was the service intended. Was this supposed to comfort the families or ease the minds of management?

Once outside the church, the family members began to mingle among themselves, comparing notes and stories. It appears some were told one version of the horrible incident and others a completely different one. I could plainly see what was happening. Yet, Ackley and Reddick seemed unaware of the families' wrath. Perhaps the executives simply did not want to deal with it. In my mind it all just stoked the fires of the madness that seemed to be closing in on me.

Why didn't Reddick just take a knife and slit his wrist? I thought. This memorial service and the way it was planned was really a stupid idea. Then the old priest came out of the church.

"We are locking up now. Everyone will have to vacate the premises." The black robe disappeared back inside as I heard the sound of the lock put in place. Heaven forbid some poor soul would be seeking sanctuary this night.

"Yeah, take your stupid grief elsewhere. What do you think this is, a house of God?" I became twisted once again, unable to deal with the folly of it all. Regaining control, I located Ackley who was becoming aware and concerned with the loud voices of the family members as they vented their frustrations. They were now exchanging phone numbers and promising to keep in touch. I silently wished them luck and tried to remain unnoticed as I did not want them approaching me with questions, at least not at this time. In my quest to find answers I determined that I would be better off working alone. More importantly, I never wanted to be put in the position of having to tell these poor souls the truth on specific matters. I had *some* of the main pieces to this awful puzzle but knew it would take the whole truth to complete the picture.

As I was about to leave the church grounds, I caught the attention of Señora Torres. She had finally realized who the young stranger at her daughter's graveside was. She stared at me intently as she approached me and placed her hands gently upon my face.

"Thank God that you are still alive." The blessing touched my soul but the growing hatred inside, the circumstances that broke this woman's heart, smothered it. It would not be allowed to take seed. I could only bow my head in respect, believing that Senora Torres somehow understood everything fully. Here was a mother in the midst of trying to cope with her own great loss, yet was able to find courage to express genuine happiness to one whose survival she may very well resent.

And where was Reddick? He had left, leaving his subordinates to deal with what remained. My suspicion was that he would begin to sweep this mess under the rug as quickly as possible. He was being assisted by the ongoing Iran-Hostage crisis, which diverted the media's attention for now.

Emotionally exhausted, I drove home down Pacific Coast Hwy., hoping that when I arrived home, I could be alone with my thoughts. Upon entering the front door, I found myself inside a house in shambles. A person or persons had turned my residence upside down. Papers and files from my desk were scattered about. Assuming it was a random break-in, I started to call my brother Mike, but I hesitated, then reconsidered. What if it was related to the crash? Who did this and what were they looking for? Were they lawyers? What if it was the handy work of Chávez? I hung up the phone, for the last thing I needed was to bring more attention to my situation.

Don't be stupid, Eddy. I scolded myself as a chill ran up my spine. It could have been any number of people representing any number of vested interests. I also did not want in any way to involve my immediate family in this mess, especially if this was a result of the vindictive comandante. No matter who the instigators were, I thought my best option would be to get the heck out of Los Angeles.

"Where can I go, who can I call?" I was at a loss. "Kyle!" I remembered my good friend from training. I quickly searched for his number and contacted him in DEN.

"So, what did you do to piss off Mexico?" Kyle knew me all too well.

"What *didn't* I do to piss them off?" I replied.

"Anyone in particular?"

"Yeah, one Comandante Primitivo Chávez De León."

"Who? Even his name sounds ugly."

"You don't want to land in a Mexican prison, Eddy," he warned. I wholeheartedly agreed. I briefly explained the complicated situation. I was confused and unsure as to who broke into my home and was frightened.

"It could even be worse." Kyle stated. "If someone thought you to be a liability or an obstacle in their way, especially if it involved a lot of money, your disappearance could be arranged." Kyle made sense. "Your body could wash up on the beach down the street and people would just say you couldn't handle it." I was dumbfounded but I trusted Kyle. Ackley, Reddick, the media and the voices in my head were all leading me in a bad direction. "Get your ass out of town for a while, Eddy." Kyle's words rang true. "Any place you know where you could disappear for some time?" I was desperate and considered Kyle's suggestion.

"My uncle has a large ranch at Todos Santos on the Pacific side of Baja, across from La Paz. I could blend in there." There was a long silence.

"That's jumping from the pan into the fire, Eddy. If discovered, they could grab you and wouldn't have to answer to anyone." There was another long pause as suddenly something sparked in Kyle's mind. "Listen Eddy, I know a beautiful little island in the Pacific that has a north coast where vehicles can't travel. The only access is by foot and there are secluded valleys where you can hide ten, eleven miles inside. The Na Pali Coast of Kauai is where you need to go."

"I am not exactly fit to hike," I responded.

"Take the trail slow and you should be okay. Besides it beats the alternative, sticking around waiting for who-knows-what."

"Kauai, huh?" I contemplated his suggestion.

"It's the perfect hiding place and the fewer people that know, the better."

I sorely wanted my old life back. But If I needed to isolate myself on an island in the middle of the Pacific to get it back, so be it. I quickly packed my suitcase with hiking clothing, shoes and tools I thought I would need. In the morning I could catch the first flight out to HNL then have to catch a commuter over to Kauai, the Garden Isle as it was called. Across my living room I spotted the sleek glistening knife that was presented to me by Lonnie, my body surfing buddy on Oahu. I grabbed it and buried it deep at the bottom of the suitcase. I also tossed in the documented pilot report McKay had given me. Come early morning I was going to be out of here. The company, lawyers, investigators could all be damned; my priority was survival.

Upon arriving at the flight attendant lounge below Terminal 5 at LAX I discovered that "Edmundo's" mail drawer was stuffed with material. The majority of correspondences were from well-wishers, mostly fellow flight attendants expressing their kind sentiments. One peculiar letter postmarked from Oregon was from what I perceived was a cultist. The gist of the content was that I was some sort of demon, born in the ashes of the fire, and he was quoting verses from the book of Revelation to support his theory. I could not crumble the sheets of paper fast enough but wondered about the possibility of demons within me. Another

272

letter was postmarked Kansas City and was from a woman who begged the survivor for his assistance in curing a serious ailment of her granddaughter. The distraught woman seemed to believe I could use whatever magical powers that saved me to help heal her loved one. There was a proposal of marriage from someone with a Buffalo, New York postmark. There also was a company letter addressed to all associates stating that "the investigation into the crash of Flight 2605 will take time," an official response to the concern of the crew members. Like coins that are lost in in the sands by the seaside, there was little chance of recovering the truth as the inevitable conclusions seemed clear. Yet, I realized that there were those in the company, the pilots especially, who would demand they be told the truth. Ramifications be damned.

While in the flight lounge, I also checked the Flight Benefits Manual to see what options were available for getting me from Honolulu to Kauai. I was relieved to discover Princeville Airways, a small commuter airline which flew the Twin Otter aircraft. They offered airline employees a generous benefit. Upon presenting my airline I.D. at their counter I would be offered a stand-by seat, if available, for the sum of $10. I was ecstatic.

Kyle informed me that the entrance to the Na Pali Coast was at the north end of Highway 56 in Haena. There I would find the start of the Kalalau Trail that snaked its way along the coast and steep mountain terrain for over 11 miles to the secluded Kalalau Valley. This was the perfect isolated location where Kyle was certain no one could find me. The short hop from HNL would deposit me directly at the Princeville Airport where it was even possible for me to rent a vehicle just a short distance from the start of the trail. The plans for my total escape were now well laid and there was one last thing to do as I entered Daisy Ackley's office.

"I'm sorry Daisy but the current events have been overwhelming. I won't be able to join you for the meetings at the other bases." I was pleased but surprised to discover that Daisy was not disappointed by my decision. I also discovered she was incorporating Skip into the program. The wounded F/A was now well enough to travel, and I wholeheartedly agreed with this plan.

"Yeah, take him with you. He'll be great." I was sure the powers-that-be had to find out exactly what he knew. Would he side with the airline or would he pose a problem? After speaking with him for some time both at the hospital and at Cary Diller's memorial, he seemed to have remembered very little. I was happy for him, for my ability to remember was becoming an affliction.

Let him shine in the limelight, I thought. I was now focused on just falling off the face of the earth. I thanked Daisy for all her assistance and informed her that I would be going to visit, local relatives for a few days for some much-needed rest. In reality I had no idea how long I would be gone. My true plans were thrown together in great haste and most likely were inadequate for my needs.

"Passenger Valenciana!" The smiling gate agent called my name as I waited patiently with all the other "non-revs" hoping to get on the HNL bound DC-10.

As we took off, I was lucky no one was seated next to me, which allowed me privacy. Once we leveled off, I immersed myself in the pilot report Jack McKay had given to me. I was intimately introduced to the cockpit crew of Flight 2605.

Carl Herbert Sr., fifty-two, was a U.S. citizen. He had a total flying time of 31,500 hours, 2,248.38 of which were on the DC-10. He held FCC restricted radio operator license No. 11E2770; pilot certification No. ATP 403815 with aircraft multi-engine landing rating: B-707/720 L-88, DC-3, DC-6, DC-7 and DC-10. He had a flight engineer certificate dated February 27, 1971. He had accumulated 28 landings as pilot-in-command into Mexico City, 11 of which were during the month of September and four in October 1979.

The numbers were impressive, but they gave no idea of the humanity of the man or of the family he left behind. I closed my eyes, remembering the night of October 30th.

The priority of an all-night flight for an F/A is to be sure that the coffeemaker is continually brewing. Whether one drinks coffee or not, it is part of the necessary equipment. I recalled standing by the jumbo jet's open door, 2L. Suddenly, a tall figure dressed in a military-style dark blue uniform appeared at the entrance. By the four stripes I recognized him as the captain of our flight. I also noticed that he looked tired but then again, who didn't that night.

"Care for a cup, Captain?" Carl Herbert nodded his head. He remained in the service area for only a second, sipping his black coffee and seemingly without anything specific on his mind. I recalled thinking that he fit the image of a commander whose knowledge and bearing went with the reputation of a seasoned captain.

He had come a long way in the industry and all his achievements were accomplished through his own determination. He was known as a captain who went strictly by the book. Even if there seemed to be an easier way, Carl would do things as he knew they should be done. There had never been a silver spoon in his mouth, no large trust fund or bank account providing the means for his flight training.

Carl was only fourteen when he got the notion to join the National Guard. He was impressed by those military parades on the silver screen during the mid-thirties and especially in the forties after Pearl Harbor. Young Carl lied about his age to join the guard and quit school. Tall for his years, he enlisted and easily fooled his superiors, drilling impressively with the 160th division. The uniform symbolized the respect he desired and commanded, but Carl's mother was not at all delighted. She wanted her son where she felt he belonged. In school! Carl knew, however, that his mother's concerns were sparked more by the fact that his division was about to be activated due to the start of the Second World War. Nevertheless, she got her way.

A determined young Carl did not give up. Discontentment at home led his quitting school again to enlist in the Marine Corps at the age of fifteen-and-a-half. The difference this time was that his mother also lied about his age so he could join the Corps. Herbert was assigned as part of a Marine detachment on the U.S.S. North Carolina, yet the young marine felt frustrated as his first love was a desire to fly. He vowed to pursue his dream at the first available opportunity.

After the war, there was a glut of out-of-work pilots, yet Carl would fulfill his dreams with the same dogged determination he had shown throughout his young life. With the aid of the G.I. Bill, he began training to be a pilot. He would wash planes after-hours in exchange for cockpit time. Once certified, he took flying jobs in which the only payment would be the opportunity to log more flight hours.

After a small stint with Trans World Airlines, he joined our airline. Long years and hard work had raised him not only to the position of Captain but also to that of a well-respected safety-inspector pilot. As Captain Herbert thanked me for the cup of coffee that October night and made his way to the cockpit, one got the feeling our flight was in the best of hands.

Placing the intriguing document down for a moment, I gazed out the window at the vastness of the Pacific Ocean. I began to study the interior of the massive jet and flashed back to the burnt remains of Carl Herbert's last command. It was truly amazing how fragile this masterfully designed aircraft, this great bird of mankind was, when it all began to go so wrong.

I returned to the report and was now introduced to Flight 2605's First Officer. German-born Dieter Reimann, forty-three, had received his initial flight training in the U.S. Air Force. Undergraduate Pilot Training under an agreement by which the United States Air Force trained pilots for the Federal German Air Force. Though based in Los Angeles, Dieter lived in Seattle, Washington. It was his custom to sleep during the afternoon when he was scheduled for an all-night flight. The report went on to state that a Los Angeles Chief Pilot called Dieter the morning of October 30th, the day prior the fateful crash. The superior had issues over a discrepancy report filed by Captain Herbert concerning Dieter's on-duty appearance that month. The words jumped out at me! I put down the report and recalled what I had witnessed. I remembered Second Officer Sam Wells seemed reluctant to open the cockpit door for me when I had presented the proper sequence of coded chimes.

"That's it. That's it damn it!" I again saw Carl's anger directed at the First Officer. I would later discover that it was a known fact among the company's LAX-based pilots that Dieter was in the middle of a rather nasty divorce. During that period Captain Herbert had written him up, reporting that First Officer Reimann had lost some twenty pounds. He had sent his company uniforms to be altered which, earlier that month, resulted in reporting for duty attired in the bare minimum of required company apparel. Apparently, the old marine, Captain Herbert, simply was not satisfied by whatever excuse Dieter had given concerning his improper dress. The first piece of a large puzzle was falling into place for me. At a vital moment when the company hierarchy should have stepped in and dealt with the issue, they simply looked the other way and whitewashed the whole affair, banking that nothing significant would result from their petty feud.

My first reaction was to take the report and share it with the families of the flight crew, but common sense made me rethink my options. How did the feud directly contribute to the cause of the incident, if it did at all? I needed more proof and that information lay in the hands of the Mexican officials. Then there was the CVR Recorder, which they were not about to present to me as a gift.

The information on Second Officer Sam Wells, thirty-nine, did not reveal anything more than a career as a highly respected pilot. He just happened to be in the wrong place at the wrong time. He was putting in his hours which were required before one became a captain, before being allowed to sit in the coveted left seat. Sitting in first class flying high above the Pacific, I realized that the information McKay had supplied produced more questions than answers. This only strengthened my determination to uncover the truth.

Upon deplaning in HNL, I hurried over to the small outdoor counter of Princeville Airways. The information I had obtained in the flight lounge was indeed accurate. With my seat belt tightly fastened, the small Twin Otter rose through a steep climb as it lifted up over HNL. If I had felt anxiety with each tremor of the DC-10, the fear was even greater in this prop aircraft. But the peace that eluded me since the moment of impact aboard 2605 soon returned as I gazed out the window and beheld the majestic terrain of my island destination. It was familiar. In some way, I was coming home. It was tremendously comforting.

I rented a car and began making plans trek while driving past Princeville. I was not capable of doing this hike alone, and I was in no condition to attempt survival in the wild. I needed help.

Passing a shopping center, I spotted two unique figures at the corner, hitchhiking. My first reaction was that it was 1967 once again, "the summer of love," as the slim man and lady had that look. I screeched to a halt.

"Hey brother." The smiling lady said.

"Hop in guys. Where you off to?" The slim fellow seemed a bit older than I and I was amazed by his lean, firm structure with minimum fat. The symmetry of his muscles was very distinct and taut. Vegetarians? By the look of the worn backpacks they loaded into the trunk of the vehicle, I determined they were experienced naturalists.

"Can you take us to the end of the road at Ke'e Beach?" The woman asked.

"Certainly. I'm headed to the same destination." With olive skin she retained a natural appearance, crowned by dark rich hair spreading like branches of a tree. She had an appealing, savage beauty. Their clothing was minimal and essential. These two individuals might just be the best source of information regarding the tough terrain I intended to confront. They introduced themselves as Erich and Katherine.

"I'm originally from the west coast," Erich stated. "Attended USC. The outside world got too crazy for me, so I came to Kauai." In the quaint town of Hanalei, we sat upon a wooden picnic table, shaded by a blossoming plumeria tree. Across the lawn I spotted a small boy enjoying a rainbow-colored shaved ice.

"I'm from the east coast," Katherine added. She rose to pick a fresh flower from the tree and placed it behind her ear, the perfect accent for a jungle girl. Like Erich, she too had decided to leave behind the traditional lifestyle. Both seemed very intelligent, though their appearance might have led some to think otherwise.

"I just survived a major airline crash and I'm running away trying to find some semblance of normalcy." The words came out, just like that. I felt embarrassed but saw no reaction from my new friends.

"I'm sure you experienced some terrible things." Erich was sympathetic. Somehow, I knew I could trust them. Without warning, I began to cry. Katherine reached out across the wooden table and grasped my hand. "You're wounded and need to begin to heal."

"The Garden Island is a special place. Allow her to nurture you." Erich and Katherine resided in the Na Pali and I was grateful that they seemed to care enough to help me get started on my journey.

I reached out to them and indeed felt fortunate to be in their company. I discovered they were extremely knowledgeable on all aspects of this magnificent island. They had a certain aura about them. I could trust them. They seemed at peace, something I dearly wanted. Now a new challenge awaited, a difficult hike along the trail I wasn't sure I could handle.

"I think we need to get you some proper equipment," Katherine said while examining the items I had packed for the trip. My initial selections were of course inadequate. Driving along the beautiful coastline towards Haena, Erich directed me to a plantation-style wooden house, their friend's home where I was able to leave my belongings and borrow a sleeping bag along with other essential items. Parking the car at the end of the road I viewed a sunset at Ke'e Beach that was a feast for my eyes. I sat on the sand, looking up and discovering animal shapes in the billowy clouds. Later that night while sleeping in the open I was treated to a spectacular ceiling of celestial delights. Our trio departed up the trail early the next morning.

"We need to cover as much of the trail as possible before the sun comes over the mountains," Erich said. The steep angles of the trail in the beginning, combined with the humidity, gave new meaning to the words "work out." From the start my greatest effort paled in comparison to the ability of my guides. With the strength of mountain goats and the stamina of distant runners, they effortlessly covered the red dirt pathway. Much of their time was spent stopping at one point and then another to wait for me. By the time we had hiked two miles to Hanakapiai Beach it was clear to all of us that I did not have the ability to keep up. Resting on the beach, Erich suggested that I go up the valley along the river to a plateau, where I'd find a beautiful waterfall.

"Its waters cascade down upon a clear, cool pond. The steep volcanic cliffs provide added shelter against the elements," my learned friend informed me. They intended to escort me up there where they would set up a camp site for me before continuing on their way. There were still wonderful, selfless people on this planet after all. They secured me near the base of the majestic falls where the random beauty was so stunning. I was ready to admit that it was probably the artistic result of Divine expression.

On the island I could rest. I could heal and be motivated to believe again. Katherine provided the basics: dried ahi, smoked marlin, dried fruits and a multitude of seeds. Water was available in abundance. On the island the sinister voices were silenced. I could read the report and not be tormented by negative energy ripping at me, scolding viciously. There was serene peace at Hanakapiai Falls and I felt totally protected, wrapped in a blissful, tropical cocoon. If the days were an eye's paradise the nights offered their own version, with a never-ending starry display. That evening, sitting in a cool tranquil breeze, I also added another phrase to my growing vocabulary, "pakalolo."

I finally descended the mountainside after running out of supplies, although I deeply wished to remain there longer to concentrate on the issues that were before me and try to determine a positive resolution. Before leaving I made sure the camp was dismantled and the site properly restored. Before leaving Kauai, I stopped at the home of Keoni, Erich's and Katherine's friend, to return his gear.

"If you ever return you are welcome here," the local man assured me.

"Mahalo, my friend."

The small Twin Otter glided on the trade winds back to HNL. I no longer felt paranoid, regaining much of my confidence despite the break-in. Was it Comandante Chávez? More likely, a bold, paid investigator. Upon arriving in HNL, I again promised myself to keep seeking the truth. I had to admit that, as much as I hated him, "Edmundo" still had the best chance of extracting information from those in the know.

I desperately wanted to listen to the CVR recording. Wish as I may, it was obvious that was not going to happen. In this case it was the Mexican Government who controlled all the strings. They were conducting the "official" investigation; all I could do was hope that fate would provide an opportunity.

Boarding the DC-10 made me even more determined. Then as the gate agent sealed the door at 2L and the craft pulled back from the gate, my anxiety returned. The jumbo jet lifted up and turned east into the skies over the Pacific Ocean and I began to panic. Luckily, I found reassurance in the familiar faces of the HNL-based cabin crew once the airplane leveled off.

"Hi Eddy. You look so tan! Let me know if you need anything at all," Camille, the senior F/A said. Later, as the passengers watched the movie I lingered with my fellow associates in the mid-galley, "talking story." Camille approached me.

"The cockpit would like you to call them," she said while reaching to adjust my tie. Then she headed back to first class.

"Okay, thanks." I was stunned. "What did I do wrong now?" I stated as the crewmembers began to laugh. I grabbed the phone at 2L and punched the secret coded chime that connected me with the cockpit.

"Aloha. I mean yeah, ah this is Eduardo." I stumbled badly with my words.

"Yes. Eduardo, this is Captain Weathers. I was glad to hear you were on board, traveling with us today." I struggled frantically to put a face with the name but came up blank. I froze as the captain hesitated, expecting a response from me. "Ah, Eduardo?"

"Ah, yes captain I'm here. I'm just a bit surprised by the call."

"Yeah, well, I was one of the investigating pilots in Mexico. Listen, could we get together and talk for a bit once we get on the ground at LAX?"

"Certainly captain, no problem. I'll wait for you in the flight lounge, sir." I hung up the intercom phone, bewildered by the exchange and becoming anxious. I wandered over to door 2R and stood alone listening to the echo of the air whistling by outside. What did the captain want from me?

Captain Weathers was a highly esteemed check pilot based at LAX. He was tall, strong and projected that positive military image. As one of the investigating pilots in Mexico City shortly after the incident, it had been his intention to look me up as soon as possible. Fate once more had intervened.

Upon arrival, I waited in the flight lounge. Soon I received a jovial greeting and a firm handshake from Captain Weathers who then directed me back to a private meeting room at the far end of the terminal building. His cordial demeanor quickly turned serious.

"I understand you were in the cockpit during the Mexico City flight?" As I sized up the captain the words just came out.

"Yes, there was an argument in the cockpit that night." Whoa! What had I done? Initially, I had thought to keep that to myself but realized now that it had to be said if I were to get to the truth. Captain Weathers looked shocked. In an instant, I realized my words had hit a nerve. The captain seemed unaware that I was in possession of the disciplinary report. He continued,

"What makes you so sure there was an argument that night?" He was testing me.

"Oh my God, the charade must continue," I whispered to myself. I wondered if the captain was going to try convincing me that I somehow misunderstood what had taken place. I was desperate for answers, which was motivation enough to play along. I'm sure he would have preferred dealing with the compliant Edmundo. Of course, the preferable alternative was that we speak openly and honestly, man to man. Suddenly the door to the room opened and in came a colleague of Captain Weathers, a younger handsome man who was assisting him in the investigation, First Officer Spencer Edwards. I looked from one to the other. "I constantly keep hearing the term 'pilot error.' Was it?"

"At this point, we really don't know, Eduardo." Capt. Weathers had earned a bit of my respect for saying my name correctly.

"Why not?" I pressed. He carefully selected his words.

"When an incident of this nature occurs on foreign soil, one is somewhat limited as to one's ability to fully investigate and recover all the facts." Officer Edwards then interceded.

"The Mexican authorities get first shot at the evidence, so our access is at their discretion." I began to chuckle.

"In other words, Gringo go home." The pilots made no reaction to my cynical statement.

"You may have heard that two of our associates were expelled from Mexico shortly after they arrived. They did not heed the government's directive and were quickly escorted onto a plane after they were found walking about the crash site unescorted." Captain Weathers' face now turned to frustration. "If certain officials did not want you to see something, you didn't." There was no need for him to explain further. I turned away, then faced them again.

"Look," I began. "From what I understand, Carl and Dieter were both prideful people, maybe sometimes even arrogant, but that night something happened." I freely related my encounter in the cockpit of 2605: the problem with the door opening, the reprimand and the eternal silence that followed. It was crystal clear that Captain Weathers knew there would be no swaying this F/A from what he had experienced.

"Carl and Dieter were not getting along." I was surprised to hear that from Spencer Edwards. He was validating me, hopefully making it easier for me to get to the truth.

Captain Weathers proceeded to inform me that Carl had gone so far as to "write up" Dieter, just days prior to the fateful flight. We were all aware that a "write-up" action is usually the last resort.

"Can any blame lie with Mexican Air Traffic Control or the controller in the tower at the airport?" I asked.

"We don't know yet. We haven't been permitted to speak with the controller on duty that night and are not sure we ever will," Edwards replied. Immediately I recalled my encounter with Señor Estrada in the waiting area of the office of the Minister: *"I was the controller on duty that night."* I was trying desperately to remember all his words. *"It was not that man's fault."*

"Yes!" I said loudly.

"What? Something you remembered?" Captain Weathers looked at me intently.

"No! Oh no, nothing, just a thought, it's really nothing." I fumbled my words badly and the pilots knew it. They could see there was something I was hiding. I quickly changed the subject. "What about the CVR Recorder?"

"Like I told you -- the Mexicans have it." The Captain showed his disgust. He quickly ended the meeting. "I may be calling upon you in the near future, Eduardo." Heading back to the flight lounge, I had one thing on my mind -- how can I listen to the CVR from 2605?

There was no tangible evidence pointing to Carl's and Dieter's confrontation as a factor in the crash of the jumbo jet, yet there was something that nagged at me. It was something I read while at my campsite by the waterfall. I took a seat in the flight lounge, removed the document and quickly glanced through it again looking for verification. There it was in black and white. Captain Weathers had been the Supervising Pilot who had spoken to Carl and Dieter just hours prior to boarding the DC-10 on October 30th. It was *his* decision that allowed them to continue flying together. Does he have blood on his hands? Perhaps my situation was not so bad.

I quickly checked my mailbox, which was full. Most messages were gracious, expressing relief at or thanks for, my survival. There were even greetings from flight attendants of other airlines: Lufthansa, Iberia, Pan Am, TWA. This reinforced my belief that when any aircraft goes down, it's an extended family matter. All crew members throughout the industry feel some sense of pain and loss. I felt deeply touched by the sentiments of those in my chosen profession.

"You don't deserve it, you little shit!" The vicious voices began scolding.

Regaining my composure, I noticed that the next letter was postmarked Kansas City. Instantly, I recalled a previous letter from a troubled grandmother in Kansas City who wished me to intervene and assist her ailing granddaughter. I quickly opened the envelope hoping there may have been some improvement in the child's condition. The very woman who earlier begged for intervention from the magical "El Gato" was now cursing my very name. The little girl had died. The woman attacked my lack of compassion, my refusal to act on behalf of her grandchild.

"May you feel such pain," were the words that jumped off the page to hurt me once more. I can't control the crazies. Madness has many subordinates. As a result of the newscasts, I was now receiving mail simply addressed to "the guy in the accident" or "the survivor from the crash." There were also letters from within my company, however, that put me on guard, like those who meant well but were putting me on an undeserved pedestal. They adorned someone or something that did not exist. No matter what I might say or do, they persisted. I began to dread my return to work.

I wandered out to the company bus stop to get a ride to the employee parking structure. I had my suitcase in one hand and all the mail in the other, clumsily dropping one letter and then another. When I arrived at the waiting area I dropped the whole lot.

"You getting fan mail now, Eddy my boy" The familiar voice brought a smile as I looked up to see Dwayne Foster, Captain "Rangoon" Dwayne himself. He acquired his unique nickname because of a concoction of various "chemicals" he bore in a special black briefcase. He christened the beverage a "Rangoon Ruby."

"You'd be surprised by the things I am receiving these days," I countered. Dwayne's jovial demeanor suddenly changed.

"One hell of a mess you were in, lad."

"And I came out in one piece for the most part. You know I could have used a Ruby right after crawling out of that fiery hole." Captain Foster chuckled, then reached out to gently pat my cheek.

"Oh, good of you to say so, son." There was a slight blush on the older man's pale face, so I fished for a reaction.

"You know, Dwayne, some strange things did occur up there." The captain nodded, then replied, "I wish I had Carl and Dieter right here in front of me. I would grab them and bang their thick skulls together. What the hell were they thinking?" Just then the clanging sound of the company tram broke the conversation, but he had already confirmed what I witnessed.

Reaching my car, I threw my suitcase in the trunk and decided I'd drop in on Jack McKay. I owed him thanks for his support. Walking in unannounced, I found him busily at work at his large wooden desk. His face lit up as I entered.

"Well my good friend, no more cane I see. Healing up I hope?"

"I just spent time on the island of Kauai."

"Oh, such a beautiful place," the Vice-President mused as he offered me a chair. I sat silent for a moment then opened up.

"Is pilot error the final verdict?" McKay turned away for a bit, his mood somber.

"It sure looks that way. People like us have to work within the system." I appreciated his honesty and understood what was on the line. The Mexican minister had made it clear that all the partners had to cooperate for the good of economic gain. Jack suddenly brightened up. "I almost forgot; I have something here I want you to see." He hurriedly searched through his top desk drawer and handed me a post card.

"Greetings from Waikiki," it stated in gold print with an aerial view of the historic pink Royal Hawaiian Hotel. As I turned the card over, I was dumbfounded to see a message from Dr. De Jesús, the doctor in the morgue, thanking Mr. McKay for all his help. He was the drunken physician who had threatened to tell the media there was alcohol in the blood of the pilots. McKay retained his smile as he shook his head. The postcard was just a final act of impudence by the despicable physician.

Nightly visits by a confused and tattered Javier now became a regular event. While awake my paranoia increased. Then there were the phone calls from those looking to make money.

"There could be a substantial payday for you if only you affirm the mistakes, we believe the pilots made that night," one caller assured me.

"You need to be vigilant. You deserve to be in agony. Your crew-mates would have dealt with this situation far better than you," the inner voices scolded. And again of course the shame, and the difficulty of separating dreams from reality.

I finally sought the company and comfort of an admiring fellow F/A. It was a mistake. I put an end to the evening's proceedings and politely, but swiftly, showed my lovely associate the door. Once alone I became overwhelmed. My body convulsed as I fell and lay there trying to regain my composure. I would fall asleep on the living room floor.

"Eddy, it's time to board the flight," the soothing, familiar voice called out. I listened intently as again she called my name.

"It's Reina's voice." I frantically looked about the dark room hoping to see her familiar smile. The frightened child within me forced my face into my knee. Gripped in fear, I struggled to my feet only to find myself in a fog as twisted, charred metal lying about.

"You belong dead...with them." It was the vile comandante's voice. The whine of a jet engine began to increase in volume. I cupped my ears with my hands to lessen the deafening sound. Then, all at once it went silent. The cruel Aztec master began to laugh in satanic pleasure. Like a wounded animal I ran and fell at the base of a doorway and reached for the frame with my scorched hands, struggling to pull myself forward.

"Help me. Mama, help me!" I placed my hand on my forehead, trying to focus on a figure and realized that the tiny image which appeared was small, a mere child. Flames suddenly shot forward and, in a moment, I recognized it as that of Javier. His body was charred almost beyond recognition. The helpless child while in flames struggled to offer his little hand. I looked and there on his distorted face, with flesh dripping off, was a tear. All at once Javier was sucked back into the depths of the inferno.

"No!" I wailed bitterly. "Please forgive me!" I awoke drenched in sweat and my heart pounding.

The anguish in my soul was taking its toll on my body. All my efforts to keep myself physically fit were useless. It sickened me to think that the powers that be, the moneyed barons and the corporate entities, were going to sweep this affair nicely under the carpet. They would turn their backs and walk away from the families and myself.

"Dealing with it, that's the real trick isn't it?" I recalled Hugo Garcia's wise words. I was starting to recognize that perhaps I was stricken by something I was simply not able to understand, but I was going to solve the puzzle regardless. My initial determination was to enforce more discipline upon my rebelling body.

"You'll never be good enough," the voices insisted. I obliged by restricting my diet even more. Discipline! That is what I believe I needed. Egg whites, boiled fish and chicken breast became my diet, with tuna packed in fresh water for a snack.

I do not know what was more annoying: the phone calls, notes left by the lawyers and investigators, or the confusion in my own mind. If I ever slightly considered the notion of enjoying a slice of pizza, ice cream or some sweet delight I would be reprimanded, the muscles of my throat tightening and nausea gripping me, and abruptly reminding me to reconsider such a pleasurable thought.

It all became too much as the desire to escape again took hold. I knew there was only one place I could go where the voices would not haunt me. I quickly decided to return to Kauai.

As I rode the company tram along the runways and pathways at LAX there were pilots with me. There we sat, the four of us alone except for a faceless driver. I heard the names Carl and Dieter.

"Those two should never have been flying together."

"Everyone knew what was going on." I sat there listening carefully and as we arrived at the tram stop at terminal 5, I spoke up and asked for their opinions concerning 2605's cockpit crew.

"Were your statements pretty much the consensus among most pilots?"

"Yeah," stated one, "but that's off-the-record of course."

I was in for another shock that day as I opened my mailbox in the flight attendant lounge. It had to do with my paycheck or lack of one of any value. Since I had not flown after the accident, I had not worked and that was reflected in my pay.

"Did you apply for disability?" Ackley placed the blame squarely back on me when I approached her concerning the matter.

Disability? To hell with disability. Make this right and do it soon. Have I not played ball with the company? Have I not agreed to be supportive in all matters? After all the crap I've gone through and now you guys turn your heads away. Of course, this is what I <u>wish</u> I had said but again I held back.

"So, you got a small paycheck." The voices shamed me. "Señora Torres got her daughter back in a box!" The chastising continued. If I had to restrict my diet, I certainly could restrict my living allowance. At that moment I reluctantly accepted living below the poverty line. I was being strangled by my own hand. It wasn't worth complaining to Ackley right now. The question of my pay would be extremely slow in being corrected. I justified the immediate divergence by convincing myself that I really did not need money while on the Na Pali Coast.

It wasn't long before I was standing on the tarmac of the Princeville Airport. I could not recall the last time I smiled so broadly. The devilish voices were again banned from the island. I rushed to get to Keoni's home to gather the necessary equipment.

"Eddy-Boy. Back again, Brah." The local man's white teeth were in sharp contrast with his brown face.

"Mahalo brother for all your help. Time again to get my mind straight."

"No better place to do that than the Na Pali," the local man replied. I was far more prepared this time for my trek into the jungle. Keoni freely offered whatever supplies I needed and gave me vital information regarding the trail. "Watch out for da centipedes and no swimming in the ocean. The current strong, you land up at Poli Hale beach." Many an expert swimmer had made the ultimate mistake, being seduced by the forbidding ocean, never to make it back to shore. I started out at the trail head in Haena with a clear mind, a set plan and, for the first time in a while, a stronger body. I climbed, struggling and sweating heavily in my efforts on the red dirt pathway. The view above the seacoast was stunning, helping to relieve the stress in my wounded soul. The majestic cathedral cliffs were inspiring as they emerged from the depths of the ocean straight up into the rich blue tropical skies. Certainly, if that God of love did exist, this island was His signature. Perhaps a trace of His compassion could be found somewhere in her majestic elegance.

I was able to hook up with Erich and Katherine along the coast of the Kalalau Valley and they immediately and graciously offered to be of assistance. With confidence I occasionally wandered off to explore, to meditate and re-evaluate my situation.

Some days under the serenity of a clear blue sky I would sit upon one of the large gray boulders that lined the riverbed flowing down the volcanic hillside. Shaped and smoothed by the waters over thousands of years, the rock contained cool green moss which grew on its top and sides, making it an inviting spot to rest, to think, to try and understand. I marveled at the cycle of life that played out over the island. By the heat of the sun, the cool fresh waters rose up from the depths of the Pacific Ocean high into the heavens. The moisture-filled clouds would gently glide westward on the strength of the trade winds, entering the cooler air and falling back upon the rich soil as rain, nurturing the island and cascading down in abundant waterfalls to the valley below. Nature indeed could rejuvenate one's spirit.

By day the rich glow of the golden sun warmed me; by night I could enjoy the stars, brighter than I had ever witnessed as they slowly voyaged across the sky. The cool breeze serenaded a gentle song and allowed me to rest peacefully without disturbance. There were no flashbacks, no voices of rebuke or nightly visits from the sadistic comandante.

In the beauty of the island I caught glimpses of what I perceived could be Divine mercy. I did feel comforted, soothed by the island's repose. My skin had become tanned and caked with the rich red soil of the volcanic island. I became lost in time forgetting for now what was happening on the outside. In the lush volcanic surroundings of Kauai, I found acceptance, regardless of all my imperfections. She allowed me to grieve, something I felt I had not been allowed to do: not by the Mexican Government, not by the airline, not by the attorneys, and not, at least in the past, by this God who chose to be silent.

But one morning I awoke in a daze, my eyes squinting at the glow of the rising sun. Letting my guard down I began to cry like a child. This all seemed like an unreal dream.

"Persevere!" I had to purge myself of all negative distractions if I hoped to survive. My diet was minimal. After a short period of time on the Na Pali Coast I took at times to discarding all clothing, like some others I encountered in the valley. Like a solemn prayer ending with moments of abundant joy, I embraced the healing essence of Kauai. Like some Franciscan monk I thought to restrict myself, seeking to nourish myself only with what the island could provide, distancing myself from a world ruled by lies and mistrust. In pushing the envelope on such feelings there was always the danger of falling off the edge. There was the real possibility of total failure and eventual madness. Then I would be at the mercy of the vultures.

Was Reina now free from such vile torment? Even while in the high mountain passages the Muerto seductively called my name, seeking to draw me out. I ventured to the base of the forty-foot cascading falls. My body's thirst was quenched the moment I stepped under the thundering downpour of majestic grace, its waters of life refreshing my parched throat. The cool spray of the shower clung to my leathery dried skin. I also wanted so much to wash that inner filth, to cleanse the choler, to clear my mind. The clean waters fell in a rhythm like glistening pearls. Its grandness eased my stress and dispelled the distrust I had felt. I looked upward, straight into the waterfall above me becoming lost in the abundance of blessings that fell upon me. I began to give thanks, feeling protected by that Divine graciousness I had turned my back on.

I was startled from my daydream by a distant whirling sound that echoed off the cliffs. I quickly turned and my worst fears materialized. I cried out in panic as a helicopter hovered above, neither advancing nor retreating. I caught sight of the pairs of arms holding cameras pointed in my direction. The dark leathery skin of the jungle man under the falls must have blossomed with radiant colors through the lens of the tourists. The imagined multiple clicks of the shutters careening down the valley, echoing to the ocean. It was one of the many helicopter tours that violated this sacred domain. I clenched my teeth as a vision of the airline crash, the fire, reporters and police flashed before my eyes. The shutters continued to whir in the rhythm of rapid shots. I had to escape as I dove hard and deep into the pool. When I came up the copter had retreated.

Now I had to be constantly on alert for intruders as mistrust once again seemed to be my sole companion. As evening fell, I returned to my small encampment which I christened my "lair." The days and nights of solitude and mistrust began to take their toll. My self-imposed isolation made it clear that the real world was void of any compassion. So, I had to change the rules of the game.

That night's tribal ritual became part of a new routine. I took great pains in mixing the colored powder inside the coconut shells I had carefully placed upon the red dirt. The texture of the tints had to be just right. Bright crimson, "rojo" in one, the other filled with "blanco," the purity of white to purge my soul. This flight attendant made broad vertical strokes upon a sun-dried torso, first the pectorals then the abdominal. Another was made across my brow. I wore the distinct visible logo of my airline dead center across my dark chest. I proudly wore these colors, but not in the same manner as before. This was different, an abstract declaration of war. Had those at home been able to see me now, they would not understand.

As I had done in the streets and in the alleyways of my old neighborhood, I concocted imaginary training courses through the dense shrubs and inclines of this pristine valley, a physical test. Now, by the light of a full moon I had evolved into a menacing dark figure, sprinting up a slope and gliding through the trees. I leapt across a stream, laying siege against imagined corrupt enemies: corruption, deceit, intrusion.

All at once, a rustling in the foliage interrupted my eccentric rituals. The jungle man froze in fear. Who or what was it? From under the dark brush a wild angry-looking sow and her three piglets emerged. I smiled in relief and kept a safe distance. Her sharp teeth could inflict great pain if she felt her piglets were in danger. Any medical assistance was non-existent in this remote location.

"Todo está bien, mamá," I stated as the sow and her brood slowly passed some distance downstream. I was the trespasser, so I showed respect. Then I realized I had addressed the pigs in Spanish. Why? I shrugged and resumed my wild journey releasing a loud yell in pursuit of invisible enemies.

As a child I was always mimicking the yell of the Tarzan character played by the actor Johnny Weissmuller. I relished the opportunity to hike up to a plateau on the volcanic wall protruding over the valley just enough for me to stand and deliver a blood-curdling cry in the middle of a calm, quiet night. Word later spread by those who frequented the Kalalau about the poor, wretched soul lost deep in the jungle, plagued by his demons. One story related that "the screamer," as he was being called, was a Vietnam vet tormented by anguished memories of dead comrades left behind in the rice fields of a faraway country. In reality these statements were not far from the truth regarding dead comrades and a distant land. Those in the know swore they encountered the mysterious character once, his body covered in sun-baked red mud, standing in the distance along the winding trail. When they looked up again, he was gone like an illusion in the midday sun. If the stories seemed fabricated to heighten the adventure of those experiencing the Na Pali Coast, there were always the echoing screams in the middle of the night for verification. Of course, I knew there was no denying that the source of the yells was one lost soul.

The sun rose gently, breaking over the crest of the 4,000' volcanic steeples that encased the lush valley of the north shore on the 5,000,000-year-old island. The stream flowed swiftly from the pond below the marvelous falls, running toward its rendezvous with the deep blue waters of the Pacific Ocean. The morning's tranquil peace was broken once again by the screamer, this time trying to dispel the emotional pain. I would learn later that the loathsome infliction my body wished to exorcise from within with such intense convulsions had a name: "survivors' guilt." It is vicious no matter how it manifests itself.

...

"What the hell was that?" Kekoa, a stout, muscular local stood surprised on the red dirt trail. Although the 24-year-old claimed to have the blood of the Hawaiian Ali'i royalty in his veins, his facial features more resemble the Portuguese side of his father's lineage, fair skin with curly hair.

"That's our boy," replied Kaupena, a native Hawaiian who ran a tour company on the island. The pair had been hired by my airline to track down their wayward child and get him on a plane back home to LAX. Tall and strong at 36, the older man had been raised on the ancient trails of the coastline and so was a more knowledgeable tracker. The Hawaiian noticed my belongings at the ridge by the side of the falls.

"It looks like that buggar is close by," Kaupena told his trainee. Kekoa still seemed confused by this assignment.

"What the hell this guy doing up here anyway?"

"From the information I got he thinks he's one jungle man - you know dakine. The wahine from the airline said they were pretty sure this is where this guy keeps running away to. He's supposed to be some survivor from one big plane crash. I don't know, a bit "lolo" in the head I think."

"At least he's not one of those growing paka lolo out here. Suckers who shoot first and ask questions later," the uneasy young man stated.

"Hell, I wonder if this guy was in Nam?" Kaupena responded. "He sure acts like one of those guys." The two locals stood about my make-shift campsite looking for any clues that could lead them to me. Frustrated, they continued their search through the thick brush.

"This guy could be anywhere, do anything." Suddenly, the silence was broken by cries of torment. The spooked duo stopped and listened once again as, yet another cry echoed down the valley.

"That's him alright." Kaupena rushed to reach the ledge. "Let's hike up there and take a look." The younger lad was not so eager.

"All pau," He stated. "I need to take one rest."

"Hey brah, we rest when we get back with 'Mr. Lolo.' The wahine boss said get him no matter what and they gonna pay through the nose." Kekoa reluctantly followed Kaupena up the trail, kicking debris and cursing my existence.

"Damn, just what we need - one more crazy haole."

Up on the ridge I sat delirious in my visions and daydreams, painted from head to toe in the colors of my airline like some deranged cannibal off the pages of National Geographic. I held a wooden stick in my right hand and took to jumping around like a primate, grunting and groaning, with pain. Death laughed with delight as he pulled the strings that made me dance his primeval jig. Muerto, the demon jester, egged me on as I gave in to the insanity. Reaching the top of the ridge, the two men spotted their prey and Kaupena instantly yelled out.

"Hey, dude!" I fell flat on my stomach and slowly started to crawl into the underbrush. All at once I stopped and began to regain my senses. I turned, sat up and softly responded.

"Yeah, who's there?"

"Hey brah, we've been looking for you all day, man. Your airline hired us to track you and bring you back down off the valley. We gonna get you on a plane back to the mainland."

I rose, embarrassed, trying to wipe the acrylic paint and baked mud from my face. The hired "guns" paid by my employer now seemed relieved and a bit surprised that the object of their hunt, who they feared might be wily and elusive was now simply docile. Early the next morning, like a timid child being taken to his first day of kindergarten, I was led out without resistance along the Na Pali Coast.

"You tell anyone where you were going?" Kaupena asked.

"No need," I stated. "Hell, I've only been gone, what? Eleven, twelve days?" I struggled to calculate. Kaupena stopped mid- trail and turned with a puzzled look. "That haole wahine told me that no body seen you now for over twenty-six days."

"What month is it?" I asked with concern.

"It's January, brah." The Hawaiian's statement just about floored me for I had been absent for Christmas and New Year's. I was certain my parents were beside themselves with worry. "The people at the airline are thinking you went lolo, maybe had do yourself in, brah." I could only stare out at the ocean's horizon.

"Twenty-six days?" I was bewildered. Had I really lost my mind?

"Hey, brah, you must be one important dude for them haoles to want you back so bad. What's the reason?" Kekoa asked as I struggled in my half-naked state to keep pace.

"Money, brah. It's all about money," I said. We hiked the rest of the afternoon until finally reaching Ke'e Beach. I suppose I had failed in my attempt to fall off the face of the world. Now, these two local boys were sending me back to so-called civilization, the outside, into chaos once again.

I was to receive another shock once we had stopped at the small plantation house of my friend, Keoni, who also had been concerned for my well-being.

"Erich and Katherine were taking care of me." I tried to reassure him.

"We gotta get him on a plane this evening so we can get paid," Kaupena whispered to Keoni.

"That buggar can't get on no plane looking like that," Keoni observed. I climbed upon the small lanai at Keoni's wooden house and looked at my reflection in the windowpane.

"Dear Lord!" I remained standing and staring in disbelief. I had not shaven nor had a proper bath in some time. I had lost weight: twenty-one pounds to be specific. My fat content had diminished, evident by my waistline. I was beginning to resemble the evil skeletons on El Día de Los Muertos, back in Mexico City. I was beginning to look like Death.

Keoni was kind enough to allow me to "freshen up," even providing me with a fresh pair of shorts and a shirt. The clothing

I had originally arrived with no longer fit. The local boy also allowed me to make a long distance collect call so that I could ease the pain I had caused my family. Needless to say, my mother was happy and relieved to hear from me.

"Are you sure you are okay, mijo?" I felt deep shame for the torment I had caused her. I assured my parents that I was boarding a plane soon and would be back in Los Angeles in a couple of days. Once again, I was escorted to an airport and boarded a plane, this time to HNL. In the morning I would connect with a company DC-10 to ferry me back to LAX where I would have to face my superiors.

"Aloha and welcome aboard." The smiling F/A directed me to my seat. With that, I had just over five hours, gliding at thirty-six thousand feet above the Pacific Ocean to plan my defense.

Flight Manager Daisy Ackley had never been married, opting to dedicate her life to the career and industry she so desperately loved. Once informed of my discovery she was heard to say that there was no need for her to have children - she had Eddy. In order to survive the questioning, I decided to utilize Edmundo, the very ploy that seemed to continually get me out of difficulties. That personality was taking over my life.

Upon the aircraft's descent over East Los Angeles, I thought I recognized our family's neighborhood, including the house I had grown up in with its back yard of lemon, peach and avocado trees which I used to climb, then scream like Tarzan. My mother and father were no doubt very disturbed by the actions of their son. The wayward child had run away for almost a month. I may have felt no regret for the trouble I caused the airline, but I was deeply ashamed of the pain I had caused my family.

"I lost track of time." That was not going to cut it. I was resolving that Eddy, not Edmundo, would have to face the music and truly make amends as my family home, quickly slipped back into obscurity as we glided on final approach to LAX.

The gracious crew wished only the best for me as I gathered my belongings to leave. The ladies in their red-and -blue Aloha outfits flashed the biggest smiles as I stepped into the jetway at Terminal 5. I took a few steps up the metal footpath when things began to go very wrong. Any confidence I had gathered suddenly abandoned me. I became dizzy and almost stumbled as

I struggled to make it into the terminal. The main floor was packed with passengers moving to and fro like an ocean tide, going in one direction then another. Small children grasped the hands of parents who were standing and gazing at the arrival and departure boards high above the terminal wall.

I quickly fell forward onto a blue vinyl seat, trying to regain my focus as I glanced across to the far side of the building, locking eyes with a small boy who I guessed to be about six years old with shaggy blonde locks under a little red baseball cap. The child held a small dinosaur figure in each hand and did not move a muscle as, for some reason, he seemed hypnotized by the sight of me.

All at once I felt like I was going to convulse. I tried to find a private corner facing the white concrete wall and crouched down to control myself. Panic rose in me as I looked all around at the moving tide of people. I ran to the large destination board desperately looking for the time and gate of the next flight to HNL. The very aircraft that had ferried me to LAX was being readied and serviced to return once again to paradise.

I returned to gate 58 while constantly looking over my shoulder for the shadow of Muerto. I tried to control my anxiety as I stood in line with the ticketed passengers, eager to speak to the gate agent who was occupied with the boarding process. I flashed my employee identification and asked her if I could stand by for the flight.

"Do you have a ticket?" The dark-haired lady inspected my ID.

I began to speak quickly and softly.

"I did not have time to put in for a documented pass you see, and I need to get over to Hawaii. It's very important." I gazed nervously about. "I thought... I mean... I wondered if I possibly could get on the standby list with just my company ID." The patient agent listened while examining my airline badge once more.

"Excuse me one second." She walked over to another agent positioned by the jetway door. The passengers were getting restless.

"If you just step aside for a minute Eddy, we are trying to see what we can do for you," She said with a smile.

"I'm busted," I told myself as I grabbed my meager belongs and retreated to one of the familiar blue vinyl chairs to await my fate.

"Eddy." I turned to see that the agent held a company phone in her hand. I approached the woman as she gestured that I should take the phone.

"For me?"

"Hello? This is Eddy."

"Eddy, this is Daisy. I hear you are trying to get back on the flight to Hawaii." There was a long pause as I quickly realized that I had better say something. The silence was making me look stupid.

"Oh no Daisy, I was just trying to say hi to one of the crew members on board....... you know, going outbound." My words made me look even more stupid. I slapped my right hand against my moist forehead and a small stream of sweat began to run down the side of my face. Once again there was silence on the other end of the phone.

"Well, why don't you come downstairs to my office." My superior was making a conscious effort to not sound threatening. I knew my ass was grass. I slowly gathered my composure and belongings and headed for the flight lounge.

"I think you need to get back to work, Eddy." Her plan for dealing with the little company "headache" was in motion and she would set the "little shit" straight. "Your legs are all better even though you never went back to the doctor the company sent you to. When can we put you back on Reserve?"

It had been a few months since the accident, and this was the established time off one received. Forget about the suffering under the comandante and his merry band of men. I thought about the complexities of returning to the flight line, but buckled under Daisy's intimidation. I smiled and allowed Edmundo to wrangle a few more day's leave.

"I need a bit more time to settle things with my family."

It was now very apparent that my actions were making people take notice. What image was going to be projected when I got back online? How would I respond while sealed in the cabin of a craft filled with all that jet fuel, and trying to be responsible for the safety of my passengers, a responsibility I believed I had failed miserably in before? How could I do an effective job? It became apparent that Eddy, at least the one I recalled graduating from Flight Attendant Training, would never return to the flight line again. The only option available seemed to either return to being the hero or the madman. I was becoming convinced that trying to live up to the first image would only lead to creating the second. Hugo's words rang loudly in my mind: "That's the trick. Since you are the one who experienced the crash you are the one that must determine the outcome." How I so missed my good friend as I contemplated what lay before me.

Back in the flight lounge I quickly filled out a few flight pass requests to hold in reserve as I boldly scribbled LAX-HNL-LAX. I wanted to make sure I had a back-up plan if things got ugly and I needed to escape. In my company mailbox there were my airline pay receipts. They were blank, for there was no income earned. I caught the red-and-white employee tram back to the parking lot. It was going to be hard to regroup because I was dead broke financially.

Upon approaching the front door my home in Manhattan Beach, I discovered that it had been shimmied open.

"Christ! Not again!" Maybe it was a local thief. The more I studied the scene it became apparent that truly nothing of value was missing. All shelves and drawers had been messed with but the TV and stereo were untouched. This was not the work of desperate druggies looking to pawn something for quick cash. I noticed that my mail that had accumulated over a period of time was scattered across the living room floor and had been opened. I was overwhelmed and just sat on the sofa with the front door wide open. I did not call the police or make any type of report. What was I going to report and to whom? I just cleaned up the mess, trying to pretend that nothing had happened.

Chapter XIV

It was an anxious world I had returned to, filled with international tension, mainly involving Iran. America's TV anchormen routinely counted and displayed the number of days our citizens had been held hostage by the Revolutionary Guard of the new Iranian government. Any hope that President Carter could negotiate their release anytime soon was slim at best. Military intervention seemed a more likely scenario. Any scenes of DC-10 NW903 broken and burnt in pieces on the tarmac in Mexico City were long gone from the television screen but they remained extremely vivid in my mind.

"Eddy, Sister Marie Inez is coming to visit the family," my mother told me once I contacted my parents. "I expect you will be there."

"Of course, mom." Sister Inez's visit took priority over all family issues including my recent disturbing disappearance. My parents tried to rationalize it as nothing more than childish behavior. Their disappointment in me could be overlooked if I behaved myself at the family gathering.

As the extended family readied themselves for the first home visit by our dear aunt, I made sure I was well-groomed and in a good frame of mind. I would do anything my parents asked, for my shame lingered and I owed big-time. At one point in the visit Sister Inez asked to speak to me in private.

"Oh, Dear God, the Cardinal." This could only mean that she got word about having met His Eminence on my flight. "What did I screw up?" I tried to think back to the flight.

"We give thanks to God for returning our Eddy safely. Our Lord has something special in store for you," my dear aunt stated in prayer.

Don't you understand? I can't live up to that expectation! The words only formed in my mind.

As she was ready to leave, Sister Inez informed me that His Eminence Timothy Cardinal Manning had contacted her, aware of my involvement in the airline disaster. The Cardinal wished to see me again if I could spare the time. After she had left I sat on the couch, hoping I had eased the minds of my parents concerning my mental stability. The problem was, I knew that in reality I was losing my grip.

I dreaded going back online, fearful of how I would react once put into a position of authority and made responsible for the safety of my assigned passengers.

"Your last passengers died!" The voices returned with a vengeance. I recalled how right out of training I had enjoyed being so inconspicuous in performing my duties. I would melt into the routine of a flight and few would notice me. Now, it was as though everyone knew who I was. Once back on reserve, everything I did would be scrutinized.

"Is he going to be able to cut it? Will he be able to put aside everything he experienced?" There were those that doubted. I was about to bet against myself. "What will he do when he has to fly the all-nighter back to Mexico?" I dreaded the thought. The reality was that I was broke, and I needed to draw a paycheck again.

I made clear in a conversation with Daisy that, as my first assignment back, I would embrace the Mexico City all-nighter once again. I was not about to wait around by the phone on pins and needles worrying whether I would be assigned the night owl on any given day. I was going to try and tweak Muerto. In reflection, I believe it was a combination of a slight amount of machismo and a whole lot of stupidity. I concluded that being Hispanic, Catholic and male gave me three reasons to seek martyrdom.

Before going back online on Flight 605, LAX-MEX. I took great care to make sure the crease on my company shirt was just right, long and straight. I recalled how I took little interest in my appearance on the night of October 30[th,], thinking about how Gary Rollings had taken his position as Senior seriously, looking so impeccable. I owed it to his memory to make an effort this night.

"Wasn't Gary Rollings more worthy to survive than you? The voices saw an opportunity.

"Yes."

"Did you look like a total slob that night in October?"

"Yes." I became annoyed with their antics. I put on my blue jacket and polished my flight wings, trying to distract my frustration.

Okay, if Muerto wants to grab me tonight then bring it on. I dared Death to make a reappearance. I was depleted by this chaotic experience and wished to create a final confrontation.

At the crew meeting in the flight lounge I discovered I was assigned the mid-galley position. I was designated an "extra" so I would not be bidding for a door station on the DC-10. I was befuddled. I was not told this beforehand by scheduling. Was management afraid I would crack in mid-flight and go berserk?

"To hell with everyone, let us all die in a fiery blaze of glory!" I imagined myself running and screaming through the cabin, trying to open one of the jumbo jet's doors at thirty-three-thousand feet. But I calmed myself down and realized that everyone was just trying to make the first flight back easy for me.

As hoped, the flight proved to have no sinister demons aboard to settle the score with me. I looked hard across the darkened cabin for that thick atmosphere that had lingered on 2605. There were no premonitions or renditions of a crew-member's fearful dreams. Everyone in the cockpit and cabin was professional and orderly. No matter how hard I searched there was absolutely nothing out of place.

Upon final approach into the Mexican capital I found myself surprisingly in control, despite descending onto the very runway that changed my life forever. Divine intervention or twisted fate? Is there a purpose to one's life?

Reina believed, but I want more proof.

"Bravely stated asshole, the flight is already over," the voices whispered. The DC-10 gently touched down on Runway 23-Left at Benito Juárez Airport.

Once parked at the terminal building and door 2L opened, the gate agent on duty was surprised to see "El Gato." Her bright smile reminded me how I so loved the Mexican people. Then I remembered something very important. "¿Señor Garcia?" I asked. "¿Trabajando?" Through the bodies that were deplaning, and the short, dark-haired agent indicated with hand gestures that she was not sure but would find out for me. She returned and

302

stated, "Este día, no!" I was greatly disappointed by the news but asked her to please give Hugo my best regards.

The passenger load on the flight down had been light. Although I had been up all night, I was not tired. Russ, another F/A assigned to the flight was a lanky, blond who I had developed a friendship with early in my career and had worked this flight with me. He liked muscle cars and owned a '65 Chevelle that could be heard rumbling through all levels of our employee parking lot. Russ saw the old Eddy in me when I returned to the flight line.

"Hey Russ, you want to come with me on a little expedition?"

"What do you have in mind?" I had piqued his curiosity. I asked the Senior F/A if it was okay if we deplaned for a bit as it would be another hour before the passengers would start to board. Permission was granted and we hurried down the outside stairs of the jetway onto the tarmac.

"Where the hell we going?" Russ inquired.

"I want to see what is left of the crash site." by his looks this is not what Russ wanted nor expected to hear.

I was not sure what I was looking for or what I would find. I supposed that the site would have been cleared of all traces of the accident. After all, it had been several months since the crash. Hastily moving through a variety of ground obstacles and dodging vehicles, we steadily continued in the direction I was sure the final impact had occurred. I kept a look-out for the foundation of the maintenance building we had struck and the large depression that was created across the street and imagined a scorched, black tarmac and concrete, a result of the tremendous heat from the flames.

I suddenly came to a stop. What I saw was completely unexpected. A big charred pile existed on the concrete beside the crumbled foundation of a what had been a cement building before being struck by the DC-10. Various pieces of aircraft wreckage had been removed but a huge pile of "leftover" material remained in the ashes. I would later discover that the remains of the aircraft had been hauled away and sold as scrap. The sale was explained to the stockholders through the year-end receipts as due to "an involuntary adaptation of aircraft DC-10 NW903." At that moment I wished I had perished along with my crew. If I had, then perhaps a fitting inscription on my tombstone would be, "Here lies 'Edmundo' Valenciana who died as a result of an involuntary adaptation."

Russ came to a halt beside me. There in front of us, among other things, were burned out passenger seats from 2605. I should have known better, but I approached the pile anyway, squatting down at the edge of the fired rubble. I picked up a plastic airline passenger information card with the proud company logo showing through the soot that covered it. Then there was a mangled tray table sticking out of the pile which I estimated to be about 30' - 40' around and 10' high. Neither of us could speak. Not a word was said. Russ walked around one side while I circled the other.

"¿Que pasó?" The words of the werewolf'-masked figure from October 31 flashed through my head. I spotted a child's shoe wedged in the debris. Whose? In my mind's eye all I saw was Javier. Then again, the tattered shoe could have easily belonged to anyone. It may have been that of one who crossed the airport lines that morning desperately searching for loved ones. Perhaps a frantic mother, dragging along her child, running through the inferno.

Cabin interior material from the shattered craft was part of the debris: the remains of cabin seats, carpet, window shades, seat belts, galley panels, meal carts, the half-burned company in-flight magazine. There were great amounts of crushed and broken concrete mixed into the heap, coated in black. Then the unspeakable occurred to me: more than likely there were probably some traces of human remains in this pile. I immediately flashed back to the three young "chavalitos" making a hideous game of catch with the severed human hand. I gazed down at my own blackened hands and began to shake as I quickly backed away from Death's inferno.

"I don't think you should stick around here, Eddy." It was Russ who had caught the panic in my face and his words made sense. I looked up at my friend with my blackened hands still held high.

"Let's get out of here." We left and I did not look back.

"Four months." I said out loud. "They have left that shit sitting out there for four months." Russ looked at me, nodding in agreement.

"Are you going to be okay?" I nodded my head but inside I had my doubts as I frantically struggled to erase the grime from my soiled hands. Russ offered me a clean handkerchief and kept a close eye on me the whole way back. There was still another leg we had to work, and my good friend would be there for me if the need arose.

The experience was just another cruel joke bestowed upon me by Muerto. As Russ and I climbed the steel stairs on the exterior of the jetway, I reminded God and Reina that there was still nothing that had happened this day to indicate a Divine presence or a sliver of hope.

Upon entering the jetway at door 2L I was met by a group of individuals huddled, talking as one of them turned to me.

"There he is." The Senior F/A directed the attention of the others. Several company gate agents approached and offered the traditional abrazo as an act of respect, then they stood aside to reveal a shy, hesitant figure.

"Look Eduardo, it's Penelope." There shifting uncomfortably, was the lovely young lady I had seen boarding Flight 2605 the night of October 30th at LAX. I now vividly recalled her walking aft down the left aisle to take her window seat. This was the same young lady whose mother had desperately asked me for help once I was in the operations room at Benito Juárez Airport. I flashed back to that conversation.

"She is nineteen years old."

"Yes, I remember her, she was in the rear section, she had a better chance of making it out." I tried to assure her mother.

Now, here standing before me was that precious daughter, Penelope Anderson, and in the midst of my cynical skepticism I was given the gift of another survivor.

"Thank God you are alive," she exclaimed, as if she had just witnessed a miracle. But at the same time, she must have been fighting extreme anxiety. This was to be her first flight since the morning she had miraculously escaped Muerto's grasp. Just as I was reluctant to enter the aircraft when it came my turn to leave the Mexican capital, Penelope also seemed hesitant during her pre-boarding process. She was aware who I was and the role I played in our shared ordeal but did not know that this was my first assignment since the two of us had escaped Death. What were the chances, I wondered? I was assigned a random flight back to Mexico City while Penelope was allotted the same flight for her return to California. I approached her and gently clasped her hand, urging her forward as we entered together.

"Thank you," she replied, appreciating my encouragement.

The unique situation was explained to my Senior F/A and since the load was light for the return to LAX, I was allowed to sit beside Penelope in the cabin once we were in the air and the craft leveled off. We mostly just stared at each other. Finally, I asked what everyone else had avoided bringing up.

"What do you remember, Penelope?" The lovely lady stared straight ahead for some time, then spoke. "There was a massive jolt, then the ceiling fell on top of me." Her beautiful dark eyes grew wider. "There was so much on top of me, I'm not sure exactly what or even who it may have been." She had my complete attention. "There was fire everywhere and then someone grabbed me and dragged me out." She didn't seem to remember much detail. She was put in a vehicle and whisked away, and the next thing she recalled was being in the hospital.

We were mostly silent during the three-hour flight, smiling at each other, just grateful for each other's survival. The young woman was to be reunited with her baby daughter from whom she had been separated for so long. LAX would not be her final destination; there would be a long drive to her home in Central California. Two survivors, one a crew member and the other a passenger, thrown together on the same day: Divine intervention or twisted fate, and for what reason? Later I would reflect that perhaps our meeting was meant as an opportunity to offer each other hope. At the time I was still not convinced, for I could see that this lovely girl was just beginning to heal. Her journey would take a different direction than mine.

Once on the ground Penelope was met by two LAX gate agents who escorted her to waiting family members. I watched them leave through the terminal toward the next leg of the journey, her second chance at life. It was obvious to me that there were going to be terrible obstacles ahead. For the first time in a long time I prayed, asking this God to see that she would make it through in one piece.

"Welcome home, Eduardo." That voice could only belong to one person. Shana, my supervisor, had been assigned to greet me at the gate upon my return from MEX. I was not surprised, understanding the company's anxiety concerning my state of mind on my return to the flight line. She tried to make small talk as we slowly walked to the stairwell leading to the flight lounge. I had hoped her approach was going to be subtle as she evaluated me, trying to determine if my completed assignment affected my stability. But it was not. Hell, I shouldn't complain because she got my name right this time.

"Are you sure you are okay?"

I played it cool and bit my tongue until I could get down to Daisy's office and in private get a few things off my chest.

"They left that burnt rubble sitting there out in the open for four months," I yelled. My frustration was obvious, and I assumed she would be just as upset.

"Are you sure it was rubble from the accident?" She seemed almost indifferent.

"Look, I don't mind being back online Daisy, but no more Mexico all-nighters for me." I slammed my fist on her desk. "I don't care, tell Scheduling to send me to Acapulco, Guadalajara, anywhere but Mexico City." I turned and left immediately. The anger had boiled over, but I felt I was totally justified. I rushed out and jumped on the employee bus where I sat angered and bewildered.

Each time I thought I was making progress something always came out of nowhere to smack me down, destroying what little confidence I had gained. Maybe I should consult a professional in these matters, a psychiatrist perhaps? Certainly, considering my situation, there would be no shame in wanting to make that choice. There was also the little matter of past family history: Schizophrenia. I was twenty-seven and perhaps the flashbacks, the convulsions, the voices in my head were not just a result of survivor's guilt. Just maybe, it was heredity.

"It would serve you right, you little shit." The voices wished to stoke the flames of fear and
shame again.

"Consult a priest." My mother immediately expressed *her* preference. I did have a standing invitation to consult more than just a priest, so I made a call to the diocese and set up an audience with Timothy Cardinal Manning. Perhaps, he could plead my case before this silent God. Maybe I could find some solace in His Eminence's words.

...

"You will sign the f###### paper."

"No!" I rose up in my own bed, in my own house, once again panicked and sweating. I looked across the room at the statue of the Blessed Mother compassionately gazing downward.

There was no time. I had to hurry. The previous night, Scheduling allotted me a flight on the 10, LAX-SEA-ANC. It included a 24-hour layover attached at the Captain Cook Hotel in downtown Anchorage. The facility had a nice weight room where I could try to eliminate the mounting anxiety. Alaskan air space was notorious for creating turbulence when flying into ANC, which I was sure would add to my burdens.

The flight crew assembled at Terminal 5. Most of my fellow associates seemed pleasant and sincere. One young lady I was to fly with spoke the dreaded words to me:

"God has something great in store for you, Eddy." I smiled, nodded and walked away. I would try and keep my distance from her during this three-day assignment. I was assigned to work the 1R position, First Class. As we boarded the DC-10 I resolved to concentrate on my duties. I very much wanted to adhere to the high standards of hospitality my airline expected. Upon catching sight of the forward position, I froze, focusing on the jumpseat at 1R. It was becoming apparent that nothing would be the same, ever!

"Can I work the 1R position, Eddy?" I flashed back. It was twenty-year-old Karen Smitt speaking. "Please, please, PLEASE," her sweet voice begged. No matter how hard I tried to dismiss the idea, jumpseat 1R would always belong to Karen.

"You okay, Eddy?"

"Oh, yeah." It was Debra, the senior F/A who would be working across the aisle from me at 1L. I quickly scrambled to store my personal belongings, trying to act normal. Once the ship was loaded and, on the runway, I desperately wished we were heading to Hawaii.

The flight and service to SEA went on without a hitch. Once mid-flight to ANC the passengers were settled and I found a bit of time to rest, finding peace sitting with the drapes closed in my small cocoon that was at 1R. With the first-class galley directly aft of my jumpseat, I could sit and embrace my isolation.

"Hi, Eddy." I suddenly had a visitor. The sweet blonde F/A who had hinted about God's plan for me had come forward once everything was calm in the cabin. I had to try hard to be pleasant.

"I gotta give it to you Eddy, coming back to work must be tough." I merely smiled and nodded. "Have you ever thought about why you were spared?" My back stiffened.

"Oh dear Lord here it comes," I whispered to myself.

"You must be a Christian." My fellow associate explained that she was "born-again" and a member of a well-known Evangelical church in Orange County, California.

"You know," I wanted to say, "I can see where this conversation is going, and I really do not want to be judged on my personal religious beliefs." But as usual I said nothing, keeping a stoic face. Carol wanted so badly to believe that I, with my so-called exploits, had to be a fellow Christian, a *stalwart disciple* of the word of Jesus Christ. Why else would God favor me so? I could see that this conversation wasn't going to go anywhere.

"What church do you attend, Eddy?"

"I was raised Roman Catholic." As my words sunk in, her radiant smile slowly evaporated.

"Oh," was her only response. There was a long pause as she seemed to be in momentary deep thought. She gazed downward, frowning. I could read her thoughts so clearly. Perhaps the Lord did not have so grand a plan for me after all. Perhaps my ordeal was a warning from the one true God to repent for my wicked, wicked ways. Yes, that had to be it. Her cheerful demeanor returned as she presented me with her company business card and an invitation to visit her church. And with that she was gone. I watched her prance down the aisle back to her designated station in the aft, and I retreated into my little enclosure. I just wanted to throw up. I was angry. Then the no-smoking sign went on and the captain came on the intercom.

"Ladies and gentlemen ah, we're gonna ask our flight attendants to secure the cabin and take their seats for the remainder of our descent into Anchorage." Now the fun would begin. I battened down the hatches, securing galley, then strapped myself into the jumpseat as tight as I could. The runaway coaster was descending, and I was helpless to prevent it.

"Control myself. Control myself." I knew the others would wonder how I would react under the pressure of intense turbulence while not saying a word. I could not let the insanity win the game. I mustered up the appearance of Edmundo and the pantomime began. No matter how strong the winds were that hit the massive jet, the forced smile never vanished from my face.

Once at the Captain Cook Hotel I quickly head to the gym to try and relieve the stress. I exhausted myself, seeking normalcy, but unfortunately on this night it would not happen. As if still caught in the turbulent struggle from the flight, I again felt the anger brewing just under the surface. In my room I showered and methodically prepared to venture out, dressing warmly for the brisk weather. Leaving the comfort of the hotel I just needed to walk. I pounded the pavement feeling disgraced.

After some time, I realized I had walked into what can be called the skid row area of Anchorage. There, on the sidewalk and doorways, lay the wretched, poor souls who were emotionally engaged in their own wild roller coaster rides, a journey likely to lead into the hands of Death.

"Who's to say yours won't?" The voices made a very distinct point. A great number of the plagued and abandoned around me that night were indigenous people. I began to look for Muerto for I was sure he was about to manifest himself. Suddenly, ahead of me two men began fighting. One, a skinny guy who could have been Alaskan, found something on the ground, a container of liquor I assumed, and a much taller and stronger Anglo man began to beat on him.

"Cut this crap!" I interceded. "Get the hell out of here!" The startled Anglo backed away and stumbled off. The skinny guy held the prize close to his chest, then stood up and quickly fled.

Perhaps I *had* wandered into Death's arena and I desired to confront him.

I continued walking and ended up in front of an establishment with lights promising music and dancing. It was The Seafarer. Through the smoke were silhouetted figures at a long bar, most hunched over. I squeezed between two of them.

"A beer, please," I requested from a husky, tattooed barmaid.

"Are you lonesome tonight,

Do you miss me tonight?

Are you sorry we drifted apart?"[7]

On the juke box "The King" tried to soothe the wounded patrons who occasionally took long draws on their cigarettes, reminding me of the evil Comandante. One guy sat comatose, holding a smoke practically all ash, still intact and burning. I quickly downed my glass of suds.

"A shot of tequila!" I requested of the haggard barmaid. "Add a beer chaser."

"Sure thing, honey." I finally found a seat at the bar with the rest of my fellow damned, feeling a sense of belonging.

Many hours later -- I don't recall -- I would re-enter the Captain Cook Hotel, quite intoxicated, as I am sure the security guards could attest. Fortunately, this was a long enough layover for me to sleep it off.

I was on time for the crew shuttle to the airport and as usual, my fellow crewmembers were asking each other how they spent their long layover?

"Mary and I rented a car and drove along the coastal highway," a cheerful F/A shared. Her companion raved about the great view.

"I went fishing," an aviator declared.

"What did you do, Eddy?" I was afraid someone would ask.

Well, I took a nice long scenic stroll amongst the intoxicated and homeless of Anchorage. I joined my fellow lepers in cocktails at the distinguished Seafarer Club in the heart of the town. My rogue compatriots and I proceeded to get shit-faced till the early morning. Instead, I made up some pleasant story to

---

7 Are You Lonesome Tonight? Elvis Presley

311

tell them about staying in my room and only venturing out to have a king crab dinner.

The flight home started well enough and the weather cooperated, but I was destined to encounter a different sort of turbulence. Maurice was an F/A, tall and olive skinned. I initially liked him because like me, he traveled a lot on his time off.

"Eddy, can I speak with you?" We met at the mid-galley. Instead of telling me about his latest adventure abroad, he asked, "Listen, is the company taking care of you?" His inquiry caught me off guard.

"Well, yeah, they made sure I saw the best physician concerning my leg and..."

"No, Ed." He cut me right off. "I mean, have they given you any money?" Maurice would have the distinction of being the first associate to stoop so low, and I was shocked. I did not respond.

"Heck Ed, if it were me, I would have made them sign over a check for a million dollars." I just stared at him in bewilderment. Maurice, the ladies' man, most likely imagined himself sunning on a beach in Rio, surrounded by beautiful women, burning hundred-dollar bills to light his expensive Cuban cigars. I pitied the fool. He knew nothing of my torment: the fire, the severed heads, the smell of the burned bodies or the sounds of those in the grasp of Death. He would never be awakened by the painful screams of the child Javier in the middle of any given night. He had no idea of the shame and guilt, the evil voices. In his mind, it was just all about the money.

I exited the craft at LAX completely disgusted. I hastily walked to the men's room located in the middle of terminal 5, went into a stall and locked the door. Sitting in isolation, I tried to gather my emotions. I could not contain myself, so I wept.

Why couldn't I have been taken with my crew?

"You were not good enough." the voices scolded. I heard an announcement calling for the boarding of the day's last flight to HNL.

To hell with this. I had a collection of passes I had stockpiled so I left my hiding place and hurried down to the flight lounge, then contacted Flight Attendant Scheduling and informed them I was taking myself offline due to illness. Elaine, the scheduler was initially silent then responded,

"I understand, Ed, let us know when you are feeling better." I was relieved by her reply. It seemed that at least one person in the company understood what I was dealing with.

Soon I was in the air again, up over the Pacific, escaping once again to paradise.

The cabin crew must have been a bit puzzled as I sat in the first-class cabin in full uniform, carrying my regulation raincoat while bound for the Tropics.

My decision to run away was again an emotional reaction, so not only did I have the wrong attire for sunny Hawaii, but also very little money to my name. Once seated and calm at 35,000' reality set in. I was not even sure I could afford a low-cost hotel room once I arrived on Oahu. Somehow, I didn't care, I was heading back to Hawaii.

"Eddy, what are you doing here?" The voice was familiar as I turned and saw Caitlyn standing in the aisle next to my seat. "Are you working right now?" I just lowered my head and did not answer. I had not seen her since the first company meetings when I had just returned from MEX.

"Listen, Caitlyn, I need to ask you about Reina." I knew the F/A was a good friend and a witness to Reina's premonitions.

"Come back after the meal service," my smiling friend informed me. "We can talk then." My spirits lifted as she headed back to her station at 4R. I felt better about deciding to get on this flight. I wanted to compare notes. I needed to reaffirm that all I had experienced was truly real and not some chaotic dream. I looked out the window at the vista below me, the billowy clouds floating gracefully above the massive waters while the sun was fading in the far west. The light bestowed its spectrum of colors creating a phenomenon of orange, pink and lavender splendor.

Why did I survive?

With the in-flight movie under way I made my way to the aft galley where Caitlyn and a couple of other crew members had gathered to take a break, enjoying left-over first-class meals.

"2, 6, 5, those were the numbers she told me concerning the flight in her dreams," Caitlyn spoke freely in front of the two other F/As. I was a bit embarrassed at first since I assumed we would talk about this privately. But since it did not seem to bother her or the other ladies I just decided to listen.

"How did she know, Cait?" One auburn haired F/A named Natalie asked as they continued eating.

"She always had premonitions. She tried to get on with several airlines before being hired by our company. We used to fly to Mexico together and it was during the layovers that she mentioned the details."

"Wasn't she scared to fly?" A tall, brown-haired girl named Janette spoke up. "Heck, if I knew that kind of information I would have quit and found another job."

"She showed no fear even when we were on final approach," I stated matter-of-factly.

"You mean she mentioned this on the flight?" Natalie's eyes grew wide as she stared right at me. Dear Lord, I had said too much.

"She told you she was gonna die?" Janette now inquired. I became very uncomfortable as I just looked at Caitlyn who signaled me that it was okay that I tell the truth.

"She mentioned that flight could be the one."

"I just got chills up and down my spine," Natalie said as she crossed her arms and rubbed her shoulders.

"What did you do when you heard that?" Janette stared intensely, wanting to hear each and every detail of what I might reveal. I became uneasy. They had no idea what was going through my mind.

"You may have heard that I had strapped myself into the jumpseat and tightened the straps so tight I could barely breathe." Three heads nodded. "Well, now you know why. Excuse me." I pretended like I had just recalled something I needed to see to. I went back to my seat in first class, leaving it to Caitlyn to fill in the details. I was once again frazzled. I sat for a long time and pondered. I knew that someday I would have to testify in the court cases that were being lined up against the airline. What kind of impact would there be when I started to ramble on about premonitions and visions? *"Oh yes, even Tamlyn knew it was coming. That is why she tried so hard to transfer out of flying."* Oh yeah that's gonna go over big! This was insanity. Then, the no smoking sign illuminated indicating our descent into Honolulu International Airport.

The crew wished me a good time as I said good-bye and left. I was totally unprepared to venture on to Kauai: wrong clothes, bad timing and a short budget. I figured I would look pretty foolish toting a heavy raincoat in 82 degrees of tropic jungle. Deciding to stay on Oahu, called my friend Lonnie Grimes who lived on the windward side of the island. We hadn't not spoken since the accident.

"Hey, gosh, I saw it all in the newspapers and on TV." He was speaking of the short window allowed in the media before the Iranian Hostage situation took over the news. "Eddy, you still there?" My anger for the media triggered me into silence.

"Yeah, I'm sorry…. I'm here in Honolulu and…"

"Well come on over, you can stay here."

"Yeah?" Off I went to Waiamanalo.

The next morning the sun shone brightly along the coastline. With Makapu'u Beach just down the road I was able to unload the pressures inside by riding perfect waves, ideal therapy a wonderful method of distraction as the wind cooled my mind for someone like me

Leonard was a master at body surfing, commanding the powerful swells with graceful swirls, cutting through the wall of cascading water. I, on the other hand was not. I continued to "eat it" big time, getting taken right down and tumbling along the sandy bottom. I would pop up out, determined to try it again in even deeper waters. I am sure there were more than a few local guys out there who were entertained by the "poor bugga" who seemed determined to punish himself. Lonnie finally swam over and suggested we go have lunch. Back on the beach I stood exhausted and bruised but it didn't matter. I felt wonderful.

We ate at a fine lunch at a Mexican restaurant and yes, they served Bohemia. Instead of asking what the crash was like, Lonnie focused on what was important.

"Shit, you're still in one piece!" We were soon joined by some of his friends. The sincerity of my island friend emphasized what he believed to be the bottom line. We were soon joined by local friends and Lonnie immediately shared with them our conversation.

"You hit the jackpot," someone exclaimed.

"I never met anyone who won the lottery," a local Japanese man replied with a grin. They sat amazed while I just smiled and nodded. Later, in private, I would give Lonnie some specifics.

"It's the investigators and legal representatives who I just can't deal with," I said.

"Well, you always have that special knife I gave you." Lonnie smiled to lighten the conversation. I laughed and finished my bottle of Bohemia.

"Yes, I do have the knife," I reassured him. My words jumped out and stuck in my memory.

"You gonna stay a few days?"

"Got to get back to L.A. I have an audience with a prince of the Holy Catholic Church." Lonnie's eyes widened with curiosity.

"Is he gonna hear your confession?" We laughed and I we grew silent.

"Perhaps he should," I whispered to myself as I grabbed another bottle of beer.

Arriving back at LAX I stood to deplane the DC-10 when I felt a hand slap me on the shoulder from behind.

"Glad you made it, buddy." I turned to see a familiar face, but I knew him only by sight. The name on his work shirt said Raul. He would board on any given assignment to clean as I was deplaning, but we had never spoken before.

"Thanks," I replied with a shy smile. His sentiment was pure and genuine. Just like the people in Mexico, I knew he was sincere. It was the simple people who seemed to really understand, and their words meant so much. And they would continue: a baggage man, a caterer worker, a janitor. I truly appreciated it, but I was growing weary of the magnificent Edmundo. I'll say one thing though - I certainly had more acquaintances since the accident although some of them I could have done without. Once in the employee parking lot after a flight my emotions peaked, and I became violently nauseous. My body would be hit with convulsions and the wonderful first-class meal I consumed on the flight was solemnly left upon the concrete floor. Driving home, I would be accompanied by the "fallen angels," as I took to calling the voices in my head.

"You Pussy," was the last taunt I heard before falling into bed.

There were a few moments when being the company's little hero had some benefits. I was able for example smooth out the wrinkles with Ackley although the concern could always be heard in her voice. Certainly, some of my recent actions and decisions could have been grounds for termination or at least suspension for any other flight employee. I realized they were stretching the rules for me, yet there was a big part of me that didn't care. I wanted to be defiant, to cause a problem for those who didn't seem to want to get to the truth concerning 2605. They might as well have suspended me. I wasn't getting much of a paycheck, anyway. Drifting with my emotions, I punished myself. Prompted by my financial situations, I ate tuna packed in water. At times it became a feast. A peach or pear became a delicate dessert. Heck, if I needed to eat snails for the protein I did it. It was the right thing to do, to suffer in silence.

"You deserve to be miserable." The voices were at it again as I drove to downtown Los Angeles for my appointment with Timothy Cardinal Manning. I desperately hoped he could help.

Climbing the stairs of the Spanish-style building with its Moorish pillars I was expecting to hear a lecture warning me that Satan is never idle. Maybe there would be a reminder to stay the road to salvation, following the path of the straight and narrow through sacrifice and denial, the regular religious admonitions. I was to be proven so wrong.

Cardinal Manning appeared and offered sincere compassion and understanding. He would have none of this falling to one knee and kissing the ring. Timothy Manning, the man and the pastor was who I was blessed to meet. But even this scholarly man of faith admitted to being at a loss to explain God's greater plan in this affair.

"The only thing I do know, Eddy, is that God's love is total and eternal." These words dared me to hope. Then the time came for my confession. I knelt to one knee and blessed myself.

"Bless me father for I have sinned. I lived," I whispered to myself.

When our time was almost up, I was introduced to a Father Riley, a man about my age and obviously well-regarded by the Cardinal.

"I thought about how best to console you and encourage you to continue to believe, and I think Father Riley would be someone you might want to speak with from time to time." The young priest was a walking advertisement for the church's efforts in recruiting young men to a religious vocation. The Archbishop excused himself and left the two of us alone. My faith in my church gained a boost. I was not sure which Pope had ordained Timothy Manning a Cardinal, but it certainly was the right decision in my humble opinion. I spent the afternoon with Father Riley in the lush gardens outside.

"I don't know how Father, but Reina knew." I poured my heart out. I continued the confession I had begun with His Eminence

"It seems it all has come down to money, Father. I wish I had done more before it was all swept under the carpet. Then there are the nightmares." The priest became concerned.

"Have you considered getting professional help?" Father Riley's question caught me off guard. My mother had led me to believe that the subject of mental illness was taboo in my family and I guess I went along with it. Anyway, how would I find the right doctor? As if on cue, Father Riley provided the answer.

"There is a wonderful man who heads up the psychiatric wing at the U.C.L.A. Veterans Hospital named Joseph Ramljak. He does a lot of work with returning Vietnam vets who are finding it hard to fit back into society. I have recommended quite a few to him." What would my dear mother have thought about the advice I was receiving from a priest?

Suddenly it was time to leave. As I was about to exit through the iron gate at the top of the stairs Father Riley began to bless me, and under the authority of God, again forgave me my sins. I left the meeting in good spirits. I was especially happy that neither clergyman stated that God had some great plan for me. As I drove the crowded freeway back towards the South Bay, I was grateful that Father Riley, my new friend, had given me absolution. I would have been even more pleased had he done something about the dreams and voices.

I vowed to have a new resolve as I was placed back on the reserve list, determined to focus on my duties and nothing else. I wished to exhibit greater fortitude in embracing my duties.

There was also the fact that I was broke and half-starving, trying to keep my head above water and not lose my home.

"Sequence 140," the scheduler announced. Upon checking my F/A bid sheet I spotted the assignment. LAX-ACA-LAX. Yes, Acapulco. I was going back to Mexico, but I was relieved it was not Mexico City or a DC-10. I would be working the smaller Boeing 727. The turn-around flight would have me back home in the evening.

I was more upbeat, smiling and interacting with others in the flight lounge, both cabin and cockpit crews. One time. I was extremely surprised to find a written communication, in my mailbox, from Barry Lane, the company's Vice President of In-Flight Services. Along with his gracious best wishes, Mr. Lane understood that I was an admirer of some of the old big band music from the forties. Music of that era, the favorite of my parents, was played often in the family home while I was growing up. Inscribed in the Vice President's handwriting were the first four lines of an old Johnny Mercer tune.

"You've got to accentuate the positive,
  Eliminate the negative
  And latch on to the affirmative,
  Don't mess with Mister In Between." Included in the letter was a cassette recording of the old tune by Johnny Mercer and the Pied Pipers, circa 1945.

Barry Lane showed real class in reaching out to me in this manner. Sure, I may have wanted to be a big pain in the butt to Ackley and Shana, but I had no desire to be twisted with Mr. Lane. His message made perfect sense and his personal touch made it more enduring. It told me that this was a man I could approach, a voice of authority who I felt would be fair and honest. Barry Lane became that tinge of hope.

The take-off over the Pacific shores was becoming routine. When we hit a bit of turbulence on our way to Acapulco I neither cringed nor felt fear. It was completely the opposite, often exhilarating. My crewmates for this run were a pleasure to work with. The service went like clockwork as we streaked down the coast into Mexican air space. We were greeted by the rugged desert of Baja California, heading to cross the Bay of Cortez. Most of the passengers were Americans looking forward to a

319

sunny holiday on the beaches of the resort city, as well as natives returning home.

Working the aft cabin, I noticed a Hispanic family, of two men and a woman. The elderly man on the aisle seemed fast asleep. I assumed him to be the father of either the man or woman. His wrinkled face and gnarled hands betrayed a life of struggle and hard work. I elected to serve the others around him without disturbing his serenity. It was not until the collection of the trays did I bother to speak to them.

"Would the older gentleman like something to eat?"

"I think he will be fine," the younger man stated.

"Going to visit family?" I inquired.

"Yes, my wife's family lives in Acapulco." His head leaned toward the quiet woman who smiled and nodded.

"And the sleeping gentleman?"

"He is her father."

"Oh, going back to join the family, should be very special for him." He sat back perfectly still, almost rigid with a frozen smile on his face. "Heck, hasn't moved a bit." He retained that same smile for a long time. "Is he okay?" I asked.

"I think he is dead," the man responded, and my jaw dropped open.

"This must be another cruel joke being played on me by Muerto," I thought. I looked around to find him, searching up and down the aisle, assuming he was disguised. I began to attract attention, but I still scanned the cabin and quickly studied each face. Finally, I checked for a pulse on the elderly gentleman.

"Has he been ill?"

"Cancer." One word told the story.

"Do you want me to see if I can revive him?" I couldn't believe I was asking this. The man turned to his wife and asked her permission.

"Certainly." She indicated. "If something can possibly be done then go ahead and try." I released the seat belt of the elder gent. It took tremendous effort to move his body to the galley floor where CPR could be performed. I alerted the rest of the flight attendants and they, in turn, informed the cockpit who passed the message on to Mexican Air Traffic Control and the tower at ACA. Just like October 31, the training kicked in as one of the young ladies working the flight assisted in CPR. I vigorously performed the compressions and lung inflation. I kept hoping to feel him breathing on his own, but no. Instead, as soon as we landed and the door was cracked, the paramedics boarded the craft. I had been performing CPR for over an hour on a dead man.

"You f##ked up again didn't you?" Shame had a voice and it was ruthless. "Why do people around you end up dead?" Muerto had been lurking in the cabin after all.

As soon I entered the flight lounge upon our return to LAX, I discovered word had already spread of about what had happened during our flight. Edmundo was hailed and congratulated for his actions and decisions. Ackley reminded me that I needed to write an account of what happened. Usually I would have been annoyed by the request, but I could only think about this poor Mexican family losing their parent. I imagined some slimy attorney presenting the promise of big cash if they simply twisted the facts a bit and sued the airline. Perhaps that crash survivor, Edmundo or whatever his name, was to blame. Had he really tried to save the man? I was sure some people might jump at the opportunity, but that noble family was not one of them. They made sure to thank me for my effort, but I could only stare at them, wondering why they had not asked for help when they thought he was dead. I signed the "incident report" and walked away, trying to feel positive about how I had performed my job.

I tried hard not to let that incident or anything else derail my efforts. I was arriving on time to my assigned flights, making a serious attempt to fulfill all my responsibilities, remaining in total control while in uniform and on duty. It was no longer always necessary after a flight to hurry to the parking lot, kneel by my car, and throw up.

"You'll never be good enough."

But fearing a recurrence of such a vulgar act because of the elderly man's death, I decided to break my regular routine. I exited the employees' bus early to stop at the company cafeteria, hoping a ginger-ale might settle my anxious stomach. I carried my regulation suitcase as I walked across the large hangar floor, and lost in thought about my dead passenger, I heard voices calling out behind me.

"Edmundo...…..Edmundo," I turned to see figures in suits across the massive space. One tall individual was also waving to get my attention. I squinted to see CEO Mario Reddick in the distance. He was mouthing something, so I walked a bit toward him.

"I had a good work-out this morning Edmundo." He then flashed a thumbs up as his subordinates stood silently, waiting for Reddick to lead them back to the executive offices. I waved and smiled, the perfect image of who Edmundo was perceived to be.

I imagined Mario Reddick pumping iron, maybe appearing in his Speedos, all oiled up, flashing his poses as the latest company jingle played in the background. I had to give him his due. He was in decent shape for his age and wore that expensive business suit well. He was no demon and I knew it. I was sure he'd had a few of his own nightmares over this crash, yet I wished he could have been witness to some of the people burning, listening to their awful screams. Maybe everyone connected with this mess, cover-up and the grab for money should all have been witness to the horror.

"Assholes!"

No matter how I tried to resist, ginger ale or not, the ritual purging was still performed on the concrete of the parking facility. Then I headed home, totally disgusted with myself for losing control. I do not remember falling asleep that night, but I awoke the next morning to a phone call from Scheduling advising me that I would be working a two-day trip with a long layover in Portland, Oregon. I must have gone through the motions of getting ready, packing my suitcase, but have no memory of either doing that or driving down Pacific Coast Hwy. to the airport.

"I would have had the company write me a check for a million dollars," The words of suave Maurice kept reverberating in my head and distracting me. LAS was the first leg of that two-day trip and I hardly spoke to anyone, whether passengers or crew.

"Are you okay, Eddy?" The concerned senior F/A asked.

Alright? Do I look f####ing alright? The blood suckers are not satisfied with pillaging the remains of my aeroplane, my friends. No! Now they want to tear my heart out. That's how I wanted to respond, but instead I remained silent.

"Eddy, I asked if you are okay." I snapped to.

"What? Oh, yeah I'm fine, tired from a heavy workout that's all." I quickly walked to the back of the jetliner to find seclusion and calm myself.

That night in Portland the four off-duty cabin crewmembers decided to have dinner together. We were joined by Gretchen, another F/A who lived in PDX but was an SFO commuter. She was a senior gal, well-known and liked. As was par for the course when I went out with the crew on any given layover, the atmosphere seemed very tense to me, like everyone was walking on eggshells.

Gretchen was a free spirit with a broad smile. She had a relaxed professional manner that was highlighted by her rousing laughter that made her curly hair shake. As a result, she would constantly be having to adjust her bifocals.

We enjoyed a fine meal and had a few glasses of red wine. Then, sweet-faced Tory spoke up.

"I don't know how you still get on the plane after what you went through."

I have to, I'm broke. The company has not been paying me for the time I've missed since our 10 crashed and burned. Of course, Edmundo would never make such a statement to please his crewmates. Instead, I offered this bull shit; "When you fall off a horse you just have to get back on."

"If I were you, I would be down on my knees every night thanking God." This was Gretchen's response as she stared intently at me, smiling. I had to control myself. Sure, it was obvious she only wished the best for me, making a statement that was shared by those at the table and so many others. But Gretchen, like Maurice before her, was making an assumption about a situation she could not fathom even in her worse nightmare. To my well-meaning associate it was a simple matter of life and death. By her speculations, her God, had intervened in a grand manner to save me. It was that simple.

323

"Why don't you girls ask me if it is true that the massive "G" forces caused passengers to be decapitated?" Edmundo of course would not allow such discussion at the table nor would he allow any word concerning my treatment at the hands of the heinous comandante or my nightmares of Javier screaming. Also, none of these dear friends sitting comfortably at the hotel restaurant in PDX that night wanted to be told that several of their fellow flight attendant's families would not be compensated financially because the deceased had been in their probationary period.

"I think about God a lot," I finally responded. What I did not add was that I wondered where the hell this God was on the morning of October 31. I slowly picked up the glass of wine in my right hand and stared into the deep rich color. I gazed back at the four faces that waited for me to finish my statement. "Believe me Gretchen, I spend a lot of time at night on my knees." I finished the last of the wine. The ladies seemed pleased with my answer.

I exited the aircraft at LAX, again with smiles and well wishes. I quickly headed for the flight lounge wondering when the next flight for HNL was. Robert, a young, good looking F/A who had graduated from training just a few classes behind mine, joined me on a sofa where I was trying to compose myself.

"Now that's not such a pleasant look for such a handsome man." Yes, Robert was gay and proud of it, and always a fun person to work with on any given flight. He was easy-going and didn't let any caustic aspects of life burden him. He was honest, a character trait I found missing in some people these days.

"I need a break from all this crap," I blurted out in frustration. Robert just laughed.

"Stop the world and let me get off," he declared with an animated gesture. "You got any days off?" I looked at my friend with a mischievous glare. "Me and eight others are catching the flight to Acapulco and you're welcome to join us. We're ready to invade the Mexican Riviera." I was going into days off, had my stack of hoarded passes and just enough time to drive to my nearby residence to change.

"Sounds good. I'm in!"

I drove fast through the tunnel underneath the runways at LAX on Sepulveda Blvd., anticipating another unique adventure. I wondered what my dear mother would say of my impulsive decision.

"Hey mom, I will be out of town for a few days. I am going on vacation with nine gay guys."
I laughed with glee, I figured this escapade or at least the tequila enjoyed would grant me some peace if only for a while.

Eight of my cohorts were F/A's, five were based with me at LAX, two were from SFO and the ninth was a partner of one of the SFO guys. Arriving at the gate for the flight, I was struck by the reaction of the passengers who sat waiting to board, particularly the women. Each of my travel partners would be considered by most as extremely good-looking men. Dressed with style, they would easily catch one's eye. I saw ladies, some young, some not so much, whispering to each other. Two girls were overheard, wondering if the boys were models maybe, traveling to some photo shoot on the beaches of Acapulco. Little did they know that my friends would be more interested in meeting their brothers instead. I just sat enjoying the show.

One thing became very clear after take-off, I was simply Eddy, one of a group on holiday. Edmundo was left stranded at the gate.

"I'm a flight attendant also, and I would like to know some of what you know," said Gilbert. "Someday that information could be very beneficial if I find myself in an emergency situation." I welcomed his refreshing sincerity. Maybe they figured that in order to relax I needed to talk. I wasn't sure.

"We all know you have been through a lot of crap and we respect you for that," Jason, another of the F/A's offered. I felt these eight were men of true character and was happy to be in their company.

On the streets of Acapulco, the reaction from women, both local and tourist, was a kick. Nine handsome, well-groomed male figures turned heads as we strolled along the seashore. I took to lagging a few steps behind the pack to enjoy the people's reaction. It was even more evident at night when the finely dressed men entered a nightclub. We walked into the ballroom of El Pajarito Azul, a disco warehouse with flashing and spinning lights of every sort and color and a constant rhythmic beat. The ladies went wild. Within a few minutes, the clan was surrounded by a horde of women- short, tall, blond, brunette and redhead, all beautiful. I was amazed as I never saw anyone pick up women so fast or so efficiently. I was impressed. The boys all danced exquisitely, and they had the girls virtually waiting in line for a turn. I sat alone in silence, both amazed and amused.

I noticed Gilbert speaking to an admirer, whispering in her ear. Suddenly Gil pointed at me and the beautiful girl gazed at me with a puzzled look.

"Gay?" I saw her mouth the question in disbelief. She quickly looked back at me, then back to Gil. Each woman looked astonished as word quickly spread throughout the club. More confusion followed as one of the F/A's informed two of the admirers that I was the only straight guy in the group.

"All your friends gay and you, no?" One sweet girl dressed in a stunning, tight-fitting gold dress reacted in dismay. I smiled and gave her a nod. The result was that the entire harem was left in my hands to deal with. What a perfect set-up.

We all had a glorious night on the Mexican Riviera. No one knew my past. No one looked at me differently, nor asked imposing questions. There were no references to the hand of the Almighty nor was I judged for actions that were beyond my control. I felt alive and was grateful to be in the company of such true friends.

Returning home, I felt reinvigorated, in a positive state of mind and dedicated to settling down into a healthy routine. My time in the weight room kept a leash on the anxiety. On one particular morning after a refreshing swim by the Manhattan Beach pier, I returned home where I was surprised to find a lovely young lady knocking at my door: early twenties, beautiful eyes, long flowing light-brown hair and dressed professionally. From behind I watched her stretching to peek in the window.

"Are you a peeping Tom?" I asked trying to be witty. Surprised, the lady turned and smiled, seeming a bit embarrassed, getting caught in the act.

"Do you know *Mr. Valencia*, the person who lives here?" She jumped and turned around; no doubt embarrassed about being caught in the act.

"Yeah, I do," I stated in a sassy manner. With only my swimwear on I thought this could get very interesting. She pouted her lips.

"Well, where is he then?" She came right up to me as I looked into her eyes and said,

"Right here." She giggled, tossed her hair back and reached into her pocket. She pulled out a very official looking envelope,

"Consider yourself served, ah, *Mr. Valencia.*" She placed the envelope onto my open hand and was off. She turned one last time and flashed a little wink. I opened the envelope while still standing outside, and its message was like a punch in the gut.

The document informed me that I was named in a lawsuit against the airline by legal representatives of a certain passenger who just happened to survive. His survival was partially thanks to me, as I remembered this guy very well. Nevertheless, his attorney went on to accuse me of being derelict in my duties as a flight attendant the morning of October 31, 1979. I was being accused of deliberately ignoring injured passengers who could have been saved because I was only interested in trying to save my fellow crewmembers.

"I wish I had died with my crew!"

Chapter XV

I sat on my bed and gazed at the statue of the ever-concerned Holy Virgin. I removed the knife I had received from Lonnie and gripped its handle, relishing the feeling of brass knuckles in my right hand. I sat for the longest time simply staring ahead, holding the weapon and continually pounding the butt into the palm of my left palm.

The following morning, I called Scheduling to report myself sick and hurried to the airport where I once again boarded a flight to HNL. Upon landing I caught a Princeville Airways flight to Kauai, seeking the sanctuary of the Na Pali. To anyone at the airport I looked perfectly fine, but inside the anger was eating me alive.

On this trip I added the stern, metal blade to my sparse belongings. The weapon became the object of my total focus once I was back on the island, as I carried it through the lush valley of the Kalalau. My recollection of persuading that particular businessman to change seats on the flight and his arrogance and rudeness consumed me with resentment and shame. They unified to destroy any sense of hope I may have mustered in the previous days. The end result was a gut full of bile for the money seekers.

"It's all your fault anyway." The voices once again brought me to tears, but now they were tears of regret for not being able to join my crewmates who had crossed over into a world of peace. They were in a place forbidden to me. The consolation prize was that I had been granted a new life. That is how everyone else saw it, or maybe as the good nuns used to teach, perhaps I was now cast into the vexation of Purgatory. Yet, as I looked around at the magnificence of my island retreat, I could not help but wonder if there just might be an exit from this despicable imprisonment. Thankfully, the tranquility and soothing nature of Kauai slowly began to chip away at my scorn. This enabled me to gather some of the pieces of my shattered emotions. All too soon my time in the sanctuary came to an end. Like it or not I had to go home and face the consequences of my most recent disappearance.

Exiting the trail at Ke'e Beach I showered and readied myself for the short hop back to HNL. Later, I once again strolled along the open walkways at the Honolulu airport, looking smart and feeling refreshed. I was on stand-by, hoping for a first-class seat back to LAX. Quietly sitting on a blue vinyl seat in the gate area and close to the podium where the company agents scrambled to assure an orderly boarding procedure, I listened to the chatter of those around me as they waited for their assigned section to be called for boarding. A blond woman in aloha wear struggled to keep her little ones in check as they ran about, hyped up by all the activity. An elderly couple wore matching red Hawaiian print shirts that screamed "tourist". I assumed it was their first trip to the islands. I smiled as the man leaned over and gave the elderly woman a kiss on her lips. Perhaps they were on a long-postponed honeymoon. Then it happened. I saw the dead of Benito Juárez where a moment before sat the elderly couple.

"Death will ride with you today." The message was loud and clear in my head. I struggled to remain calm in the midst of so many people then turned to view the nose of the jumbo jet through the massive windows. I strained to view the movement in the cockpit of those who would control the mighty bird this day. There I saw a faint, skeletal image attired in Captain's cap and four stripes clearly visible on the shoulders. The master of deceit turned to look in my direction and raised his ridge-like hand in recognition. The voice of little Javier entered my mind and began to plead Death's case.

"Why didn't you help me, Eddy?" I arose in panic trying hard not to bring attention to myself. Looking up and down the concourse, things began to close in around me. I tried to find a place to be alone and spotted a lavatory. Carrying my belongings, I quickly ditched into the last stall and locked myself in, sitting upon the stool and raising my legs in the fetal position.

"Will we ever be good enough?" The lost child demanded an answer.

"I don't know. I don't think I will ever know." The psychosis struck deep as the terminal intercom announced that my flight was boarding. Opening my suitcase and reaching deep into a pouch, I felt the nasty blade. I searched from side to side with my hand until my fingers felt an herbal roach. Certainly, a bit of pakalolo would calm my nerves enough to let me board without causing a scene.

Much more composed, I returned to face the agents at my gate who smiled and handed me my boarding pass. Now I was almost in a state of euphoria, being careful not to make eye contact with any one person. Once in the cabin I glanced up and down the aisles and recognized the faces of the HNL crew, then calmly walked to my front cabin seat and stored my belongings in the appropriate manner. Feeling much relieved, I sat and buckled my seat belt. Even though we hadn't moved an inch from the gate, I was already "in-flight!"

I sat sedated unaware that the slight pungent aroma of pakalolo began to fill a portion of the first-class cabin.

"Do you smell anything?" I picked up on the conversation of the F/A at 2R as he confronted another associate who was walking aft from first class. I gritted my teeth.

"Oh shit!"

"No, what are you smelling?" I sensed a split second of relief as the passengers were now boarding. The cockpit door was still open, the pilots performing their pre-flight duties. I sat motionless when a gate agent rushed up the aisle to first class accompanied by a flight attendant. He opened the commode as the captain now appeared at the entrance of the cockpit and engaged in conversation with the F/A and gate agent. All at once they turned in unison and looked straight at me. I tried to ignore the obvious, but the gate agent walked over and stood over me.

"Will you please exit the craft with me?" There was no denying what was about to occur. I was going to be tossed off the flight and I was sure my airline career was "*fin*." Then, a female F/A interceded and whispered something to the gate agent. Scowling, he hesitated for a second. Then instantly, his demeanor changed. I glanced up to see the passengers staring at me.

Who is this man being confronted? Is he a madman? Is the flight in danger? Do I want to be on the same plane with him?

The agent studied the passenger manifest list then leaned forward and whispered to me.

"Ed, you want to come join me out on the jetway?" I was sure I was busted as I stood and started to gather my personal belongings. "That won't be necessary." He moved aft motioning me to follow him. All eyes on the aircraft were on my pitiful self yet I noticed that the cabin crew ignored my movement and continued to see to their duties. "So, what's going on?" The agent was trying to be understanding. I spoke the truth.

"I'm going through a lot of shit."

"Why don't you get some help?" We both understood that he meant psychological. Just then we were joined by the captain, fortunately for me he, too, tried to be understanding.

"What's happening, son?" I told him about the nightmares, the flashbacks and even touched on the lawsuits that I realized I would have to deal with eventually.

"Damn it, Captain, I'm tired of all this crap and I want it to stop." I fell silent and felt utterly defeated as he listened and sympathized.

"Captain, here is the new unit to be replaced." Suddenly, a company mechanic appeared in his red jumpsuit and held a new replacement part. With a nod from the captain he headed for the cockpit.

"Why don't you get some help?" came the standard but sensible question.

"I'm trying to make things happen," I replied, realizing that I was barely getting started. The Captain gestured for me to re-board his aircraft. As I did, I was greeted by the stares of all the seated passengers. I regretted what I had done and was so grateful for the compassion I was shown by the agent and the captain.

We were told over the intercom to announce that the delay was due to having to replace a vital instrument in the cockpit but now we were ready for departure. After take-off and once settled in at a cruising altitude, the focus on the idiot in the first-class cabin diminished. I imagined the incident would sure make for some good small talk amongst the cabin crew during the six-hour flight. Once the meal service was over and the cabin was secure, I decided to go mid-galley and face the music. The HNL crew members were saying nothing, for which I was grateful. I turned to one of the male F/As, with whom I was antiquated. I threw my arms up and twisted my face in confusion.

"Tell me the truth Fred about what just happened," I asked. He just stood there in deep thought, then said,

"You know at first I said 'what a jerk, why in the hell is he doing something like that?' Then I thought longer." I listened intently. He shifted his body once again. "I realize I have no idea what he went through down there in Mexico and if it happened to me how do I know I wouldn't be doing the same?" He chuckled slightly, a reaction that relieved me somewhat. He presented me with a sliver of hope. I had brought shame to my chosen profession and I swore that it would not happen again. I began to wonder if there truly had been a need for an instrument change in the cockpit, or was it merely a ruse to mask my bad behavior? Either way I was grateful.

I would remain an object of curiosity to the restless passengers around me and was glad to hear that, assisted by the winds, we would eventually shorten my flight of embarrassment by twenty minutes. I settled into my seat trying to discard the previous vision of Muerto at the controls of the jumbo jet. My actions had made me wish I could die but I was wise enough to know that Death never comes to he who asks for it.

Once on the ground at LAX I was actually surprised to find no company supervisor waiting to greet me at the gate. I slunk through the flight lounge like a disobedient child, expecting my punishment from a disappointed parent.

"Surely they had to know by now." I was referring to the powers that be: Ackley, Barry Lane and most probably Mario Reddick. I was sure that my company's golden boy image was greatly tarnished. How was I going to face them with this latest incident? This dishonor became new fodder for the demons tearing at my soul.

"Certainly, none of the other crew-members of 2605 would have behaved in such a manner if they had survived. You are worthless." The fallen angels' voices were back. I arrived home to find a company envelope waiting for me. The formal letter was from my supervisor, Shana James, informing me that due to my succession of canceled availability I was in danger of possible suspension and/or termination. Although Shana's signature was at the bottom of the document I wondered if it was Ackley who was pulling the strings. I sat on my bed and looked once again at the stoic image of the Holy Virgin. I was truly lost.

"Yeah, Ed, sequence 174." The following day I vowed again to clean up my act. I resolved to be the best flight attendant the company had as I boarded the Boeing 737 at LAX, for an excursion on the "prairie patrol." This was a journey through the western deserts, mountains and grasslands of our nation. ending up with a layover in Idaho Falls. My confidence was boosted when I discovered that the master in command was Captain Dwayne Foster.

"Eddy boy, you look great, still hitting the gym?" His jovial attitude brought a wide smile to my face, something that had been dearly lacking in recent times. I wanted to tell the captain that my slim physique was due partly from staving, since I was receiving minimum pay. I bit my tongue.

The hot air rising over the desert created the perfect atmosphere for a rolling ride in the small twin-engine jet as we headed for LAS, our designated first stop.

"Can I offer you something to drink?" I exhibited sincere courteousness to the half-sickened passengers as they gripped their arm rests. The 737 rose, only to drop in an instant with the unstable air. One fellow crewmember had to endure the process in high heels, clinging to the beverage cart as we gently swayed in all directions. In an unusual reaction I felt elated with the turbulence for it presented me with another opportunity to thumb my nose at Death. I silently dared him to intervene. *Kiss my ass, Muerto,* I thought as I passed out a lot of ginger ale to the ailing passengers. My defiance was strengthened by the belief that my life was in good hands with Dwayne Foster at the helm.

Once back home I resumed my routine at the gym, which refreshed me. My body had healed and with a little more money coming in I evolved from my usual tuna-in-fresh-water cuisine. I kept in touch with Father Riley whose counseling was a great help to me. My relationship with my parents had been mended, especially with my mother who heard through Sister Inez that I was continuing my visits with Timothy Cardinal Manning. I had a few more successful flight assignments under my belt and thought perhaps the worst was behind me. Whoever trusts in his own mind is a fool.

"I have a flight for you, Ed," the pleasant voice of the scheduler informed me as I held the Flight Attendant Bid Sheet as reference.

"Ah, sequence 190." I froze. There was no need to reference the bid sheet. I was all too aware of that sequence, LAX-MEX-LAX, the all-nighter.

"Excuse me, I'm sorry, I really am sorry." I fumbled the words as I began to shake. "Ah, I don't do the Mexico City all-nighter." I was sure there was a mistake. Certainly, with my recent behavior they were not about to send a perceived madman back on the journey that instigated his madness.

"I'm sorry, Ed, I have my instructions." It became very clear. This was the supposed tough love action of Daisy Ackley. The scheduler continued. "If you refuse the assignment, I am directed to pull you off the reserve list."

"Your beloved airline just stabbed you in the back." The fallen angels laughed and gloated. I could not speak. Had I not proven my devotion to my company, my profession? Yes, I was having difficulties, but wouldn't anyone? The voices became relentless, "None of the other crew-members would have exhibited dysfunctional behavior if they had survived." But whatever I felt, it was being overshadowed by the pure anger.

That night I sat stoically on the long, green sofa, one of several in the flight lounge. I was dressed immaculately in my pristine uniform, nicely pressed and shoes stunningly polished. Now my anger was turning to rage – rage and a determination to survive this shit, even if it required retribution. The airline could no longer be trusted. I would never deny that there were still good people in the company, individuals with clout. Jack McKay certainly was a man I still admired, but when it came to being up-front, could I trust anyone?

"Hey, Eddy, how are you doing?" My good friend Michael Lottergan spoke up as he took a seat next to me. Mike was always upbeat, had a zest for life, and happened to be my union rep. "Where you off to?" he inquired.

"Mexico City." The words popped out as I turned to see his merriment vanish and his jaw dropped.

"The all-nighter?' he asked. I nodded, just staring straight ahead. Michael thought for a moment. "Is this your choice?" I simply shook my head. "What happens if you refuse?" My friend's mind began to problem-solve. I rose and simply drew my hand across my throat indicating my termination. I stood up as it was time to board my aircraft. "You need to call Reva," were the last words I heard. Michael was right; he always made good sense when faced with a sticky situation, but his wise advice came too late to overcome the obstacle now before me.

If my fellow associates had any misgivings about flying with me, they disguised them well. At the crew briefing I chose 4R as my working position. Why not? Certainly, there was not going to be a repeat of the Halloween disaster. It just made common sense to pick that space. While storing my belongings by my station, I was approached by William, a tall, handsome associate who had selected the workstation right across the cabin from me at 4L.

"You know, Eddy, I have no problem working this flight. The way I figure it, you are probably the safest guy to fly with. It's not going to happen to you again." He chuckled, grabbed my arm, and gently slapped me on the back. I turned slowly and looked at him.

"Well if it does happen pray you don't make it out." His smile quickly vanished as he hesitantly walked back to 4L.

I sat staring blankly, strapped to my jumpseat. Once in the air however, I was determined to concentrate on my duties, although I chose to remain isolated for most of the all-night journey across the Bay of Cortez to the Mexican capital. As usual, the majority of the passengers slept, and I felt no apprehension. Instead, I was still dealing with my anger towards the airline. I recalled how devastated Diego had been when he discovered he had been lied to regarding the runway lights. Thankfully, my fellow crewmates respected my isolation during both legs of the trip.

Upon arrival at LAX I was still fuming. I decided to go hit the gym even though I had been up for over twenty hours. The adrenaline flowed the anger grew as I rode the company tram to the parking facility. Perhaps I should just get as far away from the airport as I could. But my disease had other plans.

"Oh, dear God," I gasped as soon as I reach my vehicle. I fell into a seizure of convulsions that paralyzed me.

"You worthless piece of shit." The voices clamored for my submission. I lay on the concrete, unable to gather my emotions or my strength to lift myself out of the vomit. All at once my wrath discharged.

"No. No. No. I will not allow this to happen again," I scolded myself. I picked myself off the pavement, tossed my flight gear into my vehicle, cleaned up my uniform as best I could and walked off in the direction of the Executive Offices.

"God damn it! I am going to see Barry Lane right now no matter what!" My resolve was clear. "I keep hearing how he is the one executive who lends his ear to the common employee. Well, I hope he has a big one because I have a hell of a lot to get off my chest." I stormed up the stairs and rapidly made my way across the marble floors and straight into the waiting area of the office of the Vice-President of Inflight Services where I was greeted by Barry Lane's secretary, Grace, who sat staring at me in disbelief. She rose and slowly approached me, looking as if she were about to cry.

"I want to see Mr. Lane," I blurted out as I rushed to take a seat and raising my hands to my face as I began to break down. Grace came to my side and put her hand gently upon my shoulder.

"I'm sorry, Ed, but Mr. Lane is currently in Salt Lake City." Her words crushed whatever hope I had gathered. Suddenly, from inside Barry Lane's office, another person appeared seeking the source of the ruckus. I glanced up while trying to wipe away the tears my despair and saw the imposing figure of Robert Eldrich, who I think was an Executive Vice-President. He immediately invited me into Barry Lane's office making it very clear from the start that he was available to listen, console, or assist me in whatever way he could.

"I just got off the all-nighter from Mexico," I began, holding back the rage. Mr. Eldrich was dumbfounded. His head jerked back, and his eyes widened. "Look sir, I can't do what they expect. I am trying to get it together, but it has only been a few months since I had to see my flight, my crew, dying in the flames."

"No, Ed, you shouldn't push yourself. These things can take years to resolve." His words flowed so freely from his mouth, yet I had a hard time accepting what he was saying. Yet he was able to put me at ease and the voices of my mind fell silent. If he was swayed by what seemed logical to both of us the only problem that remained was to eliminate the hassles from Shana and Daisy.

I still carried the court summons I had been served with and presented it to Mr. Eldrich. He was quite surprised I was being singled out in the lawsuits against the airline.

"I am sorry all this has happened to you, Ed. I will certainly contact Mr. Lane and inform him. I also assure you that this airline will stand with you regarding any court situation. We are all proud of the actions taken by you during this horrible event in Mexico City. Rest easy and give us a little time. You know, Ed, this whole process is all very new to us, also." With that being said I thanked Mr. Eldrich and Grace and calmly walked out with a sliver of hope. I went home and slept for the next sixteen hours.

My next assignment sent me across the southwest desert to PHX, ending up in DEN for the night. The final leg of the second day brought our Boeing 727 into SLC where I learned we were to board special passengers. I was surprised to discover that Barry Lane and his wife had entered the coach cabin rather than take First Class. I was unsure if he knew of my meeting with Bob Eldrich, but he put me at ease by immediately informing me that he had.

"Please be patient, Ed. A fair solution addressing these issues is in the works. You will soon be advised of a meeting." He gave me a nod and shook my hand. I admired his straightforwardness and was content to wait and see what lay ahead.

It was just a matter of days before I found myself heading to the executive offices once again. Upon entering the meeting room I immediately spotted both Shana James and Daisy Ackley seated at a large table. While Daisy smiled and welcomed me, I sensed she wasn't entirely sincere. Perhaps my behavior had resulted in an intervention by the powers that be, a scenario indicating an inability to keep her own house in order. I personally was not at odds with Daisy and had only the greatest respect for her as my superior. I was one of the few people who witnessed the ordeal in assuming the task of morgue duty in Mexico City. The sight of mangled body parts could not be dismissed so easily from one's memory.

Shana, on the other hand, paid little attention to my presence, seemingly engrossed in a large file of papers that she ruffled through, stopping at times to examine specifics on each sheet. I hoped that the large file was not mine, a detailed reflection of my recent flight cancellations. I was certain that if there was to be an evaluation of my recent behavior Shana was surely confident that she had the ammunition to shoot down this insubordinate fly-boy. I envisioned her standing and reading straight from the Flight Attendant Manual.

"Regulation section 1.2.8. Maintaining acceptable attendance is an important aspect of your job as a Flight Attendant. Please be aware that failure to improve and maintain a satisfactory record could result in stronger disciplinary action up to and including termination." The anticipation gave me shivers.

I did not arrive empty-handed. Along with a series of commendations I received from civic and private institutions corresponding to my actions on October 31, I also brought along a letter from Mario Reddick. He applauded my "performance" during the entire ordeal concluding with the following remark: "This airline can always use bright individuals as yourself in our future."

I was convinced that Barry Lane did not arrange this meeting so that we could butt heads. This was not his style. The Vice-President and Grace, his secretary, arrived with two other individuals who I recognized as being from both the Legal Department and Public Relations.

"This airline and you, Eduardo, have a responsibility to each other." Mr. Lane made it clear *that* was going to be the focus of any resolution. I was very pleased to hear those words for I wanted nothing less. Although I believed Shana wanted to inform those in attendance of my indiscretions, I was pretty sure that Mr. Lane was aware of my unacceptable conduct and did not need Shana to refresh his memory.

"Would you like to inform us of what you have been experiencing, Ed?" With that I slowly rose and decided to let go of the anger.

"I'd like to thank all of you for attending this meeting to help me in finding solutions to a multitude of problems I am currently plagued with. You all know the specifics of the tragedy so I will be brief. I would like to tell you something you may not know about, the behavior and outcome of one passenger." I slowly and articulately expressed my encounter with the rude businessman during flight 2605, recalling his outburst and my effort to patiently diffuse the situation to his liking. I recounted his deep displeasure in having to relocate to a seat in the aft section, an action that saved his life. Then, I removed from my pocket the court summons I had recently received, unfolded the legal papers and held them high for all to see. I then continued.

"I have received accolades for my actions and decisions while in the service of this company during the ordeal that ensued and afterward. Here I hold in my hand a legal document naming me as an incompetent crew-member who among other horrendous assertions is being accused of making a conscious decision to bypass injured passengers who could have been saved." I slowly rotated my body to allow all present to view the subpoena. "The passenger who survived, due in part by my allowing him to relocate on the aircraft, will most likely be awarded hundreds of thousands of dollars from our carrier's insurers once the frenzy for money is concluded." I then reached into another pocket, removed and unfolded another document and held it high in my other hand for all to see. I proceeded. "I, on the other hand, who supposedly performed my duties in the highest tradition of my profession, have been threatened with possible termination by my supervisor Shana James." Not a sound was heard.

Barry Lane quickly seized the initiative as he sensed things were becoming uncomfortable. He had thought long and hard on the situation prior to this meeting and had come up with a plan that he emphasized more than once would be fair.

"Concerning your lack of pay, the airline would allot you maximum hours flight time each month, whether or not you flew those hours. For this consideration Eduardo, you will be required to undergo psychiatric therapy by a physician to be agreed upon by you and the company." He went on to mention that the physician would then advise the airline in the person of Barry Lane, of my progress. The selected physician's initial report would dictate the direction the company would take in the future. Mr. Lane also added that for the present, I was to be kept off the Mexico City all-nighter.

While some may have thought this was too generous and I should have been fired, others surely thought I deserved much more.

Maybe it wasn't a bad idea to seek professional help, especially when it became clear that my F/A insurance was going to cover the cost. I looked forward to the therapy. I remembered nothing in the Flight Attendant Manual discussing "Crew Insanity."

"Who could I contact regarding information and assistance in this matter?" I knew I needed some advice and guidance, then I recalled Mike Lottergan's advice to get in contact with Reva. Yes, it was time to tap into AFA. I recalled how the feisty union rep told me back in Mexico City that I did not have to speak to the company. I knew she was based in SFO and made it my business to get her contact number. I figured she would help if I should have to clash with the airline regarding these issues. There was no need to fill Reva in on the specifics. She was there in the middle of it, she saw the chaos, she could relate. Considering what I had gone this F/A deserved to have the best psychiatric assistance and Reva was going to make sure I got it.

"There is just one big loophole concerning the union's contract with the company though, Eddy." The lady was on top of things. "In wording concerning mental illness and therapy the contract states that the three parties involved: the patient, the company and the insurer covering the cost, each get to select the name of a physician. In almost all contested cases, the company's doctor and insurance's doctor overrule the patient's doctor." Her voice became very soft and the words came through very slow. "Eddy, we have got to figure out a way you can get the airline to pick the doctor *you* want."

If *I* made the choice my selection would be wasted, and down the road that could come back to haunt me. I recognized that it was now time to survive in the maze of a bureaucratic grinder, the world of insurance, diagnosis, expertise and the cost of it all. Another mine field now appeared, and I had to be extremely cautious.

"Edmundo" entered Daisy's office at Terminal 5 with a smile, and projected naivete and vulnerability.

"Gosh, this is all new to me Daisy, I've never seen a psychiatrist." My superior was prepared and had done her research well, even asking fellow associates what physician might be best for me. But what would they know unless all of *them* had been on the couch? I believe she perceived that my recent behavior reflected the possibility of a devastating eruption on a future flight if I went over the edge. The list of doctors she compiled was impressive. There, near the bottom of the alphabetical list, was the name Ramljak. I fixed on the name and my eyes widened, which caught Daisy's attention.

"Have you heard of that doctor?'

"No, I just am trying to pronounce his ethnic name," I quickly replied.

"He's a good doctor," she stated much to my surprise.

"You know him?"

"Not personally, I know someone who sees him and she raves about him."

"Yes, three diagnoses determine the validity." I remembered Reva's words. Now the company was about to give me *their* selection. I was filled with excitement. I pretended to study the list and "Edmundo" continued.

"Do you believe this Doctor Ramljak can help me?"

"I believe he can." Daisy assured me. "I'll make the initial appointment for you."

"I will trust your recommendation Daisy and I promise things will be like before." I walked out of the flight lounge knowing damn well that things would never be like they were before. Never. Ever. Yet, I felt confident in knowing that I had eliminated a possible future legal ambiguity.

Dr. Joseph Ramljak had done significant work with the Vietnam era vets, many who had endured far greater suffering bedlam than I could ever imagine. Post-Traumatic Stress Disorder was in its infancy of being accepted as an accepted mental disease. Joe Ramljak, M.D. was at its forefront of its recognition. I respected Father Riley's opinion of the man for the priest was wise beyond his years. I supposed that is what could happen when you finally achieve the balance of body and spirit. I would remember the physician's name mostly because I kept rhyming it with Applejacks.

My decision to seek therapy created another dilemma. There were those in my family who strongly advised that the only thing to do was to put the whole affair as far behind me as possible and get on with my life.

"It was a gift." Those who believed they could see the *whole* picture advised me so. I could agree that I had received a gift, but it seemed flawed by tremendous pain. The fallen angels' voices argued for another path.

"You're worthless!" There were facts I could not ignore like the report on Carl and Dieter. There was also the memory of the faces of the mothers at the crew memorial services. Eventually the opinion in my family softened with some satisfaction that I was making progress toward the return of the old "Eddy." Attending family functions now added a new twist as the issue of the schizophrenia in the family history played heavily on my mind. I was the right age and the flashbacks, convulsions and voices reflected a text-book description.

I entered the second-floor corner office of my new physician in West Los Angeles on the designated date and was met with a mountain of paperwork to be completed. As always, I tried to hide my ignorance and my fears with a defense of sarcasm.

"A penny for your thoughts." A voice whispered as I stared upward, fatigued from completing the necessary documentation.

"I wish I were high on the mountaintops of my island," I replied, never turning to face the man who quickly approached and put a hand on my shoulder. Doctor Joseph Ramljak had strong, reassuring hands. He had seen others before me beaten down by flashbacks and things no one should be meant to witness. His positive nature and big smile projected a warmth and nurturing I so desperately needed.

"I feel like a screwball, Doc. So, what's the verdict, am I a nut case?" These were the first words out of my mouth once inside his private office.

"No," Dr. Ramljak simply replied. "My initial thought from what little I know about you is that you most likely are suffering from Post-Traumatic Stress Disorder, "PTSD." You experienced an out-of-the-ordinary tragedy and shoved the details of the experience down into your subconscious. You need to find a positive way of releasing it, and I believe you can because you are a survivor." The stout man who was perhaps in his early sixties impressed me with his candidness. There would be no need for my silly games or the appearance of the universally admired Edmundo. I knew that Dr. Joe had my ticket. Any jostling on my behalf would only be foolish antics that would delay the true purpose of my being there: to get well. I had to let down all the barriers for it was evident that I was no match for what was eating me alive. In those first few minutes I felt as though this kind, honest man had come into my life for a reason.

I was pleased to discover after the second session that a great portion of the therapy would be conducted through hypnosis. Dr. Joe saw the potential of further trauma by reliving the experience in conscious mode. This approach allowed me to suppress the anger and limit the anxiety while relating detailed specifics. I was becoming very impressed with "Dr. Applejacks," who I thought possessed a magnificent mind and a big, gentle heart. Once again, a helping hand had been extended to pull me out of this chaos, and everything told me to latch on to him and heed his advice.

"I feel like I am always locked in a hideous void, a black box if you will, and I am afraid I will never break out of it,"

"Why?" asked Dr. Joe. I gazed up at the ceiling and hesitated.

"Because for the first time in my life, I truly recognize how things are on the outside of that box. The reality of greed and pain are there clearly to see. The truth of the matter is that I not only gained a new life in the accident, but a different frame of mind."

"Do you believe in God?"

"I did once."

"I can diagnose and suggest, but only your God can cure you." I could only frown at his words. I had experienced what God's hand had accomplished. Did God bring Javier safely out of the fire? I wondered how such a deity could take a radiant angel like

Reina, and in an instant snuff out her life. My anger started to
bubble up.

"You are in a state of comorbidity," the doctor explained.
"You are stuck in an array of circumstances creating a mental
loop, never progressing positively or having the ability to exit."
This struck a chord. I perceived I was trapped. The nightly
visits by Javier took their toll in denying me of valuable sleep.
The added stress I put on myself of trying to live up to the image
of a heroic crew member greatly added to an acute feeling of
worthlessness. Even when I did gain some small measure of
confidence, which was mostly after an intense workout, the
negative voices would often try to reassert themselves.

"Is there anything you might consider that could relieve you
from this corrosive cycle?" I sat in the lush chair and wondered.

"Why did such an experienced pilot land his aircraft on a
supposedly closed runway?" My statement kindled Doctor
Ramljak's curiosity.

"Do you think it would be beneficial for you to read the
investigation reports?" I felt my anxiety rise and thought. You
don't get it, Applejacks, there is no investigation report! There
was no professionally guided investigation as is expected with
such aviation accidents.

"Chaos conducted the investigation." Doctor Joe just
assumed that serious aviation experts had been dispatched to
assist in determining what exactly caused the crash. "Hell,
Doctor, the crash site was contaminated within hours of the
explosion." It irked me that I was put in this position to try and
explain the facts to everyone. "That is not the way things went
down."

"What do you mean?" The doctor was, of course, puzzled
whenever I tried to explain the truth.

"You're perplexed? Well how in the hell do you think I feel?"
It should not have been my responsibility to explain these things.
I told the doctor this only heightened the trauma and anger for all
the principal participants of this tragedy who wanted the issue to
be discussed only in whispers.

"So, you're still surviving and functioning in that mode?"

"It doesn't end. When I think I've got it covered, it re-
surfaces." The jungle man of Kauai now appeared before the

gentle therapist. I informed him of my wild island antics. Ramljak would eventually have an interesting interaction with Edmundo, also. After a period of time, it became clear that it had been the right decision to trust this guy. He could see that I was holding onto stability by my fingertips.

"Where can you go to find out what really happened?"

"That was the $351,000,000 question!" I told Dr. Joe about the lawsuits. I pushed aside my disgust and tried to think of an answer to his inquiry.

"The truth can only be found on the Cockpit Voice Recorder, but where would the so-called black box be?" The Mexican Government had released a small segment of the CVR recording soon after the incident, which caused North American pilots and investigators to believe *that* version had been spliced. Where could I go to get even the slightest chance to hear the un-edited conversation between the cockpit and the tower?

"Diego!" I shouted, startling Dr. Joe as I sat straight up. "Doc, listen, I have to go back to Mexico." My therapist raised his thick right eyebrow and just stared at me.

I sped south down the 405 freeway at a high speed, filled with a new sense of hope. If the accident had occurred on U.S. soil the investigation would have been conducted by the proper authorities who would never allow a surviving flight attendant to have access to any vital information, much less the CVR Recording. In Mexico I believe that much of what gets accomplished "officially" is due to an individual having the proper connections. I had to contact Diego, but this clandestine effort had to be planned delicately. The "powers that be" at the airline would consider my actions as just another misadventure, unnecessarily rocking the boat and possibly ending any hopes of getting to the truth if I were caught. Ackley would certainly put an end to it if they discovered my intentions. I would need a lot of help if I had any chance of getting anywhere near the flight recorder. That evening I made a long-distance call to the Distrito Federal de México, but it was directed to someone I knew I could fully trust.

The international operator informed my party that she had a call from Los Angeles and immediately a surprised Hugo García answered.

"¿Eduardo, qué tal?" Was this silent God of mine finally coming through?

"I wish I could tell you that all is well mi amigo, but the reality is that I am twisted up in a web of horrid nightmares, voices and bureaucratic bullcrap. I need to return to Mexico; I need to meet with Don Diego once more, but this all has to be arranged confidentially. Can you help me?"

"Certainly, El Gato, but have you been contacted by Victor Estrada yet?"

"What? Who?" I strained my brain and after a second recalled the friendly face of the Mexican controller who manned the tower the morning of October 31. Hugo continued.

"Victor and his family are currently in Los Angeles. His infant son is having treatment at a children's hospital in the city. I think it would be beneficial for you to speak with him before coming to Mexico."

"Can you arrange for him to contact me?"

"Certainly, y vaya con Dios my dear friend." I hung up the phone and began to contemplate a meeting with the man in the tower that Halloween morning. I understood the Mexican Government had not allowed any American investigator to speak with him during the first few vital days after the accident. I then became afraid to think of what he might reveal.

Manuel's El Tepeyac Mexican Restaurant is an East L.A. institution, located on Evergreen Ave., about a half mile from Our Lady of Talpa Church where I attended elementary school. There is always a colorful array of customers lined up early to get a seat in the small café or to order take-out of their delicious cuisine. On a sunny day in the barrio, in between the café's rush hours, I entered the popular eatery to the jukebox sounds of mariachi music by José Alfredo Jiménez y Amelia Mendoza. There I was greeted by the friendly face of the man I believed could perhaps solve the mystery that plagued me so dreadfully. Abrazos where exchanged as both of us Mexicans sized each other up. Suddenly we were approached by the proprietor of the restaurant, Manuel Rojas, who demanded that we begin our reunion by having a shot of tequila with him, a common tradition for his friends at El Tepeyac.

"How is my friend, El Gato? a jovial Victor asked once the formalities were concluded.

"I think I've used up four or five of my nine lives since we last met, Señor."

"Please Eduardo, call me Victor. I was quite surprised when Señor Garcia contacted me. I did not know whether you were aware that I was presently in Los Angeles."

"I have been having a rough time trying to sort everything out in my mind, Victor."

"Yes, Señor García has told me of your difficulties. Señor Hugo is a very wise man."

"How is your son, Victor?"

"Doing very well, gracias a Dios." I decided to cut to the chase.

"Victor, what did you mean when you told me it was not that man's fault that day in the office of El Ministerio?" I looked deeply into his eyes trying to gauge his intent. I began to study the lines on his face. He rubbed his chin and became serious, recollecting the details of the fateful day. In his face I saw someone with a good heart, a man I could trust.

"I think it all started with my young son." My weary-looking friend began to tell his story. "I had been on duty in the control tower at Benito Juárez that night for nearly sixteen hours. Unlike your federal rules and regulations that govern the job here in Los Estados Unidos, such luxuries do not exist in Mexico."

"How did you put up with that crap?" I inquired.

"Remember amigo, at any given time much of Mexico's work force is unemployed, so that job was a treasure. I had high aspirations when I first took the position, a career." Victor's face filled with disappointment while reflecting. "At any rate, about twenty minutes before the scheduled arrival of 2605, I received an emergency call. My baby son had somehow fallen out of his crib. I'm still not sure how it occurred. There was a pool of blood beneath him on the floor, Madre de Dios." Victor blessed himself.

"Is he okay?" I wanted to assure myself before he proceeded for the strain was very visible.

"Yes. It seems yours was not the only soul God smiled upon that day, but a replacement for me was needed in the tower as quickly as possible. I hurriedly gathered my belongings to leave for El Centro, the hospital. Señor Rodríguez, a new hire, had been contacted and was running up the stairs as I departed. The Mexicana DC-10 from Los Angeles had landed on Runway 23-Left and taxied to the gate. It was hard to see because the fog was really rolling in. I worried because all aircraft with instrument landing capabilities were being directed to Runway 23-Left, the only runway with the beacon to guide the planes in." I began to fall under the spell of his story, grasping each word as he slowly re-told it.

"That runway had been closed to traffic for three weeks, according to the Minister of Transportation," I stated. "I understand the Minister of Transportation even *signed an affidavit* to that fact." Victor shook his head.

"The runway was closed, then opened, then closed, depending on the availability and amount of traffic. There was construction going on and then 'poof,' the workers would stop, and all would be cleared on the tarmac. A plane would land on the runway and be cleared to taxi to the terminal and 'poof,' once again the trucks and tractors would be back, all without a word or telephone call to us in the tower." I could not believe what I was hearing!

"What a shit, and the paying public did not have the slightest knowledge of it." I felt a chill and thought back to that awful morning, becoming nauseated recalling the stench of burning flesh. I turned to view a sinister-looking Hispanic man enter the restaurant. He stood for a moment by the entrance looking about, finally taking a seat at the counter nearby. My paranoia persuaded me that it was Muerto himself, making his presence known as Estrada continued.

"The tractors rushed up and down the paved surface till the early hours of the morning of the 31st. The runway at that time was closed, but the morning rush was beginning and there had not been enough time to brief Señor Rodríguez concerning the status of the runway or the fact that work had momentarily stopped. The workers, in their vehicles, were taking a short nap. Not realizing the state of 23 Left, Rodríguez turned the runway lights on about the time your aircraft was making its final approach. Down by the employee parking area I could see a large object coming out of the sky as the runway lights made the entire fog bank glow brightly and only the craft's silhouette was visible." The mariachi music stopped in my mind and was replaced by the sound of jet engines slowly rising. "I saw the jetliner hit something on the runway as there was a large spark of fire for a second, then the wing seems to clip a tractor on the edge of the runway. Suddenly the huge plane lifted up back into the sky. My eyes followed the jet in disbelief as it banked to the right and her tail began dragging, heading straight for the maintenance buildings. A great ball of fire rose upon impact. Her entire rudder and wing broke away, flying far into the neighboring homes. It was horrible." I listened silently but intently.

"Did you tell any U.S. investigators what you have told me, Victor?"

"I was not allowed by my superiors to speak to any Norte Americanos. I was taking a chance conversing with you when you went to la oficina del ministerio." Victor's voice revealed the trauma he was feeling as he once again re-lived the tragedy. This good and innocent man was also burdened by Muerto's heavy yoke of guilt, a victim of nightmares like those that plagued me.

"How did you know I would be at the minister's office?" I inquired quickly to keep my new friend talking, hoping in that way to keep him from completely falling apart.

"Señor Hugo," Victor replied. My mind was racing as here was the opportunity I hoped would come.

"Listen Victor, I need your help. I'm going back to Mexico to try and hook up with Diego Suárez de la Vega. I share your hideous dreams even though I was spared, given a new life, but I have found that it comes with a terrible price." Victor was taken aback by what I shared.

"Pero Eduardo, Señor Don Diego is not himself anymore. This tragedy has taken a heavy toll on him as well, plus have you forgotten about Primitivo Chávez?" That name! Not again!

"You know about that? How?

"Señor Hugo." I thought maybe guardian angels exist after all, and mine would be Senor Hugo if I decided to return to Mexico City. Victor reached out and put his arm around my shoulder, his deep, dark eyes reflecting both guilt and compassion.

"I, too, must make amends my dear friend." Here was a true hero willing to risk his own safety and perhaps his life, feeling a responsibility to help me.

I again found myself racing down the 405 freeway soon after I had thanked Señor Estrada for his graciousness. Redondo Beach and the home of Tommy Acoba was where I needed to go, for I did not have the strength to return to Mexico's Distrito Federal on my own. Good friends ignite an inner determination that is usually absent when alone. This was going to be a dangerous adventure and if I happened to run into my old friend the Comandante, things could get difficult. Tommy's sharp mind and ability to think quickly would compensate for what I lacked, and I knew exactly what I had to say to get him to go with me.

"Hey, Tommy, what was one of Trotsky's greatest accomplishments?" He was enjoying a rather large can of Foster's Lager. He sat in his music room below a painting of Lenin created in a radiant Soviet propaganda style. Acoba was no admirer of Bolshevik Communism, but rather its antagonist. He pushed himself to know everything concerning the military of the old Soviet Union. To Tommy, they were his opponent in an elaborate chess game. With his hair in a mess he pondered my question and then responded.

"Trotsky fought three different wars on three different fronts against three different enemies and won?" I saw my opportunity.

"Hey Tommy, wasn't Trotsky assassinated in Mexico?"

"Yeah, got a big ice ax in the middle of his head."

"Hey Tommy, wanna go to Mexico City?" He stared at me trying to make the connection, then replied with a grin,

"You buying the beer?"

"You got it."

"When do we leave?"

"Tomorrow night?" Acoba look at me in puzzlement for only a second then by a slight tilt of the head he agreed. My backbone instantly stiffened as I imagined the impossible. What if I really got an opportunity to listen to the CVR? I filled him in on the information Victor Estrada had provided, and we discussed our strategy as Frank Zappa serenaded us in the background.

"St. Alphonzo's' pancake breakfast, where I stole the margarine...."[8]

The one set back in my plan was having to take the all-nighter to MEX. Tommie was extremely curious to experience that flight. On the plus side there would be fewer people at Terminal 5 at that hour, lessening the possibility of arousing the suspicion of either the Mexican government or my airline company suspicion. When we approached the departure gate the following night I recognized the ticket agent, a sweet woman who was very surprised to see me.

"Please, I do not want anyone to know I was here." I came right out and asked for her silence. By her word I knew my secret was safe. Once in the air my privacy was respected by the F/As who knew me. Traveling with my dearest friend certainly lessened my anxiety and with several bottles of Bohemia consumed I hardly noticed the descent and final approach into Benito Juárez Airport.

Acoba and I waited till all the passengers had deplaned, then were met with reactions of shock from the MEX gate agents.

"¡Eduardo! ¡Bienvenidos!

"You are back! Who is your friend?" Their kindness reminded me of the gratitude I have for them, the Mexican people, the down-to-earth folk who truly cared for me those first few awful hours after the disaster. The agents graciously escorted us through customs, and we were quickly out the terminal doors looking for a cab.

We situated ourselves at the Maria Isabel Sheraton, off the Paseo de La Reforma, and rested that day. In the late afternoon I made the call to the one man who I believed could provide us with solid answers. Hugo García had alerted Diego of my plans, so Deputy Minister immediately arranged for Tony and I to be received at his office.

"So, para las Gracias de Dios, El Gato returns to us. Y qué dices?" The Deputy Minister was very excited to see his old friend.

---

8 Frank Zappa 1973

"Por favor Don Diego, con su permiso, yo puedo presentar mi compadre, Tomas Acoba." My colleague stepped forward and offered his hand.

"A sus ordenes, Señor." Diego was impressed and amused by our uncommon effort in showing proper Mexican deportment.

"Good to meet you my friend. But please, sit down. Something to drink, un refresco perhaps? And of course, you must join me for dinner tonight. I know a place where the enchiladas verde are magnificent." We were impressed by Diego's elegance but still I remained tense.

"I'm looking for answers, Diego. I need answers." Diego's happy mood quickly changed. Tommy put his hand on my shoulder indicating he believed I was moving too quickly. My Mexican host took a cigarette from an engraved silver box on his desk and lit it, taking a long drag, holding it for some time, then raising his chin to release the smoke into the air. I knew that all the while he was trying to formulate an answer.

"The whole damn thing was a real mess, my friend. Thank God it's over."

"Not for me Diego, it just continues on and on." I spoke the truth and he knew it, shifting uncomfortably in his chair.

"I'm ready for cocktails." Tommy's request broke the tension and Senor Suárez de la Vega reacted.

"Certainly, I am forgetting my manners, anything for my Norte Americano compadres. Let us head out to La Zona Rosa." We departed in Diego's large American-made governmental vehicle. "Made in the U.S.A!" The deputy joked as we sped off.

Diego was an official well-known by many, and a regular at Bonaparte's Restaurante in the center of the Zona Rosa. The valets hurried to assist him, opening the doors with speed and efficiency. The jovial manager welcomed the honored guest and his friends with great respect and enthusiasm.

"Ah Julio, mi amigo." Diego shone with the talents he had polished over the years.

"Don Diego joven, y sus padres?" The elderly manager welcomed him with an abrazo and a handshake.

"Todos son bien Julio, por favor estos son mis amigos Norte Americanos," gesturing toward us, "Dales lo que quieren." Diego turned to assure us, "They will take care of you gentlemen, please excuse me while I use the lavatory." Tommy and I, almost embarrassed by the elegant greeting, were directed to a table where two waiters stood waiting.

"We've got to get him to tell us more," I whispered to Tommy.

"First things first. Tres Bohemias por favor." Tommy was cool and calm, a contrast to me. In the moments we were alone Acoba tried to get me to settle down and realize that patience and a well-laid plan would garner the results I so desired. "Look, he wants to tell us more," my chess master advised me. "I can feel it. Diligence is the key. I say we get him drunk." My vexation subsided as I began to see the logic in Tommy's plan.

"What if he drinks us under the table?" I asked. Acoba looked straight into my eyes for my inquiry insulted his intelligence.

"Tres Centenarios también," my calculating friend informed the second attendant as the first was returning with the beer. As Don Diego approached the table the bartender spoke up to ask,

"Para usted, Don Diego?"

"Ah, Serafino, un vino blanco."

Tommy reacted quickly.

"No, no, please. Since we are in Mexico, I insist we have Centenario con una Bohemia." Don Diego took a step back for a second, then found this idea to be whimsical and a pleasant surprise.

"You know my friends, this could be quite a lethal combination but what the hell, it is not every day that I get to spend time with El Gato, the man with nine lives." I glanced over at Tommy who just smiled. Our trio enjoyed the drinks the waiters swiftly delivered to the table. Cerveza, tequila, sal y lima.

"¡Salud!" After a couple of shots with beer chasers I began to relax.

"What really happened down here, Diego?" The official took his time to light another cigarette, keeping me on edge. He contemplated what to say. Tommy was convinced Diego wanted to unload his conscience and threw in his support.

"What happened Señor?" The diplomat took a deep breath, then exhaled.

"Well, as you know, it was determined to be pilot error."

Tommy's response was immediate.

"Was it?"

Diego raised his hands.

"I don't know, I don't want to think about it anymore."

"Diego, I must know." I again was persistent. The torn diplomat didn't know where to start.

"I can't believe how crazy things got. There was the man who died twice, a young Mexican national." Diego seemed deeply fixed upon this situation. He gazed toward the ceiling, traveling into some void. "He had been working on a farm in California, "un bracero," and had been killed accidentally by farming equipment. Since he and his two brothers were in Los Estados Unidos illegally, this posed a problem not only for them but also for the farmer who had hired them unlawfully. Fearing problems with "la migra," immigration, the brothers were compensated by the farmer, booked to travel on your flight, and were returning to Mexico with their deceased sibling in the hold of the aircraft."

"It truly was El Día de Los Muertos," I blurted out. Diego locked eyes with me as he extinguished his partially smoked cigarette.

"Indeed, it truly was for those poor souls. His brothers died once, and he was made to die twice." I glanced at Tommy who managed to keep his poker face.

"Then there was the case of the two Sandinista gentlemen." Acoba's eyes grew large, I felt my heart leap up into my throat. "One of those two deceased individuals had eight different passports on his body. This caused a lot of debate. That dog Chávez!" Diego hesitated as he saw the reaction on my face. "Well, Chávez was sure the crash was some clandestine act of your Central Intelligence Agency, to kill the two Nicaraguan agents. Who's to say? But shortly after, officials from Los Estados Unidos arrived in town and took the bodies of two other gentlemen that were not even listed on the manifest of the flight. So, they were not counted among those that had perished."

"You mean their bodies disappeared?" Tommy sat up intrigued.

"I was informed by the Minister himself that as far as we were concerned, those two bodies never even existed.

"C.I.A." Tommy nodded with a sly smile on his face.

"The black box, Diego, what is on the black box?" I urged my friend to continue.

"It was a strain trying to listen to it as the box was damaged and there is a continuous loop of gaps on the recording. Es muy terrible my friends. The pilots knew it was coming." I began to tremble with impatience, almost ready to cry. Tommy leaned over to whisper in my ear.

"Take it easy cabrón. keep cool." A nervous Diego went on with his story.

"You know, there is this unusual sound at the end of the cockpit tape, no one can figure it out. For only a scant moment, it sounds like a multitude of voices crying out." He shrugged and shook his head.

"The pilot's crying out?" I rationally assumed. I had to maintain my cool, despite re-living the nightmare.

There was a pause as more tequila y cervezas were brought to the table. Tommy signaled for me to go with the flow. He had no doubt that our blue-blooded friend would reveal all. Just be patient.

A penitent Don Diego resumed his dialogue.

"You know my friends; the Minister called a news conference three weeks after the accident. My superior assured everyone that all the bodies of the passengers had been accounted for. Yet, later on that very afternoon of the conference, the clean-up crews discovered another body." Tommy sensed that the liquor was accomplishing its task.

"To His Excellency, The Minister!" Tommy raised his glass in a salute. Diego was obliging.

"The big fart!" Evidently, Diego was still bitter for being lied to. Tony continued to push new drinks forward.

"Ay, otra vez? What the hell, I'm my own boss." I kept pressing for more information.

"What else Diego?" The slightly intoxicated official took another shot of tequila perhaps to either numb the pain or get up the courage to continue.

"For your own sake, forget about this mess." I freaked, thinking we had reached a dead end. But I couldn't stop now and pressed on.

"Where is the black box?" Diego thought for a second.

"Ah, put away in the Ministry offices."

"Is there any possible way I could listen to it?" The question nearly made my host spit up his beer.

"No, no, no, I don't think that would be a good idea. It would not be healthy for you, just forget about it." Tommy kept his composure, trying to keep the conversation and drinks flowing. He rose to make another toast.

"To the Black Box!"

"¡Salud!" The manager politely approached the table.

"¿Para comer, Don Diego?"

"Sí Julio. Enough about Death, my friends, for he will come soon enough. Let us celebrate life. Tres platos de enchiladas verdes. Serafino, por favor, cánteme algo especial, es una fiesta. Would you care to be serenaded, Señor Acoba?" A tall, lean figure bartender untied his apron and approached the table of the "caballeros." From the other room a trio of mariachis appeared. "What is your pleasure, Señor Acoba?" Tommy did not have to think long.

"Llego Borracho, El Borracho." The traditional song of twisted fate echoed through the night air of La Zona Rosa, now inebriated, Diego rose from the table, grabbing my hand as us two Mexicans danced and stumbled about. The plaintive ballad concluded just as the entrees arrived. We paused to cheer the talented Serafino, then sat to enjoy the marvelous cuisine. But I soon grew restless and wanted more information.

"Tell us Diego, about the crash." My Mexican friend took a deep breath, put down his Bohemia. He rose to grab the back of my head and to my great surprise gave me a big kiss on my cheek.

"You must know mi amigo; you are one lucky S.O.B." With a lock of my hair tightly in his grasp he continuously shook my head in a rhythmic beat. He grinned wildly. Suddenly he released his hold, fell back into his chair and became somber once again. "Everything got so crazy, bodies were everywhere. One was given here and another one there." Tommy and I looked at each other, as the revelation threw us into disarray. Diego was feeling no pain and seemed determined to free his soul of all sins, real or imagined. "There was no effort made in the beginning to screen the families effectively when they came to claim their loved one. There was this Norte Americano on the plane, tall man."

"Yes, I remember!" I could see the man's image clearly. Diego was in deep thought, looking as if he was trying desperately to concentrate. "Anyway, so many families were coming to the morgue area, all of them in shock, out of control, not wanting to believe their wife or child was in pieces. They were clamoring forward screaming, swearing in the name of God that the bodies with the least injuries had to be their loved one. The imbecile initially assigned to handle this delicate matter ran the facility like un rastro...how you say?" Tommy quickly interjected.

"A flea market." Diego looked at him and nodded.

"Yes, yes, a damn flea market. Senor McKay was there when a man came looking for his deceased brother. The tall Americano I spoke of earlier had supposedly already been claimed by the dental expert sent by his family in Vermont or somewhere up there, old money, they had it." Diego's eyes widened as he tried to emphasize his statement. "But I believe another body was bagged by mistake because after many days we still had this tall cadaver." Acoba and I were riveted. Diego stopped briefly to take another shot of Centenario, savoring the tequila. He closed his eyes and shook his head as he struggled to remember where his conversation left off. "Here was this gentleman who stated that none of the bodies still procurable were his dead brother. When we asked how he could be so sure, especially because of the condition of the bodies, he stated that his brother was an avowed homosexual and that his genitals attested to his lifestyle.

"WHAT???" Tommy and I responded at the same time. The young aristocrat kept shaking his head denoting that his facts were true.

"Please don't ask me for details regarding his lifestyle" The Deputy Minister shook his right hand in an action reflecting lunacy. "It's just that all the remaining corpses all had their genitals intact and he was convinced none were his brother. This did not sit well with his Excellency the Minister, who informed the man that his claim for $70,000 in compensation, as is the law in Mexico, could not be paid without a body, suggesting that the grieving brother claim the larger remains and have a closed casket ceremony. Senor McKay subsequently informed his Excellency the Minister that he sounded like some damn used car salesman. The brother's initial reaction was to be greatly offended but finally settled down and started to evaluate his circumstances. Apparently, the brothers had three sisters and the man was concerned about the effects upon the women if he was to be discovered pulling off a stunt like the one the Minister had suggested. He needed time to contemplate his options and promised to return. Three days later he did return and took the body of the tall cadaver, choosing a closed casket funeral on the pretense that his brothers' body was too mangled by the crash. Soon after the man was paid his settlement."

"And the Mexican body?" I inquired. The Mexican official shook his head.

"Resting in peace up in Vermont, I presume." Tommy and I could barely believe what we were hearing. I took a deep breath, sat back and began to contemplate the whole affair. Airplane crashes are not supposed to be like this. The experts arrive upon the scene, everything is conducted in the most professional manner, and within a period of time a final report is issued, and all the victims are accounted for. The more I delved into the specifics of this affair the more chaotic it became.

"Don Diego," I respectfully said in a calm voice. "Was it pilot error?" He looked up at me as if he did not understand the question, but of course he had. His conscience, character and social status required him to tell me the truth.

"I don't know my friend."

"Listening to that tape is not the most pleasant thing you want to do." He had a point. "What facts are to be found? Who's to say?"

"Diego, if a more thorough investigation had been done, perhaps one could say." He looked and over my head, speaking as if thinking out loud. "You understand that there was much that would be jeopardized if it looked like the Mexican Government had contributed to this terrible incident."

"That is why they kept trying to get me to sign a false affidavit stating I had served liquor to the pilots." I became stern and reflected my hurt.

"You recall the explanation of the Minister himself," I nodded my head in agreement. "Did you know that your airline was buying its fuel from Mexico, PEMEX?" The change in direction of conversation caught me by surprise. I struggled to recall the process of a Mexico City flight.

"I know that we have three flights a day to Mexico City from the West Coast, DC-10s."

"Yes," Diego quickly interceded. "And those flights along with all the others make the journey with just a sufficient amount of fuel to safely complete the journey. You should thank your creator!" He turned to take another swig from the bottle of Bohemia. "Can you imagine the fireball and carnage had the tanks been full?" I flashed back to the morning of October 31 and I could smell the jet fuel. It instantly became almost overwhelming. Among the fumes people screamed and cried and died. He continued, "That jumbo jet was scheduled to be fueled and sent back north. When payment was arranged, those that are unscrupulous could find a hundred different ways to skim off the top."

"WHAT?" Acoba and I reacted in unison again. "Send the money through Panama and deposit it in European accounts." My intoxicated amigo was venting and getting a lot off his chest. I admired him but sympathized for I recognized the pain. "There are many powerful individuals on both sides of the border who have their hand in that cookie jar." I looked over at Tommy as we both shrugged. "There are a multitude of reasons why, for all concerned, a more thorough investigation is not a good idea and that goes for you my Chicano friend. Even that dog Chávez gets his cut of the booty."

"I recalled the day I departed Mexico City there was a delay regarding the fueling of the aircraft." The memory was vivid. "Once up in the air we had to divert to ACA and get fuel there." Diego understood my confusion.

"Your accident provided an opportunity for the union of the fuelers." I did not understand his meaning. Diego raised his eyes, adjusting his posture to simplify the statement for me.

"You see, the union gets its cut from the price of the jet fuel, so if your airline wants the fuel at that moment at that time, then they must agree or delay their journey. In this particular circumstance because the airline was experiencing some difficult situations, the union bosses decided to go on a timely strike. The game is played with all the airlines. It was due to the quick thinking of Señor Valenzuela to call Acapulco and see what they would settle for to fuel the jet. The boss there underbid El Distrito Federal."

"A toast to the cookie jar," Tommy stated as he raised his shot glass." The laughter warmed the room and brought us back to happier times.

"Diego, I must listen to that tape." Suddenly, Felipe entered the room seeking his boss. Spotting Diego the young assistant approached, leaned and whispered something in his superior's ear. The official shook his head and thanked him, then Felipe was gone. Don Diego was again serious as he looked at his two dinner guests.

"Tell me my friends, did you inform anyone that you were coming to the Federal District" Both Acoba and I were concerned by the question.

"No, why do you ask?"

"Well, your old friend Comandante Chávez knows you are here." The words sent a chill down my spine. I began to panic.

"What? Hey, I'm a private citizen on holiday. I haven't done anything." I tried to convince myself of half-truths. Tommy put the picture into perspective.

"Wise up Eddy, you of all people should know better than that." Diego agreed.

"Your compadre is wise. Primitivo doesn't need to justify himself to anyone. Tell me my friend, are you still sure you want to listen to that hideous tape?

"Of course I do." My wise Mexican friend leaned closer to me and reached over to grab my hand.

"Be careful what you ask for." My personal pain and need to know the truth outweighed his advice. Diego could see I was determined. "I suppose you, more than anyone, have earned the right to make that decision. Señor Acoba will go with Felipe who will return him to your hotel to gather all your belongings.

He will be transported to Benito Juárez." Diego turned to Tommy. "Eduardo will meet you at the airport in a couple of hours so the two of you can catch the first flight back to Los Angeles." Don Diego raised the tequila glass and offered up one last toast. "To the black box-may it be the key that opens the door to the peace that you seek." We finished our drinks and left Restaurante Bonaparte. I was surprised to find two cars waiting outside as Don Diego directed Tommy to one of them.

"I better see you at the airport or I'll come looking for you and beat your ass myself," my loyal companion warned. He left, still holding a bottle of Bohemia as he was chauffeured by Felipe. I waved as the black American Suburban sped away into the darkness of the early morning. A chill enveloped me which I hoped was a result of the high altitudes cool air, but in retrospect I wondered what I was getting myself into.

Chapter XVI

In another corner of Mexico City, a confident and amused officer of La Policía Federal sat at a large table, lecturing two underlings. The imposing figure puffed on his rancid cigarette and carried a white handkerchief to place over his mouth. He coughed heavily as a result of his four-pack-a-day habit. Sensing the possibility of having another shot at making me shiver, he felt in good spirits.

"So, the mouse has come back for the cheese? I must admire el pocho's efforts. When all have been willing to forget and sweep this mess under a rug, that little Chicano es como una pulga." The career policeman continued to lecture his two assistants who stood listening, stone-faced.

"You have to keep an eye on these Norte Americanos. You can never trust them. Como los investigadores that came soon after the crash, wanting to see everything, know everything: here to assist us. When has Los Estados Unidos ever assisted?" The cunning lawman slowly rose to answer his own question. "Dominate! Takeover is more like it. Those so-called investigators, those mentirosos, looking down at our agents from La Navegación en el Espacio Aereo Mexicano. They believed their agency the F.A.A. should be in charge. ¡ES MÉXICO!" The wild comandante suddenly erupted, screaming with rage and misguided pride. "We're no two-bit banana republic they can push around." His agitation increased, which frightened his two young officers who were well aware of "el jefe's" reputation.

The comandante rambled on. "Los inteligentes in Washington, they know the truth. Los Norte Americanos need our petroleum, natural gas, and with that Mexico is once again important to them. They're not going to let a little thing like this silly plane crash be an obstacle to the agreement Presidente Portillo negotiated on our behalf. Unfortunately, for those poor souls in la aerolina, it was simply a matter of being in the wrong place at the wrong time." Chavez realized he was digressing and returned to the matter-at-hand. He grabbed his sport coat and carefully put it on, then quickly adjusted his tie. "Vámonos caballeros, we have a mouse to catch." Primitivo Chávez de León and his foot soldiers hastened out into the cool morning air onto the streets of the federal district. Suddenly a subordinate came running out of the nearby police precinct looking for him.

"Jefe, por favor, teléfono." The young officer informed his commander that it was a high-ranking official on the line. The two young assistants waited in the street, smoking those filthy cigarettes. Soon, the comandante was back on the street, much more subdued.

...

"I'll reveal the evidence you so desperately wish for," Diego assured me. We were sitting in the rear of a small black and yellow taxi that Julio (the reliable manager of Restaurante Bonaparte) had summoned for us. I began to become fearful, for weren't we on our way to some unknown location where I could listen to the CVR Recording once or possibly twice? Did Don Diego have another agenda? I sat silent and just listened. "Most likely, El Gato would have used up all nine lives." Diego smiled. "You'll be fresh meat for that dog Chávez." He chuckled. Was he kidding? This drive with Diego was distinctly different than what I had anticipated. The driver was in a hurry, darting in and out through the streets of Mexico City. I gazed out at the urban landscape, my thoughts reverting back to *that* Halloween day.

"What is your mother's name? What is your father's name?" Primitivo's raspy voice demanded my attention. I was losing my nerve. Maybe I was pushing things too fast. Diego turned and studied my face. He placed his hand firmly on my thigh, a gesture to fortify my backbone. "You're not afraid?" I tried to muster my courage, display a posture of confidence, but it was a poor endeavor and so I lied.

"No!" I shouted.

"Maybe you should be," the deputy warned. "Do you have faith in God?" The question caught me off guard.

"I did...once."

"Well, maybe it is time you reconsider?" The taxicab approached the airport and Diego directed the vehicle to the gate of the ministry grounds. The lone security officer on duty at this early hour seemed surprised while admitting us onto the grounds. Who would be coming here at this time?

As Diego and I entered the offices I was taken back in time by the dark, cold rooms. Don Diego hurried to his office as I stood shivering in the corridor, glancing from up and down through the empty hallways. I flashed back to the morning I was summoned by the Minister of Mexico himself. The reporters lined these very walls as they pressed to get information from me.

"Valenciana, Valenciana, did you serve the pilots liquor?" I held my head as the voice of Muerto returned.

"You're worthless. You are the one who deserves to be dead." I slowly turned and saw viewed a small shadowy figure at the end of the corridor. What was happening?

"Will I ever be good enough?" I recognized the voice as Javier's. I stared open-mouthed.

"Eduardo?!" I turned to see Don Diego at the entrance to his office staring at me. I turned again to look at the boy but there was only an empty corridor.

"Eduardo, are you okay?"

"Yeah, I'm fine, just got carried away in thought." How do I try to explain the inexplicable? I followed Diego into the ministry office. Once inside he quickly started gathering and examining documents in assorted envelopes. He would spend a few seconds viewing the contents of one paper, then place it in a relevant cardboard box. It was only after some time that I began to realize that these important records were intended for me. Were we going to sit and listen to the CVR Recording? All at once Diego held up a medium-size envelope and partially removed its content for my benefit. I could see a medium size recording reel with a masking tape label that read "2605."

"This is for you." He placed the envelope into the box with the other documents. "Take this material and get your ass out of Mexico. Felipe has taken care of the specifics for your passage and that of Señor Acoba. Your friend will be awaiting you on the aircraft. Get on the plane and do not disclose to anyone what transpired. I am taking a big gamble Eduardo, but maybe it is the least I can do on behalf of those poor souls who perished." I fumbled clumsily as he handed me the box. As we stepped into the hallway and he locked up his office, I wondered if I had the wits and the courage to pull this off.

We descended the few stairs out onto the compound where I was surprised and relieved to find a faithful Felipe awaiting us. Felipe informed Diego that some of Comandante Chávez's cronies were indeed seen in front of Benito Juárez Airport, lap dogs definitely on the hunt. Diego chuckled obviously taking pleasure in putting one over on his sadistic adversary.

"Felipe will drive us directly to your gate through the back entrance." As we entered the government vehicle, I intentionally forced myself not to consider the contents of the box, focusing instead on the important matter at hand: getting out of the federal district in one piece. Felipe drove the official vehicle along the airport tarmac turning his head once to smile and give a nod of assurance that all was well. I spotted our DC-10 in the distance. The gleaming white jumbo jet with the distinct red logo never looked so good. I felt like some refugee fleeing for his life from a country in chaos.

Felipe slowed the car as we approached the plane. Suddenly I noticed a lone figure at the bottom of the stairs who seemed to be awaiting our arrival. I almost wept as I recognized the tall figure dressed in the company uniform. The sedan was still moving as I swung the door open and rushed onto the tarmac to give this man a huge abrazo!

"Hugo! Mi amigo." He smiled and continually shook his head as he patted my back in our embrace. "Hugo García, what a wonderful name." He smiled broadly. Señor Hugo, a simple man with simple desires who carried a wealth of goodwill in his heart and soul.

Suddenly, underneath the jetway I recognized a large familiar figure lumbering out of the shadows. It was Montoya, the Mexican federal agent, the block of a man. Filled with fear, I slowly backed away from Hugo's embrace as my compadres became aware that we were not alone on the tarmac.

"Caught, como un ratón," a delighted Comandante Chávez appeared from the shadows, his laugh quickly turning into a hacking cough. Regaining his composure, the prideful bastard rapidly approached me. I continued to back away, but he reached out and grabbed me by the arm. To my shock, he simply wanted to pinch my cheek sternly while letting out another hideous laugh.

"¡Alto Comandante Chávez!" Don Diego quickly stepped between myself and my antagonist. Primitivo was surprised by Diego's bold interference. We were now surrounded by more federal officers.

"Ah, the hidden accomplices. Can you comprehend what a blow this all would be to your shining career, Don Diego?" The sadistic comandante bowed in an animated fashion as he mocked Diego.

"What do you mean Señor?" Diego countered. Primitivo began coughing, then after regaining control became serious.

"Don't insult my intelligence, Señor Suárez, your kind think they're so smart just because you have a silver spoon in your mouth. I've had to work hard for all I have."

"Yes Primitivo, we all have seen the result of your work. What do you intend to do?" Chávez was relishing his position and paused to enjoy the moment.

"What are we to do about this little problem, Don Eduardo?" Primitivo approached me once again, taking an interest in what the contents of the cardboard box I was clutching may contain.

"Stop stalling, what are your intentions...what will you do?" Diego interjected to regain the advantage. The comandante grinned widely, assuming, I hoped, that the contents were nothing more than my personal belongings. Primitivo Chávez de León reached out once more and put his hand upon my shoulder. If I did not know better, I would have thought that the executioner had developed a sense of affection for his prey. Primitivo turned toward Don Diego still hacking every few seconds.

"Nada, Señor De La Vega, nada. As you so often have reminded me, Señor Valenciana is a guest of the people of Mexico and a citizen of the mighty Estados Unidos." My compadres and I looked at each other. Had we heard his words correctly? Diego continued staring at the comandante as if daring him to make a wrong move. Primitivo Chávez began to laugh and cough uncontrollably.

"Eduardo, go with Hugo, the plane is holding for you." I gave my benefactor a quick abrazo before Hugo and I ran up the jetway stairs, leaving Diego to deal with the semi-crazed comandante who suddenly had seemed to lose his mind, rambling on incoherently.

"Ah, Madre de Dios," was all the guffawing Primitivo seemed to be yelling.

"Quick, Eduardo, here is your boarding pass. You must board the plane. Señor Acoba is already on board." The agent stood ready to close the door at 2L.

"Gracias, Hugo, mi compadre."

"And the next time you take a vacation my friend, go to Hawaii!" I entered the cabin of the craft as the door was being shut and locked. I hesitated for a moment still clutching the cardboard box thinking that once again, men of honor and integrity had come to my aid. They were not just friends but mentors, persons of such character whose bravery would be remembered during difficult times ahead. I turned and proceeded to first class as our jumbo jet backed away from the gate.

"I was getting ready to get off this plane and start looking for your ass," an irritated Acoba said, greeting me with a hug.

"Here," I tossed the box of documents on his lap, "Something for you to read on the flight home." My learned friend look looked in disbelief at the reel marked "2605."

"Is this what I think it is?"

"You look through the box. I'm too exhausted to concentrate." I collapsed onto my assigned seat and tightened my seat belt. And with that I closed my eyes and tried to start breathing normally. I fell into a deep sleep at 30,000' above the world, gliding once again over the Sea of Cortez. Occasionally I would be aroused by Acoba's reaction to the documents he scanned.

"Crap, you won't believe what's in this shit." His words should have been a forewarning, but I took them instead to mean that perhaps I could finally find the peace I so desperately sought now that I had the CVR recording. I was so naive.

"Good morning Mexico Tower, Flight 2605 is inbound for 23."

"2605 report over Mike Echo final approach navigation point, wind calm."

"Roger, 2605. Over Mike Echo."

"Will I ever be good enough?" I awoke abruptly, disoriented and in a panic. I reached out for something, for someone, then recognized my own room in my own house. I was up late at night since arriving back home from Mexico, listening to the CVR tape. Diego's words of warning had become very apparent. The black box had sustained damage when the massive forces tore open DC-10 NW903. There were indeed lapses in the conversation every few seconds and it would take painstaking attention to decipher every word. Also, another problem became evident immediately. I was a certified flight attendant, not a pilot, and I had neither the knowledge nor the skills to accurately interpret the audible exchanges of the cockpit crew. If I was to learn the truth surrounding the crash, I needed to educate myself without anyone knowing what I possessed.

It was obvious I could not trust anyone from the company or the government to assist me. Through the help of a trusted friend who worked at the McDonnell Douglas plant in Long Beach, however, I was able to obtain the operation manuals of the DC-10. In return he insisted he be allowed to listen to the recording. Desperately needing those handbooks, I relented. He listened to it only once and told me he wished he never had. I on the other hand had to listen to it over and over despite the pain. Like a lethal drug which becomes addictive after the first ingestion, the CVR recording enticed me to listened to it over and over, and each time it took a piece of my sanity. Only someone with a deep desire to be driven mad would continue on such a path.

"2605 advise runway in sight. Do you have the lights?" The directions from the tower, according to Victor Estrada, came from a Señor Rodríguez whose voice seems strained while trying to advise the cockpit crew. He also clearly states that the runway lights of Runway 23-Left may be on, a system the Mexican Government adamantly insisted had been nonfunctional and undergoing repairs for the three weeks prior to October 31. The loop silence which surfaced every few seconds demanded that I strain to listen then carefully rewind the tape to assure that I had truly heard what was being said. The Mexican Tower advised once more. *"2605 you are left of the track."* Instantly I recognized the voice of Captain Herbert responding.

"Just a bit." The tower shot right back.

"Advise runway in sight, there is a layer of fog over the field."
"Roger."
"2605, do you have approach lights on left in sight?" The voice from the tower seemed confused, uncertain.
"Negative," responded Captain Herbert.
"Okay sir, approach lights are on Runway 23-Left but that runway is closed to traffic." I did not have to be a pilot to understand that a runway which supposedly had been closed for weeks, a runway that had neither had the mandatory "X" at each end nor its light system in disabled, the governor had claimed, was, as the saying goes, an "accident waiting to happen" for even the most seasoned of pilots like Captain Herbert. I became very nauseous and the convulsions paralyzed me as I fell to the floor.

I couldn't understand it. If a regular flight attendant could see the discrepancies between the Mexican Government's conclusion of "pilot error" and the CVR recording, why hadn't the aviation experts of my airline, spoken up about such abnormalities?

"Don't be stupid, Eddy." It was Tommy who brought me back to reality. "It's the world of politics and big corporate entities."

"So, the victims, my fellow crew members, they are the sacrificial lambs that are paying for the silence the power brokers demand?

"Yeah, something like that."

"Why must we surrender life to the brutes and fools?"

The truths of the genuine world were too much to bear. I knew what I had to do. I called Scheduling and canceled my flight availability, packed my bag and headed for the airport. Arriving at LAX with plenty of time to spare, I focused all my energy in trying to forget the confidential facts I had learned from the tape: the information this airline apparently wanted to keep secret. Checking my mailbox, one envelope stood out. It was from the Chief Executive Officer of the airline and I was bewildered as to why Mario Reddick would be sending me a note. The brief note requested that I contact his office at my convenience. I approached the F/A supervisor office with apprehension, holding up the letter.

"Shana, can I use your phone?"

"Sure, Eddy." She gathered her things and left the office to afford me some privacy.

"Mr. Reddick, please." I could barely get the words out.

"Hello, good afternoon, ah, this is Eduardo Valenciana."

"Yes, Ed," the assistant stated. "Mr. Reddick is anxious to speak with you, just one moment." Maybe it was no big deal. Maybe our CEO wanted me to perform some minor public relations duty?

"Ah, Eduardo," My stomach tightened.

"Yes, Mr. Reddick, how are you this fine day, sir?" I tried to display the phony cordial manner Edmundo would have offered.

"Yes, Eduardo, I understand you recently returned from a profitable journey to Mexico City." I froze as he spoke the words. Jesus! How the hell did he know what I had done? I tried to downplay the experience.

"Ah yes, sir, a friend and I decided to go see the sights, you know the pyramids and all." I was failing miserably at my attempt.

"Seems like you got a lot of people down there upset. You know, Ed, ah, we can do all we can to see to your well-being up here but we have no control over what some of those people down there may do." There was a long pause as neither party knew where to go. "I think it best you stay away from Mexico City, at least for the near future. Do you understand?"

"Clearly sir."

"Good, that is all I wanted to tell you. You have a pleasant day."

"You also, sir." The Chief Executive Officer hung up the phone and the anger deep inside me rose. I boarded the DC-10 bound for Honolulu still fuming yet realizing that it might be a good idea to get out of town.

...

"We're cleared on the right; we're cleared on the right. No, this is the approach to the god-damn left." I awoke deeply shaken by the recurring dream gazing up into the dimly lit spectral sky over Kauai. Nestled in the warmth of the sleeping bag at the base of the majestic falls, I smelled the morning dew. I had been induced into a deep slumber, exhausted by the combined effort of the hike up to the Hanakapiai Falls and my mental exhaustion

370

from re-hashing the disciplinary report regarding the two pilots. One significant point in that document that had never really come to light in any conversation before was the fact that the session with the Supervisory pilot occurred just hours prior the departure of the ill-fated jumbo jet. Who in their right mind holds a hearing regarding the personal conflicts of two proud, former military pilots, then give the green light for these two choleric individuals to lock themselves in a small cockpit together and expect them to work together to guide a jumbo jet to a safe landing on a fog-shrouded runway?

"Okay boys, have a nice flight." It puzzled me even more that no one suspected that such animosity between the two aviators would have been a contributing factor in the accident. As I set myself upon a large rock by a large oval pond, I recalled the voices of the CVR tape.

"We're cleared on the right; we're cleared on the right." Were Captain Herbert's words not not a statement but rather a question? Regardless, there were two distinct immediate responses.

"The right one."

"The other runway." Those were the responses from F/O Reimann and S/O Wells. Were those themselves questions, or an indication that both processed the correct information regarding which runway the craft was supposed to land on? Was this information Captain Herbert seemed uncertain of at a vital time in the landing procedure?

Crap! The frustration just grew. Diego was right. In my desire to hear the recording I ignored the warnings of my dear friend.

"Be careful what you ask for." There was no resolution to be had only more confusion. Even if I was to discover anything significant what credible aviation organization going to be swayed by the opinion of a flight attendant?

I decided to vent my frustration by repeating the ritualistic role I had adapted when on Kauai previously. Here, high in the vegetated valley of the Na Pali, I could live out my wild fantasies. Though they be irrational to most, I found solace in such behavior. My bizarre conduct included rising at all hours of the night to relieve my pain with a Tarzan war cry that echoed down the valley to the tranquil beach. But this, along with the painted body and savage grunts, was the catharsis of a troubled soul.

I would run down the valley and leap onto large stones across the river and scramble up one elevated side of the wall, then back midway to the river. I would then leap from rock to rock back to the other side of the river, starting the whole ritual over again. The grunts and shriek intensified as I gathered momentum. At one point I lost my footing on the soft mountain trail and went tumbling out of control down the wet hillside. A fresh mud puddle softened the landing as I sat momentarily dazed. With my adrenaline rushing I refocused just in time to see a wild piglet in the distance staring at me. The little porker seemed to snort her approval of the jungle man's tumble, then turned and scurried off into the dense bush. I jumped to my feet and stealthily moved through the branches, vainly searching for my little antagonist. I waited, intending to have the last laugh on the piglet, keenly aware of the danger if a vicious mother was near-by. Suddenly the crackling of leaves on the trail announced the little squealer's arrival. Encased in a coat of drying mud the jungle man leapt out of the brush and onto the trail, letting loose a blood-curdling cry. In an instant, the valley echoed in response. Before me terrified hikers, clinging to the cliff wall in shock. I was no less shocked than they.

"It's the jungle wild man," one young man uttered.

"I read about you," clamored the other. Their female companion meanwhile was still too startled to let loose from the nearby tree *she* clung to.

"Excuse me, I'm sorry, I mean." Embarrassed, I fumbled my speech trying to explain what at that moment seemed pretty stupid. "I'm just a guy having some fun." I stuttered, "I'm on vacation like you guys." The hikers glanced at each other, then at my tanned, mud-covered body. They finally regained their composure, although the young lady would never completely let her guard down. Slowly, we managed to communicate. I dispensed with the wild jungle man and reverted to the tour-guide/flight attendant, willing to help and provide information in an instant. "Welcome aboard and if there is anything we can do for you on this majestic volcanic trail, please don't hesitate to call upon us." They must have wondered who "we" is! I'm sure they still didn't completely trust me. But they were not about to go home empty-handed.

"Hey, could we have a picture?" One of the guys asked while raising his camera. I jumped at the opportunity to put these visitors at ease.

"Sure!" That broke the ice.

"Stand over by the trail," He directed, trying for the best angle for such a prized photo as his hand worked the lens for the proper focus. "Look vicious," he commanded. If these tourists were to bring back proof of what they had claimed to find, they were not willing to settle for just some-meek looking madman. The colors pleased him. The bright green backdrop provided a perfect setting. The red dirt caked upon the jungle man highlighted the wilted leaves that covered his nakedness. In an instant, that moment was recorded forever.

"Do you think you guys could send me a copy?" I requested. We exchanged mailing information and they were off once more.

The chance meeting put me at a disadvantage. What if the tourists started telling people of the demented individual they had confronted? Later that evening my mind returned to the CVR recording that only created more questions. The airline was probably aware of my covert activities, attorneys were still wanted to talk to me and certain individuals in Mexico were pissed at me. I desired nothing more than to remain secluded in the valleys of the Na Pali.

I needed to get some sound advice, but I'd known that for some time. Of course, Dr. Ramljak immediately came to mind. Gathering my belongings, I began my exit along the majestic coastline. Later, showered and clothed, I boarded the propped twin otter of Princeville Airways and departed the Garden Island.

"This is the approach to the god-damn left!" The haunting voices echoed then died in the second-floor office of Dr. Ramljak in Westwood. The damaged tape demanded his full attention and I could see the strain on the good doctor's face as he tilted his head at a distinct angle, grasping what he could from the panicked voices of the doomed airliner. All the while he kept his eyes on me, taking in my reaction.

In the cockpit of the DC-10, Captain Herbert struggled to keep up with the rapid pace of events. Doctor Joe could plainly see that the tape had totally taken over me I silently murmured each sound, each moment. I was once again a passenger inside the cockpit of my aircraft.

"The thick fog was totally unexpected," I reminded the doctor. In the cockpit, Captain Herbert was calling for a missed approach.

"Take her up to 8500," Then there was panic and chaos. The Captain brought full throttle back on, just as he had been trained to do. The engines immediately responded.

"Get her up! Get her up!" First Officer Dieter Reimann begged his superior. *"You're starting to bank! You're banking!"*

"Oh Jesus Christ! Oh fuck!" Captain Carl Herbert Sr. suddenly became aware of the inevitable. *"I can't, I can't get her up!"* Then the shrill sound of alarms as Muerto entered the cockpit to take over.

"Get her up, Carl!" S/O Wells now pleaded, Carl Herbert, refusing to accept the inevitable, fought with all his might as the fog cleared revealing to the three stricken aviators their inescapable demise. Out the forward windows, a two-story building appeared in the path of our aircraft. The doomed ship was gliding 35' above the pavement of Benito Juárez International Airport, while one could hear the chaos of numerous voices screaming almost in unison. Then dead silence. I put down the recording device and glanced at Doctor Joe. He seemed deeply concerned by the price my mind was paying.

"How is this knowledge going to allow you to heal?" I was caught off guard by his question and could not immediately answer.

"In an earlier portion of the tape, Mexican Air Traffic Control advises the crew to expect a 23 Left approach into the airport," I finally offered.

"How is this information going to allow you to heal?" My wise mentor would not allow me to deflect his inquiry. Again, I had no answer.

I headed back to Manhattan Beach in a daze. I thought about the large cast on Skip Mitchell's leg, the physical injuries and multiple surgeries he had already endured. Yet, he remembered little if anything from the whole affair. I later discovered that others, like the passenger who lost both arms and was terribly scarred by the flames, also recalled little if anything. I wept silently, recalling those who had praised a gracious God for allowing me to, as they saw it, emerge from the fires virtually untouched. No, this God was continually playing a cruel joke. Like a Frankenstein monster I was given a new life embedded with a demented mind filled with horrors, lies and deceit. Like the fabled beast of Shelley's creation, I saw myself destined for destruction.

At home I sat staring at the pilot's disciplinary report on the table but avoided touching it. I thought again about my deceased crewmates and imagined how they might have handled my situation. The fallen angels always convinced me that each of them would have done a far better job. I remembered how not one of the F/A's had left a child.

"We were all so young at that moment of impact." I spoke without intending. "I want a child; I want a son."

I returned to the flight line disappointed that my covert mission to Mexico City had not eased the deep pain inside my soul. The effort had the complete opposite effect. The temptation to sit and listen to the CVR recording was enticing and was an addictive drug that took a piece of my soul every time. I found solace in the company of Tommy Acoba.

"Don't give in to it. You will eventually come full circle." His words were direct and logical as always.

"You're right Tommy. I have a feeling that things *are* going to turn around for me." Was my response just to appease Tony?

I left alone for a refreshing walk along the beach. The morning revealed radiantly clear skies along the coast of the South Bay of the basin as I descended the long flight of stairs from Avenue C to the sand. The wind was brisk as I gazed out upon the sunlit beauty of the vast Pacific. In an instant, I somehow believed I was supposed to be here. I was filled with a sense of peace, a luxury I had not enjoyed in some time. I did not want these feelings to fade. Someone or something was about to reach out to console me. Then slowly turning I saw her. She gracefully descended the steep incline. Long brown hair and olive-skinned, she was the first real angel I had the fortune to see after months in the company of wretched demons.

"I'm Eddy." I said, extending my hand.

"I'm Sofia." She replied with a smile.

A whirlwind romance was sparked that spring morning along the beautiful coastline. Sofia lived in the nearby community of Torrance. Yes, it struck me as odd that this lovely Italian young woman had come into my life when I just had told Tommy that I believed things were going to turn around for me. Every time I tried to dismiss our meeting as coincidental, I recalled Reina's premonitions. She had always believed that we were meant to be at a certain place at a certain time in our lives. My connection with Sofia seemed to have that feeling.

The courting process was quite unusual for the lovely lady. With my new freedom established freedom in the company I could offer her the skies of our airline routes. A night on the town was not restricted to the City of the Angels as SFO, SEA and of course HNL became destinations to kindle the hopes and dreams of our relationship. I was now spotted at Terminal 5 with my young sweetheart, the gossip and rumors flew. I took little notice as I was simply in love. Sofia's tenderness and compassion would make her a wonderful mother while also giving me a second chance at life.

I found myself relishing the duties of being a flight attendant once again. My relationship with Sofia seemed to have relegated my past into nothing more than a bad dream, although there still existed a tinge of guilt for surviving.

"Why should you bask in the warmth of a love affair? Your friends are cold and dead." Would the voices ever leave me alone? I was torn.

Through her warm smile and tight embrace, Sofia was supportive from the beginning. Yet each time I was assigned a flight I knew I owed something to the families that were left without closure regarding the circumstance surrounding the loss of their loved ones. How close had my family, my mother in particular, come to having to mourn and fret over all the legalities that overwhelmed these families? I knew that I would never be free to go forward in my blossoming relationship with Sofia if I did not try to make a difference to the others. So, I decided I had to confront the airline.

Returning from a HNL flight, I looked forward to a few days off, my mind filled with only thoughts of Sofia. I picked up the mail as I entered my home and noticed a large manila envelope, assuming it was most likely another request from an investigator. I knew not when, but was well aware of the litigation ahead, and the ordeal it would be. As I opened it, I was pleased to see that the trio of hikers I had encountered in the Na Pali had kept their word. The glossy print revealed a half-naked figure plastered in red dirt, muck, paint and vegetation; a wild man possessed. I stared at the demented fiend I now wanted to put forever in the past.

...

A determined young man wandered through the executive hallways of the airline. He carried a box filled with the documents and evidence that could prove that the crash and deaths of those on board was far more complicated than just "pilot error."

I deeply resented "Edmundo," the persona I had adopted so many times. I was certain of the conspiracies orchestrated by the Mexican Government to sweep the true facts under the carpet, while assuming the airline's participation in this deplorable cover-up. I so wanted to believe that there was no underhandedness on their part, but logic was telling me otherwise. What exactly I was looking for I really did not know. For myself, I was determined to come away this day with a definite answer of some sort, a firm foundation by which I could try and construct my new life. I decided I would no longer settle for this chaotic existence. It was a poor substitute even though everyone insisted I should be thankful. I brought along a small cassette player and was ready to force my superior to sit and listen to the agonizing dialog, alarms and screams. In my mind there was only one man I could approach in hopes of receiving a straight answer, Executive Vice President, Barry Lane.

"Anything I can help you with, Eduardo?" Mr. Lane was a diplomat of the airline industry, dignified and professional. The former airline ship cleaner was a humble gentleman recognizing instantly that I was deeply troubled, and he always correctly called me by my correct name, Eduardo.

"Have you listened to the CVR recording from flight 2605?" I went straight to the point.

"Yes, I have, Eduardo."

"Not very pleasant is it?"

"No, it is not." There was a long pause.

"You know. Mr. Lane, I have the recording."

"I am well aware of that fact." I instantly froze. His stark honesty made me uneasy. I arose from my seat and began to walk about his office, noticing the usual aircraft models on his desk and shelves. Mustering up the courage, I turned and faced him.

"Was it pilot error?" Mr. Lane took a deep breath and clasped his hands together.

"You probably know just as much as any of us in that regard." I was relieved. His answer reinforced my trust in him. I continued.

"There was so much crap down there, dishonesty at every turn. Then there was the incident with the Federal Police."

"You're right, Eduardo, I have spoken with Jack McKay concerning the things you had to go through."

"There is also the conflict between Carl and Dieter which I partly witnessed in the cockpit early that morning. All this shit that none of the employees know about. What about the families of my fellow crew-members?"

"You speak the truth about all of this, Ed, but really what are we to do? Mexico is pulling all the strings."

"I could go public with the tape."

"Yes, you could and that would be your right to do so." Once again there was a pause as I tried to absorb what he had just said. But he wasn't through.

"But what would be the result of such an action? You must understand the company is having a difficult time as a result of deregulation in the industry. Last year took a significant toll on the company and this year has been no kinder." I <u>was</u> aware. Under the protection of government regulation and with former systems in place, since the dawn of passenger aviation, there was prosperity for our regional airline. Now, anyone wishing to own a passenger aircraft could start an airline.

Our CEO, Mario Reddick, helped the airline reach the prosperity it formally enjoyed using old tried-and-true formulas which succeeded under federal protection of routes. Unfortunately, he and his subordinates continued to use these methods through the alteration that now produced a free market. This would quickly prove unsustainable, as many established regional airlines were now being forced out of business. Bankruptcies and mergers with larger, financially stronger airlines were now the norm.

"But what about the families of my deceased crew-members? Don't I have a responsibility to them?" I was looking at him straight in the eye.

"What about the associates of this company, Eduardo? What would be the effect on them? Possibly you and many of your friends could be out of work." As always, Barry Lane was honest and practical. "What good would it be for everyone involved to bring all of this mess to the forefront?"

"How will this knowledge help you to heal?" I muttered Doctor Joe's words, shaking my head.

"What?" The airline executive didn't quite hear. I looked up to explain.

"I was just repeating what Doctor Ramljak had asked me. He wanted to know how the tape and the other revelations would help me in my healing process." Barry Lane seized on this.

"And what is the answer to that question?"

"I'm not sure knowing these things could ever be a positive factor in trying to get better."

"Then toss it aside, lad. You have your whole life ahead of you. Perhaps you are to some degree at a crossroad in your life. Is Doctor Ramljak helping you?" The last remark hit a chord.

"Oh yeah, he has really made a difference."

"Then let him guide you so you can go forward. Do you have a girlfriend?" I hesitated and thought how Sofia was making a difference in my life.

"Well yeah, I recently met someone who I believe is special."

"Then reap the graces God has given you. You have been given a rare gift and the knowledge that goes with it. Embrace your new life, get married, have children."

"You don't deserve it." The fallen angels attempted again to derail my new-found desire to actually hope. But I fought back. I thought about Reina, Tamlyn, Karen and the rest of the cabin crew. They left no children.

"Yes, Mr. Lane, I will get married and have children." The company Vice-President was pleased with what he thought he had accomplished and came over to shake my hand. I know he wasn't simply trying to prevent me from possibly embarrassing the airline. He was a good and honest man who was genuinely concerned for my well-being.

"Continue your sessions with Doctor Ramljak, get back to work, and I guarantee you will see brighter and happier days."

I left the executive offices, returned home and gathered up everything I had accumulated related to the crash, then tucked them away in my bedroom closet. I decided to walk away from whatever responsibility a survivor inherits. My avowed loyalty to the airline took priority and offered the best opportunity in achieving the goal of a fruitful life. I once again returned to the flight line as my courtship with Sofia blossomed. With Doctor Ramljak's guidance I sculpted out a healthy relationship. Fortune also bequeathed that when the time came to proceed with the proper introductions to my family, I could proudly declare that my betrothed and her family were Roman Catholics. My mother couldn't wait to tell Sister Inez!

Part III
A Nest of Ashes

Chapter XVII

I carefully walked the crowded streets of Hell's Kitchen in New York, the city that never sleeps, first looking around like some bird of prey and then ducking into a pizzeria to watch and wait.

"Want a date?" A familiar solicitation phrase on the streets was ignored by some and caught the interest of others. A pack of five young men, possibly college students, stopped and showed interest in the teenager's proposition. The leader of the group began haggling with the young street walker which brought laughter and ridicule from the others. Seemingly filled to the brim with liquor and false bravado the small, burly student seemed to be making some headway in his negotiations when his taller, less-intoxicated friend stepped forward and wisely yanked his friend away, rapidly reprimanding him for the error of his ways. Soon, the rowdy rogues disappeared among the crowd that flowed through the streets and the young coquette instinctively turned her attention to other prospective customers.

The time had come for action, so I calmly rose and went into the washroom of the small eatery to refurbish the smeared, fading colors on my face, my visual declaration of war. I carefully sketched the white and bright red of my airline logo, an evolution for an avenging muse. Completing my metamorphosis, I then reached behind and fondled the cold metal hand grip of my precious knife I had strapped to my back.

What would my crew think of my illicit intent? I thought of Gary Rollings, his strong character and demeanor making him the perfect candidate for leadership, a company man till the end. "He deserved to live. Not me! Not me!" I was engrossed with self-pity which fired up my hatred and a desire for blood.

All at once I sensed someone behind me, then turned and stood face-to-face with a middle-aged smiling intently at me. As I gazed down, I witnessed the fool holding what pitiful manly presence he could retain. Such a sinful act was the fatal spark that lit an enormous detonation. Rage was unleashed as the perverted victim hit the floor in a flash, blood running down the side of his face. I instinctively readied myself to strike again.

"YOU FUCKING LEECH!" In this pathetic soul I saw them all, Chávez, Montoya, the politicians, the lawyers, the money men. He represented all the bloodsuckers that drained the life and decency from all of us: me, my friends, the victims and their families, the eternal wounded who would never taste the sweetness of life again. I struck again with a vengeance before he was able to turn and try to pull the door open. I retrieved the large knife from its sheath and directed it at my quarry.

"SIGN THE FUCKING PAPER!"

...

Stop! I'm getting way ahead of myself. I promised Barry Lane I was going to make a true effort at putting this madness behind me. And I was in love. I was going to marry Sofia, have children. You must understand that I did take Mr. Lane's advice. I tried with all my heart and soul to do what was right. Unfortunately, I as yet could not understand that this plague, the evil Muerto, those fallen angels, would always exist in the shadows, waiting. Sofia deserved the happiness I promised to give her the day we said our vows."

"Let us raise out glasses to the new Mr. and Mrs. Valenciana. May their lives together be filled with peace and contentment." So was the "Salud" that was presented by Tommy Acoba after Sofia and I had received the blessing of the Holy Mother Church. The reception went on into the early morning hours as family, friends and airline associates ate, danced and bestowed their well-wishes.

"You really have the world in the palm of your hand," a co-worker assured me. Sofia and I embarked on an elaborately planned honeymoon tour. The first stop had never been in doubt. I was filled with excitement to share the radiant beauty and tranquility with her of the Garden Island of Kauai with her. This time there would be no trekking through the red mud to some isolated campsite. Instead we enjoyed amenities of a well-known resort on the coast of the north shore. It was the ideal place for me to forget the past and look forward to this new relationship.

The happy newlyweds returned to the City of Angels, tanned and content, for a small reprieve in an ambitious agenda. Next, the capitals of Europe beckoned. Madrid and Vienna were wonderfully romantic cities, not to mention spectacular for a first-time traveler like Sofia. The grand finale was a two-week Christmas holiday in the Tyrolean Alps of Innsbruck Austria, where the sight of Hawaiian t-shirts over our ski attire caught the eye of our European host.

"You are from Hawaii?" One gentleman asked in a German accent.

"We just came from there."

"I would have remained there!" He replied with a smile as he shivered in the cold. Sofia and I looked at each other and laughed too, barely noticing the chill, for we were lost in a dream, entranced by our love for each other. Since the proclamation of husband and wife by Father Riley, Sofia and I had ventured into a mythical world of enchantment. We glistered in jubilance. I slept soundly those nights, gratified to be in the arms of my adorable new wife.

As we glided high over the Atlantic Ocean, I pondered our new way of life, but it was also a different world we were returning to. Jimmy Carter had failed in his bid for re-election and Ronald Reagan assumed the Presidency with a promise to return America to a place of prominence in the world. The Iran Hostage ordeal would end.

"No one wants to remember." The voices were stern, yet for this one time I heartily agreed. I wanted to forget. I looked over at Sofia who gently slept on my shoulder. She stirred a bit, then fluttered her sparkling eyes and smiled as the jumbo jet settled into its final approach into LAX. Neither of us wanted the dream to end.

"Honey, after we land let's go home and rest. Tomorrow let's return and stand by for the flight to HNL and head over to Kauai for a few more days." The new Mrs. Valenciana contemplated my suggestion for a second, then smiled broadly and nodded with approval. Just like that the fanciful fable continued.

A few weeks later while Sofia and I were still setting up our first home together, I was scheduled for LAX-MIA-LAX.

"Sofia, they are sending me to Miami, and I have a 30-hour layover. I checked the load on the flight, and it looks a bit light, you want to come along?" My blushing bride sat proudly at gate 58, Terminal 5 as I entered the DC-10 with my crew. Sofia would get the opportunity to see her husband at his best as we shared the night flight across the southern stretch of the country. The airline supplied the layover hotel room upon arrival, and we picked up where our fairytale honeymoon had left off. Sofia joined me on my next trip to NYC, where we marveled at the field of endless lights from a balcony at Radio City Music Hall.

"It seems like married life is agreeing with you, Ed," Doctor Ramljak said as I sat in his office. "You seem to be on the road to healing."

"Thanks, Doc." It was true. I was meeting the goals I had set for myself in my effort to be a good flight attendant. Meanwhile Sofia was delightful, sincere, and worked hard to make a comfortable, welcoming home.

"Well, I'm pregnant," Sofia announced joyfully one day as she exited her doctor's office. We hugged each other tightly and it felt so good. The proud father-to-be found great satisfaction in spreading the news -- on the company bus, in the terminal and in the cabin of the aircraft.

But there was another reality that was catching my eye, the diminishing number of passengers on our flights. Deregulation was brutal on our proud airline and it was obvious that other companies in the industry were now taking a piece of the lucrative pie, our routes. I had a child on the way and my job security was in question. My family responsibilities would take took priority, or so I thought. Over any other issues, I believed that I could keep the vile issues of my crash bottled up forever. I was foolish.

On January 23, 1982, a World Airways DC-10 with 212 passengers slid off the runway at Logan Airport in Boston. The pictures on the TV screen were sucking me in again. The jumbo jet sat tilted downward at the end of the runway with its nose in shallow water. The cockpit crew had landed the craft off the mark. Unlike flight 2605, this incident truly did seem like pilot error from the beginning.

I went to bed that night unable to sleep, visualizing a long assembly of frightened passengers and crew. They were awaiting their turn to board their own personal roller coaster that was screeching to a halt to load the new passengers. Each poor soul boarded the mad amusement ride which was destined to bestow misery upon them. I imagined the attorneys congregating to create boundaries from which these survivors would have to choose sides. Only the cabin crew had no advocates. I wondered if the flight attendants of the World Airways crash were unionized. I was pretty sure that the captain's fate would be a sentenced of slow death by guilt. His career was over. I finally fell asleep feeling sorry for them all.

"Good morning Mexico Tower, Flight 2605 is inbound for 23."

"2605, report over Mike Echo final approach navigation point, wind calm,"

"Roger, 2605 over Mike Echo." The CVR's haunting dialogue returned to wake me up. I looked over at the slumber of my expectant wife. The curvature of her body revealed the young child that would soon arrive to be greeted, loved and nurtured. There was a lot at stake, and I became afraid.

Cristiano Valenciana made his appearance at a sizable 9 lbs., 9 ounces. Family members were ecstatic. In Hispanic tradition, the arrival of a male child who will carry on the family name is always greeted as a blessing. I felt deep gratification in the fact that Sofia and I were able to produce a child, one that could represent the cabin crew of 2605. I proudly spit in Muerto's face and mocked him for his failure.

The airline industry was falling into disarray as prior boundaries dissolved. With much smaller loads being transported the once vibrant company suffered. Flight Attendant Training abruptly discontinued new training classes, and employees throughout the system feared for their jobs. Although my particular situation with the airline was somewhat vague, I tossed aside any fears regarding my career in favor of relishing my new-found status as a father. While other crewmembers discussed the concerns of empty flights, I spent my layovers finding special toys for a boy I determined would be "a child of the world." A stuffed bear in a crate from Anchorage would remain one of his favorites.

Sofia visited her older sister in HNL to alleviate the physical and emotional stress of giving birth. Since Cris was a strong baby I had no worries about letting her travel with him just after turning one month old. I discovered a Star Wars diary book in a Portland department store with colorful drawings and wise proverbs by the Jedi Master Yoda, an ideal child's aviation logbook. I intended to document each flight Cris took and hoped there would be many. The Yoda logbook would be sent up to the cockpit where the pilots would document miles and flight times with signatures and personal messages.

I carried a feeling of pride in the workplace, sharing new photos of Cris with every flight crew. Focusing my mind on my fast-growing boy distracted me from my deepest worries. Returning to LAX from a three-day trip, I found a letter from Reva, the Flight Attendant Representative for our AFA union. Apparently, the association was inviting a congregation to their headquarters in Washington D.C. where the actions of those involved in our incident, especially Reva, were to be acknowledged. Surprised by the invitation, I felt a bit awkward as I had never filled out an application to join the union.

"Sofia, would you mind if I went to Washington D.C. for a few days?" The request was not well received.

"It's bad enough that you are gone a great deal as it is." Her point was well taken. "Go ahead. I'll have my sister stay with me while you are gone." I should have read between the lines of her statement, but I did not. I went to D.C.

...

"Skip. Good to see you brother." I was excited as Reva, Skip and I were accompanied by Mike Lottergan and another dear F/A friend, HNL union rep Tim Blackman. Skip and I had never really had the time to sit down and discuss any specifics on what either of us may have remembered from our ordeals. I refrained from asking what he recollected. But he and I were on the same wavelength. Thoughts of partying in Georgetown filled our mischievous minds as we boarded the company craft bound for the nation's capital.

"Remember guys, I'm a family man now, no hijinks on this trip," I warned.

"Oh sure, don't worry, Eddy, we will take good care of you," replied Mike with a devilish smile. Somehow, I knew I was in trouble.

This AFA event was designed to be a safety conference involving many flight crews from various airlines. There was a great atmosphere of camaraderie as all flight attendants were housed in the on-site dormitories at the union's training center. Experts from all aspects of aviation safety would be conducting seminars over three days. There were representatives from the Federal Aviation Administration (FAA) and the National Transportation Safety Board (NTSB). Although the flying public rarely can view the real reason F/As are stationed on their flights, the union headquarters provided an institution and a learning center dedicated to the main focus of our career, safety.

At the conclusion of the conference, Skip and I joined other F/As on a panel to discuss our involvement in various incidents. The AFA director, who presided over the panel, started the discussions.

"Let's hear from each of you now. What happened and how did you deal with it?"

"A woman's water broke right in the middle of the flight," Peggy, a petite F/A employed by an east coast airline recollected. "The Captain was required to make an emergency landing at a non-scheduled airport. I am happy to tell you that mother and child are doing well."

Another woman from a southern-based airline described the fear and anticipation of an emergency evacuation when, on take-off in a DC-9 aircraft, smoke came billowing out of the left engine.

"Grab ankles! Stay down! Stay down!" Hers was a story of a dash to evacuate the cabin once the plane came to a complete stop. "The slides at each exit were deployed and an orderly evacuation was conducted." The raw emotion and anxiety of the incident surfaced in her narrative. "Fortunately, the pilots had shut the engine down and no further danger was projected."

"What about you Skip?" My fellow crewmate was surprised by the director's sudden attention. I could see that he became nervous and I wondered what he would say. I saw his mind working as he tried to remember events that I was very aware were not pleasant.

"There was a huge shifting of the aircraft, a flash of light and fire. I just remember crawling." My dear friend then fell silent as he struggled to hide what was now obvious, a blank period in his consciousness.

"Eddy? What about you?"

"The aft section of the craft shifted and broke into three sections as the number two engine exploded and a fireball shot forward through the fuselage." There was a unified chorus of alarming gasps from all in attendance. Their eyes grew wide and mouths dropped as they looked at each other and tried to imagine the scenario. I looked at Skip who seemed just as interested, as if he had not been part of it. I continued to speak frankly but calmly. "I was fortunate to see Skip's hands waving by the firelight right after the werewolf guy had run up to me screaming in Spanish, wanting to know what had happened to the aircraft."

"Werewolf guy?" The participants were on the edge of confusion.

"Oh shit," I murmured. Then I recalled a conversation I had some time back with Jack McKay.

"Remember Eduardo, there are only a few of us that know the true nature of what went on down there. Your supervisors, associates and the general public are unaware of the facts of this beast. Toss it aside and get on with your life." Like a Pandora's box that had been unexpectedly opened my calm descriptive words escaped.

"The Mexicans never roped off the crash site. There were ice cream and balloon vendors hocking their wares as the general public rustled through the luggage. No U.S. investigators were allowed on the site. And you know, somebody stole the left landing gear from the destroyed jumbo jet."

"I think we should move on now." The words shot forth from the AFA director. I doubt she believed a single word of what I had related. Airline crash sites are handled delicately and overseen by experts of the industry. Certainly, my narrative could not be true. Perhaps the survivor of 2605 was suffering from that PTSD, which was not unimaginable in these circumstances, but a political cover-up? No. I recognized how complete the cover-up was, orchestrated by the Mexican Government with the blessing of the airline and U.S. Government.

"I would like to hear more about your ordeal if you don't mind." A man in a suit stood before me as the conference was breaking up. "I have spoken to a number of investigators who went down to Mexico after the crash and were stonewalled at every step." Grant Greenly was with the FAA in Washington and took great interest in my story. "I've tried to look into the specifics of your crash but there is very little information on file at our bureau. It is my understanding that the Mexican agency conducted the investigation,"

"La Navegación en El Espacio Aereo Mexicano," I interjected. Greenly paused for a moment.

"Yeah, those guys, they still have not released their findings." The rest of the afternoon was spent discussing specifics which Grant found intriguing. I developed a friendship with the investigator and our relationship offered me an open door to the agency's headquarters, an opportunity to examine files and evidence of other airline crashes. I was eager to expand my personal knowledge of aviation accidents and the industry as a whole. On the flight back to the west coast I wondered why my crash had dissolved so totally into oblivion. But deep down I knew.

"Perhaps if the cabin crew had not been so junior," I whispered to myself. If the flight attendants had recognized faces with established years in the company maybe there would have been a greater outcry by the associates. Such cries may have forced the airline to reveal more of the specifics. Then again as others would remind me,

"It's a huge motherhood/sisterhood from airline to airline. If anything, the youth of the crew made it more disturbing." I recalled the angelic face of Karen Smitt, the "baby" of the crew.

"Please, please, please," she begged. If my own union was expressing doubt about my affidavit, then there was truth in Jack McKay's words. My mind drifted to my lovely, gracious wife and my sprouting baby boy. I resolved to toss this whole affair to the side. For them, for me.

With Doctor Ramljak's guidance I was able to dislodge much of the vulgar malady that infested my subconscious. I blossomed in my duties as a respected flight attendant and Edmundo the Magnificent slowly gave way as time passed. New sincere work relationships developed. If there was a kink in the chain that bound my life in tranquility it was the fact that my job required, I be in an environment filled with a multitude of possible triggers.

"We're cleared on the right, we're cleared on the right?"

"The other runway."

"The right runway."

"No, this is the approach to the god-damn left!" The words of the CVR were never far below the surface.

"Will we ever be good enough?" Whenever things started to get dicey, the weight room was always my first choice, followed by body surfing near the pier at Manhattan Beach. But the best remedy and greatest pleasure was with Cristiano who was full of energy, testing limits of his parents' energy. He was a good boy and the love he projected dampened my pain. Cris was my joy. He reinforced a belief that perhaps this dormant God really was listening. My son was a living example of hope and I cherished him dearly.

"How about New York? It's a 28-hour layover," offered the scheduler. I was delighted but Sofia wasn't for it meant that her husband was dashing off once more while she remained home to care for an overactive Cristiano. Her arguments had merit. One spouse would be enjoying the fast pace activities of the city that never sleeps, the other would struggle with little sleep, changing diapers and seeing to the needs of a feisty little boy. Sofia began to feel neglected.

But once at the airport any guilt from leaving was diminished by my crewmates who were very excited about the amount of free time we would have in "The Big Apple."

Our anticipation grew on final approach when our DC-10 circled high above the massive concrete skyscrapers of Manhattan.

"Want to hit the city with us, Eddy?" An F/A extended an invitation as we rode the crew bus to the hotel by Shea Stadium.

"No, no I'm going to get some much-needed sleep tonight. I will see you guys tomorrow." I begged off not really knowing how I intended to spend the layover. But upon checking in at the front desk of the hotel the Captain in command of my flight stepped forward to introduce himself.

"I've been anxious to meet you, Eduardo." I was surprised he was not calling me "Edmundo."

"I'm Ron Banner. I headed up the investigation on 2605 for ALPA. (Air Line Pilots Association)." I stood silent, perplexed because I thought I was aware of all the primary players in this probe. "I'd like to speak to you if you have the time. I have some material concerning the crash I would like to share with you."

"If I have the time? Are you kidding me?" I couldn't believe this!

"Let's say we get together in the bar in about 30 minutes?" I could not get to my room fast enough as I stumbled about to change and freshen up, then I quickly returned downstairs to the facility's hotel lounge and the promise of answers from the most reputable source I had yet encountered. As we enjoyed a couple of cold beers the chief pilot disclosed that he was still trying to sort out all the details of what had happened.

"Have you read the Mexican final report?" Captain Banner inquired.

"I wasn't aware it was out." He put down his drink, opened a briefcase he had brought with him, reached in and grabbed a document and laid it upon the table.

"That's for you." I nearly peed in my pants. He gave me a hard look. "Its conclusion was 'pilot error' of course."

"Was Carl sucked into the wrong runway?" My frank question produced a frown on Captain Banner's face. He had been a close friend to Carl and the family, still in close contact with Carl's widow, Heidi.

"It sure looks that way, Ed, but because of the restrictions put upon those of us trying to get answers at the scene it would be hard to prove at this point. But ALPA simply could not sit idle. The union simply refuses to accept the Mexican document." Wow! Finally, I was speaking to a man of quality who represented an organization which now seemed to be saying, "Enough is Enough!"

"I've recently completed work on an independent report on the accident." he added. My eyes grew wide. Captain Banner had been given the thankless job of cleaning up the mess. "I have an extra copy." I could hardly control myself. "This is for you, Ed, and I hope you are able to find a sense of peace in its contents." Captain Banner presented the blue folder to me as I sat frozen. The hair on the back of my neck rose as I grabbed the icy glass of beer and finished it in several hurried gulps. I felt relief. Here was an expert that seemed to be saying, "No you are not crazy, you seem to have perceived the entire ugly affair in a rational and acute manner."

"I'm not a bonehead flight attendant," I whispered. "We flight attendants are not air heads."

The mindless chatter with myself continued.

"What was that?" The captain asked.

"Oh, nothing. Listen captain, how could something like this have happened in the first place?"

"I don't know, Ed, I just hope it never happens again." He shook my hand and departed to retire for the evening.

I hurried to my room and first examined the Mexican report. I found it to be ten pages of confusion. I was disgusted to see the report state that Skip Mitchell had died in the tragedy and Reina Torres had survived. I recalled how in the international agreement governing airline accidents on foreign territory, the airline and host nation of the company have the right to question any irregularities in a final report. There were plenty in the Mexican account yet both entities remained silent and blind to the obvious. I became frustrated and tossed the report aside, then I grabbed the ALPA report.

I held the document and realized that I was shaking uncontrollably. Sitting on the bed I opened Captain Banner's evaluation and was struck by the very first sentence.

"After an extensive investigation, the Air Line Pilots Association is unable to determine a precise cause of this accident."[9]

"So, what's new," I thought, but then continued on.

---

9   ALPA Report

"But because investigators were withheld from making a complete and thorough examination of the aircraft wreckage, crash site and airport facilities, it will never be accurately determined to what extent the aircraft or the approach facilities contributed to this disaster." If my airline or the U.S. Government needed a reason to confront the findings of La Navegación en El Espacio Aereo Mexicano, there it was. But I wasn't stupid: I had long ago realized that politics and big money were going to determine what caused the crash of flight 2605.

The deeper I dove into Captain Banner's assessment the greater my anger swelled. The senior pilot had done a good job and sacrificed none of the truth. It led to where he had his suspicions, although he was far more diplomatic about pointing the finger than I certainly would have been. The flight was cleared to descend to 13,000' and proceed directly to the Tepexpan radio beacon, the blue folder revealed. It further implied that the cockpit crew of 2605 was to expect an INS approach to Runway 23-Left. Even an amateur pilot could have seen the ramifications of such instructions. The Captain and the F/O agreed at that time that they would make a Tepexpan approach, which is the transition that leads to the INS approach for Runway 23-Left.

It was there in black and white. Bits of the puzzle that were confusing before now began to fit.

"Carl was suckered in!" I stopped reading for a time to concentrate and recall that fateful morning. Obviously, my friends, my co-workers were all dead as a result of stupidity. The Mexican Government knew it, the airline knew it and so did the politicians in Washington.

But why such an elaborate cover-up? Then I remembered that conversation with the Mexican minister.

"Your own airline, Señor Valenciana, is a working partner with our government in creating economic success…all our partners are in agreement, working in harmony and not making waves."

There had been widespread rumors that the Mexicans had tampered with the CVR Recording once it was retrieved from the scorched wreckage. Maybe that's what Captain Banner was referring to when he said that he wished he knew the entire truth?

I found no proof of tampering in the tape Diego had given me but certainly was no expert in such matters. I placed the report gently down on the table, treating it as a precious ancient manuscript. Feeling depressed I stood and walked over to the mirror focusing on the lines and shapes of my face. So, the destruction of my jumbo jet had all been a very sad mistake with apologies to be offered by all involved. All that was left was to ante up the thirty pieces of silver that created a sweet sound once buried deep in the pockets of the moneychangers. With that, my mind became transformed by hate and the reflection now in front of me was that of someone I did not recognize. It had my face but stood with a much more committed demeanor.

"Who is watching out for your interest, Ed?" My jaw dropped as I could swear the figure in the mirror had just asked me a question. "Those who were to blame for this tragedy stand to lose much if the truth is revealed. Do you think that buffoon, Edmundo, is going to help you? I will take care of you; the world be damned." The sight of Señora Torres kneeling at her daughter's gravesite came to mind. The memory haunted me as I turned away from the mirror and faced the door that led to the hallway. I slowly unlocked and opened it, walking out and turning to peer down the corridor. There at the end of it stood the young Mexican child, Javier, his arms reaching for me.

"Will I ever be good enough?" I clenched my hands into a fist, gritted my teeth then howled in pain. The hotel operator's board must have lit up with numerous calls. I assumed the security staff would check out the guests' concerns, but they would find nothing.

"Got to get out of here!" I gathered some belongings and ran out the door and down the stairs onto the rain-soaked sidewalk, stopping only through pure exhaustion.

"Dear God, why do you abandon me?" I bent over to catch my breath and gain some composure. Not paying attention to where I was running, I looked up and realized I was standing at the entrance to the New York City underground. It looked enticing, a dark refuge, a place to hide and I ran down the steps.

"Welcome aboard Flight 2605." The announcement rang loud and clear, through the catacombs of the NY subway. "We'll be traveling at 37,000 feet and will arrive in Mexico City at approximately 5:45am. We invite you sit back and enjoy your flight. If there is anything we can do to make your flight more enjoyable…" the voice became ugly and gross, "…please don't hesitate to call upon one of your friendly flight attendants." I ran through the shadowy corridors impatient to catch the next available train with no regard to destination. When one finally came to a screeching halt in front of me I rushed in, falling into a seat exhausted. As the doors shut and we lurched forward I heard a familiar voice.

"Welcome aboard sir." It was Reina! Suddenly, the strong image of myself I had viewed in my room appeared, seated right across from me.

"Can't you see, Ed? Peace equates to death." A new and more lethal idea developed. "Reina found peace in her faith, Tamlyn in her recent marriage, Gary in his plans to transfer to Denver and Cary in the rekindled relationship with her husband. Now, they are dead. Only I can protect you."

"NO!" I screamed. The image vanished. I looked about the subway car knowing I was the focus of uncertain stares. I became ashamed thinking about Sofia and Cris.

"Now there is even more to lose," I muttered in a semi-fetal position. The few passengers in the car kept staring. I murmured unintelligible words and sentences. "Cleared to land 23-Left. The other runway. Why? Good enough? Look what happened to my friends!" All at once I became aware of my fellow passengers looking at each other and indicating I must be crazy. Then out of the corner of my eye I spotted a Mexican campesino sitting at the end of the subway car. Across from him appeared two young passengers from 2605, Ronald Daily and his young Mexican friend. The three men smiled and glanced in my direction.

"Hey dude, got any more Bohemia?" I swallowed hard and turned away trying to ignore the request. The sounds of the rushing train increased in volume and I could hardly think. I glanced to the other end of the car where sitting passively were the Mexican sisters I had given cocktails to, on 2605. One of the kind women sat busily knitting a child's sweater, the other one just smiling at me. Suddenly the train sped up again.

"Ah, this is your captain speaking." The voice echoed through the car as the side lights blinked off and on. "We've been advised to expect some moderate turbulence as we descend, please make sure that your seat belt is tightly fastened, thank you." I gazed out the window just as we entered a tunnel. I think we were under the East River heading for Manhattan. The train jerked and swayed. Was I going to end up on the tarmac? Finally, it slowed and rolled to a screeching stop.

"TIME SQUARE!!" A voice yelled out. I remained still as others hurried out, then I rose and decided to follow them. They guided my trek through the corridors of the catacombs. Then the crowd I had embraced emerged above ground to a unique terrain and diverse culture, one that stirred rapidly, enticing yet fearful and tremendously inviting. Peril seemed to loom everywhere, and this delighted me. I remained standing stoically as everyone and everything rushed by me. I glanced skyward to the heavens, viewing pinnacles of concrete towers, attesting to the efforts of man challenging the forces of nature. Their tilted slopes reminded me of the volcanic mountains of the north shore of my island. What shot skyward here was every bit as exciting, but this was not a peaceful jungle. Instead, it offered the twisted opportunity I somehow had been seeking.

"Vengeance, that's what you want." The voices egged me on. Oh, I so desired it. Elated by the prospects, I became very observant. An elderly woman across the street in a worn gray coat struggled to escape the harassment of three youths who toyed with their prey. A tall balding man stood defiantly in the cool night air in the middle of the street, engaged in an argument with a short taxi driver who looked to be of Middle Eastern descent. The late night suddenly erupted with the blaring of car horns from those trapped by the dispute. Like a child in a candy store I marveled at the possibilities and walked slowly on to 42nd St., distracted by the radiant, colorful lights that made the night seem like day.

"You buy some coke?" A dark figure in a long blue coat whispered as he approached me. I took no notice and just continued on. Others flashed jewelry set upon their arms as I smiled, fascinate. I was not there seeking bargains or illegal chemicals; in fact, a great part of my being seemed to be laying down defined ground rules for a very guileful and deadly game. The more I walked, the more this persona took delight in the fantasy my vile thoughts were constructing.

Then I found myself in Hell's Kitchen, home to the city's castoffs. For some reason I began to feel comfortable among them! Who protected them? Society's easiest prey. I saw the vultures among them. All that I perceived as foul concerning my ordeal, I specifically related to them.

"Hey, want a date?" In my absorption I barely heard the invitation. "You want a date or not?" She stood facing me in a short black dress with high heels that made her a good three inches taller. Underneath the caked make-up I could see a trace of sweet Karen.

"How old are you?"

"You got fifty bucks?" She got right to the point. "I'm old enough!" I could feel the anger and disgusted. "Who did this to you?" The person I view in my hotel room mirror and then again in the subway car began to take over. He would without hesitation readily attack anyone trying to steal the innocence of this girl. The frustration overwhelmed me.

"First this society lets children burn then they allow them to prostitute themselves to eke out a pitiful existence."

For whatever reason, the young lady continued to badger me, solicit. This flight attendant on layover was ill prepared to deal with what was facing him. I had to escape, ducking into an adjacent pizza shop until the spaced-out pathetic child wandered off. I ordered a beer and took a seat by the front window settling down staring out at this concrete jungle where everyone was expendable.

"Prey for vermin." I said the words easily and with no regret. Suddenly I spotted the young woman across the street. "No rest for the working girl." She seemed so wasted. Some of her associates, not much older than she and dressed in lavish bright colors, tried to help her walk straight. All at once, a brazen young man in a white shirt and dark dress pants pushed his way through the group and forcefully grabbed the black-haired teenager by the arm.

"Possibly her brother?" I knew better. I recalled television reports about the young street people of this area, mostly runaways, and the leeches that were waiting for them as they stepped off the bus. Needing a friend in the big city, they let their guard down and make a pact with Death's henchmen. They get hooked on drugs and are forced to sell themselves to the bloodsuckers, working for the pimps. But it wasn't my problem, not my responsibility even though I desperately wanted to walk across the street and break his face. I watched him strong-arm the girl, yelling obscenities and slapping her about as she struggled to protect herself. No one bothered to help, including myself. Most residents of this hellhole struggled to deal with their own personal miseries. Perhaps I was one of them! Then the voice dared me,

"Go ahead, Ed, kill the bastard." I quickly rose and hastily made my way back to the subway station. Suddenly my anxiety was tempered by the thought of Cris. I had responsibilities; I had my flight duties to attend to on the return trip home. I could not get involved. I returned to the underground and went back to the hotel.

"Would you care for a cool drink?" I politely asked an elderly woman on the flight home. I worked the cabins of the DC-10 like a diplomat. There was little indication to the passengers who relaxed comfortably during the six-hour flight to the west coast that they were being attended to by a man dangerously on the edge. But Edmundo made sure the smile did not fade away.

"So what conclusions have you drawn by your experiences in New York?" Doctor Ramljak's face looked concerned.

"Well Doc, when Eddy died in the plane crash Edmundo was born. Personally, I can't stand the bastard. Someone has now come along to see to my interest."

"Oh yeah? Who is that?" I swallowed hard and tried to be make logic out of the absurd.

"It is said we all have a dark side. Carl Jung called it 'our shadow self.' Light and dark, good and evil: yin and yang: matter and anti-matter. The airline's boy, the good Edmundo has a dark side." I sat staring as Doctor Ramljak thought for a moment then scribbled some notes on his yellow pad.

"And if you had to give this new friend of yours a name what would you call him?" I thought for a split second.

"Antimundo!"

"Why that name?"

"Because in Spanish it means 'opposing the world.'"

"Is Antimundo in you right now?"

"More and more each day."

"Doesn't this frighten you?"

"It scares the crap out of me."

I fought hard in the gym to disavow this deplorable persona and his impulses. With the guidance of Doctor Ramljak and the support of Sofia and my family, I tried to settle into a productive routine of work and home life. My role as father to Cristiano strengthened my desire not to relapse. There were moments when I was all too willing to drop my personal inquiries, continue on the road of therapy and enjoy the fruits this second chance at life was offering. But as I said before, beware of the triggers.

The time finally came for me to testify the court cases. They needed my testimony; I also knew there were some in the executive offices that were worried about what I might say. I began meeting with the airline's legal department.

Corporate economics were at stake and the wrong word or phrase from me could cost the airline hundreds of thousands of dollars. It was no longer a question of fault as the Mexican Government had the upper hand. The U.S. Government had looked the other way and the airline danced its jig of submission. The only thing that remained was to try and lessen the blow. How much of a payoff? The crash of Flight 2605 came down to an intricate game of chess, but the company's lawyers were considered the best at their craft,

Dennis McDonald was a top corporate attorney with the airline. He would join with Andrew Jawkins, whose primary employer was the insurance company holding the policy on DC-10 NW903. Yet from the beginning I was nagged by ill feelings.

"If we are on the same team, why do I mistrust McDonald so much?" I was unsure of how much information he believed I knew. The only people in the company I had leveled with were Barry Lane and Jack McKay. I wished to believe that neither of these men of good character would have sat down with McDonald to warn him that I may be problematic.

Upon arriving at the executive offices McDonald seemed very at ease as we sat face to face.

"Well, Edmundo, perhaps we can finish this up in ten or twenty minutes," McDonald stated as he gazed at his watch.

"First, I would like to ask *you* a few questions," I requested of the attorney.

"Certainly,"

"Was it really pilot error?" My inquiry was expressed with innocence. A small request from a simple-minded F/A. My host readjusted his posture.

"Well Ed. from all indications and the official investigation it will probably end up that way." The anger swelled. I had heard this bullshit before but that did not make his words any more palatable. I continued my probe to see the quality of the man who would ultimately represent me in court.

"I understand that the lights on the closed runway 23-Left were lit when we approached for landing. Did this lead Carl into believing he was on the correct runway?" McDonald remained calm while trying to answer.

"Well, there is no evidence whatsoever that would support that."

"I heard that there was a problem between Captain Herbert and First Officer Reimann; any truth to that rumor?" He looked me squarely in the face and did not bat an eye.

"No, Ed! There is *no* evidence whatsoever suggesting that type of problem existed that night." His words seemed more like an admonishment.

"Oh yes there was, and I was witness to it in the cockpit." I hit the airline's counselor right in the face with the bomb he did not want to hear. He did not respond then reached for the phone to make a call. We sat just staring at each other for the longest period until we were joined by Andrew Jawkins, the ultimate professional, who had handled several such cases in the past. The most recent being the horrible tragedy of the American Airlines DC-10 in Chicago where the left engine fell off the wing during take-off. Everyone was instantly incinerated when the massive aircraft fell to the ground. With Jawkins present, McDonald asked me to continue with my revelations. So, I did.

I told them everything, the feelings I had in training, the premonitions of Reina. Tamlyn's desire to stop flying. I recalled the businessman who was fortunate that I forced him to change seats and who was now accusing me of negligence. My mind fell back into the dancing shades of white, yellow and orange as the fires feasted on the dead and dying.

"There was the werewolf, witch and esqueleto (skeleton) on the site." I revealed to these legal minds the images of El Día de Los Muertos. I elaborated on my experience in the cockpit and my knowledge of the prior history that existed between Carl and Dieter. After some time, I was done, but informed the lawyers that what I had given them was merely an overview of what I knew. "Upon a request I could provide far greater specifics for you if you wish." I slumped in my seat. A great silence engulfed the room. Dennis McDonald looked emotionally exhausted while Jawkins kept his cool. I never told them them that I possessed the CVR recording.

McDonald gave a serious glance over at Jawkins who did not respond.

"Let's call it a day. We'll be in touch with you Edmundo." Dennis McDonald quickly rushed off. Exiting, I became curious about the fact that Jawkins did not seem rattled by what I had revealed.

"Are you surprised with what I said regarding the premonitions of the crew?" Jawkins shook his head slowly.

"Not at all. I have represented quite a few companies over the years in a variety of terrible incidents and in my examination of each there have been similar instances such as your crew-mates' foreboding. Some of the premonitions have been discovered in letters by people who knew their time was short, others related their concerns from dreams. I can't explain it but I have come to expect it in each instance." I was now the one listening intently: Andrew Jawkins was showing a true understanding of my plight.

"I feel very comfortable with you on my side," I confided with a smile. Jawkins just chuckled as we left the office and went our separate ways.

Once at home I patiently waited for the next call from the legal department. Cristiano was walking now which added to my workouts in trying to keep up with my active son. The unconditional love I received from my son was unlike any sense of comfort I had ever known. All my wounds were instantly soothed by his smile and hugs. He knew nothing of the greed, lies and deceptions that I was dealing with. I longed to view the world once more through his innocent eyes for is that not what someone was to hope for when given a second chance at life?

Sofia had taken Cris to shop with her sisters one day as I sat outside and enjoyed the smell of the ocean breeze, appreciating my loving wife, a beautiful young son and the support of a family that wanted nothing more for me than to put aside the difficulties from my past. Then the phone call came.

"Hello...Eddy?" The female voice was gentle but hesitant. I was not prepared for the words that came next.

"Eddy, this is Becky Devita's mother." I instantly tensed, transported back to the evening of October 30, 1979, envisioning the beauty that was young Becky with her soft light hair, fair skin and dressed impeccably in her company uniform. "Hello? I'm sorry, have I caught you at a bad time?"

"No. I'm sorry, yes, it's okay, I'm not busy right now," I fumbled.

"I'm sorry to bother you, Eddy, but we are at our wits' end. I have been as patient as I can be, but I can't seem to get any straight answers from the airline." Her words cut deep but the sounds of her struggling with her emotions was even more devastating. "We need your help, Eddy."

"Go ahead, I'm listening." She had my ear.

"The airline has stonewalled us at every point. You know Eddy, Becky was not working on that portion of the flight. Why did she have to die?" She continued, "I realize that you are probably under pressure from the company not to say anything. Did they ask you to remain silent?"

"Oh my God" was all I could mutter to myself.

"Eddy...help us. What happened down there in Mexico?" I was trapped. What could I say? I was not going to lie to her, yet I had to be careful.

"There were a lot of things that went wrong down there," I began. "I am currently preparing to go to court to testify. I can't really say anything now, but I promise I will get back to you at their conclusion." It was the best I could do for the grieving woman. I hung up the phone and was so pissed at my company. "Why in the hell is it my responsibility to have to explain to my crew-mates' loved ones the real reasons they died?" I felt as if the oath of loyalty I swore had been trampled on and those responsible had no honor. Becky's mother's words remained in my mind which ignited instantly into a fire of a magnitude I had not known previously. I angrily grabbed the phone once again and made a hasty call to the company's legal department

"Dennis McDonald please, this is Eduardo Valenciana," I tapped my foot uncontrollably as I waited.

"Yes, Edmundo, how can I help you?"

"Damn it, Dennis, my name is EDUARDO. Can't you guys get it right just once?"

"Sorry, what can I do for you?" I tried to cool down with little success.

"I just got off the phone with Becky Devita's mother. What the hell have you told her, or more like *haven't* told her? The poor woman is in such a panic that she is reaching out to *me* for answers?"

"The lady called you?"

"Yeah."

"Today?"

"Just right now. What the hell is going on?" There was a long pause.

"She's trying to cause trouble. Look, if she calls again just hang up on her." I heard the words, but my heart and soul refused to accept them. Did he really tell me to hang up on Becky's grieving mother? I stared off through my large living room window into the blue eternal sky, said nothing more then slammed down the phone.

I knew there were some in the industry who saw me as a walking time bomb. I wasn't about to let Sofia or Cristiano witness the explosion. Quickly gathering belongings, including my knife, I made plans to catch the next flight to Kauai. That was the only place I could possibly avert a catastrophe.

"We need your help, Eddy." Becky's mother's words rang clear as I boarded the jet bound for HNL.

"What a piece of shit." The grieving mother and the blood sucking attorney. Neither were aware I was lifting off into the spacious skies over the Pacific,

"It was not my responsibility, not my duty." Deep inside I knew I was running away from having to do what was right. My body was twisted. I erupted into convulsions. I raced into the first-class lavatory to the dismay of the flight attendants who were still strapped into their jumpseats. The craft was in a steep climb. Once we leveled off, I returned to my seat. My kind associates said nothing.

...

The long trek up the slopes to the waterfalls could be difficult but the trails had become very familiar and I quickened my pace, desperately wanted my sanctuary. Damn airline! I sat alongside the majestic falls, in the depths of the valley, hypnotized by the falling beads of clean water splashing into the glistening pond. The serene atmosphere kept my demons contained, allowing me to focus on my young son. I dreamed of never returning to the mainland, perhaps bringing my young boy here to live in the bosom of the island. I envisioned us running together along the hillside trails, chasing piglets upstream and counting the endless stars each night. Oh, what a grand time we would have! Then I came falling back to earth for his mother would never approve.

"Damn. I forgot about Sofia." How in the hell am I going to explain my disappearance to my dear wife?

Seeds of despair began to take hold causing me to contemplate abandoning my responsibilities, possibly not return to LAX. Maybe I won't appear at the court proceeding.

"Help us, Eddy." Becky's mother's plea haunted me. She needed closure. Perhaps it was time for some payback to the indifferent One. "We need your help..." I arose in a rage.

"Ask this silent God to help you, lady!" I screamed as my words echoed off the volcanic walls. I no longer wanted to think, only react by instinct, reverting once again to cries heard throughout the jungle.

As the sun set, I decided to strengthen my resolve and invited Antimundo to join me. Removing the shiny metallic weapon from my backpack, I raised it up and admired its design, its long smooth lines, then began to dance about and singing a familiar tune.

"I've never been lost like this, I've never been lost like this and I wouldn't be happier anywhere else."[10] I had packed only the white body paint, forgetting the red. I thought of possibly using the red tinge from the natural volcanic dirt, but its shade was nowhere near the bright red of my airline's logo.

Suddenly, there was a faint rustling in the foliage nearby and I discovered a fat little porker. Instantly a vile fantasy took hold and all dreams turned sour.

"That's the ticket. I'll take care of it." I had the solution. *"Sometimes the innocent are the ones who pay the highest price."* With my knife and I slipped silently into the bush. Survival can be a bitch. It was purely a selfish need for blood. We were drunk with hate and Muerto was delighted.

Finally, I lay on the ground exhausted and mesmerized by the cascading falls, I fell asleep and dreamed. Then Reina's voice.

"Find faith, seek hope."

"I wanted to go with you!" Suddenly the crows of roosters woke me. Shame put an emphasis on my previous night's behavior. My mind had cleared as I broke camp, cleaned up and began to hike out of the valley. Again, it was time to face the consequences back home.

"You're really sick, Eddy." Sofia lashed out when I returned, and her anger was justified. Cristiano sat in the middle of the living room floor crying. Who could blame them?

"You worthless scum." The fallen angels joined in.

"Promise me you won't take off to Kauai again." She was adamant. "Promise me!" I walked over and picked up my sniffling child and held him close to me the rest of the evening.

"You don't know how close you came to not being here, son." Exhausted, I slept peacefully with my son that night as the cool breeze swept in from the ocean.

Sofia was not the only frustrated person I had to make amends with. Daisy Ackley had become aware of my recent misadventures plus I had also skipped an appointment with Doctor Ramljak.

---

10   Oingo Boingo

"Really Daisy, everything is fine. I just went to Kauai to blow off a little steam before I was to testify." I don't think she believed me. And the legal department of the airline was up in arms.

"We've been trying to get ahold of you. You need to be available as this thing is far too important. Do you understand?" Dennis McDonald was adamant.

"Yeah, I understand. I'm fine now." I felt a sense of shame in my company's lack of confidence in me. When we met again Dennis tried to stiffen my resolve.

"You're part of the team, right?"

"Yeah, I am part of the team."

"Good, we all need to be on the same page."

Whether I liked it or not I had to focus on the immediate obstacle facing me, the legal interrogations. At least Jawkins seemed confidant.

"You know Ed, the opposing attorney is going to use every means possible to trip you up and pick at any inconsistencies in your statements." I recalled the comandante:

"Sign the fucking paper!"

"Ed, did you hear what I said?"

"Yeah, I understand. It's not hard to figure, with so much money to be had at stake; I expect they will try and bulldoze right over me."

"You can't get emotional on the stand, Ed."

"No, no, I realize the importance of remaining composed. Remember guys, I'm just the simple flight attendant who was lucky to survive. What would I know that would be of vital interest in this case?" In my mind I knew that is what they wanted. Yet, Jawkins had one other concern:

"Please relate to me once again how you got into the cockpit that morning, why you were there and what you saw."

It was apparent that everything I witnessed in the cabin of flight 2605 - Reina's visions, Tamlyn's desire to transfer jobs and the uncertain atmosphere -- had zero value in the courtroom. The activity in the cockpit was a different matter. The opposing side would see it as a gold mine of information.

"Take your time, Eduardo, I wish to know every detail you recall, no matter how minor."

"I walked forward and instigated the coded chimes that would allow me entrance." I spoke slowly.

"Does every crew member know this code?" Andrew Jawkins was playing the opposing lawyer.

"That's it! That's It!" I concluded my account by quoting Captain Herbert's display of anger and the deafening silence that followed. Jawkins scribbled down notes.

"Those two guys were really pissed at each other," I blurted out after a long pause.

"What?" Dennis McDonald went ballistic. "You don't know that. How do you know that?" The frantic attorney recognized the potential damage such a statement could make in a court of law. I remained calm.

"They were pissed, Carl even wrote up Dieter a short time prior. Dieter's discipline hearing was just hours before he piloted the jumbo jet to Mexico."

"How do you know this?" He remained agitated and was leaning forward.

"I have the damn disciplinary report."

"Where did you get that?" McDonald was not happy. Jawkins wisely interceded.

"That's not important. Ed, you must realize how, under pressure, some of the things you are telling us can be detrimental. What if they ask you about this information? You know they will twist and distort your words." I hesitated. He had a good point.

"Isn't that what the Federales and the press tried to do to me in Mexico City? I did okay."

"What if the attorney asks you how you got into the cockpit, what you saw and heard while in there?" Jawkins inquired.

"Don't worry gentlemen, I have something special planned if that situation should arise. Remember, I'm part of the team." My sarcasm was appropriate. Even after all I had been through in this messy affair I felt as though the company still refused to give me what I felt I had earned, belief in my character. But then again, my recent behavior was a good argument against it.

I felt the burden of this court date while on the flight line. The outcome seemed clear, very clear indeed. Barry Lane, Jack McKay and Captain Ron Banner all indicated that pilot error was

408

inevitable. If so, what was the purpose of me having to testify in a court case? Surely, the company and its insurer had made very generous offers to the remaining parties seeking restitution. The obvious was staring me in the face: The only reason my testimony was needed was so the money could be properly divided by the opposing attorneys. My so-called valuable contribution of the truth would be brushed aside. I had been reduced to a cog in a machine meant to gather up any money that remained. This really pissed me off.

"You don't deserve anything!" The voices again. "It's been a couple of years now since the incident, Edmundo, you should have your act together by now." After everything is resolved, what if Management starts looking for a reason to dismiss me?

During a rainstorm one morning I sped dangerously down the 405-freeway headed for Westwood and the offices of Doctor Ramljak. I was thinking of my splendid Roman Catholic wedding and marriage Sofia and I had shared with even the blessing of His Eminence Timothy Cardinal Manning. This union was now crashing in violent flames like 2605 and the tremendous pain I was imprisoned by was projecting its madness on those I loved so dearly.

I rushed up the stairs leading to Doctor Joe's office and hit the front door with the weight of my shoulder as I grabbed and turned the knob and was stopped cold. The green wooden door was locked.

"NO!" I crumpled upon the hallway floor and began to weep. "Not the doctor, too? Had he betrayed me also?" Then Antimundo spoke up.

"I have the solution." I thought of entering Terminal 5 at LAX and creating a violent scene, the innocent shocked in panic, running in all directions to escape a vengeful madman.

"That's it boy," Muerto gladly joined in.

"I'm sorry I'm late, Ed." I was jarred from my demented dream by the voice of the good doctor walking down the hallway. "The weather made the traffic miserable. I am glad you waited for me." I got up and casually followed him into his office as if nothing had happened. The hypnosis session he utilized in my medical care that day did dissipate the awful anxiety that plagued me. But shame prevented me from revealing to him the deplorable vision I imagined while waiting for him.

Heading back to Manhattan Beach, I struggled to try to find a solution to this dilemma. There was a real threat of losing my wife and son, and once the cases were settled, possibly my job.

"Ten confianza en Dios" Reina spoke.

"Sí, mira lo que te pasó a ti," I replied defiantly.

…

I was called to the cockpit on the final leg of a 3-day trip.

"Someone is going to meet you at the gate, Ed," Captain Jeffers advised me. Did my airline want to make sure I did not rush off to another gate, fleeing once more to my island retreat? The reality was that this <u>was</u> my first impulse. Ackley was indeed waiting patiently when I disembarked. I struggled to remain composed.

"You are being released from duty until the conclusion of the court proceedings," Daisy informed me. "Get a good night's rest, Eduardo."

"Stop pacing and come to bed." Sofia was frustrated and frightened. "I hope this court thing is not going to make you run away to the jungle again." The only facet of my life that did not seem to be affected was the unconditional love of my young son. Cris was what was good about my new life. He was living proof that Muerto's grip on me was not secure. The young child *was* hope.

Chapter XVIII

I entered the courtroom the following morning with my legal team, knowing that what the airline wanted was the dim-witted Edmundo. I believed they asked for too much. If it wasn't for the disdain, I had for the opposing side I might have finally let loose on someone.

"A man must do what a man must do, Eduardo," Jack Mckay stated early on in this ordeal. He was damn right. My only loyalty was to my wife and child. After all this legal bullshit and mudslinging was concluded I had no idea what condition I would be in. There was certain to be a mental lashing from the fallen angels. I had to steady myself to relive the unbearable.

Judge Casey entered, followed by a sharply dressed lawyer with a briefcase, I tried to put in chronological order the events of that terrible day.

"I am my parents' son." I had to be truthful. Andrew Jawkins was to sit beside me while Dennis McDonald and the legal assistants took a back seat to this presentation. I imagined what the reaction would be if my learned team viewed the jungle man of the Na Pali entering the courtroom? I laughed. This whole affair really was a circus.

"Eduardo Valenciana." The clerk articulated my name correctly, even adding the Spanish accent.

"Why was it so damn hard for anyone at the airline to pronounce my name?" I whispered.

"What?" my murmur concerned Jawkins. I stared right into his bright blue eyes and he smiled. He knew what a fiasco this ordeal was and he was a master at his game. I would be in good hands.

Andrew Jawkins' face beamed with confidence which calmed me greatly. He was a sly devil and just before the proceedings were about to start, he leaned over to whisper into my ear,

"By the way, this guy represents that jerk who claimed you were incompetent." I was surprised that I was not instantly incensed by my counselor's words. Instead, his statement strengthened my resolve.

"You swear to tell the truth the whole truth and nothing but the truth?"

"Globos, rojo y azul."

"Nieve, chocolate." In my mind the courtroom suddenly became an extension of the carnival on the tarmac that Halloween morning.

"I do," I softly responded.

"You are Eduardo Valenciana?" My antagonist started on a methodical plan of attack.

"I was....I mean, I am." My opponent gave me a quizzical look.

"Have you ever been arrested, Mr. Valenciana?"

"In this country or another?" My expression remained austere.

"Anywhere?" The attorney reflected a hint of annoyance.

"No!"

"Do you speak Spanish, Mister Valenciana?" I paused then replied.

"I was raised in a household where English was the primary language."

"What are your parent's names?"

"Alicia and Reynaldo." The counselor seemed surprised at this answer.

"Are you married?"

"Yes."

"What is your wife's name?"

"Sofia." The attorney was again surprised.

"Alicia, Reynaldo and Sofia?" My inquisitor stared.

"Is there a question in there somewhere counselor?" Andrew Jawkins entered the confrontation.

"Well yeah, with Spanish names like those are we supposed to believe that he does not speak Spanish?" While asking this, the opposing attorney threw up his arms indicating his displeasure. Judge Casey quickly brought the room to order and instructed my inquisitor to continue. The perturbed man took his time as he reviewed a portion of prepared notes.

"Where in the aircraft were you sitting upon impact?"

"Door 4-R!"

"Did you have any warning that the plane was going to crash?"
"Yes!" My antagonist was thrown a bone, obviously surprised by my answer. He gazed over at Jawkins who was just as calm as I was. He continued.
"Oh? In what way?" I hesitated before answering.
"Reina Patricia Torres, one of my fellow flight attendants, had maintained and believed that she would be killed in a plane crash, having had these premonitions since childhood. She expressed concern that 2605 was the flight." Silence! Instead of a bone, I threw my inquisitor a curve! He decided to change the subject.
"You were in the cockpit that night, were you not, Mr. Valenciana?" The trap was being set.
"I was."
"How did you get into the cockpit, Mr. Valenciana?" I took my time, then turned to the judge.
"Your honor, I refuse to answer the question."
"What? What does he mean? What do you mean?" The attorney twisted and turned in a slight effort to stand only to sit down once more. "You have to answer the question, it's the law." The flustered lawyer looked towards Jawkins in hopes that he'd advise his client concerning proper legal protocol. His effort was met with silence, a classic method of stonewalling. Finally Judge Casey calmly intervened.
"On what grounds do you base your refusal, Mr. Valenciana?"
"Your Honor, I base my refusal to answer on Section 4.2.7 of the United States Federal Aviation Manual. It states as follows; "No person may have admittance knowledge to the flight deck of an aircraft unless the person is....
1.) A crewmember.
2.) An F.A.A. air carrier inspector, or an authorized representative of the National Transportation Safety Board.
3.) Any person who has the permission of the pilot in command and is specifically authorized by the certificate holder management and by the administrator of the airline." I hesitated then slowly leaned forward towards my inquisitor. "I don't believe you qualify for any of those categories, gringo." The shit hit the fan.

"It wasn't *my* airline that caused the death of so many innocent people," the attorney shot back. I simply sat back and kept my mouth closed. I assumed that the judge would realize the fact that anyone who had survived such a vicious ride would have some type of mental imbalance, so, perhaps she would not be so angered by one misstep. My adversary was livid. Jawkins was amused. McDonald was a wreck.

Order was demanded and the proceedings went on.

"So, after you entered the cockpit, what did you see or hear, Mr. Valenciana?" I took a deep breath and focused on an image of the serene coastline of the Na Pali in my mind as a way to help me relax.

"I heard the captain say, 'That's it,' then he repeated those words. That's all."

"What else did you hear?" Jawkins immediately jumped in.

"Look! He said that was it, what part of that answer do you not understand?" The courtroom was again filled with confusion. I chuckled and shook my head recalling how all the lawsuits against the airline mounted to $351,000,000. I pitied these brilliant minds of the law haggling for the plunder. There would be no mention of Reina, Javier, Tamlyn, Gary and all the rest who took perished. I thought about Ronald Daily and his Hispanic friend to whom I handed over bottles of Bohemia. They had all been so alive, full of promise. This courtroom was merely an assemblage to determine merit and worth. Jawkins stated outright the airline's willingness to accept responsibility and the opposing sides were at odds to the final numbers to be put on the checks.

"Did you ever see any signs that the aircraft was in difficulty?" I lurched forward in my seat.

"Yeah Einstein, when we hit the fucking building."

"That's enough Mr. Valenciana," the judge would not tolerate what she saw as my impudence.

"Isn't it true you by-passed injured passengers while exiting the plane that morning?"

"No."

"Were you not more focused of just trying to save your crew-mates?"

"No!" The lawyer was trying to up the ante for his clients, and of course himself.

"Your Honor, it was not me or my clients that were so careless with the flying public." It was all such a game. I leaned over towards Jawkins and felt embarrassed.

"I'm sorry," I whispered to my adviser.

"I'm enjoying myself," he replied with a smile.

"While in the cockpit did you view anything that was wrong?"

"Sir, I am not qualified to give an opinion as to what constitutes a problem on a DC-10."

"Look," Jawkins spoke up. "Do you think we can finish this in a reasonable amount of time? The airline has accepted the cause as 'pilot error,' why in the hell are you putting this poor guy through the ringer?"

"It was your airline and the crew that caused the death of all those innocent people. Your company should not be allowed in the skies if this is how you run an airline." The jostling went on and I began to wonder where I'd go from here. All this bickering was pointless. In the end, the checks would be signed and cashed. What would the pay-out to my parents have been if I had died?

It was obvious that the opposition would get what they wanted in the end. The airline could ill-afford a prolonged fight, especially with the damage that deregulation was already having on the bottom line.

The proceedings broke up with the promise of another day of continued confrontation. The company's lawyers escorted me out of the room and into an elevator. As the door closed, one of the younger colleagues said,

"Great job, Ed!" giving me a slap across my shoulder to emphasize his satisfaction. Jawkins also gave a broad smile.

"Did you see the look on that jackass' face when Ed hit him with that federal regulation bullshit?" The attorneys were laughing. Even McDonald looked relaxed at this point.

"Hey, Ed, did you ever consider becoming a lawyer? I'm sure you can get the airline to pay for your tuition to law school." I continued to just stare at Jawkins who gave me a slight nod. Somehow that meant so much more to me than all the back-slapping praise from the others, yet I remained confused. The attorneys seemed to feel that I had devised some sinister plan to derail the opposing attorney when, all I wished was to tell the truth. Jawkins informed me that my testimony had probably saved the insurer and the airline a "hunk of change." Dedication and loyalty seemed to have been forgotten, and nothing would ever be done to correct the wrongs done to the families of the deceased crew. Their relatives would receive pennies in comparison. The "why" of the accident was not raised during the proceedings.

I returned to my family assuming my participation in the legal process was now over. I tried to imagine a period where I could leave the past behind, to fully center my attention on Sofia and Cristiano. I wanted to prove to myself that I could emerge from this terrible mine field which surrounded me. Just a few days after my court appearance the phone rang in our home.

"Hola Eduardo, este es la Señora Torres." I glanced down at Cristiano playing joyfully with his mother in the living room, recognizing the absence of such joy in the heart of the dear woman who was on the other end of the phone.

"Eddy, we need your help." The tone in her voice concerned me.

"¿Señora, cómo le puedo ayudar?" We have hired a lawyer. He wishes to file a lawsuit against the airline." She was joining forces with Becky Devita's mother in seeking answers that were not forthcoming. I truly wanted to reach out to this poor gentle lady but was hamstrung. I recalled the information my own attorney, David J. Brooks had declared: From a legal standpoint, any employee would have little chance of being awarded more than the meager amount the insurance policy indicated.

"I have called the airline over and over again. I get no response to my inquiries." My mind flashed to the image of my own mother, one of the very few who experienced relief after the crash. Her child came back home in one piece. "I live with a heart that is broken," she sobbed. "I will never find peace without the answers I need." In that moment, I hated the company.

I could foresee the possibility of the families coming to me for answers. They had to find some solace to carry on. Their faces at the multiple funerals I attended testified to the need for the truth if there was to be a livable future. After Reina's service I made a promise to myself to avoid the families because I never wanted to commit the vile sin of having to lie to them. Now the one woman I respected and felt so much compassion for was asking me for aid.

"We believe the airline paid you to remain silent." My heart sank. This blow to my spirits was as devastating as being accused of negligence in my flight duties. I wasn't sure I could ever convince this grieving mother that such a thing was not true. Who, more than me, wanted truth? Now the surviving families believed me to be a sell-out. "Mi hija y yo queremos encontrarnos con usted." I was not about to deny this request, and so a time and place to meet was arranged. I cursed the airline I loved so much. Once again, I could be jeopardizing my job and my family.

How could I convince Señora Torres that my sympathies were with her and the other families? What would it take for her to see that I had been left on the wayside regarding any financial payout? What in the world can I tell her that would be of any significance in her efforts to attain justice for her lost daughter? These were the questions that occupied my every waking moment up until the day of our meeting.

"Hello, Mom?"

"Hi, mijo."

"Mom, I need your help." My dear mother Alicia Sr. was an honest person. "Mom, would you come with me to meet Mrs. Torres?" She was fluent in Spanish and I needed her to translate. I'd tried to keep my family out of this nasty affair, yet I needed her.

Mrs. Torres and her daughter seemed surprised as I approached the meeting place with my mother.

"Alicia Valenciana a sus ordenes," my mother stated, extending her hand to this distraught woman.

"Eduardo, we need your help. The company refuses to give us any facts regarding the details of the plane crash."

"Señora, whatever information I could provide for you, be it the truth, will not bring you any happiness." I could see Señora Torres was not willing to accept this, and her daughter Theresa, stepped right in.

"Was it truly pilot error?" I took a deep breath while realizing that my words would come as news to my mother.

"The Mexican Government who conducted the official investigation has stated that it was, and this conclusion, flawed that it may be, has been accepted by the United States Government and the airline. No matter what you or I say, that determination will not change." The words did not satisfy Reina's sister. She confronted me squarely.

"Did the airline pay you to keep silent?" My mother was taken aback and looked at me in confusion. Before I could respond, she took charge.

"No, he has not received any payout. My son would not lie to you." Her defense of my integrity was heartfelt. Señora Torres and my mother stared at each other in silence for a moment.

"Has the company been lying to us?" La señora persisted.

"If you have been dealing with their attorneys, then I believe they have." I assured her.

"Will you help us?"

"Ladies, I am still an employee of the company. I am married now with a young son. I have a responsibility to them so I cannot directly confront my employer. But I promise that I will not lie to you about anything you may ask regarding my recollection of the facts." Theresa quickly interceded.

"Will you speak to our lawyer?"

"No." The two women stared at me, open-mouthed. There was a long pause and I decided that I could not leave these ladies just hanging without hope.

"Listen, there is one man with influence at the airline, an honest man who has helped me immensely. His name is Barry Lane. He is the Vice--President of In-Flight Services, so he was Reina's boss. Go see him, he will not lie to you."

I turned to my mother on the drive home.

"Thanks for coming, Mom."

"Of course, mijo."

"I feel a little guilty."

"Why, son? You told them the truth." I fell silent. I should not have dumped this delicate issue on Mr. Lane but then it should have never fallen to me to be the one from whom the families sought the truth. It was obvious that the airline and the

U.S. government were strong-armed by the Mexicans, but these facts needed to be voiced by the airline, not by me. Once again, I glanced at my mother, I suspect she had discovered more about this affair than she wanted to know.

Sometime later I learned that Barry Lane had indeed met with the Torres'. His quality as a good man shone through, I am sure, but unfortunately, he was hamstrung legally because an attorney was a required presence at their meeting. It was clear that the Torres Family was on a wild ride that dispensed nothing but heartbreak and disappointment. Muerto's signature was visible. He toyed with them as expertly as he manipulated me. I could only wish the best for them.

When it came to compensation, the young flight attendant crews and their families were getting the short end of the stick. Their hands tied by regulations, the Torres' united with the Surutan-Bailys and the family of Becky Devita. Perhaps their grief had turned to anger which gave them strength and resolve, but for them, too, closure was not within reach.

An answer would come in a ruling from the United States Court of Appeals. Justice seemed to have turned its back on the burned and dismembered bodies. I was destined to imagine the smell of jet fuel for years to come, if I made it that far. My minor experience in the courtroom was nothing compared to the injustice done to the victims' families.

The claim of Devita's family had more substance. Becky was deadheading the flight, traveling as a passenger to be available to work the next segment. The argument was that Becky was legally a passenger not sanctioned under the codes for employees. The counter-argument which I imagine came from a team that may have included Andrew Jawkins and Dennis McDonald was that Becky was working and assigned to be a passenger for just that particular leg. The courts conclusion?

"The plaintiffs were limited to the exclusive remedies provided by the California worker's compensation statute Cal Labor Sec. 3201-3213."

The maximum anybody was going to receive for each deceased child would be around 75 thousand dollars. Many nights I dreamt seeing my own parents in a similar setting. The mad ride just continued on. All the free trips in the world could

419

not remove the scars and the bitterness. With the company's continued silence on an affair all parties now considered closed, the persona I named Antimundo returned to seek vengeance.

Returning to my duties on the flight-line each day as Edmundo, the pantomime became intolerable. I was competent at wearing this mask well, then disposing of it in a pool of vomit in the parking lot at trip's end.

My wife Sofia could not handle my walking a fine line between sanity and emotional breakdown.

"You need help, Eddy." I so yearned for the majestic slopes of Kauai, the Garden Island. The company had three flights a day to HNL. It would be so convenient to push aside all the responsibility, evade the unceasing torment and just go. I held back, just barely.

"Comorbidity" had been a term Doctor Joe used concerning the never-ending confusion that gripped my consciousness. The abuse in my mind contributed to the self-abuse of my body. This combination made it difficult to figure out what was right and what was wrong. I came to the conclusion that I could not take on the airline and Sofia's displeasure at the same time. Then, without warning, came an unsuspected disorder.

"Dear God, help! Javier is screaming. He's dying!" I scrambled out of bed.

"Eddy! Eddy! No! No! It's Cristiano who is crying. Wake up!" Sofia pleaded. Her eyes wide with fear, she sat on the bed shaking. I shook my head and looked at my dear son crying, his face replacing that of the helpless Javier. My poor young wife was at her rope's end. Things were unwinding quickly.

"I have a flight for you, Ed." Marlene from Scheduling happened to call with an assignment that would open Muerto's door to the next level of chaos. Checking the sequence, the letters jumped out at me, LAX-JFK-LAX. The layover was twenty-eight hours. Now was the time. I was being offered a new jungle, one made of concrete and iron.

That evening I took great care ironing two uniforms, one issued by the airline and an extra one that would serve Antimundo. He wanted vengeance and this uniform would serve his persona in the dark corners of the city. Along with the essentials for my regulation suitcase I added extra items for this particular trip. Appropriate footwear for prowling the streets, fatigues, the body-paint and an indispensable bandanna to highlight the morbid ceremony. Now it was time for others to feel the abuse. Now it was time to put an end to those who would take advantage of the innocent.

During the flight to the concrete jungle, my anxiety rose. While the passengers watched the featured film, I hid away in the downstairs galley for a time with my suitcase, blocking the elevators from operating so I would not be disturbed. I opened my bag and carefully removed the steel knife from its leather sheath which was now tinted in crimson from the red dirt of Kauai. I held it high to gaze upon the glistening light as it was reflected from the smooth metal. The handle fit perfectly into my sweat-filled hand. The arched alloy of the weapon's brass knuckles covered my grip well,

"The perfect tool for a desperate man." Antimundo whispered. But within minutes of returning to the upper cabin, the hands intent on ferocity were now utilized in the company's elegant first-class service.

"Would you care for white or red wine?" My passengers enjoyed the attention. "Thank you for traveling with us, have a good day."

Once on the ground I wore my poker face well. Some in my crew spoke of taking in a Broadway show. With twenty-eight hours of free time they knew there would be lots to do and lots to see. They sought fun and excitement while I sought something else.

That evening I sat for some time with Antimundo, boxed in a room at a Marriott Hotel. We wanted to allow my fellow F/As time to leave the premises or settle in for the remainder of the night. Like a surgeon carefully preparing his tools, I slowly opened the case, gently removed the contents, and aligned them carefully upon the bed. I took great care to bathe slowly and thoroughly, like some High Priest preparing for a ritual, applying the crimson and white paint, the airline's colors, upon my face. Somehow it was fitting in my mind that I remained the company man to the very end.

I lost myself in thought over Reina's premonitions. What was lacking in her predictions was the injustice that would be done to those she loved. But now she could depend upon me to seek retribution. I headed out the hallway, down the back stairs feeling exhilarated. Only in New York could an oddity such as me venture into the night without being seen as particularly odd.

With the large blade strapped to my back under my regulation raincoat, I descended into the underground and headed for the city. My destination was Spanish Harlem, an area few outsiders could comfortably blend into. I emerged from the subway catacombs up to the excitement of the cool night's breeze, taking in the whole scene: the constant motion, the flashing lights and the overwhelming noise, a world far away from flight crews and fancy hotels. Within this urban jungle lived every type of vice imaginable, available all around me, and it was exhilarating. Overwhelmed by the level and dynamics of the constant motion, I took a curbside seat and made myself as comfortable as if I were in a lush movie theater anticipating a heralded film.

From the corner of my eye I spotted a lean young black boy attempting to drag a large suitcase across the busy street toward my side. It amused me to watch his efforts. With much exertion the young lad finally made it and took a seat on the same curb not far from me. I was fascinated by him. He could have been no more than eight or nine, not that much older than Javier and his brother.

"What you be starin' at?" The defiant child shot me a menacing glare without showing an ounce of fear. For an instant I was intimidated. I shook my head, rose up and walked to a nearby liquor store, returning with a six-pack and laughing as I opened the first can of many that night. "What be so funny?" The little man was not amused. I hesitated for a second, then turned and looked the boy straight in the eyes.

"I have some white friends that would simply freak out if they found themselves here." The child let my words stir his imagination and revealed a wide grin.

"What's your name?" The boy demanded.

"My name?" I responded with great zeal. "You wish to know who I am?" My new little friend smiled, chuckling at my antics. "Well, my dear friend, you happen to be in the presence of Antimundo."

"You P.R.?"

"P.R.?" I was confused by his inquiry while opening another can.

"Yeah, a Puerto Rican, a laughing P.R." The boy said, laughing himself.

"No, no my good fellow, I happen to be of Mexican descent." The brew began affecting my perception. The curious boy shook his head.

"Okay, you be Messican if you wanna be but I wouldn't want to be no beaner." Surprised at his words I spit up what liquid was left in my mouth

"Excuse me young man, I do take issue with your statement." The streetwise boy just sighed. The child seemed like a prudent elder about to explain the true facts of life to a silly, painted up beaner. Captivated by my new friend, I listened intently.

"The first time I be called nigger, I ask around." The pint size wise man continued. "I find out what that be and the next thing I be doin', I be asken what everybody else be called." I would find that in his dysfunctional world there was some sense of logic. "You know it be just like learnin' one of them different tongues. You know how it be, the way people be learnin' all the dirty words first. I'm a nigger, you Messicans be beaners, Ricans be spics, docs be quacks, lawyers be shysters, cops be pigs, women be sluts and teenagers be punks." Suddenly he ended his lesson, looking around impatiently as if looking for someone. I had empathy for the lad and realized that Death was playing with his head as well. I then asked him a question.

"What about children? What do you call children?" The little man looked at me with a frown and I knew he was looking for an answer.

"Man, why you gotta be askin' such a hard question?" The inquiry had hit a chord with the little warrior who I knew had to fight his battles daily. I actually had great respect for the kid as I turned away and continued to guzzle the beer. There we sat as the world rushed by in an array of sounds, colors and motion. Who are they? Where are they going? And for what reason? My juvenile friend could not care less, for survival demanded much more of him, complete attention to the perils in such surroundings.

"What you all painted up for anyway, like some fool on Halloween?"

"I am the image of Halloween past," once again speaking to the child in him.

"Hey little man, you want a soda?" I respectfully offered.

"Soda?" The boy was insulted.

"What's your name?" I inquired.

"Jerome." Soon I found myself relaxing as the kid and I engaged in conversation, exchanging insights on survival. He was competent at trading playful insults, but the details of his short life were truly sad.

It would not be a pleasant tale about his mother, who I assumed by his words was a prostitute and drug addict. He never knew his father. He had a handful of siblings, but he really never knew half of them. Yet somehow the little man seemed to deal with it in stride. Through our conversation I came to realize that this child was a courier for a drug merchant. The clever dealers would use the young and innocent to transport their South American resources from place to place in the concrete jungle. The children could be busted fifty but because of their age, there would be little consequence from the law. Jerome bragged how the money was good.

I lowered my head into my F/A issued raincoat. My mind went back to training, regulation 1.2.10., Flight Attendant Conduct while in uniform: "Flight Attendants will present a professional, businesslike appearance/manner." I thought about my job and the "survivor" tag that had been placed upon me. Here, sitting alongside me was a true survivor whose childhood was being robbed. It was a truly depressing to realize that the boy's chances for survival were not very good. Finally, the painted flight attendant rose and bid farewell to the little man. From a distance I watched Jerome continue on to his appointed time and contact. I liked the little guy; even more, I respected him.

I wandered the streets in a daze for some time. How fortunate indeed I was and gave thanks that my son would not have to confront such a childhood. I thought about Cristiano and Jerome. Naturally the street boy was older, but I was more perplexed by the poker hand the Almighty had dealt out to these two. From Jerome's perspective this did not reflect an all-loving God.

Suddenly, there was a big commotion as a blue police sedan raced through the streets and screeched to a halt just ahead. I began to weave through the thick crowd to where the chaos was about to commence.

"They were chasing him," a woman blurted out. A disturbance was occurring in the semi-circle of bodies positioned in the middle of the action. A young Puerto Rican lay pinned to the street by a cop's knee.

"Why did you run? Why did you run?" Everyone gawked as the man was hauled away. Soon, they all dispersed.

"It don't mean a thing." Antimundo began to harden my heart. I suddenly felt no sympathy for those thrown so callously into this cruel roulette wheel of life by this silent God.

"Put your faith in His divine intervention." I smirked at Regina's advice to me. The people I viewed around me would most likely be destined to experience dire disappointment. I froze and realized this deity's lack of concern for my lost crew.

"Those assholes never even found the stolen left landing gear. Who in the hell loses an entire landing gear?" I then thought about the poor Mexican families who were at end of the line when compensation was being given.

"Yeah, we were able to take care of two families for less than seven thousand dollars," one airline lawyer boosted. "That's right. Just enough money to buy a couple of burros."

"What gives the fools of the world the right to kill us?" I screamed out loud on the street, but no one took notice of my words. Yet, it was happening all around me. I could take no more. I retreated into the underground to find a safe haven, selecting an isolated corner in the long subway platform to catch my breath. No one took notice of the figure hunched in the corner, a derelict fool who deserved not a moment of their acknowledgment. Like a wounded animal disguised in a posture of humility, the thirst for fresh blood beckoned. I resigned myself to Antimundo. On this brisk night, there was no doubt about what his intentions were. The circumstances and atmosphere paired in an eruption of clear hate which fueled the fire in my blackened heart. I caught the train that would take me

425

downtown, knowing where one such bottom-feeding bastard dispensed his unique variety of evil-doing could be found.

Like an impatient marauder I emerged onto the streets heading for Hell's Kitchen. My eyes scanned the crowd of faceless figures seeking only to find the young streetwalker. If I could not find her, I was sure I would find a substitute for there were many more like her in this awful cauldron of despair. Entering a liquor store, I bought another six-pack and guzzled one after the other, the perfect elixir for this grievous blood sport. I thought about Mr. Reddick with his initialed clothing and Ackley with her persuasive manner. The spectrum of chaos I now viewed *was* reality, these streets I roamed.

"There she is." Antimundo spotted the now-familiar adolescent, our intended bait. My heart beat faster as I hid inside a pizzeria, watching and waiting.

"Want a date?" A familiar solicitation phrase on the streets was ignored by some and caught the interest of others. A pack of five young men, possibly college students, stopped and showed interest in the teenager's proposition. The leader of the group began haggling with the young street walker which brought laughter and ridicule from the others. Seemingly filled to the brim with liquor and false bravado the small, burly student seemed to be making some headway in his negotiations when his taller, less-intoxicated friend stepped forward and wisely yanked his friend away, rapidly reprimanding him for the error of his ways. Soon, the rowdy rogues disappeared among the crowd that flowed through the streets and the young coquette instinctively turned her attention to other perspective customers.

The time had come for action, so I calmly rose and went into the washroom of the small eatery to refurbish the smeared, fading colors on my face, my visual declaration of war. I carefully sketched the white and bright red of my airline logo, an evolution for an avenging muse. Completing my metamorphosis, I then reached behind and fondled the cold metal hand grip of my precious knife I had strapped to my back.

"What would my crew think of Antimundo's illicit intent?" I thought of Gary Rollings, his strong character and demeanor making him the perfect candidate for leadership, a company man till the end. "He deserved to live. Not me! Not me!" I was engrossed with self-pity which fired up my hatred and a desire for blood.

All at once I sensed someone behind me, then turned and stood face-to-face with a middle-aged smiling intently at me. As I gazed down, I witnessed the fool holding what pitiful manly presence he could retain. Such a sinful act was the fatal spark that lit an enormous detonation. Rage was unleashed as the perverted victim hit the floor in a flash, blood running down the side of his face. I instinctively readied myself to strike again.

"YOU FUCKING LEECH!" In this pathetic soul I saw them all, Chávez, Montoya, the politicians, the lawyers, the money men. He represented all the bloodsuckers that drained the life and decency from all of us: me, my friends, the victims and their families, the eternal wounded who would never taste the sweetness of life again. I struck again with a vengeance before he was able to turn and try to pull the door open. I retrieved the large knife from its sheath and directed it at my quarry.

"SIGN THE FUCKING PAPER!"

"I don't have any paper," he pleaded. "Please, I'm sorry just leave me alone." Those outside the restroom no doubt heard the commotion. I stopped and tried to clear my head. Shame overcame me as I saw the deep fear in the face of the unfortunate man helpless on the ground. Antimundo was delighted.

"Yes, good. Now run and find another." I ran into a back room, knocking over a shocked and frightened young worker in a white apron. I sprinted through an alley filled with garbage, boxes and the smell of urine. No doubt those who worked the flight with me were returning from an evening at the theater or a night of fine dining, seated in a clean taxi going to a warm hotel to rest up for the return duty home. I, instead, had opted to be among the filth and vermin. I slipped calmly into the faceless crowd, suddenly thinking about the love that had first brought Sofia and I together. Although nothing definite had been determined, I was sure it was gone forever.

"Hey, you wanna date?" The familiar voice of the girl stopped me in my tracks, asking the familiar question of no one and everyone.

"What's your name?"

"Suzanne."

"Where you from anyway?" I inquired. Confused by my question, she answered anyway.

"Minneapolis, you wanna date or not?"

"Then we're gonna get your ass back to Minneapolis." Up close I could see that she was physically ill. The drugs, the beatings by her pimp, the entire lifestyle were evident. We walked across the street where I beheld the ever-watchful eyes of the young panderer who pulled the strings of her life. She was his meal ticket and he would not want to let her loose. Heading towards the Port Authority depot I led Suzanne, who still seemed in a cloud of intoxication and confusion into a dark alleyway. I was certain the punk would follow, in fact I was counting on it. I let go of Suzanne and removed my weapon from its sheath as I hid in the darkness, preparing my ambush.

"Now get the hell out of here," I whispered to the young girl. She stood frozen with fright. "Go, home, get on a bus and get out of here. I handed her a one-hundred-dollar bill. "You deserve to live. I am the one that belongs with the dead." Suddenly a light seemed to illuminate in her degraded mind.

"Home?" She struggled to decipher the concept.

"Yeah, go home, find joy once again." I pointed to an outlet in the distance. "Go!" The frail figure backed away, glancing back and paused, finally disappearing into the shadows.

"Suzanne." The pimp called out as he slowly approached. I was totally focused on him, ready to execute my plan. I whispered.

"Psycho-killer qu'est-ce que c'est, fa fa fa fa, fa fa fa fa fa far better, run run run run run run run away."[11] The street-wise punk kept advancing, unaware of me and therefore unprepared.

"Suzanne. Where are you girl?"

"PENDEJO!" I cried and attacked. He never saw the blow coming that hit him squarely in the face. As he fell to the ground bleeding, I threw off my raincoat and danced about. "DO YOU BELIEVE I AM STUPID? YOU FAKE! YOU LIAR!" The surviving flight attendant from 2605 had lost his mind and was about to lose his soul. Muerto roared with delight, applauding from the shadows and urging me on. I continued to hit the

---

11   * Psyco Killer, Talking Heads, 1977

pimp's bleeding face with the brass grip of the knife. "YOU KNOW YOU SERVED LIQUOR TO THE PILOTS DURING THE FLIGHT!" I pulled his head up by the hair as I placed the blade at his throat. "YOU GONNA SIGN THE FUCKING PAPER? I ORDER YOU!" My victim cowered in fear, pleading with eyes close,

"Please don't hurt me anymore. I'll sign anything. Don't hit me anymore, please."

I stood helpless, frozen and in a stupor, realizing I had been beating a mere child himself. Children selling children. The boy's blood was smeared on my hand as I clutched the knife. Hoping he would make no effort to stand, I slowly backed away and quickly sheathed my weapon. Muerto was not pleased. Unsurprisingly, the young girl reappeared and knelt down to comfort her handler. I felt dirty and wanted to distance myself from my sin. I simply had lowered myself to the level of those I despised. I began to weep as I ran to blend in with the crowd on the street, then stumbled back down into the darkness of the subway.

"You pussy!" Antimundo shamed me to no end. I continued to cry as I reached the train platform and huddled into a fetal position in a dark corner. My body convulsed and I rocked uncontrollably back and forth. Death was having his way with me once again.

"Reina, Reina," I sought her comfort in my deterioration.

"Can you forgive yourself?"

"Never, not one bit." Even in the midst of such a failure my heart remained hardened. I sat in the subway car traveling back to Queens, clinging to my defiance. I continued to embrace the poison and condemned myself to the inevitable pain that accompanies it. Muerto was again delighted.

"2605, do you have approach lights in sight?" The voices echoed through the rail car. *"2605, approach lights are on 23-Left."* The rhythmic beat of the wheels on the tracks echoed like a shot in competition with the tower and cockpit. I sat quietly trying to keep myself under control.

"We're cleared on the right; we're cleared on the right. This is the approach to the god-damn left."

"Oh Jesus Christ! Oh Fuck!"

"Get it up Carl, you're banking!"
"I can't! I can't!"

Emerging from the station, I sprinted up the subway stairs and ran all the way back to the hotel, in the shadow of Shea Stadium, hoping to enter unnoticed. There would be no time for sleep as I spent the better part of the morning removing any trace of Antimundo.

"Hi Eddy." A crewmember greeted me as I entered the van.

"We had fantastic seats." I listened while one lady raved about her experience in the big city. "A glorious theatrical production," raved a blond associate.

"We made the reservations a month ago," stated another F/A talked about some classy restaurant. "The cuisine was fabulous."

I really fucked up a sleazy pimp last night. The urge to speak was disgusting yet I was tempted. I finally began to settle down as I walked down the jetway at JFK.

Entering the DC-10, the first one I saw in First Class was none other than Shana James.

"Hi Edmundo. Ready for a check-ride?" Perhaps it was karma for my misdeeds the night before, but I didn't contest it. I had been assigned the F/C position at 1R and I made every effort to store my suitcase with its illicit contents across the cabin aft, as far away as possible from my illustrious supervisor. When the gate agent came aboard to announce boarding, each of the crew members secured their positions. From 1R I witnessed Shana get up from her first-row position, and head directly for a seat in the last row in F/C. There, just inches beneath her posterior, in my suitcase, lay my knife.

I breathed deeply and resigned myself to getting through the six-hour flight without incident. Surprisingly I never felt any fatigue considering the lack of rest after my misguided escapades. I assumed there was still a good amount of adrenaline in my system keeping me alert. Once the plane had leveled to its cruising altitude, I noticed Shana writing in her yellow pad, a short scribble here, a longer observance there.

"You know, I may have the makings of a pretty decent Flight Attendant," I spoke to myself in jest but then reality gave me a swift kick in the rear.

"You're a walking time bomb." The voices chimed in. How could I hope to continue to fly? Doctor Joe had warned me and was very concerned about the possible triggers, the unexploded mines I had to negotiate on any given flight. Any fool could see that a detonation was inevitable. Par for the course, I dismissed the warnings and focused on Shana. She seemed completely annoyed by the steady-drinking middle-aged man seated next to her trying to put the make on her. A company woman to the end, Shana endured it. I could have quietly walked down the aisle and eased rescued her by inviting her up to the front galley, even grab my suitcase in the process. I imagined her seated on the jumpseat at 1R as I ceremoniously removed my glistening blade. Waving the instrument forward and aft I could instruct her on the proper way to hold the brass-knuckled handle. I could demonstrate the best angle by which to seriously wound an opponent. Or, I could just leave her to fend off the horny drunk. I decided not to interfere.

"I can't believe you, Eddy." The remarks came from a pretty F/A on the tram headed for the parking lot. "A cute wife, a son, you have the world on a string."

"Thank you, Marsha." Little did she know my marriage was in a downward spiral and the reality was that I was in fact hanging by a string, inches from total self-destruction. The only true joy and anchor in my life was my young son Cris. He was giving me the emotional support I sorely needed.

I would continue to fulfill all assignments from Scheduling, relishing those with a long layover in urban areas. Antimundo would continue to wander through darkened alleys of lost souls. I considered myself their companion. Dressed for battle, in various cities I would enter a number of shady dives with such names such as Club Deuce, We Love Dirty Blondes, and Dead-End Row. Some promised much more than they could ever deliver with names like Happy Angels and Shangri-La.

"Excellent, this is where you belong," the voices would reassure me. On most occasions a skirmish would occur. One person or another with a gut full of liquor could not resist commenting on Antimundo's attire. Here was a phantom spoiling their ritual descent into inebriation and after the insults there would sometimes be blood. The first rays of the morning sun would find me hurrying back to safety, to the well-respected hotel which housed the rest of my unsuspecting crew. There was the surge of shame, creating a great amount of anxiety and regret as I hurried to cleanse myself of the stains of illicit behavior.

I would always arrive at the lobby on time, dressed in my uniform. I took great pleasure during the ride to the airport listening to fellow crewmembers discuss their layover time. One girl found bargains at the most elegant retail store while two others attended a musical concert.

"How about you Eddy, what did you do?" I glanced at them and smiled.

"Penance." The ladies all laughed.

Chapter XIX

On a bright, sunny day across the basin of the city of the angels the actualities of what was called "deregulation" in the industry came a-knocking at the executive offices on Avion Dr. In recent times, the ever-shrinking passenger loads on all flights across the system became a disease for our airline. The flying public was now more interested in saving a few bucks, choosing to patronize no-frills start-up airlines. The protective shield that had guaranteed the prosperity of many regional companies had been dismantled and prime vacation destinations were now up for grabs. Something had to give, and the changes were drastic.

My airline came within five days of declaring bankruptcy. No one was a bit concerned about the buried truth concerning 2605; they were all too worried about whether they would still have a job. In one swift act the majority of management was swept away. Mario Reddick, who took the brunt for what was perceived as the company's failures, was heckled out of the employees' cafeteria in one of his few remaining days in power. The CEO scheduled a trip to Hawaii, but the bag handlers were a group full of scorn. One clever associate in a regulation red shirt and blue pants made sure Mr. Reddick's bags landed in Bangkok.

"Gosh, all those initialed dress shirts were on their way to Thailand," I thought when informed of the "mis-direction." But Mario Reddick wasn't a bad guy. In his time, he was a master of his game in the industry: brilliant, cordial, intelligent, with a knowledge and taste for fine wines, but the world had changed. Ackley was gone. Shana James would be asked to exit in a not-so-polite manner. Jack McKay went off into a well-deserved retirement.

"The only people with any kind of a smile these days are the ones in uniform," observed an F/A on the tram soon after the massive purge. Everyone was devastated and I now had to survive in this new and uncertain environment. A situation which should have pushed me into a panic, somehow didn't. I was comforted by the fact that I had the CVR recording. If I had to use it as a threat to secure my position, then I would.

"If they screw you over you must go to the media." I found myself agreeing with Antimundo's words. I had to do whatever it took to meet the needs of my wife and son. But for now, the plan was to just lay low. Then rumors began circulating about someone who had been brought in to save our ailing company.

Uncle Dale, as some took to calling him, was a successful businessman from the Pacific Northwest. I was optimistic when I heard he had retained the services of Barry Lane. The new CEO arrived with just one idea in his mind: cut all possible fat throughout the system and systematically reshape the airline into a united "air force" of no frills. The routes the company had secured decades before were still a highly-prized commodity. Uncle Dale was sure he could still make a buck on each and every seat. Naturally there was the usual call for the unions to convince its members that concessions would have to be made, and nothing was off the table. ALPA, the entity that governed the pilots, might believe they had the most to relinquish but the losses would be no more painful than those suffered by the workers in the company's cafeteria. AFA was also resistant to Uncle Dale's cutbacks.

Ironically, I found this period to be quite a reprieve for my personal battles. No one cared to stop and ask me difficult questions and I was able to focus more time on Sofia and Cris. Family trips were taken, things slowed down and I dared to hope that the end of my difficulties was possibly in sight.

The letter came on a normal day while I oil painted, a needed outlet to express my feelings. It was obvious the document was of some importance. I was informed that my medical coverage would no longer cover the cost of my therapy with Doctor Joe. The demons deep down stirred. I was pissed but it was not unexpected. Reva, my smart union rep was right on target. As predicted, the insurer was guided by the employees' agreement with the airlines. I spoke on the phone to a lady from the underwriter; I would be evaluated by a second physician. Any payments to Doctor Ramljak would be immediately suspended. Like it or not, I had no choice.

"Doctor Joseph Ramljak was the recommended physician to see and that decision was made by the airline representative, Daisy Ackley." I hesitated in revealing the ace I had up my sleeve. I would wait patiently for the right time to break the news to the insurer. But then I thought that seeing another doctor, even though he may be a "hatchet man" working for the underwriter, would allow me a different perspective on my therapy with Dr. Joe.

If a guy who comes out of a crashed, burning jumbo jet is evaluated and determined <u>not</u> to be dysfunctional, what could other patients with deep personal scars hope for? I decided to play by the rules and an appointment was made to travel to Sherman Oaks for the evaluation. Doctor Ramljak was far more concerned than I about this second evaluation. I should have taken note, but I stupidly dismissed his warnings.

Doctor Sidney Hackle was a piece of work. If one looked up the word "greed" in the dictionary, his picture would be under it! Arriving for my appointment, I was directed by his assistant to a room where I would spend the better part of two hours completing a series of tests. I was asked to draw a picture of the perfect family on a sheet of white paper and express whether I felt overwhelmed by life.

"Is he kidding?" Instantly, I found myself standing in the burning mound of charred metal.

"*¡Mi mamá! ¡Mi mamá!*" The sights sound and smells of that horrible day were just below the surface. Have I not been on the edge of insanity? Of course, the insurance company would not simply take my word, and after a period of waiting I stood face to face with Sidney.

"Mr. Valenzuela have a seat," he said, gesturing to a white sofa. I ignored the mispronunciation of my name. The physician sized me up from behind his thick bifocals. It appears the man was following a routine.

"So, what type of injury do you have?" He was serious.

"I was in an accident."

"What type of accident?" Was the scrawny man in the white coat for real? "Do you have my file? Did you read up on anything regarding my medical claim?" Dr. Hackle was apparently not use to being challenged and his face reflected his embarrassment. Sidney returned to his monologue.

"Exactly what type of accident was it?" I was somewhat confused.

"What do you mean?" Now it was frustration on top of the embarrassment.

"What happened?" Finally, I realized that this supposed doctor had no idea what the specifics of my case were. The only thing that seemed certain was that he was going to find absolutely nothing wrong with me, details be damned. My anger swelled.

"I was on a fucking jumbo jet that slammed into two buildings." The hatchet-man was unimpressed. "There was a massive blow to the ship. We first hit a dump truck which tore our right landing gear from our belly. I crawled out of the burning rubble to a scene of total devastation. You don't think that fried my brain? I was then subjected to the death cries of two young boys." The tears welled up. I found myself lost in my oral declaration. Suddenly I turned to find my esteemed evaluator with eyes closed, seeming to be fast asleep. Now what? I coughed loudly and awakened him.

"Ah yes, I think I've heard enough." The determination was a done deal, but unfortunately not to my benefit.

I drove away from Sherman Oaks cursing myself for not listening to Dr. Joe's advice. If anything, now I knew why there is the term "hatchet man."

"How bad could his evaluation be?" I comforted my mind with false hope. Certainly, with the likes of Doctor Ramljak and his impeccable reputation, we would be able to logically explain any minor differences Sidney might express. Until Dr. Hackle's final evaluation was available, payment for my therapy with Dr. Joe was on hold.

"I will see you next week Ed," Doctor Joe stated as we ended our session.

"You're not getting paid, Doc," I blurted out, reminding him of the carrier's actions. He stared at me and gave a sly smile, an indication that I would not stand alone. Perhaps it did not take a genius to determine what they were doing to me was wrong. I left his office sure he had seen this type of action by the corporate entities before and he would continue to guide without receiving a penny. I was grateful.

In time, the report from Sidney Hackle arrived and it was no surprise that his decision had gone against me. What was astonishing was the length that the sleepy hatchet man had gone to in order to destroy any evidence that might indicate that I had a valid case. Page after page carefully outlined his determination that I had not suffered one bit of psychological trauma. Reflecting upon my experience, this determination was actually scary. Dr. Sidney could have screwed me big time. If I had not manipulated the system on the advice of Reva, I could easily have been left out in the cold, making my situation even worse. This physician was dangerous, and no doubt may have destroyed the lives of many who were broken and ignorant of the system.

Instead, I remained calm and logical, sticking to my plan. Dr. Joe was not about to say, "I told you so." My intelligent physician examined Sidney's document with interest.

"You were smart to foresee the complications the system can present." Ramljak was impressed by the ploy.

"I need to thank my AFA union rep Reva; she is the one who had the insight." Dr. Joe peered at me above his glasses.

The underwriters were quick to arrange a conference call once Sidney's report surfaced. Doctor Joe and I waited patiently in his office when the call came in.

"According to the flight attendant contract," a Ms. Harlington began, "we have the evaluation of our physician Doctor Hackle and your physician Doctor Ramljak. Now what is needed is a third opinion by…." I cut the polite woman off.

"Excuse me, Doctor Ramljak is not my physician." There was a long pause as I spotted a little smile on the face of my psychiatrist. He was enjoying himself.

"He is not your Doctor?" Ms. Harlington was obviously confused.

"No," I slowly responded. "Doctor Ramljak was selected and recommended to me by the airline. In fact, they are the ones who contacted him and arranged my initial session." Another long pause.

"Is this information correct, Doctor Ramljak?"

"Indeed, it is," my hero responded. "According to the company contract with the Association of Flight Attendants, a third evaluation is needed by a reputable physician selected by Mr. Valenciana, is that not correct?"

"Ah, yes," the corporate ploy was shattered, and Dr. Joe took control of the situation with an immediate response.

"I will see that Mr. Valenciana proceeds with this evaluation as soon as possible so that we may accelerate the process and confirm his status with regard to his therapy." Another long pause on the other end, then:

"Ah, yes, that is the correct procedure and we will await the third evaluation." In concluding the conference call, I began laughing and danced about the office.

Once I settled down, Dr. Joe indicated he had a colleague in San Bernardino who would be the perfect selection to validate my medical claim.

"Now, tell me the reasons why you are roaming the streets, putting yourself and others in harm's way during your layovers?" My doctor was not going to let me off the hook and the therapy continued.

Although the airline and my job security teetered on the brink from day to day, the period in which Uncle Dale guided the company brought a sense of tranquility to my life. All the associates had much more important issues on their minds. The crash and its survivor no longer mattered. Eddy Valenciana was once again allowed to join the flight line in lieu of Edmundo, allowing me to quietly fade into the background and simply do my job. It was wonderful.

While under the care of Doctor Ramljak my employment status was still formulated by the guidelines set by Barry Lane. I still did not have to fly Mexico City and had the ability to remove myself from the reserve flight list without repercussions. With the airline in such dire straits, no one in the new management team seemed interested in my comings and goings. Most likely, no departments other than Scheduling and Payroll even knew of my specific circumstance.

But try as hard as I could to recapture the carefree attitude of my pre-accident flying days, I still felt a contempt for those complicit in the lies and dis-respecting the families who had lost loved ones.

"Let it go."

"Get on with your life."

"You have a lovely wife and a beautiful son, don't let anything destroy that." The arguments were quite logical and were sincerely presented by individuals who truly cared for my well-being. Yet, the words were spoken by those whose minds did not carry the memories of the dancing flames or the torn, broken bodies. Their ears did not have to listen to the screams of lost loved ones. Their hearts were not filled with shame and hatred. So, many layover nights were still being spent seeking vengeance.

My list of hunting grounds covered the spectrum of designated cities. PHX, PDX, SEA, LAS, DFW and DEN were just some of them. I sought to mingle with the cursed and forsaken, in the dingy dives and bars where the helpless sought escape. For there were always vulture-scum nearby whose ambition was to pick the bones of the defenseless.

"Hit him again," Antimundo directed. As time went on, I never seemed content with the initial damage inflicted. I would justify my sin by convincing myself my victims were "not good enough" and deserved more.

Roaming the limitless backstreets and alleyways enhanced the pleasure in Antimundo's desire, seeking a greater degree of danger. I wanted to spit in the face of Muerto not because I was brave or noble, but because I was so damn incensed by the injustice of it all. When the night of vengeance was over I returned to the hotel and re-packed my brass-knuckled knife. Soon, once again, Edmundo would be standing by the aircraft entrance.

"Welcome aboard, we are so happy to serve you."

. . .

In time the honeymoon between the airline and its new leader, Uncle Dale, began to sour. With the future of the airline still in doubt, the associates had enough and took action.

With the aid of massive union concessions from all ranks in the company, the 10,000+ employees became the helmsmen of their own destiny; they became owners of the airline. With such a bold move the new board of directors needed a strong leader who could not only guide and motivate but also have the insight to deliver the company from the verge of bankruptcy. He would have to bring her back to profitability, which at the time was seemingly impossible. This required someone who could navigate the airline through the ever-turbulent waters of deregulation. So, Barry Lane, the Vice President of Inflight Services, the man who was a ship cleaner in 1946, put aside a well-earned retirement to become the Chief Executive Officer.

Barry greeted the obstacle just like great men do, with courage and faith. With all these important issues to deal with he still had the compassion to reach out and assure me that he remained my advocate. The company would continue to endorse any situation that favored my healing process. Despite all my deplorable behavior, I was not deserted by him. His actions humbled me.

"I got really lucky," I reminded myself. In studying the reports of most other air disasters and seeing the way in which other companies dealt with survivors and crewmembers, I discovered most of their actions to be swift and heartless. There were efforts to terminate any relationship with those perceived "not to be in line with the program.".

I certainly had no intention of trying to approach Mr. Lane early in his tenure as CEO but to my amazement he called me up to the Executive Offices one morning. Appointments with Dr. Ramljak were being missed as my resentment had taken the upper hand and my desire to heal was fading. I was embracing the demon I was becoming. The good doctor was concerned and acted and Barry Lane was made well aware of my plight. I felt like a mischievous child, embarrassed for having let both men down.

"What's holding you back Eduardo?" The CEO asked as a friend and mentor. "What can we do to help you along?" My head fell with shame.

"I need to tell the truth." I quickly regretted my statement. Perhaps I was overstepping my bounds.

"Go ahead, say your piece."

"Hell, nearly everyone in this company has been lied to, directly or indirectly, by the withholding of specific information." That's all I could get out at the moment.

"You want a chance to express yourself to the new board of directors?" I could not believe my ears. "Look, you get back to seeing Dr. Ramljak and I will arrange for you to meet and speak to the board sometime soon." Mr. Lane was a busy man and I had been graciously given precious time. I left the executive offices in a fog for I still could not believe what I had heard. It was Barry Lane's personal choice to support me. No one demanded he do this. Gathering my thoughts, I wondered what was I going to tell the directors?

I returned to the beach house optimistic, but Sofia was distant and silent. Anything related to the crash was the last thing she wanted to hear. I sympathized with her. I was still in deep trouble.

"Will I ever be good enough?"

Barry Lane was a good man who believed it would be in my best interest to find a way to just move on from this torment. I also believe he came to realize that I was determined to see this thing through to its conclusion. And he reasoned correctly in perceiving the conclusion could be disastrous. He was providing me with opportunities, but more importantly he reintroduced me to hope.

I sat in the large conference room, nicely dressed and extremely uncomfortable, tapping my foot in a continuous beat. Once the director's meeting had come to order, Mr. Lane turned in my direction.

"As you can see, today we have a visitor." I nodded to the group which also included a flight attendant and a pilot. Some on the far side of the polished table stretched their heads to get a glimpse of me.

"Yes, it's your buddy, Edmundo," I murmured to myself. I slowly walked to the side of my advocate, at the head of the table. The smiling faces gave me their full attention. And so, I began.

"You all know me because of the terrible tragedy that occurred in Mexico City on October 31, 1979." I paused because I sensed an unholy presence enter the room. I imagined Muerto taking the exact same seat I had previously occupied. I lost my perspective. "Oh, damn it, screw protocol, Suzette, you represent the flight attendants, right?" My question caught her by surprise, but she quickly nodded. "Remember when Ackley promised us at the company meetings that vital details regarding the accident would be forthcoming? It was all bullshit, a straight-out lie. Imagine, several of the F/A's that perished in that fiery wreckage were so junior, still in their probationary period and not covered by the flight attendant insurance plan. Their families were initially offered zero compensation along with no response to their inquiries as to why such a tragedy happened. It was not until these families lawyered-up did they discover that, by law, they would be limited to what workers' compensation offered. In their desperation some of the despondent mothers reached out to me for help, but what was I supposed to do? Why was it my responsibility to have to deal with such delicate issues?" I stopped, then began to walk about the room as the heads turned to follow.

"Just hang up on her." That was the suggestion from the company's lawyer when a grieving mother called me seeking answers." I cringed at the recollection. I lost focus and jumped to another matter.

"Gary Rollings. That man took so much pride in that 2605 was his initial flight serving as the senior F/A. His shoes were polished liked glass." I glanced to my side and saw that Mr. Lane's face revealed a look of deep concern. He remained silent, keeping to his promise of letting me have my say. "Do any of you know that right after the crash as people screamed and burned and died, others were engaged in stealing the left landing gear of the destroyed jumbo jet?" A soft gasp could be heard as some of the faces at the table reacted with surprise. "Yeah, that is how chaotic the situation was. This is how tormented my mind becomes each time I have to remember and believe me there were many, many more horrible scenes I could relate to you if I wanted."

I paused to let everyone including myself regain a bit of composure. Then I slowly removed a small piece of paper from my dress pants and continued.

"Did any of you happen to know that the company actually made a profit off this flight? The scrap metal, minus the left landing gear, was sold and the net income from the sale was described in the yearly report in the following manner: "an involuntary adaptation of a DC-10." One female board member became teary-eyed, but I needed to continue.

"Did the company bother to tell you how all the bodies were stripped, and their belongings looted of valuables?" It was obvious that some around the table did not want to hear any more, but I couldn't stop. "Then there are the pilots," I stated with sarcasm. The silent tension in the room was becoming unbearable. "I was in the cockpit, right there in the middle, witnessing the unthinkable" I reached into my coat's inner pocket and removed a condensed copy of the disciplinary review of Dieter Reimann. I tossed the folded papers onto the center of the table. "Proof is in the documentation. Carl had officially written up Dieter earlier in the month of October. Most of the pilots based in LAX are well aware that friction rode jumpseat that night. What was the company's solution for such a lethal situation? It was simply to have one good old boy conversing with another and verbally assuring each other that all was well. Despite the obvious differences the two men had, management decided things would be just fine. Was this disciplinary review and subsequent decision to let them continue to fly together, was it made weeks or days prior? No, the entire procedure and final determination was conducted just <u>hours</u> before the departure of 2605. It's obvious to me that both carried the mutual contempt with them into the cockpit. If you doubt me, listen to the CVR recording of 2605 yourself." Reaching into the left pocket of my pants I removed a cassette tape and lightly tossed it also onto the middle of the polished table.

"Listen to it if you have the stomach. It's ugly! I have it constantly playing in my head." Finally, as I looked at the faces around the room I realized that I was beating up the wrong people. These were individuals who could help me but my anger had kept me from realizing it. The need to speak my mind was greater. "Forgive me my friends but there were a whole lot of unscrupulous people on both sides of the border who created by design a gross cover-up of the true facts. This was done because economics determined what was in the best interest of the countries, the airline, and the industry. My crew and the other victims paid a terrible price and their families still don't know why."

My voice rose in pitch. "Hell, it was not my responsibility to be the bearer of information regarding how this disaster occurred! I went through the damn fire, what the hell more do you want? This company dropped the ball on this matter. Do you want to know what a phone call from a grieving mother does to me when she is begging for a bit of the truth and I am afraid to reveal it?" I couldn't look around the table. I just kept venting.

"And what did our company gain with our reluctant resistance and our deafening silence, not challenging the official report by the Mexican Government? Some see it as a real blessing that our newly restructured airline is now the only U.S. carrier who has been given landing rights into three of the most lucrative vacation destinations on the Mexican Riviera." I was now becoming emotionally exhausted.

"I am glad I survived but my new life also came with a terrible burden." I turned slowly and looked down at an obviously stressed and stoic Barry Lane, who sat through this tirade because he would not go back on his promise to allow me to be here and tell my story. This was part of a healing process he knew I badly needed.

"This man is the only one who has been honest with me. His personal support beats all the free flights this airline can offer me. This man gave me hope."

From the side of the room Muerto had heard enough. He rose and quickly walked out the door.

"How am I going to get out of this maze?" I softly asked. I became confused and a chill came over me. The faces at the table....

"Will I ever be good enough?" I shook my head as no one moved. I heard another woman weeping as I stood overwhelmed. I had enough. I turned and quickly left the room, hurrying down the hallway. I just needed to leave the company grounds, right now! I sped out of the employee parking lot and headed down the Pacific Coast Highway. I met Tommy at a well-known watering hole overlooking the Manhattan Beach Pier. We drank and sang America the Beautiful as the sun disappeared into the Pacific, then we drank some more.

444

Barry Lane's generosity in allowing me to purge my demons before the board of directors was incredibly unique in the industry. The action spoke more about the character of the man that was now leading our fragile company than anything else he could have done or said. He believed in my ability to overcome the complexity of my wounds more than I did. I felt some satisfaction after my meeting with the board, but it quickly faded. Returning from a three-day assignment I was informed that there was a message for me to call Mr. Lane's office – from Grace, his secretary, to be exact.

"Eduardo, Mr. Lane wanted me to advise you that along with your continued therapy with Doctor Ramljak, the company would like to extend the same type of assistance to your wife Sofia with a therapist of her choice." I could barely hold back the tears of gratitude, for there was no limit to the CEOs decency. Here was the chance for Sofia and me to heal our deteriorating relationship. I returned home filled with excitement. My optimism was totally shattered when Sofia and Cristiano were nowhere to be found. Soon I discovered that Sofia had decided to make her own exit from the mine field.

"Eduardo Valenciana?" a finely dressed young man stood at my door a few days later.

"Yes." I opened the screen door as he presented me with a very legal-looking envelope.

"Sir, you have been served." He turned and slowly walked away. I remained frozen.

Sofia's desire to dissolve the marriage was painful but did not come as a surprise. What astounded me as I reviewed the legal papers was that she was petitioning the court to grant her full legal and physical custody of our son. Muerto was playing his trump card as the hatred in my heart returned with a vengeance. This dormant God must have been fully amused. Whatever hope I had been given by Barry Lane was crushed that awful morning.

Gripped by uncontrollable grief, I found myself wandering the halls of the company on Avion Drive. My instincts led me to the Flight Attendant Training offices where a surprised staff tried to console me.

"Oh Eddy, I am so sorry." I cried uncontrollably. My tears flowed. My dear friend Tim Blackman was a new addition to the training staff and tried his best to help.

"I can't continue on." That's all I could say. After some Tim insisted, I join him for lunch at a nearby restaurant.

"This is when your son will need you more than ever," Tim began. "You have come so far, and you will get through this mess, also." I did not respond but merely jabbed at the paper casing of a straw that had come with our soft drinks. "Look at yourself, Eddy. Look at what all of this is doing to you." I ceased my anxious behavior and glanced up at my friend.

"What? What did you say?" Tim became very concerned.

"My dear El Gato, you are wasting your nine lives very quickly." He was right.

There was one glimmer of promise for saving my relationship with my son, the services of attorney David J. Brooks.

In her effort to escape one complicated situation, Sofia inadvertently thrust herself onto another. The few initial court-supervised conversations Sofia and I had proved fruitless. She was adamant about cutting me out of the picture completely.

"You deserve this." The vicious voices were relentless. The break-up of our marriage convinced me I was headed for a relapse, maybe a severe one. The love for my son Cristo was all the stability I had going for me right now.

I would be lying if I claimed that at this point, I had strengthened myself for the court battle. The opposite was true. I had received the deposition for family court at the end of September, right about the time retail stores began decorating for the Halloween season. I retreated into the locked seclusion and darkness of my beach home and began to listen once again to the CVR recording.

"Oh Jesus Christ! Oh fuck!"

"Get her up Carl!"

"I can't!" Then the screaming. I downed another bottle of Bohemia.

"Scream all you want Carl, those assholes suckered you in and now they all just want to wash their hands of the matter."

Then, once again the abnormal sound revealed itself in the final seconds of the recording. It was distinct and perplexing.

This unison of many voices rising in pitch and then instantly terminated. I listened to the strange sound over and over until I passed out.

"Why didn't you help me?" Young Javier pleaded his case again as he stood in the burning wreckage, fully engulfed in flames. Suddenly there was a loud pounding at my front door.

"Eddy! Hey, Eddy, open up!"

"Go away!" I commanded. I was in no condition to see anyone. The pounding continued. "Whoever you are, go away!"

"Hey Papa!" That distinct greeting meant it could only be my friend Jean Pierre Donici, a flight attendant with Pan American Airways who was based in London. With reluctance I finally opened the door. J.P. as we called him, stood staring at me.

"You want a beer?" I offered in my intoxicated state. J.P. was taken aback, having never witnessed me in such a state.

"No, no, no Papa, you have had enough, we need to get you cleaned up. This is not good for you." In my stupidity I resisted and became arrogant.

"Hey, you want to listen to the CVR recording? You want to hear them all screaming bloody murder? Come on, let's have some beer and listen to people dying. It's okay, nobody else seems to care anyway. Hey, a whole bunch of people made a lot of money from it, didn't you know?" J.P. dragged me into the shower and forced into me several cups of black coffee. He got me semi-sober and dressed.

"This is not going to end well for you, Papa. You need to change direction." J.P.'s parting words as he left for his hotel, did little to help me. I finally sobered up just in time for my next assignment from Scheduling and the whole cycle of despair and self-abuse began once more in a city far away.

I would later learn that my words to the board of directors contributed to a positive break from industry protocol. For the first time ever, a major airline voted to create a financial reserve separate from any union agreement, available for the assistance of any crew member on an aircraft that "went down." Barry Lane had attended all the funerals and I also spotted him at some of the post-service gatherings one at which he met with Mrs. Torres. Mr. Lane had known the young F/As who were still in their probationary period. I believed it ate at his soul, what the system dealt out to those grieving families. I wondered if that was his plan all along when he allowed me access to the board of directors. But it didn't matter because what was voted by the new board was a very good thing and I hoped that such funds would never have to be accessed. The details of the plan were of no interest to me. I was glad for the program but was sorry it was all done too late to help me.

The dates and times, monies and possessions regarding temporary sharing of Cristiano were set up and arrangements for a court hearing were established. Sofia was not happy. I began to care less about her feelings once I had been served with the divorce papers. The rules and playing field had changed drastically. In my eyes it was now all about Cristiano.

I paid strict attention to the regulations as I entered the court room. "Every other weekend and one day mid-week" were new terms which demanded the reorganization of my schedule. On the court-appointed days of custody with Cris my house was swept of Muerto's stench, and the relentless voices were banned with the boy's arrival. I had him all to myself and with our flight benefits we had limitless boundaries for a playground. Cris became my flying partner. I am a strong believer that travel is an education. The boy was beaming as my fellow crewmembers showered him with attention.

Once, after a Utah ski adventure, my excited three-year-old was invited into the cockpit of the soaring jet by the friendly captain.

"You want to sit in the Captain's chair and fly the plane?" Cris could hardly contain himself. Still in his ski bibs, he was lifted onto the left seat and his small hands gripped the controls. He looked back at me with the widest grin! The jumbo jet was on auto pilot, but the gesture spoke volumes of a different time in the industry.

As it came closer for the court proceedings, I straightened myself out physically and mentally. This was far too important to leave anything to chance. I forced myself to memorize one phrase and I repeated it over and over.

"The judge has the last word."

Whether in the gym or strapped in my jumpseat, I spoke it like a silent prayer: "The judge has the last word." The specifics of the case were overwhelming, but I was determined to see this through to a favorable end, which was simply to have the court award Sofia and me joint legal and physical custody.

The tall, glass windows of the Torrance Municipal Courthouse rose high into the ceiling. This is where "Edmundo" had been summoned to just "look pretty and keep his mouth closed" according to David Brooks. I was smart enough to let David take control.

"The judge has the final word," I repeated one more time, and so it began.

A smiling white-haired magistrate entered. The near empty room was divided only by the opposing sides and a confident David turned to me and nodded. Judge Robert Stifler began the proceedings.

"So, Mrs. Valenciana, I see that in your petition for divorce you do not wish to agree to a legal joint custody of your son with your husband, is that correct?" Caught off guard, Sofia hesitated.

"Yes," she responded weakly.

"Do you know what that means?" inquired the judge.

"We have expressed our desires in our petition your honor," her counselor interjected himself quickly.

"All right," the magistrate cleared his throat. "Why are you so adamant about not sharing physical custody of the boy with your husband?"

"Your honor, that man has not been the same nor will he ever be the same since his accident." Sofia gave me an admonishing look. The magistrate looked confused.

"What accident? Was he in some type of automobile accident?"

"No, No. He's a flight attendant. He was involved in a plane crash." I immediately put my hands to my face as I leaned over and whispered to David.

"Wasn't this supposed to be just about the marriage and the custody of Cris?" My attorney simply raised his hand and dismissed my concerns, for he was on top of the matter.

"I don't quite understand, Mrs. Valenciana. Does he have a private plane that he crashed?"

"No, he was on a DC-10 that smacked into a couple of buildings," Sofia calmly stated. She smiled broadly as she related the now-familiar story. At that moment her soft long hair and sweet looks had me convinced of her intentions, protecting her son from a supposed madman. The judge slowly pulled his glasses down to stare at me as I was twisting in my seat. I began to notice more people continually filtering into the courtroom. I recognized no one as the room slowly began to fill up. Mr. Stiles, Sofia's attorney, continued his questioning with more vigor.

"Do you believe he would be harmful to your son?"

"Yes, ever since our son was born, that's when the chaos started. He might steal our son." The judge seemed shocked by her statement and intervened.

"Why? Has he ever threatened to take the boy?"

"No, but he might."

"Has he ever done anything that would indicate that the boy would be in peril while in his care?"

"He acts weird." For a moment no one spoke.

"Your honor," Stiles rose. "I would like to introduce a photo into evidence. I cringed when I realized that it was a copy of "the wild jungle man of the Na Pali" taken when I had come upon the three hikers. Stiles approached the bench, handing the glossy print to the judge. To make matters worse, once he had examined the photo, he held his arm high so that all could see me in my glorious make-up.

"Your honor, that photo is the personal property of my client and was obtained without his permission." David confronted the legitimacy of presenting the photo into evidence.

"Oh, I don't think a little look will hurt anybody." He allowed David to approach and examine the print.

"This is no proof of anything," David explained. "Your Honor, what madman poses for a photo?" The thoughtful judge seemed to have come to a similar conclusion.

"You do this out on some island in the Pacific?" The direct question caught me off guard as every eye in the room was upon me.

"Ah, yes I do, yes Sir." Judge Stifler raised an eyebrow and scratched the base of his broad chin.

"Huh, it looks like fun," he stated to my surprise.

"Oh my," I murmured as my head fell forward. With the judge's dismissal of the jungle man as a threat, the supposed damaging tool was made null and void. Regardless, I felt like a wreck at this point and was ready for the proceedings to be concluded, for now the courtroom was filled with curious on-lookers. I turned and spotted Muerto's image in the crowd, accompanied by a woman in the face of a darling "calavera" or skull, wide-eyed and smiling with dark black lines bordering many vivid colors. The carnival had arrived and the audience in the bleachers wanted to hear more. The judge also seemed to become more and more fascinated.

"She believes he will kidnap the boy." Sofia's brother was now on the stand. I leaned over toward David who was taking some notes on his yellow legal pad.

"You got to do something, I am being skinned" Once again, he dismissed me with a movement of his hand. I gazed up at the clock, then at the gawkers in attendance.

"Globos, rojo, azul, y amarillo." (Balloons, red, blue and yellow). The Mexican vendors now plied their wares in the courtroom when an object flew passed me. Across the room a young teen caught it then dangled it with great delight.

"Es de su novia," (It's your girlfriend's) he chuckled. I looked deeper and recognized it as a severed hand. The circus was complete. Death sat across the room some rows back and followed the testimony with interest.

"He seemed to leave the load of the work to Sofia." I once more concentrated on brother-in-law's testimony.

"That will be all Your Honor." The petitioners seemed satisfied with their effort.

"He chewed you up like you deserve," the voices now joined the chorus. David J. Brooks did not rise, he simply placed his right hand onto his temple and thought. The judge just stared at him indicating that it was his turn. Would there being a questioning of this witness? I sat there feeling helpless.

"Sir." David hesitated once more then looked straight at the man. "Is Eddy a good father?" A short, direct approach caught Sofia's brother off guard. David leaped at the chance. "Is Eddy a good father, yes or no?" The honest brother turned and stiffened his spine.

"Yes."

451

"I have no more questions, Your Honor." My brass-knuckled knife could not have cut any more sharply as David Brook's skills as an attorney. He once again directed the case back to the focal point: what would be in the best interest of the child. Over a series of court-ordered dates, David was able to eliminate the court's concerns. Doctor Ramljak, Timothy Cardinal Manning and Barry Lane were all steadfast in their support on my behalf, submitting letters to the court vouching for my character. Muerto left the final proceedings disappointed.

Now, I could continue my adventures with Cris as my flying partner. Up there in the skies, inside a DC-10, we would not have to deal with the distrust of the world below. Once Cris would be returned to his mother and I was alone in my beach home however, demons would come forth.

"Get her up Carl, you're banking." I once again listened to the CVR recording. On the tape, First Officer Dieter Reimann's attitude changed quickly once our aircraft hit the dump truck on runway 23 Left. It's funny how one can go from disliking an individual to cheering for him in a split second when one's ass is on the line. It also became apparent to me that with all the commands and screaming that went on in those final moments, were loud enough to be heard by the crew and passengers in first class. I recalled being able to understand some conversation coming out of the cockpit on certain flights while strapped to the jumpseat at station 1L or 1R. I tried to take solace in the fact that most of the passengers would have been asleep. Yet, I was certain the flight attendants up front, Gary and Karen, would have been wide awake, especially after the jolt when striking the truck.

"It should have been you." The whispers tormented me. "You should have been seated at 1R." In the darkness, when the doors and windows were firmly locked, I found myself very alone, afraid to go to sleep, and the night belonged to Muerto. If I were to close my eyes, I knew I would have to face Javier's pleas as he was consumed by the flesh-eating flames.

"Why couldn't I save him?" I downed another Bohemia.

I found myself becoming complacent in my duties on flights. Although I was aware of the ramifications of the unthinkable, I now felt secure being locked in the tubular aircraft. At 35,000' I was protected from the people I despised on the ground. Although I had found some contentment in my "presentation" to the company's board of directors, I soon fell back into a shallow pool of resentment. Sure, other associates did sympathize, but I was the one who was expected to retain the secrets.

"Get on with your life" was the consensus. Initially it sounded like a good idea but as Dr. Joe realized early on, it was a nearly impossible task. He indicated that my salvation lie in the ability to purge my sub-conscious, which held so many self-destructive memories. I found myself more willing to express specific details of the incident when continually questioned by fellow crew-members eager to learn something that might benefit their own survival.

The pilots would always invite me to visit the cockpit to enjoy the view. They had been one of the few to be told specifics.

"Many of the F/A's were so junior, their families were not eligible for any financial compensation."

"Are you shitting me?" One senior pilot was in disbelief and assured me that <u>he</u> would have immediately gotten himself a good lawyer.

"It would not have done any good. The appellate court shot down their claims because of workman's compensation." This particular discovery I kept to myself. Repeating it over and over would just re-kindle the resentment. But no matter what disturbing facts I decided to share with my crewmates, the reaction was always the same: a cringing of the facial muscles, a look of disbelief, then a sobering moment of contemplation.

"Please tell me what you can Eddy," some sincerely asked. Others who perhaps wanted the whole affair buried forever simply avoided me at all cost. Either way, my continued presence on the flight line began to take a toll on me.

"2605, expect an approach to Runway 23 Left," so said the Mexican Air Traffic Controller. The hours I spent listening to the CVR recording were draining, but also educational. If I was indeed suffering from Post-Traumatic Stress Disorder as Doctor Joe had indicated, I had to be sure about what I believed truly happened, clear on the facts I was relating to those who were interested.

After one night of familiar visits from the dead, I was awakened in the early morning hours by a phone call.

"I am a Senior Producer of the Oprah Winfrey television show," she informed me. "I would like to extend an invitation to be part of a panel of "Whistle Blowers" on a show based on that subject."

"My God, I can finally dump this crap on the side of the road," I thought. As the producer spoke, I envisioned myself speaking to the general public across the country. "You want to know what these assholes are responsible for?" I broke into a rare smile. Why shouldn't I? But the producer's words suddenly rang through.

"You will be part of a panel." That meant I would have just a few minutes to make my case.

"Who is he?" they would ask. I was no aviation investigator. Once on the air the audience would only see a regular flight attendant, a disgruntled one at that. This was complicated. My explanations to the public would only be taken seriously if supported by an expert pilot.

"We would like to send the limo tomorrow morning to take you to the airport where transportation to Chicago will be arranged."

"Go ahead, make a bigger joke of yourself than you already are." The fallen angels chimed in. My mind was racing. Oprah would certainly not be airing the ghastly screams of the black box. What harm would I be doing to my airline? A swift emotional explanation was not the solution to my issues. What a disappointment I would be to Barry Lane who had worked endlessly and was seeing positive results in the resurrection of the company. Another problem was the show's subject.

"Excuse me, I am not a whistle blower. I am a survivor." I had to think this process through. "Please relate my gratitude to Oprah but my story just requires a different format." After I hung up the phone, I continued the self-abuse.

"Psycho Killer" by Talking Heads became a theme song for my shameful expeditions. Antimundo loved the tune. If there was a dim cave, darkened tunnel or hollow spot under a rusted bridge, in any town, he sought to be there. If there was a down-trodden bar, he found it. If he mingled with the self-condemned

454

who inhabited these domiciles of despair, he embraced it. If through the implementation of these action there happened to be misfortune for the fools and bloodsuckers, so be it. Late one night I returned from a SEA trip, heading to my car. Suddenly I fell to the ground convulsing. In the past there would be vomit or just dry heaves, but this time there was the distinct color of red.

"Stop!" This was my message to Flight Attendant Scheduling. "I am not going to work another assigned flight. I don't care who knows, I'm not doing it." I was taken off the flight line. It would be foolish to think that none of my fellow crew members never suspected my strange behavior on layovers. I no longer cared.

Days passed as I sat alone, isolated in the beach house. My spirits were lifted when Cris would arrive for our arranged time together, but his inevitable departure always reopened the door to the chasm where I would merely exist. The company continued without me, emerging from near bankruptcy to financial strength under the new management team.

My basic needs continued to be met. What did not change was the deep-rooted guilt and resentment. One morning I was again summoned to the executive offices. It was a mentally and physically beaten down flight attendant who faced CEO Barry Lane.

"Learned Helplessness," I sighed.

"What?"

"Doctor Ramljak told me I am in a state of learned helplessness, like a rat running on a spinning wheel. I am going nowhere but must continue to run."

"Perhaps we could find an alternative solution," Barry suggested as he rose from his desk, grabbed a chair and sat beside me.

"What do you want to do with your future, Eddy?" His inquiry caught me off-guard.

"I suppose if I had the opportunity, I would like to return to school. There is power to be found in education."

"And the possibility of healing also." He jumped on my words. "So why don't you do it?" Mr. Lane was serious. My spine stiffened and I sat erect.

"Do you know how much it would cost me for college tuition these days?" I began to chuckle.

"That is exactly what I am talking about." Barry Lane responded seriously. It went clear over my head.

"What?"

"Listen Ed, the board has recently allotted funds to aid employees who are victims of a crash and I believe you qualify in that category. The airline is in a much better financial condition and I believe you have earned this opportunity" Mr. Lane rose and slowly escorted me to the door. "Do some research and determine what you would like to study and where. The airline will continue to see to your financial needs and when you come back, I am sure we can come to an understanding." Like a devoted father, he placed his hand upon my shoulder as we walked past his smiling secretary. "Thank you for coming by today, Ed, and I expect to hear from you soon." All at once I found myself standing alone in the hallway, in a totally different place. While feeling a rush of adrenaline, I tried to process what had just taken place.

"Yes!" I screamed. I sped out of the employee parking structure pondering the possibilities. The voices were not so trusting.

"It's just a ploy to get you away from the workplace and those associates who simply want to know the truth. Get it all on paper." I listened to them but then reflected on Barry Lane, whose character was beyond reproach. He was going out of his way to personally help me when he didn't have to. His guidance was a true blessing, but the voices had a point. It made sense to have all the proceedings legally documented.

Chapter XX

Dr. Judy Bishop PhD. was Director of Continuing Education at Loyola-Marymount University, just a few miles from LAX. She had worked endlessly to establish a program for women who had been absent from higher education for at least ten years. The prestigious private Catholic institution certainly would be met with great approval by my family and the location was ideal. Cris, my home and the gates at Terminal 5, for I still retained my flight benefits, were all but minutes away. I needed a good reason for the Jesuit institution to admit me and Judy needed a reason to expand her program. I met all the requirements regarding the continuing education syllabus with the exception of one: I was male.

I was soon back in the executive offices with a plan for my continued education. Barry Lane seemed quite pleased that I had acted on his advice and he supported the plan I had made.

"With this agreement, your career as a flight attendant will be terminated." The finality struck me. I would be designated as a full-time employee with all such benefits and privileges, with the title "Assistant to the CEO." I had no office, no workstation nor would I be expected to appear at the company headquarters on Avion Dr. My only assignment was to attend school on full-time and continue my therapy with Doctor Ramljak. Any advisement or rescheduling of said company duties would be at the discretion of Doctor Joe and Barry Lane.

Forfeiting my flight attendant certifications would be a personal difficulty after all that had occurred. The airline offered me one last flight assignment, a farewell trip, with an extended layover in HNL. For once my mind was crystal clear on the matter; my flying career had truly ended the morning of October 31, 1979 amidst the terror, screams and walls of flames. Everything since had been a forced pantomime.

I embraced the airline's generous offer and tried getting used to my new career as a college student. At the beginning of the school year I strolled tentatively on the clean concrete sidewalk along the neatly-trimmed lawns that sprawled across the campus. There were new challenges to be met. The obvious was that the students were a good 10 to 15 years younger. Then there was the selection and scheduling of classes. Gone were the tailored flight uniforms and regulation accessories. The sleek, tubular lines of the DC-10 were now replaced by the aged structures of an institution with a highly-accredited past.

Of course, the majority of friends and relationships I had developed at the airline were now in the past. It seemed as though I was just plucked out of the flight line, never to be seen again. I saw familiar faces only when Cris and I flew off to some exotic destination. There was always Tommy and David, but there was no longer a workplace environment of people my own age. I had to adjust, adopt my surroundings and remain physically and mentally healthy.

One day on a campus bulletin board I spotted a flyer inviting students interested in trying out for the university crew team to meet the next evening. Rowing was a sport I never envisioned doing, yet the challenge and training intrigued me. A man in his early thirties certainly would not be considered for a collegiate sport.

"They're not looking for an old man." The menaces in my mind accompanied me to school. I sat with all the young jocks in the auditorium where we were directed to meet the following morning at the LMU boat house in Marina Del Rey. Energetic and determined I hoped my strength would be an advantage. The coach, who seemed to be in his early twenties used my age to his benefit.

"Come on, Ed. Don't let these little pimple face brats show you up." He shouted. The pace, routine and repetitive actions in guiding the boat was what I needed. After learning the basics, swiftly gliding along the ocean waters on the lean, sleek craft was thrilling. Across the marina lay a strip of well-known restaurants and bars. The chatter and laughter could be heard across the canal where we practiced.

"Another Bohemia," I envisioned my request to a bartender. I wondered if there might be any flight crew I would know over there, enjoying a relaxing afternoon after a three-day trip.

Instead, my circumstances had offered me another path where my physical strength might keep me competing where my mental endurance had failed. I felt a sense of accomplishment when I learned that I had made the team, although there was a hint of a possible motive in their acceptance of me.

"He's old enough to buy beer for our parties," one young optimist observed. I smiled, happy to go to crew each day after classes. It calmed my demons.

I relished the opportunities provided to me in the classroom and although it had been more than a decade since I had been a student, I held my own. I was not twenty-one years of age nor did I want to be. I would return home and spend my evenings studying. With time it turned into a lonely existence.

In another generous gesture from Mr. Lane, my flight benefits for Cristiano, myself and my parents would now include extra "companion passes." I was being given the opportunity to bring along a friend or a date, if the load factor of any given flight allowed it. With several weeks off at a time from classes I once again could be found wandering the world. But soon, a wrinkle appeared in this fanciful lifestyle. In these ventures I was fortunate to meet a host of new and interesting people. They had a job, a schedule to keep and, friends. What I offered was different.

"Well, you see, I work for this airline, but I really don't have to go to work, I mean." The whole attempt at trying to explain my situation sounded suspicious. "I was involved in this airline disaster." Eyes and mouths would widen. What normal individual would offer to take a single female to Hawaii on a first date? But that is exactly what I suggested to someone I felt I had something in common with.

There were individuals who accompanied me on some wild and fun excursions, enjoying all the amenities, including first-class service. But it was all an illusion. I abandoned high-flying dates for more time with my son. Loneliness was becoming a menacing partner with my other issues. It was exceedingly difficult on the nights without Cris. All too often I would simply lock myself away, fearing to venture outside where people mingled, communicated and developed relationships. El Gato had no workplace to be responsible to, so the wrath inside my heart stirred. I had traveled the world and was still no closer to answering the troublesome question.

An ugly issue was now spoiling the compassionate plan Barry Lane had initiated for my benefit.

"Oh, so the company bought you off." The statements differed slightly in their presentation, but their interpretation added up to one thing in my troubled mind: my hands were stained with blood money. No matter how hard I tried to explain or justify the significance of the help I was receiving, the conclusion by others led in one direction.

"Where do I sign up for such a deal?" A foolish acquaintance joked. Astounded by his ignorance, I could only sneer at the impudent ass.

With few people of my age to associate with at the university, I fell deeper into isolation. I resisted leaving my home except for school. My saving grace was my court appointed time with Cris. I perfected the procedure of travel as a single parent. Along with my regulation F/A suitcase, there was the backpack with the necessities of Cris. Including were various toys to occupy his attention. We waited, finely dressed, for our names to be called at gate 56 for an over-booked flight to HNL. Fortunately, Cris and I were assigned the last two available seats in first class.

"Welcome aboard, Eddy." The friendly F/A showed us to our seats. I quickly tried to store away our carry-on luggage wherever possible. Cristiano was excited in what was now becoming a fanciful mode of transportation for the young boy. I adjusted his seatbelt and rose to remove my sport coat as the aircraft jerked away from the gate.

"Hey, did they charge you full price for the boy?" The bizarre inquiry caught me off guard as I handed my coat to one of the crewmembers and quickly sat in my seat while the DC-10 began to taxi for take-off. I looked across the aisle at a finely groomed blond gentleman who had asked the question, eyes wide with wonder, obviously waiting for a response. It is made very clear to a new associate in training that while traveling on a company-issued pass, one is to be appropriately dressed and never divulge the reason for our ability to travel, especially while seated in first class. I remained silent. "Did they charge you full fare for the boy because these seats cost a pretty penny?" The polished looking man, who seemed to be traveling with a spouse or girlfriend, would not quit. He wanted an answer. I simply smiled and focused on the flight attendants' safety demo.

"Hurray!" yelled a jubilant Cris as we rolled down the runway, the cabin slightly shuddering. He was the only child in the first-class cabin. Passengers seated nearby chuckled at his enthusiasm. The massive jet rose up into the clear blue skies, heading over the Pacific. We were eagerly looking forward to a leisurely time in paradise.

We leveled out at cruising altitude and the pleasure of being in-flight filled me once more. The fuselage had become a soothing cocoon, far more familiar and enjoyable than being on the ground. There were no demons or depraved voices to accompany me while with my son.

"Up here there can be no disagreements with his mother," I whispered to myself. The boy and I could simply board a company jet and be whisked away, feeling no guilt or the sickness of blood money on my hands. I was once again Eddy Valenciana, employee #21196-1. I came to realize that the cabin of a DC-10 felt more like a home than the earth below. At 35,000' I was grateful and content.

"What did they charge you for the boy?" The man was relentless, and contempt quickly sabotaged my joy. I simply smiled and shook my head politely.

Once the meal was completed a kind F/A, Jackie, took Cris on a walk to explore the aircraft. I walked forward for some personal time in the F/C galley at 1R. I stopped and my eyes focused in on the F/A station.

"This is where Karen was." I began to feel a great sense of peace. I wished I could be with them. There was so much I wanted to tell them, so much they could teach me. I looked around the galley and longed to spend all my time aboard the DC-10 adrift amongst the clouds, never landing.

"Karen and the rest are just fine," I said. "They reached their destination." This put a smile on my face.

"Did they charge you full price for the boy? What do you do?" The words startled me as I snapped out of my pleasant dream and was again face-to-face with my inquisitor. He had me cornered in the 1R galley.

461

"I travel a lot," I mumbled, caught off-guard. I focused on his light-colored polo shirt with its logo of a highly-regarded golf location. He also sported a pale-blue pinstriped coat and white patent leather loafers.

"Yeah, we have a condo on the islands," the talkative stranger carried on. I was blocked with my back against the fuselage and unable to make an escape. I fidgeted and squirmed but still he would not set his captive free.

"Yeah, we usually spend all our time on Maui." He would not shut up. I adjusted my tie and found myself sweating and getting agitated, feeling penned in.

I began to recall being trapped, surrounded by fire in Mexico, and once again smelled the foul odor of jet fuel. I could see the traveler's lips moving but I was now deaf to the outside world.

"Mi mamá, por favor." Words seemed to echo off the curved sides of the cabin wall.

"Help me! Help me!" The screams began but just as quickly began to fade.

"Played golf at Poipu Bay, great course. So, what do you do?"

"Huh?"

"Your line of work?" His eyes widened and eyebrows rose high atop his head. I waited for a moment and thought.

"I am in import/export," I stated nonchalantly. My words triggered an immediate response.

"Yeah, what kind, high end automobiles?" I could see I had piqued his interest, so I did my best to dampen it.

"Ah, no, I deal strictly with Colombia." His square chin fell like an elevator whose cables had been severed; all the way to the ground. He fumbled badly in an effort to continue our conversation.

"Well, I better get back to the little lady." And he was gone.

My son and I were in our element on the beaches and streets of Waikiki. Cristiano also bonded with Uncle Lonnie, my friend on the windward side of Oahu. If a fundamental sense of family stability was beyond me, then I would bestow the gift of travel to the boy combined with unconditional love. This provided an arena that was most consistent in our unique situation. It certainly would not have been my first choice in the development of a son, but his adventures provided a pathway to strong character, confidence and knowledge. The pages of his flight Yoda logbook began to fill quickly. Each trip provided messages and autographs from cockpit crews of many airlines. Once it was over the boy went back to Sofia and I sunk back into depression.

On layovers my erratic and deplorable behavior continued. And no matter the city, there was always a bully present at each establishment, though his name and looks changed from town to town. There he would stand, defiantly, in the midst of the grunge gazing down like a bird of prey at the defenseless. He would be selective in his decision to punish the crippled for no reason but self-gratification and dominance. If he could snatch away their drink, food, money, drugs and eventually their soul, he would. Antimundo was not very fond of their kind and made a diplomatic effort to persuade them to change their wicked ways.

"You're going to sign the fucking paper!"

But why restrict my misadventures to the cities of *my* airline? Why not find more fertile ground for bedlam? The back streets of any major city worldwide became open for exploration. Muerto raised the stakes and I must admit Antimundo was fascinated. I had the means to prepare myself for a game of Chess with him so why not expand the playing field. During the week I worked hard, attended classes, trained on campus, rested and prepared myself. I studied the school calendar, planning my itineraries for my dysfunctional journeys. During the seasonal breaks from classes I was whisked away, foolishly, fearless of the possible consequences; but that was what was so enticing. I hurried to catch a flight to NYC. The next leg would take me to London, then onward, with a grueling flight to Bombay, India.

"Your perception has been distorted by the events of this trauma, so you need to be aware that your subconscious directs you into peril." I not only had ignored Dr. Joe's advice; I developed a fancy for the perilous. Walking out of the wreckage of a broken fuselage engulfed in flames changed my concept of mortality. It was now me against Muerto. Escaping his grip fed my adrenaline and a need for even more extreme challenges.

Misery resides throughout the world and the lost can be found in every city and in every culture. The Irish and Scots love to fight. At the drop of a hat they will rush you no matter how cockeyed they might be. The Italians would rather insult you. But in my travels around the world I saw significant differences. Many of the condemned in the U.S. had submitted to a slow process of death through the simple lack of money. In other countries the lost who had given up on life seemed to be doomed by social class. Some were poor, uneducated and denied basic opportunities. But they did not delight in punishing others suffering from the same conditions. I could have written a thesis called, "International Street Life. No matter the city, my mind and body would suffer injuries more often than not. Doctor Ramljak was becoming extremely concerned by now.

Fortunately, my finances were in order despite my behavior. I purchased a new convertible coupe, maroon with a white interior and top, an extravagant toy for "the boys." Cristiano screamed with delight driving down Pacific Coast Highway with the top down. To vent pent-up anxiety, I would sometimes park the convertible at LAX on Aviation Drive near The Proud Bird Restaurant and Bar, sitting directly under the "flight-line of approach." Cris and I, wrapped in warm coats and light gloves, would spy the lights of aircraft a great distance away to the east.

"What type of plane is it, Cris?"

"7-2-7," he called out. He began to learn the shapes of the various planes quickly.

"I say DC-8." Father and son stretched our necks and squinted our eyes, trying to determine if our guess would be proven right. The glare of the landing lights and the sound of wailing jet engines grew with each second.

"Time to put the plugs on," I yelled as we both cupped our ears with our hands. Suddenly the massive metallic cylinder roared with all its great power, just meters over our heads.

"YYYEEEAAAAHHHH!!!" We'd scream, then turn to watch the great ship land on the tarmac. Rubber and concrete kissed with friction, creating a wisp of smoke.

"Look! Here comes another one." Cristiano stood and pointed. The whole amusement ride was beginning once more. We reacted with greater frenzy when it was a jumbo like the DC-10, L1011 or 747 and I screamed at the top of my lungs:

"Screw you Muerto! Here I am, come and get me!" This favorite source of father-son entertainment did not cost a dime.

The school year was concluding, participation in Crew was done and students on the picturesque LMU campus left for the summer. I prepared to travel to Europe for the wedding of my Pan Am friend, J.P. Donici, knowing if I stayed home in hibernation I might self-destruct, despite the time I could spend with Cristiano.

On a bright day I boarded a KLM 747 for Amsterdam. My airline badge encouraged the agent to graciously up-grade me to business class.

"Am I a student, a flight attendant, a member of management, or just lost in limbo?" Being in limbo made the most sense. After two adventurous days in the capital of the Netherlands I boarded a flight to Madrid where, in a week, I would meet up with Tommy and his family. From there we would head to France together. Ah, but the voices tasked me.

"We know where you can find Muerto," they teased.

Arriving at Barajas Airport, Madrid I had one thing on my mind, a taxi ride to the Plaza Mayor for a meal and vino, then to the Atocha train station to catch the express going north. I had bought a first-class ticket to Pamplona, Basque country in the Province of Navarra, heading for La Fiesta de San Fermín. Eager to engage once again with Death: I would run with the bulls.

The festivities began on the train and an all-night party allowed no one any sleep, so I joined in on the tomfoolery. I would choose to discard common sense onto the cobblestone wayside of Pamplona in the morning, during the first run leading up to the Plaza de Toros. This was no relaxed holiday, but rather an exciting descent into total irresponsibility. I had attended the festival in the past and knew the old town's streets and back alleys, but also knew the confusion and chaos that dominates the stone pathway when the large bulls are released. Total bedlam erupts, kind of like an airline crash.

In the morning, with little sleep and hung over, I positioned myself into the thick mass of bodies on the street with other drunken individuals with the same craving, a testosterone driven instinct for bravado. The music blared as I squeezed a rolled-up newspaper, my only protection. If cornered by a fierce bull, a hard rap upon his sensitive nose was the only way to ward him off, otherwise his sharp horns and sheer weight could tear the flesh and crush the body of anyone unable to get out of the way. This is exactly what I desired.

The Medieval clock high above the historic city hall revealed that just minutes remained before the first fireworks would explode, signaling the gate keepers to release the impatient bulls. The crowds gathered tightly behind the barriers along the pathway while some hung out the windows and off balconies of the old buildings that lined the route: a spectacle of vivid colors swaying with excitement high above. The red scarf of a maiden momentarily caught my eye.

"You're cleared on the right; you're cleared on the right." The Mexican Tower whispered anxiously in my head. Individuals wearing large, paper mache masks from medieval times whirled in exhilaration. I glanced around at the participants, many dressed in the traditional white pants and shirts with red beret and sash, still drinking heavily. Long streams of red wine squirted down from their full "bota" bags straight into their mouths. The bags, made from hide, were also used to spray the unsuspected: those who were determined to be too well-dressed or too clean by festival standards. The atmosphere was made complete with the echo of blaring trumpets, pounding drums and the exited yelling in languages from all over the world. There was French, German, Eastern European, and of course Spanish. I became dizzy as I briskly made my way through the thicket of people.

"Who looks overweight or slow?" I asked myself. "Who looks like they might fall on the route and become an obstacle?" There had to be a game plan. "Where are the emergency exits?" One had to be quick and nimble to stay alive.

Suddenly there was the crackle of fireworks and the mad race was on. At first the participants gently pushed forward while anticipating the horde of muscular "Bos Taurus" coming our way soon. I jogged along near the fence that held back the onlookers.

"Viva San Fermín!" I passed a lovely Basque girl with soft dark hair and stunning features screaming at the top of her lungs.

"Viva España!" echoed a deep voice. Cries from the crows indicated that the bulls were right behind us, and the pace quickened up the corridor. Suddenly, there on the corner, leaning on the top wooden rail of the fence, I saw him. Muerto simply gave a slight smile and rhythmically waved his boney hand back and forth. The game was on and I was filled with adrenaline. The crowd moved rapidly now, as to my left a large man tumbled. I raced on, slipping through those in front of me when I could. I paused for a split second to determine by the reaction of the crowd on the street and above, the location of the bulls. My first estimation was about fifty to sixty yards, not a safe buffer with speed of these animals. Still clinging to my rolled newspaper, I did not see the young man fall right in front of me. I stumbled over him and quickly tumbled to the side, hugging the wall of a merchant's store. Looking up I saw the panic in the eyes of the participants. This was truly a confrontation with Death, and I loved it.

I tried to stand but was pushed down again by the rushing crowd as the first bulls came into view. A young man with bell-bottom jeans and lying in the middle of the cobblestone street seemed to be singled out by one drooling beast. The animal was enormous but magnificent. I was mesmerized by his structure; every muscle was visible. The bull snorted, raised his head in defiance and quickly turned in my direction. I instinctively ditched into a doorway, but it was too late; in a second he was confronting me. In a panic, I raised my arm and swatted his wet nose as hard as I could with my funnel of newspaper. He froze, just standing and perhaps laughing at my futile gesture.

"¡Eh, coño!" Two brave teens yelled at the beast from behind and startled him as one jumped forward and swatted the bull's massive hind end. Before retreating to safety, the boys raised their tanned faces and smiled at me in celebration of their bravado. The black bull turned and charged up the street.

"He must be the first bull" I thought, but then viewed the scene approaching from behind: a wave of black with a glistening from those opalescent lethal horns. Human bodies were swirling like an ocean current, swaying from one side to the other, working their way up the incline to the plaza. The mass swept over anything or anyone in its path. The smart thing to do was to huddle in a doorway until the immediate danger passed. But I was not that smart. The desire to directly confront Muerto was too great. Like a drug, the hysteria drew me into the swirl of the thundering mass as it turned the corner, trampling and stomping whatever obstacle was in the way.

"¡Madre de Dios!" In a split second saw a human body tossed in the air by the first herd of bulls. I sped recklessly trying to distance myself from the deadly horns. The pack ahead suddenly came to a stop as someone leapt from one side of the road or the other. The group resembled a human zipper ripping open and I saw the reason for the panic. The first arrogant bull that had cornered me decided to change direction. The muscled male was retreating down the hill and woe be to whoever failed to see him. The beast snorted insults to us all.

"¡Eh, toro! ¡Toro!" A man stood in defiance. Others dared to come close to swat the animal. I spotted two young boys lying on the stone avenue. One, wearing a blue and yellow shirt, was doing the right thing. He huddled motionless in a fetal position with his hands protecting his blond head. The bull acknowledged his submission, then turned his thick-necked head to the other lad who looked of North African heritage. This poor boy's fear appeared as defiant to the animal. He tried to quickly crawl to the fence, but the beast jumped to block his escape. Luckily, a brave Spaniard in the traditional white garb took command, confidently leaping between the boy and the bull.

"¡Fácil, toro!" He gracefully slid along the length of the bull. He lightly laid the palm of his hand along the broadside muscles distracting the animal away allowing the boy to escape.

"¡Viva!" The crowd roared as arms and hands reached down to pull the boy from danger.

I, on the other hand, cowered against a wall. I sorely wanted to challenge Death once again but had no aspirations of being gallant or elegant in the process. In fact, it was the opposite. It was now total stupidity that directed my decisions. The beast trotted forward, continuing his journey up the hill while the screams of the observers signaled another wave of bulls approaching. Bodies began to move more rapidly now toward the bull ring, the only immediate place of safety. As we passed the renowned bust of Ernest Hemingway at the entrance of the Plaza de Toros, the street dipped down to the tunnel into the open ring. Descending into the darkness, the screams and yells became deafening as they echoed off the concrete tunnel walls.

"I'm home free." I relaxed as the bright sunlight expanded while I approached the open ring. But suddenly one person went tumbling, then another. All at once, the whole group fell forward, becoming an immovable wall of human flesh. Hands of all shades rose up in panic. Arms and legs jerked in an eternal knot, blocking the exit for the fast-moving wave of bovine right behind us. Finding myself on the top of this pile of lost souls, I thought it simple enough to roll forward, down the few feet of rapidly growing human barricade. I lurched forward but was unable to move. I looked down and found myself seized by the hands and the arms of the people below me, all grasping in panic. I found eyes, light and dark, wide open in desperation. One man's teeth were capped; I noticed the gold during his plea for help. There were limbs in an orchestration of various colors. Blue jeans of all shades squirmed like a giant snake. There were piles of muscle and bone twisting, seeking self-preservation. Their motions gave life to the walls of the arena. I looked around and envisioned flames around us.

"Why didn't you help me?" Young Javier's voice rang clear.

"My daughter! My mother!" A woman's voice echoed. Was I back on the tarmac? The herd now entered the tunnel and I knew I had to act. Unceremoniously wrenching open the fingers of some man who was gripping my jeans, I kicked aside the entangled legs and slipped off into the open ring just as the pack hit the barrier with great force. I ran to the nearby ring wall, ready to leap to safety. Frustrated, the scared and angry animals tried to retreat, going backwards on the roadway once again, but then forced to push forward by the incoming crowds. I looked up into the stands of the packed arena and spotted Muerto. He was filled with delight as he orchestrated the chaos.

Some died that hot, muggy day in the streets and bull ring in the Province of Navarra, but I and thousands of fellow revelers had survived. We all drank, feasted and danced through the streets of the old Basque town throughout the night. In the morning my head swirled like a beehive, a result of the wine, cognac and anise. Stupidly, I convinced myself to challenge Muerto once again.

Have fun but don't get idiotic, I told myself over and over as I hurried down to the plaza. I became careless, or was it what I intended all along? The lines of subconscious and reality were becoming blurred. That morning I allowed myself to be cornered on the final turn leading up to the arena. With a swift kick of a rambunctious young bull's hind leg, I ended up on the cold cobblestones, my head ringing and throbbing. A faceless voice inquired,

"¿Estás bien, hombre?" I arose and staggered to the fence. That festive night there was a commemorative nasty bruise on my brow for all to see. The obvious decision at this point should have been to leave Pamplona, meet up with Tommy in Madrid and continue the rest of my journey. I did not make that decision. Instead, the contusion was looked upon by my fellow celebrants as a badge of honor, one that was worth celebrating. Death was throwing a party and I was an honored guest.

After six days of celebration and debauchery I was barely able to climb onto an old bus for and an eight-hour ride to Madrid. It was the middle of July and hot!

"Please make sure your seat belts are tightly fastened. I just wish to advise you that there will be no air-conditioning available on this segment of your trip. We sincerely apologize if we have inconvenienced you." The large red-and-white coach pulled out of the Pamplona depot and my head and body made it very clear that payment for my behavior was now due. Being severely hung over, I suffered for my iniquities.

Caked in dirt mixed with wine and unshaven, I gingerly held on and stepped off the bus in Madrid looking like a homeless vagabond. I moved slowly through the bus terminal, turning the heads of the "Madrileños" as I reached the exit. My bruised body struggled along the Gran Vía towards the hotel where Tommy and his wife Takako were staying.

"The obvious result of liquor." I heard one woman deliver her verdict in Spanish as the doorman, with a badge indicating the name "Ignacio" stared at me suspiciously. The majority of the well-dressed patrons did not notice me at first as I moved to the front desk where a man began to repeat a memorized speech.

"Bienvenido, señor." He stopped in mid-sentence as all at once I was surrounded by a security man, Ignacio and the manager on duty. None of the distinguished Spaniards seemed pleased by my presence.

"Por favor, Señor Tomás Acoba." I requested. Not a word was spoken as a clerk looked at his manager, hesitated, then began to look for Tommy's name. I turned and faced my inquisitors.

"Sign the fucking paper!" I was in a foreign country once again, subject to their laws, looking like a rodent. I should not inhabit such space. I took out my passport from my pouch and offered it up in submission.

"San Fermín," where the only words I could speak. The doorman's angry face began to slowly soften.

"¿Fuiste a Pamplona?" The security man raised his hand and pointed at me. I nodded.

"La Fiesta de San Fermín." They relaxed, and I became one of the boys. The manager chuckled shaking slightly. Ignacio placed his hand on my shoulder, my six-days-dirt-and-wine-caked shoulder. These finely dressed men were looking at me almost in awe. The Magnificent Edmundo in Madrid! Then my Admirers resumed their professional demeanor. Certainly, I could not be left in the large white lobby with its high ceilings and artistic trim. The manager urged the clerk to work faster in contacting "Señor Acoba" so I could be on my way as quickly as possible.

"Holy shit!" Tommy was as cordial as ever. "You need a shower and a beer. Well maybe not the beer but the shower for sure."

I would eventually regain respectability after a shower and a cold San Miguel with my dear friend. Tommy tolerated my behavior because that is what true friends do. His intellect allowed him to always find the humor in my journey, insuring me that I would find a way out of the bewilderment I produced. He, along with Takako, provided stability at this point in our trip. They certainly deserved my best behavior as we jointly traveled on to Barcelona. With Tommy, I always felt safe.

Leaving Barcelona, we boarded a train heading north into France focused on another grand celebration Le Festival d'Avignon. Before we knew it we were dancing on the courtyard of a Medieval Gothic structure known as Palais des Papes (the palace of the popes). Takako was wise enough to not let the two of us get carried away.

A few days later we boarded another train to attend the wedding of our friend Jean Pierre Donici, a flight attendant with Pan American Airways. His fiancée Carine lived in Sur Sallon, our destination. The ceremony was performed at the Cathedral of St. Vincent and all guests were then bused to the Château Rully for the reception. There were attendees from fifteen countries and five religions. Most of the non-locals were airline employees. Pan American, Air India, Iberia Airlines, Pakistani International, Trans World Airlines, United Airlines and my own were represented. The faces were intriguing and the languages fascinating. The variety was a testament to the limitless boundaries an airline position afforded an individual. The champagne flowed and the music echoed through the valley and lush hills of the French countryside. The setting sunbathed the courtyard with hues of yellow and orange.

"Eddy is also a flight attendant," J.P. announced as I turned and stood face to face with two Pan Am F/As. The statement stung me. It triggers the voices to be uninvited guests to this celebration.

"You are not a flight attendant, not anymore." I had not flown a flight as a working crewmember in a long time. The two ladies smiled, waiting for me to respond to the introduction.

No, I'm not a flight attendant, I am a full-time student. I am employed by an airline, a really good one, but I never go to work, you know? Of course, that wasn't the response I gave.

"I fly," I muttered.

"Do you work the DC-10? Where? Out of LAX?" Other F/As wanted to compare notes and discuss their latest adventures to exotic locations, whether on a pass or assigned layover. I no longer fit in and that hurt because often the only place I felt I truly belonged was with my crewmates from 2605. I envied them, the dead.

The evening's festivities continued far into the wee hours with the music and screaming guitar blaring above the partygoers. Usually I would overindulge, but this night I hesitated, even though I so wished to anesthetize my guilt.

I was soon swept up by a group of inebriated flight attendants who decided to take a late night stroll up an old dirt road to a hilltop overlooking the moonlit valley. With wine bottles in hand a couple yelled a salute in French.

"Hourra pour J.P. et Carine!" A chorus of happy songs ensued as the mixture of locals and F/A's settled us on a grassy knoll. We became mesmerized by the valley's radiant beauty and serenity.

"Qu'est-ce que c'est?" (What's that?) Across the landscape, on the opposite rim of the hills was an unusual sight. It looked like a large glow worm making its way laterally along the hillside and gradually turning in our direction. The uncertain spectacle was divided into sections each challenging the darkness with its own luminescent colors. I so wished to partake in this glow worm's journey through a filament of emptiness where I felt no pain. As the fanciful light moved closer, we all realized it was, in reality, the late-night express train from the south of France heading north to Lyon and possibly on to Paris. Tommy and I and Takako would also be heading soon to the French capital.

Paris, in the company of the of dear friends, was splendid. We shared intellectual conversations, fine dining, and an appreciation of the culture and artistry. But just at the crest was trouble, for Muerto waited patiently.

Now, away from the solid anchor of Tommy Acoba, I returned to Amsterdam. I sat in a smoked-filled hashish cafe considering the challenges that might soon confront me. There was a continually growing part of me that wanted to go over the edge, to see exactly what Muerto had in store. In some ways I wanted to refuse to acknowledge the blessings of life I had been granted.

It was soon time to return home. I was extremely anxious to see Cristiano, I had missed him dearly. On the flight home I fantasized that one day when he was a grown man, we could come back to relive these events. Well, maybe not all of them. Pamplona certainly would always be a consideration.

Sitting aboard a KLM 747, I also felt strongly motivated to continue my studies. I needed to show the airline, Barry Lane in particular, that the company's resources were being wisely used. There was also the opportunity to return to the crew team enjoying vigorous workouts that settled my troubled soul.

No one at the airline other than Berry Lane knew what was going on with me. I had kept the specifics of my contract with the company secret even from my parents. They asked no questions. They seemed bit fearful to know what ensued. It was all so confusing. Eddy was here one day and gone the next.

"Limbo," I whispered to myself at 35,000', at Our Lady of Talpa School in Boyle Heights, the sisters taught us early on about Limbo.

"Limbo is where the innocent goes when they die but never had the opportunity to be baptized." It really was a smart move by the airline. I had become unstable and by isolating me from my strongest support, other crewmembers, I could not "infect" them with a messy situation. There was also the added danger that I was volatile and could possibly lose it. It was best that such an occurrence not happen at 35,000'! On paper, the opportunities and benefits looked like a single man's dream. Unfortunately, it came with skeletons and demons attached. "Yes, I had to be in Limbo."

Arriving at LAX I rushed over to Terminal 5. These days I noticed a more buoyant attitude amongst company employees. It cheered me to see how the airline had rebounded. I entered the lounge and was struck by the number of new uniformed crewmembers that were about. Many F/A classes had been conducted since my "exile" and the faces of the new hires reminded me of that initial feeling of invulnerability.

"I am gonna fly, high, fast and with just a tad sense of irresponsibility. I am going to enjoy every second of it." I remembered the feeling. In my company mailbox there were no personal letters on my paycheck.

"You can't complain with the deal you got out of this," the voices lectured. "The airline has given you a free ride, much more than you deserve." Yes, my financial needs were being well met. My education was being provided. If Cris or I got sick, there was health care. The airplanes were always available. I supposed that no one in the company actually cared what arrangements were made for me. Under my paycheck was a small company envelope: I recognized the handwriting of Mr. Lane's secretary. The note inside to me to contact Mr. Lane's office at my convenience. My rehab plan had been running efficiently, so what could this be?

Contacting Barry Lane's office, I hurried to catch the bus back to the executive office and a meeting with my benefactor.

Yeah, I may be screwed up in the head, but I would do anything for Mr. Lane. I smiled and let the thought linger. *"The Kindly Executive and the Lunatic."* What a duo. I thought it sounded like a bad movie title as I once again walked the marble floors, peeking in on the adjacent offices but not seeing many familiar faces. There was a new regiment of soldiers planning, sharing information and seeing to the needs of the airline. It seemed I had entered a rift in time. I was a full-time college student now. These were the real employees. Even with the deal I had, I did not feel right.

Entering Mr. Lane's office, I was surprised to see another gentleman with him.

"Eduardo. Please come in." Barry rose to greet me, courteous as ever. "What happened to your head?" Embarrassed, I stood shifting from one foot to the other.

"It is a long story, sir. Really, I am okay." I quickly focused my attention to the other individual whom I did not know. He seemed friendly enough, an elder gentleman with reddish hair, rimmed bifocals, confident looking in the typical Brooks Brothers suit.

"Ed, this in Robert Wilcox." I looked at his eyes and tried to read his expression, sensing no hostility. Once we were all seated, Mr. Lane verified the rumor that had been running through the offices and the terminals. He was leaving to enjoy a well-deserved retirement.

"Bob here will be seeing to your needs." Mr. Lane said as the new Executive Vice-President extended his hand.

"My door is always open to you, Ed." I shook Wilcox's hand but had my suspicions. But I wasn't worried; our contract stated that Doctor Ramljak made all the final decisions. As I sat with my superiors, I mused that Doctor Joe would not be too pleased with me these days.

When Barry Lane rode into the sunset, he earned the right to leave with a feeling of great self-satisfaction and accomplishment. The airline was just days away from closing the doors when he took the reins. Now the company was financially sound. He had taken on a great task and completed it, leaving a few extra bucks in the pockets of us all, the associates and owners of the airline.

At home I re-focused my attention on Doctor Ramljak. I had left for Europe abruptly without letting him in on my itinerary, as I was sure he would frown on my adventure in Pamplona. My forehead still bore a bruise where the bull kicked some sense into me. Prior to my leaving for Europe I had also missed a session, something I had never done in the previous years. I knew my behavior was irrational and I was not smart enough nor foolish enough to try to deceive the wise man. I had just avoided him and run off.

"Where were you on the 29th of last month?" Finally pressed to face the music, I sat placidly facing his inquiry. I squirmed a bit as I sat down, there was no use trying to lie my way out of my indiscretions.

"On the 29th I was in Amsterdam smoking kief." My usually smiling mentor tilted his round head forward looking at me, just above the frame with his glasses, eyebrows raised high. He hesitated a bit, then continued.

"Where were you on the 9th of last month?" He looked down at the calendar on his wooden desk.

"On the morning of the 9th I was half-intoxicated from two solid days of drinking and dodging bulls through the streets of Pamplona." Dr. Joe once again just stared. The room grew very silent and I grew nervous with my mentor's silence. "I even got kicked by one nasty critter while I was there." I leaned forward so he could inspect the bruise. He was not impressed.

"Are you abusing substances?"

"Yes,"

"Are you abusing alcohol?"

"Yes,"

"Are you out of control when abusing these substances?"

"Yes."

"Does your ex-wife know you are abusing these substances?"

"No."

"Does anyone at the airline know of this behavior?"

"No."

"Is this the reason you have missed your appointments?"

"Yes." There was another pause. Dr. Joe's demeanor relaxed.

"You know that these substances disturb your level of adjustment." I remained silent, head down.

"Such activities are high-jacking the pleasure centers of your brain. You will be worn down and suffer."

"Maybe that is what I deserve."

"What about this program you received from the airline? Isn't that worth fighting for?"

"Hey, my grades at LMU have been solid. Not bad for a guy who had been out of school for so many years." I tried to deflect the truth.

"Do you like your airline?" The question hit me. I raised my head and stared at the man squarely. Was he questioning my loyalty after all what I went through in the name of that company? "Look here Doc, I was branded that morning in October of '79. Even if I wished to distance myself from that name and logo it would be impossible. My only alternative is to somehow find comfort in my loyalty. That comfort was Barry but now he is leaving." I fell silent and lost my train of thought. Dr. Joe stared. I had not answered his question.

"Hell yeah, I care for that company." I continued, "I am also very angry with the airline."

"Why are you angry at them?"

"I am angry that they backed away and did not stand firm and issue a challenge to Mexico's final report. I am angry that they lied to the families of my crewmates. I am angry that they swept the whole thing away, very neatly. I am angry that I had to be witness to all of this and more." I was shouting as if speaking to a large audience. Perhaps I truly wanted to. I viewed the dark silhouette of Dr. Ramljak against the glistening sunlight as he listened intently.

"I see bright colors and the logo of one of our aircraft lifting off the concrete, soaring up into the sky, catching great lift from the streaming winds coming off the ocean. Then, at night, the twisted flaming metal glowing. I can feel the heat and see the blood. I am angry at my airline for condemning me to re-living these memories." I became flustered. "I should have gone with my crew!" The doctor jerked forward.

"What do you mean?"

"I had the right – No!...to just fade away with them."

"Explain."

I hesitated for a moment trying to fathom the dimension of death. My first thoughts were of my poor mother, good hearted and loving, standing at the foot of my grave. I most likely would have been remembered by the family with a photo, dressed in my F/A uniform, placed proudly on the dining room wall. Through her faith, prayers and love, I perhaps would have been raised to near sainthood in her eye's, though most family members and friends would know better. My thought then wandered to Cristiano and I instantly began to weep.

"This battle you are waging," my doctor rose up to offer me a tissue as he spoke. "This battle with Muerto? You know, this type of behavior is to his advantage. Maybe we can figure out a way to get back on the positive." Dr. Joe let me know he with me no matter what. For a man condemned, I truly was blessed.

I felt encouraged by the doctor's insistence on more frequent appointments. He wanted a tighter rein on me, and with good reason. He also encouraged me to return to the gym in earnest.

"I want you to resist going out of the country for the time being," he requested. I flinched, but he made it clear that I limit my travels.

"What about Kauai?"

"What?"

"What if I promise to limit my travels to Kauai?" Dr. Joe thought for a moment.

"Ok, but no jungle man!"

"Okay, I'll try to straighten up my act."

As I drove down the 405-freeway heading to the South Bay with a piece of resurrected resolve. I took my studies seriously although I was not sure where such a degree would lead me. I doubled my efforts in the gym. The demand for a disciplined routine helped to ground me. But life's events, even in the most positive of circumstances, delivered Muerto's scorn.

The TV screamed the tale of Japan Airlines Flight 123. The 747 was crippled by a blast, then floundered across the skies above the Japanese homeland. The crew had no sense of direction or the ability to correct the damage to the ship. Muerto would toy with the victims for some time, like the sadist that he is, before slamming the jumbo jet into the ridge of a high mountain. Five-hundred-and-five passengers perished along with fifteen crew members. Instantly I was back on the tarmac at Benito Juárez Airport trying to deal with the flashbacks and of course the trauma. Soon, the media blared once more with the destruction of Air India 747 Flight 182 which blew up over the Atlantic claiming three-hundred and twenty-nine victims. Muerto was busy gathering bounty in the friendly skies. I was believing he was still annoyed by the fact that I had slipped away. Once again, Antimundo emerged, filled with hatred and a desire for vengeance.

Death was not finished. He struck again; this time much closer to home. An Aeromexico DC-9 on descent into LAX had its tail sheared off by a Piper PA-28-181 Archer. Both planes went down; the DC-9 while in flames plummeted into the local community of Cerritos. Sixty-seven in both planes and an additional fifteen on the ground paid the ultimate price. The scenes from the TV screen put me right back in there, next to the flames, the charred bodies. Again, I heard the endless cries of the damned and smelled the odor of jet fuel and burning bodies. That night I discovered a 24-hour weight room, a place to exorcise my demons. I listened to the grieving survivors who would soon suffer what I and the families of 2605 had endured. But I had to heal, especially for Cris. There was no other option except my self-destruction.

Chapter XXI

Al Greenleaf now ran the airline, a strong leader determined to continue the airline's recovery. Yet, this in itself brought new concerns to the employees. Financially weak airlines were being "assimilated" into bigger, stronger companies. Many of the famous airlines that were there at the dawn of commercial aviation ceased to exist. Our now-healthy airline, with all her lucrative destinations, made the bigger carriers lick their chops. One such suitor who arrived at Avion Drive was an economically solid company based in the South. Their domestic routes stretched mostly through the eastern sector of the country, so our beloved airline would be a fine addition, doubling the other carrier's territory. People were put into play, jostling for the right time and right approach to make things happen.

For the rest of the summer I would retain primary custody of Cris and, since I had no work hours or classes, I could devote all my time and attention to his needs - a blessing for us both. I adhered to Doctor Ramljak's advice to stay away from international travel, and rented a house in Poipu, Kauai where Cris and I indulged ourselves in a playground of a majestic setting by the beach. The nurturing spirits of the island soothed and eased my troubled soul.

Sofia would have Cris one weekend during that period. This was not a problem as my son, and I would simply board another DC-10 from HNL to LAX. Cris visited his mother and I visited Doctor Joe. It seemed as though things just might be falling into place. The guiding light was Joseph Ramljak.

"One day you will control it," Dr. Joe encouraged me. "You can keep it in a box if you wish, file it away and if you deem it right, take it out anytime. Then, close it up and file it away once more." The jovial man with his plump features and gray mustache approved of my recent efforts. He meant so much to me. On that Monday morning we would soon be lifting into the skies once more, back to Kauai. When I finally did return to the

480

mainland Cris was returned to Sofia and I prepared myself for my final semester of school.

There would be instances when I did choose to open the box and listen to the CVR Recording. I wanted to satisfy my need to know the truth. I also studied the APHA report by Captain Ron Banner. He had showed true compassion for my plight. The report, certainly the best written to that point, made it clear that the investigators' inability to get on the crash site hindered any complete, detailed explanation of the truth. It was truly a mystery and the healthier I got, the greater my understanding developed.

In the final split second of the CVR recording there remained the sound of multiple voices screaming almost in unison. There were only three individuals in the cockpit at the time of the impact. I was befuddled. Perhaps it was an electrical glitch. With time I began to feel I understood the sequence of events that Halloween morning. The carefully designed aviation industry safety system that should have prevented our crash, failed. The mistakes were obvious. Even a mere flight attendant like myself could see the truth. The sad part was that I was but one of a few who knew, and the powers-that-be, expected me to remain silent.

My life became fruitful and I began to believe I could, at will, toss to the wayside the events of that horrible day. This "second life" now offered a glimmer of possibilities. I filed away all the material I had accumulated over the years related to the incident. I carefully documented all that had happened up to that point in an organized manner. I turned my attention to trying to understand this strange disease of PTSD recognizing that it was an ailment that one suffered alone and writing down my thoughts provided another tool to ease the burdens. Then my nemesis returned in the Fall.

Like it or not, October 31st will always be difficult, sometimes impossibly difficult. On the first anniversary of the crash, I was confused, not knowing how to react. Would I mourn for my crew mates? Should I allow myself to celebrate my survival? That was what most people thought I should focus on. But I did not mourn, nor would I for many years. I did nothing but feel enormous shame, anger and hatred.

Halloween increasingly became a bigger burden. It was unrelenting as the retail displays rammed it down my throat and Muerto was of course pleased. I would prepare weeks in advance to lessen the impact. Now, with Doctor Joe's help, I was going to meet this year's encounter with a renewed resolve for I had an appointment with him on October 31st. I wouldn't have to deal with it alone in some stinking bar, drinking with Antimundo who would continually bait me.

"This year I am going to beat it." I kept telling myself. I planned to turn the tables and try to concentrate instead on Cris in his little pirate outfit. "This day should be about living!" I felt energetic and reassured as I pulled off the 405 freeway and headed to Westwood. The previous night had been free of cries from the child Javier, ablaze. There was no visit from Reina with pleas for repentance. I drove the convertible coupe with the top down, enjoying a sunny day, heading to my appointment with Doctor Joe.

I grabbed the brass knob of the heavy green door and shoved my hip into it as I had done numerous times. I was stopped cold. The door wouldn't budge. I backed away puzzled, rubbing my hip which was now sore. It was the right time and certainly the right day. Perhaps the Doc was running late or just forgot? I sat on the floor not really knowing what to do.

"You think you're so smart, got everything figured out. Well, you don't. It's October 31st, the day people become dead." The voices emerged viciously. Doctor Ramljak will be here soon, I told myself, sat and tried to relax but Dr. Joe did not arrive, nor did the voices subside. After an hour I could stand it no more and ran down the steps to the photo shop that sat below his office.

"You got a pay phone?" I asked of the proprietor. He simply pointed to the telephone on the wall.

"Yes, I am a patient of Doctor Ramljak. I had an appointment an hour ago, but the door is locked. Can you page him?" The young woman hesitated then put me on hold.

"What is your name?" she asked with a bit of concern. Perhaps I got the days wrong? Wait a minute, I thought. This is definitely Halloween and we made the appointment well in advance.

"Ah, Mr. Valenciana, Doctor Ramljak is not available." The statement was brief.

"Is that all you are going to tell me? What do you mean? I have an appointment." My impatience grew. "Listen, is something wrong?" I became insistent. "Look, this man is my doctor, but he is also my dear friend, I have the right to know." Once again, I was placed on hold.

"Damn it, what the hell is going on!"

"Mr. Valenciana?"

"Yes?" I became more hopeful.

"Ah, Mr. Valenciana?"

"YES?"

"Doctor Ramljak suffered a stroke and I am sorry to have to tell you that he passed away. I'm sorry we were not able to inform you." I stared at a green wall, trying to process the information. It was Halloween and Death had struck hard. Once again, someone close to me was snatched away in an instant.

"Hello, hello, Mr. Valenciana are you alright?"

"Ah, yes, I'm fine. Thank you for the information."

I hung up the phone and slowly walked to the door. I became a zombie. I stopped at the entrance and laid my head against the windowpane, nearly losing consciousness as reality sunk deep in. I gazed up at the outside world. Vehicles drove by and people moved about as normal. There were school children dressed for the festivities of the day. There was a small fairy princess and a boy in a lion suit with a brown fluffy mane on his head. A feisty child in his red devil costume was chased by a woman who I supposed was his teacher. She corralled the active boy and led him back in line with the rest of the children as they came to the busy corner and waited for the light to change. There standing behind the brood was Muerto grinning widely, satisfied with his latest handiwork. I stared into his hollow eyes.

"Are you okay, sir?" I was startled to see the proprietor standing next to me.

"Sorry, ah, no, I mean yes, I am fine, thank you." Still looking concerned, he turned and went back to tending to his shop. I turned quickly and looked again across the street. The children were there but my nemesis had disappeared.

My dear friend Dr. Joe was gone and possibly along with him any chance that I might escape from this mine field I was exiled to. I was devastated. Arriving back at my beach home I rushed inside, closing all the blinds and locking all the windows and doors in an attempt to protect myself.

"Death will surely take me this time."

Josef Ramljak was one of the wisest, kindest people I had ever known. He was snatched away in an instant just like the others. I sat motionless and silent on my sofa in the middle of the living room, in the darkness, awaiting my fate. I focused on a ray of light as the sun began to set over the Pacific Ocean. Yellow and orange filtered through the side slits between the shades. I wanted this day to quickly end. The slivers of light began to fade rapidly, giving way to what was going to be a black night.

"Trick or treat!" the faint echo of children's voices made their way from outside.

"Trick or treat, trick or treat." The voices cried out in cadence to create one sound. I remembered the CVR recording and how the voices blended together at the very end, right on impact. My home stood in the dark, not a single bit of light visible from the outside. The children left, perhaps they fearing my dark house contained some hideous monster inside, and perhaps it did.

"Trick or treat." It was Muerto this time. Soon it became clear as I sat motionless, hiding with fear, he was going to toy with me and watch me squirm. Then I realized he was seducing me to come to him. His power over me had to be complete, desiring my death to be by my own hand.

"Trick or treat."

I was awakened the following morning by the knock on my door. Getting up slowly from the sofa I glanced through the front window and saw an excited little figure by Sofia's side. The devastating news of Doctor Ramljak had so occupied my mind that I forgot Cris would be coming. Hope was now running to embrace me as he rushed in and gave me a big hug. I held him tightly, hoping he could get me through November 1, All Saints Day, alive.

We were soon headed to a theme park in the Los Angeles basin.

"Doctor Joe just died, and you should follow him." The vile voices slammed back at me.

"No! I'm staying with the living," I whispered in response. "There has already been too much pain this Halloween."

"Who you talking to, Daddy?"

"No one son. We're going to Magic Mountain!" I was soon watching Cris on the kiddie rides. He rode a red helicopter and any aircraft he saw. There were also miniature motorboats to enjoy, turning the wheel in make-believe control of the vessel. Cris was indeed getting me through the day.

The amusement park had a reputation for offering some of the latest and most daring roller coasters. Although Cris was far too young to be a passenger, I decided it would be fun anyway to watch. We sat on a bench beside the roller coaster named "Colossus."

Father and son sat close together and studied the white, wooden structure in all its geometric glory. High above was the pinnacle of the ride. The cars were slowly cranked up one side to be released into the grip of gravity and plunge downward. This is where the screams and facial expressions were the most amusing.

The first compartment crept over the top pulling the others behind and gaining momentum. The eyes of men, women, girls and boys all widened at the same instant. Each car released waves of screams that were unnaturally warped, just a split second after the cars sped by.

"I know that sound." I was struck with a truth and I instantly hoped I was wrong. Cristiano unaware clapped with excitement.

"Again!" He requested. I was feeling nauseous. The long, caterpillar-like object slowly crawled up the incline once again. I could see a boy waving to someone on the ground as he first car showed its wide-eyed passengers. A blond man in the first-class cabin threw his arms up in complete submission. Then each coach section revealed itself with terror orchestrating the passengers. The screams followed in unison, filling the air with that familiar warped echo. Then it instantly faded, and the *aircraft* gained distance.

The screams on the tape! It was the passengers of 2605! I sat on the bench at Magic Mountain with my happy little boy when I finally figured out the final scenario of the doomed aircraft. "Dear God!" There were only three people in the cockpit at the moment of impact but the cockpit CVR microphone remained on for the entire period of destruction. The first-class cabin came crashing through the destroyed cockpit and the last screams and cries of the dying were recorded. I remained on the bench unable to get away as the jumbo jet raced by on the rails of Colossus, its death screams trailing behind. But I wanted the screams to return. Cris was next to me, innocently enjoying the show. The young child could not realize that his father was teetering on the verge of insanity.

I faintly recalled driving Cris home. I know I hugged and kissed him as he ran into the arms of his mother. I wondered if I would ever see my son again. Once home, I walked to a wooden cupboard and removed a full bottle of Gran Centenario Tequila.

"Hecho en México," the label read, "100% de agave." The self-destruction began. The more I indulged the more I retreated inward. I locked the windows and doors and continued the abuse in darkness. Only the vivid scenes of hideous pain and sorrow remained. Once again, I was treated to the cries of pain and the smell of burning flesh among the wreckage.

"Mi hijo, mi hijo," I saw a woman on her knees, weeping in despair, reaching out, obviously in great pain.

"Mom," I whispered calmly. It was my mother and then her face suddenly changed. Now, she was Becky's mother. The woman's anguish never subsided. After a few seconds she was Tamlyn's mother and finally Reina's. I realized that all the unfortunate mothers were my mother. They had no one to accept their petition for justice. As a group they were lied to and dismissed. There were those in the company who made a great effort to comfort them, to sympathize and serve, but the mothers never received an explanation of the truth.

I noticed that the bottle of Mexico's finest was half-empty.

"Gosh, it went down so smoothly," I thought. It steadied the demons temporarily, but it also assisted them to slowly rise again, and when they did the result would not be good. "To hell with this glorious life of the cursed and damned." There were so many to blame: the air traffic control for directing the craft to Runway 23 Left, the tower for clearing the flight onto the runway, the airline for allowing two angry men to fly together. Then the *insult* came when the airline and the United States Government became complicit in either hiding or ignoring the truth.

I wanted my contempt for all of them to become stronger. Another shot of Centenario would do it.

"The tape." I stood and realized that there was one thing missing from my little party.

"I need to listen to the tape." I set myself up for a one-way ticket back to hell. Only this time I agreed to let Muerto pilot the craft.

"You're left of the runway."

"Just a bit." The calm before the storm was seductive. I imagined myself in the cockpit, studying their faces and reactions. I imagined Captain Herbert becoming confused with the untimely direction from the tower.

"We're cleared on the right; we're cleared on the right?

The other runway." The impact into the parked truck on Runway 23-Left is clearly audible. Once again, I was on board, strapped to jumpseat 4R.

"Oh Jesus Christ, Oh FUCK!" The captain screamed. I became completely limp, letting the sounds overwhelm me. The tape concluded with the now familiar frantic voices of the victims from First Class. Then silence. I sat in the midst of smoke and flames. The distinct rancid smell of jet fuel surrounded me as I choked and struggled to release my safety harness. I stood in the middle of a horrible catastrophe, knowing in my heart the others had perished.

"Don't leave me behind," I demanded. There was no response. I was left to wander among the carnage. There I sat in my home in Manhattan Beach totally defenseless.

I belong dead. It certainly would get everyone's attention." My eyes widened and I saw a distorted potential solution to everything.

"Why did he do it?" Those I left behind would try to fathom it. The press would certainly jump all over it:

"Maybe we should all take another look at what really happened to drive this former flight attendant to such drastic measures." More appealing to me was that I would finally be gone, joining Muerto and his rogue crew forever. At least I would be out of this tormenting mine field.

"Will I ever be good enough?"

"NO!"

So, there I stood at the end of the Manhattan Beach pier, gazing into the skies along the coast toward LAX. *"If you survive a plane crash you will be better equipped to save others."* It was Mari's voice from training in my mind. I studied her face as her nostrils stiffened in determination, emphasizing the seriousness of the subject matter. After a pause she continued to speak. *"If you survive, others can live but you will really be fucked up in the head forever."*

I left the Pier for LAX with a destructive purpose. I walked down the jetway at Terminal 5 carrying my regulation F/A suitcase as I approached the open door at 2L of the DC-10 and stopped at the entrance. I popped my head into the cabin and gazed forward, up the left aisle of the jumbo jet then aft, finally boarding the plane destined for MSP. This evening, I harbored a very intense desire to take one final journey to self-destruction.

"Hi, Eddy." The bright, petite brunette stewardess startled me. "You coming with us tonight?" she inquired. I fumbled for my boarding pass and quickly rushed forward to the First-Class seat I had been assigned, excusing myself by saying I was tired. I stored my suitcase underneath the seat in front of me so it would be readily available at the proper moment. I had been allowed to pre-board the aircraft; the other passengers had yet to follow. There could be heard the pleasantries of the young flight crew in the galley as they laughed and joked, anticipating this jaunt to the Twin Cities. Days of sleeplessness and self-medication were now taking their toll on me. I studied the layout of the first-class cabin, doors 1L and 1R, the front lavatories and the cockpit door, fixating on its color-coated pattern with metal framing. Fear gripped my throat as the other passengers began to board the aircraft, stowing their carry-ons and seating themselves for the late-night flight.

"Can I take your coat, Eddy?"

"No!" I snapped rudely at the blonde young lady assigned to my section. She seemed to understand the root of my discourtesy, or so she thought. "I'm sorry, I'll be okay," I stated. She gently rested her hand on my shoulder and lowered her head toward mine.

"Anything you need just ask for it, okay?" she whispered, and started down the aisle to assist the regular passengers. Sure, it would all be just fine. She wasn't surprised at what Edmundo the survivor was exhibiting acute anxiety: a normal reaction to an abnormal situation. Perhaps that is exactly what the rest of the cabin crew also surmised.

"Prepare for departure," the cockpit crew advised the flight attendants as they armed their respective exit doors. There would be the usual safety demonstration, seat belt fastening request, proper storing of personal items and final preparations as the large craft jolted back from the gate. Much of it wasn't registering however as I was in a daze. The F/As positioned themselves on their jumpseats and into their seat harnesses, just like I had done so many times before. I looked down at my suitcase, satisfied I had carefully prepared the metallic ordnance resting inside. I was suddenly pushed back in my seat as we roared down the concrete runway and gradually lifted up into the darkness over the vast Pacific. I just sat there smiling.

Once the large transport finally leveled off at her cruising altitude I had only one desire, I wished to fan the flames that totally consumed me. Beer, and lots of it, was ordered and would be served by a gracious crew who knew of my ordeal and the perceived demons that came with it. This outweighed their sensibility to step forward and cut me off. The chemicals I had absorbed over the last three days ensured that the brew would have little effect at that moment on my already morbid brain. I would remain stoic for a while with no outbursts or rude behavior. I chuckled ominously, drinking, never even noticing the occupants of the sparsely filled aircraft, wondering if they realized that they booked passage with a mad man.

"Ask anyone," I blurted out for no apparent reason. I quickly turned to see if anyone had heard me but as is typical on a "red-eye" everyone was hunkered down-asleep or trying hard to be. I calmly drank the remaining lager and it was not long before a male attendant placed another cold one brew on my tray table. As I grasped the icy can I noticed that my server took a step back and was smiling. He nodded in recognition and then was off. I shrugged my shoulders, then realized I had seen that same look before. "He could see right through me," I said to myself.

I was suddenly distracted by the occasional conversation and laughter that filtered through from the mid-galley area just aft of first class. It was the cabin crew, my fellow flight attendants engaging in small talk while the majority of the passengers on board slept. I really did love the job. I was given the opportunity to travel the world. And the camaraderie, that was truly special. These were the things that were priceless.

"My behavior is so disgraceful," I whispered to myself. There was a time when I took great pride in every aspect of my duties as a crewmember. I had spent countless hours in conversation and laughter with my beloved associates as I knew was occurring right then in the galley. That's where I needed to be, that's where I had found comfort in the past. The flight attendants were all my supporters. I seized the now empty can sitting on my tray table and decided to join my compatriots in the galley. My torn heart began to soften. Perhaps I should abandon my woeful plan?

I found it difficult to stand due to the recent days of ill-treatment and little sleep. I grunted as I stretched and made it to my feet. The adrenaline surged at the thought of joining my mates. I turned down the right aisle of the craft and slowly made my way toward the galley. Their conversation, their words became clearer.

"I think Eddy is doing darn good considering all he has been through." I determined it to be the petite brunette girl who had greeted me upon boarding.

"I certainly could not have gone through that," another female voice joined in. I stopped and positioned my body alongside the galley wall, just out of their view. Although I was mere feet from them, they had drawn the galley curtain closed to limit the amount of light shining into the cabin.

"I give him kudos for what he has had to endure," another female expressed. All at once there was a deep silence. Not a sound could be heard so I moved forward a bit more.

"I don't know." It was the voice of the male flight attendant who had brought me my can of beer and delivered a calculating glance. "Somewhere, sometime," he continued, "he's going to cross the line, go over the edge big-time and it's going to be ugly." My God, he was referring to me. I was devastated. I struggled to make it back to my seat while fighting back the tears. Then anger began to swell. If they wanted ugly Antimundo can deliver ugly.

"Grab the gun. End it all now, right in First Class!" The voices saw their chance. In my mind's eye I envisioned me placing the weapon to the side of my head and doing the unthinkable.

"What if the bullet continued on?" I murmured to myself. I imagined a rapid decompression of the cabin at 35,000', the noise, the panic as passengers who were fast asleep were jolted awake, desperately reaching for the yellow oxygen masks released instantaneously amid the chaos. Either way I would have put an end to my misery.

"But no! What about the poor ship cleaner who would have to clean up the mess, the skull fragments and brain matter?"

"Eddy, wake up." I felt a hand on my shoulder shaking me. The voice rallied me from my nightmare.

"Yeah, I'm here." I slurred my words.

"You okay?" The sweet brunette inquired. I was afraid I may have drawn attention to myself.

"Yeah, I'm fine, what's up?" I sheepishly asked.

"The captain has extended an invitation to join him in the cockpit," she announced.

"What?" I shuddered in surprise.

Her sweet brown eyes wide with approval. She nodded in recognition of the honor and dashed off back to mid-galley.

"Ah, thanks," I replied seconds after she'd already left. I leaned forward, rubbing my chin. "What if the captain had found out what I had in my suitcase? But if he did, why would he want me in the cockpit?" For the first time in so many dark days I began to see just how unstable I was.

I slowly approached the cockpit door and initiated the combination of coded chimes to the crew inside. The door swung open to almost pitch darkness. Then I heard a self-assured voice with a distinct drawl.

"Eddy, my boy." The greeting was upbeat and sincere. "Have the jumpseat behind me, Eddy, take a load off." As the pilot turned, we locked eyes.

"Captain Foster." I chuckled with delight. It was "Rangoon Dwayne" himself. I could hardly believe it. Hell, he's one of the good guys.

Man, I can't blow my brains out on this guy's flight, I thought to myself. After a few seconds the magnitude of that last statement registered. That flight attendant in the galley behind me was right. I had stepped over the line. I briefly glanced over at the other two aviators. I didn't recognize their faces, but I was sure they knew who I was.

"What takes you to the Twin Cities Eddy?" Captain Dwayne inquired.

"A lady," I stated. The pilots laughed and nodded with approval.

"Sounds good to me," said the white-haired captain with four stripes on each shoulder. I had lied but knew that's what pilots liked to hear.

Should I tell them I'm really running away after a three-day binge with initial thoughts of ending my life in First Class while 35,000' above the earth. No, probably not.

"You're welcome to stay with us for the remainder of the flight, Eddy boy. Buckle up and enjoy the ride." My God, had I heard right? The evil crept back into my soul. I was losing it. How easy it would have been to kill myself and everyone else with a couple of well-placed shots in the cockpit! I began to sweat and tremble. I thought I'd make small talk, let the flyboys see that I'm just one of the guys.

"I thought you only bid to fly the 737, captain?" I asked.

"Thought I'd try something a little different," he replied.

"Is there much difference?"

"Heck, the Boeing 737 is like maneuvering a forklift," he explained. "The DC-10 is like driving a Cadillac." His subordinates nodded in agreement. I could tell by the plane's pitch that we were beginning our descent. The multi-colored lights on the black panels began to blink and flutter. The noise,

492

the rush of air outside, became more intense. My anxiety began to rise.

"Weather in Minneapolis is minus-twenty degrees with a half mile visibility," the first officer reported.

"Tell the flight attendants to store away the carts, tighten up things and get strapped into their jumpseats for the remainder of the flight," Captain Foster cued the flight engineer who immediately grabbed the phone and rang the cabin crew.

"You're gonna have to learn to recognize certain facets of your life Eddy that may pose as dangerous triggers." Doctor Joe's voice advised me. *"Avoid anything you believe might bring the awful experience back alive from your sub-conscious to the conscious."* Then the first jolt of turbulence hit. The jumbo jet bucked and although I was bound in my seat with a harness, I experienced that split moment of weightlessness, the instance your stomach rams up into your throat. I glanced over Captain Dwayne's shoulder. We were descending fast past 20,000'. The skilled crew giving their full attention to guiding the DC-10 through some nasty skies. Dr. Ramljak's words filled my head: *"Avoid potentially harmful situations that may initiate flashbacks, Eddy."*

"Yeah, fat chance, Doc," I blurted out but the other three in the cockpit were too occupied to have heard me. The plane dropped, then rose again only to fall once more like a runaway roller coaster. Although I was on the verge of total panic, Captain Foster remained calm and in total control. I gazed through the cockpit windows as the jet traveled through one massive haze after another. The conditions outside had turned downright foul. The giant airship, fighting for stability, finally dropped below the clouds. Things suddenly settled down nicely.

"Take her in for us, Jim," the captain told the first officer. Grasping the controls firmly, it was evident that the subordinate officer relished the opportunity to guide us home.

The recent turbulence had rattled my nerves. The cockpit became alive with commands and actions, the Minneapolis tower also chiming in and the crew responding but I closed myself off from the activities. I just wanted off this mad ride. The first officer called out for flaps, and the proper rotation and adjustment of the elevators made. The landing gears were lowered, and the shining runway lights guided us in. An extended coat of pure white across the frozen landscape was visible.

"One-sixty, one-forty, one-twenty," the captain called out the altitude as we drifted down in a controlled fall from the sky. The touchdown onto the runway was flawless as the crew initiated reverse thrust of the engines. In a matter of seconds however it became clear we were not slowing down.

"Apply brakes!" the captain ordered. The first officer executed the command, but the aircraft did not react. "I need those brakes, Ken." The captain's voice showed concern as the pilot in the right seat furiously stomped down again and again in a fruitless effort to slow the careening jumbo jet.

"We don't have any brakes, they're locked, probably frozen!" The airship lurched and began to swivel in a change of direction.

"Oh Jesus Christ, here we go!" Capt. Foster instantly assessed how to deal with the obvious. The huge aircraft began to shift to the right of a runway that was covered in a layer of ice, causing us to slide at high velocity, heading for a potential disaster. Captain Foster quickly grabbed the wheel in an effort to save his plane. I just freaked and raised my legs as I huddled in a fetal position clenching my hands into tight fists and crossing my arms around my legs in horror.

"No, not again," I pleaded in prayer, but the dormant God remained silent. What about the fuel? How much jet fuel remained in the wings? Even if we slid off into the ditch, there was sure to be fire.

"Come on baby, come back to papa." The determined captain used all his strength to recover control. Ever so slowly the jumbo jet reacted to the captain's efforts as he coaxed her back from catastrophe. Finally, the DC-10 came to a rolling stop and the four of us breathed a sigh of relief. After a second or two the three aviators turned their heads in unison to view me frozen in my seat. Their stares were met with silence, yet I could see that they waited for some type of reaction from me.

"I've been through worse," were the only words to come out of my quivering mouth. The pilots began to laugh and shook their heads in disbelief.

"Indeed, you have, Eddy my boy, indeed you have." Captain Foster became upbeat. "Time for a Rangoon Ruby," he announced in half jest. He immediately went on the intercom to assure the passengers that everything was perfectly normal. He was merely taking all precautions and determined it would be better to be towed to our arrival gate. Because of the early morning darkness and since everyone was probably still groggy, no one suspected that they were party to a massive "slide for life" upon landing. Since the flight attendants were facing aft in their jumpseats they too had no idea as to how close they came to having to conduct an emergency evacuation.

Stranded on the concrete runway is where we remained until a tug could be brought to our assistance. The cockpit crew took delight in having been put to the test and coming out as winners. They had been given a small glimpse of what they'd trained and prepared for year after year yet never expected. The two younger pilots were almost giddy about the experience. Captain Foster was more reserved, having logged many more flight hours in his time. I was sure that he had gone through his share of close calls and had learned to deal with such occurrences in the most professional manner.

I on the other hand was pissed. I said not a word as I struggled to unclench my hands which seemed as frozen as the barren landscape on the other side of the fuselage. My insidious mind determined that I had once again been the butt of a sick joke, afflicted upon me by a God who neither cared nor listened.

The tug arrived and we inched our way toward the gate. Once the plane was secured the flight crew became occupied with post-flight duties. I quickly undid my harness and silently slipped away, taking one last glance at the display panels in the cockpit. I truly had a love/hate relationship with the DC-10. In the passenger cabin I stopped at my original assigned seat to gather my suitcase and the personal belongings I had stored in the pocket in front of me. The stupidity of my actions finally registered as I felt my mind and body begin the process of crashing. All my endorphins had been spent bringing with it a feeling of disgrace.

"Thank you for traveling with us this morning." Janice, the young, petite brunette who manned the exit at door 2L, displayed her pleasantries to the passengers disembarking. "Bye Eddy have a good stay," she called to me. I merely nodded my head and proceeded up the jetway towards the terminal building, half dead from days of physical self-torment and trauma of our landing. Upon entering the greater passenger waiting area, I saw the start of a swirl of energy as the dawn was lighting the open space. I picked out the far corner of the waiting area and sat in the last seat in the last aisle of identical blue vinyl-covered seats. My head hanging down between my knees, I began to weep, placing my shaking hands over my face.

There I sat. I was physically and mentally shattered, taunted by Muerto who laughed with glee. If it wasn't for the fact that Dwayne Foster happened to be the captain on my flight to abomination, the mass media would soon be screaming about the maniac who took his life in mid-flight. I wanted to vomit. I tried to keep my focus on my surroundings, tried to retain some semblance of composure. There were gate agents scurrying about, dressed neatly in their freshly pressed uniforms, a couple of them comparing notes and forming their game plan for the morning rush of passengers streaming in.

"Flight 67 to Las Vegas is now boarding at gate 54." Announcements rang throughout the terminal. Another agent with an air of urgency warned the late arrivals that this was the last call for a flight to SFO. All about they scampered. People scampered about, including an older man who ran to a pay phone, making one last call before boarding.

"Jack, you get back here this instant!" A woman was losing her patience in an effort to lasso her rambunctious little boy. And all around were the flight crews, including captains with four embroidered stripes on their sleeves. Some carried themselves with that aura of authority. Nothing had changed. Sensing Muerto was nearby and I corralled a cab and got a room at the nearest Marriott Hotel. Once in my room I made a feeble attempt to remove my clothing, but my burdened body flopped upon the bed. I slept for forty-four hours straight.

A few days later I boarded a DC-10, unarmed, bound for LAX. I was a shadow of the man I had once been struggling with the pestilence of withdrawal and shame. It was evident from take-off that I would spend more time in the first-class lavatory than my assigned seat. Once the aircraft leveled off however, I was able to settle my nerves. I could not focus on any one individual, formulate a face, a movement or their speech. I wanted to give in to Muerto who I believed was riding somewhere in coach. It was no mystery to me that I would submit myself to the *inevitable* at some point and Death would be the final victor.

Who can I go to? I could think of no one with enough wisdom and insight to rescue me from myself. Suddenly it happened. "Rachel Ramos." I had called out her name.

Rachel was my father's first cousin. Although older than I she had been a regular presence in my life. Rachel was a bright, beautiful woman who was raised in the old neighborhood. Outgoing and energetic, she had been able to rise above the negative elements of our neighborhood. A registered nurse, Rachel was also a wife and mother but knew next to nothing concerning the specifics of my situation. She had always been kind, logical and compassionate. Arriving at LAX I rushed to find a pay phone. My hands shook and my heart raced as I tried to make the call. I danced from one foot to the other as the ringing continued.

"Come on, answer." I yelled in desperation.

"Hello?"

"Hello, Rachel?"

"Yes?"

"This is Eddy, I am in trouble." She immediately took charge.

"Can you make it to my home? Come now if you can."

"Are you sure it is okay?"

"Yes, come right now." I hung up the phone and for one of the few times in my new life, I was truly grateful.

Rachel was standing at her front door when I pulled into her driveway. Walking up to her I immediately started unloading my problems. The nurse in her took control.

"Do you need to go to the emergency?" She inquired.

"No, Rachel," I sighed. "I need to talk." My good cousin guided me into her house and directed me to take a seat on the sofa. I had been to her home numerous times over the years, mostly during family celebrations. As a boy I used to attend the birthday parties for her twin daughters. But this was the first time I had entered her home burdened by such grief, guilt and shame.

"What's going on, Eddy?" I sat and thought for a bit. Where should I begin?

"It's so twisted, Rachel." As I began to talk I imagined myself standing on the burning tarmac screaming defiantly at Muerto.

"That seems so long ago," I whispered to Rachel, now aware of my recent behavior. I told her about Reina and her premonitions. The time passed and I continued to fill Rachel's ears, leaving no stone unturned in my recollection. My cousin listened with great patience. At the conclusion, I lay back on the sofa in total exhaustion. Rachel remained silent, in deep concentration.

"Do you believe you deserve the suffering you are encountering?" The voices answered for me.

"You deserve far worse." I was in the hand of Death and Rachel could see that it was just a matter of time before that hand close.

"It most likely will get worse if something is not changed today," she warned me. I hoped Rachel would pull out a magic wand that could change everything with just one wave. But of course not.

"Have you asked for help from God?" I glared at my cousin. She was serious in her inquiry. My resentment rose as I sat straight up.

"God?" My face became rigid. "God? Are you referring to that deity who stood back while the children screamed as they were consumed by the flames? Maybe He's the one who abandoned my crew mates," I sat in defiance not against Muerto, but God. "Tell me, cousin, where is this God when I am paralyzed by fear and pain? Where is this God when I am crying day after day in torment?" Rachel stopped me.

"He's right next to you Eddy, crying his heart out alongside you." I stopped ranting. No one had ever said such words to me.

"Where is he?"

"He's right there sitting on the sofa." She pointed to the empty side. I turned and of course saw nothing, then chuckled.

"Rachel, the only God I know is deaf, dumb and blind. I see nothing."

"Eddy, he is right there," she insisted. I asked a logical question:

"Then why is he silent?"

"Because you have him bound and gagged with your anger and hatred." I had never heard it explained this way. "He was on the plane with you, wasn't he?" I recalled the moment before the final impact.

"Everything will be okay." I looked back at Rachel. It finally became clear to my dysfunctional brain. Perhaps the compassionate advice I was receiving from my good cousin was leading me on an unexplored path worth investigating.

I spent the rest of the day feeling safe. There was no rush to judgment by Rachel regarding my deplorable behavior. She genuinely wanted to save me. Rachel Ramos was true to her oath as a caregiver.

I began to calm down as we spoke of family and happy times. Composed, I decided to leave, which concerned Rachel.

"Stay here, Eddy. You can spend the night." I declined but thanked her repeatedly as we walked to my car.

"What do you want to happen, Eddy?"

"I want to find peace." I paused and thought. "I want a way out of this explosive mine field without having to turn on my airline." The emotions began to overcome me. "I suppose I *was* a miracle."

"I think you know where to put in your request." Rachel hugged me, patted me on my shoulder and backed away as I started to back the car out of her driveway. Suddenly she shouted, "By the way, have you forgiven yourself for surviving?" I was jolted by her words.

"What?" I asked.

"Have you forgiven yourself for surviving the crash?" I remained silent. She flashed a loving smile. "I think that is where you need to begin if you wish to heal." She waved. "Eddy, it is *good* you survived." I made no response as I drove away. I could see her figure continually waving in the rear-view mirror, a big smile upon her face. I took a deep breath and acknowledged a tinge of hope in the advice she had given me.

Sitting at the end of the Manhattan Beach Pier I struggled with the fear my recent behavior had instilled in me. If there really was a loving God wishing to extend a gentle hand it would not be through one miraculous action. I thought about the peace I embraced on Kauai. The island's beauty was awe-inspiring, yet uncomplicated. I concluded that any path to a possible solution lie in total simplicity.

Returning home, my first order of business was to gather all the material acquired over the years regarding the crash. I sorted the various reports, photographs, newspaper and magazine articles. There was the report regarding the cockpit crews' disputes, government documents I had obtained through the Freedom of Information Act, and of course the CVR recording. I carefully placed everything related to the crash in a large cardboard box, sealing it tightly. I placed the box in a closet where it would remain available if needed but I was determined to eventually get to a point where that decision would rest with me and not the voices. Next, I sat down and began to draft a daily schedule that would be beneficial physically and mentally; A routine based on simplicity.

"Take care of yourself Eddy." Rachel's voice resonated.

"Take it day by day, or hour by hour, or even minute by minute if necessary," I told myself. Do whatever it takes to evade the triggers that allow the anger and hatred to control you.

In the initial development of my plan there were long, dark nights where I would set the alarm on my airline wristwatch for a period no longer that ten minutes. I would struggle desperately with the urges, then the sharp tones of the alarm would startle me back to reality. I would reset the watch once again for another ten minutes, continuing my resistance. Many a night the struggle would only subside with the faint rays of the rising sun coming into my bedroom window.

I remained dedicated to my classes at Loyola-Marymount. Knowledge always equates to freedom. The rest of the day was devoted to the upkeep of my physical health in the gym, on a bike, or running on the soft sand at El Porto Beach or bodysurfing at Manhattan Beach. I embraced a healthy diet and dedicated myself to quality sleep when I could get it. But the of my *simple* life was my time with Cristiano. There were no longer trips to some exotic location. Quality time was reserved for my immediate family right at home. Now my young son would really get to know his grandparents more intimately. Family functions were now placed high on my priority list.

I believe petitions to God could only be presented with a heart filled with humility and the willingness to be patient. Above all, I visited LAX only on rare occasions.

At the airport, in the Executive Offices of the airline, job security was on minds of most associates. Even before Barry Lane departed, employees who had been with the company for many years were being shown the door. The few that were left began to figure it out.

I think Barry always believed his decisions would only delay the inevitable. A small number of airlines grew stronger while others were falling by the wayside. Perhaps his goal was to revive the company and get her healthy enough to attract a suitor who could ensure employment for the remaining employees. On a clear sunny day at LAX, suitors from a financially solid Southern-based airline came calling with hopes of courting and acquiring our airline.

"Why don't we just buy you, and by combining our systems we will solidify a huge chunk of the industry?" I am sure the conversation in the executive offices was much more detailed but essentially, that was the bottom line. Al Greenleaf would remain to be the closer.

"Consultants who weren't consultants, were brought in from the outside," one former employee related. "They showed up previously in the management line-up of other failed airlines who were absorbed or went bankrupt." Those associates lucky enough to remain in their positions saw the writing on the wall. Speaking up led to a quick termination.

Our airline would be slowly assimilated into the greater entity. Our large red logo would cease to exist in the skies it had flown for over sixty years. The culture and daily interaction for the remaining associates would be drastically changed. Some would spend years of "being perceived as an adopted child," as one worker expressed. There was a secure promise of jobs for those in uniform. For the others, the outlook was not so bright.

"It's more than a merger, it's an All-Star team." The public relations machine went to work. Two of the former giants in the industry were combining to create a massive airline. The new masters wanted to put a positive spin on the marriage, tasteful to the eyes and ears of the flying public.

"The best gets better," was the message from the southern based company. An upbeat tune ensued. In reality, it was all just another form of survival. Many non-crew employees were offered positions with the new family in remote locations. Others would find themselves in lesser, lower-paying positions, and others were simply terminated.

I was sitting in my living room when I heard the news of the merger for the first time on TV. Surprisingly I was not shocked, I had enough conversations with Barry Lane to have picked up on what was over the horizon. I believe he graciously was forewarning me. Then it suddenly hit me.

"I'm not a part of that southern-based company." I sat up and my eyes widened. "I'm not a part of that airline." A huge grin donned my face. "I have no allegiance to them." A powerful chill shot through my body. "I don't owe them a thing." My eyes began to fill with tears. Now a great burden had been lifted from me! I had kept my vow of loyalty to my airline. I fell to my knees upon the wooden floor and bowed my head as I wept. I was free to speak my mind, to speak the truth!

With regard to my association with the new company, I was once again in limbo. But I was not concerned for I had a rock-solid contract. I knew they had to honor it. I would continue to receive my pay and benefits in exchange for services. What exactly those services were was "complicated" and I was sure would raise the eyebrows of my new superiors when it was brought to their attention. Still, I wasn't worried.

I continued to receive tuition for my education, so I was quite content to let things be. I prepared myself to play the game once again when someone in the new administration happened to *find* the contractual agreement. I could wait and would be prepared when that day arrived. For the first time I saw a light at the end of the tunnel. It was still some distance away, but I saw it.

I began to formulate a plan as to how I could get out the truth about 2605. Throughout the years bits of information had slipped out in subtle ways. There were many in the airline who were aware of the "dispute" between Captain Herbert and First Officer Reimann, but it was only discussed internally. And there were those who had their suspicions concerning the truthfulness of the Mexico's official report, but it, too, was never discussed openly.

Periodicals were also occasionally interested in hearing my story. A couple of noted journalists contacted me over a period of time wanting to discuss a possible story. I was always curious to hear their approach and potential angle in documenting my experience, but most of the time, once their presentation was concluded, I would shy away. What *I* needed was a reputable organization that had the resources and ability to conduct an objective investigation of the entire matter. There were television programs with a news magazine format, but I didn't know how to get their attention or how to persuade them to take me seriously. The bottom line was that I was not yet a stable person and was afraid I may come across that way on TV, especially when I began to tell such a gut-wrenching story.

When I was finally ready to speak, I put the word out to individuals I knew had connections in the media. I believed any such collaboration would come. The first obvious task was to deal with the airline, but the powers-that-be were too busy with their merger to pay attention to some former flight attendant. But one day I did receive a phone call.

"Ay-ed-moon-do?" a high-pitched female voice with a southern twang was on the other end. In that very moment I knew exactly what kind of people I was dealing with. "I'm calling on behalf of Mr. Carlton Cleburne. He'd like to meet with you." A time and date were set for a meeting at the Avion Drive HQ.

"Be smart, don't get foolish." Being once again physically healthy I determined I owed the new overseers not a thing. Finding myself in a circumstance of strength for once gave me faith.

Carlton Cleburne came into the waiting area of an office I had been in numerous times prior but now it was *his* office. The fair-haired, short, bottom heavy man extended his hand.

"Edmundo!" I focused on his eyes and he was immediately sizing me up. I'm sure he was thinking, "How in the hell did this little shit get such a plum deal from the airline?" He seemed genuinely interested in sitting down with me and getting as much information as possible, see where my weakness might lie.

"You know, Edmundo, this airline would be proud to have you return to duty as a respected flight attendant. Mr. Mitchell has decided to join us and will be returning to work soon." The information about Skip caught me by surprise. I initially did not realize that Carlton was trying to find a simple way of voiding my contract. I fell deep in thought as the airline executive rambled on. Finally, I spoke.

"That's good about Skip,"

"What?" He stopped and stared.

"I'm happy for Skip. I wish him all the best, he deserves it." I was being cordial. Carlton returned to his prepared oration. Soon it became quite evident that the airline executive was at a loss as how to resolve my situation.

"By all accounts I understand you were a good flight attendant." He was playing me. Certainly, the new masters would be delighted if the solution was as simple as me agreeing to return to the flight line. That would free them from any legalities related to seeing to my well-being.

"Be careful what you ask for," I blurted out. Carlton looked surprised. Sure, there would be no monetary settlement, but putting a walking time bomb into their newly re-painted fleet of jets could be disastrous.

"Welcome aboard, if there is anything we can do to make your flight more enjoyable, please don't hesitate to ask," I thought as I envisioned Antimundo mocking the pleasantries. I was healing and with my mind being much clearer now, I could foresee trouble. The fork in the road before me became obvious. It was time for me to leave the industry, but the manner in which I would exit had to be dealt with delicately. I promised Mr. Cleburne that I would deal with him in good faith: that is what Barry Lane and Doctor Ramljak would have wanted me to do. But I was not going to trust him.

I finally decided to get an evaluation of my situation by David J. Brooks. Brooks determined that they most likely want to settle obligations with me monetarily.

"It's quick, it's pennies in a pocket to them, and you're gone forever," he stated. David mentioned the possibility of substantial financial gain if the negotiations with the airline were handled correctly. The next move had to be planned very carefully. One afternoon I received a phone call.

"Hello, Eduardo, this is Mazie, Cary Diller's mother." I hadn't spoken to her in a while but had met her on two separate occasions. She was a strong, wise woman and I remember her facing the tragedy and its aftermath with grace and dignity.

"Yes, Mazie, how can I help you?"

"Eduardo, I don't know if you were aware, but soon after the accident the company offered the parents of the crew-members that were lost the privilege of obtaining one free travel pass a year."

"Yes. I had heard something of the sort. It was great of the company to do that." It sparked fond memories of my airline that was no more.

"Well, we received a letter from the new airline, and they are revoking this one little pleasure we look forward to each year." The good woman became distraught. "This kind token was a way of reconnecting with Cary." I could hear her sobbing. This meant so much to her.

"Did you get the initial promise of passes in writing?"

"No." I understood that. In the culture of the old airline, most employees would never hesitate to take the company at their word. Why not, when it was only a couple of tickets a year? "Who should we call in the new administration who could assist us?"

"Mr. Carlton Cleburne," I blurted out without thinking.

Soon I was summoned again to the corporate building on Avion Drive. It became apparent from the start of our conversation that Mr. Carlton, the southern gentleman had done some research.

"You know, Edmundo, (I did not bother to correct him) returning to the flight line as one of our respected flight attendants would ensure you job security." Of course, he failed to mention that such a decision on my part would also be the most convenient solution for the airline. He was being condescending, lessening the possibility of any other options on my part.

"Who knows, Edmundo, perhaps being a flight attendant is just a starting point with the new company." He seduced me with the possibility of perhaps climbing that corporate ladder if I played ball. I sat there remembering the first time I had entered this very building years before, filled with excitement and anticipation. I had considered the prospects for a grand future back then. That office was just down the hallway. Now I was in *their* building, the one with a large new name painted on the sides of the various hangars.

I want no part of this, I thought.

"Hey, is it true you guys revoked the yearly single travel pass privileges of the parents of my deceased crew-members?" Carlton's piercing blue eyes shot right through me. His body language and facial features revealed anger. A cold stare telegraphed his disapproval. "Is this the wrong time to bring up this matter?" Yes, I was sarcastic and as a result, abruptly shown the exit with no word of a future date or time to meet again.

I marched down the hallway with a smirk on my face. I didn't care. It was obvious that I needed to place the task of my resolution in the hands of David J. Brooks. My focus needed to be on maintaining my mental health through this process.

For the first time since October 31, 1979 I was fully confident. I was free to discover the limitless possibilities of being granted that second chance. There, first and foremost, was a promise of joy to be found for myself and my son.

It was now time to reestablish my relationship with the island of Kauai. On the Na Pali Coast I could find the serenity I needed while my lawyer worked on my behalf. I packed my gear and I drove to the employee parking structure the following day. On this particular morning I was surprised to find a line of cars waiting to enter the multi-floor complex. As the slow-moving traffic brought me to the entrance, I found a security guard with a clip-board checking each vehicle and occupant, but I wasn't concerned. I had my airline I.D. though it was from the former airline it still granted me entrance onto the company grounds.

With the assimilation process just beginning new identification badges had not been issued.

"I.D please." He looked intensely at my red and white plastic card then quickly gazed down at a list on his clipboard. All at once he looked up at me, frowning. He knew who I was and was obviously uncomfortable. He had a duty to do and clearly, he did not like it. Suddenly he just looked up at the sky and said, "Go ahead, Ed. Next!" He let me slide and I was not sure what had just happened.

I entered the flight lounge under Terminal 5 at LAX to find small groups of crewmembers in intense discussion. The faces were familiar and missed very much. I had not been in or near the lounge for such a long time. Caroline, a cheerful brunette with whom I had worked with in the past, was obviously surprised to see me and broke into a big smile.

"Eddy it's good to see you. How did <u>you</u> get through?" I just stared at her. "Don't you know?" she asked. I threw up my arms. She quickly put her hand on my shoulder and led me to a more secluded area near the mailboxes. "There is a list of people that are banned from the property."

"Yeah, so?" Caroline just stared.

"Well, your name is on it." I was stunned. That explained the behavior of the security guard. Caroline began to chuckle at the absurdity of all this. Then I began to think of my last meeting with Carlton. Since I did not bend to their preferred conclusion of our issues, perhaps it was better to demonize this F/A little shit. I began to chuckle, too. I truly felt honored.

"So, they consider me an antagonist." The thought was entertaining.

"I wonder if they will let me on the flight to Honolulu! The gate agents must have the list." Once again Caroline and I began to laugh.

Change can be a painful experience that I suppose incites fear. I assumed the nervous would begin to see threats in darkened corners. Maybe Carlton just wanted to be a big dick and teach me a lesson, make things difficult so I would relent, settle, and just disappear.

"Insanity!" For now, I just wanted to get to Kauai, a serene island I now believed would paint a portrait of a promising future.

I stood by the gate, patiently waiting for my name to be called.

"Valenciana -- here's your seat." I boarded the aircraft but could not relax until the aircraft backed away from the gate. Now I was safe. I smiled and settled back in my comfortable seat.

"A-l-o-h-a."

Chapter XXII

It was clear that the process to exorcising what pained me would be a lengthy one. Doctor Joe believed I could do it and finally now, so did I. Sure, it was at a snail's pace, but things seemed to be moving it the right direction. Still recognizing the danger of my past behavior, I felt confident in exiling myself to the Garden Island.

The splendor of Hanakapiai Falls soothed my soul. Days were filled with meditation and reflection. For the first time I allowed the word "forgiveness" into my conscience. At the top of that long list of names for consideration for absolution was me. My own actions could arguably be considered the most vile behavior of all.

"It is your own anger and hatred that shackled God." I recalled Rachel's words. The most insidious revulsion of feelings was reserved for me, which made the final chapter, still to be played out, all that more important.

Sometime later and being well rested, I boarded the flight HNL-LAX. At 35,000' I fantasized how some lawyer for the new airline might receive a call from David, hang up and shout,

"How in the hell did that flight attendant get that attorney?" When asked by his superiors to examine my case what would his recommendation be? "Settle the matter and move on." That was a pleasing thought.

I met with Carlton after taking a couple of days to gather my thoughts. The corporate hallways were now decorated with new signs and photos. The beloved posters of the white fuselage and red logo of a McDonnell Douglas DC-10 were gone. In their place were the blue, red and white images of the Lockheed L1011 jumbo jet, the preferred wide body of the new airline. To my amazement Carlton greeted me with a smile. I was surprised to see that Mr. Wilcox, Barry Lane's former assistant, sitting at Carlton's desk.

"I'll leave you two alone," Carlton said. He was wise to leave the office.

"Whatever had occurred prior was a misunderstanding," Wilcox explained. Here was a face from the deceased airline. "Certainly, we both can resolve our differences in a logical manner. We can settle this matter today if you wish, Eduardo." Mr. Wilcox wrote a monetary amount on a white piece of paper and coolly slid it across the polished desk at me. Surprisingly, the offer was fair. I kept my poker face.

"It's good to have a starting point, sir."

I had no great demands upon the inheritors of my contract nor was there any desire to lash out at them. I made it plain to Mr. Wilcox that I wanted to walk away with nothing more than an earned sense of respect, fair monetary compensation, and the ability to begin again on a clean slate.

"We want no less, Ed." It was easier for the new airline to open the purse strings than to deal with the itch of this pestering mosquito.

"I will seriously consider your offer, Mr. Wilcox, and get back to you." We rose, shook hands, and I headed for the door. Suddenly, I stopped, turned and popped a sly little smile.

"By the way, what about my flight benefits?" I caught Wilcox off guard. He raised his hand to his chin and thought for a moment. I became impatient.

"I want them." Wilcox's eyes grew big. We had a problem.

I left the airport facility and soon received a call informing me that any travel benefits would be terminated by our agreement. The new company had a long set rule of never bestowing benefits to survivors of any airline incident.

"Sorry to hear that. It looks like we are back to square one." I felt so empowered when I was able to say those words to my superiors. It once again became a waiting game, but I was enjoying it. I felt at peace and re-invigorated. I was back at school, back on the crew team, in the gym, enjoying the ocean and eating healthy.

"Hit them up for big money." There was always an abundance of wise guys who believed they knew better. If only they had been the survivor! They would have walked into the sunset with tons of money, a beautiful girl on each arm, and many other well-deserved perks. But I saw it differently. True riches lay in having wonderful, compassionate people in my life like Barry Lane and Joseph Ramljak. True riches were found in simplicity. And I needed that simplicity in my life once negotiations were over.

"Take what's rightfully due and walk away with your pride intact," I said to myself. I could imagine Barry and Dr. Joe telling me to leave the trash behind. I could wait. I was getting a paycheck and still had my benefits. The time had come now to seriously consider the prospect of going public. The truth had waited long enough!

Once again, I gathered, sorted and reviewed every piece of information with regard to 2605, then tactfully informed contacts I had encountered over the years that I was now ready to speak. Some were journalists, aviation enthusiasts, pilots of all forms of aircraft and those who were just curious. Like before, I knew I could possibly come out of this looking like someone mentally deficient, but hell – I had to take the chance. There was no turning back.

"Tell me about the crash in three sentences." A new phrase entered my vocabulary as interested individuals in different media wanted information. Along with my studies at Loyola-Marymount I now undertook learning the business of the media. The fact that the official report was such a sham and never released publicly really stoked the interest of many who at first had only a peripheral interest in my story.

The 400+ days of the Iranian hostage saga seemed to have completely erased the memory of the crash.

"He has the CVR Recording?"

"A flight attendant?"

"Why have I never heard of this crash?" No matter how hard the initial inquirers dug they could <u>not</u> find a thing published on the incident. The NTSB, the FAA, the manufacturer of the aircraft all came up empty for specifics. All these institutions could acknowledge was that the accident had indeed taken place.

"The flight attendant?" I understood their hesitancy. It was going to take work and patience to find an appropriate organization willing to take up the investigation.

On a lovely sunny day, I received a call from New York. A guy in Sherman Oaks, CA knew a lady in Manhattan, and someone called someone who spoke to another highly placed lady at the American Broadcasting Company. The Executive Producer of the News Magazine 20/20 was intrigued with the story she had been told.

"Can you possibly send me an overnight package detailing your involvement in this incident?" an executive secretary politely asked. "Send it FedEx." Information was exchanged and I assured her that I would comply.

How is this going to happen? This could be very beneficial or very destructive. I contemplated the possibilities and it unnerved me.

"You still have other unfinished business to deal with in the airline, so focus." The voices had been silent for some time, so I was able to let the fear go and regain my confidence.

"We are very interested in this story." A phone call clear from across the country finally threw open a door that let in an abundance of light. ABC was sending a senior producer immediately to Los Angeles to meet with me.

I would like to thank the American Broadcasting Company for agreeing to fly with me. Please make sure your seat belt is tightly fastened and that the tray table in front of you is in the up and locked position. I would only get one shot at this. I needed a plan.

Within 48 hours I was pulling up to the entrance of the Sheraton Isabella at LAX. All I had was a name, Kurt Lappert. I asked a lady behind the front desk if she could please let Mr. Lappert know I had arrived. I sat in the bustling lobby scrutinizing the various businessmen. I made a game of trying to see if I could spot the senior producer upon his entrance into the lobby. Suddenly in front of me stood a tall middle-aged gentleman in a black suit.

"Eduardo?" Hey, he got my name right! I was pleased. The man from New York recognized me from the brown leather flight jacket I said I'd be wearing. His grip was strong and firm as we shook hands.

"So, how are you? How's your family?" Mr. Lappert's greeting indicated a feeling of awkwardness, not quite knowing how to begin our conversation.

"We are going to dinner, mi amigo." I took the initiative. "First we eat and drink then we can talk business."

"Sounds good," I think I impressed him. I was sure he assumed we would patronize one of the high-scale restaurants in the area but I had other plans. I intended to see what Kurt Lappert was made of.

"Ever been to East L.A?" I was asking the man from the City That Never Sleeps. I went screeching out of the hotel's driveway and soon we were headed northward on the 405 freeway.

"Do you still correspond with Skip?" That caught me by surprise. The reality was that Skip and I had drifted apart. I remained silent, so I said nothing. "It was not a full flight that night, right?" This guy had done his homework. I was impressed. I certainly did not mind conversing with someone who was well-prepared but first I wanted to know more about his character. Was he someone I could trust? The well-respected news magazine he represented reached millions of households every week and they had the means to revisit specifics of the accident. I just hoped they also had the balls to do it right and get to the truth. But I had my misgivings. I was not a Kennedy or a Rockefeller. I was just some guy from East Los Angeles who got caught up in an awful mess.

"Can I hear the tape?" Kurt was ready to get to work!

"Patience my friend, first things first. I would like to see photos of your children. You have children, yes?" Kurt looked at me a bit perplexed. Exiting the freeway, we entered a unique little enclave of the City of the Angels filled with history, tradition, celebration and, if you're not careful, danger. Kurt Lappert was out of his element. Sure, he was from New York, but this was different. He gazed with curiosity at the old fluorescent lights and worn buildings: nighttime in the barrio. A crowd of campesinos stood on a corner by a local market.

"Day laborers celebrating," I assured. My gringo friend nodded lowering his window to take in the mariachi music which rang loud and clear from a bar whose colorful name read La Copa de Oro, (The Golden Cup). "You want to go in there for a drink?" I joked. He tried to force a smile. The half-drunken hooligans who lingered on the sidewalk, their faces and manners seemed filled with anger and hatred. It struck me instantly that not long ago I had sought out such places and mingled my anger amidst similar lost souls.

Manuel's El Tepeyac Restaurant in the old neighborhood would provide the perfect setting to begin any conversation concerning 2605.

"It all begins here, Kurt," I explained. "I was born not far from here, went to grammar school down the street. To understand me you have to see and experience where I came from."

"¿Joven, quieres tequila?" The proprietor, Manuel Rojas, offered. Just hours after landing at LAX the Senior Producer from ABC was downing shots with the best of the barrio. My guest seemed more relaxed. A sad Spanish song of lost love serenaded from the jukebox and there were the familiar pictures on the wall of Our Lady of Guadalupe alongside one of President Kennedy. As I finally secured a table, I noticed Kurt was taking in the scene in the small dining area. He liked what he saw.

"The children?" I inquired.

"What?" He did not understand. "The children. I was serious about wanting to see photos." The man from Manhattan quickly removed his wallet and laid it open on the table. Amidst lively conversations and festive music, I began to develop a broader picture of who Kurt Lappert was. With the arrival of his large hot plate of chile rellenos, a Manuel's specialty, the Senior Producer dismissed any thought of engaging in specifics of a plane crash. I had a smile watching him savored the melted cheese as it strung from his chin to his fork.

Suddenly, angry words were being exchanged by two patrons. One sentence concluded with the usual Spanish vulgarity and then it was on. Chairs went flying and tables crashing as the two young bucks in rival dress and colors collided. Everyone gasped and retreated from the action. A split second before the pandemonium reached our table, Kurt snatched up his oval plate and backed away, guarding his culinary booty at all cost.

"¡Chinga tu madre!" (Fuck your mother.) The combatants crashed to the floor drenched in a mixture of red chile sauce, soft drinks and broken plates. All at once the small figure of Manuel, the proprietor, leaped into the struggle. He was going to teach these young "chavalitos" a lesson. I turned back and viewed the Senior Producer casually watching the mayhem while stuffing his mouth with the appreciated contents of his plate. The atmosphere in the room had gotten a little "tense" shall we say, yet Kurt Lappert was enjoying himself.

"Wow! This kind of reminds me of Beirut," Kurt reminisced in wide-eyed excitement. I would come to find that in his various posts with the network, Beirut was one of his favored. I liked this guy. Barry Lane and Joe Ramljak were mentors who kept me going. Was Kurt Lappert such a man? Was he here to help me or hurt me?

The next morning, I maneuvered a cart loaded with my suitcase and boxes into the room at the Sheraton Isabella.

"I need to get this done, Kurt." I turned to face him. "I can't afford for this to turn on me." He thought for a second.

"All this time you have been told to keep quiet concerning this issue, right?" I nodded. "Then, let's start by you telling me what happened to Flight 2605." We each pulled up a chair to a round table in the room and I began.

As an employee of the industry, one becomes a number. Eduardo Valenciana was designated as associate 21196-1. Numbers determine everything related to one's job in the industry. Flight 2605 was the result of a designated sequence #190 in the Flight Attendant Bid Sheet for the month of October 1979. The human face of the airline was too often suppressed by the company, or in some cases, the cockpit crews. Some of the most respected individuals I was acquainted with were airline pilots, men of high intelligence and strong character. Yet some of the most disgusting words and actions I had been witness to had also come from airline pilots. Over the years the industry had been conducting business concerning cockpit crews through a "good old boy" network. I believe this process hindered the actions of the men in the cockpit that Halloween morning.

Carl Herbert was a Marine, not an Air Force pilot. Whether one liked Carl or not, he had become one hell of a pilot and one could not have put himself in safer hands. Dieter Reimann had earned his wings in the post-war era of the German Luftwaffe.

As a boy of ten, he and his family had suffered much, especially during the last days of the Third Reich. He had come a long way.

With ten years in the company, Sam Wells was the rookie by seniority standards. There was no doubt in his mind that the prize of securing a place in the left seat, the captain's seat would one day be his. Here were three distinctly different men who were all good pilots, especially Carl Herbert yet they seemed unable to work together on flight 2605, October 31, 1979.

The last resort by anyone dissatisfied with the performance of a co-worker is to do a "write-up." Herbert did just that days prior to the scheduled flight. The First Officer he shared the cockpit with had gotten under his skin. This allowed trivial feelings of disdain to ride jumpseat that fateful morning. The airline industry would argue that there are effective methods for dealing with tension in the cockpit. The reality is that the systems in place at the time resulted in a Check Pilot "jawing" with the combatants individually, one good old boy talking to another.

There were red flags that were visible to other pilots dissatisfied with the performance of a co-worker in the company long before October 31. Dieter's personal life was turning inside out. A strained divorce had forced his back against the wall. He supposedly had lost more than twenty pounds, one individual stated,

"He was becoming defensive concerning the world around him." Company regulations meant little to someone suffering from what Dieter was going through. To make matters worse, he was scheduled to fly as First Officer to a prim and proper "fly by the book" captain. Other pilots saw the problem and discussed it, then someone finally suggested that the check pilot should have a little talk with the pilots. McKay's file indicated that Dieter had gotten into the habit of arriving for work without his uniform jacket and pilot's cap, which Carl seemed to resent. Others saw something deeper.

"They should not have been flying together," one well-respected captain put it bluntly. A conversation ensued between the Supervisor, a Check Pilot, and each pilot individually. The Check Pilot was greeted by angry men who masked their true feelings as was pilot protocol. Neither would dare let it be known that he may be willing to back down, a critical mistake.

The moment I spotted sequence 190 in my Flight Attendant Schedule I knew that I'd be in for a hard night-and-day service. One's body can play games on you. By the time the three-and-a-half-hour flight arrived in Mexico City, one felt as though one had worked a Trans-Atlantic day flight.

Carl Herbert was 53, certainly not old for a captain. But when a person's body wants to sleep, it is often hard to take no for an answer. The industry's solution was to keep those coffee pots continually filled. Flight 2605 took off after an unscheduled delay and equipment change.

Captain Herbert guided his DC-10 southward, a familiar route he had successfully completed to Mexico City 351 times prior. As the flight attendants prepared to serve the midnight snack, the cockpit crew sat back to what seemed like an ordinary flight. One pilot is heard on the CVR recording expressing the fact that he had not slept in three days.

Regulation 1.2. 1-4 from the Flight Attendant Flight Manual states "Sleeping, dozing or action by the F/A that gives the impression of sleeping is cause for immediate dismissal." One can assume that the regulation was even stricter for pilots.

Dieter lived in Seattle and commuted to LAX for the all-nighter. Carl had spent the time prior to the assignment flying many hours in his personal aircraft. Fatigue with personal animosity can be a disastrous combination. Disdain became an unwanted companion in the cockpit, despite the combined skills and experience of the three men. Then, Mexican Air Traffic Control would make a fatal mistake that skill and experience was unable to overcome.

According to experts such as Captain Ron Banner, Runway 23-Left was the most desirable operating runway at Mexico City because it was the longest and widest and had the only precision approach and approach light system (ALS) available. Approaching Mexico City as the CVR recording revealed, Mexican Air Traffic Control cleared the flight to descend to 13,000 ft. and proceed directly to the Tepexpan radio beacon. They were further told to expect an instrument landing system (ILS) approach to Runway 23-Left. The Captain and First

Officer agreed at the time that they would make a Tepexpan approach, which is the transition that leads to the ILS approach to 23-Left.

Analyzing the cockpit recording and using Greenwich Mean Time, one can deduce that fatigue and animosity begin to manifest themselves. At 1134:07 on the audio tape, after being guided toward Runway 23-Left, Second Officer Sam Wells has misgivings about the Captain's planned approach. He speaks up.

"Charlie, do you realize that you're in INS?" When assurance is received from the captain, he becomes apologetic (1134:19 on the tape). *"Just checking up old buddy, to make sure."* Conditions in the cockpit deteriorate rapidly. Procedures in the tower and instrumentation in the cockpit are part of the problem. Carl Herbert is being sucked into a "black hole" condition and no one speaks up. Almost six minutes and thirty seconds of crucial time pass before Carl correctly recognizes the problem. At 1140:48 of the recording he inquires:

"We're cleared on the right, we're cleared on the right, is that correct?" Both Dieter and Sam respond immediately. The First Officer contradicts:

"The other runway!" The Second Officer agrees:

"Yeah, the other runway." Captain Herbert makes the proper adjustments but by then it is too late. Who would have thought that construction workers would be allowed to park their trucks on an on-again-off-again runway, to take a "siesta"?

The replacement control tower operator had mistakenly reported visibility at two-and-a-half miles. In reality, it was at *zero*. The fog had crept in from the dried lakebed to camouflage the dump truck that stood directly in 2605's path.

Did resentment between the captain and first officer prevent effective communication? I must consider such a possibility after what I experienced in my visit to the cockpit during the flight. Sam Wells may have suspected the fast-developing dilemma but may have been reluctant to speak because of cockpit etiquette. Did Dieter's resentment toward the captain keep him from speaking up? If so, it may have cost him his life. Of course, any theory regarding to what extent their conflict was a factor would remain hypothetical. These are just the questions put forth by a surviving flight attendant.

Carl Herbert relied heavily on those skills he had sharpened over the many years in the sky. He played by the rules but was unaware that the rules were about to be breached on his final flight. He struggled to save his ship to the very last second, but this time his skills were not enough. Three men might have done the job but the company failed to recognize that in some rare situations it takes all three, working in compatibility. The airline and the lords that guided the company dictated policy in cliques. The printed laws of the industry are impressive as stated in the manual. Regulation 1.3-E "In conjunction with the Captain's authority and the established chain of command, each crew member has the direct responsibility to perform their duties <u>as a team</u> to insure a safe and comfortable flight." Of course, seldom is the real world so harmonious. The needed regulation and those like it were often tossed by the wayside by a caste system that existed in the skies. Up to that time the industry seemed to fail to see the power of an individual to rise to a challenge. The airlines were solely to blame, management in particular, and rarely did the scenario ever change.

My airline, a company with an excellent safety record, found itself in deep shit. Once it was made clear that Mexico would control the investigation, the airline scrambled to salvage what they could. They would cooperate with the Mexican Government. Those who tried to seek the truth would be stone-walled. There were many in the industry who felt the company was rewarded for its willingness to go along by being promised valued routes along the Mexican Riviera once all the lawsuits were settled.

The United States Government's NTSB sent their skilled investigators down to the Mexican Federal District, but none were ever permitted to speak to various ground crews. Civilian witnesses were segregated from the Norte Americanos. No real evaluation could be conducted. "Higher ups" in Washington would be restrained in their questioning.

"This should be a Mexican show," reliable sources claim to have been told. Besides, the U.S. had just received a much-needed agreement with Mexico allowing her to be the recipient of the country's newly discovered wealth of oil and natural gas. The deaths of passengers and crew were not enough to stop U.S.

political leaders from turning their heads the other way on this one.

Many discoveries by experts representing interested parties were immediately brought to the attention of El Servicio a La Navegación en el Espacio Aereo Mexicano (SENEAM). In fact, representatives of the U.S. agencies remained in Mexico City for some time to help correct obvious faults in Benito Juárez's flawed systems. The airport was not a pilot's favorite by any means. Mexican airspace, for that matter will always test the skill of the most experienced pilots.

Why didn't the crew see the trouble mounting? For one thing, the crew could not get a visual on the runway. The last report they received stated that there was one-mile visibility. Neither Los Angeles Flight Control nor the Mexican Air Traffic Control Center at Mazatlán or Mexico City ever tried to update the reports for 2605. At 1135:15 of the CVR recording, the cockpit finally received an update from the Mexico City Terminal Arrival Center:

"Two six zero five, tower advises, ah, ground fog...the runway and two miles visibility." It was the wrong information. The instrumentation for weather at Benito Juárez was situated in an extremely awkward spot. It took time to secure a proper reading. The fact of the matter was that the fog rolled in two miles *away* from the instruments and locked in the approach area.

Benito Juárez had been designated with the infamous "black star" rating from ALPA. The dishonor is reserved for the worst facilities. It was also a common practice to keep only one air traffic controller on duty all night in El Distrito Federal. Señor Estrada's testimony concerning himself and Señor Rodríguez could not initially be confirmed at the time of the incident. The claim has been made that officials altered the tower logbook and no one was permitted to question the discrepancy.

Why did Carl Herbert land on a closed runway? On the 18th of October, SENEAM released a summary of Notice to Airmen (NOTAM) in relation to the closure of Runway 23-Left:

"23-Left will be closed for construction work until further advised." Later that same day, they revised the message.

"23-Left open all length." The work on the runway was sporadic in days leading up to Halloween. On Captain Herbert's

prior flight into Mexico City, he was cleared to land on Runway 23-Left although there had been evidence of continuing work on the site. First Officer Dieter Reimann guided the DC-10 into Mexico City via 23-Left on the 19th and 24th of October while Carl was off sick. Even though there were continuous closings of 23-Left, planes were landing on that runway.

Were the approach lights illuminated on 23-Left the morning of the crash? The control box for such lighting was located quite far from the tower. The controller had to call a technician who would then walk some distance to the control box. Seeing the cables sliced, as I did while accompanied by Diego, showed evidence of tampering. One U.S. investigator also discovered the cables sliced. Mexican officials calmly advised the investigators that the lights had been inoperable since the 24th or 25th of October. In an adjoining area lay numbers of runway edge light fixtures. The same officials assured the Norte Americanos the equipment had been removed long before the tragic episode. U.S. investigators were given a statement signed by the Technical Deputy Manager of Mexico City Airport stating that the lights on 23-Left had been removed along with all approach light systems *well before the accident.* On the CVR recording, controller Señor Rodríguez could be heard telling the cockpit crew that "the lights are on Runway 23-Left."

Why didn't the captain use his instruments aboard the DC-10 to bring the craft down safely? The McDonnell-Douglas DC-10 is equipped to practically land itself. The CVR recording clearly reveals that the Mexico Air Traffic Control Center told 2605 they should expect a landing on "two three left." Later Mexico Tower requested that 2605 report over Mike Echo, the normal ILS, 23-Left final approach fix. This is the only runway at Benito Juarez so equipped. Under extreme conditions, Carl did land. He landed the craft half on and half off 23-Left. His last-minute decision to abort the landing took the DC-10 airborne once again. If there had not been the truck but ten feet further down the runway, all that has been disclosed would not have occurred. Upon investigation of the airport, U.S. representatives discovered the ILS 23-Left localizer and glide slope did not correspond with the instrumented final approach course of 23-Left. With

American assistance, the course was later corrected by four degrees.

The angle by which 2605 touched down initially started a rumor which was used to support the "pilot error" verdict. Some Mexican officials claimed that Carl Herbert was in the middle of a "side-step maneuver," a landing simply consisting of the using two runways. A pilot may bring an aircraft with instrument assistance onto one runway, bounce back up and manually skip it over to actually land on another. Prior to the incident, there was no existence of such a maneuver at Benito Juárez in the Jeppesen Flight Manual carried by all U.S. commercial pilots in the cockpit at all times. After the accident, such a procedure was worked out.

Representatives of McDonnell-Douglas, the maker of the destroyed DC-10, arrived in the Mexican Federal District to see to their interests. Was the aircraft a contributing factor in the incident? Perhaps more about the aircraft would have been discovered if investigators had been permitted to examine the accident site. Yet again, the CVR recording revealed a hint at what may have been a definite problem. At 1139:15, the captain is heard complaining of radio failure: *"the whole thing just quit!"* One company investigator did disclose that navigational instruments in the cockpit were giving erroneous information. The DC-10 certainly had its detractors. Insiders had complained that on impact the entire cabin floor simply gave way due to rapid decompression. Upon releasing myself from my harness at what was once door 4-R, I found myself in the midst of an inferno of rubble at ground level.

How did the plane crash? Once the craft was airborne, after the captain called for a missed approach, the plane's right landing gear struck the first dump truck, snapping the gear backward and completely off along with much of the right horizontal stabilizer. Flight 2605 was doomed at that moment. At the same instance, it can be speculated that the Second Officer proposed a much more logical solution than the one made. He wanted Carl to "take it straight down the runway" and ride it out, *"Carl cut the…"* Instead, the captain tried to take the wounded plane back up into the sky, away from the danger. The power in the engines increased to one hundred percent but it would only be a matter of time before the craft would come crashing down. The aircraft proceeded down the runway in mid-air heading directly to the main terminal building. Suddenly, the right wing that was dipping twelve degrees clipped an operator cage area on a backhoe excavator sitting aside the runway. The jumbo jet was once again redirected. The wing would then be struck by a stationary telephone junction box sparking the first of a thousand fires. Flight 2605 then smashed into a garage then ground vehicles and parked trucks in an airport parking area. There was instantaneous combustion. The jumbo jet finally crashed into some concrete steel-reinforced buildings. The carnage continued. Undetermined numbers of buildings and vehicles were destroyed. A wing flew into an adjacent neighborhood and combusted. The entire incident took 28 seconds.

"The noise, I am still afraid of the noise," I stated in an interview. Through all my training nothing had prepared me to deal with the volume of dissonance created by the crash.

Thus, the damning label of "error de piloto" was bestowed upon Captain Carl Herbert, Sr.

"It was his ship, it was his command," the ignorant insisted. Where really does the blame belong? Perhaps it lies with us all when the flying public becomes complacent. To quench the hunger for economic profitability, or mere survival in a vicious industry, many airlines and airport facilities are constantly looking to cut corners. Do we look the other way for the right price on a cheap ticket? Yet, each time a plane takes to the air, the dormant subject (of safety) is hidden in the back of our minds.

"Will it be today?" The voice may persist.

Finally, just days after the tragic crash, fate played another cruel joke. The Iran Hostage saga began. Its effect was to detract from any legitimate journalistic scrutiny of the investigation and the eventual final report presented by SENEAM. The tense siege at the U.S. Embassy half a world away allowed the accident to be neatly swept away and forgotten. Many months later the airline and the U.S. Government had the opportunity, dictated by international law, to challenge the final conclusion based on the many inconsistencies. They had the right to ask for a new investigation but did not. Why not? Politics and money?

Kurt Lappert sat speechless, struck by what he heard. The following days were spent helping him digest eight years of information.

"We're cleared on the right; we're cleared on the right. No! This is the approach to the goddamn left!" I assumed that in his foreign assignments Mr. Lappert had been witness to other awful events. He was familiar with the dealings of Muerto, perhaps under a different name and disguise. Still, the CVR tape could bore a hole through the thickest of mental armor, right to the core of one's soul.

"Ouch," was the only expression Kurt could mutter at times. He spent much of his time reading, and then there were the questions, the same ones I had answered numerous times in the past.

"Why did they accuse you of serving liquor to the pilots?"

"Because in the midst of total confusion, government representatives panicked and tried to grasp any opportunity to shift the blame elsewhere."

"Even though the runway had been declared closed, they were still allowing planes to land there?"

"A Mexicana DC-10 flight landed on 23-Left just twenty minutes before we arrived." So many questions, yet in responding to his inquiries I felt that *this time* my words were going to be taken more seriously. The Senior Producer was taking it all in. He would stare straight ahead in deep thought, then put his nose back into any given document. He worked at not reacting positively or negatively regarding my answers. I could not deduce an opinion one way or the other whether the journalist agreed with my conclusions.

Then finally: "I believe much of what you have presented, Ed." It came out of nowhere as I sat patiently in the hotel room. The New Yorker was fascinated by the story. He could hardly conceal his excitement. "What about the Herbert family? Have you spoken to them?" Kurt was formulating a plan.

I told him no. Because of what I experienced I have made an effort to avoid the families of the victims. I never wanted to be put in the position of having to lie to them. I especially avoided Captain Herbert's family. Kurt remained silent for a moment, but his mind was racing. From the wooden table strewn with papers, Mexican newspaper reports, transcripts and airline documentation he grabbed the blue-covered ALPA report published three years after the incident. The document was commissioned not as an addition to the official report but as an alternative to the SENEAM report which the American Airline Pilots Association could not accept with a clear conscience.

"The one hitch I see in this story is what you saw in the cockpit. But still, you've done a fine job in accumulating all this material and I am still amazed that you have the CVR recording. By the way how did you get it?"

"You don't want to know." The journalist smiled. The sleeves on his white dress shirt were rolled up to his elbows.

"All of this is coming from the flight attendant, not the NTSB or the FAA, but a flight attendant." Kurt held the ALPA report as he faced the window just as a Boeing 727 was gliding in the distance, descending, seconds from touchdown.

"We need a knowledgeable expert who can verify all that you have told me today." I chuckled. This was a vexing dilemma I had experienced from the beginning.

"The man you want is Retired Captain Ron Banner, the man who authored the report that is in your hand."

"Do you have a contact for him?" I slowly nodded. I left the Sheraton Isabella with a sense that Kurt Lappert would be able to persuade his superiors at ABC in New York to run with the story. I drove away filled with hope and anticipation.

"Dear God, we may actually get this thing done."

I assumed that the wheels which drove the news magazine back in New York rotated very slowly. Sure, there was a story and certainly enough there to make one want to dig deeper, to see what this bizarre incident was really about. It would be six months at best, I believed, before hearing whether the network would commit itself. A crew would have to be gathered and schedules considered. Then there was the unfinished business with my superiors at the airline. I resigned myself to waiting, being patient.

I was very surprised when I eventually received word that the new airline agreed to continue the flight benefits for both Cristiano and me in addition to a monetary settlement.

"It could not be that simple." I hung up the phone fully perplexed. Could there be some deception I was unaware of? The reality was, I was not that important. I was merely a pesky mosquito that came with the great package they had inherited.

"Eduardo, are you ready to go back to Mexico City?" I knew it was coming. I remained numb, motionless for a few seconds. Kurt Lappert let it be known that the network was moving swiftly on the story. There would be filming in Los Angeles and LMU as they developed a story line. We only had eighteen minutes of on-air time to explain what seemed like a lifetime of drama.

"We've got Captain Banner on board with us and I have contacted the Herbert family. They are extremely happy that someone has finally taken an interest in this crash." The process was in motion and speeding up. I was not used to good things happening consistently like this.

Guilt remained, however. I supposed the new airline might feel betrayed, me going public so quickly. But I was willing to be guided by Kurt Lappert.

The crew and staff from the American Broadcasting Company were wonderful! The interviews for Captain Banner and Carl Herbert Jr., the captain's son and family spokesman, were done separately. The quality of the investigation was first-rate. I was never pressured, and all consideration was given respecting my privacy. And no! I was never financially compensated in any way for my participation.

"¿Quieres tequila, joven?" The jovial voice of Manuel Rojas rang clear. While filming in Los Angeles I would have the pleasure of treating the crew from New York to a pleasant meal at El Tepeyac. Things were going perfectly.

But despite everything, doubts still lingered and although Carl Lappert informed me that ABC would supply the airline tickets for me to Mexico City, I refused, preferring instead to use my flight benefits.

The new company would ferry me across the Sea of Cortez and over the desert and mountains of greater Mexico. I wondered if we would be able to get anyone to speak to us. After studying Kurt Lappert and the camera crew, I saw that there was a method to his approach. He was patient, and with the arrival at Benito Juárez Airport of the field reporter, who would present the story to the public, I could see the greater plan. Once in the city, I was delighted to find myself again in the lobby of El Presidente Hotel, Chapultepec. There would be time before filming, and I had priorities.

I was honored to greet two gentlemen to whom I will always be grateful, Hugo and Diego. Both had aged some. The three of us sat in the plush cocktail area of the hotel, frosty glasses of Bohemia before us on the table. At first, we didn't have much to say. Words seemed unnecessary to express the joy of this reunion. We just stared with a sly smile on each of our faces.

"Hugo García, that's a good name." I remembered the day I first said that, as they ushered me into the back of the ambulance.

"You know he's gone now." It was Diego, the well-dressed diplomat. He was trying to tell me something.

"He's gone? Who?"

"Primitivo, he's gone." My eyes widened and a chill went down my spine with just the mentioning of his name. I stiffened and gazed over at Hugo.

"Lung cancer, such a terrible death."

"When?"

"About three months ago, I believe," Diego said, looking over at Hugo for confirmation. I then gazed up at the high wall of the hotel where suddenly I saw the comandante. He was standing, leaning on a bar counter, looking at a pack of those vile cigarettes he held in his hands. Removing and placing one in his mouth, he frantically searched his pockets for a light. I noticed he was, as usual dressed impeccably. A large shadow him approached from behind. The familiar dark figure then stood beside Chávez and ignited a flame with the snap of his bony fingers. He graciously offered it to the comandante.

"Gracias mi amigo," Chávez said and then began to cough heavily.

"It is my pleasure," Death replied. Muerto chuckled in delight as the two walked away into a black void.

"Eduardo, you okay?"

"What? Oh, yeah." I laughed and I was fine. I recognized it was simply my imagination. Yet, I wondered. Perhaps Muerto had finally captured the soul he sought!

I ventured away from Chapultepec in the late afternoon while the television crew was out. It was mid-December and the air at the high altitude was chilly. The city was alive with colorful lights and decorations commemorating the season. A shop's showcases once filled with the dispiriting figures of El Día de Los Muertos were replaced with the Three Wise Men along with various versions of the Nativity and archangels.

"Una para la señora," a butcher in a blood-stained white apron offered as ladies pressed tightly against his glass case. Each woman eyed their personal choice, looking to get just the right cut of meat for their holiday meal. On the streets, the children played and ran about, some stopping to view gifts displayed in one store, then another. A slim young boy focused on controlling his soccer ball with his foot. He balanced it masterfully, kicking it up, then again with his knee and finally sending it to a comrade with a perfect header.

I worked my way through the crowd. There were no grand marionettes of the sinister Muerto being manipulated, leering down at us on the streets. All about was the essence of life and a spirit of promise. Although not rich in material possessions, the people of the city were indeed rich in love, respect and family. I thought about Cristiano and hoped that my collaboration with the 20/20 crew would allow me to follow a path that emphasized those same virtues.

With the episode "in the can," I returned to Los Angeles to wait and prepare to deal with the outcome, one way or the other.

"What Happened to Flight 2605?" would be presented to the nation on the evening of January 15, 1988. That morning I awoke, showered and dressed very nicely. I pinned my flight wings onto my flight jacket and headed inland of the basin to the city of Whittier near East Los Angeles. I drove up the wide asphalt road of Rose Hills Memorial Park, surrounded by beautiful green lawns. I arrived at the grave site, now marked by a strong young tree.

"I desire to be a part of life once more in another form," were Reina's words. The tree stood guard over her with a sense of tenderness.

Like a door that suddenly is slammed and instantly startles, so it was with the story presented in the 20/20 episode. It left no doubt.

"The first process in healing is to grieve." Dr. Joe's words rang clear from above. He understood my dilemma. In over eight years I had not grieved.

"Cascadas de su alma," (Cascading falls of your soul) my mother stated. I wept for months. When I regained my strength and composure, I retreated to the cascading falls of the Garden Isle. Soon, Cristiano would join me there on a permanent basis.

"Will I ever be good enough?" Most likely not, but it really didn't matter anymore because with time, the deep-rooted pain in my soul was lifted by the Grace of God.

Made in the USA
Las Vegas, NV
29 May 2021